S0-BYB-250

A COMPANION TO CLASSICAL MYTHOLOGY

ROBERT J. LENARDON
Ohio State University, Emeritus
MARK P. O. MORFORD
University of Virginia

With contributions by
MICHAEL SHAM
Siena College

New York   Oxford
OXFORD UNIVERSITY PRESS

Oxford University Press

Oxford   New York
Athens Auckland Bangkok Bogotá Buenos Aires Calcutta
Cape Town Chennai Dar es Salaam Delhi Florence Hong Kong Istanbul
Karachi Kuala Lumpur Madrid Melbourne Mexico City Mumbai
Nairobi Paris São Paulo Shanghai Singapore Taipei Tokyo Toronto Warsaw

and associated companies in
Berlin Ibadan

Copyright © 1997 by Oxford University Press, Inc.

Published by Oxford University Press, Inc.
198 Madison Avenue, New York, New York 10016
http://www.oup-usa.org

Oxford is a registered trademark of Oxford University Press

All rights reserved. No part of this publication may be reproduced,
stored in a retrieval system, or transmitted, in any form or by any means,
electronic, mechanical, photocopying, recording, or otherwise,
without the prior permission of Oxford University Press.

ISBN: 0-19-514725-1

Printing (last digit): 9 8 7 6 5 4 3 2 1

Printed in the United States of America
on acid-free paper

Contents

Preface, Bibliography, and Acknowledgments

The content and design of this <u>Companion</u> are meant to serve several purposes.

Perseus. Primary has been the preparation of the computer disk to accompany the text, with the formation of Paths that relate the extensive information in the Perseus program 2.0 to Chapters 1 though 23 of Morford and Lenardon, <u>Classical Mythology</u>, fifth edition. Perseus does not include material for Chapter 24 on "The Nature of Roman Mythology." Organized access is afforded to its computer resources for Greek mythology from vases, coins, sculpture, architecture, archaeological sites, maps, and ancient and modern texts.

Content and Format. For several years we have been asked for a shorter and simpler version of <u>Classical Mythology</u> that isolates the significant details. The abbreviated text presented here responds to that request and also provides essential background for anyone following the Paths that we have created in Perseus. By isolating the important information, we hope to provide a quicker and firmer grasp of essentials for an easier understanding of the riches that Perseus offers and so that more time and energy can be devoted to the meaning and interpretation of the myths and their impact upon subsequent literature, art, music, and film. The capitalization in the text of the important names allows for emphasis and ease in the learning of basic facts and mastery of the material. The pronunciation guide alongside these designated names will at least indicate where the accent belongs in English (for the marking of macrons one must go to the Index in <u>Classical Mythology</u>). The Roman names for the Greek gods are provided in parentheses. Alternative Greek spellings are also included in context because they have now become the vogue, and ready comprehension of both Greek and Roman forms is indispensable for the user of Perseus.

Translations and Tests. The translations from ancient authors omitted from the fifth edition of <u>Classical Mythology</u> are included: Mimnermus (Chapter 1); Homer, <u>Odyssey</u>, Menelaus' outwitting of Proteus (Chapter 5), and Seneca and Lucian (Chapter 13). The new translations added are: Catullus (63), "Attis" (Chapter 7), and two selections from Vergil's <u>Georgics</u>, on Aristaeus' consultation of Proteus (Chapter 5) and the story of Orpheus and Eurydice (Chapter 14). The objective sections of the Test Questions can be answered from the information in each chapter of the <u>Companion</u> (an answer key is given). The essay questions often look to the more complete discussion in <u>Classical Mythology</u> and beyond, and encourage further reading; some of them could become themes for written papers or oral reports.

Mythology in Music. Another major purpose has been to expand our exploration of the inspiration of Greek and Roman mythology in Western civilization; and we have done this in various ways. Each chapter has a list of compact discs of pertinent music available. We have tried to list all the works on mythological themes on CD, with comments on some of the more important. Yet, as we write, two new obscure and tantalizing pieces have just appeared: Benjamin Britten, <u>The Rescue of Penelope</u> (Erato), and Granville Bantock, <u>Atalanta in Calydon</u> (Albany Records). Each recording listed has a number linking it to the Discography, which offers full bibliographical information. The date of individual compositions is not given, but the Discography includes the dates of the classical composers to establish the period of a composition. The hundreds of musical works on classical themes not yet on CD have not been mentioned. The brief survey of this vast topic provided by Chapter 26 in Classical Mythology will have to suffice for the time being.

Mythology in Art and Literature.   There is a final section for each chapter with the heading Interpretation. The reader must not conclude that no interpretative material and commentary are included elsewhere, but in this section we have singled out topics that we find interesting and significant. We also offer information about literary treatments, and most important of all, we discuss many illustrations of Greek and Roman mythology in art throughout the ages. The ancient works included will be particularly helpful as a supplement for what can be found in Perseus.

The indispensable work of reference is Jane D. Reid, The Oxford Guide to Classical Mythology in the Arts: 1300s to 1900s, 2 vols. (New York: Oxford University Press, 1993). For Greek art the brief and very selective guide by T. H. Carpenter: Art and Myth in Ancient Greece (New York: Thames & Hudson, 1990) will be most helpful. The basic work of reference is the Lexicon Iconographicum Mythologiae Classicae, 7 double volumes, with the eighth and final volume due to appear in 1996 (Zurich: Artemis, 1981-1996). This huge work will be available only in reference libraries, but it is indispensable for research, and it includes Roman works and appearances of Classical mythological figures in cultures other than those of Greece and Rome. Carpenter is limited only to Greece. An unassuming, reliable, and exceedingly helpful work of reference is Frances Van Keuren, Guide to Research in Classical Art and Mythology (Chicago: American Library Association, 1991).

For the interpretations in art and literature, the authors' method has been to review the listings in Reid and LIMC and to supplement them with Carpenter and other works on ancient art, especially for Greek vase-painting. These reference works have been extensively supplemented by our own experience and knowledge, and most of the illustrations in the fifth edition of Classical Mythology have been included.

Videos.   The section Videos for each chapter lists only those films that are available on VHS. We have not included laser discs. A brief survey of film and Greek and Roman Mythology is to be found in Chapter 26 of Classical Mythology. Listed below are some of the major sources (but certainly not the only ones) for the purchase of the videos that are identified in the text.

Facets Multimedia, Inc., 1517 West Fullerton Ave., Chicago, Ill. 60614. Phone: 800-331-6197.
A vast catalogue of videos for both purchase and rental (by mail). One should check with Facets (or with a similar company offering access to movies worldwide) before settling for the prices of some more limited, esoteric catalogues.

Corinth Video, 34 Gansevoort St., New York, N. Y. 10014. Phone: 800-221-4720. FAX: 212- 929-0010.
Their catalogue specializes in videos on opera, drama, and dance.

Films for the Humanities and Sciences, Box 2053, Princeton, N. J. 08543-2053. Phone: 800-257-5126 or 609-275-1400.
A mixed bag of offerings. Some videos are of poor quality both visually and in terms of content, while others are acceptable; all are expensive. There are a few gems which it seems cannot be acquired elsewhere, e.g., the superb BBC television production of the Theban plays of Sophocles. All tapes should be previewed before purchase.

Insight Media, 2162 Broadway, New York, N.Y. 10024. Phone: 212-721-6316. FAX: 212-799-5309.

In many respects like Films for the Humanities (caveat emptor), with a wide range of videos, some of which are available elsewhere for less money. Among its varied collection are invaluable items, e.g., Michael Wood's In Search of the Trojan War.

Institute for Mediterranean Studies, 7086 East Aracoma Drive, Cincinnati, Ohio 45237. Phone: 513-631-4749. FAX: 513-631-1751.

Offers unique, indispensable documentation about the excavations of Troy and a series of videos beginning with Pandora's Box. Those who contribute in support of the Friends of Troy receive important updates on the world of Bronze Age archaeology.

Lyric Distribution Inc., 9 Albertson Avenue, Albertson, N.Y. 11507. Phone: 800-325-9742 or 516-484-5100. FAX: 516-484-6561.

Offers in addition to performance on CD and cassette tape, videos of operatic performances difficult, if not impossible, to find elsewhere. Although quality varies widely, particularly in terms of the visual, prices are reasonable and their catalogue is worth investigating. These videos are not listed in the text.

Sinister Cinema, P.O. Box 4369, Medford, Oreg. 9751-0168. Phone: 541-773-6860. FAX: 541-779-8650. World Wide Web: http://www.cinnemaweb.com/sinister

Many astounding B films about the ancient world (not only those about Hercules), difficult to find, are reasonably priced.

Video Yesteryear, Box C, Sandy Hook, Conn. 06482. Phone: 800-243-09877. FAX: 203-797-0819. E-mail: video@yesteryear.com

A few videos of interest for mythology.

BIBLIOGRAPHY

In addition to the bibliography mentioned above for mythology in art and literature, works will be referred to in individual chapters. Important are the bibliographies in Morford and Lenardon, Classical Mythology, 5th ed. (New York: Longman, 1995) (referred to in this Companion as M/L), especially those for Chapter 25, "The Survival of Classical Mythology in Literature and Art" (pp. 593-594), and Chapter 26, "Classical Mythology in Music and Film" (p. 613). To these we add:

Dance Film and Video Guide, compiled by Deirdre Towers for the Dance Films Association, Inc. A Dance Horizons Book (Pennington, N.J.: Princeton Book Company, 1991).

Mercedes Roshelle, Mythological and Classical World Art Index (Jefferson, N.C.: McFarland, 1991).

For the Glossary of Mythological Terms and Phrases in English:

Dale Corey Dibbley, From Achilles' Heel to Zeus's Shield (New York: Fawcett Columbine, 1993).

Michael Macrone, By Jove! (New York: HarperCollins, 1992).

———. It's Greek to Me! (New York: HarperCollins, 1991).

ACKNOWLEDGMENTS

We should like to acknowledge our gratitude. Charles Alton McCloud has offered freely of his extensive knowledge of the history of theater, music, and dance, and been most painstaking in the reading of the text. All those at Longman who have participated in the production of this book deserve our sincere thanks: in particular we are indebted to the friendship and support of Ginny Blanford, whose expertise we could not have done without; also we are grateful to the sympathetic encouragement of Roth Wilkovsky and the arrangements made with Yale University Press for the use of Perseus. Our association with Michael Sham has been invaluable: the translations from Vergil's <u>Georgics</u> are his and he has contributed the substance of the "Glossary of Mythological Words and Phrases in English" and the Test Questions; his expert knowledge of the computer has been indispensable for our creation of the paths in Perseus, and he has been the principal creator of the printed guide to Chapters 3A and 3B.

CHAPTER 1

Myths of Creation

GENESIS FROM CHAOS

Hesiod in his epic poem the <u>Theogony</u> offers the earliest Greek version of genesis. CHAOS (meaning a yawning void) provides the beginning for creation. Out of Chaos the universe came into being. Later writers interpret Chaos as a mass of many elements (or only four: earth, air, fire, and water), from which the universe was created. From Hesiod's Chaos came Ge, Tartarus, Eros, Erebus, and Night.

- TARTARUS [tar'ta-rus] or TARTAROS. Tartarus, which came out of Chaos, was an area in the depths of the earth, which became a place of punishment in the Underworld; EREBUS [er'e-bus] or EREBOS, its darkness, became another name for Tartarus itself.

- EROS [er'os] (CUPID). From Chaos came Eros, the potent concept of Love, which is fundamental.

- GAIA [gi'a] or GAEA, GE. Most important and first, Gaia, the earth, fertility mother, came from Chaos. Contemporary feminist approaches to mythology lay great importance on the fact that many early societies first conceive of deity as a woman.

THE HOLY OR SACRED MARRIAGE OF EARTH AND SKY

URANUS [u'ra-nus] or OURANOS. Of the elements that Gaia, earth, produced on her own, most significant is Uranus, the male sky or the heavens, with his lightning and thunder. The deification of the feminine, mother earth, and masculine, god of the sky, is basic to mythological and religious thinking. Their marriage is designated as a HOLY or SACRED MARRIAGE, a translation of the Greek HIEROS GAMOS [hi'er-os ga'mos], which has become the technical term.

THE CHILDREN OF URANUS AND GAIA

The holy marriage of sky and earth produced:

- The three CYCLOPES [si-klo'pez] or KYKLOPES. Each CYCLOPS [si'klopz] or KYKLOPS, meaning orb-eyed, had only one eye in the middle of his forehead. They forged lightning and thunderbolts.

- The three HECATONCHIRES [hek-a-ton-ki'rez] or HEKATONCHEIRES, "Hundred-Handed," strong and monstrous creatures.

- The twelve TITANS, six brothers and six sisters, who mate with each other.

SOME TITANS AND THEIR OFFSPRING

Deities of Waters. The Titan OCEANUS [o-se'an-us] or OKEANOS was the stream of Ocean that encircles the disc of the earth in the early concept of geography. He is the father of the many spirits of waters (rivers, springs, etc.), the OCEANIDS [o-se'an-idz], three thousand daughters and three thousand sons.

Gods of the Sun. The titan HYPERION [hi-per'i-on], god of the sun, was father of HELIUS [he'li-us] or HELIOS, also a god of the sun. Later the god APOLLO [a-pol'lo] became a god of the sun as well. The sun-god dwells in the East, crosses the dome of the sky in his chariot drawn by a team of four horses, descends in the West into the stream of Oceanus, which encircles the earth, and sails back to the East to begin a new day.

The Son of a Sun-god. PHAËTHON [fe'e-thon], son of the sun-god, whether he be called Hyperion, Helius, or Apollo, wanted to be certain that the Sun was really his father and so he went to the splendid palace of the Sun in order to find out. The sun-god assured Phaëthon that he was his father, swearing a dread oath that the boy could have anything that he desired. Thus Phaëthon was granted his adamant request that he be allowed to drive the sun-chariot for one day. Too inexperienced to control the horses, Phaëthon created havoc, and in answer to the prayers of Earth, he was hurtled to his death by the lightning of the supreme god, Zeus or Jupiter. This tale illustrates the brave folly of youth, the conflict between parents and their children, and the search for identity.

Goddesses of the Moon. SELENE [se-le'ne], goddess of the moon, is a daughter of the Titan Hyperion, and she drives a two-horse chariot. Later the goddess ARTEMIS [ar'te-mis] (DIANA) becomes a moon-goddess. Selene (or Artemis) fell desperately in love with the hunter ENDYMION [en-di'mi-on] and used to abandon her duties in the heaven to visit the cave of her beloved. In the end, Endymion was granted perpetual sleep and eternal youth.

Goddess of the Dawn. EOS [e'os] (AURORA), goddess of the dawn, was a third child of Hyperion. She, like Selene, drives a two-horsed chariot. Eos fell in love with the mortal TITHONUS [ti-tho'nus] or TITHONOS and carried him off. The supreme god Zeus granted her prayer that Tithonus be made immortal and live forever. Poor Eos forgot to ask for eternal youth for her beloved. Tithonus grew older and older, finally being turned into a shriveled grasshopper, while the passion of the eternally beautiful goddess became cooled to dutiful devotion. A tragic story illustrating how our ignorant wishes may be granted to our woe and illuminating the contrast between lovely and sensuous youth and ugly and debilitating old age.

Eos and Tithonus had a son named Memnon, who is killed by Achilles in the Trojan saga (Chapter 17). The amorous Eos also carried off other lovers, including Cephalus, who became the husband of Procris in Athenian saga (Chapter 21).

CASTRATION OF URANUS AND THE BIRTH OF APHRODITE

Uranus hated his children, and as they were about to be born, he hid them in the depths of their mother earth, Gaia. The mythic image is Hesiod's poetic merging of vast sky and earth imagined, at the same time, as man and woman, husband and wife. Her anguished appeals for revenge were answered by the last-born, wily Cronus. He agreed to accept the jagged-toothed sickle that his mother had fashioned and, from his ambush, he castrated his father as he was about to make love to his mother. The severed genitals of Uranus were cast upon the sea and from them a maiden grew, APHRODITE [af-ro-di'te] (VENUS), the powerful goddess of beauty and love.

THE TITANS CRONUS AND RHEA AND THE BIRTH OF ZEUS

CRONUS [kro′nus] or KRONOS (SATURN) and RHEA [re′a], two important Titans, had several children, who were devoured by their father as they were born. Cronus, who had castrated and overthrown his own father Uranus, was afraid that he too would be overcome by one of his children. Therefore, when their son ZEUS [zoos] (JUPITER) was born, Rhea contrived that his birth be hidden from Cronus. She bore Zeus on the island of Crete and gave her husband a stone wrapped in baby's clothes to devour. Zeus was hidden in a cave and grew up eventually to overthrow his unwitting father; he will marry his sister HERA [he′ra] (JUNO) and they will become secure as King and Queen of the gods.

TRANSLATION

A Greek poet of the seventh century (Mimnermus, frag. 10) provides a description of the sun's daily journey across the sky, with poetic emphasis upon the endless and wearisome labor involved.

> *Helius has as his lot toil day after day and there is never any rest either for him or his horses, when rosy-fingered dawn (Eos) leaving the stream of Ocean makes her way up into the sky. But a beautiful hollow cup, winged and of precious gold, fashioned by the hands of Hephaestus, bears him, sleeping deeply, from the land of the Hesperides to the country of the Ethiopians, where he makes his swift chariot and horses stand, until rising dawn comes. Then the son of Hyperion mounts his chariot.*

COMPACT DISCS

28. Britten, Benjamin, "Phaethon," for solo oboe, from <u>Metamorphoses after Ovid</u>.

58. Converse, Frederick Shepherd, <u>Endymion's Narrative: Romance for Orchestra</u>. Inspired by Keats, "Endymion, A Poetic Romance."

66. Dittersdorf, Carl Ditters von, <u>Symphony in D Major</u>, The Fall of Phaëthon.

117. Haydn, Franz Joseph, <u>The Creation</u>. Oratorio, in which the orchestral Introduction is a Representation of Chaos.

156. Lloyd Webber, William S., <u>Aurora</u>. Short tone poem by the father of Andrew.

160. Lully, Jean-Baptiste, <u>Phaëton</u>. Operatic elaboration of Ovid.

192 and **193.** <u>Music of Ancient Greece</u>, <u>Hymn to the Sun</u>.

178. Mondonville, Jean-Joseph Cassanéa de, <u>Titon et L'Aurore</u>. This opera about Tithonus and Aurora has a prologue concerned with Prometheus and the creation of mortals.

180. Montéclair, Michel Pignolet de. <u>Pan et Sirinx</u>. Cantata.

244. Saint-Saëns, Camille, <u>Phaéton</u>. Symphonic Poem.

251. Schubert, Franz, "Aus 'Heliopolis' I." Song about Helius the sun.

288. Wakeman, Rick, and Ramon Remedios, <u>A Suite of the Gods</u>. New Age songs for tenor, keyboards, and percussion, which include "Dawn of Time," "Pandora's Box," "Chariot of the Sun," and "The Flood."

291. Winter, Paul, <u>Missa Gaia (Earth Mass)</u>. New Age work inspired by universal, ecological concerns expressed in both words and music and set in the context of the Christian Mass. Sections entitled "Return to Gaia" and "Dance of Gaia" are a modern celebration of the Earth, highlighting connotations in the Greek concept of all-embracing Gaia.

VIDEOS

<u>Pandora's Box, The Roles of Women in Ancient Greece</u>. Institute for Mediterranean Studies Video Lecture Series, Vol. 1. A perceptive introduction by Ellen D. Reeder (Curator of Ancient Art, The Walters Art Gallery) to women in mythology and society that highlights important feminist themes, especially "Women and the Metaphor of Wild Animals," and "Mythic Women as Images of Apprehension."

INTERPRETATION

This first chapter provides ample material for testing the most persistent of interpretative theories (M/L Introduction). Here are myths predominantly about nature, which accord with the analysis of Max Müller, although we need not, like Müller, argue that all subsequent mythological stories must be interpreted as allegories of cosmological and natural phenomena.

Feminist concerns are deeply nourished: mother Earth is the first and most prominent deity, and the feminine will always remain aggressively assertive, if not always dominant, in Greco-Roman mythology; but it is encroached upon by masculine conceptions of the divine, as patriarchy in both society and religion gains supremacy over matriarchy.

Most apparent is the constant interweaving of structuralist and psychological motifs. The dualities (binary opposites) of Lévi-Strauss are everywhere: chaos/order, male/female, sky/earth, youth/age, and beauty/ugliness. Freudian sexuality is blatantly manifest in the castration of Uranus, and the subconscious motivations of the psyche reveal themselves in the recurring pattern of the victory of the ambitious son in his battle for power against his ruthless father. The Jungian archetype of the holy marriage that is enacted three times (by Uranus and Gaia, Cronus and Rhea, and finally Zeus and Hera) is equally fundamental and universal. And the characters in these conflicts in the beginning of things are themselves archetypes: earth mother and queen, sky father and king, vying for control and settling for an uneasy and sometimes bitter reconciliation between the sexes.

Above all, these stories are etiological, beautiful and powerful mythical explanations of the origins and nature of the universe and the devastating physical and emotional force of Love.

Representations in Art

Creation Myths. Creation myths are not shown in Greek art. In later Western art, even when it has been most clearly influenced by classical myths and models, biblical stories are likely to be the artists' sources—for example, in Michelangelo's frescoes of the Creation in the vault of the Sistine Chapel (1506–1512). Similarly, the preeminent musical representation of the Creation, Haydn's oratorio, <u>The Creation</u> (<u>Die Schöpfung</u>, 1798), was set to words based on Milton's <u>Paradise Lost</u>. Nevertheless, the "Representation of Chaos," with which the work begins, is profound and moving, and it shares in the spirit of the Greek creation myth, whose purpose is to show how order emerged from Chaos (i.e., the void). The English painter G. F. Watts in 1896 painted "Chaos," part of a design for his projected history of man, called <u>The House of Life</u>, and he painted several other works about the creation of the universe.

The Birth of Aphrodite. The birth of Aphrodite has been portrayed in all ages. Eros was shown receiving her on the base of the throne of Zeus at Olympia (ca. 450 B.C., known only from literary descriptions). On the altar known as "The Ludovisi Throne" (ca. 460 B.C., whose marble reliefs are in Rome and Boston), Aphrodite is shown rising from the sea, attended by two women on shore. This relief (now in Rome) is the most beautiful of all ancient representations of the scene and it is the canonical version from which many later artists have derived their inspiration. Of later versions by far the most famous is that of Sandro Botticelli (1486, in Florence), which shows Aphrodite standing on a shell being propelled toward the shore by gentle breezes. There female attendants wait to clothe her. Whatever the allegorical meaning of the painting, its classical inspiration is undeniable. A second very beautiful representation is the oil-sketch by Peter Paul Rubens (1636, now in Brussels), which shows Aphrodite as a young woman wringing out her hair on the shore after emerging from the sea. This sketch was prepared for the decorations of the Torre della Parada near Madrid illustrating (for the most part) Ovid's Metamorphoses.

The Children of Uranus and Gaia. The children of the sacred marriage of Uranus and Gaia are frequently shown in art. Depictions of the Titans Hyperion and Prometheus will be mentioned below. In the nineteenth century the Titans were the subject of several paintings: notable are The Titan's Goblet by Thomas Cole (1833, in New York) and the designs by G. F. Watts for his House of Life series (1882, one in Liverpool, and another in London), and other studies of various dates (now at Compton in Surrey). The Cyclopes are shown in scenes of the forge of Hephaestus, usually as muscular blacksmiths. A memorable example is The Forge of Vulcan (1630, now in Madrid) by Diego Velázquez. The Hecatonchires are shown as part of the Titanomachy (the battle of Zeus against the Titans), possibly the subject of the west pediment of the temple of Artemis on Corfu (ca. 580 B.C.). A fine representation is an oil-sketch by Rubens (1636, now in Brussels) of The Fall of the Titans.

Hyperion. Hyperion has some importance in literature, and many artistic representations of the sun could as well be depicting him as Helius or Apollo. John Keats wrote two epic fragments (1818–1819), Hyperion and The Fall of Hyperion, which are allegories (possibly about poetry and poetic inspiration) that take as their starting point the fall of the Titans. The love of Selene (the moon, later equated with Artemis and Diana), daughter of Hyperion, for Endymion is the subject of a beautiful painting by Poussin (ca. 1630, now in Detroit). Quite different is the striking small painting by G. F. Watts (1873, in a private collection) on the same theme. The horses drawing the chariot of the sun rise from, and those drawing the chariot of the moon sink into, the sea on the east pediment of the Parthenon at Athens (ca. 440 B.C.), thus setting the birth of Athena in cosmic time. The fall of the son of Helius, Phaëthon, has been popular with artists at all times: representative are the oil-sketch by Rubens (1636, now in Brussels) and a series of paintings by Odilon Redon (1896–1910). Eos (the dawn), also the daughter of Hyperion, is shown in Greek vase paintings watching her son, Memnon, fighting Achilles at Troy, or mourning over his corpse (best known is a vase by Douris, ca. 490 B.C., now in Paris). The myth of Cephalus and Aurora (Eos) was especially popular with artists in the seventeenth century, for example, Poussin (ca. 1625, now in London) and Claude Lorrain (1645, also in London). Aurora (Eos) is also the subject of a watercolor and gold paper collage on silk (ca. 1820, now in Williamsburg) by an unknown New England artist.

Uranus and Cronus. This subject has been painted by few artists (e.g., Giorgio Vasari in Florence, 1556), and the myth has been less popular than that of Cronus devouring his children. Saturn (i.e., Cronus) Devouring [One of] His Sons has been most memorably painted by Rubens (1636, in

Madrid) and Goya (1821, also in Madrid). Rhea offering the stone in place of the infant Zeus is shown on a Greek red-figure vase (ca. 450 B.C., now in Paris).

The Nurture of Jupiter. Of many post-classical representations of the childhood of Zeus on Crete, an exceptionally beautiful one is The Nurture of Jupiter by Poussin (ca. 1635, now in Dulwich).

CHAPTER 2

Zeus' Rise to Power: The Creation of Mortals

THE TITANOMACHY: ZEUS DEFEATS HIS FATHER CRONUS

This epic battle was waged for ten years between Zeus and the Olympians and Cronus and the Titans. Cronus fought from Mt. Orthys; his allies were the Titans except for Themis and her son PROMETHEUS [pro-me'the-us]. Prometheus' brother ATLAS [at'las] sided with Cronus.

Zeus fought from Mt. Olympus, and his allies, in addition to Themis and Prometheus, were his brothers and sisters, who had been swallowed by Cronus but later regurgitated, namely: Hestia, Demeter, Hera, Hades, and Poseidon. Also on his side were the Hecatonchires and the Cyclopes.

Zeus was victorious and the Titans were imprisoned in Tartarus, guarded by the Hecatonchires; and Atlas was punished with the task of holding up the sky.

THE GIGANTOMACHY: ZEUS DEFEATS THE GIANTS AND TYPHOEUS

Giants, called GEGENEIS [je-je'nays], since they were "born from the Earth," challenged Zeus and the new order of the gods. They were defeated in a fierce battle and were imprisoned under the earth. Volcanoes, when they erupt, reveal the presence of the giants below.

TYPHOEUS [ti-fe'us], also called TYPHAON [ti-fa'on] or TYPHON [ti'fon] was a ferocious dragon-god, whom earth produced to do battle with Zeus, either separately, or alongside the Giants in the great Gigantomachy. Zeus' triumph singles him out as an archetypal dragon-slayer.

- The giants, OTUS [o'tus] or OTOS and EPHIALTES [ef-i-al'tez], in a separate attack, failed in their attempt to storm heaven by piling Olympus, Ossa, and Pelion one upon the other.

- The Titanomachy and the Gigantomachy are often confused in literature and art, and details vary considerably.

THE FOUR OR FIVE AGES

There are several conflicting versions of the creation of mortals. According to the myth of the ages of humankind, men and women are the creation of the gods or Zeus himself. The following is a summary of Hesiod's account. Ovid describes only four ages, omitting the Age of Heroes. This tale of human degeneration mingles fact and fancy in an astonishing manner, for ages of bronze and of iron are historically very real indeed.

The Age of Gold. In the time when Cronus (Saturn) was king in heaven, the Olympian gods made a golden race of mortals, who lived as though in a paradise, without toil, trouble, or cares. All good things were theirs in abundance and the fertile earth brought forth fruit of its own accord. They lived in peace and harmony, never grew old, and died as though overcome by sleep. The earth covered over this race, but they still exist as holy spirits who wander over the earth.

The Age of Silver. The Olympian gods made a second race of silver, far worse than the one of gold. Their childhood lasted a hundred years and when they grew up their lives were short and distressful. For they were arrogant against one another and refused to worship the gods or offer them sacrifice. Zeus in his anger at their senselessness hid them under the earth, where they still dwell.

The Age of Bronze. Zeus made a third race of mortals, a terrible and mighty one of bronze. Their implements and weapons were of bronze and they relentlessly pursued the painful and violent deeds of war. They destroyed themselves by their own hands and went down to the realm of Hades without leaving a name.

The Age of Heroes. Zeus made still another race, also valiant in war but more just and more civilized. This was the race of the heroes, also called demigods, who were involved in the legendary events of Greek saga. They fought, for example, at Thebes and in the Trojan war. When they died, Zeus sent some of these heroes to inhabit the Islands of the Blessed, a paradise at the far ends of the earth, ruled over by Cronus (Saturn), who had been deposed and freed by Zeus.

The Age of Iron. Zeus made still another race, that of iron, troubled by toil and misery, although good is intermingled with their evils. It is in this age that the poet Hesiod lived, and he exclaims in woe: "Would that I were not a man of the fifth generation but had either died before or had been born later." He predicts further moral and physical disintegration and annihilation through war until Zeus will finally destroy human beings when it comes to pass that they are born with grey hair on their temples. More and more will this become an age of wickedness, strife, and disrespect for the gods, until Shame itself and righteous Retribution will abandon mortals to their evil folly and doom.

PROMETHEUS OUR CREATOR

Dominant in the tradition about creation is the myth that Prometheus (not Zeus) was the creator of human beings from clay and Athena breathed into them the divine spirit. In the version of Hesiod, although his account is far from logical and clear, it seems that Prometheus fashioned only mankind. Womenkind was created later, through the agency of Zeus, in the person of Pandora.

PROMETHEUS AGAINST ZEUS

Although Prometheus had fought on the side of Zeus in his war against Cronus, the two mighty gods soon came into conflict once Zeus had assumed supreme power.

The Nature of Sacrifice. Their antagonism began when Prometheus dared to match wits with Zeus. There was a quarrel between mortals and the gods, apparently about how the parts of the sacrificial animals should be apportioned. Prometheus divided up a great ox, and for his creatures, us mortals, he wrapped the flesh and the rich and fatty innards in the ox's paunch. For the gods, however, he deviously and artfully wrapped up the bones of the ox in its enticing, rich white fat. He asked Zeus to take his choice between the two portions, and Zeus, fully aware of Prometheus' deception, chose the bones attractively wrapped in fat. Thus it was that when the Greeks made sacrifice to the gods, they enjoyed feasting upon the best edible portions of the animals, while only the white bones that remained were burned for the gods.

The Theft of Fire. Zeus was enraged at Prometheus' attempt to deceive him and wreaked his vengeance upon mortals, the creatures of Prometheus. He took away from them fire, essential to their livelihood and progress. Prometheus, defiantly our champion, once again tricked Zeus (who this time was presumably at first unaware?) by stealing in a hollow fennel stalk fire from heaven and restoring it to earth. Zeus was stung to the depths of his heart by Prometheus' outrage and "contrived an evil thing for mortals in recompense for the fire," namely, the woman Pandora.

The Punishment of Prometheus. A further defiance of Prometheus was his refusal to reveal to Zeus a crucial secret that he knew and Zeus did not. If Zeus mated with the sea-goddess Thetis, she would bear a son who would overthrow his father. Thus Zeus faced the terrible risk of losing his power as supreme god, like Cronus and Uranus before him. The outcome of Zeus' anger against Prometheus for his rebellious championship of mortals and his obstinate refusal to warn Zeus about Thetis was a dire punishment. Zeus had the wily and devious Prometheus bound in inescapable bonds to a crag of the remote Caucasus mountains in Scythia, with a shaft driven through his middle. And he sent an eagle to eat his immortal liver each day, and what the eagle ate would be restored again each night. Generations later, however, Zeus worked out a reconciliation with Prometheus and sent his son Heracles to kill the eagle with an arrow and release Prometheus. Zeus avoided mating with Thetis, who married a mortal, Peleus, and bore a son, Achilles, to become mightier than his father.

PANDORA

The woman that Zeus sent as a beautiful and treacherous evil to mortals in punishment for their possession of Prometheus' stolen fire was named PANDORA [pan-dor'a] ("all gifts"). He had Hephaestus fashion her out of earth and water in the image of a modest maiden, beautiful as a goddess. Athena clothed her in silvery garments and her face was covered with a wondrously embroidered veil. She placed on her head lovely garlands of flowers and a golden crown, beautifully made and intricately decorated by Hephaestus; and she taught her weaving. Aphrodite bestowed upon her the grace of sexual allurement and desire and their pain. Hermes contrived in her breast wheedling words and lies and the nature of a thief and a bitch. All at the will of Zeus.

Zeus sent this snare to the brother of Prometheus, named EPIMETHEUS [ep-i-me'the-us], who received the gift even though his brother had warned him not to accept anything sent from Zeus. The name Prometheus means forethought, but Epimetheus means afterthought.

Pandora's Jar. Zeus sent with Pandora a jar, urn, or box, which contained evils of all sorts, and as well hope. She herself removed the cover and released the miseries within to plague human beings, who previously had led carefree and happy lives: hard work, painful diseases, and thousands of sorrows. Through the will of Zeus, hope alone remained within the jar, because, without it, life would be hopeless, unbearable in the face of all the horrible woes unleashed for poor mortals. In Hesiod, Pandora is not motivated to open the jar by a so-called feminine curiosity, whatever later versions may imply.

Pandora, the First Woman? The most obvious interpretation of Hesiod is that Pandora, for the Greeks (like Eve in the Bible), was the first woman. Thus the world previously was populated only by men—an extremely difficult concept. Yet Hesiod's account is riddled with contradictions and difficulties because various stories have been awkwardly but poetically conflated. Embedded in the tradition (discernable from a careful reading of the <u>Theogony</u> and <u>Works and Days</u>) was the belief that both men and women were created at the same time and that Pandora was sent by Zeus primarily to release among these happy men and women (whether their creator was Zeus or Prometheus) evils which they had never known before; and so women were not originally molded in the archetypal image of Pandora but, after her dispensation of evils, at least some of them, if not all, partook of her characteristics and became her descendants. After Pandora a golden age, a garden of Eden (however paradise is to be named), was no more, and women became evil, but also so did men, as is implied in the Greek tale of the various ages, where neither god nor a woman is blamed for our fall.

AESCHYLUS' PROMETHEUS BOUND

In addition to Hesiod, Aeschylus' play <u>Prometheus Bound</u> is fundamental for an understanding of the archetypal Prometheus. Aeschylus powerfully establishes Prometheus as our suffering champion who has advanced human beings, through his gift of fire, from savagery to civilization. Furthermore, he gave us the hope denied to us by Zeus, which, however blind, permits us to persevere and triumph over the terrible vicissitudes of life. Prometheus is grandly portrayed as the archetypal trickster and culture-god, the originator of all inventions and progress in the arts and the sciences. At the end of the play, Prometheus is still defiant, chained to his rock, and still refusing to reveal the secret of the marriage of Thetis. The conflict between the suffering hero and the tyrannical god was resolved in the lost plays of Aeschylus' <u>Prometheus</u> trilogy (i.e., group of three connected plays). In that resolution, Aeschylus presumably depicted Zeus as a god of wisdom who, through the suffering of Prometheus, established himself in the end as a triumphant, almighty god secure in his supreme power, brought about through his divine plan for reconciliation.

Io. This divine plan of Zeus for reconciliation with a defeated Prometheus entailed the suffering of IO [i'o], a priestess of Hera who was loved by Zeus. Hera found out and turned Io into a white cow. She appointed a guard to watch over Io, a very good one indeed, since he had many eyes (perhaps as many as one hundred), and his name was ARGUS [ar'gus] or ARGOS PANOPTES [pan-op'tez] ("all seeing"). Zeus rescued Io by sending Hermes to lull Argus to sleep and cut off his head. Henceforth Hermes was given the title ARGEIPHONTES [ar-ge-i-fon'tez] ("slayer of Argus"). Hera set Argus' eyes in the tail of a peacock, her favorite bird, and continued her jealous persecution of Io by sending a gadfly to drive her mad. In a frenzy, Io in her wanderings over the world encountered Prometheus. In Aeschylus, these two "victims" of Zeus commiserate with one another. We learn, however, that Io will find peace in Egypt where she will be restored to her human form and bear a son, EPAPHUS [ep'a-fus] or EPAPHOS, a name which means he of the touch. Io had become pregnant, not through sexual rape, but by the mere touch of the hand of god, and among the descendants of Epaphus would be mighty Heracles to bring about the release of Prometheus. The fulfillment of the will of Zeus was in the end accomplished.

THE FLOOD

Lycaon and the Wickedness of Mortals. In the age of iron, Zeus took the form of a man to find out whether reports of the great wickedness of mortals were true. He visited the home of LYCAON [li-ka'on] or LYKAON and announced that a god was present, but Lycaon, an evil tyrant, only scoffed and planned to kill Zeus during the night to prove that he was not a god. Lycaon even went so far as to slaughter a man and offer human flesh as a meal for Zeus, who in anger brought the house down in flames. Lycaon fled but was turned into a howling, bloodthirsty wolf, a kind of were-wolf in fact, since in this transformation he still manifested his human, evil looks and nature. Disgusted with the wickedness that he found everywhere he roamed, Zeus decided that the human race must be destroyed by a great flood.

Deucalion and Pyrrha. Zeus allowed only two pious mortals to be saved, DEUCALION [du-ka'li-on] or DEUKALION (the Greek Noah), the son of Prometheus, and his wife PYRRHA [pir'ra], the daughter of Epimetheus. When the flood subsided they found themselves in their little boat stranded on Mt. Parnassus. They were dismayed to discover that they were the only survivers and consulted the oracle of Themis about what they should do. The goddess ordered them to toss the bones of their great mother behind their backs. Deucalion understood that the stones in the body of earth are her bones. And so the stones that Deucalion tossed behind his back were miraculously transformed into men, while those cast by Pyrrha became women. In this way the world was repopulated.

Hellen and the Hellenes. Deucalion and Pyrrha had a son named HELLEN [hel'len]. The ancient Greeks called themselves HELLENES [hel'len-ez] and their country HELLAS [hel'las] and so Hellen was their eponymous ancestor.

COMPACT DISCS

14 and **222.** Beethoven, Ludwig van, <u>The Creatures of Prometheus</u>. Music for a ballet about the creation of mankind by Prometheus, ending with his apotheosis.
12. Barber, Samuel, <u>Incidental Music for a Scene from Shelley</u> (act 2, scene 5 of <u>Prometheus Unbound</u>).
66. Dittersdorf, Carl Ditters von, <u>Symphony in C Major</u>, "The Four Ages of Man."
154 and **222.** Liszt, Franz, <u>Prometheus</u>. Symphonic Poem, depicting a humane and suffering Prometheus, inspired by the play, <u>Prometheus Unbound</u>, by Johann Gottfried Herder.
178. Mondonville, Jean-Joseph Cassanéa de, <u>Titon et L'Aurore</u>. Opera about Tithonus and Aurora, with a prologue about Prometheus and the creation of mortals.
179. Monk, Meredith, <u>Atlas</u>. Multimedia, very avant-garde opera, whose title is based on the meaning of Atlas as map and then travel and therefore peripheral to the legend of Atlas. It relates the travels of a female explorer, Alexandra Daniels, and her companions, which become a metaphor for the spiritual quest of the soul.
197 and **222.** Nono, Luigi, <u>Prometeo</u>, Opera and Suite, portraying Prometheus as perpetual wanderer and "the force of non-violence," which includes vocal settings of texts by Walter Benjamin and Hölderlin.
251. Schubert, Franz, "Der Atlas" and "Prometheus." Songs; the text for "Prometheus" is by Goethe.
255 and **222.** Scriabin, Alexander, <u>Prométhée, Le Poème du feu</u>. Symphonic portrayal of Prometheus as the bringer of fire and light.
288. Wakeman, Rick, and Ramon Remedios, <u>A Suite of Gods</u>. New Age songs for tenor, keyboards, and percussion, which include "The Flood."
295. Xenakis, Iannis, <u>Phlegra</u>, for chamber orchestra. Phlegra is a battleground between the Titans and the new Olympian gods.

VIDEOS

<u>Seize the Fire: Prometheus Bound</u>. Modern version of Aeschylus by Tom Paulin. Insight Media. DP605.

INTERPRETATION

Archetypal themes once again abound and, embedded in many of them, a mythological etiology, causes and explanations for such eternal mysteries as: What is the nature of god or the gods? Where did we come from? Do we have a dual nature, an earthly body and a divine spirit? What is the source of and reason for evil? Who invented the wheel? Here are some important motifs.

- Prometheus, the trickster.
- Prometheus, the culture hero, inventor of language, mathematics, the arts, and just about everything.
- Promethean fire, the symbol of defiant progress.
- The nature of sacrifice.
- The creation of mortals with a body and a soul.
- Rivalry of gods, with human beings as their pawns.
- The loss of paradise and degeneration.
- Evolution from savagery to civilization.
- The first woman, bringer of evil.
- The nature of hope.
- The wickedness of mortals and the flood.

The universality of these themes is confirmed by the many parallels, particularly in the mythologies of the Near East (M/L 71 and 75). A dominant motif common to them all is that of succession to power. The flood archetype is particularly fascinating for the evidence of its recurrence *worldwide*, studied in a collection of essays, <u>The Flood</u>, by Alan Dundes (Berkeley: University of California Press, 1988).

We may listen to the grandeur of the creative spirit of Prometheus, expressed by Beethoven in his music (especially the overture) for the ballet <u>The Creatures of Prometheus</u>, and by Schubert in his setting of the fine poem by Goethe (1749–1832) <u>Prometheus</u>, expressing not only the defiance of the Titan but also the independence of mortals from the Olympian gods (M/L 574). Other symphonic music listed above is worth hearing, particularly that of Lizst. The extant <u>Prometheus Bound</u> by Aeschylus (of uncertain date between 472 and 457 B.C.) presents a Prometheus defiant against the tyranny of Zeus; but in the lost plays of Aeschylus' <u>Prometheus</u> trilogy Zeus must have been the victor. This same defiant Prometheus is the hero of P. B. Shelley's dramatic poem <u>Prometheus Unbound</u> (1820), in which Prometheus, the champion of humanity, is freed and Jupiter (Zeus) is overthrown! The great American composer Samuel Barber has written music for Shelley's poem.

Representations in Art

The Battle between the Olympian Gods and the Giants. This was an important theme in Greek art. It was shown on the north frieze of the Siphnian Treasury at Delphi (ca. 525 B.C.) and appears in vase paintings in Attica twenty-five years earlier. The origin of the giants and the earlier Hecatonchires can be readily explained as volcanic phenomena, consistent with the myths of the imprisoning of Enceladus and Typhoeus under Mt. Etna and the showers of rocks hurled by the Hecatonchires. But allegorical interpretations of the battle and the victory of the Olympians chiefly account for the popularity of the myth in Greek art, above all for the purpose of expressing Greek self-awareness. Most commonly the Gigantomachy signifies the victory of civilization over disorder, especially the triumph of Greek over barbarian culture. (It shares this allegory with other battle-myths, in particular those of Centaurs and Lapiths and of Greeks and Amazons.) It was shown in the sculptures of the west pediment of the temple of Apollo at Delphi (ca. 520 B.C.), one of the most important of Greek religious centers: the pediment is described by Euripides in his tragedy Ion (412 B.C.). After the Greek victories in the Persian wars (480–479 B.C.) the Gigantomachy was an impor-tant political and cultural allegory, especially at Athens. It was shown on the eastern metopes of the Parthenon (ca. 440) and was painted on the inside of the shield of Pheidias' statue of Athena Parthenos. It was the subject of the great frieze of the altar of Zeus at Pergamum (mid–second cen-tury B.C., now in Berlin): the victory over the giants was won with the aid of Heracles, the father of the mythical founder of the royal house of Pergamum, Telephus. This is an early example of the myth being used for the political purpose of glorifying a ruler and his family, rather than a people or a city-state. The Gigantomachy continued to be popular into Roman times—for example, on a sar-cophagus from the mid-second century A.D. in the Vatican—perhaps as an allegory of the victory of the soul over death. There are many representations in later art, where inevitably the theme of the fall of the Titans becomes confused with the Christian theme of the fall of Satan and his angels and with representations of the damned in scenes of the Last Judgment.

Typhoeus. Other monstrous opponents of the Olympians include Typhoeus, from whom, says Hesiod, "arise the winds that blow the mighty rains." His origin, then, is in the violent storms of nature, but he, too, comes to represent violence and disorder overcome by reason and order. He is, like the giants, represented as a human upper half joined to a serpentine lower half, for example, on shield-bands and vases in the sixth century B.C. Like many polymorphous monsters in Greek mythology, he has developed from eastern imaginary monsters, found in the arts of the early king-doms of Asia Minor and in the "orientalizing" vase paintings of seventh and sixth century Greek art.

The Four or Five Ages. The myth of the ages of humankind has attracted poets from Dante (1314) to W. H. Auden (1964), and artists from Lucas Cranach (1530) to Henri Matisse (1906), whose paint-ing The Joy of Life evokes the innocence of a Golden Age.

The Creation of Mortals. Of the several myths of the creation of mortals, the creation by Prometheus and by Deucalion and Pyrrha are especially popular. The fine poem by Goethe (1749–1832), set to music by Schubert, has been mentioned above. Deucalion and Pyrrha's act of cre-ation has attracted artists as different as Hendrik Goltzius (1589), Peter Paul Rubens (1636), and Pablo Picasso (1930). There is little in the early stages of Greek myth that emulates the first creation myth in the biblical Genesis, although later Greek authors (for example, Plato) composed their own allegories of creation.

Prometheus. The most complex of the Titans is Prometheus. The many facets of his character (identified above) have made him one of the most popular symbols in art, poetry, and music. His punishment is shown on Greek vases in the early sixth century B.C., most notably on a vase from Sparta (ca. 560) now in the Vatican. The rescue by Heracles is also frequently portrayed on archaic Greek vases (seventh century through the end of the sixth century) and it was the subject of a fifth-century painting in the temple of Zeus at Olympia, where Heracles had an important role in myth, cult, and artistic representations. The rescue was portrayed in a sculptural group attached to a wall in the sanctuary of Athena at Pergamum from the second century B.C. Among the countless works of art inspired by Prometheus, three very different versions are representative of their variety: first, Prometheus Bound, by Peter Paul Rubens and Franz Snyders (1611, now in Philadelphia), which focuses on the cruelty of the eagle's tearing at Prometheus. Second, the abstract head Prometheus by Constantin Brancusi (1911, marble version in Philadelphia, bronze in Washington). Third, the gilded bronze figure of Prometheus with the torch by Paul Manship (1934) in the Rockefeller Center complex in New York.

Io. In the Prometheus Bound of Aeschylus, Io appears as another victim of Zeus. The best-known version of her legend was told by Ovid in the first book of the Metamorphoses, from which many artistic works have taken their inspiration. The slaying of Argus by Hermes is the commonest theme, for example, in the oil-sketch by Peter Paul Rubens (1636, now in Brussels; the final version is in Madrid). Impressive also is Juno Discovering Jupiter with Io, by Pieter Lastman (1618, now in London). Unique are the large panel paintings by Bartolomeo di Giovanni (1488, now in Baltimore), in which the whole legend is shown sequentially, with the divine figures in Renaissance dress and Io's human form emerging from the body of the cow in the final transformation scene.

Pandora. Hesiod tells the myth of Prometheus in both of his major poems, the Theogony and the Works and Days, and as well that of the woman Pandora, sent by Zeus with her jar of evils to be an affliction for mortals because of Prometheus' sins. Pandora has been a rich source of inspiration for artists. Her birth was shown on the base of Pheidias' statue of Athena Parthenos in the Parthenon. In an Athenian vase from about ten years earlier (ca. 450 B.C.), Pandora is shown rising from the ground. Of the very large number of paintings of her legend, that by Odilon Redon (1910, now in New York) is exceptional in its evocation of dreams and emotions which at that very time were being explored by Sigmund Freud. Like the myth of Eve, the myth of Pandora expresses fears and prejudices that are expressed as myths in many cultures.

The Flood. Representations of the Flood in later art are dominated by non-classical sources, above all, the biblical narrative of Genesis. The classical figures of Deucalion and Pyrrha appear regularly in illustrations of Ovid, who tells their tale in the first book of the Metamorphoses. Representative examples are the engravings by Hendrik Goltzius (1589, now in London); the oil-sketch by Rubens (1636, now in Madrid); the etching by Picasso for the edition of the Metamorphoses published at Lausanne in 1951. The myths of Lycaon, the flood, and Deucalion and Pyrrha are shown compendiously in the full-page engraving that illustrates George Sandys's translation of the Metamorphoses, published at Oxford in 1632.

CHAPTER 3

The Twelve Olympians: Zeus, Hera, and Their Children

THE OLYMPIAN DEITIES

APHRODITE [af-ro-di′te] (VENUS)
APOLLO [a-pol′lo]
ARES [ar′es] (MARS)
ARTEMIS [ar′te-mis] (DIANA)
ATHENA [a-the′na] or ATHENE (MINERVA)
DEMETER [de-me′ter] (CERES)
DIONYSUS [Di-o-ni′sus] or DIONYSOS (BACCHUS)
HADES [ha′dez] (PLUTO)
HEPHAESTUS [he-fes′tus] or HEPHAISTOS (VULCAN)
HERA [he′ra] (JUNO)
HERMES [her′mez] (MERCURY)
HESTIA [hes′ti-a] (VESTA)
POSEIDON [po-si′don] (NEPTUNE)
ZEUS [zoos] (JUPITER)

- The fourteen major deities are listed above, alphabetically.
- Zeus is the supreme god and his wife is Hera; they are king and queen, father and mother of gods and mortals.
- Zeus, Poseidon, and Hades are the trinity who control the important spheres of power: Zeus, god of the sky, Poseidon, god of the sea, and Hades, god of the Underworld.
- Apollo has the same name for both the Greeks and the Romans.
- The fourteen deities are reduced to a canon of twelve Olympians: Hestia is removed from the list and so is Hades, whose home is not Mt. Olympus but the Underworld.

HESTIA, GODDESS OF THE HEARTH AND ITS FIRE

HESTIA [hes′ti-a] ("hearth") was the august and revered goddess of the hearth and its fire, which was considered sacred and a symbol of both the home and community. She remained a virgin and was a goddess of chastity, just like Athena and Artemis. For the Romans she was the goddess VESTA and vestal virgins attended to her worship.

ZEUS AND HERA

ZEUS [zoos], "bright" (JUPITER), originally a god of the sky, became the supreme god with final authority. He appears as a bearded, regal figure with a scepter and a bolt of lightning and thunder in his hand. He often carries his shield, the aegis, which is also an attribute of his favorite daughter, Athena. He married his sister HERA [he′ra] (JUNO), originally an earth mother goddess. As the wife and consort of Zeus, she retains much of her inherent dominance to become a difficult partner.

The characterization of Zeus is most complex. On the one hand, he mirrors the harassed, philandering husband, who has countless affairs and is upbraided and intimidated by a self-righteous, nagging wife. On the other, he emerges as the almighty god of morality and religion, a just god who rewards the good and punishes the wicked.

THE SANCTUARY OF ZEUS AT OLYMPIA

The most important sanctuary of Zeus was at Olympia beside the river Alpheus in the territory of the city of Elis in the northwestern Peloponnese. Here the Olympic games originated in 776 B.C., said to have been founded by Zeus' son, Heracles. Among its many buildings was an imposing temple of Hera, but the temple of Zeus was the most magnificent, adorned with the following sculpture:

- West pediment—the battle of the Greeks and the centaurs at the wedding of the Lapith king Perithoüs (a son of Zeus). Particularly impressive is the central figure of Apollo (another son of Zeus) with arm outstretched, imposing order on the scene of violence and chaos (see Chapter 23).

- East pediment—the fateful chariot race between Pelops and Hippodamia and her father Oenomaüs; the central figure of Zeus assured Pelops' victory in the coming race and the winning of Hippodamia as his wife (see Chapter 16).

- Doric frieze—metopes (relief sculpture) depicting the twelve labors of Heracles.

- The cult statue of Zeus in the naos (or cella), made by the Athenian sculptor Pheidias. It was huge, with its surfaces inlaid in gold and ivory. This regal Zeus was seated on a throne that was elaborately decorated with various mythological motifs.

THE SANCTUARY OF ZEUS AT DODONA

Dodona in northern Greece was another significant sanctuary of Zeus. Here, however, the oracle of Zeus was the most important element. Private individuals and political representatives came to Dodona with questions of every sort. The god answered by means of various omens (such as the rustling of the leaves of his sacred oaks) and eventually through a priestess (in a manner similar to that at the more famous sanctuary of Apollo at Delphi).

CHILDREN OF ZEUS AND HERA: EILEITHYIA, HEBE, HEPHAESTUS, AND ARES

EILEITHYIA [i-li-thi′ya or i-li′thia] was a goddess of childbirth, like her mother, Hera, and Artemis.

HEBE [he′be], "youthful bloom," was a cupbearer of the gods. She became the wife of Heracles.

HEPHAESTUS [he-fes′tus] or HEPHAISTOS (VULCAN) was sometimes considered to be the son of Hera alone. He was lame from birth, and Hera, ashamed of his deformity, cast him out of Olympus; we are also told that once, when he interfered in a quarrel between Zeus and Hera on behalf of his mother, Zeus hurled him down from Olympus and he landed on the island of Lemnos, which became his cult-place. In either case, he was restored to Olympus. Hephaestus was above all a divine artisan and smith, a god of the forge and its fire, whose workshop was said to be in various places, including Olympus. Assisted by the three Cyclopes, he could create marvelous masterpieces of every sort, among them the shield of Achilles.

ARES [ar'es] (Mars) was the virile and brutal god of war, associated with the area of Thrace.

HEPHAESTUS, APHRODITE, AND ARES

The wife of Hephaestus was APHRODITE [af-ro-di'te] (Venus); theirs was an archetypal union between the lame intellectual and the sensuous beauty. Aphrodite turned to the handsome and whole Ares for sexual gratification (playing out yet another archetype); but military Ares and promiscuous Aphrodite were outwitted by the ingenious and moral Hephaestus, who fashioned unbreakable chains that were fine as a spider's web and hung them as a trap on the bedposts above his bed. Thus he ensnared the unwitting lovers in the midst of their illicit lovemaking and summoned the gods down from Olympus to witness the ludicrous scene. Ares and Aphrodite were released from the chains only when it was agreed that Ares should pay an adulterer's fine.

For the Romans the relationship between Vulcan (Ares) and Aphrodite (Venus) was of serious political import. Their union represented allegorically the conquest of war by love with Roman peace (pax Romana) the happy and noble result.

GANYMEDE

Zeus in the form of an eagle or a whirlwind carried off the handsome Trojan GANYMEDE [gan'i-meed] to be a cupbearer to the gods like Hebe. The <u>Homeric Hymn to Aphrodite</u> explains:

> *Zeus in his wisdom seized and carried off fair-haired Ganymede because of his beauty, so that he might be in the company of the gods and pour wine for them in the house of Zeus, a wonder to behold, esteemed by all the immortals, as he draws red nectar from a golden bowl.*

Zeus took pity on Ganymede's father, who mourned for his son who had mysteriously disappeared, and gave him the gift of wondrous horses and sent Hermes to explain how Ganymede would never grow old but would be immortal just like the gods. And the father rejoiced.

The innocence of this depiction implies the joyous calling of a young man chosen by god for a special immortality. The sensual appreciation of beauty, on the other hand, encourages another intrepretation: the passionate, homosexual love of the supreme god Zeus for the young and handsome Ganymede.

THE NINE MUSES, DAUGHTERS OF ZEUS AND MEMORY

Zeus mated with MNEMOSYNE (ne-mos'i-ne), "memory," to produce the nine MUSES [muzez] ("reminders"), patron goddesses of the arts; thus allegorically god and memory provide creative inspiration. They live in Pieria in northern Thessaly (and are called the PIERIDES, pi-er'i-dez) or near the fountain Hippocrene on Mt. Helicon in Boeotia. Their spheres are sometimes specifically assigned:

CALLIOPE (ka-li'o-pe), epic poetry
CLIO (kli'o), history, lyre playing
ERATO (er'a-to), love poetry, hymns to the gods, lyre playing
EUTERPE (u-ter'pe), lyric poetry, tragedy, flute playing
MELPOMENE (mel-pom'e-ne), tragedy, lyre playing
POLYHYMNIA (pol-i-him'ni-a), sacred music, dancing

TERPSICHORE (terp-sik'o-re), choral dancing, flute playing
THALIA (tha-li'a), comedy
URANIA (u-ra'ni-a), astronomy

THE THREE FATES

The three Fates, the MOIRAI (moi'ri), the Roman Moerae, were the daughters of Zeus and Themis (or Night and Erebus) and imagined as three old women spinners, who control the thread of life and thus each person's destiny:

CLOTHO (klo'tho), "spinner," spins out the thread of life.
LACHESIS (lak'e-sis), "apportioner," measures the thread.
ATROPOS (at'ro-pos), "inflexible," cuts the thread.

COMPACT DISCS

22. Bliss, Arthur, <u>The Olympians</u>. Libretto by J. B. Priestley. Comic opera with a play within the play, <u>The Comedy of Olympus</u>, involving the amusing antics of Diana, Bacchus, Mars, and Jupiter.
36. Campra, André, <u>Hébé</u>. Cantata for soprano and continuo.
49. Chadwick, George Whitefield, <u>Euterpe: Concert Overture for Orchestra</u>.
123. Holst, Gustav, <u>The Planets</u>. Although Holst explains that his work is inspired by astrology and not mythology, it is difficult not to think of the gods when listening to "Mars, the Bringer of War" and "Mercury, the Winged Messenger."
127. Hovhaness, Alan, <u>String Quartet No. 1, Jupiter</u>. The subtitle "Jupiter" is derived from Mozart's Symphony no. 41, which also includes a four-voiced fugue. Hovhaness's fugue was reworked for orchestra to become *Prelude and Quadruple Fugue*. Many recordings are readily available of Mozart's Jupiter.
174. Leo, Leonardo, <u>L'Olimpiade</u>. Opera to a libretto by Metastasio, like the more famous one by Pergolesi, below.
192 and **193.** <u>Music of Ancient Greece</u>. <u>Hymn to the Muse</u>.
214. Pergolesi, Giovanni Battista, <u>L'Olimpiade</u>. The setting of this opera is the Olympic games and the plot is inspired by Herodotus' tale of Cleisthenes of Sicyon and the suitors of his daughter.
221. Porter, Cole, <u>Out of This World</u>. This delightful musical, loosely based upon the legend of Amphitryon, includes amusing songs for Jupiter and Hera: "I Jupiter, I Rex," and "I Got Beauty" (M/L 606).
231. Rameau, Jean Philippe, <u>Platée</u>. In this operatic comedy, Platée is a reed-nymph who through the trickery of Mercury believes that Jupiter wants to marry her.
250 and **251.** Schubert, Franz, "Dithyrambe" and "Die Götter Griechenlands (songs about the Olympian gods); "Ganymed" (Ganymede's ecstatic hymn, with text by Goethe, extolling his loving union with his beloved god the father); "Der Musensohn" (a song sung by a poet, son of the muses); "Uraniens Flucht," a lengthy song set amidst the festive life of Zeus and the gods and recounting the dramatic return of Urania (a goddess as conceived by the poet Mayhofer).
293. Wolf, Hugo. "Ganymed." Song, like Schubert's, using Goethe's poem.

VIDEOS

<u>Down to Earth</u>. Rita Hayworth stars as the muse Terpsichore, who comes to earth to make a Broadway producer fix a new musical because she is irate that she is portrayed as too modern and sexy. Directed by Alexander Hall. RCA/Columbia Home Video.

<u>In the Paths of the Gods</u>. Films for the Humanities AGU6210. A series of eight videos on the gods: <u>Zeus, King of the Gods</u>; <u>Athene and Aphrodite</u>; <u>Dionysus, The Joy of Life</u>; <u>Demeter, The Miracle of Fertility</u>; <u>Poseidon, Master of the Seas</u>; <u>Artemis, The Forces of Nature</u>; <u>Apollo, Light and Harmony</u>; <u>Ares and Eris</u>. Tapes may be purchased individually at greater expense. The primary asset of this series is the narrator Peter Ustinov.

<u>The Seven Wonders of the Ancient World</u>. Questar Video QV2226. One is the statue of Zeus at Olympia and another, the temple of Artemis at Ephesus, both illustrated and discussed with theatrical flair for a general audience.

INTERPRETATION

The life of Zeus illustrates special motifs that appear again and again in the lives not only of other deities but also in the mortal lives of the heroes of saga, to be sure with infinite variations and amplifications:

- He is the child of extraordinary parents; both of Zeus' parents are gods.
- The circumstances of his birth are unusual or difficult. He must avoid being swallowed by his father.
- He must be brought up in secret and he leads a charmed and idyllic childhood, amidst nature. This motif is that of the "Divine Child."
- Upon reaching manhood, he must come into his own by overcoming challenges and adversaries: his father Cronus and the Titans, the Giants, and Prometheus.
- He must kill the real and symbolic dragon (Typhoeus) to achieve the archetypal status of Dragonslayer.
- In the end, he is the victor and wins a bride, a kingdom, and power. Zeus triumphs to become almighty god, although his exploits and trials are by no means over.

The carrying off of Ganymede by Zeus introduces yet another significant motif, reflecting Greek society in particular and human life in general, the motif of homosexuality. Since the supreme god is created in the image of man, inevitably he must embrace all the passions of man.

The story of Zeus and Ganymede illustrates succinctly the wide variation of interpretation and reinterpretation that these myths are capable of inspiring—a principal reason for their immortality. As seen above, the earliest version of the tale tells a simple story of how wise Zeus singled out beautiful Ganymede to grace Olympus as cupbearer and live there forever, immortal, like a god.

The spirituality and also the sensuality of the myth emerge with sublimity in the poem by Goethe, especially in its musical settings by Schubert and Wolf. The incident is seen from the point of view of a devoted Ganymede. Amidst the glowing sun, beloved spring, and burning love, Ganymede ecstatically cries to the descending clouds to carry him aloft: "In your lap/Upwards/ Embracing, embraced. Upwards to your breast, loving father!"

For a different artist, the homosexuality latent in the myth may offer amoral or non-moral testimony to the fact of a physical relationship, and not a religious calling. Another may tell the story to prove a divine vindication of male relationships. Yet another may vehemently identify the myth as the Rape of Ganymede by Zeus—accusing god of the sin of rape, an idea so inconceivable to the poet and philosopher Xenophanes. Or the tale may become (as in the case of the Roman writer Lucian) a divinely amusing, sophisticated, satiric jest.

There is, of course, no single "correct" interpretation of a great myth. Myth is protean by nature; most gratifying because it forever changes through the personality and genius of each and every artist, in any medium at any time, to provide pleasure and enlightenment in our search to find our own individual enrichment.

Representations in Art

The Twelve Olympians. The twelve Olympians, each with a clearly defined personality, were worshiped individually in particular city-states and sanctuaries—for example, Athena at Athens, Hera at Argos, Apollo at Delphi, and so on. As a group they are described in the Iliad as feasting on Olympus, much in the manner of Mycenaean aristocrats, and debating in assembly under the presidency of Zeus. In Greek art they appear together as guests at the wedding of Peleus and Thetis, shown by the painter Kleitias on the François Vase (ca. 575 B.C., now in Florence), where some ride in chariots and some are on foot, led by Iris, their herald and messenger. The same scene is shown on a slightly earlier black-figure Athenian vase signed by the painter Sophilos. Groups of the Olympians are often shown as onlookers of particular scenes (e.g., the birth of Athena) but, in general, representations of all of them together are comparatively unusual. In 522 B.C. the Altar of the Twelve Gods was dedicated in the Agora at Athens, decorated with reliefs of the Olympians. Exceptional is the assembly of seated Olympians on the east side of the frieze on the Parthenon at Athens (ca. 440 B.C.), where their attendance at the presentation of Athena's peplos honors the city whose citizens are shown on the same frieze. Above this scene were the sculptures of the east pediment, showing the birth of Athena from the head of Zeus, attended by Hera and Hephaestus, while other Olympians are present as spectators. (Nearly all of the surviving pediment sculptures and panels of the frieze are now to be seen as the Elgin Marbles in London.) Athens was exceptional in its claim, expressed in public art, of special closeness to the Olympians. There, and in other Greek city-states (and also at Rome), the Olympians were identified with the vitality of the state and its citizens. As the power, pride, and energy of the city-states declined, so the Olympian gods' role was weakened.

At Rome, where the Olympians (other than Apollo) took the names of Italian gods, they were placed in pairs on couches (lecti) in a ceremony called the lectisternium (first celebrated in 399 B.C., but changed in 217 B.C. to honor the twelve Olympian gods), at which a banquet was offered to them as the priests, on behalf of the state, made solemn supplications. The images of the Olympians were also carried in procession at great public festivals, for example, at the opening of the games in the Circus Maximus. At the foot of the Capitoline Hill at Rome, facing the Forum, was a portico in front of which stood gilded statues of the twelve Olympians (whom Varro calls "the urban gods, six male and six female"). These were called the "Twelve Unanimous Gods" (Divi Consentes; the meaning of the second word is uncertain). A different group of twelve gods was worshiped by Roman farmers, and of this group only six are Olympians.

The Twelve Olympians in Western Art. Representations of the Olympian gods together are frequent in Western art. They are shown most commonly banqueting, reclining at tables among the clouds and served by their cupbearers, Ganymede and Hebe. Usually Heracles is added to their number. Sometimes the feast of the gods is shown for its own sake, especially in ceiling frescoes. More often it is shown as a counterpart to activity on earth, for example, in a painting by Gerard de Lairesse, Hermes Ordering Calypso to Release Odysseus (1669, now in Cleveland). Unique in its satirical wit and beauty is The Feast of the Gods by Giovanni Bellini, with additions by Titian (1514, now in Washington), in which the feast is associated with Ovid's legend of Priapus (see Chapter 7). The feast is often shown in representations of other myths: popular were the Wedding of Peleus and Thetis (as in the François Vase mentioned above), and the Introduction of Psyche to Olympus (see below, Chapter 7), painted in a tapestry-like fresco by Raphael in 1518 for the Villa Farnesina in Rome. More often the Feast (or the Council) of the Gods is used allegorically, most skillfully by Rubens in his series on the life of Marie de' Medici (1622–1625, now in the Louvre at Paris), in the paintings of The Apotheosis of King Henri, and The Council of the Gods (The Government of Marie).

Zeus in Literature and Art. In Homer Zeus presides over a sometimes quarrelsome assembly of Olympians and he himself is liable to human passions. He is the father of innumerable children (and gives luster to families claiming descent from his children), and his conquests are told with wit and brilliant narrative skill in Ovid's Metamorphoses, which is the source for a large number of works of art. Long before, however, his metamorphosis into a bull had been shown in a metope representing the myth of Zeus and Europa at Selinus in Sicily (ca. 540 B.C., now in Palermo). Increasingly he comes to be identified with Justice and Fate: the Athenian poet and statesman Solon (ca. 595 B.C.) focused on the former aspect, and the Roman epic poet Vergil (died 19 B.C.) on the latter. As the gods of the city-state declined in vitality, Zeus survived as the supreme god, as, for example, in the Hymn to Zeus of the Stoic philosopher Cleanthes (ca. 250 B.C.). In the Roman world he was identified with various non-Roman gods—for example, under the title of Jupiter Dolichenus, with the Syrian god Baal. The custom of identifying a Roman god with a foreign god is called interpretatio Romana.

In art he is a mature bearded man, often seated on a throne holding a scepter and a thunderbolt and accompanied by an eagle. He is shown in archaic Greek art in the myth of the Birth of Athena, who springs fully armed from his head (as in a black-figure vase, ca. 550 B.C., now in Boston). This was the subject also of the east pediment of the Parthenon, in which Zeus was the central figure. He was also the central standing figure in the east pediment of his temple at Olympia (ca. 460 B.C.), in a scene showing the preliminaries to the chariot race of Pelops and Oenomaüs. Inside this temple was his seated chryselephantine (i.e., with surfaces made of gold and ivory) statue, the masterpiece of Pheidias (ca. 440 B.C.) and known only from literary descriptions. Zeus held a figure of Nike (Victory) in his right hand and in his left a scepter on which perched the eagle. The throne included representations of Heracles fighting the Amazons, several of the labors of Heracles, and Heracles freeing Prometheus. On the base was carved the birth of Aphrodite. One of the most successful post-classical paintings based on Pheidias' statue is Jupiter and Thetis by J. A. D. Ingres (1811, now in Aix-en-Provence), a vast canvas that shows the god enthroned among the clouds with his scepter and eagle, while the Gigantomachy is shown on the base of the throne. Less happy was the statue of George Washington by Horatio Greenough (completed in 1839 and still in Washington), in which the American hero is shown seated and half-robed in the manner of Pheidias' Zeus.

Hera. Hera in ancient art is most commonly portrayed on a throne near Zeus, as, for example, in the Parthenon frieze at Athens, where she turns toward Zeus holding her veil open in a wifely gesture. In post-classical art she is often painted with Zeus as an allegory of marriage: this use is seen, for example, in Rubens's Medici cycle (1622–1625, mentioned above) in The Meeting of Marie and Henri at Lyons. In many paintings she is shown with her attribute of peacocks, in whose tails were set the eyes of Argus, the guardian of Io. Many artists have represented her anger against Zeus: a dramatic representation is the painting by Pieter Lastman mentioned in Chapter 2, Juno Discovering Jupiter with Io (1618, now in London), and in the Ingres painting of Jupiter and Thetis she looms threateningly on the left of the picture. She has been comparatively little portrayed in art since the early nineteenth century.

Eileithyia and Hebe. Of the children of Zeus and Hera, Eileithyia and Hebe are fairly insignificant in art. Eilieithyia is often shown helping at the birth of Athena, for example, in a black-figure vase (ca. 540 B.C., now in Richmond, Virginia). Hebe's duties as cupbearer to the Olympians are taken over by Ganymede, but she is often shown as the bride of Heracles among the Olympians, for example, in a red-figure vase from southern Italy (ca. 350 B.C., now in Berlin), in which she is the central figure. In the eighteenth century, painters liked to portray their sitters as the goddess of youth: for example, Joshua Reynolds painted Mrs. Pownall as Hebe (1762, privately owned).

Ares. Ares appears with the other Olympians in group representations (e.g., in the Parthenon frieze), but in ancient art usually he is shown as a warrior in battle scenes (for example, Gigantomachies) or as an onlooker of heroic combat. He was far more important at Rome, where he was identified with Mars. In post-classical art the myth of his love for Aphrodite, told in Book 8 of the Odyssey, has been very popular, usually with the Roman names of the gods, Venus and Mars. One example from many is Sandro Botticelli, Mars and Venus (1485, now in London). The myth has frequently been used as an allegory of love overcoming strife. Ares himself appears also in allegories of the horrors of war: a superb example is The Horrors of War by Rubens (1637, now in Florence), where (as Mars) he is shown bursting out of the temple of Janus and away from the arms of Aphrodite (Venus). He is pulled onwards by the Fury Allecto, and underfoot he tramples on the arts of peace.

Hephaestus. Hephaestus is often shown in ancient art assisting Zeus at the birth of Athena, as in the sculptures and vase paintings mentioned above. At Athens he shared his temple, the Hephaesteum (ca. 445 B.C.), with Athena, in which his bronze statue stood beside hers. On one pediment was shown the apotheosis of Heracles, and on the other, the battle of Lapiths and Centaurs. The labors of Heracles and of Theseus were shown on the metopes. Thus Hephaestus, the god of creative fire, was associated with the triumph of civilization over disorder: he shared his temple with the goddess of wisdom and the crafts and with the heroes whose deeds benefited human beings. In post-classical art he is shown in his forge making the thunderbolt for Zeus or the fine net in which to entrap Ares and Aphrodite, as in Velazquez's painting mentioned in Chapter 1. He is frequently painted (as told in Book 18 of the Iliad) making the armor of Achilles at the request of Thetis or its counterpart (from Book 8 of the Aeneid), the armor of Aeneas, at the request of

Aphrodite. François Boucher painted or designed the latter scene repeatedly with exuberant enjoyment of the contrast between the voluptuous goddess and her muscular husband: an example is Venus at the Forge of Vulcan (1757, now in Paris). Finally, an especially popular scene in classical vase-painting was the Return of Hephaestus to Olympus. Here he is usually shown drunkenly riding on a donkey or a mule, accompanied by Dionysus and dancing satyrs: one example is a black-figure vase in New York (ca. 550 B.C.) painted by Lydos, and the scene appears on the François vase (ca. 575 B.C., now in Florence), painted by Kleitias.

The Nine Muses. These daughters of Zeus, as a group or individually (according to the particular genre of art represented) have been shown at all times as allegories for the inspiration of poetry, drama, art, and music. All nine are shown, for example, in a Roman mosaic (4th century A.D.) in Trier. In Raphael's fresco Parnassus, painted in 1510 for the Stanza della Segnatura in the Vatican, they accompany the central figure of Apollo. In the eighteenth century (as with Hebe) sitters were often painted as Muses, for example, Mrs. Siddons as The Tragic Muse by Joshua Reynolds (1784, now in San Marino, California). In the twentieth century the Muses have been repeatedly reinterpreted by the sculptor Constantin Brancusi (e.g., Sleeping Muse, 1910, now in Washington) and by the surrealistic painter Giorgio de Chirico (e.g., The Disquieting Muses, 1918, now in Milan). The Muses still inspire creativity in the arts and literature.

CHAPTER 4

Anthropomorphism and Greek Humanism

THE NATURE OF THE GODS

Anthropomorphism. The Greeks and Romans (like most peoples) conceived of their deities as anthropomorphic, that is, human in form and character. These gods and goddesses are idealized mortals in their physical beauty (although Hephaestus is lame), human beings made larger than life through the intensity of their emotions (however grand or petty these may be) and their superhuman powers. They perform extraordinary feats, change shape, become invisible, and fly. On the other hand, they appear tragically human in their pain and sorrows, their rivalries, and their sins. Ichor, not blood, runs through their veins, and they feast not on the food of mortals but instead drink nectar and eat ambrosia. In the last analysis, proof of their divinity lies in their immortality.

Olympian Deities. The major deities have as their home Mt. Olympus, where they dwell in splendid houses and enjoy opulent feasts in halls that echo with their inextinguishable laughter. Individual gods and goddesses frequent favorite cult places or cities. These immortals are worshiped by mortals in temples and honored with statues, altars, and animal sacrifices. Priests and priestesses serve them and officiate at celebrations; at an oracular shrine such as Delphi, they convey god's responses to the prayers and inquiries of suppliants.

Chthonic Deities. Those gods and goddesses who are primarily associated with the Underworld are called *chthonic* ("of the earth"). Although Hades is an Olympian, he is primarily a chthonic deity because he is king of the Underworld, and so is his wife and queen Persephone, for at least the part of the year that she is with him. Hecate and the Furies are other examples of important chthonic deities.

Nymphs. Among the various lower echelons of divinity are spirits who animate aspects of nature, all of whom may not necessarily be immortal but merely long-lived. The feminine spirits are often imagined as attractive nymphs, called Naiads, if they inhabit waters, and Dryads, if they inhabit trees.

Zeus and Greek Monotheism. Within the polytheistic cast of Greek and Roman mythology and religion, there is a strong element of monotheism from the very beginning. In Homer and Hesiod, Zeus is unquestionably the sovereign deity, and he is very much concerned with moral values. Yet his monotheism and patriarchy are severely tested by other divinities, especially goddesses. Hera's power is able to thwart Zeus' plans. Aphrodite can bend all the gods to her will, Zeus included, except for the three virgins, Hestia, Athena, and Artemis. Demeter, angry at the rape of her daughter Persephone, forces Zeus and the gods to come to her terms. And Zeus must yield to fate or the fates, although this need not always be the case.

At the same time, in the evolution of Zeus as the one supreme god, he became the almighty god of morality and justice until he could be referred to without a name and simply as god in an abstract, rather than specific, anthropomorphic conception. This greater sophistication in thought, which gave Zeus a more unquestionable, absolute authority, came about through the writings of religious poets and philosophers. Ultimately in the sixth century B.C., Xenophanes argued against the folly of conceiving deities as human beings and insisted (frag. 23) that there is "one god, greatest among gods and mortals, not at all like them, either in body or in mind."

Greek Humanism. A belief in the inevitability of fate or the fates created a particularly somber mood for the development of Greek literature. This sense of predetermined destiny for each individual was analyzed in terms of the meaning and possibility of free will and independent action. There also developed a strong and realistic awareness of the miseries, uncertainties, and unpredictability of human life, ordained by the gods. If we are lucky, our lives will be more blessed by happiness than doomed to misery; still, the terrible vicissitudes of life lead to only one conclusion: it is better to be dead than alive.

In opposition to this pessimism was an uplifting faith in the potential of human endeavor to triumph, against all divine odds. According to the fifth-century philosopher Protagoras, "Man is the measure of all things," meaning that mortals, not gods, are the arbiters of the human condition. In this optimistic mood about the hope and achievement possible in this life, Achilles, in Homer's Odyssey, cries out that he would sooner be alive, the slave of a poor man, rather than dead, a king in the Underworld.

These two seemingly irreconcilable views account for a unique humanism originated by the Greeks, with its emphasis upon the beauty and wonder of mortal achievement, attained in the face of horrible disasters which a vindictive god may dispense at any moment.

THE LEGEND OF SOLON AND CROESUS

Herodotus presents in the context of his History of the Persian Wars a brilliant crystallization of the tragic, yet uplifting nature of Greek humanism, which can only be truly understood through the emotional and intellectual experience afforded by great art.

Tellus the Athenian. After a year of office in Athens with extraordinary powers (594–593 B.C.) in which he wrought many political and economic reforms, the wise man SOLON [so'lon] set out to see the world. Among those he visited was the rich and powerful CROESUS [kre'sus], or KROISOS, the king of Lydia, whose capital was at Sardis. Croesus tried to impress his guest with a tour of his vast treasures, before he asked Solon the question, "Who is the happiest of human beings?" Croesus, of course, expected that he would be so designated, but Solon, surprisingly, identified an unknown Athenian, named TELLUS [tel'lus] or TELLOS. His reasons for the choice were as follows. Tellus came from a prosperous city and was prosperous himself (by the standards of Athens, not Lydian Croesus) so that he could fulfill his full potential as a human being. He had beautiful and good children, to whom he saw children born and all survive. Finally he died gloriously fighting on behalf of his family and his city, and he was honored with burial at public expense in the place where he fell.

Cleobis and Biton. Despotic Croesus, taken aback, persisted in asking, who was the second happiest, fully expecting that he would, at least, win second place. But Solon refused to flatter or be intimidated and named two young men from Argos, CLEOBIS [kle-o'bis], or KLEOBIS, and BITON [bi'ton], who had won prizes in the athletic games. Their mother was a priestess of Hera, who had to be present at the festival of the goddess. Once when the oxen did not arrive in time, her two sons yoked themselves to their mother's chariot and brought her to the temple, a journey of five miles. The whole congregation marveled at this deed, congratulating the youths for their strength and their mother for having such fine sons. She was overjoyed and prayed before the statue of the goddess to give her sons the best thing for human beings to attain. After they had sacrificed and feasted, Cleobis and Biton went to sleep in the temple and never woke up. The end of their lives was the very best, and thereby god showed clearly how it is better to be dead than alive. Statues of the brothers were set up in Delphi, since they had been the best of men.

The Nature of God and Human Life. Angrily Croesus asked why his happiness was dismissed as nothing and he was not even put on a par with ordinary men. Solon explained. All deity is jealous and fond of causing trouble. For in the length of a lifetime of seventy years there is much that one does not wish to see, and not one of the days in all those years will bring exactly the same experiences. A human being is completely a thing of chance.

A human life cannot be judged happy until it has been completed. The one from whom fate has kept most evils and misfortunes and to whom fate has given most blessings and good fortune, this one is the happiest, provided as well that the end of death is good. It is too soon to judge Croesus happiest because his life is not yet over and cannot be reviewed in its entirety. A rich king seemingly blessed with happiness now may at any time in the future meet with disasters, just like any other ordinary mortal.

Croesus considered Solon a fool, but Nemesis (Retribution) punished him for his hubris in thinking that he was the happiest of mortals.

Croesus and his Son Atys. Croesus had a fine son named Atys [a'tis], "the doomed one," in whom he placed all his hopes. A dream came to Croesus as he slept and foretold that Atys would die, struck by the point of an iron weapon. Croesus forbade his son to engage in any further military activity, removed all weapons from the men's quarters, and arranged that his son should get a wife. In the midst of preparations for the marriage, an unfortunate suppliant polluted by blood arrived and begged Croesus for purification. His name was ADRASTUS [a-dras'tus], or ADRASTOS ("the one who cannot escape fate"), a Phrygian from a royal family; he had killed his brother unintentionally and had been driven out by his father. Croesus benevolently purified Adrastus and accepted him in his palace.

The Mysian Boar Hunt. It happened that the neighboring Mysians were unable to overcome a monstrous boar that was destroying their lands. They appealed to Croesus that he send his son with an expedition to come to their aid. Croesus, remembering the dream, refused, but his valiant son, anxious to help the Mysians, convinced his father to allow him to go. Atys argued that the fight was not against men but a boar; since a boar did not have hands or an iron weapon, how could he possibly die by the point of an iron weapon, if he went on the hunt?

Croesus was won over but nevertheless still concerned about his son's safety. And so he asked Adrastus that, in return for the great kindness that he had done him, he go along with Atys to act as his guardian. Adrastus, although reluctant, could not refuse Croesus' request.

In the midst of the hunt, as the attackers hurled their weapons against the wild beast, Adrastus missed his aim and hit instead Atys, and killed him. The prophecy of the dream was fulfilled.

The Suicide of Adrastus. When the expedition arrived home, Adrastus stood before the corpse and begged Croesus to kill him. But the bereaved Croesus answered that it was the god who had warned him of this evil who was responsible. And he forgave Adrastus. Yet Adrastus could not forgive himself. Alone at the grave of Croesus' son Atys, whom he had murdered, he slaughtered himself on the tomb, realizing that he was the unhappiest of mortals, most oppressed by misfortune.

In the final scene of this tragedy, we cannot help but contrast the unfortunate and most unhappy Adrastus with Tellus and Cleobis and Biton, the happiest of men, who ended their lives well.

The Defeat of Croesus by Cyrus the Great. CYRUS [si'rus], or KYROS, THE GREAT, king of the Persians, had been carving out a vast empire to the east. Now, however, he threatened Croesus' kingdom of Lydia to the west. Croesus sent magnificent offerings to Delphi before consulting the great oracle of Apollo there for advice. The ambiguous answer given by the god was that if he marched against Persia, a great empire would fall. Croesus foolishly did march against Cyrus, but it was his own Lydian empire, not that of the Persians, which fell.

The Enlightenment and Salvation of Croesus. When Sardis, the capital of Lydia, was captured, Cyrus had a great pyre built and Croesus placed upon it. As Croesus stood on the pyre, about to be burned alive, he now understood that the words of Solon about the nature of happiness for mortals were inspired by god. Croesus called out the name of Solon three times, and Cyrus, who heard him, was perplexed, and Croesus explained the truth expounded to him by Solon: No one can by judged happy until dead. After the fire was lit and the flames began to burn the outer edges of the pyre, Cyrus, fearing retribution for himself, ordered the fire quenched and Croesus saved. When Croesus realized Cyrus' change of heart and saw that the men were unable to put out the fire, in tears he called to Apollo; and the god answered him by sending out of the clear and calm sky, torrents of rain that extinguished the fire.

Cyrus knew then that Croesus was a good man and beloved by god and made him his wise and benevolent counselor. Later Croesus inquired at Delphi why Apollo had deceived him by his oracle. Apollo, his savior, answered that it was Croesus' own fault for misinterpreting the oracle and not enquiring for further elucidation; and Croesus agreed.

COMPACT DISCS

136. Keiser, Reinhard, <u>Croesus</u>. Opera about Croesus, Solon, and Cyrus, inspired by Herodotus' story; the complete title is <u>Croesus, Haughty, Fallen, and Again Exalted</u>. (For other operas inspired by Herodotus see Chapter 3, Leo and Pergolesi.)
139. Korngold, Erich Wolfgang, <u>The Ring of Polycrates</u>. Of related interest, since this opera with its modern setting cleverly incorporates the legend of the tyrant Polycrates from Herodotus, which is similar to the legend of Croesus in its theme of the inevitability of fate.
192 and **193.** <u>Music of Ancient Greece</u>. <u>Hymn to Nemesis</u>.
256. Sibelius, Jean, <u>The Dryad</u>. Tone-Poem.

INTERPRETATION

Herodotean themes are the themes of Greek tragic literature: fate, god, and guilty mortals, who by their own actions try to avoid their destiny, only to further its fulfillment. Most significantly, Croesus, like Oedipus, can learn through sin and suffering to triumph against adversity and win reconciliation with god. There is not a single Greek tragedy that does not echo either implicitly or explicitly the admonition of Solon, "Never count a person happy, until dead," with its twofold connotation: the happiness of human life cannot be judged until the entire span of that life has been lived, and death is to be preferred to the vicissitudes of life.

Herodotus, like most Greek writers and artists, takes his philosophy from Homer. In the last book of the <u>Iliad</u> (see Chapter 17), Priam, great king of Troy, comes alone as a humble suppliant to the Greek hero Achilles, in order to beg for the body of his son Hector, whom Achilles has killed. In the course of their interview, Achilles, who has also suffered much because of the death of his beloved Patroclus, divulges his conclusions about human existence.

No human action is without chilling grief. For thus the gods have spun out for wretched mortals the fate of living in distress, while they live without care. Two jars sit on the doorsill of Zeus, filled with gifts that he bestows, one jar of evils, the other of blessing. When Zeus, who delights in the thunder, takes from both and mixes the bad with the good, a human being at one time encounters evil, at another good. But the one to whom Zeus gives only troubles from the jar of sorrows, this one he makes an object of abuse, to be driven by cruel misery over the divine earth.

The once great Priam will soon lose everything and meet a horrifying end, and Achilles himself is destined to die young. His fatalistic words about the uncertainty of human life are mirrored in the sympathetic humanism of Herodotus and echoed again and again by the Greek dramatists, who delight in the interplay of god and fate in human life and the tragic depiction of the mighty fall of those who were once great.

Jack Miles, a former Jesuit, provides a brilliant, Pulitzer-prize-winning study of the anthropomorphic God of the Tanakh (the Hebrew Old Testament). His literary portrait depicts God as a fictional character with many facets. (*God: A Biography*, New York: Alfred A. Knopf, 1995. See especially pp. 397-408.) To show that the Tanakh is a "character-dominated classic," Miles retells the biblical story by presenting "the several personalities fused in the character of the Lord God" as separate characters. The result is a tale that reads very much like Greek and Roman mythology.

Yet there is no need to retell the story of the Tanakh polytheistically in order to reveal the essential similarity between the God of the Hebrews and the Greek Zeus. It is true that the Tanakh, with its plot "trapped within the principal character" of God, illustrates an absolute monotheism that appears more all-pervasive than that of the Greeks. Yet if we modify the major contention of Miles that for the Hebrews "all depends on a frighteningly unpredictable God" to read "all human happiness and misery depend on a frighteningly unpredictable God," we are describing the god of Homer and Herodotus.

Representations in Literature and Art

The portrayal of the Olympian gods in classical and post-classical art has been described in Chapter 3. That they have continued to be important is evidence of their unique power as universal symbols of humanity. As early as the sixth century B.C., philosophers were criticizing the myths of the Olympians on moral grounds, yet these very myths continued to be central to the life of Greek city-states and to take on new life in the Roman world. After a period of eclipse, the Olympians returned in their classical form in the Renaissance, and during the sixteenth and seventeenth centuries the gods and their myths were the subjects of narrative works of art, music, drama, and poetry, or, more frequently, as political and moral allegories. Peter Paul Rubens (1577-1640) was unequaled in the allegorical use of classical myths, and his genius was equaled by the austere and spiritually profound work of his younger contemporary Nicolas Poussin (1594-1665). These two great artists have been the most sublime interpreters of classical mythology since the Renaissance.

Solon and Croesus.   As we have seen above, the Greek historian Herodotus (ca. 484-430 B.C.) tells how Cyrus ordered Croesus to be burned alive on a pyre. Croesus called on Apollo to save him, and the god caused a miraculous rainstorm to extinguish the fire. The scene of Croesus on the pyre is shown on an Athenian red-figure vase by Myson (ca. 500 B.C., now in Paris) — evidence for the close relationship between history and myth. Evidence is found for the Argive heroes, Cleobis and Biton, the second happiest of men, according to Solon. The Argives dedicated two statues of the young heroes (as Herodotus states) shortly after 600 B.C., which still can be seen at Delphi. In addition, the "historical" boar-hunt of Herodotus recalls the famous legendary Calydonian boar-hunt (see Chapter 23).

The story of Croesus was also narrated in a poem by the lyric poet Bacchylides of Ceos, written in 468 B.C. In this version Croesus himself ordered the pyre to be lit, but Zeus extinguished the fire, and Apollo took Croesus to live happily forever among the Hyperboreans as a reward for his piety.

CHAPTER 5

Poseidon, Sea Deities, Group Divinities, and Monsters

MAJOR DEITIES OF THE SEA

We have already met some of these many deities of the sea.

POSEIDON [po-si'don] (NEPTUNE) became established as the mighty god of the seas. His wife was AMPHITRITE [am-fi-tri'te].

PONTUS [pon'tus] or PONTOS ("sea"), produced by Gaia in the first stages of creation.

OCEANUS [o-se'an-us] or OKEANOS, the stream of Ocean, and his mate Tethys, titans who produced thousands of children, the Oceanids.

TRITON [tri'ton], son of Poseidon and Amphitrite, a merman, human above the waist, fish-shaped below (many male deities of the deep are often so depicted). His most distinguishing characteristic was that he blew on a conch shell, and thus he was known as the trumpeter of the sea.

PROTEUS [pro'te-us], a pre-Olympian deity who became an attendant or son of Poseidon and Amphitrite, was an old man of the sea who could foretell the future and could also change his shape at will.

NEREUS [ner'e-us] was another old man of the sea and, like Proteus, could foretell the future and change his shape. He was a son of Pontus and Gaia. Nereus mated with one of the Oceanids (Doris) and became the father of fifty daughters called NEREIDS [ner'e-idz]; three of these are important: THETIS [the'tis], GALATEA [gal-a-te'a] or GALATEIA, and AMPHITRITE [am-fi-tri'te]. Nereids are beautiful and often, but not always, depicted as mermaids; and usually they can change their shape.

PELEUS AND THETIS

Zeus learned from Prometheus the secret that Thetis was destined to bear a son mightier than his father, and so he avoided her. Instead a mortal named Peleus wooed and won her, not without difficulty, because she changed herself into all sorts of things, a bird, a tree, and a tigress. The wedding of Peleus and Thetis was one of the most famous in mythology, and their son Achilles (the hero of the Trojan war) did become mightier than his father.

ACIS, GALATEA, AND POLYPHEMUS

The second Nereid, Galatea, fell in love with ACIS [a'sis] or AKIS, the handsome son of a sea-nymph, daughter of the river-god Symaethus, in Sicily. To her dismay, she was wooed by the Cyclops POLYPHEMUS [po-li-fe'mus] or POLYPHEMOS, son of Poseidon. This monstrous and boorish giant, with one eye in the middle of his forehead, tried to mend his savage ways, but to no avail. Galatea would listen to his love songs, cowering in the arms of her lover Acis. Enraged with jealousy, Polyphemus finally turned on the two lovers. He pursued Acis and hurled a jagged mass, torn from the mountain, which buried him completely. But with the help of his beloved goddess of the waters, Galatea, Acis was transformed into a river-deity, fulfilling his ancestry.

POSEIDON AND AMPHITRITE

The third Nereid, Amphitrite, became the wife of Poseidon, and herein lies her importance.

Poseidon himself looks very much like his brother Zeus, a majestic and bearded king, only more severe and harsh. He can be identified by his trident, a long, three-pronged fork resembling a fisherman's spear. Poseidon has many moods, just like the sea that he controls. He is often ferocious and relentless in his hostility, as in the case of his devastating anger against Odysseus for the blinding of his son the Cyclops Polyphemus.

Poseidon, as the earthshaker, was a god of earthquakes as well as of storms. His virility and power are symbolized by his association with horses and bulls.

SCYLLA AND CHARYBDIS

Poseidon made advances to SCYLLA [sil'la], or SKYLLA (a granddaughter of Pontus). Amphitrite was jealous and threw into her bathing place magic herbs, which turned her into a vicious monster, encircled with a ring of dog's heads. She lived in a cave in the stormy Straits of Messina between Sicily and Italy. With her was CHARYBDIS (ka-rib'dis], daughter of Poseidon and Gaia, an equally formidable ally, who drew in mountains of water and spewed them out again. Scylla and Charybdis were a menace to heroes such as Odysseus.

Another version of this myth has become famous because it is told by Ovid. A mortal, GLAUCUS [Glaw'kus] or GLAUKOS, was transformed into a sea-god. He became enamored of Scylla, who rejected him. He turned for help to the sorceress Circe; but she fell in love with him, and through jealousy poisoned the waters of Scylla's bathing place.

IRIS

Many were the progeny of the sea; some of them we shall meet later in saga, for example, the Graeae, the Gorgons, and the Harpies. Progeny of the sea often appear grotesque or fantastic. At this point, however, we single out only IRIS [i'ris], a beautiful descendant of Pontus and Gaia. Iris, fleet-footed and winged, is the lovely goddess of the rainbow, the meaning of her name. She is also (like Hermes) a messenger of the gods, only Iris often becomes the particular servant of Hera.

TRANSLATION

We have two classic accounts of Proteus, which give wonderful insight into the ancient conception of divinities of the deep and their habitats: Homer (*Odyssey* 4. 363-570) and Vergil (*Georgics* 4. 386-528).

Homer relates that, on his return voyage from Troy, Menelaus, king of Sparta, was unduly detained on an island off the coast of Egypt (Chapter 18). In his distress (for provisions were almost gone) he was anxious to know why he was prevented from returning home. As it turned out, he and his men would not be able to proceed on their way until great sacrifices had been made to the gods. Menelaus learned about this fact only after he had consulted Proteus, the old man of the sea. Proteus' daughter EIDOTHEA [i-do-the'a] or EIDOTHEIA took pity upon him and gave him the directions necessary for finding out the truth. Menelaus and three of his best companions were to lie in ambush to ensnare Proteus. Here is how Menelaus tells of Eidothea's assistance in tricking her father, the immortal and infallible old man of the sea, who can readily assume countless changes of form (*Odyssey* 4. 435-450):

> *Eidothea dived down into the vast cavern of the sea and brought out of the depths four skins of seals; all were freshly skinned, for she was planning to trick her father. After hollowing out in the sea-sand four beds for us, she sat waiting; and we came right up to her. She placed us in our beds, one after the other, throwing a sealskin over each of us. A most horrible ambush this was; for the pernicious odor of the sea-nurtured seals was dreadfully oppressive. For who would like to lie down beside a monster of the sea? But she herself helped us out and contrived a great boon: she brought ambrosia and placed it under each of our noses; its very sweet fragrance eliminated the seal smell.*
>
> *All morning we waited, steadfast in spirit: the seals emerged from the sea in a swarm and then they lay down side by side to sleep on the shore of the sea. At midday the old man came forth from the deep and sought out his well-nourished seals; he went round and counted them all; in his reckoning we were the first, but he did not suspect any treachery. Thereupon he himself also lay down. And we rushed upon him with a shout and threw our arms about him; but the old man did not forget his devious arts. First off he became a thickly maned lion, and then a serpent, a leopard, and a great boar. And he became liquid water and a tree with lofty branches. But we held on to him firmly with steadfast spirits. Finally the devious Proteus grew weary and answered Menelaus' questions about his return home.*

Vergil's depiction of Proteus begins (*Georgics* 4. 315) with ARISTAEUS [a-ris-te'us] or ARISTAIOS (the son of Cyrene and Apollo), who is distraught because his bees are sick, starved, and gone. He fled to the source of the river Peneus and complained to his mother Cyrene, who allowed him to enter the depths of her watery home.

> *Cyrene bid the deep waters to recede and make a broad swath that the youth might approach. And the waters, bent back like a bow, towered over him like a mountain, received him in their vast embrace, and drew him beneath the flood. Now, in awe of the halls of his mother and her liquid realm, Aristaeus reached a pool shut up in caverns and echoing groves. He was dumbfounded at the immense movement of waters, as he watched all the rivers in their separate beds gliding under the great earth. . . .*
>
> *Then he entered her cavernous chamber with stalactites of pumice. Cyrene knows the vain tears of her son. Her sisters pour clear spring-water over one of his hands and then the other; they carry towels with a closely clipped nap. Some load tables with food and refresh brimming cups. Altars burn with perfumed Panchaean fires.*
>
> *"Lift your goblets of Maeonian wine and let us pour a libation in honor of Oceanus," Cyrene says. She herself invokes Oceanus, the father of the world, and the nymphs, her sisters, who watch over a hundred woods and a hundred rivers. Three times she sprinkles clear nectar over the gleaming fire. Three times the flames blaze up anew and lick the ceiling. Strengthening her resolve by this omen she begins.*
>
> *"There is in the Carpathian gulf of Neptune a dark blue seer, Proteus, who traverses the great surface of the sea with fish and a chariot yoked with two-hoofed horses. He is now paying another visit to the harbors of Emathia and his homeland Pallene. Even we nymphs and aged Nereus himself venerate him. For the seer knows everything: what is, what was, and what is being drawn out for the future soon to come. Indeed thus it seemed good to Neptune, whose great herds and shapeless seals he pastures under the swell.*

"First, my son, you must bind him in chains that he may explain the full cause of the sickness and favor the outcome. For without violence no instruction will he give and you will not prevail upon him by entreaty. Exert hard force and chains when he is taken. His empty stratagems at last will break around these fetters. When the sweltering sun has reached its zenith, when the vegetation becomes parched and the flocks find the shade more pleasant, I will lead you to the secret lair of the old man, where, tired from the buffeting waves, he refreshes himself, so that you may easily approach him as he lies asleep. But when you hold him bound fast in chains, then his many appearances and faces of wild beasts will sport with you. For he will suddenly become a bristly boar and a black tigress, a scaly serpent and a lioness with her yellow neck. Or he will give forth the crackling sound of a flame and thus slip out of his fetters. Or he will melt into clear water and escape. But the more he transforms himself into every shape, the tighter, my son, you must draw the shackling bonds, until he is in his final metamorphosis just as you saw him when he closed his eyes and sleep first took hold."

This is what she said and poured forth the pure scent of ambrosia, which she rubbed over her son's entire body. But the sweet perfume wafted down upon him from his smoothed locks and a supple strength invigorated his limbs.

There is an enormous grotto in the hollow flank of a mountain, where many waves are driven by the wind, and drawn back into a bay, they are broken up; it was once a most safe harbor for sailors who had been overtaken by storm. Within, a great rock as a barrier, Proteus hides away. The nymph brings her son out of the light of day into this hidden retreat, while she herself retires at a distance, shrouded in mist. Now swift Sirius, the Dog-Star, parching India dry, was glittering in the sky, and the fiery sun had reached the middle of its arc. The vegetation was withering, and the rays of the sun were boiling the deep-channeled streams, warmed in their courses dried to clay, when Proteus, seeking his usual lair, departed from the waves. Around him the watery race of the vast sea gamboled and shook off a spray of brine. The seals lay scattered about the shore in sleep. As a stable watch in the hill country, as soon as night returns the calves from pasture to their stalls and the lambs arouse the wolves with their noisy bleating, he himself in their midst sits down upon a crag and surveys their number. And since the opportunity for capturing him presented itself to Aristaeus, he had barely allowed the old one to relax his weary limbs, when he rushed upon him with a great shout and took hold of him with fetters as he lay. Now Proteus, not unmindful of his art, transforms himself into all manner of wondrous disguises: fire, a terrifying beast, and a running stream. But when no deceit afforded escape and he was beaten, he returned to himself and at length spoke with a human voice.

"Who ordered you, my most reckless lad, to approach our dwelling? What do you want here?"

"You know, Proteus, you of all people know. Nothing can deceive you. Stop your questions. I have followed the commands of the gods and have come here to seek answers to my sagging fortunes."

That was all Aristaeus said. Finally the seer at these words with a great force rolled his eyes burning with a green cast. He gnashed his teeth violently and loosened his tongue to the fates. "No god's anger makes trial of you. You are atoning for great wrongs. Orpheus, wretched, though undeserving of it, stirs up these punishments against you, unless the fates should oppose it; he rages terribly for his wife who has been snatched from him. The truth is, while she was running from you in headlong flight along the rivers, her death almost upon her, that girl did not see in her path the monstrous serpent keeping to the banks in the tall grass. But a chorus of Dryads, all alike, filled the mountain tops with their cry.

Proteus then continues to recount the myth of Orpheus and Eurydice, which is translated in Chapter 14. Then the story of Aristaeus continues as he learns of the solution to his woes:

When Proteus had finished, he dived into the deep and in his wake turned the water to foam around his head. But not Cyrene. With a mind to address her trembling son, she said:

"My son, you may lay aside sorrowful cares from your mind. This is the entire cause of the sickness. For this reason the nymphs, with whom Eurydice used to dance in the deep groves, sent destruction to your bees. As for you, seek peace with them, and as a suppliant bestow upon them gifts and worship the kindly nymphs of the wooded dell. For they will grant pardon for your vows and relax their wrath. As for the manner of your entreaty, I will first tell you step by step what it should be. Choose four splendid bulls of unblemished body, which now pasture on the heights of verdant Lycaeus, and the same number of young cows that have never worn the yoke. For these build four altars by the lofty shrine of the goddesses, let stream the sacred blood from their throats, and leave the carcasses of the cattle in a leafy grove. Later, after nine days, at daybreak, you will sprinkle Lethean poppies, the funeral offerings to Orpheus, you will sacrifice a black sheep, and you will revisit the grove. You will worship Eurydice and she will be placated with a slaughtered calf."

Aristeus immediately obeyed the instructions of his mother, and when he revisited the grove, he witnessed an awe-inspiring miracle.

. . . . within the entire cavity bees buzz throughout the liquefied entrails of the cattle; they burst forth from the broken side; huge clouds are drawn out; they crowd together at the top of a tree, and let down a cluster from the pliant branches.

COMPACT DISCS

98 and **97.** Handel, George Frideric, <u>Acis and Galatea</u>. Masque. Particularly moving is Galatea's final address to Acis: "Heart, the seat of soft delight/Be thou now a fountain bright." Handel also has a dramatic cantata, <u>Aci, Galatea e Polifemo</u>, on the same subject.
134. Ireland, John, <u>Tritons</u>. Symphonic Prelude evoking sea-poetry.
138. Koechlin, Charles, "Le Cortège d'Amphitrite." Song.
146. Leclair, Jean-Marie, <u>Scylla et Glaucus</u>. Opera inspired by Ovid.
257. Sibelius, Jean, <u>The Oceanides</u>. Tone-Poem.
282. Uttini, F. A., <u>Thétis and Pelée</u>. Opera.

INTERPRETATION

Representations in Art

Nereus. Among the pre-Olympian gods of the sea, Oceanus, Proteus, and Nereus are the most important and are sometimes confused. Heracles (see the Apples of the Hesperides labor in Chapter 20) is shown wrestling with Nereus on sixth-century black-figure vases; there is one in Paris by the Gorgon painter which shows him with a serpentine body. In red-figure vases he is human in form but holds a fish, as in another version of the struggle with Heracles (ca. 490, also in Paris).

Thetis. Of the Nereids the most important is Thetis, who also could change her shape, and her mortal husband, Peleus, had to wrestle with her to win her, a scene that was ingeniously painted on several Athenian vases, e.g., two black-figure vases from the sixth century now in London (see Chapter 23.) For the wedding of Peleus and Thetis see Chapters 3 and 17, and for her part in the Trojan saga see Chapter 17.

Acis, Galatea, and Polyphemus. The myth about the Nereid Galatea is narrated by Ovid in Book 13 of the <u>Metamorphoses</u>, the source of a very large number of paintings, among which the fresco by Raphael of <u>The Triumph of Galatea</u> (1511, painted for the Villa Farnesina in Rome) is preeminent. The transformation of Acis is the subject of powerful drawings by Nicolas Poussin (ca. 1620, now in Windsor), and Poussin's painting <u>Landscape with Polyphemus</u> (1649, now in St. Petersburg) is a profound meditation on the coming tragedy.

Amphitrite. Bacchylides has a beautiful description of the submarine home of the Nereid Amphitrite in his dithyramb that narrates the myth of Theseus and Minos (see Chapter 21): a red-figure vase by Onesimos (ca. 500 B.C., now in Paris) shows her giving her wreath to the boyish Theseus as Athena looks on. Like Galatea, she is primarily shown in post-classical art riding over the sea in triumph, her chariot drawn by dolphins and escorted by Poseidon, sea-horses, Nereids, Tritons, and other sea-gods, while cupids fly around her. The outstanding example of this genre is the exuberant painting of <u>The Triumph of Amphitrite</u> by Poussin (1637, now in Philadelphia).

Oceanus and the Oceanids. The chorus in Aeschylus' drama <u>Prometheus Bound</u> is made up of Oceanids, and Oceanus himself and Oceanids (or Nereids) escort Marie's ship in <u>The Disembarkation of Marie at Marseilles</u> in Rubens's Medici cycle (see Chapter 3). Oceanus is described in the <u>Iliad</u> as a river encircling the earth on the shield of Achilles. In vase-paintings he has the same appearance as Nereus: on the vase by Sophilos (before 575 B.C.: see Chapter 3) he replaces Nereus in the wedding procession of Peleus and Thetis, even though Nereus is the father of the bride. He appears frequently in Roman mosaics as a bearded old man, for example, in a second-century-A.D. mosaic from Verulamium (St. Alban's, England), where he is horned and has seaweed for hair. In later art and music he symbolizes sea-power and is so shown in the design by Rubens for the title-page of the <u>Pompa Introitus Ferdinandi</u>, the book published at Antwerp in 1641 containing the designs and Latin inscriptions for the ceremonial entrance of the Cardinal Infante Ferdinand into Antwerp in 1635. Shelley introduces Oceanus in the third act of his <u>Prometheus Unbound</u> (1820), where he foretells an end of battle and bloodshed on the sea.

Poseidon. Poseidon is regularly shown as a bearded man, robed and wielding a trident, and on one early red-figure vase also carrying a fish (ca. 520 B.C., by Oltos, and now in Copenhagen). He is also shown on horseback or riding a hippocamp (sea-horse), as in a black-figure vase (ca. 490) now in Oxford. The statue of the nude god known as the <u>Zeus of Artemisium</u> (ca. 460, now in Athens) could also represent him, if the missing weapon which the god is throwing is a trident rather than a thunderbolt. Poseidon's most important appearance in classical art is on the west pediment of the Parthenon (ca. 440 B.C.), which showed his contest with Athena for control of Attica. He is also shown on vases in association with Theseus. In post-classical art, usually with his Roman name, Neptune, he is very common as a symbol of water, or of sea-power, or of storms. There are many paintings and engravings which show him as the escort of Amphitrite, or calming the storm that wrecked Aeneas (Book 1 of the <u>Aeneid</u>), or favoring some historical figure sailing across the sea. A representative example of the first motif is Poussin's <u>Triumph of Amphitrite</u> (see above); the second and third motifs are combined in Rubens's oil-sketch <u>Neptune Calming the Tempest: The Cardinal</u>

Infante Ferdinand Sailing from Barcelona to Genoa (1635, now in Cambridge, Mass.: the large painting from this sketch is now in Dresden). Originally Rubens designed this scene for one of the three paintings on the Arch of Welcome at the Entry of Ferdinand into Antwerp in 1635, and it was engraved for the Pompa Introitus Ferdinandi (1641: see above). The references to Neptune calming the storm in Book 1 of the Aeneid have also led to this painting being erroneously titled Quos Ego, a quotation from Neptune's speech at Aeneid 1. 135. The painting is a compendium of marine mythology: in it are Neptune, hippocamps, Triton, Nereids, and, above, Boreas (the North wind) and smaller figures of two other winds. All these classical figures and allusions are used by Rubens for the purpose of contemporary political allegory.

Triton. This snake-bodied sea-god is generally made out to be the son of Poseidon and Amphitrite, whom he escorts as they ride over the sea. He is memorably described by Ovid in the first book of the Metamorphoses, blowing his conch-shell to order the Flood to recede, and these lines have inspired countless paintings and other works of art. Triton is also a significant ornament in gardens, parks, and city squares: a famous example of an urban fountain is the Fontana del Tritone in the Piazza Barberini in Rome, designed by Gian Lorenzo Bernini in 1642.

The many other sea-gods and sea-monsters, whose forms are limited only by the imagination of artists and poets, will be discussed later as they make their appearance in saga.

CHAPTER 6
Athena

THE BIRTH OF ATHENA

Zeus swallowed his consort METIS [me'tis], "wisdom," after he had made her pregnant, because he feared that she would bear a son who would overthrow him. And so ATHENA [a-the'na] or ATHENE (MINERVA) was born from the holy head of Zeus, and Hephaestus with his ax may have facilitated the birth. The occasion was awesome, as Athena sprang forth fully grown, a beautiful young woman in full armor, fearlessly announcing her arrival with a thunderous war-cry.

CHARACTERISTICS OF ATHENA

Athena's birth allegorically proclaims her essential character: her divine wisdom drawn from the head of god; the special bond of affection between father and daughter; her championship of heroes and male causes, born as she was from the male, and not from a mother's womb. A dread goddess of war, she remained a virgin.

APPEARANCE OF ATHENA

Athena bears an aloof kind of loveliness, akin to the beauty of youthful masculinity. She is associated with the owl and the snake. She is usually represented with helmet, spear, and shield or aegis that bore a depiction of the head of Medusa. With her there may be a female winged figure (called NIKE [ni'ke], "victory"), bearing a crown or garland of success. Athena herself as victorious war goddess was called Athena Nike, and the simple but elegant temple of Athena Nike stands to the right of the entrance to the Acropolis.

THE CONTEST BETWEEN ATHENA AND POSEIDON

Athena and Poseidon vied for control of Athens and its surrounding territory, Attica. The contest took place on the Acropolis. Poseidon struck the rock with his trident and produced a salt spring or a horse. Athena brought forth an olive tree from the ground by the touch of her spear and she was proclaimed the victor. The olive was fundamental to Athenian economy and life.

   Angry at losing, Poseidon was appeased and continued to be worshiped in Athens, especially in conjunction with the Athenian hero Erechtheus (see Chapter 21). In his lovely temple the ERECHTHEUM [e-rek-the'um] or ERECHTHEION on the Acropolis, just across from the Parthenon, the marks of the blow of his trident supposedly could be seen, and nearby the olive tree that Athena had produced continued to grow.

THE PANATHENAEA OR PANATHENAIC FESTIVAL

The PANATHENAEA [pan-ath-e-ne'a] was an annual festival celebrating the birthday of Athena; every fourth year the celebration of the Great Panathenaea was especially splendid. Important in the ceremonies were sacrifices and games; the prizes for winners in the games were special Panathenaic amphoras, vases inscribed and decorated with a depiction of Athena and containing sacred olive oil.

A Panathenaic procession wound its way through the city ending with the presentation of an embroidered robe (*peplos*) to Athena on the Acropolis. Athenians (young and old, male and female) carrying sacred implements, leading sacrificial animals, with chariots or on horseback, figured in the procession.

THE PARTHENON AND ITS SCULPTURE

The PARTHENON [par'the-non] is the great temple to Athena Parthenos on the Acropolis of Athens that was built in the fifth century B.C. Parthenos [par'the-nos], an adjective meaning virgin, was a standard epithet of Athena. It is a most beautiful Doric temple (even in its ruined state today), and its sculpture (created under the aegis of the great Athenian sculptor Pheidias) bears tribute to Athena herself and her city and all that they mean forever.

- East pediment—the dramatic moment of the birth of Athena, who stood in the center before the throne of Zeus, from whose head she had just spring, fully grown and fully armed. Other divine figures are present at the miracle, and at the corners, the horses of Helius and those of Selene set the momentous event in cosmic time.

- West pediment—the contest between Athena and Poseidon, decribed above; these two central figures pull away from each other as they produce the gifts with which they vie. On either side figures of Athenian divinities and heroic kings are witnesses.

- Doric frieze—on the exterior are metopes (relief sculpture) depicting four subjects: the battle between the Lapiths and Centaurs; the sack of Troy; the Gigantomachy; and the battle between the Greeks and the Amazons.

- Ionic frieze—in the interior, on the outer wall of the naos (or cella), continuous relief sculpture renders the splendid Panathenaic procession described above. Athenian men and women are shown as marshals, attendants, horsemen, hoplites, and assistants in the worship, with the animals of ritual sacrifice. At the climax the ceremonial robe is presented to a priestess of Athena while, on either side, enthroned Olympian deities witness the joyous celebration of civic piety.

- The Athena Parthenos—this monumental statue of Athena stood in the cella (or naos). The surfaces of the standing goddess were made of gold and ivory, and she held a figure of Nike (Victory) in her right hand; she wore a helmet and the aegis with the head of Medusa, and a spear and shield are at her side; elaborate decorative reliefs enhanced the statue, which has not survived.

A fuller description of the Parthenon and its sculpture appears below (see Interpretation, Representations in Art).

PALLAS ATHENA TRITOGENEIA

Athena is often called Pallas Athena, and sometimes she is given the obscure title TRITOGENEIA [tri-to-je-ni'a or tri-to-je-ne'a], which suggests her links with Triton, a river-god. Triton had a daughter named PALLAS [pal'las] who used to practice the arts of war with Athena. As the result of a quarrel, Athena impulsively wounded Pallas. When Pallas died, Athena was distraught when she fully realized what she had done. In her sorrow, she made a wooden statue of the girl which was called the PALLADIUM [pal-la'di-um] or PALLADION. Through the agency of Zeus this Palladium fell into the territory of the Trojans, where as a talisman it carried with it the destiny of their city. The word Pallas probably means maiden and designates Athena's virginity, like the epithet parthenos, "virgin."

THE INVENTION OF THE FLUTE: ATHENA AND MARSYAS

Athena invented the flute after she heard the lamentations and the sound of the hissing of the serpent hair of the surviving Gorgons, after Perseus had killed their sister Medusa (see Chapter 19). She quickly grew to dislike her invention because her beautiful cheeks became distorted when she blew into the instrument, and so she threw it away. The satyr MARSYAS [mar'si-as] picked up the flute and became so excellent a player that he dared to compete with Apollo in a musical contest, with dire consequences (see Chapter 9).

ATHENA AND ARACHNE

ARACHNE [a-rak'ne] was born in a lowly family, but her skill in spinning and weaving was extraordinary. When Athena (or Minerva in Ovid's account) learned that Arachne's fame as a worker of wool rivaled her own, she was determined to destroy her. Arachne was foolish enough not to admit that Athena was her teacher and challenged her to a contest. Disguised as an old woman, Athena warned Arachne about the danger of her hubris, but Arachne persisted. Athena in anger threw off her disguise and accepted the challenge. She wove at her loom, with surpassing skill, a tapestry depicting noble scenes from mythology. Arrogant Arachne, on the other hand, wove into her tapestry scenes of the gods' less honorable amorous conquests. Athena was furious, particularly since she could find no fault with Arachne's excellent work. She tore up the embroidered tapestry and beat Arachne's face with the shuttle. Grief stricken, Arachne strangled herself with a noose, but Athena took pity and transformed her into a spider; as such, she and her descendants practice the art of weaving forever.

COMPACT DISCS

55. Christiné, Henri, Phi-Phi. An operetta about Pheidias (nicknamed Phi-Phi). M/L 605.
254. Scott, Stephen, Minerva's Web, for grand piano, bowed and plucked by ten musicians; inspired by Ovid and thematically related to Scott's The Tears of Niobe.

VIDEOS

Athens and Ancient Greece (Great Cities of the Ancient World). Questar Video QV2337. A tour of the Acropolis and Athens and other major sites: Olympia, Delphi, Mycenae, and Santorini.

INTERPRETATION

A study of women, cloth, and society in early times, Women's Work: The First 20,000 Years, by Elizabeth Wayland Barber (New York: W.W. Norton, 1994) presents insights into how women's textile arts function as analogy and metaphor in mythology and illuminates the importance of Athena as the goddess of the "central womanly skill of weaving" (p. 242). Athena represented not only skill but also cunning, and so weaving became a metaphor for human resourcefulness as illustrated by clever Penelope, a wily wife, just like her wily husband Odysseus. The related theme of life as a thread, created by women and controlled by the feminine fates, receives scrutiny. Barber makes us realize that weaving, however necessary, was also revered as a most respected art which belonged to the arete (excellence) of a woman as opposed to the different arete of a man.

The character of Athena as a war goddess and her close relationship with her father Zeus resemble the depiction of Brünnhilde and Wotan in the Teutonic and Norse mythology of the epic *Nibelungenlied*. An enriching experience is to explore these parallels in Richard Wagner's opera, *Die Walküre*. One can believe that Athena's mighty war-cry sounded very much like a Greek rendition of the triumphant "hojotoho" of the Valkyrie Brünnhilde. That Hera and Fricka have very much in common would also become all too apparent, and Loge as a god of fire would suggest contrasts with Hephaestus. The exploration of *Die Walküre* provides an easy and enjoyable beginning for a later study of Wagner's entire cycle *The Ring of the Nibelungen* (there are plenty of excellent recordings and videos) to afford comparison with figures, concepts, and themes in Greek and Roman legend. Siegfried, after all, is yet another in the long tradition of archetypal dragon-slayers.

Representations in Art

Depictions of Athena. Athena is shown in the earlier stages of Greek art as a woman dressed in a long robe, e.g., on the François Vase (ca. 575 B.C.), where she also is the driver of the chariot in which she is riding with another goddess (perhaps Artemis, who is named as her passenger on the vase by Sophilos (see Chapter 3).

With the wide-reaching political changes at Athens, after about 560 B.C., she is portrayed as a warrior goddess, still robed, but wearing helmet and aegis and carrying shield and spear. She is so shown on the Boston vase depicting her birth (see Chapter 3) and on countless other Attic vases. A red-figure vase (ca. 520 B.C., now in Berlin) by the Andocides painter shows her watching the struggle between Heracles and Apollo for the tripod, and the snakes and Gorgon's head of her aegis are vigorously painted. She is often shown with an owl, which was regularly stamped on the reverse of Athenian coins. In about 460 B.C. she is shown on a relief (still in Athens) as a young woman, robed and with spear and helmet (but without shield or aegis) standing in an attitude of mourning before a stele (i.e., an upright stone marker) on which the names of Athenian citizens killed in the previous year's battles are inscribed, an expressive example of the intimate connection between the goddess and her citizens.

The armed Athena (Athena Promachos, "the Defender") was portrayed on the vases given as prizes at the Panathenaic games from ca. 560 B.C. for four centuries, always in black-figure technique (most major museum collections have examples). A huge statue of Athena Promachos stood opposite the Propylaea at the entrance to the Acropolis.

As a virgin and warrior goddess, Athena could not be shown as a mother. Nevertheless, the myth of Erichthonius (see Chapter 21) shows that she was once a mother-goddess. In a red-figure vase (ca. 400 B.C., now in Richmond, Virginia) she is shown receiving the infant Erichthonius from Ge (Earth). Usually, however, artists focus on the finding of Erichthonius, as in Rubens's painting of The Discovery of the Infant Erichthonius (1616, now in Vaduz), in which Athena does not appear.

The Birth of Athena. The commonest myths of Athena in art are those of her birth and her contest with Poseidon (see Chapters 3 and 5). The former is especially popular in Attic black-figure vases of the sixth century, which show her leaping fully armed from the head of Zeus, while other Olympians assist at the birth (Hephaestus or Eileithyia or both) or are observers (most commonly Hermes and Ares). The most sublime representation of her birth was undoubtedly the sculptures of the east pediment of the Parthenon, of which the central figures have been destroyed. The remaining figures (part of the so-called Elgin Marbles in London) transform the archaic motif of the spectators of the birth into the groups of watching goddesses, to whom Iris brings the news. Other figures, including Dionysus (or Heracles) are present, and at each corner are the horses, respectively, of the sun and moon (see Chapter 1).

The Contest between Athena and Poseidon. The contest with Poseidon was again most memorably represented on the Parthenon, this time on the west pediment, of which little now remains. The olive tree and the salt-water spring (with the marks of Poseidon's trident), as well as the mark of the thunderbolt of Zeus, were shown in the precinct of the Erechtheum, the temple dedicated jointly to Erechtheus and Athena Polias (i.e., goddess of the city), which was rebuilt in 421-406 B.C. (see Chapter 21). Neither the birth of Athena nor the contest with Poseidon have inspired many significant post-classical works.

Athena Parthenos. The rebuilding of the Athenian acropolis after the Persian sack of Athens in 480 B.C. centered on the Parthenon, which housed the immense chryselephantine statue of Athena, a masterpiece by Pheidias, like that of Zeus at Olympia (see Chapter 3). It is now lost, but there are accurate reconstructions in Toronto and Nashville, the latter a full-size one. Athena was standing, holding in her right hand a figure of Nike (Victory), with her left hand on her shield, while her spear rested against her left arm. She was robed and helmeted, and on her breast she wore the aegis with the Gorgon's head. On the exterior of the shield were reliefs of the battle of the Amazons, and on its interior was painted the Gigantomachy (see Chapter 2). On the rims of her sandals were reliefs of the Centauromachy (see Chapter 23), and on the statue's base were reliefs showing the creation of Pandora (see Chapter 2).

Metopes of the Parthenon. The three battle scenes (the battle of the Amazons, the Gigantomachy, and the Centauromachy), together with the sack of Troy, were also the subjects of the 92 metopes that formed the outer frieze: of these the only extensive remains are those of the Centauromachy originally on the south side (now part of the Elgin Marbles). The association of Athena with the myths of violent battle was, like the west pediment of the Temple of Zeus at Olympia, symbolic of the triumph of Greek (and, specifically, Athenian) civilization over barbarism, which at Athens was taken particularly to refer to the victory over the Persians in 480–479.

The Panathenaic Procession. The rebuilding of the Acropolis was begun in earnest after the formal ending of the Persian Wars in 449. Athena, as patron goddess of Athens, was closely involved in the economic prosperity and success of her citizens. This was shown vividly on the inner frieze of the Parthenon (also part of the Elgin Marbles), on which the procession of Athenian citizens made its way to present the robe (*peplos*) for the cult-statue of the goddess housed in the Erechtheum. At the climax of the procession, shown on the same scale and in the same plane as the human participants, were the seated figures of the twelve Olympians.

Athena and Arachne. This contest has been popular in post-classical art, sometimes as an allegory of pride and its punishment. Exceptional examples are the oil-sketch by Rubens (1636, now in Richmond, Virginia) and the complex painting by Diego Velazquez <u>Las Hilanderas</u> ("The Spinners," 1647, now in Madrid).

Athena, Champion of Heroes. Athena is shown as the helper of many heroes in poetry and art. She is particularly close to Achilles in Book 1 of the <u>Iliad</u>, and to Diomedes in Book 5, and she is the constant helper of Telemachus and Odysseus in the <u>Odyssey</u>, in which she puts an end to the fighting between Odysseus and the relatives of the dead suitors (see Chapter 18). She is hostile to Ajax, and friendly to Odysseus, in Sophocles' tragedy, <u>Ajax</u> (ca. 455 B.C.). She is shown in vase paintings of the sack of Troy as angry with Ajax (son of Oileus) for his rape of Cassandra. With Apollo, she protects Orestes after the murder of Clytemnestra and presides at his trial before the court of the Areopagus at Athens, pronouncing the verdict of acquittal (Aeschylus' <u>Eumenides</u>, 458 B.C., see Chapter 16). She assists Heracles in his labors, as in the metopes of the Temple of Zeus at Olympia (see Chapters 3 and 20); to a lesser extent she is the helper of Theseus. She is one of the three contestants in the Judgment of Paris—the only myth whose artistic representations show her unclothed (see Chapter 17).

Minerva. Athena was identified with Minerva at Rome, and shared the Temple of Jupiter Optimus Maximus on the Capitoline Hill with Jupiter (Zeus) and Juno (Hera). The Palladium, which was believed to have been brought by Aeneas from Troy, was housed in the Temple of Vesta beside the Forum and was one of the most sacred objects in Roman state religion. It is shown in the beautiful oil-sketch by Rubens (1617, now in Vaduz) showing <u>Mars and Rhea Silvia</u>. Minerva was especially worshiped by the emperor Domitian (A.D. 81-96), who built a temple with an open space (*Forum Transitorium*) in her honor. The colonnade of the Forum Transitorium was decorated with a frieze showing Minerva as the patroness of the arts and crafts, which included a scene of the myth of Arachne.

Athena in Western Art. In post-classical art Athena symbolizes wisdom and intellectual activity, the arts and crafts, and orderly government. In these aspects she was especially significant in the seventeenth century, and appears frequently in the political and intellectual allegories of Rubens. She is the teacher of Marie in <u>The Education of Marie</u>, one of the cycle of the Marie de' Medici series (see Chapters 3 and 4) and appears as the queen's supporter or counselor in several other paintings of the cycle. She is shown as <u>Minerva Conquering Sedition</u> in the ceiling paintings for the Banqueting House in Whitehall, London (1634, and still in place). Her intellectual patronage is shown in several of the designs for title-pages by Rubens (e.g., the <u>Opera Omnia</u> of Justus Lipsius, published at Antwerp in 1637), and she appears as the symbol of the Stoic virtue of wisdom (<u>Sapientia</u>) on the title-pages (not designed by Rubens) of the <u>Opera Senecae</u> edited by Lipsius and published at Antwerp in 1605 and 1615. She represents the figure of Virtue in the scene of the Choice of Heracles from the <u>Pompa Introitus Ferdinandi</u> (1641, see Chapter 20). While Rubens was but one of very many artists to represent Athena (Minerva), he is preeminent in his allegories, which in themselves form a compendium of post-classical images of Athena.

CHAPTER 7

Aphrodite and Eros

THE DUALITY OF APHRODITE (VENUS)

Aphrodite Urania. We know that Aphrodite arose amidst the foam (*aphros*) from the severed genitals of Uranus cast upon the sea. Hesiod's account of her birth allegorizes the powerful sexuality of her nature. Yet this APHRODITE URANIA [a-fro-di'te u-ra'ni-a], born from the male alone and not as the result of sexual union, came to be characterized as the goddess of pure love that has as its end not physical satisfaction but spiritual gratification. The sensual Aphrodite Urania, sprung from Uranus, god of the heavens, became the HEAVENLY or CELESTIAL APHRODITE of philosophy and religion.

Aphrodite Pandemos. In stark contrast to celestial Aphrodite, another Aphrodite was identified, the daughter of Zeus and his mate Dione, about whom we know little. Their daughter was APHRODITE PANDEMOS [pan-de'mos], APHRODITE OF THE PEOPLE or COMMON APHRODITE, the goddess of sex and the procreation of children, whose concerns are of the body and not of the mind, the spirit, or the soul.

- This duality in Aphrodite's nature came to be described as sacred and profane love, the most universal of all archetypal conceptions.

- Aphrodite received two epithets in connection with her birth on the sea, CYTHEREA [si-the-re'a] or KYTHEREIA and CYPRIS [si'pris] or KYPRIS, since she was brought first to the island of Cythera and then Cyprus, the latter especially associated with her worship.

THE CHARACTER OF APHRODITE

In general Aphrodite was the captivating goddess of beauty, love, and marriage, and her power was very great. Her universality led to a gamut of conceptions of this goddess, who presided over everything from hallowed married love to temple prostitution. Depictions of her in art, literature, and music reflect not only the duality but also the multiplicity of her nature.

ATTENDANTS OF APHRODITE

The Three Graces (CHARITES, kar'i-tez). These are feminine personifications of aspects of charm and loveliness.

The Hours or Seasons. The name of these daughters of Zeus and Themis is HORAE [ho'ri] or HORAI, meaning hours and then time and then seasons. Their number increases from two to four, and they represent the attractive attributes of the various times of the year.

THE ITHYPHALLIC PRIAPUS

PRIAPUS [pri'a-pus] or PRIAPOS, the son of Aphrodite, personifies the elemental, sexual side of his mother's nature. He bears a huge and erect phallus and began as a respectable fertility god bringing good fortune for crops and procreation. He developed into an erotic and sometimes obscene inspiration for later art and literature.

PYGMALION

Ovid's story of PYGMALION [pig-ma'li-on] is most influential. Venus, enraged because the women of her own cult-place of Cyprus denied her divinity, caused them to be the first women to prostitute themselves. The sculptor Pygmalion would have nothing to do with these licentious women. In his loneliness, he fashioned an ivory statue of surpassing beauty, so realistic that he fell in love with his creation and treated it as though it were alive.

On the feast day of Venus, Pygmalion timidly prayed to Venus that his ivory maiden would become his wife. He returned home to find that his lovely statue was alive. He gave thanks to Venus, who was present at the marriage of the happy couple. The son of Pygmalion and GALATEA [ga-la-te'a] (her name is not in Ovid) was Paphos [pa'fos], after whom Venus' favorite city in Cyprus was named.

APHRODITE AND ADONIS

The classic version of this myth is by Ovid. CINYRAS [sin'i-ras] or KINYRAS (the son of Paphos) had a daughter named MYRRHA [mir'ra], who fell in love with her father. The faithful nurse of guilty Myrrha prevented her from committing suicide by convincing her to satisfy her passion. So Myrrha carried on an incestuous relationship with her father, who was unaware of her identity. When Cinyras found out, he pursued his daughter, who fled from his rage. In answer to her prayers, Myrrha was turned into a myrrh tree. She had become pregnant by her father, and from the tree was born ADONIS [a-don'is], who became a most handsome youth and keen hunter.

Aphrodite fell desperately in love with Adonis and warned him of the dangers of the hunt, but to no avail. While he was hunting a wild boar, it buried its deep tusk into his groin and Adonis died in the arms of a grief-stricken Aphrodite. The goddess ordained that from his blood a flower, the anemone, should arise. Here is allegorized the important recurrent theme of the Great Mother and her lover, who dies as vegetation dies and comes back to life again.

This motif of death and resurrection becomes even clearer in the following variation. When Adonis was an infant, Aphrodite put him in a chest for Persephone, the queen of the Underworld, to keep. But Persephone looked upon the child's beauty and refused to give him back. It was agreed that Adonis would spend one part of the year below with Persephone and one part in the upper world with Aphrodite. Celebrations honoring the dead and risen Adonis share similarities with Easter celebrations for the dead and risen Christ.

CYBELE AND ATTIS

The myth of the great Asiatic mother goddess called CYBELE [si'be-le] or KYBELE in the Greek and Roman world and her consort, Attis [at'tis], is another variation on the archetype of the Great Mother and her lover. Cybele originally was a bisexual deity who was castrated. From the severed organ, an almond tree arose. Nana, daughter of a river god, put a blossom from the tree to her bosom; it disappeared, and she became pregnant. The beautiful Attis was born, and when he grew up, Cybele fell passionately in love with him. But he loved another, and Cybele, because of her jealousy, drove him mad. In his madness Attis castrated, himself and a repentant Cybele obtained Zeus' promise that the body of Attis would never decay.

Religious ceremonies in honor of Attis celebrated resurrection and new life, through the castration and death of the subordinate male in the grip of the eternal, dominant female. This is the powerful theme of Catullus' great poem, translated below.

APHRODITE AND ANCHISES

The Homeric Hymn to Aphrodite tells how Zeus put into the heart of Aphrodite an overwhelming desire for the mortal Trojan ANCHISES [an-ki'sez].

Using all her wiles, Aphrodite seduced Anchises by tricking him into believing that she was a mortal. Discovering that he had slept with a goddess, he was terribly afraid that he would be enfeebled, "for no man retains his full strength who sleeps with an immortal goddess." Here is yet again the eternal theme of the Great Mother and the castration of her lover, only in a more muted form. The son of Aphrodite and Anchises was AENEAS [e-ne'as], the great hero of the Romans.

EROS

As with Aphrodite, there are various facets to the character of EROS [e'ros] (CUPID). He came out of Chaos, and he attended Aphrodite after she was born from the sea-foam. He (or a different Eros?) was said to be the son of Aphrodite and Ares. Eros was a young handsome god of love and desire in general but by the fifth century B.C. had become very much the god of male homosexuality.

The Symposium of Plato. Plato's dialogue presents a profound analysis of love, the topic of this famous dinner-party. Two among the speeches are particularly illuminating.

The Speech of Aristophanes. Since this speech is by the famous writer of Greek Old Comedy, not surprisingly, it is both amusing and wise. Aristophanes explains that originally there were not just two sexes but a third, an androgynous sex, both male and female. These creatures (all three sexes) were round in shape with four hands and feet, one head with two faces exactly alike but looking in opposite directions, a double set of genitals, and so on. They were very strong and they dared to attack the gods.

Zeus, in order to weaken them, decided to cut them in two. So all those who were originally of the androgynous sex became heterosexual beings, men who love women, and women who love men. Those of the female sex who were cut in half became lesbians and pursued women; and those bisected from the male became male homosexuals who pursue males. Thus, like our ancestors, according to our own nature, we pursue our other half in a longing to become whole once again. Eros is the yearning desire of lover and beloved to become one person not only in life but also in death.

Aristophanes by his creative humor has given a serious explanation through mythic truth of why some persons are heterosexual while others are homosexual; he also articulates a compelling definition of love, reiterated throughout the ages: Eros inspires that lonely and passionate search for the one person who alone can satisfy our longing for wholeness and completion.

The Speech of Socrates. The great philosopher Socrates elucidates Platonic revelation about Eros. Socrates claims that his wisdom on the nature of love came from a woman from Mantinea named DIOTIMA [di-o-ti′ma]. A new myth is created about the birth of Eros to explain his character. He is squalid and poor, not beautiful himself, but a lover of beauty and very resourceful, forever scheming and plotting to obtain what he desires passionately but does not himself already possess—beauty, goodness, and wisdom. This is the Eros who must inspire each of us to move from our love of physical beauty in the individual to a love of beauty in general and to realize that beauty of the soul is more precious than that of the body. When two people have fallen in love with the beautiful soul of each other, they should proceed upward to pursue together a love of wisdom.

Platonic Ero is   lov inspire in th beginning by the sexual attraction of physical beauty, which must be transmuted into a love of the beautiful pursuits of the mind and the soul. Although Socrates' discourse dwells upon male homosexual attachments as his paradigm, his message transcends sexuality. Platonic lovers of both sexes driven by Eros must be capable of making the goal of their love not sexual satisfaction at all nor the procreation of children, but spiritual gratification from the procreation of ideas in their intellectual quest for beauty, goodness, and wisdom.

Cupid. The Greek Eros develops into the Roman Cupid, still a very familiar deity today. This mischievous little darling with a bow and arrows, who attends Venus, can inspire love of every kind, often very serious or even deadly, but usually not intellectual.

CUPID AND PSYCHE

The canonical version of this famous tale comes from the Roman novel <u>Metamorphoses</u>, or <u>The Golden Ass</u>, by the African author Apuleius. Thus Eros is called Cupid, who appears as a handsome, winged youth. PSYCHE [si′ke] means soul, and here is an allegory of the union of the human soul with the divine.

Once upon a time, a king and queen had three daughters, of whom Psyche was so beautiful that Venus was jealous. She ordered Cupid to make Psyche fall in love with the most vile of creatures, but instead Cupid fell in love with Psyche himself. She was transported to a magnificent palace, where each night an anonymous bridegroom (Cupid himself) visited her and departed quickly before sunrise.

Psyche's two sisters, who were very jealous, visited her. Cupid warned of their treacherous purpose to persuade Psyche to look upon his face. He told her that she was pregnant and that she must keep their secret. Nevertheless, Psyche was tricked by her sisters into believing that she was sleeping with a monster, and, at their advice, she hid a sharp knife and a burning lamp with the intention of slashing her lover in the neck when he was asleep.

In the night her husband made love to Psyche and then fell asleep. As she raised the lamp, knife in hand, she saw the gentle and beautiful Cupid. Overcome by desire, she kissed him so passionately that the lamp dropped oil on the god's shoulder. Cupid leaped out of bed, and as he flew away, Psyche caught hold of his leg and soared aloft with him. Her strength gave way and she fell to earth, only to be admonished by Cupid for ignoring his warnings. In her despair, Psyche attempted unsuccessfully to commit suicide. As she wandered disconsolate she encountered her two evil sisters and lured each to her death.

When Venus learned from Cupid all that had happened, she was enraged and imposed upon Psyche four impossible tasks.

First, Psyche had to sort out a vast heap of a mixed variety of grains. She did this successfully with the help of an army of ants.

Next, Psyche had to obtain the wool from dangerous sheep with thick golden fleeces. A murmuring reed told her to shake from the trees under which the sheep had passed the wooly gold clinging to the branches.

Then, Psyche was ordered to climb to the top of a high mountain, face the terrors of a frightening dragon, and collect in a jar chill water from a stream that fed the Underworld river of Cocytus. This she accomplished with the help of Zeus' eagle.

Finally, Venus imposed the ultimate task, descent into the Underworld itself. Psyche was commanded to obtain from Persephone a box containing a fragment of her own beauty. As Psyche, in despair, was about to leap to her death from a high tower, the tower spoke to her and told her to take sops to mollify Cerberus, the dread hound guarding the realm of Hades, and money to pay the ferryman Charon; most important of all, she was not to look into the box. Of course Psyche looked into the box, which contained not the beauty of Persephone but the sleep of the dark night of the Underworld, and she was enveloped by this deathlike sleep.

At last Cupid flew to the rescue of his beloved. He put sleep back into the box and, after reminding her that curiosity once before had been her undoing, told her to complete her final task. In the end, Venus was appeased. Psyche became one of the immortals, and on Mt. Olympus Jupiter ratified the marriage of Cupid and Psyche with a glorious wedding. A daughter was born to them called Pleasure (*Voluptas*), and they lived happily ever after.

Here are some of the universal motifs in this tale which are common to mythology and particularly folktale.

- The element of romance with a happy ending.
- The fairy-tale atmosphere.
- The beautiful princess awakened from sleep.
- The wicked sisters.
- The mysterious lover.
- The bride who is too inquisitive.
- The imposition of tasks or labors.

As will become apparent from a study of saga, usually the hero, not the heroine, must perform extraordinary labors, especially the conquest of death by a visit to and return from the Underworld.

THE APHRODITE OF SAPPHO OF LESBOS

Female homosexuality in Greek and Roman mythology and society is as important a theme as male homosexuality, but it is not always as visible. Sappho, a lyric poetess from the island of Lesbos (sixth century B.C.), in a fervent and moving poem, invokes Aphrodite's help to win back the love of a young woman with whom she has been involved. From Sappho comes the term Lesbian and the association of Aphrodite with Lesbian love.

Lesbianism is a latent motif in stories about the strong bond of affection among Artemis and her band of female followers, which we shall encounter in the next chapter. The atmosphere is virginal and the relationships pure, although the success of Jupiter with Callisto when he takes the form of her beloved virgin goddess Diana makes one wonder. It seems appropriate that Aphrodite, not Artemis, presides over more sensual female relationships.

TRANSLATION

The myth of Cybele and Attis has inspired one of the greatest of all Roman poems, the <u>Attis</u> of Catullus, his 63rd poem, remarkable for the interaction of its meter, language, and subject-matter. Cybele's eunuch priests are called Galli (feminine, Gallae). Dindymus is a mountain in Mysia sacred to Cybele.

Attis was whisked over the deep sea in a swift ship. As soon as he set foot in the Phrygian woods, eagerly and quickly he entered the shadowy forest-crowned haunts of the goddess. Then and there, driven by a frenzied delirium, Attis, out of his mind, hacked off the burden of his genitals with a sharp piece of flint. And so when she (no longer he) sensed that her manhood was gone, while still staining the soil of the earth with fresh drops of blood, she impetuously took up in her snowy-white hands your light tambourine, Cybele, took up your mysteries, O Mother. Shaking the hollow ox-hide of the tambourine with delicate fingers, tremulously she began to sing this exhortation to her companions.

"Gallae, come and go to the forest-heights of Cybele, all together, together go, you wandering herd of the Lady of Dindymus, you, who sought alien lands, like exiles, and followed my rule with me as your leader. My companions, you endured the rapid sea and the turbulent deep because of your inordinate hatred of Venus. Delight the heart of your Lady by your headlong pursuit. Dismiss any thought of tardy delay. Together come and follow to the Phrygian home of Cybele, to the Phrygian forests of the goddess, where the clash of cymbals rings, where tambourines resound, where the Phrygian flute-player blows deeply on his curved reed, where ivy-crowned maenads toss their heads wildly, where they brandish their holy emblems with piercing cries, where the wandering cohort of the goddess is accustomed to range. To this place it is right that we rush in swift dances."

As soon as Attis, not a real woman, finished this song to her companions, the holy band of followers suddenly cried aloud with tremulous tongues; the light tambourine resounds, the hollow cymbals renew their clash, the rapid chorus on rushing feet ascends verdant Mount Ida. At the same time, their leader Attis, frenzied, gasping, and bereft of sense, wanders through the shadowy forests to the sound of the tambourine, just like an untamed heifer avoiding the burden of her yoke. The swift Gallae follow their fleet-footed leader. And so, as they reached the home of Cybele, all worn out after too strenuous exertion, without food, they seize upon sleep. Deep exhaustion covers their eyes drooping with weariness, and the mad fury of their minds is dispelled in restful peace.

But when the sun with the radiant eyes of his golden countenance illuminated the clear aether, hard earth, and wild seas, and dispelled the darkness of night with his vigorous, tramping horses, then Sleep in flight quickly left Attis awakened and the goddess Pasithea (Sleep's wife) received him in her tremblinbg breast. So after gentle rest and freed from fierce madness, as soon as Attis himself realized in his heart what he had done and saw with mind clear where he was and what he had lost, with a surge of emotion he rushed back to the sea-shore. There, looking out over the vast expanse of water, miserable, with eyes full of tears, she spoke to her fatherland in a pitiful voice.

"O my country, land of my birth, my country, my fatherland, which I, poor wretch, abandoned, as runaway servants desert their masters. I made my way to the forests of Ida so that I might be amidst snow and the cold haunts of wild animals and, in my madness, might frequent all their lairs. Where, in what region, do I think that you, my fatherland, are situated? My very eyes desire to direct their gaze upon you while, for a brief time, my mind is free from wild madness. Shall I be borne from

my home into these remote forests? Shall I be away from my fatherland, possessions, friends, and parents? Shall I be away from the marketplace, the wrestling ground, the racecourse, and gymnasium? O wretched, wretched heart, you must bewail again and again. For what form of human being is there which I have not had? I, now a woman, I, who was once a young man, an adolescent, and a boy. I was once the flower of the gymnasium. I was once the beauty of the wrestling-ground. For me, doorways were crowded, for me, thresholds were warmed by lingering crowds of admirers, for me, the house was decked with garlands of flowers, when I had to leave my bedroom each sunrise. Now am I to be called a handmaid of the gods and a female slave of Cybele? Am I to be a maenad, I only part of myself, I a man barren? Am I to live in the frigid snow-clad regions of verdant Ida? Am I to live my life under the lofty summits of Phrygia, where the hind dwells in the woods, where the boar wanders the forests? Now, now I am sorry for what I have done. Now, now I am full of regret!"

As this cry quickly rose from his rosy lips, bringing news of a change of heart to both ears of the gods, then Cybele loosened the fastened yoke of her lions and goading the one on the left, enemy of the flock, speaks as follows:

"Come on now," she says, "be fierce, go, and see to it that madness drives him on, see that by a stroke of madness he makes his return into the forests, he who too freely desires to flee from my domination. Come, lash your back with your tail, endure your own tail-lashes, make all places resound with your bellowing roar. Fiercely shake your ruddy mane on your brawny neck."

Cybele utters these threats and with her hand frees the lion from the yoke. He, urging himself on, incites his heart to rage. He rushes, roars, and breaks through the brushwood with his speeding paws. But when he approached the watery stretch of the white shore and saw tender Attis by the marble surface of the sea, he makes his attack. Attis, out of his mind, flees into the wild woods. There, always, for the whole span of his life, was he her handmaid.

Great goddess, goddess Cybele, goddess, Lady of Dindymus, let all your fury be far from my house. Drive others to frenzy, drive others mad.

Many powerful emotions and questions are evoked by this masterpiece. Why does Attis succumb to such fanaticism? Does his fanaticism relate to fanatical obsessions today? Why his regrets? How is mother Cybele characterized? How is she different from the Venus for whom Cybele's followers have an inordinate hatred?

- Much of Catullus' poem is in the text of Johann Mayhofer, set to music by Schubert.
- The worship of Cybele with her mysteries is not unlike that of Dionysus. See Chapter 11.

COMPACT DISCS

5. Bach, Johann Christoph Friedrich. Pygmalion. Cantata for bass and orchestra.

19. Bernstein, Leonard. Serenade. After Plato's Symposium, for solo violin, string orchestra, harp, and percussion. Sections are entitled: Phaedrus, Pausanias; Aristophanes; Erixymachus; Agathon; Socrates, Alcibiades.

24. Blow, John, Venus and Adonis. Masque (M/L 597).

37. Campra, André, La Dispute de l'Amour et de l'Hymen. Cantata.

54. Cherubini, Luigi, Pigmalione. Opera.

68. Donizetti, Gaetano, Il Pigmalione. Operatic scene between Pygmalion and Galatea.

78. Franck, César, Psyché. Symphonic Poem for chorus and orchestra.

93. Gounod, Charles, Sapho. This first opera of Gounod revolves around the legendary, tragic love of Sappho for Phaon and her suicide.

113. Harrison, Lou, <u>A Summerfield Set</u>. For solo piano and inspired by lines from the invocation to Venus, at the beginning of Lucretius, <u>De Rerum Natura</u>, depicting Mars seeking love from Venus.

138. Koechlin, Charles, "Hymne à Vénus." Song.

150. Lerdahl, Fred, <u>Eros</u>. Variations for mezzo-soprano and chamber ensemble on a poem "Coitus" (in <u>Lustra</u>) by Ezra Pound.

155. Lloyd, George, <u>The Vigil of Venus</u>. Lovely setting of the late Latin text of <u>Pervigilium Veneris</u> for soprano, tenor, chorus, and orchestra. A romantic peom about springtime and love.

157. Loevende, Theo, <u>Venus and Adonis</u>, for five instruments. Written for a stage production of Shakespeare's poem.

158. Loewe, Frederick. <u>My Fair Lady</u>. Lyrics by Alan Jay Lerner. Great musical starring Rex Harrison and Julie Andrews, replaced for the movie by Audrey Hepburn. See Video below.

159. Lully, Jean-Baptiste, <u>Atys</u>. Opera about Attis and Cybele.

161. Magnard, Albéric, <u>Hymne à Vénus</u>. Symphonic poem.

193. <u>Music of Ancient Greece</u>. <u>Epithalamium and Hymeneal</u>, by Sappho, <u>Partheneion</u>, by Alkman.

198. Nono, Luigi, <u>Fragmente-Stille, An Diotima</u>, for string quartet. Short quotations from the poetry of Hölderlin are written into the score, twelve of them from the poem "To Diotima," in which Hölderlin evokes his beloved Susette Gontard as Diotima.

202 and **203.** Orff, Carl, <u>Trionfo di Afrodite (Triumph of Aphrodite)</u>. Scenic cantata. Settings of texts in the original Latin and Greek of Catullus and Sappho presenting a wedding ceremony with a concluding apparition of Aphrodite. Orff's <u>Catulli Carmina</u> (a setting of some of Catullus' love lyrics) and his popular <u>Carmina Burana</u> (songs to medieval texts) are of related interest.

205. Pacini, Giovanni, <u>Saffo</u>. Opera (like Gounod's) about Sappho's tragic love for Phaon.

227. Rameau, Jean Philippe, <u>Castor et Pollux</u>. The prologue to this opera deals with Venus' subjugation of Mars.

232. _____, <u>Pygmalion</u>. Acte de Ballet, with a text.

247. Satie, Erik, <u>Socrate</u>. For voice or voices and chamber orchestra or piano, entitled a <u>Dramatic Symphony</u>. Texts (in French) are drawn from Plato's <u>Symposium</u>, <u>Phaedrus</u>, and <u>Phaedo</u>.

249. Schoeck, Othmar, <u>Venus</u>. Opera based on Mérimée's <u>La Vénus d'Ile</u> and Eichendorff's <u>Das Marmorbild (The Marble Statue)</u>, about a statue of Venus that comes to life.

251. Schubert, "Atys." Song of the Catullan Attis.

275. "Stupid Cupid." Very popular song sung by Connie Francis.

276. Suppé, Franz von, <u>Die Schöne Galathée</u>. Delightful comic operetta about Pygmalion and Galatea (M/L 605).

284. "Venus." Very popular song sung by Frankie Avalon.

285. "Venus in Blue Jeans." Very popular song sung by Jimmy Clanton.

290. Weill, Kurt, <u>One Touch of Venus</u>. Musical.

For Richard Wagner's <u>Tannhaüser</u>, not listed in the Discography but readily available on CD, see Videos.

VIDEOS

<u>One Touch of Venus</u>. A statue of Venus comes to life. Based on the novel <u>The Tinted Venus</u>, with music by Kurt Weill, starring Robert Walker and Ava Gardner, and directed by William A. Seiter. Republic Pictures Home Video. NTA Home Entertainment VHS V3060. The forty-fifth anniversary issue VHS 5558.

Mannequin. An artist falls in love with the department store mannequin he has created, a master-piece that comes to life. Video Treasures. M920.

My Fair Lady. Celebrated movie of the Lerner and Loewe musical based on Shaw's *Pygmalion*, star-ring Audrey Hepburn (her singing voice is that of Marni Nixon) and Rex Harrison and directed by George Cukor. CBS/Fox Video 25th anniversary edition 7038; 30th anniversary edition 81166.

Pygmalion. Excellent film adaptation of George Bernard Shaw's play, starring Leslie Howard and directed by Anthony Asquith and Leslie Howard. Embassy Home Entertainment 6018; also Video Yesteryear. It is enlightening to compare parallel scenes with the musical version, My Fair Lady.

Songs of Sappho. A recreation of song and dance as imagined on ancient Lesbos, with Andrea Goodman as Sappho, and chorus. In ancient Greek with English subtitles. The New York Greek Drama Company, Box 2113, Hartford, N.Y. 12838.

Tannhäuser, by Richard Wagner. An operatic tour de force (with its depiction of a voluptuous Venus and her abode) that delineates, unforgettably, the conflict between sacred and profane love.

Bel Canto Paramount Home Video. Cassilly et al., Metropolitan Opera Orchestra, cond. James Levine.

INTERPRETATION

Aphrodite has been the inspiration of more works than any other personage in classical mythology, and only a very few works can be mentioned here from the thousands that could be listed.

Aphrodite Urania and Aphrodite Pandemos. Examples of the many works of art inspired by Hesiod's myth of the birth of Aphrodite from the sea have been discussed in Chapter 1. The alter-nate myth, which names Zeus and Dione as her parents, is alluded to in the east pediment of the Parthenon, where Dione is one of the seated goddesses receiving the news of Athena's birth. Aphrodite's rule over the island of Cythera is exquisitely recalled in two paintings by Antoine Watteau, Pilgrimage to the Island of Cythera (1717, now in Paris, and a second version, 1718, now in Berlin).

The duality of Aphrodite is continued in the post-classical (and especially Renaissance) theme of Sacred and Profane Love. Urania is shown naked, Pandemos robed in luxurious clothing. The most famous such representation is Titian's Sacred and Profane Love (1514, now in Rome), a com-plex painting whose meaning is not fully known. The dual nature of Aphrodite extends also to the allegory of the Choice of Heracles (see Chapter 20): indeed, in Rubens's design for the Pompa Introitus Ferdinandi, a Cupid, accompanying Pleasure, is trying to pluck away the hero's club and lionskin.

The Range of Artistic Depicitions of Aphrodite. Pre-Greek sculptures, which emphasize female sexual attributes, from the Aegean islands are given the title "Aphrodite" or "Venus," which is an anachronism. In archaic Greek art Aphrodite is shown clothed, whether seated with other Olympians (as in the east pediment and inner frieze of the Parthenon at Athens) or standing or rid-ing in a chariot, or even (as on a red-figure vase from Cyprus, ca. 440 B.C., now in Oxford) on a swan. After about 400 she begins to be portrayed nude in statues, but not in vase-paintings. The most famous of these statues is the Venus of Cnidos by Praxiteles (mid-fourth century B.C.; copy in the Vatican), which is known, like other famous versions derived from it (the Medici Venus, etc.), from Roman marble copies from the second century A.D. onwards. A second type is a half-draped Venus; the most famous is the statue from Melos (Venus de Milo, now in Paris), the original of which might also have been by Praxiteles. A third type is a crouching nude statue, of which the bronze original may have been by Doidalsas (ca. 200 B.C.; Roman copy in Paris). All these types have been the inspiration of countless post-classical renditions.

Many paintings include a statue of Aphrodite as a reminder of her power to affect the action of the painting: this is the case in Watteau's paintings mentioned above; another example is Rubens's The Garden of Love (1633, now in the Prado), where the statue's position and attributes reflect the urgency of the lovers in the garden. More subtle, and perhaps satirical, is John Singer Sargent's Breakfast in the Loggia (1910, now in Washington), where behind the two elegantly dressed women at their meal is a statue of Aphrodite similar to the Venus de Milo. Of the countless representations of reclining Aphrodite it will be sufficient to mention Titian's three masterpieces—Venus of Urbino (1538, in Florence); Venus at her Toilet with Two Cupids (1555, in Washington); Venus with an Organist (ca. 1550, in Madrid). In eighteenth-century France at th courts of Louis XIV and Louis XV Venus was the subject of paintings, court ballets, and operas. François Boucher (1703–1770) painted a large number of works which were variations on the theme of Venus: many of them, genuinely inspired by their classical origins, are masterpieces which are in collections in Paris, London, New York, and many other cities; many however, are superficial even if technically accomplished.

The Graces. Among companions of Aphrodite in art, The Graces (Charites, but often confused with the Horai, Seasons) are especially popular. They were usually portrayed as three clothed young women and appeared on the statue of Zeus at Olympia (see Chapter 3). At Rome, in a painting of the fourth style from Pompeii, they were shown naked and linked together. This pose has been popular with many post-classical artists: of hundreds of representations the preeminent one is The Three Graces by Rubens (1635, in Madrid).

The Range of Literary Depictions of Aphrodite. In Homer Aphrodite fares badly when she takes part in the *theomachies* (fighting between gods), and she is even wounded by a mortal hero, Diomedes, in Book 5 of the Iliad. She also can show terrible anger, as she upbraids Helen in Book 3 of the Iliad when Helen resists her command to make love to Paris. Her anger is shown also in Euripides' tragedy Hippolytus (428 B.C.), in which she speaks the prologue and reveals her plan to destroy Hippolytus by means of Phaedra, because of his refusal to worship her. In Book 14 of the Iliad, she assists Hera in the deception of Zeus by lending her the *kestos* (usually translated as "girdle," although Homer says she takes it from her breasts), in which lie all the charm and power of sexual attraction. Her role in the Aeneid is far greater, where she repeatedly appears to comfort, advise, and help her son Aeneas. Because of her success in the Judgment of Paris (see Chapter 17), she supports the Trojans in the Trojan war. The myth of her love for the Trojan prince Anchises is told in the Homeric Hymn to Aphrodite (No. 5): a fine post-classical representation is the painting by Annibale Carracci (1600) of Venus and Anchises in the Farnese Palace at Rome. This Hymn and the very beautiful and subtle Invocation to Aphrodite by Sappho (ca. 600 B.C.) in their different ways express the power of the goddess. A distant echo of the ancient hymns is heard in Palamon's prayer to Venus at her temple in Chaucer's The Knight's Tale (ca. 1387).

Priapus. This fertility god, Aphrodite's son, was worshiped especially at Lampsacus, a Greek city on the Hellespont, where his ritual included the sacrifice of a donkey. Ovid (in the Fasti) twice tells the tale of the reason for the hostility of Priapus to donkeys, and it is a principal theme in Bellini's painting The Feast of the Gods (1514, now in Washington), discussed in Chapter 3. Priapus' importance to the fertility of nature was indicated by his statues, which displayed a huge erect phallus and were common in Greek and Roman gardens. A sub-genre of poetry, ranging from the lyrically erotic to the obscene, called Priapeia, was popular in the Roman world, and the wrath of Priapus is a leading motif in the Latin novel Satyricon, by Petronius (d. A.D. 66).

Pygmalion and Galatea. From Book 10 of Ovid's Metamorphoses, this popular myth is readily interpreted as an allegory of the inspiration and achievement of the artist, or as the fulfillment of desire by lover or spiritual pilgrim. Both allegories appear in the cycle by Edward Burne-Jones (1868–1878, now in Birmingham) based on a poem by William Morris. The titles of the four paintings indicate the nature of the allegories: The Heart Desires, The Hand Refrains, The Godhead Fires, and The Soul Attains (in the fourth painting, the statue comes to life and is embraced by the artist). For the comedy by George Bernard Shaw and other modern adaptations, see Compact Discs and Videos.

Venus and Adonis. The myth of Adonis is most important for its influence in ritual and religion, as well as in art and poetry. Innumerable post-classical works of art are based on Ovid's full account in Book 10 of the Metamorphoses. Adonis is an Asiatic vegetation deity, the consort of the goddess of creative Nature (Astarte being one of her many names in the East), who dies each year and is resurrected. Sappho (ca. 600 B.C.) refers to his death and the mourning of women for him: these are the basic elements in the myth, to which later are added the motifs of Aphrodite as his lover, the boar-hunt, and his birth from the myrrh-tree. The tradition of Adonis spending one-third of his time with Persephone in the Underworld and two-thirds with Aphrodite is old and appears in Greek vase-paintings, where he first appears around 400 B.C., sometimes with Eros as well as Aphrodite. In the mid-fourth century he is shown on a couch (on a vase now in Naples) with Zeus enthroned above adjudicating the sharing of his time with Persephone and Aphrodite. Earlier, however, another feature of his ritual, the "Gardens of Adonis," first appears on Athenian vases around 450 B.C.: there is a good example of ca. 390 B.C. now in Karlsruhe. At Rome he appears in wall-paintings at Pompeii, including one (now lost, but reproduced from earlier photographs) of the fourth style (i.e., ca. A.D. 65). As a dying and resurrected divinity he is an obvious source of allegory for funerary art, and on several sarcophagi the three main stages of his legend are narrated sequentially: a sarcophagus of the late second century A.D. (now in Paris) shows scenes of his farewell from Aphrodite, the hunt and the fatal wound, and the mourning over him. In post-classical art an important representation of the myth is the cycle of four paintings by Marcantonio Franceschini (completed before 1699 for the ducal palace in Vaduz, Liechtenstein, where they still are, although not in their original rooms), which show dramatically the birth of Adonis, the hunt with Venus, his death, and the mourning of Venus. Of the huge number of post-classical paintings, masterpieces, both with the title of Venus and Adonis, by Titian (1554) and Veronese (1584) are exceptional: both are now in Madrid. Titian focuses on the stage of departure, and Veronese on an earlier stage when Adonis sleeps in the lap of Venus. The stage of mourning has been especially popular in the Christian world because of its evocation of lamentation for the dead Christ (i.e., the Pietà): the Spanish painter Jusepe de Ribera (who lived and worked in Naples) painted one such scene (1637, now in Rome), and a very dramatic painting by one of his followers (ca. 1650, now in Cleveland) shows Venus descending from her chariot (drawn by doves) to mourn over the corpse. His departure from Venus and her efforts to restrain him are also popular because of Ovid, as shown by Titian's painting mentioned above, and in the Shakespeare's Venus and Adonis (1593). The myth of Venus and Adonis is similar to that of

Cybele and Attis, but Attis has not inspired many works of art; Cybele will be discussed in Chapter 12.

Eros/Cupid. Of the associates of Aphrodite, Eros is by far the most important. In archaic Greek literature, he is the creative force in nature, but potentially maddening and destructive, as Sophocles (in his <u>Antigone</u>, 441 B.C.) says in a chorus addressed to Eros. Around 400 B.C. he begins to be represented as a chubby infant, the Cupid of innumerable ancient and post-classical works. In Roman art, especially in the frescoes from Pompeii, Cupids are shown in all kinds of human activities, and they are the inevitable companions of Venus in post-classical art. Sometimes Eros appears with his opposite, Anteros, a variation on the duality of Sacred and Profane Love. Most often, however, Cupids (known as *putti*) signify the joy, energy, and hope of love, as is the case in almost every painting of Aphrodite and Venus mentioned earlier in this chapter. Veritable swarms of putti appear in paintings of the seventeenth and eighteenth centuries, for example, those by Rubens, Poussin, Watteau, and Boucher—four very different masters all using the same decorative and allegorical figures. Cupid is shown in many guises: a mischief-maker who is punished or taught by his mother; a winged archer; a child stung by a bee; a mourner or a joyful celebrant. He is perhaps the commonest of all decorative personages from classical mythology to appear in post-classical art.

Cupid and Psyche. The myth of Cupid and Psyche is an allegory of the union of the human soul with the divine. The lovers appear on Greek vases and reliefs in the fifth century B.C. and on many more in the fourth and third centuries; Psyche is a winged female figure representing the soul, and Plato in his <u>Phaedrus</u> similarly refers to the soul as winged. Apuleius (ca. A.D. 160) made Psyche into a mythological figure with her own narrative in his Latin novel, paraphrased above. In art Psyche often has butterfly wings, and in the Roman world she and Cupid are most commonly shown embracing: the best-known example is the statue now in Rome, a Roman copy of the fourth century A.D. of a Greek original of the second century B.C., in which the lovers are children without wings. This work was especially admired in the eighteenth century and copied in many media, including Wedgwood porcelain. The myth of Cupid and Psyche is also common on funerary reliefs as an allegory of the soul's immortality. Of the hundreds of post-classical representations, the cycle of frescoes by Raphael painted for the Villa Farnesina in Rome (1518, mentioned in Chapter 3) is preeminent.

Venus at Rome. Aphrodite has been celebrated in all ages as the goddess of the creative power in Nature. At Rome she was identified with Venus, the Italian goddess of neatness and fertility in gardens; despite her limited status, one of the most joyous of hymns to Venus is the opening of the <u>De Rerum Natura</u> of Lucretius (ca. 55 B.C.), imitated by Spenser in the <u>Faerie Queen</u> (4. 10. 44-47). Lucretius calls Venus "Mother of the descendants of Aeneas" (*Aeneadum Genetrix*), anticipating the claim of Julius Caesar and Augustus to be descended from Venus. Caesar's family did most to promote Venus to the first rank of Olympian deities at Rome. He dedicated a temple to Venus Genetrix in his new Forum Iulium in 46 B.C., and Hadrian (emperor A.D. 117-138) dedicated a temple to Venus and Roma in 135, one of the largest temples in the city.

CHAPTER 8
Artemis

THE BIRTH AND NATURE OF ARTEMIS

Zeus mated with the goddess LETO [le'to] (LATONA), and she bore ARTEMIS [ar'te-mis] (DIANA) and APOLLO [a-pol'lo] on the island of Delos. In some accounts, Artemis was born first and helped in the delivery of her brother. Thus she revealed at once her powers as a goddess of childbirth, which she shares with Hera and Eileithyia.

The birth of the twin deities Artemis and Apollo links them closely together from the very beginning. Lovely Artemis will on occasion join her handsome brother in supervising the dances of the Muses and the Graces, and they both delight in the bow and arrow.

NIOBE AND HER CHILDREN

The skill in archery of Apollo and Artemis is exemplified by their defense of the insulted honor of their mother, Leto. The women of Thebes greatly honored Leto and her two children. Their tributes seemed excessive to NIOBE [ni'o-be], who boasted that she was better than Leto because she was not only rich, beautiful, and the queen of Thebes, but had borne seven sons and seven daughters, whereas Leto was the mother of only one son and one daughter. Leto complained to her children about Niobe's hubris and they exacted a swift vengeance. With unerring arrows, Apollo killed all seven sons of Leto, and Artemis, all seven daughters. As Artemis was about to shoot the youngest, Niobe attempted to shield the girl and begged that this last one be spared, to no avail. Niobe herself was turned to stone and brought by a whirlwind to a mountaintop in her former homeland, Phrygia. There, tears trickling down wear away her face.

ACTAEON

ACTAEON [ak-te'on], or AKTAION, was an ardent hunter. Once when he wandered off alone, away from his companions, he stumbled upon, by accident or fate, a woodland cave with a pool of water, where Artemis (or Diana, in Ovid's version of the tale) was bathing accompanied by her attendant followers, as was their custom. When they saw Actaeon entering the cave, they screamed, and Diana, outraged that a man had seen her naked, took swift revenge. She splashed water in his face, and immediately horns began to grow from his head, and he was transformed into a stag, completely except for his mind. He ran away in fear and was sighted by his own hunting dogs, who turned on him and tore him to pieces.

CALLISTO AND ARCAS

CALLISTO [kal-lis'to], or KALLISTO ("most beautiful"), was a chaste huntress, just like the goddess Artemis whom she followed so devotedly. Zeus (or Jupiter, as Ovid tells it) no sooner saw Callisto than he fell in love with her and was determined to win her. He disguised himself as Artemis, knowing full well that in this transformation he could best win her confidence and affection. When Zeus pressed his attentions too ardently, his deception became only too clear to poor Callisto, who struggled in vain. Callisto rejoined Artemis and her companions, but eventually, when they bathed together, she could not disguise the fact that she was pregnant. Artemis was furious with Callisto for her betrayal and expelled her from the sacred group.

Hera (or Juno) had long been aware of her husband's guilt, and when Callisto gave birth to a son, named ARCAS [ar'kas], or ARKAS, she took her revenge. She turned Callisto into a bear, but her mind remained intact; thus, alone and afraid, she wandered the forests.

Arcas grew up, and, in his fifteenth year, while hunting he encountered his mother, Callisto, a bear whose human and relentless gaze frightened him. As he was about to drive a spear through her body, Zeus intervened and prevented matricide. He brought them both up to the heavens, where he transformed them into constellations.

Callisto became the Great Bear (Ursa Major); Arcas perhaps became the Little Bear (Ursa Minor) but more likely he should be seen as the Bear Warden (Arctophylax, or Arcturus, or Boötes).

ORION

Another constellation myth linked to Artemis concerns the hunter ORION [o-ri'on], whose story has many variations. He wooed Merope, the daughter of Oenopion ("wine-face"), king of the island of Chios, famous for its wines. While clearing the island of wild beasts, he encountered Artemis and tried to rape her. Enraged, the goddess produced a scorpion out of the earth that stung Orion to death. Both are seen in the sky. Others say Orion pursued the PLEIADES [ple'a-dez] (daughters of theTitan Atlas and Pleione, an Oceanid), and they were all transformed into constellations; SIRIUS [sir'i-us], Orion's hunting dog became the Dog Star.

ARTEMIS, SELENE, AND HECATE

Artemis became predominantly a vehement virgin, as the stories above make terrifyingly clear. Yet she also possesses characteristics that suggest a fertility goddess, e.g., her interest in childbirth and the young of both humans and animals. At Ephesus a statue depicts her with what seem like multiple breasts (see below). As a moon-goddess she was worshiped by women who linked her with the lunar cycle and their menstrual period. Nevertheless, above all, Artemis is the virgin huntress, the goddess of nature itself, not concerned with its teeming procreation (like Aphrodite) but with its pristine purity. Artemis, like the moon, appears as a symbol, cold, white, aloof, and chaste.

Hecate's Suppers. As a moon-goddess Artemis is linked with SELENE [se-le'ne], another earlier goddess of the moon (see Chapter 1). She is also linked with her cousin HECATE [hek'a-te], or HEKATE, a fertility goddess of the Underworld, who is depicted as a Fury (see Chapters 12 and 13), with a scourge and blazing torch, and accompanied by fierce hounds. In particular she is a goddess of the crossroads, a place thought to be the center of ghostly activity in the dead of night. Skilled in the arts of black magic, Hecate is invoked by sorceresses and murderers (e.g., Medea and Lady Macbeth). Offerings of food were made to her (called Hecate's suppers) at triple-faced statues, erected at crossroads and depicting three aspects of the moon: Selene in heaven, Artemis on earth, and Hecate in the Underworld.

EURIPIDES' <u>HIPPOLYTUS</u>

HIPPOLYTUS [hip-pol'i-tus], or HIPPOLYTOS, is the son of Theseus by the Amazon HIPPOLYTA [hip-pol'i-ta], or ANTIOPE [an-ti'o-pe]. Theseus has married Phaedra, the daughter of Minos, and

Hippolytus has grown up to be a young man, troubled by his illegitimacy and obsessed with his virginity. Aphrodite, in a typically Euripidean prologue, describes her great power and her vehement anger against Hippolytus, a hunter who hubristically rejects love and prefers to follow Artemis. Aphrodite exacts her revenge by making Phaedra fall desperately in love with her stepson, a passion impossible of fulfillment, which can only lead to tragedy. Phaedra first saw Hippolytus while he was being initiated into the Mysteries and was smitten by a hopeless lust. For two years Phaedra has suffered, and now she lies ill, overcome by her guilty secret and determined to die because she is a noble woman and cannot commit this abominable adultery, unlike other unfaithful wives who could be false to their husbands under any circumstances. She desperately desires to preserve her own honor and also that of her sons, Theseus' legitimate heirs. Her faithful nurse wrests the truth from her, and the solution that she takes upon herself determines the tragic outcome. [The well-meaning but interfering nurse becomes a literary archetype, e.g., Brangäne in <u>Tristan and Isolde</u>.]

The nurse has Hippolytus swear an oath to secrecy, but when she tells him of Phaedra's passion, he is enraged and cries out that his tongue swore but not his mind. Phaedra overhears the angry exchange and fears Hippolytus will tell all to her ruin (but he never does violate his oath). She hangs herself, but before doing so leaves an incriminating note to save herself and her children by claiming that Hippolytus violated her. Theseus too quickly believes her accusation against the protests of his innocent son, whose purity and religious fanaticism he has always resented. With a curse given him by his father, Poseidon, he orders his son into exile. Poseidon sends a bull from the sea, which frightens the horses of Hippolytus' chariot, and he is entangled in the wreckage. As he is dying, he is brought back to his father for a heartbreaking reconciliation, engineered by the deus ex machina Artemis who tells Theseus the truth and promises Hippolytus honors after his death for his devotion, and assures him that she will get even with Aphrodite. (In one version of Adonis' death, Artemis causes the boar to kill him.)

This bald summary does no justice to Euripides' play, which all must read themselves for its masterful symmetry of construction and its deceptively transparent simplicity, endlessly revealing intricate subtlety of thought and complexity of characterization. In the context of this and the previous chapter, Euripides' profound and critical scrutiny of the antithetical Artemis and Aphrodite and their worship should be primary (M\L 166-168).

COMPACT DISCS

29. Britten, Benjamin, <u>Phaedra</u>. Dramatic cantata for mezzo-soprano and small orchestra; a setting of lines from Robert Lowell's translation of Racine.

45. Cavalli, Francesco, <u>La Calisto</u>. Opera.

50. Charpentier, Marc-Antoine, <u>Actéon</u>. Opera.

66. Dittersdorf, Carl Ditters von, <u>Symphony in G Major</u>, "The Transformation of Actaeon into a Stag."

125. Honegger, Arthur, <u>Phèdre</u>. Suite drawn from music composed for the <u>Phèdre</u> of d'Annunzio.

176. Milhaud, Darius. <u>Trois Opéras-Minute: L'enlèvement d'Europe, L'abandon d'Ariane, and La délivrance de Thésée</u>. The last of these very short operas is about Phaedra's pursuit of Hippolytus, who is enamored of Aricia.

218. Philidor, François-André-Danican, <u>Carmen Saeculare</u>. Cantata for chorus. Musical setting of the Latin text of Horace's hymn to Apollo and Diana.

223. Puccini, Giacomo, "Hymn to Diana." Something classical from Puccini but dedicated to the fraternity of Italian hunters!

229. Rameau, Jean-Philippe, <u>Hippolyte et Aricie</u>. Opera indebted to Racine's <u>Phèdre</u>.
250 and **251.** Schubert, Franz, "Hippolits Lied" ("song of Hippolytus") and "Der zürnenden Diana" (a passionate eulogy "to wrathful Diana").
254. Scott, Stephen, <u>The Tears of Niobe</u>, for grand piano bowed and plucked by ten musicians. Inspired by Ovid and thematically related to Scott's <u>Minerva's Web</u>.

VIDEOS

<u>Desire under the Elms</u>. Video Film Classics. Kartes Video Communications 83227 01054. Eugene O'Neill's version of the Hippolytus story adapted for the screen, with Sophia Loren, Anthony Perkins, and Burl Ives, and directed by Delbert Mann (M/L 611).

<u>Diana and Actaeon</u>. Ballet. A. Vaganova, choreographer, with music by C. Pugni. Included in a mixed program, <u>Classic Ballet Night</u>. <u>Kirov Ballet</u>. View Video Dance Series NTSC 1203.

<u>The Seven Wonders of the Ancient World</u>. Questar Video QV2226. One is the temple of Artemis at Ephesus and another, the statue of Zeus at Olympia, both illustrated and discussed with theatrical flair for a general audience.

INTERPRETATION

The Misogyny of Hippolytus. In Euripides' play, after Hippolytus learns from the nurse of Phaedra's desire for him, he bursts out in a tirade against women as vile and evil, which has received a great deal of attention and interpretation, particularly today, because of its misogyny. Hippolytus' hatred of women is to be understood, but not necessarily condoned, in the context of his character and the play. This pure man has suffered the most traumatic shock of his young life. Sex with any woman is for him impossible. The sudden realization of the lust of Phaedra, the wife of his beloved father, strikes him as an abomination. His feelings are in some ways similar to the misogyny of another holy man, John the Baptist, in his outbursts against Salome and her mother Herodias. Hippolytus at least is in love with one woman, Artemis.

Yet some see in Hippolytus' outcry against women the expression of views generally held in Greek society, particularly in fifth-century Athens, as though somehow Hippolytus were himself a typical ancient Greek male. It is abundantly clear from the play that he is anything but that. Aphrodite herself punishes him for his aberration, and his father hates him for his religious fanaticism and cannot believe his virginal protestations; Theseus hastily convinces himself that Hippolytus raped Phaedra because he never could believe that his boy does not like women. Theseus is the archetype of the traditional, extrovert father who loves his wife and is disappointed by his son, who has turned out to be an introvert, different from him in almost every way. If one were to pick an average Athenian (a dangerous, if not foolish, game to play), it would be Theseus.

Misandry, Artemis, and the Amazons. Misandry, hatred of men, rather than misogyny is a more immediate theme in connection with Artemis, where it manifests itself in the close religious bonds of her group, which exclude the male, as made evident in the stories of Actaeon and Callisto. In this connection, the Amazons are relevant, important figures in the legends of Theseus, Heracles, and the Trojan war; they developed a society not unlike that of Artemis the huntress, which excluded men. The Amazons, however, were devoted to the pursuits of battle and determined to become invincible warriors. Their arete (excellence) was to be the same and in no way different from that of a male.

For a fascinating conception of what the Amazons might have been like, one should read the novel The Bull from the Sea by the wonderful Mary Renault, telling us about how Theseus wooed the Amazon mother of Hippolytus.

Hippolytus in Art and Literature. In the Iliad, Artemis takes part in the theomachy of Book 21 and is beaten violently by Hera. By far the most important conflict of Artemis with another divinity is her rivalry with Aphrodite in the myth of Hippolytus. The classic interpretation of the conflicting demands of sensuality and chastity is that of Euripides, as we have seen. The full title of his play (to distinguish it from his first Hippolytus, which does not survive) is Hippolytus Stephanephoros (Garland-Bearer), of 428 B.C.; in it Artemis is unable to save Hippolytus from his fate as the victim of the anger of Aphrodite. The setting is Troezen, where there was a cult of Hippolytus. Among the post-Euripidean dramas on the myth are the Phaedra of Seneca (died A.D. 65), set in Athens, which explores the psychological tensions of the myth without bringing in the goddesses; Racine's Phèdre (1677), in which Hippolytus is the lover of Aricia (see below); Eugene O'Neill's Desire under the Elms (1924), set in New England in 1850; and finally, Robinson Jeffers's The Cretan Woman (1954), a powerful adaptation of Euripides' play in which Aphrodite (but not Artemis) has a role.

A collection of plays with related essays is regrettably out of print: Phaedra and Hippolytus, Myth and Dramatic Form, edited by James L. Sanderson and Irwin Gopnik (Boston: Houghton Mifflin, 1966). It contains the plays by Euripides, Seneca, Racine, Jeffers, and O'Neill (discussed above), which so beautifully illustrate how varied, interesting, and illuminating the manipulation of the Hippolytus motif has been. Racine, by giving him a girlfriend, drastically changes the configuration of the archetype. Jeffers is closer to Euripides by keeping Hippolytus' abhorrence of sex; but when he introduces a companion for Hippolytus who is "slender and rather effeminate," he suggests another shifting of the archetype. At any rate, once Hippolytus' sexual orientation is made too explicit, the mystery of his psyche is diminished. Euripides gets everything right, a judgment made with due appreciation of the masterpieces that he has inspired. To be sure, not all adaptations of Euripides are masterpieces. In a recent music drama, Ode to Phaedra, by George Roumanis, with libretto by Frank Zajaczkowski (an Opera San Jose/KTEH Production, 1995, seen on TV), Phaedra commits suicide by poison, is brought to life by Aphrodite, and dies (again) by her own sword!

The myth has been more forcefully represented in drama than in art, but there is an impressive red-figure vase painting (ca. 340 B.C., now in London) showing the bull rising from the sea as Hippolytus drives his four-horse chariot and a Fury brandishes a torch. Episodes of the myth also have been narrated on many sarcophagus reliefs. A group of three (all ca. A.D. 300; one, the best, now in Paris) show Phaedra on the left, Hippolytus and the nurse in the center, and Theseus on the right. Of later works, The Death of Hippolytus, an oil-sketch by Rubens, is very powerful (ca. 1612, now in London).

Vergil (Aeneid 7. 761-82) and Ovid (Metamorphoses 15. 479-546) narrate how Hippolytus was brought back to life by Asclepius and "the love of Diana." He was called Virbius (as was his son by Aricia, whom he married after his resurrection) and associated with the cult of Diana near the town of Aricia (a few miles to the southeast of Rome). This legend belongs to the myths of the Roman goddess Diana (identified with Artemis), for which see Chapter 24.

Depictions of Artemis. Artemis is shown with other Olympians in group representations, e.g., at the wedding of Peleus and Thetis on the François and Sophilos Vases, riding in a chariot with Athena, and on the Parthenon frieze (see Chapter 3).

Artemis is called the Mistress of Animals by Homer (Iliad 21. 470), a title and function that may have been established in pre-Greek (Cretan) and Mycenaean cultures. She is shown holding an animal in each hand in archaic Greek art: for example, as a standing winged figure, she holds a lion in each hand on one of the painted handles of the François Vase (ca. 575 B.C., now in Florence), and holds a stag and a panther on the other handle. She both protects and hunts animals. When one of her protected animals is harmed she exacts revenge, as in the myth of Iphigenia (see Chapter 16). In Euripides' play Iphigenia in Tauris (412 B.C.), Athena foretells that Iphigenia herself will return to Greece and be the priestess of Artemis at Brauron (in Attica). The cult at Brauron was connected also with Artemis as goddess of childbirth, and young girls, representing little bears, danced for her and were dedicated to her service there for a period.

As huntress Artemis is shown with bow, arrows, and quiver, her clothing loose and her limbs uncovered: exemplary is the statue of Artemis the Huntress, a Roman marble copy of a Greek bronze (original fourth century B.C.; copy now in Paris). In her hunting she is accompanied by a band of virgins, some of whom must once have been goddesses (e.g., Callisto, whose name means "most beautiful"). Those who break their oath of chastity she punishes, as in Titian's paintings of Diana and Callisto (ca. 1559, now in Edinburgh and Vienna). A fine romantic representation of Artemis and her nymphs in a mountainous landscape is the painting by Washington Allston, Diana and Her Nymphs in the Chase (1805, now in Cambridge, Mass.).

Artemis, Goddess of Childbirth. Artemis is a virgin goddess, yet concerned with the fertility of animals and human beings, and especially with childbirth. In this aspect she was identified at Rome with Lucina. She is shown assisting at the birth of her twin, Apollo, on a red-figure vase (ca. 340 B.C., in Athens). Marcantonio Franceschini, however, paints her as a baby in The Birth of Apollo and Diana and Latona and the Lycian Peasants (1699, in Vaduz), in each case with lunar horns on her head; in Franceschini's Adonis cycle (also in Vaduz, 1699), she is shown as Lucina at the birth of Adonis (see Chapter 7).

Artemis of Ephesus. In Asia Minor she was worshiped as Artemis Ephesia at Ephesus, where her temple was considered one of the seven wonders of the world. Her statues show her standing with a long skirt on which are rows of animal heads and figures. In front of the upper half of her body she displays three rows of breast-like objects, and on her head she wears a turreted crown (in this she is similar to the Asiatic fertility goddess Cybele: see Chapters 7 and 24). These statues date from ca. A.D. 130, for example, two in Selçuk, Turkey, and one in Naples, which is made of alabaster and bronze with black skin. The many-breasted Artemis appears as a fountain-figure in Peter Paul Rubens's The Discovery of the Infant Erichthonius (1616, now in Vaduz).

Artemis and Apollo. Artemis joins with Apollo in a number of myths, especially legends of punishment. She is present when Apollo tries to prevent the attack of Tityus on Leto, in a red-figure Attic vase (ca. 510 B.C., now in Paris). Franceschini (see above) shows her joining him in killing Python. She is present at the contest of Apollo and Marsyas, for example, in an Athenian red-figure vase (ca. 400 B.C., now in London), in which she holds a torch. She is present at the contest of Apollo and Heracles for the Delphic tripod (see Chapter 20) in a red-figure vase by the Andocides painter (ca. 525 B.C., now in Berlin).

Niobe. Artemis joins Apollo in the punishment of Niobe, as shown in the red-figure vase by the Niobid painter (ca. 450 B.C., now in Paris), in which she coolly takes an arrow from her quiver to kill yet another victim. While Ovid focuses as much on the pride of Niobe as on her grief, it is her grief and the suffering of her murdered children that have dominated the artistic tradition. Both emotions are shown in the Niobe Group in Florence, large marble copies of originals of the fourth century B.C. made by Skopas or Praxiteles for the pediment of a great temple or monument. Another famous antique marble copy of a fifth century B.C. original is the Niobid (i.e., a dying daughter of Niobe) in the Baths of Diocletian in Rome.

Actaeon. On her own, Artemis punishes Actaeon, perhaps the most popular of her myths with post-classical artists. The best-known ancient representation is the vase painted by the Pan painter (ca. 460 B.C., now in Boston), on which Actaeon is still human in form as he is devoured by his hounds and shot by the arrows of Artemis. Titian's Diana and Actaeon (ca. 1559, now in Edinburgh) shows Actaeon unwittingly coming upon Artemis bathing, while Rubens (in an oil-sketch of 1639, now privately owned) shows him already transformed. Ovid tells the story of Actaeon and the anger of Artemis most fully (Metamorphoses 3. 158-255), and Apuleius (ca. A.D. 150), in Book 2 of his novel Metamorphoses (The Golden Ass), describes a statue-group of Diana and Actaeon (already turned into a stag) that stood in the atrium of the house of Byrrena, as a foreshadowing of the consequences of the curiosity of the novel's hero, Lucius. Shakespeare likens the lovesick Duke Orsino in Twelfth Night (1. 1) to Actaeon turned into a hart pursued by the hounds of his desire. The myth has been repeatedly portrayed by storytellers, poets, and artists to the present day. The Italian-American painter Bruno Civitico, in his 1983 work Diana and Acteon (sic), depicts the myth in a park-like setting whose woods in the background alone hint at the tragedy that is to come. A vivid re-telling is the fate of Larry Actaeon in the first part of John Cheever's Metamorphoses (published in The Stories of John Cheever, 1978).

Orion. Like Callisto and Arcas, another victim of Artemis, Orion, became a constellation, mentioned by Homer in the Iliad (22. 29); this is the context in which he is most frequently mentioned in astronomical poems (e.g., the Astronomicon of the Roman poet Manilius, ca. A.D. 15) or portrayed in Renaissance sky-maps. In the Odyssey (5. 121-24), however, Calypso refers to him as a victim of the jealousy of the gods, and Odysseus sees him as a hunter in the Underworld (11. 572-75). Poussin's painting Landscape with Diana and Orion (1658, now in New York) shows Orion as a blind giant striding to the east guided by the child on his shoulder as Diana looks down from the sky. The painting is also known as Blind Orion Searching for the Rising Sun. A modern version of the blind Orion is by the English painter Stephen McKenna, The Blind Orion with Eos and Artemis (1981, now in a private collection).

Artemis, in another display of her anger, sent the Calydonian boar to punish Oeneus for his failure to sacrifice to her (see Chapter 23).

Artemis, Hecate, and Selene. Artemis is often identified with Hecate, a pre-Olympian chthonic goddess associated especially with magic, who was worshiped particularly at crossroads or places where three roads met; hence her title in Latin of Trivia (she of the three ways), and the title of George Meredith's novel (1885), Diana of the Crossways, which has nothing to do with myths of Artemis. Hecate is invoked in literary representations of magic rituals, for example, in Book 6 of Lucan's epic Bellum Civile (A.D. 65), by far the most extended narrative of its sort, and in acts 2 and 3 of Shakespeare's Macbeth (1606).

Artemis is more consistently identified with Selene, the moon, which in Latin and English poetry is therefore often called Cynthia. In art (for example, the Franceschini paintings referred to above) she is shown with lunar horns. In this aspect she was especially popular in Elizabethan and Jacobean poetry (i.e, in the period between 1558 and 1625), for example, in Ben Jonson's <u>Hymn to Diana</u>, "Queen and huntress, chaste and fair." The myth of Artemis-Selene and Endymion was represented on Roman sarcophagi as an allegory of the sleep of death and hope for a new life; she is shown, for example, approaching the sleeping Endymion in a sarcophagus (now in New York) of about A.D. 160. Preeminent among many later representations is the painting of <u>Diana and Endymion</u> (ca. 1630, now in Detroit), showing Artemis standing lovingly over the kneeling Endymion, who implores her not to diminish his human life by giving him eternal sleep (the same fear of the results of the intercourse between a mortal and a goddess is expressed by Anchises to Aphrodite: see Chapter 7).

CHAPTER 9

Apollo

THE BIRTH OF APOLLO

Zeus mated with LETO [le′to] (LATONA), who conceived the twin gods ARTEMIS [ar′te-mis] (DIANA) and APOLLO [a-pol′lo]. The lengthy Hymn to Apollo tells in its first part ("To Delian Apollo") of Apollo's birth; no mention is made of Artemis.

Leto roamed far and wide searching for a refuge where she might give birth, but the many places she approached were afraid to receive her. Finally the island of Delos accepted her, but only after she assured the island (personified in the <u>Hymn</u>) with a great oath that a sacred precinct of Apollo would be built there and that it would become a place of prosperity, wealth, and prestige.

When Leto had endured nine days and nights of labor, Eileithyia, the goddess of childbirth, was summoned by Iris from Olympus to help in the delivery. Goddesses present at the birth attended to the newborn child, and as soon as Apollo had been nursed on nectar and ambrosia, he miraculously became a mighty god who declared that the bow and the lyre were his and that he would prophesy to mortals the unerring will of Zeus. Leto was delighted with her son and all Delos blossomed with joy.

In the conclusion of this part of the <u>Hymn</u>, the poet describes the great festival of Apollo at Delos with its famous chorus of maidens who can sing in all dialects, and he identifies himself as a blind man from Chios "whose songs are the best forevermore." Some erroneously believe that this poet is Homer. Bards, who are archetypically blind, see the Muses' truth.

THE SANCTUARY OF APOLLO AT DELPHI

The second part of the <u>Homeric Hymn to Apollo</u> ("To Pythian Apollo") tells how Apollo traveled in Greece until he found the proper place for the foundation of his oracle, Crisa, under Mt. PARNASSUS [par-nas′sus], or PARNASSOS, where he laid out his temple; then he slew a dragon, PYTHO [pi′tho], or PYTHON, and thus the site was called Pytho. Apollo was given the epithet PYTHIAN [pith′i-an] and a prophetess of Apollo received the name of PYTHIA [pith′i-a]. Originally at this site there had probably been an oracle of the great mother goddess Gaia, and the slaying of the dragon may symbolize conquest by the Hellenes and their god Apollo, who thus becomes yet another to add to our list of dragon-slayers.

The OMPHALOS [om′fa-los], an archaic stone shaped like an egg with two birds perched on either side, was thought to designate the location of the sanctuary at the center of the world, for according to legend Zeus released two eagles from opposite ends of the earth and they met exactly at the spot of Apollo's sanctuary, which came to be known universally by the name of DELPHI [del′-fi], or DELPHOI, for the following reason.

After Apollo had established his sanctuary, he needed to recruit attendants. He spotted a ship sailing from Crete and he sprang aboard in the form of a dolphin. The crew were awed into submission and followed a course that led the ship to Crisa. Here Apollo revealed himself as a god and initiated them to his service, with directions to pray to him as Apollo DELPHINIUS [del-fin′i-us], or DELPHINIOS, a word meaning "dolphin," from which Crisa or Pytho received its new name of Delphi.

THE PANHELLENIC SANCTUARY AT DELPHI

The Panhellenic sanctuary of Apollo is in many ways representative of other Panhellenic sites elsewhere, for example, the sanctuary of Zeus at Olympia (see Chapter 3). Yet the sacred area and the temple built on the lower slopes of Mt. Parnassus are particularly awe-inspiring, and the many dedications made to the god remind us of how Greek religion was responsible for the development of great and universal literature, poetry, drama, sculpture, architecture, etc. The Pythian games celebrated every four years included both physical and intellectual competitions and the worship of the god.

The Oracle and Pythia at Delphi. The Panhellenic sanctuary at Delphi was the most important oracle in the Greek world. People in general and representatives of states in particular came from all over the Greek world and beyond to ask Apollo questions of every sort. The Pythia, the prophetess of Apollo, uttered the responses of the god as she sat on a tripod. Her answers came in incoherent ravings, which were transcribed by a nearby priest into intelligible prose or verse. In Plato's <u>Apology</u> we are told that Socrates learned from the Delphic oracle that he was the wisest of men, a response that this great philosopher took very seriously.

FOUR OF APOLLO'S LOVES

The Cumaean Sibyl. The general designation for a prophetess was SIBYL [sib′il], or SIBYLLA [sib-il′la]; a Sibyl at Delphi, however, was called specifically the Pythia, as we have noted.

The Sibyls at Cumae in Italy were famous. Most famous among them was the CUMAEAN [ku-me′an] Sibyl, who was Aeneas' guide in the Underworld (see Chapter 13). We learn about this Sibyl from Ovid. Apollo offered her anything that she wished, if only she would yield to him. She picked up a heap of sand and asked for as many birthdays as the individual grains but forgot to ask for continuous youth along with the years. Nevertheless Apollo would have given her long life and eternal youth if she had agreed to succumb to him. When she refused him, the god granted her original wish, and she withered away, eventually to become only a voice. This story of the Cumaean Sibyl once again illustrates how our ignorant wishes may be granted to our woe (cf. Eos and Tithonus, Chapter 1).

Cassandra. CASSANDRA [kas-san′dra], or KASSANDRA, daughter of the Trojan King Priam (see Chapter 17) agreed to give herself to Apollo, who rewarded her with the gift of prophecy. When Cassandra changed her mind and rejected his advances, Apollo asked for one kiss and spit in her mouth, thus insuring not only that Cassandra would keep her gift but also that her true prophecies would never be believed.

Marpessa. The daughter of Ares' son Evenus, MARPESSA [mar-pes′sa], was wooed by IDAS [i′das], one of the Argonauts, who carried her off in his chariot, to the anger and dismay of her father, who committed suicide. Apollo stole her away from Idas in a similar fashion, and the two rivals met face to face. Zeus ordered that Marpessa choose between her lovers. She chose the mortal Idas because she feared the immortal Apollo would leave her when she grew old.

Cyrene. Most of Apollo's love affairs end tragically. A notable exception is his success with CYRENE [si-re′ne], or KYRENE, an athletic nymph with whom he fell in love when he saw her wrestling with a lion. He whisked her away in his golden chariot to the city in Libya that would bear her name. They had a son Aristaeus, who became a keeper of bees (see Chapters 5 and 14).

APOLLO AND DAPHNE

The story of Apollo's love for DAPHNE [daf'ne], "laurel," explaining why the laurel was sacred to him, is one of the most famous and inspiring of all myths because of Ovid's version.

After Apollo had just slain the Python, he boasted to Cupid that the god of love with his bow and arrows could not compete with his glorious slaying of a dragon. Cupid got even for this slight by shooting a dull, leaden arrow that repels love at Daphne, the daughter of the river god Peneus, and piercing Apollo's heart with a bright, short one that arouses passion.

Daphne was extraordinarily beautiful but refused her many suitors. She vowed to remain a virgin, devoted to Diana, the forests, and the hunt; both her father and Jupiter respected her wishes. As soon as Apollo saw her he was inflamed by passion and he desired to marry her, but because of Cupid his hopes were doomed. Daphne fled in fear as Apollo made his appeals and pursued her. Exhausted, she reached the waters of the Peneus, and her prayer that the power of the river would destroy her too-enticing beauty was granted. She was transformed into a lovely laurel tree, and the heartbroken Apollo, as he embraced its trunk and branches, promised that since she could not be his wife, she would be his tree, and from it would come the laurel wreath, a symbol of love, honor, and glory forever.

APOLLO AND HYACINTHUS

Apollo as the archetypical Greek god also was susceptible to the love of young men. He was enamored of Cyparissus [si-pa-ris'sus], or KYPARISSOS, who was turned into a cypress tree, the meaning of his name (see Chapter 23). His devotion to HYACINTHUS [hi-a-sin'thus], or HYAKINTHOS, a handsome Spartan youth, also told by Ovid, is more famous.

The god and the youth enjoyed competing with the discus. Apollo's first throw showed magnificent skill and great strength, for he sent the discus high up into the clouds. When eventually it came back to earth, an enthusiastic Hyacinthus dashed to pick it up, but as it hit the earth, it bounced back and struck him full in the face. All of Apollo's medical arts were of no avail, and his beloved companion died. Overcome by grief and guilt, the god vowed everlasting devotion by singing of Hyacinthus to the tune of his lyre and by causing a new flower, the hyacinth, to arise from his blood. Apollo himself marked his laments on its petals, the mournful letters AI AI, and predicted the suicide of the valiant Ajax (See Chapter 17), whose initials (these same letters) would appear on this same flower, which would arise from his heroic blood. An annual festival, the Hyacinthia, was celebrated at Sparta in honor of Hyacinthus.

APOLLO, CORONIS, AND ASCLEPIUS

In the story of Hyacinthus, we see Apollo acting as a god of medicine, ineffective though he proved to be. His son Asclepius took over the role of god of medicine and seems to have been more successful than his father.

Apollo loved a maiden from Thessaly, Coronis, and she was pregnant with his child. Unfortunately, Apollo's bird the raven saw Coronis in the arms of another lover and told the god, who in a quick and violent rage shot her with one of his arrows. As she was dying she told him that their unborn child would die with her. Apollo too late regretted his anger but to no avail. He was unable through his medical arts to revive his beloved. He embraced her in anguish and performed the proper burial rites over her corpse. As the flames of the funeral pyre were about to engulf her, he saved their baby by snatching it from her womb and giving it to the wise centaur Chiron to raise. The color of the raven, which had been white, he now changed to black.

The child grew up to become ASCLEPIUS [as-kle′pi-us], or ASKLEPIOS (AESCULAPIUS for the Romans), a famous practitioner of medicine, worshiped as both a hero and a god. He had several children, among them the doctor Machaon (in the Iliad) and more shadowy figures such as Health (Hygeia or Hygieia).

When Hippolytus died (see Chapter 8), Artemis appealed to Asclepius to bring her devoted follower back to life. He succeeded and enraged Zeus, who hurled him into the Underworld for such a disruption of the natural order.

THE ALCESTIS OF EURIPIDES

Apollo was enraged at the death of his son Asclepius and killed the Cyclopes who had forged the thunderbolt. For this crime, he was sentenced to live in exile for a year under the rule of ADMETUS [ad-me′tus], or ADMETOS, king of Pherae in Thessaly. When Apollo found out that his master had only a short time to live, he induced the Fates (Moirai) to allow the king a longer life. They, however, demanded that someone else must die in his place. No one (not even his aged parents) was willing to do so except for his wife, ALCESTIS [al-ses′tis], or ALKESTIS. In the end, Heracles arrived to save Alcestis from death and return her to her husband (see Chapter 20).

Euripides' entertaining play Alcestis, however controversial, presents a touching portrait of a loving and devoted wife. Although Admetus must face the just attacks of critics for allowing Alcestis to die in his place, a case may be made that he recognized his selfishness too late, after he realized that life was not worth living without his Alcestis.

APOLLO'S MUSICAL CONTEST WITH MARSYAS

As we know, Apollo was an expert in the playing of the lyre, but two musicians, because of hubris, foolishly dared to challenge him.

Athena invented the flute (see Chapter 6) but threw it away because her beautiful features became distorted when she played. MARSYAS [mar′si-as] the satyr picked it up. Although Athena gave him a thrashing for taking up her instrument, he became so proficient that he dared to challenge the great Apollo to a contest. The god imposed the condition that the victor could do what he liked with the vanquished. Inevitably Apollo won, and he decided to flay Marsyas alive.

The earth drank up all the tears of the woodland spirits and of the gods who wept for him, and from them a stream was formed in Phrygia bearing the name of Marsyas.

APOLLO'S MUSICAL CONTEST WITH PAN

While Pan was playing a dainty tune on his pipes (see Chapter 11) on Mt. Tmolus in Phrygia, he dared to belittle the music of Apollo and engaged in a contest with the god. TMOLUS [tmo′lus], or TMOLOS, the god of the mountain, was the judge. Pan played first on his rustic pipes, and then Apollo, in the stance of an artist and crowned with laurel, followed, plucking his exquisite ivory lyre.

Tmolus declared Apollo the victor, but MIDAS [mi'das], the king of Phrygia (who now had a loathing for riches, see Chapter 11), witnessed the contest. He still had not learned wisdom. He had become a worshiper of Pan and preferred his music and declared the verdict unjust. Apollo could not endure that such stupid ears retain their shape, and so he changed them into the ears of an ass.

King Midas Has Ass's Ears. Midas hid his shame by wearing a turban. His barber, however, could not help but find out. He wanted desperately to tell but did not dare to reveal Midas' secret. Since he could not keep quiet, he stole away and dug a hole in the ground and whispered into it that his master had ass's ears. He filled up the hole again, but in a year's time, a thick cluster of trembling reeds had grown up, and when the wind whistled in the reeds, you could hear the murmur of a whisper revealing the truth: "King Midas has ass's ears."

Two archetypal motifs are dominant in this story about Midas: the garrulousness of barbers and the stupidity of some critics.

THE NATURE OF APOLLO

Apollo is a very complex deity. As a god of shepherds, he was associated with music and was a protector. He was also god of medicine, and he replaced Hyperion and Helius as a god of the sun. He is often called PHOEBUS [fe'bus], or PHOIBOS Apollo, an epithet that means bright. There is a moving tragic humanity to many of his stories. Yet he is subject to many moods and passions, not least of all, terrifying anger, however just.

Yet this same god was worshiped as the epitome of classical restraint, handsome, strong, and intelligent, preaching the Greek maxims of "Know thyself" and "Nothing too much." He can bring enlightenment, atonement, truth, and a new civic order of justice. It is because of the disciplined and controlled side to his character that Apollo can be pitted against Dionysus to encompass the basic duality of human nature, the rational (Apollonian) and irrational (Dionysian). See Chapter 11.

COMPACT DISCS

20. Bliss, Arthur, Hymn to Apollo. Bliss said that this symphonic work evokes Apollo as "the God of the healing art."
28. Britten, Benjamin, "Niobe," from Metamorphoses after Ovid, for solo oboe.
31. _____. Young Apollo, for piano and strings. Inspired by the last lines of Keats's "Hyperion."
36. Campra, André, Daphné. Cantata for soprano and continuo.
65. Diepenbrock, Alphons, Marsyas. Programmatic orchestral suite, drawn from music written for a comic play by Balthazar Verhagen about the contest between Apollo and Marsyas.
80. Fux, Johann Joseph, Dafne in Lauro. Opera about Daphne's devotion to Diana, her encounter with Apollo, and her transformation.
82. Gagliano, Marco da, La Dafne. Opera first performed in 1608. The text by Ottavio Rinuccini (based on Ovid) is the same as that of the very first opera, composed in 1594 by Peri and Corsi (M/L 596).
85. Gluck, Christoph Willibald, Alceste. Opera (M/L 598-599).
95. Grétry, André-Ernest-Modeste, Le Judgement de Midas. Comic opera about the contest between Apollo and Pan.
101. Handel, Georg Frideric, Apollo e Dafne. Cantata for two soloists and orchestra.
144. Larsson, Lars-Erik, God in Disguise. Cantata. Setting of pastoral poems by Hjalmar Gullberg

(for soprano, baritone, speaker, chorus, and orchestra) that includes Apollo's exile in Thessaly.

187. Mozart, Wolfgang Amadeus, <u>Apollo et Hyacinthus</u>. Mozart's first opera, with a libretto in Latin (M/L 599).

192 and **193.** <u>Music of Ancient Greece</u>. <u>Pindar's First Pythian; First and Second Delphic Hymn; Exercises for Cithara; Paean to Asclepius; Prosodic Chant to Apollo</u>.

212. Partch, Harry, <u>Daphne of the Dunes</u>, for eight musicians and prerecorded tape. Originally composed for a film about Daphne and Apollo, <u>Windsong</u>, by Madeline Tourelot.

218. Philidor, François-André Danican, <u>Carmen Saeculare</u>. Cantata for chorus; musical setting of the Latin text of Horace's hymn to Apollo and Diana.

226. Rameau, Jean-Philippe, <u>Les Boréades</u>. Opera about Boreas, in which Apollo has an important role. See Chapter 21.

263. "The Song of the Sibyl." Anonymous liturgical composition of the fourteenth century, which has the ancient Sibyl prophesy the return of Christ on the day of the last judgment.

268. Strauss, Richard, <u>Daphne</u>. Opera with an enchanting final scene, hauntingly evoking Daphne's transformation into a laurel tree. (M/L 601).

271. Stravinsky, Igor, <u>Apollo</u>. Ballet. See Videos.

VIDEOS

<u>Apollo</u>, dance, choreographed by George Balanchine, music by Igor Stravinsky. Excerpts in <u>The Balanchine Library, the Balanchine Celebration Part 1</u>. New York City Ballet. Nonesuch 40189-3 (excerpt also on <u>The Balanchine Library: Dancing for Mr. B: Six Balanchine Ballerinas</u>. Nonesuch 401887-3). Balanchine, in the composition of his ballet <u>Apollo</u> (original title, <u>Apollon Musagète</u>), for the first time, in 1928, collaborated with Stravinsky, who wrote the score. Balanchine later described this collaboration as the turning point in his creative life. Just after Apollo's birth, three of the Muses educate the young god in their arts: Calliope personifies poetry and rhythm; Polyhymnia represents mime; and Terpsichore combines poetry and gesture in dance. Apollo and the Muses in a final dance ascend to Parnassus. In 1979, for a revival with Mikhail Baryshnikov, Balanchine eliminated nearly the first third of the ballet; his original version is much to be preferred.

Star Trek, Episode 33: <u>Who Mourns for Adonais?</u> Paramount Home Video 60040-33. Apollo, the last of the Olympian gods, is undone (alas!) by the members of the Enterprise.

INTERPRETATION

The dramatic myth of Apollo and Daphne, with its seemingly endless inspiration for uplifting works of art, impels one to consider how one is to interpret today these many classical myths of ardent pursuit as well as those of amorous conquest. Are they religious stories, are they love stories, or are they really all fundamentally horrifying tales of victimization and rape? In the brief interpretative discussion of Zeus and Ganymede (Chapter 3), it was suggested that a story may be all or any one of these things, and interpretation depends both upon the artist and the person responding to the work of art. Gender, politics, religion, sexual orientation, age, experience and experiences—all such things and more determine the character of a creation and one's personal response. Only a few basic observations about this vast and vital subject can be made here, with the major purpose of insisting that the questions and the answers are not simple but complex.

- The Greeks and Romans were fascinated with the phenomena of blinding passion and equally compulsive virginity. The passion was usually evoked by the mighty gods Aphrodite and Eros, who could gloriously uplift or pitilessly devastate a human being and a god. The equally ruthless force of chastity was symbolized by devotion to Artemis. Usually, but not always, the man defines lust and the woman chastity. In the case of Hippolytus and Phaedra (among others) these roles are reversed.

- The motif of pursuit by the lover of the beloved with the implicit imagery of the hunter and the hunted is everywhere and becomes formulaic with the pursuit ending in a ritualistic acquiescence or the saving of the pursued from a fate worse than death, often through a metamorphosis. The consummation of sex need not be part of the scenario of this ancient motif, played upon with versatile sophistication by a civilized poet such as Ovid.

- Many seduction scenes are ultimately religious in nature, and the fact that it is a god who seduces a mortal can make all the difference. A god (usually Zeus) may single out a chosen woman to be the mother of a divine child or hero for a grand purpose intended for the ultimate good of the world, and the woman may or may not be overjoyed. These tales are told from different viewpoints, sometimes diametrically opposed. For example, Zeus took Io by force, or their son Epaphus was born by the mere touch of the hand of god.

- There is no real distinction between the love, abduction, or rape of a woman by a man and of a man by a woman. Eos is just as relentless in her pursuit of Cephalus or Tithonus as any god, and they succumb to the goddess. Salmacis attacks Hermaphroditus and wins. It is possible, if one so desires, to look beyond a romantic vision of beautiful nymphs in a lovely pool enamored of handsome Hylas to imagine a horrible outrage as the poor lad, outnumbered, is dragged down into the depths.

- The title for a famous story that has become traditional may be misleading or false. Paris' wooing of Helen is usually referred to as the Rape of Helen. Yet the ancient accounts generally describe how Helen fell quickly and desperately in love with the exotic foreigner Paris and (despite her complaints about Aphrodite) went with him willingly to Troy. Of course a different version can find its legitimacy too, if an artist wishes to depict a Helen dragged away screaming her protests against the savage force of a bestial Paris. The Rape of Persephone is quite another matter. Hades did brutally abduct Persephone, who did indeed cry out to no avail. Zeus and Hades saw this as the divine right of gods and kings. Demeter and Persephone did not agree. On the other hand, a religious poet might maintain that god's will is god's will, and it was ordained to have Hades and Persephone as king and queen of the Underworld.

The sections on Interpretation in this Companion, page after page, reveal how illuminating these Greek and Roman tales have been for our civilization. They explored countless issues and emotions (among them passion and lust), as burning for them as they are for us, in their own images, just as we explore them in ours. When one looks not only at the beauty but also the ugly horror, however revealing, so often brutally exploited in our contemporary vision, one hopes that it too will enlighten and reward future generations some two or three thousand years hence. The discussion of classical inspiration begins with:

Apollo and Daphne. Because he was the patron god of the emperor Augustus, he is prominent in the poetry of the Augustan age, particularly in Vergil and Ovid. In Ovid's <u>Metamorphoses,</u> his pursuit of Daphne is the first of the love-stories of the gods in the poem. His importance in narrative post-classical art is largely due to Ovid's poem. (Apollo's importance in Roman religion will be discussed in Chapter 24.)

Of the many individual myths of Apollo, by far the most popular with artists has been the story of Daphne. Reference is made below to Bernini's statue (1624). Other representations include ones by Antonio del Pollaiuolo (late fifteenth century, now in London) and Giovanni Battista Tiepolo (1731, now in Paris). It is still a popular subject: the setting chosen by the Yugoslav painter Milet Andrejevic for his <u>Apollo and Daphne</u> (1969, now in Providence, R. I.) is a city park, where no one notices the tragedy that is occurring. The psychological and physical tensions in this myth have fascinated painters and sculptors, and none have exploited them more profoundly than Poussin in his unfinished painting <u>Apollo and Daphne</u> (1664, now in Paris), in which the arrows of Cupid (described by Ovid) have done their work, and the god and nymph look toward each other at opposite sides of the painting. For the late-medieval commentators, Daphne was an allegory of virginity, as, for example, in William Caxton's translation of <u>Ovyde Hys Booke of Methamorphose</u> (1480).

The story of Apollo and Daphne has been of the utmost importance in the history of music. The very first opera, composed in 1594 or 1597, was <u>Dafne</u> (the second, <u>Euridice;</u> see M/L 596). In the list of musical compositions based on Ovid's tale (see Compact Discs above), one of the most inspiring is that of Richard Strauss. The final scene magically evokes Daphne's metamorphosis, and her final words affirm her triumph and joy at becoming one with the nature that she worships. She feels the earth's sap arise in her and reaches with her leaves and branches upward to the life-bringing light to become a symbol of never-ending love.

Depictions of Apollo in Art. Apollo is so many-sided and appears so frequently in art and literature in all ages that only a very brief selection from thousands of references can be given here. A recent encyclopaedia lists nearly two thousand representations of him that survive from the ancient world alone.

The birth of Apollo is shown in the same scenes as the birth of Artemis (see Chapter 8). In Greek and Roman art he is almost always shown as a young and beardless god. A bronze kouros (large standing male nude) of ca. 525 B.C., recovered from a wreck in the Piraeus and now in Athens, originally portrayed him with bow and quiver. A little later (ca. 510 B.C.) is the robed Etruscan statue of him as Aplu; now in Rome, it stood originally on the roof-end of the temple of Apollo-Aplu at Veii. As archer he is frequently shown killing the Python, an exploit sometimes shared with Artemis (see Chapter 8). In Rubens's oil-sketch, <u>Apollo Bested by Cupid</u> (1638, now in Madrid, along with the final painting by Cornelis De Vos), the death of Python is combined with Cupid aiming a golden-tipped arrow at Apollo, as narrated in Ovid's tale of Apollo and Daphne.

In archaic vases he is present at the birth of Athena (see Chapters 3 and 6); in a black-figure vase depicting the scene (ca. 540 B.C., now in Boston) he is bearded and holding his kithara. Like Artemis, he is shown in the various Olympian groups, often with Hermes. In the <u>Iliad</u> he favors the Trojans and refuses to fight in the theomachy of Book 21. He is the first god to appear in the <u>Iliad</u>, the action of which begins with him striding in anger down from Olympus and killing the animals and human beings in the Greek camp.

As Apollo Delphinius he is shown on a red-figure vase by the Berlin painter (ca. 500 B.C., now in Rome) sailing over the sea on a winged tripod, while dolphins leap around him. As Pythian Apollo, he is frequently shown fighting with Heracles for possession of the tripod (see Chapter 20).

In an Apulian vase (ca. 370 B.C., now in Naples) he is shown protecting Orestes, who is clasping the omphalos, from the Furies, while Artemis approaches and the Pythia leaves the tripod and runs away.

As the ideal of Greek humanism and moderation, he is shown standing, nude or half-clothed, as young and handsome but also a figure of authority, as befits the son of Zeus. Two representations are preeminent: he is the central figure in the west pediment of the temple of Zeus at Olympia (ca. 450 B.C.) looking to his right and by his gesture quelling the disorder of the battle of Lapiths and Centaurs. In his left hand he held his bow and arrows (now missing). About 300 B.C., a larger-than-life-size bronze statue of Apollo as archer was made by Leochares; it is lost, but a marble Roman copy (ca. A.D. 130) is the famous Apollo Belvedere, which is named after the courtyard in the Vatican palace in which it stands. Apollo's cloak is draped so as to leave his body nearly nude, and of his bow and quiver only the quiver-strap and the grip of the bow remain. Beside him is a tree-trunk with a snake upon it. He wears sandals and moves ahead confidently, gazing to his left. This statue has been the inspiration of innumerable later works of art: for example, Apollo adopts its stance as the central figure in Rubens's The Government of Marie in the Medici cycle (see Chapter 6). Jason has the same stance in Rubens's oil-sketch (ca. 1638, now in Brussels) of Jason Taking the Golden Fleece, as does Apollo in Bernini's statue of Apollo and Daphne (1624, now in Rome).

Apollo is often shown in Greek art as a somewhat effeminate young god, sometimes robed as a lyre-player. The bronze Apollo Sauroctonos (Apollo the Lizard-killer), by Praxiteles (ca. 340 B.C., now in Paris) showed him naked and looking at a lizard on the tree-trunk against which he is leaning; this is the most effeminate and the most famous work of this type.

In post-classical art, Apollo is important in allegories of political order. He appears in the Medici cycle of Peter Paul Rubens (see above) in this role, and in many of Rubens's designs for title-pages and triumphal entries.

Apollo in Greek Literature. Apollo is prominent in the Iliad (see above) and in tragedy. In the Eumenides of Aeschylus (458 B.C.), he is the protector of Orestes at Delphi and his advocate before the court of the Areopagus at Athens. Euripides is more critical of him in his drama Ion (412 B.C.). His oracle at Delphi is important in Book 1 of the Histories of Herodotus (ca. 430 B.C.), in which he saves Croesus from death on the pyre, a story also narrated by the poet Bacchylides about forty years earlier. Later he justifies his oracles in answer to the complaints of Croesus (see Chapter 4).

Apollo with the Other Olympians. Apollo's most important associations in art with other Olympians are with Artemis (see Chapter 8) and Hermes (for Heracles see Chapter 20). Among the scenes narrated in the Homeric Hymn to Hermes (see Chapter 10), the theft of the cattle appears several times on Greek vases, for example, on one by Brygos (ca. 490 B.C., now in Rome). He appears with Hermes in scenes of the birth of Athena (see above) and in pastoral and musical scenes.

Apollo and the Muses. Apollo is frequently shown with one or more Muses on Greek vases. He is a very common figure in post-classical art as the leader of the Muses and the inspiration of poets and musicians. The canonical representation is the fresco of Parnassus by Raphael (1511) in the Stanza della Segnatura in the Vatican. Poussin's Inspiration of the Poet (1630, now in Paris) shows Apollo with his lyre as the source of inspiration for the lyric poet.

Apollo is also the instructor of the young in music and the arts, a role he sometimes shares with Athena. Both gods are so shown in Rubens's Medici cycle in The Education of Marie.

Apollo and Helius. Like Artemis-Selene, Apollo is identified with Helius, usually as Phoebus Apollo. Reference was made in Chapter 1 to the <u>Forge of Vulcan</u> by Velázquez (1630, now in Madrid), in which Helius has the characteristics of the young Apollo. In a remarkable example of religious syncretism, Apollo-Helius is shown on a wall mosaic of <u>Christus Apollo</u> from a Christian house-tomb in the cemetery underneath St. Peter's basilica in the Vatican, of the early third century A.D. He rises into the heavens in his chariot, while the rays around his head are in the form of a cross, and the vine of Dionysus trails across the background.

Apollo's Contests with Marsyas and Pan. The contest with Marsyas and his punishment have also been frequently represented. A statue of Marsyas was a prominent landmark in the Forum at Rome. In post-classical art, the agony of Apollo's victim has frequently been portrayed, for example, by Jusepe de Ribera in two versions of <u>The Flaying of Marsyas</u> (1637, in Brussels and Naples). By far the most moving of the paintings of this grisly subject is the unfinished <u>Flaying of Marsyas</u> of Titian (ca. 1570, now in Kremsier in former Czechoslovakia), in which the aged artist sums up his experience of human suffering.

Apollo's contest with Pan is narrated by Ovid (<u>Metamorphoses</u> 11. 146-193). Of many post-classical representations, the oil-sketch by Rubens of <u>The Judgment of Midas</u> (1638, now in Brussels) is exceptional.

Hyacinthus. The metamorphosis of Hyacinthus has also been frequently painted. It is prominent, for example, in Poussin's <u>Realm of Flora</u> (1631, now in Dresden). More explicit is the oil-sketch by Rubens, <u>The Death of Hyacinth</u> (1638, now in Madrid).

The Cumaean Sibyl. Apollo's love for the Sibyl of Cumae is referred to in the <u>Satyricon</u> of Petronius (A.D. 66), when the Sibyl has shriveled so much that she is contained in a bottle and longs to die. Much more substantial are the <u>Cumaean Sibyl</u> and the younger <u>Delphic Sibyl</u> in Michelangelo's frescoes for the Sistine Chapel (1512). Several paintings show Apollo and the Cumaean Sibyl in beautiful landscapes—for example, Claude Lorrain, <u>Coast View with Apollo and the Cumaean Sibyl</u> (1646, now in St. Petersburg), and J. M. W. Turner, <u>The Bay of Baiae with Apollo and the Sibyl</u> (1823, now in London).

Asclepius. The chief sanctuary of Apollo's son Asclepius was at Epidaurus. In ancient art the god is shown usually as a half-nude bearded man, seated on a throne or standing, with his attributes of a staff and a serpent, as in two Roman copies of the second century A.D. of Greek originals (seated, in Copenhagen, and standing, in Rome). The remains of a relief showing his arrival in Rome in 293 B.C. (see Chapter 24) are still visible on the Isola Tiberina (the island in the Tiber) in central Rome. The birth and death of Asclepius are referred to by Hesiod, but he does not appear in Homer, who does include his sons Podalirius and Machaon in the <u>Iliad</u>. The daughter of Asclepius, Hygieia, is often shown with him in vase-paintings and statues.

CHAPTER 10

Hermes

THE HOMERIC HYMN TO HERMES

The charming, amusing, much admired, and lengthy Hymn to Hermes (4) tells the story of his birth and childhood.

Zeus and Maia. Zeus joined in love with the beautiful nymph MAIA [mi'a] or MAEA in a luxurious cave, and she bore the god HERMES [her'mez] (MERCURY). This precocious baby was born at dawn, by midday he was playing the lyre, and in the evening he stole the cattle of Apollo.

Hermes Invents the Lyre. As soon as Hermes left the cave where he was born, he encountered a tortoise and quickly devised a plan. He seized and cut up the tortoise and used the hollowed tortoise shell, along with reeds, an ox's hide, and strings of sheep gut to invent the seven-stringed lyre. In no time at all, he tuned the lyre and was singing beautiful songs in honor of his father and his mother.

Hermes Steals Apollo's Cattle. Very soon Hermes became intent on other pursuits; he craved meat and devised a scheme for stealing the cattle of Apollo. In the night, he cut off from the herd fifty head and cleverly made them walk backwards, their heads facing him, while he himself walked straight ahead, wearing sandals of wicker that he had woven to disguise his tracks. When an old man working in a luxuriant vineyard noticed Hermes driving the cattle, the infant god told him not to tell, promising him a good harvest of grapes and much wine.

Hermes Makes Sacrifice. At daybreak Hermes fed the cows well and found a shelter for them. Then he gathered some wood and was the very first to use dry sticks and by friction kindle a fire. He skinned and butchered two of the cattle (baby though he was) and divided rich parts of the meat into twelve portions and roasted them as offerings to the gods. Following the ritual of sacrifice, he as one of the gods could not eat any of the meat but could only savor the aroma. After destroying all evidence of what he had done, he returned home to his mother.

Hermes Reassures Maia. Hermes got into his cradle and acted like a helpless baby; but his mother Maia was not fooled by his display of helplessness and berated him, for she knew that he had been up to no good. Hermes answered her with clever words, assuring her that he was to be the prince of thieves and that he would win honor and riches for them both among the Olympian gods.

Apollo Tracks Down Hermes. Apollo, anxious about the loss of his cattle (which he explains were all cows), made inquiries of the old man tending the vineyard, and the old man told him that he saw a child driving a herd backwards. The sign of an eagle with extended wings told him that the thief was a son of Zeus, and when he saw the tracks of the cattle turned backwards and the tracks of the robber cleverly obscured, the ingenuity of the theft led him to the cave of Maia and Hermes.

Apollo Confronts Hermes. In a rage, Apollo faced Hermes, who sank down into his blankets with a look of baby-innocence that failed to deceive Apollo. After a search of the surroundings, he urgently questioned the child about his stolen cattle. Hermes claimed that he did not know a thing; since he was only born yesterday, it was impossible that he could have committed such a crime. Apollo, however, was not fooled, but knew Hermes for the sly-hearted cheat that he was. Their argument ended only when Apollo brought Hermes to the top of Mt. Olympus, where he sought justice from Zeus himself.

Zeus Decides the Case. Apollo spoke first and truthfully stated the facts about the theft of his cattle. Hermes' reply was full of lies, and he even swore a mighty oath that he was absolutely innocent. Zeus gave a great laugh when he heard the protests and denials of the devious child and ordered Hermes in his role of guide to lead Apollo to the place where he had hidden the cattle.

The Reconciliation between Hermes and Apollo. Hermes did as Zeus commanded, and when Apollo found his cattle, the two became reconciled. Hermes took up the lyre that he had invented and played and sang so beautifully that Apollo was enthralled and exclaimed that this enchanting skill was worth fifty cows! He promised that Hermes would become the messenger of the gods and that he and his mother would have renown among the immortals (and thus Hermes' promise to his mother was fulfilled). At this, Hermes gave the lyre to Apollo, ordaining that he should become a master of the musical art; and Apollo in turn gave Hermes a shining whip and put him in charge of cattle herds. And so the two returned to Olympus, where Zeus united them in friendship.

Furthermore, Hermes swore to Apollo that he would never again steal any of his possessions. For this Apollo gave to Hermes a golden staff, protective of wealth and prosperity, and as well another gift. Apollo alone had the prerogative of knowing the mind of Zeus and uttering prophecies in accord with his divine wisdom. This prerogative he could not share with his new friend Hermes. Yet he could and did tell Hermes about the Thriae, three virgin sisters who were masters of the art of divination, whom Hermes could consult as a source of prophetic knowledge which he could pass on to mortals, who would be fortunate if they listened.

HERMAPHRODITUS AND SALMACIS

As a result of an affair between Hermes and Aphrodite, a son was born, named HERMAPHRODITUS [her-ma-fro-di'tus], or HERMAPHRODITOS, whose name and beauty came from his parents. The most famous version of his story comes from Ovid, which not only gives an etiology for the hermaphrodite but also explains why the spring SALMACIS [sal'ma-sis], or SALMAKIS, was believed to enervate those who bathed in it.

Hermaphroditus was brought up in a mountain cave by nymphs, and when he was fifteen he left home to wander in unknown lands. When he came to Halicarnassus, on the coast of Asia Minor, he discovered a lovely pool of clear water surrounded by fresh green grass. A nymph Salmacis inhabited the pool. She refused to hunt in the woods and follow the pursuits of Artemis but instead remained at her pool, often lounging seductively on its verdant banks.

Once when she was picking flowers nearby, she caught sight of the divinely beautiful Hermaphroditus and was smitten with an irresistible desire to have him. She carefully made herself as attractive as possible before she addressed him with a fervent declaration of love that she insisted must be consummated.

The boy blushed because he did not know what love was, and when she touched his lovely neck and demanded at least the kisses of a sister, he threatened to leave. Salmacis, afraid to lose him, said that she would give him free access to the place and pretended to leave him all alone. Instead she hid behind a nearby grove of bushes to watch.

Hermaphroditus, captivated by the pool, threw off his clothes, and Salmacis was overwhelmed by the sight of his naked body. He dove into the water, and Salmacis, inflamed by passion, quickly dove in after him. She grabbed hold of him and held him, enveloping him with kisses as he struggled to be free. Salmacis clung to Hermaphroditus with her whole body, and it was as though they were one. The gods granted her prayer that they never be separated. Their two bodies were joined together, and they no longer were boy or girl but partook of both sexes.

The parents of Hermaphroditus, now a hermaphrodite, granted his prayer that any man who would bathe in this pool would emerge with limbs weakened and softened and but half a man.

THE NATURE, ATTRIBUTES, AND WORSHIP OF HERMES

Here is a litany of the attributes of Hermes:

- Lord of herds and lord of Mt. Cyllene and Arcadia, rich in flocks.
- Devious, winning in his ingenuity, and a clever talker.
- A spy in the night, a robber, and a prince of thieves.
- Slayer of Argus (Argeiphontes, see Chapter 2).
- Guide of dreams and guide of souls (Psychopompus).
- Messenger of the gods.

Very important among these attributes is Hermes as the archetypal trickster and master of persuasion. Also important is his role as divine messenger (particularly of Zeus) and as the god who guides our souls to Hades; his epithet Psychopompus means guide of the soul. Since he is a messenger and guide, he has the accoutrements of a traveler and a herald:

- The PETASUS [pet'a-sus] or PETASOS, a broad-brimmed hat, sometimes winged.
- Sandals (*talaria*), often winged.
- The CADUCEUS [ca-du'se-us], or KERYKEION, a herald's staff, sometimes entwined with two snakes (see Glossary of Mythological Words and Phrases in English).

The friends, Hermes and Apollo, have a great deal in common. They are both gods of shepherds, flocks, and music. Hermes is a teen-age Apollo, and his statues, Herms, were to be found in gymnasia.

Herms (sing. Herm). A Herm was a square pillar equipped with male genitals and with the head or bust of Hermes on top. (Herms also is the designation, in the ancient world, of such pillars with the head or bust of any person or god, not necessarily Hermes.) These statues brought fertility and good luck.

The character of Hermes and the nature of his mythology provide interesting variations of standard archetypal themes. Here is a handsome, young god, who is a charming rogue and his major quest is to steal cattle, a robbery accomplished when he is still just a baby.

COMPACT DISCS

76. "The Fountain of Salmacis." A rock song about the story of Salmacis and Hermaphroditus.

221. Porter, Cole, <u>Out of This World</u>. Hermes very wittily characterizes himself as an amorous rogue in his patter song listing his conquests through the ages, "They Couldn't Compare to You."

INTERPRETATION

Hermes is a complex god, whose pastoral and musical functions were shared with Apollo, as we have seen above. He is often associated with Apollo in art, while he takes as his peculiar and separate functions those of messenger (especially of Zeus), herald, and escort.

Hermes usually is depicted with his attributes of a herald and traveler (hat, *petasos*; staff, *caduceus*; and sandals, *talaria*, described above) He is present in many group representations of the Olympian gods (see Chapter 3): for example, on the Sophilos vase (ca. 580 B.C.), he is driving a chariot with Apollo to the wedding of Peleus and Thetis; he is present at the birth of Athena, as in the black-figure vases in Boston and Richmond, Virginia (both mid-sixth century B.C.). He escorts newcomers to Olympus (for example, Psyche and Heracles; see Chapters 7 and 20) and Olympians to meetings on earth—he escorts the three goddesses to the Judgment of Paris (see Chapter 17), as on a black-figure vase in Munich (ca. 540 B.C.).

His speed as a messenger is symbolized in the bronze statue by Giambologna (1576, one of several versions is in Florence), which has been adapted to more trivial uses by modern businesses that wish to advertise their speed of service.

Hermes' Theft of Apollo's Cattle.   Of the episodes in the <u>Homeric Hymn</u>, the stealing of Apollo's cattle has been most popular with artists. It is shown on an Etruscan black-figure vase (ca. 530 B.C., now in Paris), on the other side of which Apollo argues with Maia as the infant Hermes sleeps peacefully in his crib. In a red-figure vase by Brygos (ca. 490 B.C., now in Rome), the cattle are grazing while the infant Hermes (wearing the *petasos*) rests in a kind of basket on the ground as his mother protests his innocence to Apollo. The theft is alluded to in Poussin's <u>Apollo and Daphne</u> (1664, now in Paris); see Chapter 9.

Hermes Psychopompus.   As Hermes Psychopompus he is the escort of the dead to the Underworld, for example, on the marble relief of Eurydice's departure from Orpheus, which originally was part of the parapet around the Altar of the Twelve Gods in the Agora at Athens (the original, now lost, was of the fifth century B.C.; a Roman copy is in Naples). He accompanies Heracles in his final Labor (Cerberus), as on a Laconian (Spartan) cup (ca. 560 B.C., now in a private collection) and on a red-figure south Italian vase (ca. 430 B.C., now in Palermo). He escorts Persephone on her annual journey to the upper world on an Attic red-figure vase (ca. 440 B.C., now in New York). In the last book of the <u>Odyssey</u> (24. 1-14) he summons the souls of the dead suitors, which follow him "squeaking like bats" to the Underworld.

Quite analogous to a journey to the world of the dead is Priam's visit to Achilles in Book 24 of the <u>Iliad</u>, which would have led to his death had not Hermes escorted him (<u>Iliad</u> 24. 329-469 and 677-94). On a red-figure vase (ca. 520 B.C., now in Berlin), he stands behind Priam and gestures toward Achilles, who is lying on a couch feasting while the corpse of Hector lies underneath. By including Hermes, the Athenian artist shows the interest of Zeus and the Olympians in Priam's dangerous journey, and the gesture of Hermes focuses the viewer's attention on the arrogance of the young warrior and the pathos of the grief-stricken old king.

Hermes Argeiphontes ("slayer of Argus"). The death of Argus (for the myth of Io, see Chapters 2 and 19) is a very common subject in ancient and post-classical art. Hermes slays him on a black-figure vase (ca. 530 B.C., now in London) and in a red-figure vase (ca. 480 B.C., now in Hamburg), in which Argus' body is shown with eyes painted all over it. Nearly contemporary but very differing versions of the slaying of Argus are those by Rubens in his oil-sketch Mercury and Argus (1638, now in Brussels, with paintings in Madrid and Dresden) and Velazquez (1659, now in Madrid): the former shows the violent moment of Hermes' fatal blow, the latter the deceptively peaceful scene before the climax.

The Psychostasia (weighing of souls). The death of Memnon, son of Eos (see Chapters 1 and 17), at the hands of Achilles is related in the Aethiopis, a poem of the "epic cycle" known to us only in summaries. It was preceded by a *psychostasia* (weighing of souls) in imitation of the weighing of the souls of Hector and Achilles in Book 22 of the Iliad. On a red-figure vase (ca. 450 B.C., now in Paris), Hermes holds the scales in which the souls of Achilles and Memnon are being weighed. In the Psychostasia, a tragedy by Aeschylus (now lost), Zeus held the scales.

Hermes in the Odyssey. Twice in the Odyssey the intervention of Hermes ensures the continuation of Odysseus' journey back to Ithaca. In Book 5 (28-148), Zeus sends him to the cave of Calypso to order her to release Odysseus (see Chapter 18 and the painting by Gérard de Lairesse, 1670, now in Cleveland, in which Hermes is a prominent figure); in Book 10 he appears to Odysseus, who is walking toward Circe's palace (10. 275-308), and gives him the herb *moly* as an antidote against Circe's magic. This scene has not been very often chosen by artists, but in Hawthorne's story "Circe's Palace" in Tanglewood Tales (1851), the meeting of Ulysses and "Quicksilver" (Hawthorne's name for Hermes) is beautifully narrated.

Hermes and Dionysus. Hermes rescues the infant Dionysus from the ashes of Semele (see Chapter 11) and takes him to Zeus. After the second birth of Dionysus, he takes the baby from Zeus to the nymphs of Nysa. Both episodes are shown on the lid of the sarcophagus with The Triumph of Dionysus, now in Baltimore (ca. A.D. 175). The former is shown on an Athenian red-figure vase of about 400 B.C. (now in Berkeley, Calif.), the latter in a white-ground vase by the Phiale painter (ca. 430 B.C., now in Rome). Hermes is shown at the second birth of Dionysus in an Athenian red-figure vase (ca. 460 B.C., now in Boston), in which he holds the scepter of Zeus while the head of Dionysus emerges from Zeus' thigh. Hermes is the central figure in Poussin's painting of The Birth of Bacchus (1657, now in Cambridge, Mass.), in which he is splendidly clad in a scarlet cloak as he brings the baby to the nymphs of Nysa.

Hermes holds the infant Dionysus in the marble statue by Praxiteles (ca. 340 B.C., now in Olympia; the statue may be a copy of the original). Here Hermes is nude (except for his sandals), and the notion of the strong young male holding the baby anticipates the image of St. Christopher in the Christian tradition.

Herms. His statue was often placed in front of houses, in the form of a square pillar with the bearded head of Hermes on top and an erect phallus on the front. These *herms* became popular in post-classical art as defining or supporting elements in architectural designs, for example, in the title-page designed by Rubens for the Pompa Introitus Ferdinandi (Antwerp, 1642). Other heads could be put on the herm-like pillars (called *terms*), for example, in Rubens's design for the title-page of <u>Opera Omnia Justi Lipsii</u> (Antwerp, 1637) or Poussin's painting <u>Bacchanalian Revel before a Term of Pan</u> (1637, now in London).

Hermes and Herse.   Hermes' love for the Athenian princess Herse (see Chapter 21), is told by Ovid in Book 2 of the <u>Metamorphoses</u>. The myth was popular with artists in the seventeenth century: representative is the painting by Claes Moeyaert (1624, now in The Hague) <u>Mercury and Herse</u>, showing Hermes circling in the air above Athens.

Baucis and Philemon.   Hermes accompanies Zeus on his tour of Lycia in the myth of Baucis and Philemon (see Chapter 23), as told by Ovid in Book 8 of the <u>Metamorphoses</u>. Hawthorne has re-told the story skilfully in "The Miraculous Pitcher" (<u>The Wonder Book</u>, 1851), in which Hermes appears as "Quicksilver." In Rubens's <u>Landscape with Baucis and Philemon</u> (ca. 1629, now in Vienna), the gods are almost dwarfed by the dramatic landscape.

Mercury among the Romans.   Hermes as Mercury was important at Rome as the god of commercial gain (and of thieves: cf. Chapter 24). He has a major role in Plautus' only mythological comedy, <u>Amphitruo</u>, in which he assists Jupiter in the deception and seduction of Alcmena. The poet Horace believed that lyric poets (<u>viri Mercuriales</u>) were under his special protection, and he composed a beautiful Hymn to the god (23 B.C., <u>Carmina</u> 1. 10), in which he refers to his invention of the lyre, his theft of the cattle of Apollo, his protection of Priam, and his role as Psychopompus. Mercury plays a crucial role in Vergil's <u>Aeneid</u>, when he is twice sent by Jupiter to order Aeneas to leave Carthage (<u>Aeneid</u> 4. 222-278 and 556-570).

CHAPTER 11

Dionysus, Pan, Echo, and Narcissus

THE BIRTH, CHILDHOOD, AND ORIGINS OF DIONYSUS

There follows the traditional version of the birth of DIONYSUS [di-o-ni'sus], or DIONYSOS; the Romans preferred the name BACCHUS [bak'kus], in Greek BAKCHOS. Zeus disguised as a mortal loved SEMELE [sem'e-le], daughter of CADMUS [kad'mus], or KADMOS. Jealous Hera appeared to Semele and convinced her rival to trick Zeus into revealing himself to her in the full magnificence of his divinity. Thus Semele was burned to a cinder by the splendor of Zeus and his lightning flash. Their unborn child was saved by Zeus, who sewed him up in his own thigh to be born again at the proper time. As a divine child, Dionysus was brought up by nymphs and Semele's sister Ino on a mountain named Nysa, variously located. Dionysus came to Greece from Phrygia and Thrace; he is a latecomer to the Olympian pantheon. He brings happiness and salvation to those who accept him peacefully and madness and death to those who do not.

THE BACCHAE OF EURIPIDES

Euripides' play the Bacchae [bak'ke], or [bak'ki], is fundamental for an understanding of Dionysus and his worship (see M/L 219-237, where the major scenes of the play are translated interspersed with commentary). The summary which follows is an inadequate substitute.

Dionysus himself has come in anger to Thebes (the first city in Greece in which he has introduced his mysteries) because his very divinity has been challenged and the basic dogma of his religion repudiated. The sisters of his mother claim that he, Dionysus, was not begotten by Zeus, but that Semele became pregnant by some mortal; her father Cadmus induced her to say that Zeus was the real father, and Zeus struck her dead because of her deception.

Through the power of Dionysus, the women of Thebes have become possessed by frenzy, and dressed in fawn skins, they raise the Bacchic cry on Mt. CITHAERON [si-the'ron], or KITHAIRON, to the musical beat of tambourines, with the thyrsus (an ivy-covered pine-shaft) in their hands. Cadmus has retired as king of Thebes and his young son PENTHEUS [pen'the-us] is vehemently opposed to this new religion. Dionysus will vindicate his mother's honor and prove his godhead, with dire consequences for his enemies.

The cry of the Bacchae (the women followers of Dionysus) describes a pure and mystic joy in Bacchic worship.

> Happy is the one who, blessed with the knowledge of the divine mysteries, leads a life of ritual purity and joins the holy group of revelers heart and soul as they honor their god Bacchus in the mountains with holy ceremonies of purification.

The play turns upon Dionysus' victory over Pentheus. This hubristic and neurotic king, still in his teens, who is so violent in his opposition to a religion that he cannot understand, becomes an easy victim for the god. He is lured to his destruction through the ambivalence of his sexual identity and by his desire to see the orgies, which he imagines are being celebrated under the pretense of mystic rites. Led by Dionysus to Mt. Cithaeron, Pentheus is torn to pieces by the fury of the Bacchae, with his mother AGAVE [a-ga've] as their leader in the slaughter. She returns to Thebes with the head of her son affixed to the tip of her thyrsus and awakens from her madness to realize the horror of her deed.

In the last scene of the play (for which the text is corrupt), Dionysus metes out his justice, which includes exile for those who have sinned against him. As Agave takes leave of Thebes, she exclaims that she will go where Mt. Cithaeron will be out of her sight and where there will be no remembrance of the thyrsus. It is for others to become Bacchae and care for the things of Dionysus.

THE NATURE OF DIONYSUS, HIS RELIGION, AND HIS FOLLOWERS

Dionysus is a god of vegetation in general and in particular of the vine, the grape, and the making and drinking of wine, with the exhilaration and release that wine can bring. He is the coursing of blood through the veins and the throbbing intoxication of nature and of sex. He represents the emotional and the irrational in human beings, which drives them relentlessly to mob fury, fanaticism, and violence, but also to the highest ecstacy of mysticism and religious experience. Within Dionysus lies both the bestial and the sublime.

Essential to his worship was a spiritual release through music and dance; in the history of religion, archetypal behavior demands music and dance as essentials for the most exalted rituals. In Bacchic ceremonies, the god took possession of his worshipers, who ate the raw flesh of the sacrificial animal in a kind of ritual communion, since they believed god to be present in the victim. This ceremony was called OMOPHAGY [o-mo'fa-ge], and the religious congregation was known as the holy THIASUS [thi'a-sus], or THIASOS.

The female followers are called BACCHAE, or BAKCHAI; as we have learned, these are mortal women who could become possessed by the god. They are also called MAENADS [me'nadz], or MAINADS. These names are also given to the mythological nymphs, spirits of nature, who follow in Dionysus' retinue.

SATYRS [sa'ters] are the mythological male counterparts of these nymphs. They, however, are not completely human, but part man and part animal, with a horse's tail and ears and a goat's beard and horns. They are usually depicted nude and often sexually excited.

SILENI [si-le'ni], or SILENOI (sing. silenus), are also older satyrs, some of whom are wise. See below.

Animal skins and garlands are typical attire for Bacchic revelers; they carry a most characteristic attribute of Dionysus, a THYRSUS [thir'sus], or THYRSAS, i.e., a pole wreathed with ivy or vine leaves, pointed at the top to receive a pinecone. It can become a deadly weapon or act as a magic wand by which to perform miracles.

DIONYSUS AND APOLLO

Dionysus, with the emotional din and clash of his music and the unrestrained freedom and passion of his worship, is often presented in direct contrast to Apollo, god of the lyre's disciplined melody, reason, and self-control. These two antithetical forces of the irrational (Dionysian) and rational (Apollonian) are dominant archetypal motifs inherent in human nature, and they have attained a particular importance and influence because of Friedrich Nietzsche's study of drama entitled The Birth of Tragedy.

DIONYSUS-ZAGREUS

Dionysus is a god of a mystery religion, with a message of salvation. Mystery religions, mentioned earlier, are more fully described in Chapters 12 and 14. As god of the mysteries, Dionysus was sometimes invoked by the name of Dionysus-Zagreus, or merely Zagreus, for whom specific dogma was established through a variation of the traditional myth about his birth.

Zeus mated with his daughter Persephone, and she bore a son ZAGREUS [zag're-us] (another name for Dionysus). Hera, because of her jealousy, incited the Titans to dismember the child and devour the pieces. The heart of the child was saved; and Dionysus was born again, through Semele and Zeus, as recounted above. Zeus in anger destroyed the Titans, and from their ashes mortals were born.

This is one of the most potent and basic myths in its elucidation of the biblical teachings of mystery religions. It explains why human beings are endowed with a dual nature. Our body is gross and evil because we are sprung from the ashes of the Titans, but we have a pure and divine soul, since the Titans had devoured the god. From this evolved concepts of virtue and sin, life after death, and reward and punishment. This myth of Zagreus was incorporated into the mystery religion attributed to Orpheus.

DIONYSUS AND ARIADNE

ARIADNE [ar-i-ad'ne] gave the hero Theseus a thread by which he could find his way out of the labyrinth after killing the Minotaur. She escaped with him from Crete but was abandoned by her lover on the island of Naxos. Desperate and alone, she was rescued by Bacchus, who placed the wreath that she wore in the heavens, where it became the constellation Corona. This damsel in distress finds deliverance through a god, not a hero; and this story of salvation illustrating the love and compassion of Dionysus (the benevolent god of the mysteries) has inspired great works of art (see below and Chapter 21).

ICARIUS AND ERIGONE

Sometimes Dionysus is accepted in peace. In Attica in the days of King Pandion (see Chapter 21), the god rewarded the hospitality of ICARIUS [i-kar'i-us], or IKARIOS, by giving him the gift of wine. When the people first felt its effects, they thought that they had been poisoned and killed Icarius. ERIGONE [e-rig'o-ne], his loving daughter (with her dog Maira), searched everywhere, and when she found her father dead, she hanged herself. A plague ensued until the people instituted a festival honoring Icarius and Erigone.

KING MIDAS OF PHRYGIA

Midas and Silenus. As we know, sileni are older satyrs, often lecherous drunkards but not always; some were wise. When one of them, SILENUS [si-le'nus], or SILENOS, was captured and brought before King MIDAS [mi'das], king of Phrygia, he said that the best fate for human beings was not to be born at all, and the next best thing was to die as soon as possible—a pessimistic philosophy reminiscent of that of Solon in Herodotus (see Chapter 4). Midas recognized Silenus as a follower of Dionysus and returned him to the god.

Midas and His Golden Touch. Dionysus was so grateful to Midas for the release of Silenus that he promised to give the king any gift that he wished. Midas foolishly asked that whatever he should touch might be turned to gold. At first Midas was delighted when he saw everything turn into gleaming riches by the mere touch of his hand. Soon, however, this blessed power turned out to be a curse. Everything he tried to eat and drink was immediately turned into a solid mass of gold, and even his beloved daughter was transformed. He begged Dionysus for release, and the god took pity. He ordered Midas to cleanse himself in the river Pactolus, near Sardis, and his power of the golden touch passed from his person into the stream. Midas became devoted to the god Pan. Once again he showed his folly by preferring the music of the pipe of Pan to the lyre of Apollo, and his ears were turned into those of an ass (see Chapter 9).

DIONYSUS AND THE PIRATES

The Homeric Hymn to Dionysus (7) tells how pirates, seeing the elegant Dionysus on the seashore, thought him to be the son of a king and carried him off on their ship. When they tried to bind him, however, the bonds miraculously would not hold. Only the helmsman realized that they had tried to capture a god, but his warnings of dire consequences went unheeded by the commander of the ship.

Then wondrous miracles appeared in the midst of the astonished sailors. Wine flowed through the ship, and with it arose a divine odor. A vine entwined the mast and grew up to the very top of the sail, luxuriant with flowers and grapes. The god created a raging bear and he himself became a terrifying lion, which seized the ship's commander. The sailors, by now in a state of panic, leaped into the sea and became dolphins.

Dionysus declared his true identity as a mighty god to the surviving helmsman, who had become dear to his heart, and he pitied him and saved him and made him happy

This marvelous poem describes Dionysus' majesty and power and the essential characteristics of his religion: miracles, bestial transformation, violence to enemies, and pity, love, and salvation for those who understand.

PAN

The god Pan has much in common with the look and spirit of Dionysiac satyrs and sileni. He is part man, with the horns, ears, and legs of a goat. His mother was a nymph, variously named, and his father was often identified as Hermes; like him, he is a god of shepherds and of music. His haunts are the mountains, particularly of Arcadia, and he is usually accompanied by a group of revelers dancing to the tune of his panpipe. He was extremely amorous. As he pursued the nymph PITYS [pit'is], she was turned into a pine tree (the meaning of her name).

Pan and Syrinx. SYRINX [sir'inks], "panpipe," a lovely nymph devoted to Artemis, ran from the advances of Pan and was transformed into a bed of marsh reeds. The wind produced such a beautiful sound as it blew through the reeds that Pan was inspired to cut two, fasten them together with wax, and fashion his own musical instrument, the panpipe.

Pan and Echo. As the nymph Echo ran away from him, Pan spread such madness and "panic" among a group of shepherds that they tore her to pieces and only her voice remained.

ECHO AND NARCISSUS

More famous is Echo's love for NARCISSUS [nar-sis'sus], or NARKISSOS. In this story she is still a lovely nymph, but garrulous. She once detained Juno (according to Ovid) in a lengthy conversation so that the goddess would not be able to catch her husband Jupiter lying with the nymphs. Juno was furious and caused Echo to have a limited use of her tongue, by which Juno had been tricked. Thereafter Echo could only repeat the final words spoken by others.

The river god Cephisus and the nymph Liriope were the parents of a beautiful son named Narcissus. When his mother inquired if Narcissus would live to a ripe old age, the seer Tiresias answered, "Yes, if he will not have come to know himself."

Narcissus had reached the age of sixteen and was so extraordinarily beautiful that many youths and many maidens desired him, but they did not dare even touch him because of his fierce pride. One of his male admirers who was scorned called out to the heavens, "So may he himself fall in love, so may he not be able to possess his beloved." Nemesis (Retribution) heard this just prayer.

When Echo saw Narcissus as he was hunting, she burned with an insatiable passion. She would follow him wherever he went but could only echo the last words that he would utter. Narcissus vehemently rejected her advances and so, spurned and embarrassed, Echo hid in the woods and from that time has inhabited solitary caves.

Once when Narcissus was hot and tired from the hunt, he came upon a pool of glistening clear water amidst a lovely, cool grove. As he continued to drink, he was captivated as he gazed upon his own beauty, and he fell hopelessly in love with his insubstantial reflection. He marveled at what others had marveled at and like them could not quench his passion. As he bestowed kisses and tried to embrace himself, he could never grasp and possess his deceptive image. Gradually he was so weakened and consumed by love of his own reflection that he wasted away and died. While he was dying, poor Echo watched and felt sorry for him as she repeated his cries of woe and his last farewell. At his death the nymphs of the waters and the forest wept, and Echo sounded their laments. In the Underworld Narcissus gazed at himself in the waters of the river Styx. On earth his body had disappeared, and in its place was a yellow flower with white petals in its center.

This tragic story of madness and death has cast a particularly potent spell, not least of all because of Ovid's perceptive and moving poetry. The ominous words of Tiresias predict the tragedy in a fascinating variation of the most Greek of themes: "know thyself," preached by Apollo and learned by Oedipus and Socrates. The fact that a male lover's prayer for just retribution is answered defines the homoerotic nature of Narcissus' self-love and self-destruction. *Narcissism* and *narcissistic* have both become technical psychological terms and part of our everyday vocabulary.

COMPACT DISCS

For recordings about Theseus and Ariadne and the salvation of Ariadne by Dionysus see Chapter 21.

5. Bach, Johann Christoph Friedrich, <u>Ino</u>. Cantata for soprano and orchestra.
28. Britten, Benjamin, "Pan," "Bacchus" and "Narcissus," for solo oboe, from <u>Metamorphoses after Ovid</u>.
32. Buck, Dudley, "The Capture of Bacchus." The text of this song is a poem by Charles Swain about Dionysus and the pirates.
33. Bush, Geoffrey, "Echo's Lament for Narcissus." Song.
38. Campra, André, <u>Silène</u>. Cantata about Silenus for low voice, violin, and basso continuo.
61. Debussy, Claude, <u>Prelude to the Afternoon of a Faun</u>. Inspired by a poem by Mallarmé.
62. _____. <u>Syrinx</u>, for unaccompanied flute.
86. Gluck, Christoph Willibald, <u>Echo et Narcisse</u>. Opera.

106. Handel, George Frideric, <u>Semele</u>. Oratorio/Opera about Jupiter's wooing of Semele.

108 and 109. Hanson, Howard, <u>Nymphs and Satyr Ballet Suite</u> and <u>Pan and the Priest</u>, Symphonic Poem.

119. Henze, Hans Werner, <u>The Bassarids</u>. Opera based upon Euripides; Bassarids is another name for the Bacchae.

122. Holst, Gustav, <u>Hymn to Dionysus</u>. Setting of a chorus from Euripides' <u>Bacchae</u> (translated by Murray) for women's chorus and orchestra.

130. Ibert, Jacques, <u>Bacchanale</u>. "Quasi-balletic" symphonic piece.

180. Montéclair, Michel Pignolet de, <u>Pan et Sirinx</u>. Cantata for voice and orchestra.

195. Nevin, Ethelbert, "Narcissus." The text of this song is a poem by P. C. Warren.

196. Nielsen, Carl, <u>Pan & Syrinx</u>. Pastorale for orchestra after Ovid.

207. Pan Flute: Recordings are available by masters of the modern Pan flute, i.e., Budd, "Syrinx," and Zamfir.

213. Partch, Harry, <u>Revelation in the Courthouse Park</u>. Music-Drama (M/L 604). The plot alternates between scenes from the Bacchae set in ancient Thebes and parallel scenes in an American drama enacted in the courthouse park of a small midwestern town in the 1950s. Each major singer plays dual roles: Dionysus, god of the frenzied Bacchae, is also Dion, rock star (a pop idol archetype for Elvis Presley) with his fanatic female followers; Pentheus the youthful king is also Sonny, a young, disturbed American; and Mom, his mother, plays her alter ego Agave. Lines are spoken or declaimed with or without music (the performance of Euripides is particularly theatrical), amidst the more purely musical episodes; but it is not the music itself that matters as much as the impact of this powerful and original work. Partch explains his Americanization of Euripides: "Dion, the Hollywood idol, is a symbol of dominant mediocrity, Mom is a symbol of blind matriarchal power, and Sonny is a symbol of nothing so much as a lost soul, one who does not or cannot conform to the world he was born to." See Interpretation, below.

245. Saint-Saëns, Camille, <u>Bacchanale</u> from the opera <u>Samson et Dalila</u>.

270. Strauss, Richard, <u>Die Liebe der Danae</u>. Operatic amalgamation of two stories: Midas with his golden touch and the wooing of Danaë by Jupiter as a shower of gold (M/L 601).

287. Vinci, Leonardo, <u>La Feste di Baccho</u>. Opera.

VIDEOS

For videos about Theseus and Ariadne and the salvation of Ariadne by Dionysus see Chapter 21.

<u>Bacchantes</u>. The absurd story of the life of a dancer. Directed by George Ferroni. International Film Forum IFF2500.

<u>Ancient Greece, The Traditions of Greek Culture</u>. Volume 2: <u>Bacchus the God of Wine; Firewalking in Greece</u>. Of interest only because of the connection made between modern ceremonies of firewalking and the ancient cult of Dionysus. Volume 1: <u>Art in Ancient Greece; Mining in Ancient Greece</u> is not really about mining but about sculpture, and it confuses copper and bronze. Kultur 1457, 1458.

<u>Echo et Narcisse</u>. Opera by Gluck. Massell et al. The Schwetzingen Festival, cond. Jacobs. Home Vision The Compleat Operagoer 71. Included is Gluck's <u>Le Cinesi</u>, and the double bill is called <u>L'Innocenza ed il Piacer</u>.

The Seven Faces of Dr. Lao. This fantasy, starring Tony Randall and directed by George Pal, includes a vision of Pan (as well as Medusa). MGM/UA M600667V.

INTERPRETATION

Listed among the compact discs is a recording of Revelation in the Courthouse Park, a dramatic modern version of the Bacchae. This is how Harry Partch (an American original) explains his highly controversial reinterpretation, in which the character of Dionysus is depicted in the image of Elvis Presley: Bitter Music, Collected Journals, Essays, Introductions, and Librettos, edited with an introduction by Thomas McGeary (Urbana: University of Illinois Press, 1991), 244-246.

> *I first decided that I would bodily transfer Euripides' The Bacchae to an American setting. But in the end the better solution seemed to be to alternate scenes between an American courthouse park and the area before the palace of the city of Thebes. . . . I was determined to make this an American here-and-now drama, which, tragically, it truly is. . . . Many years ago I was struck by a strong and strange similarity between the basic situation in the Euripides play and at least two phenomena of present-day America. Religious rituals are not unknown to our culture, nor are sex rituals with a strong religious element. (I assume that the mobbing of young male singers by semihysterical women is recognizable as a sex ritual for a godhead.) And these separate phenomena, after years of observing them, have become synthesized as a single kind of ritual with religion and sex in equal parts, and with deep roots in an earlier period of evolution.*

The issues raised by Partch are perhaps more complex than he realizes. The androgynous cult figure of Michael Jackson is worshiped by members of both sexes. And what are we to say of the Dionysiac devotion afforded a female singer such as Madonna? The furor aroused in both sexes by the Beatles has been but a preliminary for an even greater frenzy evoked by subsequent rock groups and enhanced by drugs; and the fanatical attachment of some opera buffs to certain divas or divos surely must be yet another manifestation of Bacchic madness.

Religious fanaticism and political control (as illuminated by Pentheus' futile crusade against Dionysus and what he represents in human nature) is another topic to incite enlightening discussion.

Depictions of Dionysus in Art. Dionysus, like Apollo and Heracles, is one of the most frequently represented figures; only a very few selections can be given here from the thousands of surviving works of art. Dionysus begins to appear on Athenian vases in the mid-sixth century B.C.: a black-figure vase by the Amasis painter shows Dionysus with human devotees and dogs (ca. 550 B.C., now in Bloomington, Ind.). The god is robed, bearded, and wreathed with ivy, and he has a cup (in this case a horn-shaped vessel) in one hand. Another black-figure vase (ca. 540, now in London) shows him flanked by two ithyphallic satyrs carrying two maenads, one of whom plays the double flute and one the castanets. He is shown alone, holding a cup and staff, in a red-figure vase (ca. 480, also in London). In some red-figure vases he holds the thyrsus (normally an attribute of maenads), as in two red-figure vases (ca. 450 B.C.) in Cambridge, Massachusetts.

Dionysus is also portrayed as a young nude god, sometimes holding a thyrsus, as on a red-figure vase in London (ca. 340 B.C.), sometimes alone, as on the east pediment of the Parthenon at Athens (where the god seated on an animal skin has also been interpreted as Heracles), sometimes with Ariadne (see below). Remarkable recreations of the youthful Dionysus are the marble statue of

Bacchus by Michelangelo (1575, now in Florence) and the painting Bacchus by Caravaggio (ca. 1596, also in Florence).

The Birth and Nurture of Dionysus in Art. Vases depicting the fate of Semele and the birth of Dionysus from the thigh of Zeus have been mentioned in connection with Hermes (see Chapter 10), and Dionysus-Zagreus will be discussed in connection with Orpheus (Chapter 14). The lid of the Indian Triumph sarcophagus (ca. A.D. 150, now in Baltimore), to be discussed below, shows scenes of the conception, birth, and nurture of Dionysus in sequence. In post-classical art, the birth and nurture of Dionysus were frequently painted in the seventeenth century. Poussin's painting of The Birth of Bacchus (1657, in Cambridge, Mass.: cf. Chapter 10 above), shows Zeus (Jupiter) in the heavens being ministered to by Hebe, while Hermes delivers the infant to the nymphs of Nysa, as other nymphs look on, who will also be his nurses. Poussin several times painted The Nurture of Bacchus: one version (ca. 1625) is in London, and two others in France (Paris and Chantilly).

Dionysus' Arrival Depicted on Sarcophagi. The myth of Dionysus' arrival from the east (vividly narrated in the first chorus of the Bacchae) was frequently portrayed in relief sculptures on sarcophagi. An exceptionally fine one is The Indian Triumph of Dionysus, from the tomb of the Calpurnii Pisones in Rome, and now in Baltimore (ca. A.D. 150). The god's chariot is drawn by panthers, and he is preceded by satyrs, maenads, sileni, elephants, lions, and other animals. In this relief, as on many other sarcophagi, he is shown young, robed, and holding the thyrsus. One of the finest of all Roman sarcophagi is the Seasons Sarcophagus (ca. A.D. 225, now in New York), in which the young Dionysus, seated and half-robed, is shown flanked by four young men representing the fruitfulness of the seasons.

Dionysus and Ariadne. The myth of Dionysus' arrival to make Ariadne his bride was also frequently represented. On a red-figure vase (ca. 470 B.C., now in Berlin) by the Syleus painter, Theseus leaves Ariadne as Athena gestures toward him, and behind Athena Dionysus (robed and bearded) leads Ariadne away. In the next century, Dionysus is shown as the young god with Ariadne, most splendidly in the so-called Derveni Krater, a large bronze container (for ashes) with reliefs of Dionysus and his followers (ca. 330 B.C., now in Thessalonike). In the main relief the nude young god sits on a rock with Ariadne, who unveils herself in a gesture of acceptance of her husband.

Dionysus appears quite often in Roman paintings at Pompeii and Herculaneum. In the Villa of the Mysteries at Pompeii is a fresco (ca. 50 B.C.) showing an initiation rite, perhaps of a bride before her wedding, presided over by Dionysus and Ariadne. Its interpretation is still a matter for debate, but its Bacchic theme is certain.

The coming of Dionysus to Ariadne was significant in funerary art as an allegory of the waking of the soul from death to eternal life. This is the theme of a sarcophagus from the cemetery under St. Peter's basilica in the Vatican (ca. A.D. 180, still in place). The god comes in his chariot drawn by a lyre-playing centaur and preceded by a centauress, Pan, and a silenus. In the center he stands, robed and holding a thyrsus reversed, looking toward the sleeping Ariadne, near whom are maenads. On the right two maenads are about to attack Pentheus. On the lid are dancing maenads, satyrs, and sileni. This may have been a Christian burial, and certainly Dionysiac themes are common in early Christian art.

The theme of Dionysus and Ariadne is very common in post-classical art. Titian's Bacchus and Ariadne (ca. 1520, now in London) is a fine example, and it shows both the arrival of the god and Ariadne's crown (the constellation Corona) in the heavens. Of infinitely inferior quality but of historical interest is the painting by Gustavus Hesselius (1728, now in Detroit) of <u>Bacchus and Ariadne</u>, the first mythological work painted in colonial America (a companion <u>Bacchanal</u> is now in Philadephia). Dionysus and Ariadne and Theseus are discussed in Chapter 21.

The Vine of Dionysus. Like the myth of Ariadne, the vine of Dionysus has also been important in Christian art. In archaic and classical art, Dionysus or his followers are wreathed with vine leaves or ivy. In early Christian art (especially in mosaics), the vine appears as an allegory or symbol of eternal life, in part because of Christ's saying "I am the true vine." It is shown on the wall-mosaic of <u>Christus Apollo</u> in the Vatican cemetery (see Chapter 9), and the vine and the vintage are repeatedly shown in the mosaics of the fourth century A.D. on the vaults of the church of Santa Costanza in Rome, built to house the sarcophagi of the emperor Constantine's mother and family. All these images appear in post-classical art with great frequency.

Pentheus and Lycurgus. Central to the theme of resistance to the coming of Dionysus is the myth of Pentheus. Euripides' masterpiece dominates the tradition, but Ovid's narrative in Book 3 of the <u>Metamorphoses</u> has also been influential. The death of Pentheus is shown on a red-figure vase (ca. 480 B.C., now in Toronto) about 75 years before Euripides' <u>Bacchae</u>, and its appearance in the Vatican Ariadne sarcophagus has been noted above. At all times the myth has been more popular in literary works than in art.

Other opponents punished by Dionysus were the daughter of Proetus of Tiryns, the daughters of Minyas of Orchomenus, and Lycurgus of Thrace. The resistance and punishment of Lycurgus is the theme of a cage-cup (carved from a single piece of green translucent glass, which shows red when a light is placed behind it) of the fourth century A.D. (now in London). On one side Lycurgus is shown trapped in the vine that he tried to cut down, and Dionysus, Pan, a nymph, and a satyr are shown on the other side.

Dionysus and the Pirates. A special example of the epiphany of Dionysus is his appearance to the sailors as narrated in the seventh <u>Homeric Hymn</u>. One of the most beautiful of all Greek vase paintings is on the kylix by Exekias (ca. 530, now in Munich), only 4-1/2 inches in diameter. Dionysus, robed, reclines in the ship, around whose mast a grape-laden vine entwines itself. The crew have already leaped into the sea and have been transformed into dolphins. Ovid tells the story in the <u>Metamorphoses</u> (3. 582-691).

The Dionysiac <u>Thiasos</u>: Satyrs and Maenads. Just as common as Dionysus himself are representations of his <u>thiasos</u>. Maenads appear in innumerable vase paintings, usually with the god or in association with satyrs; the early painting by the Amasis painter (ca. 530 B.C., now in Paris) is a fine example. In it two maenads in long patterned robes and wearing jewelry, each with an arm round the other, dance in step toward the god (robed, bearded, and holding a wine-cup) and offer him a hare and a panther: they hold ivy tendrils. Perhaps the finest of all painted maenads is the unaccompanied dancer on the round kylix by the Brygos painter (ca. 480 B.C., now in Munich), robed and wearing a leopard-skin over her himation. She carries a thyrsus and a small leopard, and her hair is wreathed with a serpent. In group paintings and reliefs, satyrs are shown with maenads, often attacking them or carrying them off (the satyrs are usually ithyphallic) but never actually succeeding in their lustful designs. With them also may be sileni and centaurs and centauresses, as on the Ariadne sarcophagus in the Vatican. Poussin re-created the classical motif in his painting (ca. 1630, now in Cassel) of <u>A Nymph Carried by a Satyr</u>.

The Dionysiac *thiasos* appears repeatedly in post-classical art, especially in the paintings of revelers in the sixteenth century, for example, Poussin's Bacchanalian Revel before a Term of Pan (1636, now in London). In the twentieth century, Picasso has especially been fascinated by the lustful and voyeuristic nature of satyrs (and their Roman equivalent, fauns), and many of his drawings of them have been published. Examples (copies in Cambridge, Mass.) include Satyr Dévoilant une Femme (from the Vollard suite, 1936), Les Faunes et la Centauresse (1947), Faune Musicien (1948), and La Danse des Faunes (1957).

The Dionysiac thiasos appears early in Greek art with paintings of the myth of The Return of Hephaestus, in which Dionysus escorts the drunken Hephaestus back to Olympus riding on a donkey. The myth is shown on the François vase (ca. 575 B.C., now in Florence) and on a black-figure vase by Lydos (ca. 550 B.C., now in New York).

Silenus and Sileni. Silenus is a more complex character, especially as a source of wisdom. Vergil exploits this in his sixth Eclogue, where the song of Silenus is an extraordinary conflation of cosmogony, human history, epic, mythology, and Roman poetry. Sileni appear very commonly in post-classical art along with other members of the Dionysiac thiasos: unique, however, are the two paintings by Piero di Cosimo of The Misfortunes of Silenus (ca. 1505, now in Cambridge, Mass.) and The Discovery of Honey (now in Worcester, Mass.), both based on Ovid's Fasti (3. 734-45). Equally mysterious is Giovanni Bellini's Feast of the Gods (1514, now in Washington, D.C.: Cf. Chapter 3 above), in which Dionysus, Silenus, and a satyr all appear. More obvious in meaning is The Drunken Silenus by Rubens (1617, now in Munich).

The gift to Midas of the golden touch as a reward for his return of Silenus to Dionysus is told by Ovid (Metamorphoses 11. 85-193), whose narrative is the inspiration for Poussin's painting of Midas Bathing in the River Pactolus (1629, now in New York), which does not focus on the usual interpretation of the myth as an allegory of foolish greed.

Pan and Syrinx. Pan is often found in the company of Dionysus and his followers. His lustful and pastoral aspects are seen in the name-vase of the Pan painter (ca. 460 B.C., now in Boston), where he is shown pursuing a shepherd; his uninhibited lust makes all the more poignant the painting of the Death of Actaeon on the other side of the same vase (cf. Chapter 8 above), where the mortal is punished with a horrible death for his unwitting violation of the chaste privacy of the goddess. Pan appears frequently in the paintings of Poussin (see above for his Bacchanalian Revel before a Term of Pan), most splendidly in The Triumph of Pan (1636, now in London), where the garlanded term of Pan presides genially over the dancing and reveling followers of Dionysus. Pan, perhaps because of the implications of his sexual vigor, has been especially popular in twentieth-century literature in the post-Freudian age.

Ovid's tale of Pan and Syrinx (Metamorphoses 1. 689-713) has inspired a large number of works, especially in the seventeenth and eighteenth centuries. Poussin's Pan and Syrinx (1638, now in Dresden) is exemplary, and Rubens painted the story many times, for example, in 1617 (now in London).

Echo and Narcissus. Echo is said to have been torn to death by shepherds maddened by Pan. Ovid's version (Metamorphoses 3. 342-510), however, in which she fades away for love of Narcissus, has dominated the tradition. Of the very many post-classical versions, exceptional is Echo and Narcissus by Poussin (1630, now in Paris). In the painting by Claude Lorrain, Landscape with

Narcissus and Echo (1644, now in London), the landscape dominates and the mythological narrative is minimal.

Poussin associates the death of Narcissus with the birth of Dionysus in his Birth of Bacchus (1657, now in Cambridge, Mass.; see above and Chapter 10), where the dead Narcissus and the grieving Echo appear to the right of the reception of Dionysus by the nymphs. Thus Poussin contrasts the life-giving fertility of Dionysus with the sterility of Narcissus' self-love.

Narcissus alone looking at his reflection is a very common subject, for example, in paintings by Caravaggio (ca. 1599, now in Rome) and François Le Moyne (1728, now in Paris). The discoveries of Freud have led to a renewed interest in Narcissus in the twentieth century, especially in poems (e.g., by Rainer Maria Rilke, 1904). He has also appealed to the surrealists, for example, Salvador Dali, Metamorphosis of Narcissus (1937, now in London).

CHAPTER 12
Demeter and the Eleusinian Mysteries

The lengthy <u>Homeric Hymn to Demeter</u> (2) provides the most important and complete information about DEMETER [de-me'ter] (CERES) and PERSEPHONE [per-sef'o-ne] (PROSERPINA), daughter of Zeus and Demeter, and is in itself a literary gem.

The Abduction of Persephone. Persephone, the daughter of Zeus and Demeter, was also called KORE [ko're], "girl," or "maiden." While she was picking beautiful flowers with the daughters of Ocean, Earth, at the will of Zeus and to please Hades, produced a most wondrous and radiant narcissus. As Persephone reached out to pluck the flower, Earth yawned open, and Hades appeared in his golden chariot and carried her away in tears. Persephone shouted and called out to Zeus, but he did not hear her, for it was by his will that HADES [ha'dez] (PLUTO), his brother and her uncle, carried her off to be his wife and queen of the Underworld.

Demeter's Grief and Anger. Demeter heard her daughter's screams and frantically rushed after them in pursuit. For nine days she did not eat ambrosia or drink nectar, nor did she bathe, but she roamed the earth disconsolate and holding burning torches in her hands. Hecate, who had heard Persephone's screams, could not tell Demeter who had carried her off. On the tenth day, the sun-god Helius, who had seen everything, explained to Demeter what had happened. He added that Demeter should not lament. Her brother Hades would make a fine husband for her daughter, since he was a great god, who when divine power was first divided three ways was made king of the Underworld.

Now that she knew the truth, Demeter's grief was intensified, and a great anger rose up in her heart against Zeus, because he had willed the rape of her daughter. She avoided the gods on Olympus, and, disguising her beautiful appearance, wandered among mortals.

Demeter Comes to Eleusis. She came to ELEUSIS [e-lu'sis], and grieving, sat in the shade beside the Maiden Well. She looked like a very old woman, who might be a housekeeper or a children's nurse. The four daughters of CELEUS [se'le-us], or KELEUS, the king of Eleusis, and METANEIRA [met-a-ni'ra], his wife, saw her there when they came to draw water and questioned her. Demeter answered that she would tell them the truth, but instead invented a life for her human identity. Her name is DOSO [do'so], and she was carried off from Crete by pirates, from whom she escaped when they disembarked. She does not know where she has come to in her travels, but she hopes that the maidens will help her find work as a housekeeper or a nurse. Callidice, the most beautiful of the daughters of Celeus, suggested that the old woman should remain at the well until they returned home to ask their mother if they might come back to fetch her.

Demeter Arrives at the Home of Celeus and Metaneira. When the young women returned home and told their mother, Metaneira, all about Doso, she directed them to return quickly and hire the woman at any price because she cherished an only son, long prayed for, who needed care. So they brought the goddess to their house, grieving, with her head veiled and wearing a dark robe. As the goddess stood in the threshold, her head reached up to the beams, and she filled the doorway with a divine radiance. Metaneira, overcome by awe, asked her guest to be seated. Demeter refused to sit on the splendid couch offered but instead waited until a servant, IAMBE [i-am'be], brought her an artfully made chair and threw a fleece over it. Then Demeter sat down, holding her veil over her face, silent and serious, tasting no food or drink and overcome by longing for her daughter. Iambe, however, with jests and jokes (doubtless in iambic meter) caused the holy lady to smile and laugh. She refused the red wine that Metaneira offered but instead ordered Metaneira to mix meal, water, and mint for her. The great lady Demeter accepted the drink for the sake of the holy rite, i.e., to initiate and observe the holy rite or sacrament. This drink (the *kykeon*) very likely represented a kind of communion.

Demeter Nurses Demophoön. Metaneira promised Demeter great rewards if she would nurse her child DEMOPHOÖN [de-mof'o-on] (or DEMOPHON) and bring him up. Demeter took the child to her bosom, promising that he would not be harmed by evil charms. She nourished him on ambrosia, she breathed sweetness upon him, and he grew like a god. At night, she hide him in the fire, without the knowledge of his parents, who were amazed how their child grew and flourished. Demeter would have made Demophoön immortal if foolish Metaneira had not spied upon her and cried out in terror because this stranger was burying her son within the blazing fire.

Demeter Reveals Her Divinity. Demeter was enraged at the stupidity of Metaneira, who by her interference had ruined Demeter's plan to make the boy immortal. Nevertheless, Demeter would still allow Demophoön to flourish as a mortal and grant him imperishable honor because he had slept in her arms. Then Demeter proclaimed, "I am Demeter, esteemed and honored as the greatest benefit and joy to mortals and immortals," and gave her instructions for the future of Eleusis. She cast off her old age and transformed her size and appearance. Fragrant beauty and a divine radiance breathed around her, and her golden hair flowed down on her shoulders. The house was filled with her brilliance as though with a lightning flash. She disappeared, and Metaneira was overcome by astonishment and fear.

Demeter's Instructions. Before her disappearance, Demeter had ordered that the people of Eleusis build for her a great temple and an altar below the town on the rising hill above the well Kallichoron; and she promised to teach them her rites so that by performing them with reverence they might propitiate her heart. King Celeus saw to it that Demeter's will was accomplished.

Demeter's Determined Grief. Demeter, still wasted with longing for her daughter, caused for mortals a most devastating year, with no harvest. The earth would not send up a single sprout. She would not only have destroyed the entire human race with cruel famine but would also have deprived the Olympian gods of their glorious prestige from gifts and sacrifices. Zeus finally took notice. He sent Iris to Demeter in her temple at Eleusis with his command that she rejoin the company of the gods. Demeter refused to obey. So Zeus sent down all the immortal gods, who approached Demeter, one by one, offering any gifts or honors that she might choose. Demeter stubbornly insisted that she would never set foot on Olympus until she with her own eyes saw her daughter again.

Zeus' Orders to Hades. Thus Zeus was forced to send Hermes down to explain to Hades all that Demeter had said and done; and Hermes also delivered the command that Persephone must return with him out of the Underworld so that her mother might see her and desist from her wrath. Hades smiled grimly and immediately obeyed Zeus the king. He ordered Persephone to return with a loving heart to her mother; but he also told her that he was not an unworthy husband for her, since he was the full brother of her father Zeus, and that while she was with him she would rule as his queen, a great goddess. Those who did not propitiate her power by performing holy rites and sacrifices would find eternal retribution.

Persephone Eats of the Pomegranate. Joyous Persephone jumped up quickly. But (according to the poet of the Hymn) Hades secretly gave his wife the fruit of the pomegranate to eat to insure the fulfillment of his words to her as her husband: she should not remain the whole year above with her mother Demeter but would rule with him below for part of the time.

He then yoked his immortal horses to his golden chariot, which Persephone mounted. Hermes took the reins, and in no time at all they came to a halt in front of the temple where Demeter waited.

Demeter's Ecstatic Reunion with Her Daughter. At the sight of her daughter, Demeter rushed out of the temple with the passion of a maenad, and Persephone leaped down from the chariot and ran to meet her mother, throwing her arms around her neck. Immediately Demeter sensed some treachery and asked if Persephone had eaten any food in the Underworld. If she had not, she would live with her father Zeus and mother Demeter above, but if she had eaten anything, she would live a third part of the year in the Underworld and the other two-thirds in the upper world. With the burgeoning spring she would wondrously rise again from the gloomy region below. Demeter ended by asking by what trick Hades had deceived her.

Persephone said that she would tell the truth. According to her version (contradicting the description of Hades' secret deception given above), when she jumped up at the news of her return, Hades swiftly put into her mouth the fruit of the pomegranate and compelled her to eat it by force, against her will. Then Persephone painfully described how Hades had carried her off, despite her screams.

Their mutual grief was soothed by their loving and tender embraces. Hecate arrived and affectionately shared their joy. From that time on, she became one of Persephone's attendants.

Demeter Restores Fertility to the Earth. Zeus sent Rhea to lead Demeter back among the gods with the following message. He promised to grant Demeter the honors among the immortals that she would choose, and he consented that her daughter live a third part of the year below and the other two-thirds above, with her mother and the other gods. Rhea swiftly rushed down and delivered Zeus' pronouncements and encouraged Demeter to comply, first by restoring the earth's fertility for mortals. Demeter obeyed. She miraculously caused fruit to spring up from the fertile earth that had previously been barren, and the whole land blossomed with flowers.

Demeter Establishes Her Eleusinian Mysteries. Then Demeter went to the leaders of the people of Eleusis and showed them how to perform her sacred rites and taught them her holy mysteries, which no one is allowed in any way to violate, question, or reveal. After she had ordained these things, Demeter and Persephone returned to Olympus. The two goddesses send to mortals whom they love PLUTUS [plu'tus], or PLOUTOS, a god of agricultural plenty, prosperity, and wealth (not to be confused with Pluto, i.e., Hades).

The following words from the Homeric Hymn promise happiness both in this life and in the next for those who are initiated into Demeter's ELEUSINIAN [el-u-sin'i-an] MYSTERIES:

> *Happy is the one of mortals on earth who has seen these things. But those who are uninitiated into the holy rites and have no part never are destined to a similar joy when they are dead in the gloomy realm below.*

Triptolemus. TRIPTOLEMUS [trip-tol'e-mus], or TRIPTOLEMOS, is only mentioned in the <u>Hymn</u>, but elsewhere he is made the messenger of Demeter, traveling to teach her agricultural arts in a magical car drawn by winged dragons. He and Demophoön are sometimes confused.

THE ELEUSINIAN MYSTERIES

The <u>Homeric Hymn</u> is our most important evidence for the Eleusinian Mysteries. Unfortunately it cannot divulge the secrets that were only known by the initiates. Yet details in the myth as told in the <u>Hymn</u> suggest some of the rituals and the religious emotions evoked:

- Hades' violent and secret abduction of Persephone.
- The miraculous flower that deceives Persephone.
- The desperate search and fasting by Demeter, carrying flaming torches, for nine days.
- Demeter learns the truth on the tenth day.
- Demeter's arrival at Eleusis at the Maiden Well.
- Demeter's disguise as the old woman Doso, and her story.
- The dress of Demeter, a veil and a long dark robe.
- The friendly reception of Doso by the four daughters of Celeus.
- The acceptance of Demeter into the house of King Celeus.
- The jests of Iambe.
- Demeter sits only on a special chair, covered with fleece.
- Demeter institutes the drink (*kykeon*) for ritual communion.
- The parable of the nursing of Demophoön.
- The miraculous transformation of Doso into magnificent Demeter.
- Demeter's continued grief and the famine that she causes.
- Zeus and the Olympians, including Hades, brought to terms.
- Persephone's eating of the pomegranate; a taboo and its consequences.
- The emotional reunion of mother and daughter.
- The friendship of Hecate.
- The miraculous and wondrous restoration of the earth's fertility.
- The establishment of the Eleusinian rites and her temple, through the personal directions of the great goddess herself.

Through compromise, both the will of Zeus and the will of Demeter are accomplished. Demeter shares the love and the person of her daughter with Hades; Hades has his wife; Persephone attains honor as queen of the Underworld; the mystic cycle of death and rebirth is explained by a myth accommodating a specific matriarchal religious ritual, promising joy in this life and the next.

The parable of Demophoön is particularly significant. Nursed and cherished by Demeter, he flourished like a god and would have become immortal, his gross mortality burned away in the fire, if only Metaneira, who did not understand the rituals, had not interfered. If we are nourished by Demeter's truth and become initiated into her mysteries, we too shall find joy and redemption through the same love and devotion of this holy mother, lavished not only upon Demophoön but also her lovely daughter.

THE ELEUSINIAN MYSTERIES

Eleusis is about fourteen miles west of Athens, and the Eleusinian mysteries were closely linked to the religion and politics of Athens itself. There were two major stages to the rituals.

The Lesser Mysteries. Precise details about this first stage celebrated in Athens each year in the early spring are virtually unknown. Ceremonies probably focused upon initial purification.

The Greater Mysteries. These were held annually during the months of September and October. A holy truce was declared to issue invitations to individuals and states. The ceremonies included:

- Splendid processions between Eleusis and Athens in which the *Hiera* ("holy objects") were carried in sacred chests by priests and priestesses.
- Sacrifices, prayers, and cleansing in the sea.
- The singing of hymns, the exchange of jests, and the carrying of torches.
- Fasting, a vigil, and the drinking of the sacred drink, the *kykeon*.

The ultimate mysteries of Eleusis were expressed visually and orally, and their unwritten secrets have been kept, apparently forever. The heart of the mysteries involved a dramatic performance of some sort, perhaps enacting episodes from the <u>Hymn</u> (e.g., the sufferings and joys of Demeter and her miracles) or presenting a vision of the afterlife to evoke a religious catharsis.

The revelation of the *Hiera,* "sacred objects" (which we cannot identify), was made by a high priest, the Hierophant ("he who reveals the *Hiera*"), while bathed in mystic light, and he uttered words, the significance of which we do not know.

Of the many guesses made about the nature of the holy objects and the sacred words, the simplest may be correct and the most profound: at their heart was the manifestation of ears of grain, representing Demeter and Persephone's mystery, which is the mystery of all life.

In the New Testament, John 13. 24 expresses the allegory of spiritual resurrection thus: "Unless a grain of wheat falls into the earth and dies, it remains alone, but if it dies, it bears much fruit."

COMPACT DISCS

26. Bon, André, <u>The Rape of Persephone</u>. Opera set in contemporary Agrigento; Demeter and Persephone are a Sicilian mother and daughter, Pluto, a Sicilian industrialist, with Athena and Artemis, friends of Persephone.
274. Stravinsky, Igor, <u>Perséphone</u>. Text by André Gide from the <u>Homeric Hymn to Demeter</u>. A melodrama for speaker, tenor, orchestra, mixed chorus, and boys' chorus. There are three sections: Persephone abducted; Persephone in the Underworld; and Persephone restored.

INTERPRETATION

We have seen again and again variations on the theme of the dominant earth goddess and her subordinate male lover, who dies and is reborn to assure the resurrection of the crops and of the souls of mortals. Demeter's name may mean earth-mother, but her myth and that of Persephone introduce a startling and drastic variation of this eternal and universal archetype. Its sexual blatancy is replaced by a more refined and purer concept of motherhood and the love between a mother and daughter. In this guise, the mother goddess and matriarchy sustained their dominance in the ancient world.

Details of the myth continually challenge the patriarchal power of Zeus. The abduction of Persephone ordained by the supreme god so that Hades may have a wife and the Underworld may have a queen is depicted not as a divine right but a brutal rape, seen from the point of view of Demeter, who will not accept the status quo and is mighty enough to modify it.

The Eleusinian mysteries became the one universal mystery religion of the ancient world before Christianity. Worship began in Athens and Eleusis, but eventually participants came from all over the Hellenic world and the Roman Empire, and its initiates included men, women, children, and slaves. George E. Mylonas, the excavator of the site at Eleusis, in <u>Eleusis and the Eleusinian Mysteries</u> (Princeton: Princeton University Press 1961), pp. 284-285, observes that the rites at Eleusis, for some two thousand years "satisfied the most sincere yearnings and deepest longings of the human heart." Among the many illustrious Greek and Romans he elicits to confirm the nobility and humanity of Demeter's worship is the learned Cicero, who maintained "that Athens has given nothing to the world more excellent or divine than the Eleusinian Mysteries."

Matriarchy was very much alive and well in the patriarchal world of the Greeks and the Romans.

Demeter, Persephone, and Triptolemus in Ancient Art. Demeter, as the goddess of the fertility of the earth (especially ripe grain), succeeded Ge and Rhea. She does not therefore have the clearly defined mythology that most of the other Olympians have (Hestia is another exception). Her unique narrative myth is the loss and recovery of Persephone, and therefore much of her mythology is shared with or defined by her daughter.

Demeter begins to appear on Greek vases in the mid-sixth century B.C. She is seated or standing, robed, and sometimes holding a torch, a reference to her search for Persephone. She appears twice on the Parthenon sculptures: on the east pediment she and Persephone (identified by the chests on which they are seated) await the news of Athena's birth, and on the east side of the frieze she is seated between Dionysus and Ares, holding a torch.

Her role as the mother of earth's fertility, who loses her daughter in the eternal and annual cycle of death and rebirth, is most profoundly expressed in the seated statue of <u>Demeter of Cnidos</u> (ca. 340 B.C., now in London), the cult-statue from her sanctuary at Cnidos.

On a red-figure vase (ca. 440 B.C., now in New York) she is shown waiting for the return of Persephone, who rises escorted by Hermes and led by Hecate, who holds two torches.

Demeter and Persephone (the latter holding a torch) are shown instructing Triptolemus on a marble relief from the sanctuary in Eleusis (ca. 430 B.C., now in Athens). On a red-figure vase by Makron (ca. 480) she stands behind Triptolemus, while Persephone faces him and pours from a jug: each goddess holds a torch. Triptolemus is seated on a winged and wheeled throne (also equipped with a bearded snake), which is more elaborate than the wheeled throne on a black-figure vase by the Swing painter from about fifty years earlier (now in Brussels). Demeter herself is shown on several vases climbing into a chariot.

Post-Classical Demeter. A <u>Demeter</u> by David Sharpe (1982, present location unknown), while it shows that the tradition of the enthroned goddess still is alive (see <u>Demeter of Cnidus, </u>above), is both witty and disturbing. In post-classical art, Demeter (usually called by her Roman name, Ceres) is frequently represented as an allegory of the fruitfulness of the earth, as in the painting by Jacob Jordaens, Offering to Ceres (ca. 1620, now in Madrid). She so appears in the masque in act 4 of Shakespeare's The Tempest (1611), in which she is joined by Juno (Hera), who guarantees the fruitfulness of the marriage of Ferdinand and Miranda. An oil-sketch by Rubens, The Union of Earth and Water (1615, now in Cambridge: the finished painting is in St. Petersburg), focuses on the fruitfulness of the earth and the sea in the same spirit as the myth of the union of Poseidon and Demeter.

The primitive notion of the connection between the earth's fertility and human motherhood has been profoundly revived in the abstract sculpture of Jean Arp, whose marble Demeter (1960, copies in Scarsdale, N.Y., and elsewhere) by its swelling curves expresses the renewed fertility that is described at the end of the Homeric Hymn to Demeter.

Cybele, Rhea-Cybele, and Demeter. The Phrygian mother-goddess Cybele was early identified by the Greeks with Rhea and was worshiped in the Agora at Athens, where her sanctuary was called the *Metroon* (i.e., sanctuary of *Meter*, the Mother) and contained a famous statue (destroyed in the third century A.D.). Rhea-Cybele shared Aphrodite's functions as goddess of human procreation but came to be closer to the Greek Demeter as goddess of the earth's fertility. Her worship was marked by ecstatic dancing and music, sometimes culminating in self-mutilation by her followers. Cybele's consort is Attis, whose ecstasy, self-castration, and devotion to Cybele are portrayed with unparalleled emotion and profound insight by Catullus (translated in Chapter 7). Cybele is shown in art wearing a turreted crown and accompanied by lions, which may be crouching beside her throne or drawing her chariot.

Cybele came to Rome in 204 B.C., where she was known as the Magna Mater (Great Mother). Vergil (Aeneid 6. 784-86) likens the future Rome to Cybele in her prosperity, her fertility, and her universal rule. In post-classical art, Cybele is common as an allegory of political stability or human fertility; these motifs are combined in Rubens's painting in the Medici cycle (1624, in Paris) of The Birth of Louis XIII, where Cybele stands centrally behind Marie de Medici. Rubens used her in a number of designs for engravings, for example, the title-page of the Pompa Introitus Ferdinandi (Antwerp, 1642), in which her attributes (turreted crown, lion, orb, and scepter) glorify the imperial rule of Spain.

CHAPTER 13
Views of the Afterlife: The Realm of Hades

Three major ancient authors taken together provide a composite and virtually complete summary of the philosophical and religious beliefs about the afterlife evolved by the Greeks and Romans.

- Homer, Odyssey, Book 11, the Nekuia ("The Book of the Dead").
- Plato, The Republic, the myth of Er, which concludes Book 10.
- Vergil, Aeneid, Book 6.

HOMER, ODYSSEY, BOOK 11

In order to reach the entrance to the Underworld, Odysseus and his men had to go to the farthest, sunless realm of deep-flowing Ocean. Here ODYSSEUS [o-dis′e-us] (ULYSSES) dug a pit and around it poured libations to the dead; then, after many supplications, he cut the throats of the sacrificed animals so that their blood would run into the pit, whereupon a multitude of the souls of the dead swarmed up. Odysseus ordered his men to flay and burn the slaughtered animals and pray to HADES [ha′dez] (PLUTO) and PERSEPHONE [per-sef′o-ne] (PROSERPINA), the king and queen of the Underworld. Next Odysseus drew his sword and took his post at the pit of blood and did not allow the spirits to drink the blood before he had spoken to TIRESIAS [ti-re′si-as].

Elpenor and Tiresias. But the soul of his comrade ELPENOR [el-pe′nor] came up first. Elpenor had fallen off the roof of Circe's palace and died, but did not receive burial. Odysseus promised to fulfill Elpenor's directions for a proper burial. Then Odysseus spoke with Tiresias, who explained that only the souls whom Odysseus allowed to drink of the blood could converse with him.

Odysseus Meets His Mother, Anticlea. Odysseus' meeting with his mother, ANTICLEA [an-ti-kle′a], or ANTIKLEIA, is of the greatest importance; from her he learns about the mystery of existence. The hero who conquers death, like a resurrection god, experiences the afterlife and returns to this world knowing with certainty the ultimate truth about life and death, unlike us poor ordinary mortals who can never do the same. This is what Anticlea reveals to her son:

> This is the doom of mortals when they die, for no longer do sinews hold bones and flesh together, but the mighty power of blazing fire consumes all, as soon as the life breath leaves our white bones and flesh, and the soul like a dream flutters and flies away,

Many other souls come up, including a parade of beautiful heroines. Odysseus sees a group of illustrious heroes, among whom is Achilles. Their interview has become most famous because Achilles' disparaging remarks about death are thought to mirror Greek humanistic attitudes (see Chapter 4): he would prefer to be the slave of a poor man rather than rule over all the dead.

Odysseus also saw a group of sinners being punished, for example, Tantalus and Sisyphus, who will be identified below.

The Homeric Underworld. The Homeric picture of the Underworld is not clearly defined. The heroes seem to form a special group in a meadow of asphodel, but no special paradise is described like the Elysian fields of later authors. These souls are vague spirits with all the passions they had while alive, drifting joylessly in the gloom. The group of great mythological sinners identified may occupy a special hell, but this is not clear. There is no mention at all of the souls of ordinary mortals, who must also end up in this realm. This, then, is the afterlife as imagined in the eighth and seventh centuries B.C.

PLATO'S MYTH OF ER

Plato concludes his <u>Republic</u> with a religious and philosophical vision of the afterlife. A man named ER died in war; after twelve days his body was uncorrupted and he returned to life, sent as a messenger from the other world to describe all that he had seen.

After his soul had departed, it traveled with many and came to a divine place where there were two openings in the earth, and opposite were two others in the upper region of the sky. In the space between these four openings were judges who passed sentence. They ordered the just to go to the right through one of the openings upward in the sky, but they sent the unjust to the left through one of the downward openings.

Er also saw from the remaining two openings some souls coming up out of the earth, covered with dust and dirt, and others descending from the sky, pure and shining. When they were all reunited on the plain, they recounted their experiences.

The Sinners. The first group from out of the earth wept as they recounted their torments, which had lasted one thousand years. Everyone had to suffer an appropriate penalty for each sin ten times over. Those who were extraordinarily wicked, guilty of many murders and other unholy deeds (such as the evil tyrant Ardiaeus), never were allowed to return out of the earth, but wild men of fiery aspect seized and flayed them and hurled them down into Tartarus.

The Virtuous. The second group, on the other hand, who had descended from the opening in the sky, told of the great happiness that they had felt and the sights of indescribable beauty that they had seen as they completed their cycle of one thousand years.

The Choosing of a New Life. All these souls proceeded on another journey to arrive at a special place which provided a cosmic view of the universe, controlled by the spindle of Necessity and her daughters, the three Fates, and where the Sirens' song echoed the harmony of the spheres. In this place each soul had to pick a lot and choose from examples of lives before beginning the next cycle of mortality. In front of these souls were placed examples of every kind of life possible not only for all living creatures but also for all human beings. All-important was the choice that a soul would make; it must have learned from its experiences in life and in death to know the difference between the good life and the wicked, and always to choose the better rather than the worse. This is the crucial choice for a human being always, whether living or dead, and the choice is the individual's own; god is blameless.

Rebirth and Reincarnation. When all the souls had chosen their lives, whether wisely or foolishly, each was given a guardian divine spirit. After certain ordained procedures, they came to LETHE [le'the], the river of forgetfulness, where it was necessary that they drink a certain amount (some were unwise and drank too much). As they drank they became forgetful of everything and fell asleep. In the middle of the night amidst thunder and an earthquake, suddenly just like shooting stars they were carried upward, each in a different direction to its birth.

Plato has a similar account of the afterlife in the <u>Phaedo</u>. He explains that true philosophers who have lived a holy life are eventually released from this cycle of reincarnation and entirely as souls inhabit beautiful dwellings. In each of our lives in this world and in each of our periods of reward or punishment in the afterlife, we are supposed to learn and become wiser and proceed upward spiritually.

The Platonic Afterlife. Plato wrote in the fourth century B.C., and his vision of the afterlife is far different from Homer's. Not only do human beings have a body and a soul but moral and religious philosophy has developed a concept of virtue and sin which merits reward and punishment in the next life and a theory of rebirth, reincarnation, and the transmigration of souls, all of which provides dogma for mystery religions.

VERGIL'S BOOK OF THE DEAD

The fullest account of the afterlife comes from Vergil, Book 6 of his <u>Aeneid</u>, written in the second half of the first century B.C., in which this learned and sensitive poet presents the classical Underworld in its full development. The Roman hero AENEAS [e-ne'as] must visit the Underworld to see his beloved father, ANCHISES [an-ki'sez]. In order to do so he must get a golden bough, which he finds with the aid of two doves sent by his mother, Venus.

Aeneas and His Guide, the Sibyl. Aeneas' entrance to the Underworld is at Cumae in Italy, and his guide, the Cumaean Sibyl, priestess of Apollo (see Chapter 9). After appropriate sacrifices, Aeneas and the Sibyl enter the Underworld and reach the banks of the river that is its boundary. The grim ferryman, CHARON [ka'ron], refuses to take across in his boat those who are unburied; among them is PALINURUS [pal-i-nu'rus], or PALINUROS, the helmsman of Aeneas, who had not received burial; he receives assurances from Aeneas that his body will receive proper rites, in an interview reminiscent of that between Odysseus and Elpenor in Homer.

Once a reluctant Charon sees the golden bough, he agrees to ferry Aeneas and the Sibyl across; on the other shore the three-headed hound of Hades, CERBERUS [ser'ber-us], or KERBEROS, guards the realm. The Sibyl throws him a drugged sop, which he devours eagerly. As the two proceed on their way, they pass through various regions (the geography of Vergil's Underworld is quite detailed). One of these regions is the fields of mourning, where Aeneas encounters DIDO [di'do], queen of Carthage, who had committed suicide when Aeneas left her (see Chapter 24). They come to a place where the road divides; on the left, the path leads to TARTARUS [tar'tar-us], or TARTAROS, on the right, to ELYSIUM [e-liz'i-um], or ELYSION.

Tartarus (Hell). This is the place of punishment for sinners, the Greco-Roman concept of Hell. In Vergil it is a triple-walled, invincible fortress with a huge door, mighty columns, and an iron tower, and it is surrounded by a seething, violent river. One of the dread Furies stands guard. From within come horrible sounds of suffering. The Sibyl expounds to Aeneas the nature of sin and its punishment and concludes by saying that she would not be able to recount all the forms of wickedness or enumerate the names of all the punishments, even if she had a hundred tongues.

Elysium, or the Elysian Fields (Paradise). When they come to the happy places, the pleasant glades of the Woods of the Fortunate, Aeneas and the Sibyl find that all is bright, for paradise has its own sunlight. Shades wearing halos of snowy white garlands on their temples are enjoying themselves in the pleasant activities that they pursued while alive. Some delight in sports, others appreciate music and dance under the inspired direction of the bard Orpheus.

Amidst the virtuous are patriots who died for their country, priests who remained pure, and devout poets who were worthy of their god, Apollo. Vergil singles out with magnanimous insight "those who made life better by their discoveries in the arts and the sciences and who through merit made others remember them."

The climax of the scene is Aeneas' touching encounter with his father, Anchises, who reveals the mysteries of human existence. The mother of Odysseus had done the same for him, but her explanation was more personal and not nearly so civic, detailed, and philosophical. A Platonic Anchises explains that a divine spirit or mind sustains the universe, and the souls of mortals are but seeds from this divine spirit. Enclosed by the prison of an earthly, harmful, and mortal body, the immortal soul becomes contaminated and must be purified before it comes to Elysium. Anchises points out the group of souls gathered by the stream of Lethe, who must drink of this river of forgetfulness before they enter a new life. In this group Anchises identifies a long array of great and illustrious Romans who are yet to be born.

TRADITIONAL ELEMENTS OF THE REALM OF HADES AND PERSEPHONE

Hades. Called DIS, PLUTO (both names mean wealth), or ORCUS [or'kus] by the Romans, Hades is a god of agricultural plenty and the king of the Underworld. He and other deities of his realm are known as *chthonian*, "of the earth" (see Chapter 4).

Persephone. Queen of the Underworld and Hades' wife (see Chapter 12).

Tartarus. The name of the realm as a whole or the place of punishment, i.e., Hell. Called ORCUS by the Romans.

Erebus. The darkness of Tartarus or another name for Tartarus itself.

Elysium, the Elysian Fields. Paradise in the Underworld.

The Three Judges. MINOS [mi'nos], RHADAMANTHYS [rad-a-man'this], or RHADAMANTHUS, and AEACUS [e'a-kus], or AIAKOS.

The Five Rivers. STYX [stiks], the river "of hate"; ACHERON [ak'e-ron], "of woe"; LETHE [le'the], "of forgetfulness"; COCYTUS [ko-si'tus], or KOKYTOS, "of wailing"; PYRIPHLEGETHON [pir-i-fleg'e-thon], or PHLEGETHON [fleg'e-thon], "of fire."

The Ferryman. CHARON transports souls across the river Styx, or Acheron. He demands as fare the coin that is buried in the mouth of a corpse. Proper burial is essential.

Hermes Psychopompus. Hermes as "leader of the soul" takes our souls, after death, to Charon.

The Hound of Hades. The dog Cerberus guards the realm. He is ferocious and usually is depicted with three snarling heads.

The Most Important Great Mythological Sinners

- TITYUS [tit'i-us], or TITYOS. A vulture tears at his liver, which is ever renewed.
- IXION [ik'si-on] is bound forever to a revolving (fiery) wheel.
- The DANAIDS [dan'a-idz] are the forty-nine daughters of Danaüs who killed their husbands on their wedding night (see Chapter 19). They endlessly attempt to draw water in sievelike containers.
- SISYPHUS [sis'i-fus], or SISYPHOS, continually attempts to roll a rock to the top of a hill, only to have it roll down.
- TANTALUS [tan'ta-lus], or TANTALOS, is "tantalized" forever by the fruit of a tree and water from a pool, just out of his reach.

The Furies. The ERINYES [er-rin'i-ez], or FURIES, were born from the blood that fell onto the earth after the castration of Uranus, or are the daughters of Night. They are the pitiless and just avengers of crime, especially murder and blood-guilt within the family. They act as the avenging spirits of those who have been slain. In Aeschylus' Oresteia (see Chapter 16) they represent the old order of primitive justice meted out by the members of the family or clan, and they are appeased and given the name EUMENIDES [u-men'i-dez], "the kindly ones." Their primitive justice is replaced by a new era of right, championed by Apollo and Athena, approved by Zeus, and dispensed through civic courts of law.

In the Underworld itself there are three major furies (named Allecto, Megaera, and Tisiphone), who with their whips ruthlessly scourge the wicked.

TRANSLATION

Seneca. Tantalus' misery is described exquisitely by Seneca (Thyestes, 152-175):

> Tantalus stands wearied, with empty throat. Over his guilty head hangs plentiful food, quicker to escape than the birds of Phineus {the Harpies}. On each side of him close by grows a tree, with laden leaves; bent with fruit, it mocks his open mouth as it trembles. Deceived so many times, Tantalus, although hungry and impatient of delay, gives up trying to touch the tree; he turns his gaze away, and, tightly closing his mouth, restrains his hunger by pressing his teeth together. But then the whole wood lets its riches hang down closer to him; ripe apples dance on the still leaves above him and inflame his hunger, which bids him move his hands in vain. When he stretches them out and decides to be disappointed, all the fruits of autumn are snatched away on high with the moving branches. Then thirst, no less grievous than hunger, presses upon him. When it has made his blood hot and burning with fiery torches, he stands, unhappy man, trying to drink the water around him. The stream runs from him and turns the water from him, leaving a dry bed as he tries to pursue it. He drinks deep draughts of dust from the rushing stream.

Lucian's Satiric View. We should remember that there is a comic view of the realm of Hades, depicted most delightfully by Aristophanes in the Frogs. Here are two witty dialogues by the satirist Lucian, who wrote in Greek during the second century A.D.

The character Menippus was a famous Cynic philosopher of the third century B.C. The Cynics were poor and extremely frugal; their dirty and ragged dress usually included a staff and a wallet or sack; they were unconventional and outspoken in their indignation at the standard and unthinking attitudes of the individual and society. Presumably Menippus stole Hecate's supper (the meal that he offers to Charon) at a crossroads. Charon refers to Menippus as a dog, which was a nickname for the Cynics; *cynic* in Greek means doglike.

22. *Charon, Menippus, and Hermes*

CHARON: *Abominable fellow, pay up the fare.*

MENIPPUS: *Go ahead and shout, Charon, if this gives you some pleasure.*

CHARON: *Pay up, I say, for ferrying you across.*

MENIPPUS: *You can't get it from one who doesn't have it.*

CHARON: *Is there anyone who doesn't have an obol for the fare?*

MENIPPUS: *I don't know whether anyone else has or not, but I don't.*

CHARON: *By Pluto, you rogue, I'll throttle you if you don't pay.*

MENIPPUS: *And I'll smash your skull open with my stick.*

CHARON: *Then you will have made this crossing to no avail.*

MENIPPUS: *Let Hermes pay you for me, since he handed me over to you.*

HERMES: *By Zeus, I'll be damned if I am going to pay for the shades, too.*

CHARON: *I won't give in to you.*

MENIPPUS: *Then haul your boat up and stay here; how can you take what I don't have?*

CHARON: *Didn't you know that you had to bring it?*

MENIPPUS: *I knew, but I didn't have it. What was I to do? Should I have not died on account of it?*

CHARON: *So you will be the only one to boast that you were ferried across free?*

MENIPPUS: *Not free, my fine fellow. I bailed water and helped row, and I was the only one of the passengers who did not weep and wail.*

CHARON: *These things have nothing to do with it. You must pay the obol; no exceptions allowed.*

MENIPPUS: *Then take me back to life.*

CHARON: *A fine remark, so that I may get a beating from Aeacus if I do.*

MENIPPUS: *Then don't be so upset.*

CHARON: *Show me what you have in your sack.*

MENIPPUS: *Legumes, if you want, and one of Hecate's suppers.*

CHARON: *From where did you bring this dog to us? He kept babbling like this during the crossing, laughing and jeering at the other passengers; he alone was singing while they were moaning.*

HERMES: *Charon, don't you know what man you have ferried across? Scrupulously free, he doesn't care about anyone or anything. This is Menippus.*

CHARON: *Indeed if I ever get hold of you.*

MENIPPUS: *If you do, my fine fellow. You won't get another chance.*

18. *Menippus and Hermes*

MENIPPUS: *Where are the handsome men and the beautiful women, Hermes? Show me the sights, since I am a stranger here.*

HERMES: *I don't have the time, Menippus. But look over there to the right; there are Hyacinthus, Narcissus, Nireus, Achilles, Tyro, Helen, Leda, and in brief, all the beauties of old.*

MENIPPUS: *I see only bones and skulls stripped of flesh, many of them alike.*

HERMES: *These bones that you seem to despise are what all the poets marvel at.*

MENIPPUS: *But still show me Helen; for I should not recognize her.*

HERMES: *This is the skull of Helen.*

MENIPPUS: *Was it for this, then, that the thousand ships were launched from all of Greece, and so*

many Greeks and non-Greeks fell and so many cities were destroyed?
HERMES: But Menippus, you did not see the woman when she was alive; you too would have said it was worthwhile "to suffer sorrows so much time for such a woman." [Iliad 3. 157.] For if one looks at flowers when they are dry and have lost their hues, obviously they will seem ugly; but when they are in bloom and have their color they are most beautiful.
MENIPPUS: And so I wonder at this: whether or not the Achaeans realized that they were toiling for a thing so short-lived and so easily destroyed.
HERMES: I do not have the time to philosophize with you. So pick out a spot wherever you wish and be comfortable there; now I shall go to fetch the other shades.

COMPACT DISCS

191. Mozart, Wolfgang Amadeus, Il Sogno di Scipione. Opera based on Cicero's Platonic vision of the afterlife for the Romans, Somnium Scipionis (M/L 599).
246. Salieri, Antonio, Les Danaïdes. In the last scene of this opera, the Danaids are punished in the Underworld.
250 and **251.** Schubert, Franz, "Elysium, "Fahrt zum Hades," and "Gruppe aus dem Tartarus." Songs describing the Heaven and Hell of the realm of Hades and our journey there.
261. Sondheim, Stephen, The Frogs. Musical adaptation of Aristophanes.

INTERPRETATION

A consideration of how different societies and peoples at various times have viewed the afterlife cannot help but be fascinating. We all must die, and what will happen to us after death is a question that each of us has pondered deeply. Whatever our beliefs, the Greco-Roman view must stand as one of the most philosophically profound and religiously archetypal, with themes that find parallels not only with religions of the West (such as Judaism and Christianity) but also of the East (Buddhism and Platonism share basic concepts). For those who dismiss any certain knowledge of death's aftermath as futile, the artistic bequest of the ancient world can offer its own rewards.

A book that should be read by anyone interested in mythology and religion is The Formation of Hell, Death and Retribution in the Ancient and Early Christian Worlds, by Alan E. Bernstein (Ithaca: Cornell University Press, 1993). The first two parts deal with "The Netherworlds of Greece and Rome" and "The Afterlife in Ancient Judaism" and argue that both traditions "display, though largely independently, a tension between two fundamentally different views. . . . all the dead live without distinction between the good and the wicked. . . . the good are rewarded and the wicked punished." Parts 3 and 4, "Hell in the New Testament" and "Tensions in Early Christianity," show how Christianity developed its own particular views "in some measure by choosing between options" offered by the Greco-Roman and Judaic conceptions. The section (pp. 272-282) on "Christ's Descent into Hades" is relevant for its theme of the Harrowing of Hell or the Conquest of Death by both resurrection god and hero, an archetype with which we have become *very* familiar.

Dante and Vergil. The most explicit literary description is that of Vergil, and this has been the most potent inspiration for post-classical artists and writers. Dante (1265-1321) takes Vergil as his guide through the Inferno, in which many of the classical features of Hades are to be found. In Canto 1, Dante, terrified and lost in a wilderness, encounters Vergil, who becomes his guide through his

Christian Hell; lines 82-87 express Dante's intense devotion to the Roman poet, inherent in the poem.

> *"O, honor and light of all the other poets,*
> *May the long study and great love*
> *which made me pore over your tome*
> *help me now.*
> *You are my master and my authority,*
> *You are the only one from whom*
> *I drew and cultivated the noble style*
> *which has brought me honor."*

Many excerpts from Dante could be offered to show his myriad debts to the Aeneid. The depiction of Cerberus in Canto 6 is a particularly famous example. Many editions of Dante are available. A recent one, Robert Pinsky, The Inferno of Dante (New York: Farrar, Straus, and Giroux, 1994), offers the Italian text and a new verse translation with illustrations, introduction, and notes.

Spenser and Milton. Edmund Spenser twice in the Faerie Queene (1594) gives extended descriptions of the Underworld that derive largely from Vergil: in the first (1. 5. 31-36), he describes Cerberus and the sinners; in the second (2. 7. 21-35), he focuses on the personifications of evil such as Hate and Care. In a third passage (6. 1. 7-8), he makes the "Blatant Beast" be the monstrous child of Cerberus and Chimaera, "fostered long in Stygian fen".

Artistic Depictions of Hades. Hades is shown on Greek vases robed, sometimes with Persephone, sometimes as the observer of actions in his realm. He is not included in the assemblies of the Olympians or in group-scenes. On a red-figure vase by the Orestes painter (ca. 450 B.C., now in Athens) he stands opposite Demeter, holding a cornucopia, while she holds a staff and a plow. The cornucopia indicates that Hades, too, is associated with the fertility of the earth, whose riches are reflected in his Roman names, Pluto ("wealth," the Greek *ploutos*) and Dis (i.e., *Dives*, "rich"). On a terra-cotta plaque of about the same time (ca. 460 B.C., now in Reggio, Calabria) from Locri, in southern Italy, Hades and Persephone sit on thrones side by side; he holds ears of grain, a sprig of parsley, and a bowl, while she holds a cock (another cock is underneath her throne), and they face an incense-burner with a tiny cock on top. This is perhaps the best surviving representation of Hades and Persephone as rulers of the world of the dead. Hades sits alone on his throne on a south Italian vase (late fourth century B.C., now in Ruvo, Apulia), supervising the binding of Theseus and Pirithoüs by a Fury, while Persephone stands over them holding two torches.

The Abduction of Persephone in Art and Literature. The only myth in which Hades initiates action is the abduction of Persephone. It is shown in a fresco from a tomb at Vergina (ca. 340 B.C.), where the head of Hades is especially fine, with its grim expression and snake-like locks of hair. A sarcophagus-relief of about A.D. 120 (now in the Palazzo Rospigliosi in Rome) gives a lively narrative of the abduction and Athena's efforts to prevent it. In post-classical art, a fine example is the painting by Rubens (1638, now in Madrid) with its preparatory oil-sketch (now in Bayonne, France), which partly derives from drawings that Rubens made of the Rospigliosi sarcophagus mentioned above. Athena's part in the myth is also narrated by the poet Claudian (ca. A.D. 395) in Book 2 of his epic De Raptu Proserpinae. In Ovid's version (Metamorphoses 5. 346-571), Aphrodite orders Cupid to shoot an arrow into Hades as he surveys Sicily. The nymph Cyane tried to prevent the abduction, for which she was turned into a fountain.

Hawthorne re-told the myth of the abduction of Persephone in "The Pomegranate Seeds," one of his Tanglewood Tales (1851), an interesting effort to avoid the violence of the original myth in narrating the story for children.

Ancient Artistic Depictions of Hades' Realm. *Hades,* meaning the House or Realm of Hades, originally is a featureless place in Homer, but descriptions become more precise with the insights of philosophers and poets and the doctrines of mystery religions, as we have seen above. Before the fourth century B.C., Greek and south Italian vase-paintings show the ferryman, Charon, as in a white-ground vase (ca. 440 B.C., now in Munich) with Hermes escorting a dead woman to a boat poled by Charon; they show the hound, Cerberus, especially in connection with the twelfth Labor of Heracles. One of the most imaginative paintings of Cerberus is also one of the earliest, a Laconian vase (ca. 560 B.C., in a private collection): it shows the hound with rows of serpents attached to its body and heads; an Athenian black-figure vase (ca. 520, now in Rome) shows Heracles, followed by Athena, approaching Cerberus as Hades (holding his staff and white-haired) looks back next to Persephone, seated on her throne. Most commonly artists chose scenes of punishment—on a red-figure vase (ca. 450, now in London) Hermes and Ares bring Ixion before Hera, as Athena holds the wheel on which he will be tied; on a south Italian vase (ca. 430, now in Munich) Hermes escorts Cerberus and Heracles (who is threatened by Hecate), while on one side a Fury whips Sisyphus (who is straining against the rock), and on the other, Tantalus reaches up for the food he cannot reach. In the center of the painting, Hades is seated on his throne and Persephone stands in a small shrine. Around them are mythical figures associated with the Underworld, including Orpheus and Megara with her children (see Chapter 20), for whose murder Heracles performed the labors culminating in the abduction of Cerberus.

Post-Classical Artistic Depictions of Hades' Realm. Dante and Spenser are the most classical in their descriptions. Milton and other poets include many classical details, but their Hell owes as much to the Judaeo-Christian tradition as to the classical Hades (see above). This is even more true of post-classical artistic representations of Hell, most commonly in scenes of the Last Judgment—even those by the most classically inspired artists (for example, Michelangelo in the Sistine Chapel frescoes, Rubens in the Last Judgment, now in Munich). Sometimes the landscape dominates the classical details, for example, in the beautiful and mysterious landscape by Joachim Patinir, Landscape with the Stygian Lake (1524, now in Madrid). Here the Elysian Fields are on the left, and Charon takes a tiny soul over the Styx to the flames and smoke of Tartarus, guarded by Cerberus. The landscape also is dominant in J. M. W. Turner's several paintings derived from Book 6 of the Aeneid; for example, Aeneas and the Sibyl, Lake Avernus (1798) and The Golden Bough (1834, both in London), in which the Sibyl holds the golden bough that will allow Aeneas to enter the Underworld.

CHAPTER 14

Orpheus and Orphism: Mystery Religions in Roman Times

THE STORY OF ORPHEUS AND EURYDICE

The Thracian bard ORPHEUS (orf'e-us) summoned HYMEN (Hi'men), the god of marriage, to be present at his marriage to his beloved EURYDICE (u-ri'di-se). The omens, however, were bad, and the new bride was bitten on the ankle by a snake and died. Orpheus' grief was so inconsolable that he dared to descend to the Underworld, where he made his appeal to the king and queen themselves, Hades (Pluto) and Persephone (Proserpina), in a song sung to the accompaniment of his lyre. In the name of Love, Orpheus asked that his Euridice be returned to him in life; if not, he would prefer to remain there in death with his beloved. His words, his music, and his art held the shades spellbound, and the king and queen were moved to grant his request, but on one condition: Orpheus was not to turn back to look at Eurydice until he had left the Underworld. As they approached the border of the world above, Orpheus, anxious and yearning, turned and looked back, through love. At his gaze she slipped away from his embrace with a faint farewell to die a second time. Orpheus was stunned, and his appeals to Charon that he be allowed to cross the Styx again were denied. Overwhelmed by grief, he withdrew to the mountains and for three years rejected the many advances of passionate women. Thus, he became the originator of homosexuality among the Thracians.

While he was charming the woods, rocks, and wild beasts to follow him, a group of Bacchic women, clad in animal skins, caught sight of him and, angry at his rejection of them, hurled weapons and stones, which at first did no harm because they were softened by his song. As the madness and the frenzied music of the maenads grew more wild, and the bard's song was drowned out, he was overcome and killed and finally torn to pieces by their fury. His limbs were scattered, but his head and lyre floated on the River Hebrus out to sea, both all the while making lamentations. They were washed ashore at Lesbos. Here, Apollo froze into stone a serpent as it was about to bite the head of Orpheus.

Orpheus now at last was reunited with his Eurydice in the Underworld, where they remain together, side by side, forever.

THE VERSIONS OF OVID AND VERGIL

The summary above is of Ovid's version of the myth in his *Metamorphoses* (translated in full, M/L 298-302). The other classic version is by Vergil, at the end of his *Georgics* (translated below). It is rewarding to compare the poetic emphasis of each and analyze the reasons for the variations in incident, drama, and purpose; both, in different ways, immortalize the theme of tragic love and devotion. The most important difference in the story in Vergil's treatment is that he holds Aristaeus, the keeper of bees, responsible for Eurydice's death, a detail absolutely essential for the incorporation of the Orpheus myth into the thematic material of his *Georgics*, a work about farming.

TRANSLATION

Vergil (Georgics 4. 453-527) tells the story of Orpheus and Eurydice in profound and moving poetry, comprising some of the most poignant lines ever written about human loss. The context involves

ARISTAEUS [a-ris-te'us], or ARISTAIOS (the son of Apollo and Cyrene), who, desperate because all his bees have died, consults his mother Cyrene, who sends him to the seer Proteus in order to provide a solution for his problems (this first section of the episode is translated in Chapter 5). Proteus tells Aristaeus that the anger of Orpheus has led to the loss of his bees because Eurydice died of a snakebite while running away from his advances. Here, then, is Vergil's Orpheus and Eurydice, as Proteus tells Aristaeus the reason for his distress:

> "No god's anger makes trial of you. You are atoning for great wrongs. Orpheus, wretched, though undeserving of it, stirs up these punishments against you, unless the fates should oppose it; he rages terribly for his wife who has been snatched from him. The truth is, while she was running from you in headlong flight along the rivers, her death almost upon her, that girl did not see in her path the monstrous serpent keeping to the banks in the tall grass. But a chorus of Dryads, all alike, filled the mountain tops with their cry. The Rhodopeian heights wept and lofty Pangaea, the warlike land of Rhesus, the Getae, and Attic Orithyia.
>
> Assuaging his bitter love with a hollow tortoise-shell, he sang of you, his sweet wife, he sang of you to himself on the lonely shore, he sang of you at the day's coming and at its departing. He entered the Taenarian maws, the lofty portals of Dis, and the grove shadowed in black dread and approached the souls of the dead, their fearful king, and hearts not known to soften at human entreaty. But moved by his song there came from the deepest regions of Erebus flitting shades and spectral images of those who have departed from the light, in number like many thousands of birds who seek cover in the leaves of the trees when evening or a winter rain drives them from the mountains. There were mothers and husbands and the bodies of great-souled heroes which had departed from life, boys and unmarried girls, youths who were placed on the pyre before the eyes of their parents. And around these the black muck, the unsightly reed of the Cocytus, and the hateful swamp with its sluggish water binds, and the Styx, circling nine times around, hems them in. Yes, the palace itself was dumbstruck, so too the inmost Tartarean reaches of death, and the Furies, their hair plaited with dark green snakes. Gaping Cerberus held his jaws tight, and even the turning of Ixion's wheel had ceased with a breeze.
>
> Orpheus withdrew his step and escaped every misfortune, and Eurydice, now restored, was approaching the upper world, following him behind; for this was the condition Proserpina had demanded. Suddenly a madness took hold of the incautious lover (certainly forgivable, if the infernal world knew how to forgive). He stood still. Unmindful of the condition and overwhelmed by passion he looked back at Eurydice, who was at that very moment verging on the light. There all his effort was wasted and the agreement of the pitiless tyrant broken. Three times a shattering was heard throughout the Avernian fens. And Eurydice spoke:
>
> 'What terrible madness has destroyed both you and me. Hear! A second time the cruel fates call me back and sleep covers my swimming eyes. Farewell. Stretching out my powerless hands to you, I am borne away, enveloped in endless night, yours no longer.'
>
> And Eurydice disappeared from before his eyes, scattered in different directions, like smoke caught in a gentle breeze. She never saw him again, though he tried in vain to take hold of her spirit, wanting to tell her more. The ferryman of Orcus did not permit him to cross any more the barrier lake.
>
> What was he to do? Where could he go now that his wife was stolen from him again? What tears, what utterance could prevail upon the dead or the guardians of the dead? She, now cold, was sailing in the Stygian craft. They say that he wept for seven whole months in succession under a lofty crag beside the waters of the deserted Strymon and that he unfolded his story beneath cold caverns, sooth-

ing tigers and stirring oaks with his song, as Philomela, grieving under the shade of a poplar tree, laments her lost young, which a rough plowman saw unfeathered in their nest and removed. But she weeps through the night, and perched on a branch, renews her mournful song and fills up the countryside with sorrowful lamentation. No Venus, no marriage rite turns his thoughts. Alone he surveys the Hyperborean ice, snowy Tanais, and fields never bereft of Riphaean frost, bewailing his lost Eurydice and the ineffectual gift of Dis. Because the women of the Cicones had been spurned by him, amidst the rites of the gods and the nocturnal orgies of Bacchus they tore the youth apart and scattered him in pieces over the broad fields. Even then, when the Oeagrian Hebrus in the midst of its current bobbed and pitched his head, torn from his smooth, white neck, that same voice and cold tongue called the name Eurydice—Alas wretched Eurydice!—even while his soul was in flight. And the banks reechoed Eurydice along the course of the entire stream."

ORPHEUS AND ORPHISM

Orpheus of Thrace was the son of Apollo (or a Thracian river-god Oeagrus) and the muse Calliope. Through music and poetry and with extraordinary art, he delivered a persuasive religious message, the foundation of a mystery religion called Orphism. This message is linked both to Apollo and to Dionysus, gods often antithetical in nature. Orpheus is torn to pieces by fanatical Bacchic maenads; this mirrors the fate of Pentheus and suggests that his death was prompted not only by his sexual rejection of women but also because of the nature of his religious teaching.

The Orphic Bible. With its myth of creation, the Orphic bible was linked in some of its details to the Hesiodic account but differed radically in its spiritual content. The first principle is Time (Chronos), and Eros, Love, is the firstborn of the deities, called PHANES [fa'nes], and hatched from an egg. Fundamental for dogma was the myth of Dionysus (see Chapter 11), in which the infant god was torn to pieces and devoured by the wicked Titans; from the ashes of the Titans (smitten by Zeus' thunderbolt) humans were created; hence the immortality of the soul, sin and virtue, reward and punishment.

CHARACTERISTICS OF MYSTERY RELIGIONS

Christianity shares many characteristics with other mystery religions of antiquity, which are called mystery religions because of their concern with the fundamental mysteries of human existence: life and death, questions about god, the soul, and the afterlife. These mysteries also involved secrets revealed only to members of the religious group, the initiates.

Thus a form of initiation into a mystery religion was mandatory, requiring some kind of ritual such as baptism to set the initiate apart from profane outsiders. A mystery religion preached a dogma to be believed and directions to be followed for happiness and redemption. Faith in the concept of god or the gods was primary, as well as a conviction of the immortality of the human soul, which partook of divine characteristics. In conflict with the purity and immortality of the divine soul was the sin and degradation of the mortal body. Communion, the sacramental partaking of food and drink, linked the initiate with the divine.

A strong sense of virtue and sin and reward and punishment in an afterlife was fundamental, embracing various concepts of immortality, involving the transmigration of souls, rebirth, reincarnation, resurrection, and redemption.

MYSTERY RELIGIONS OF ANTIQUITY

Many mystery religions (in addition to Christianity) developed and flourished during the Roman Empire:

- The Mysteries of Dionysus/Bacchus (see Chapter 11). The vine of Dionysus (Ariadne's savior) became a symbol of renewed life and Christian resurrection and redemption.

- The Mysteries of Demeter at Eleusis (see Chapter 12).

- The Mysteries of Cybele and Attis (see Chapter 7). The priests were eunuchs called Galli, and the rites of initiation included baptism by the blood of a slain bull, the *taurobolium*.

- The Mysteries of the Persian god Mithra (Mithras).

- The Worship of Atargatis, Dea Syria (the Syrian goddess), and Tammuz.

- The Mysteries of the Egyptian deities Isis and Osiris. Most fully documented by Apuleius in his <u>Metamorphoses</u>, or <u>The Golden Ass</u>, as he describes the experiences of the initiate Lucius.

- The Mysteries of the Cabiri, called the great gods (*theoi megaloi*).

- Syncretism: In the development of Greco-Roman religious thought the process of SYNCRETISM ("growing together") becomes increasingly apparent. This term describes the harmonizing by different religions of their gods and myths into some sort of unity. In Apuleius, the great Egyptian deity Isis has absorbed the identity of other similar goddesses and may be invoked by their names, Cybele, Athena, Aphrodite, Artemis, Demeter, Persephone, and Hera.

COMPACT DISCS

17. Berlioz, Hector, <u>La Mort d'Orphée</u>. Cantata about Orpheus and the Bacchae.
40. Carter, Elliott, <u>In Sleep, In Thunder</u>. Song cycle of six poems by Robert Lowell; one of the songs, "In Genesis," relates to Orpheus.
42. _____, <u>Syringa</u>. Original setting of the poem about Orpheus by Ashbery, with added Greek texts, sung in Greek.
52. Charpentier, Marc-Antoine, <u>Orphée Descendant aux Enfers</u>. Cantata.
75. Foss, Lukas, <u>Orpheus and Euridice</u>, for two violins and orchestra, incorporating pantomime.
83. Gagneux, Renaud, <u>Orphée</u>. Opera.
89. Gluck, Christoph Willibald, <u>Orpheus and Eurydice</u>. A landmark in the history of opera (M/L 598).
118. Haydn, Franz Joseph, <u>Orfeo ed Euridice</u>. Opera.
120. Henze, Hans Werner, <u>Orpheus behind the Wire</u>. Text in five sections by Edward Bond.
126. Hovhaness, Alan, <u>Meditation on Orpheus</u>, for orchestra.
142. Landi, Stefano, <u>La Morte d'Orfeo</u>. Early opera, subtitled "a pastoral tragi-comedy."
143. Lang, David, <u>Orpheus Over and Under</u>, for two pianos.

153. Liszt, Franz, <u>Orpheus</u>. Lovely symphonic poem, with a sublime and subdued spirituality not always characteristic of Liszt.

175. Milhaud, Darius, <u>Les Malheurs d'Orphée</u>. Tableaux depicting Orpheus as a healer.

183. Monteverdi, Claudio, <u>L'Orfeo</u>. Important masterpiece in the early development of opera.

200. Offenbach, Jacques, <u>Orpheus in the Underworld (Orphée aux Enfers)</u>. Delightful operetta that introduced the cancan.

204. <u>Orpheus Suite</u>. Popular. Sections are: Descent into the Underworld, Dialog with the Devil, and Ascent from Hell.

215. Pergolesi, Giovanni Battista, <u>Orfeo</u>. Cantata for soprano, strings, and continuo.

216. Peri, Jacopo, <u>L'Euridice</u>. Earliest opera to survive in its entirety (M/L 596).

217. Perle, George, "Sonnets to Orpheus." Part 2 of Perle's <u>Songs of Praise and Lamentation</u>, for orchestra and chorus, provides a musical setting for sonnets 1, 9, 5, and 19 by Rilke.

230. Rameau, Jean Philippe, <u>Orphée</u>. Cantata.

239. Rossi, Luigi, <u>Orfeo</u>. Opera.

251. Schubert, Franz, "Orpheus." Song. Orpheus' melodic appeal to the shades of the Underworld.

253. Schuman, William, "Orpheus with His Lute." Beautiful setting for lines from Shakespeare, Henry VIII, act 3, scene 3.

273. Stravinsky, Igor, <u>Orpheus</u>. Music for the ballet, choreographed by George Balanchine. We may hope for some documentation on video of this important work, since some tapes in a series about Balanchine have been released. See Chapter 9.

Very informative is the entry on "Orpheus" in vol. 3 of <u>The New Grove Dictionary of Opera</u>, edited by Stanley Sadie.

VIDEOS

<u>Black Orpheus</u>. Award-winning recreation, set in Rio at carnival time, starring Breno Melo and Marpessa Dawn, and directed by Marcel Camus. In Portugese with English subtitles. Connoisseur Video CVC-1001.

<u>The Fugitive Kind</u>. Fascinating and challenging reworking of the myth, with a brilliant cast, Marlon Brando, Anna Magnani, and Joanne Woodward, directed by Sidney Lumet. Screenplay by Tennessee Williams from his play <u>Orpheus Descending</u>. Key Video 4677; MGM/UA Home Video M202510. Much to be preferred to the version of the play presented on stage and then made for TV and entitled <u>Orpheus Descending</u>, with a miscast Vanessa Redgrave and weak Kevin Anderson, directed by Peter Hall. Turner Home Entertainment 6165.

<u>Orfeo ed Euridice</u>. Opera by Gluck. Baker et al., Glyndebourne Festival Opera, cond. Leppard. Staged by Peter Hall. Home Vision; Kowalski et al. The Royal Opera House, Covent Garden, cond. Haenchen. Surreal version, staged by Harry Kupfer. Home Vision ORF 120. Films for the Humanities offers a performance (AGU3367) that claims to recreate the opera as staged by Appia and Dalcroze in 1912. This static amateur effort is only for the hardy.

<u>Orpheus</u>. A cinematic masterpiece, starring Jean Marais and written and directed by Jean Cocteau. In French with English subtitles. Embassy Home Entertainment 6062; also Video Yesteryear 430. Cocteau also has a play <u>Orpheus</u>, which first brought him fame; it is a fascinating, but preliminary and immature, study for the superb movie he would make later.

Orpheus Descending. See The Fugitive Kind.

Testament of Orpheus. Jean Cocteau is the writer, director, and star; as the personification of the Orpheus-archetype, he reveals that his film is "a strip-tease act, gradually peeling away my body to reveal my naked soul." Home Vision TES 010.

INTERPRETATION

In music, art, and poetry, Orpheus has been a source of inspiration for thousands of works. His myths address several of the most profound of human concerns: the power of music over animals and inanimate nature, over human discord, and over death itself; the pain of bereavement and the hope of reunion after the loss of a dearly loved wife.

Orpheus exemplifies the universal power of the artist and, in particular, music and poetry. Art eases care, makes life meaningful and beautiful, and it can instruct. Orpheus is also the archetypal religious teacher, illustrating the omnipotence of the word in music. Orpheus suffers and dies the martyr's death of a prophet and a savior. Just as potent are the eternal elements in the romance of Orpheus and Eurydice. Theirs is a moving and tragic love story that, in its endless metamorphoses, never fails to touch the hearts and minds of human beings forever.

One can listen to and see Gluck's Orpheus performed traditionally but nevertheless powerfully by a mezzo (in Janet Baker's performance) or turn to this same Orpheus sung by a male alto, Jochen Kowalski, in leather jacket and with electric guitar, pursuing his Euridice who has died in a car accident. One can study the music and text of a melodious song by Schubert or W. Schuman or explore the avant-garde, modern Syringa of Carter. One can marvel at the possibilities of a humorous Orpheus through the amusing operetta of Offenbach and consider how this most serious tale of love and devotion can be turned upside down for comic effect.

The words of Marlon Brando in the brief opening scene of Tennessee Williams's The Fugitive Kind speak volumes. The name of this Orpheus sounds like Savior, he wears a snakeskin jacket to attest to his underworld connections, and he is devoted to his guitar, "a lifelong companion." Cocteau's Orpheus is in love with Death, named The Princess, and his entrance to the Underworld is through a mirror; Black Orpheus attests to the universal humanity of the myth, which transcends race, color, locale, and time.

The Composer in Richard Strauss's opera Ariadne auf Naxos, yet another Orpheus, captures ecstatically the duality of religion and music in the archetype, declaring in the most soaring of all musical motifs: "Music is a holy art."

Orpheus and Eurydice in Art. Orpheus begins to appear in Greek art in the fifth century B.C. On a red-figure vase by the Orpheus painter (ca. 440 B.C., now in Berlin), he is shown playing the lyre to an audience of Thracians. The return of Eurydice to the Underworld was the subject of a relief (mentioned in Chapter 10, above), now lost but surviving in a Roman copy (now in Naples) made for the enclosure of the Altar of the Twelve Gods in the Agora at Athens in about 420 B.C. There are many vase-paintings of his death, for example, one by Hermonax (ca. 460 B.C., now in Paris) showing women attacking him with a rock and a pole. Finally, his oracular head is shown on a red-figure cup (ca. 400 B.C., now in Cambridge): the man consulting the oracle writes down Orpheus' words, while Apollo stands behind Orpheus.

The conquest of Hades by the music of Orpheus was used as an allegory of Christ's victory over death in early Christian painting. In the catacomb of St. Calixtus in Rome (ca. A.D. 200) is a painting of Christus-Orpheus playing the lyre. Perhaps the power of Orpheus over animals has also contributed to the tradition of St. Francis of Assisi. The myth of Eurydice has been the inspiration of a huge number of works. Three will be mentioned here. One is the painting by Poussin <u>Landscape with Orpheus and Eurydice</u> (1650, now in Paris), based principally on Ovid. The death of Eurydice takes place in an exquisite landscape, where Orpheus plays his lyre in the foreground, and in the background smoke pours from the Roman Castel Sant'Angelo, a reference to the smoky torch of Hymen in Ovid's narrative. Second, the designs by Isamu Noguchi for the ballet <u>Orpheus</u> (1948, with music by Stravinsky) express with great economy the power of music to make, as Noguchi has written, even "glowing rocks, like astral bodies, levitate." Third, Barbara Hepworth showed the power of music in her abstract sculpture of <u>Orpheus</u> (1956, versions in London, Detroit, and elsewhere), whose bronze form and taut strings recall the essential significance of the myth of Orpheus.

CHAPTER 15

The Theban Saga

THE HERO IN SAGA AND FOLKTALE: RECURRING MOTIFS

Propp's theory of the structure of Quest folktales (see M/L Introduction) applies also to the hero of saga. Nine motifs appear in the same order but not necessarily all in the same tale. They are:

1. The extraordinary birth and childhood of the hero.
2. The hero faces opposition and must surmount challenges.
3. He is set a task that defines his achievement.
4. He is helped by one or more divine or human allies.
5. He faces apparently insuperable obstacles.
6. His conflicts with opponents (divine, human, or monstrous) involve physical, sexual, or spiritual challenges.
7. He may have to observe certain taboos.
8. His final conquest is Death, achieved typically by journeying to the Underworld and returning.
9. The hero's ultimate success brings rewards, for example, marriage or political power.

- The hero's quest may also bring knowledge through suffering and spiritual enlightenment.
- These themes and their variations have been in evidence for the lives of the gods and figures such as Orpheus (see especially Chapter 3, Interpretation).

THE MYCENAEAN WORLD AND GREEK SAGA

Greek sagas are grouped in cycles (i.e., clusters of legends concerning a hero, a family, a tribe, a city, or an area) connected with late Bronze Age communities which flourished ca. 1600-1100 B.C. (see M/L Introduction, for historical background and chronology of the early Greek world). The richest of these was Mycenae. Other Peloponnesian centers with cycles of saga are Tiryns, Argos, Sparta, and the rural area of Arcadia. On the Greek mainland the chief centers are Athens, Thebes, Orchomenus, and Iolcus. Outside the Greek mainland, important sagas are connected with Troy and Crete. The saga of Odysseus is unique in extending far outside the Mycenaean world and incorporating many folktales.

Saga must be distinguished from history, even when its details can be corroborated by archaeological discoveries. Saga focuses on a few personages, divine or heroic, not on geographical, economic, and social facts.

THE THEBAN SAGA: THE FOUNDING OF THEBES

Cadmus and Europa. EUROPA [u-ro'pa], daughter of Agenor of Tyre and sister of CADMUS [kad'mus], or KADMOS, was abducted by Zeus (in the form of a bull) and taken to Crete, where she became by Zeus the mother of Minos.

Cadmus went to Greece in search of Europa. The oracle at Delphi told him not to go on with the search but instead to follow a certain cow until she lay down. There he was to found a city. The cow led Cadmus from Phocis to the place (in Boeotia) where he founded CADMEIA [kad-me′a], or KAD-MEIA, later called Thebes.

The Spartoi ("sown men"). The companions of Cadmus, needing water for the ceremony of sacrificing the cow to Athena, killed the serpent (child of Ares) that guarded the spring. It killed Cadmus' men and was itself killed by Cadmus, who obeyed Athena's command to sow its teeth. From them sprang up armed men, who fought and killed each other until there were five survivors. From them were descended the noble families of Thebes, called SPARTOI [spar′toy], "sown men."

Cadmus and Harmonia. In penance for killing the serpent, Cadmus served Ares for a year and was given HARMONIA [har-mon′i-a], daughter of Ares and Aphrodite, as wife, to whom he gave as a wedding gift a necklace made by Hephaestus. Their four daughters were Ino, Semele, Autonoë, and Agave (see Chapter 11).

Cadmus introduced writing and other arts of civilization at Thebes. After a long reign, he and Harmonia went to Illyria and finally were changed into harmless serpents.

THE FAMILIES OF LABDACUS AND LYCUS

Pentheus succeeded his grandfather, Cadmus, as king. After his death (see Chapter 11) Labdacus founded a new dynasty. On his death LYCUS [li′kus], or LYKOS, son of Chthonius (one of the Spartoi), became regent for the infant LAIUS [la′us] or [li′us], or LAIOS.

Antiope and Zeus. The niece of Lycus was ANTIOPE [an-ti′o-pe], daughter of Nycteus. Zeus made her the mother of the twins AMPHION [am-fi′on] and ZETHUS [ze′thus], or ZETHOS, who were brought up by a shepherd while Antiope was imprisoned by Lycus and his wife, DIRCE [dir′se] or DIRKE. She escaped and after a long time was recognized by her sons, who killed Lycus and tied Dirce to the horns of a bull that dragged her to her death.

Amphion and Zethus. These twin brothers became rulers of Cadmeia and sent Laius into exile. They built walls for the city, whose stones were moved into place by the music of Amphion's lyre. Amphion married Niobe (see Chapter 8) and Zethus married THEBE [the′be], after whom the name of Cadmeia was changed to THEBES [thebz].

Laius' Abduction of Chrysippus. In exile Laius lived with PELOPS [pe′lops], king of Elis, whose son, CHRYSIPPUS [kri-sip′pus], or CHRYSIPPOS, he abducted. For this transgression of the laws of hospitality Pelops invoked a curse on him and his family.

Laius and Jocasta. On the death of Amphion and Zethus, Laius returned to Thebes as king and married JOCASTA [jo-kas′ta] or IOKASTE. Apollo's oracle at Delphi warned that their son would kill his father as the working out of the curse of Pelops.

OEDIPUS

Laius ordered a shepherd to expose his infant son on Mt. CITHAERON [si-the′ron], or KITHA-IRON, driving a spike through his ankles. The baby was given instead by the shepherd to a

Corinthian shepherd, servant of POLYBUS [pol'i-bus], or POLYBOS, king of Corinth, and Queen MEROPE [mer'o-pe], who called the baby OEDIPUS [e'di-pus], or OIDIPOUS,"swellfoot."

Oedipus at Delphi. As a young man Oedipus was taunted for not really being the son of Polybus and asked the oracle at Delphi who his parents were. He was warned to avoid his homeland, since he was destined to kill his father and marry his mother.

The Murder of Laius. Oedipus therefore did not return to Corinth, and on the road that led to Thebes, he killed an old man in a chariot who had struck him and driven him off the road. The old man, whom he did not recognize, was Laius.

The Sphinx. Thebes was suffering from the Sphinx ("strangler"), a monster that was part woman, part lion, and part bird. It killed those who could not answer its riddle, "What has one name that is four-footed, two-footed, and three-footed?" Oedipus answered, "Man, who as a baby crawls on all fours, in his prime he walks on two feet, and in old age he uses a stick as a third foot." The Sphinx hurled itself to its death, and Oedipus became king of Thebes in place of the dead Laius and took the widowed queen, Jocasta, as wife.

Oedipus the King. Thebes was afflicted with a plague after many years of Oedipus' reign.   The oracle at Delphi advised the Thebans that it had been caused by the pollution of the murderer of Laius living in their city. Oedipus was determined to find out the murderer's identity, yet he refused to believe the prophet, TIRESIAS [ti-re'si-as], who told him that <u>he</u> was the murderer. A messenger (who was the same shepherd to whom the infant Oedipus had been given by the Theban shepherd) came from Corinth to announce the death of Polybus and offer the throne of Corinth to Oedipus. He told Oedipus, who refused to return to Corinth because of the prophecy that he would marry his mother, that he was not the son of Polybus. Oedipus sent for the Theban shepherd, and the truth was discovered. Jocasta had already silently gone into the palace, where she hanged herself: Oedipus rushed into the palace and blinded himself with the brooches from Jocasta's robe.

Oedipus at Colonus. CREON [kre'on], or KREON, the brother of Jocasta, became king, and Oedipus went into exile accompanied by his daughters, ANTIGONE [an-tig'o-ne] and ISMENE [is-me'ne]. He wandered eventually to COLONUS [ko-lo'nus], or KOLONOS (in Attica), and was received kindly by THESEUS [the'se-us], king of Athens.

At Colonus Oedipus bid farewell to his daughters and then miraculously disappeared from the earth, observed only by Theseus. A hero-cult was established at the place where he vanished.

THE SEVEN AGAINST THEBES

In another version Oedipus was shut up in the palace at Thebes and cursed his sons, ETEOCLES [e-te'o-klez], or ETEOKLES, and POLYNICES [pol-i-ni'sez], or POLYNIKES, for putting before him one day a less honorable portion of food. He prayed that after his death they might fight to divide the kingdom.

Oedipus died at Thebes (in this version), and his sons quarreled over the throne, agreeing finally that they should reign in alternate years while the other went into exile.

Eteocles and Polynices. After the first year, Eteocles refused to give up the throne, and Polynices raised an army with the help of Adrastus, king of Argos, to march against Thebes. This is the start of the saga of the Seven against Thebes.

The Seven. The names of the seven leaders who attacked Thebes were Polynices, Adrastus, Tydeus, Capaneus, Hippomedon, Parthenopaeus, and Amphiaraüs.

Amphiaraüs and Eriphyle. AMPHIARAÜS [am-fi-a-ra'us] was a seer and knew that the Seven would fail. His wife, ERIPHYLE [e-ri-fi'le], bribed by Polynices with the gift of the necklace of Harmonia (see above), persuaded him to go. He ordered his sons to avenge his death by punishing Eriphyle.

Hypsipyle and Opheltes. During the march from Argos to Thebes the Seven met HYPSIPYLE [hip-sip'i-le] (see Chapter 22), nurse of the infant OPHELTES [o-fel'tez], who was killed by a serpent. In his honor the Seven founded the NEMEAN [nem'e-an] Games.

The Seven against Thebes. Tydeus, one of the Seven, failed in a peace embassy to Thebes and escaped an ambush set by the Thebans. In the attack on Thebes, each of the Seven stormed one of the city's gates. Capaneus was killed by Zeus' thunderbolt; Hippomedon, Parthenopaeus, and Tydeus fell in battle; Amphiaraüs escaped in his chariot and was miraculously swallowed up by the earth beside the river Ismenus. Hero-cults in his honor were established there and elsewhere. Polynices and Eteocles killed each other in single combat. Of the Seven, only ADRASTUS [a-dras'-tus], or ADRASTOS, returned home.

Antigone. Antigone defied the edict of Creon forbidding the burial of Polynices. Obeying the decrees of Zeus, she gave her brother symbolic burial and was condemned to death by Creon. HAEMON [he'mon], or HAIMON, Creon's son and her fiancé, shared her death, and Creon, warned by Tiresias, relented too late.

Burial of the Heroes. Theseus helped the widows and mothers of the dead Argive heroes recover the unburied corpses and give them proper funerals. EVADNE [e-vad'ne], widow of CAPANEUS [cap'an-us], threw herself into the flames of his pyre.

THE EPIGONI, SONS OF THE SEVEN

ALCMAEON [alk-me'on], or ALKMAION, son of Amphiaraüs, led the EPIGONI [e-pig'o-ni], or EPIGONOI ("the later generation"), in a successful attack on Thebes, which was abandoned by its inhabitants.

Alcmaeon and Eriphyle. Alcmaeon killed his mother, Eriphyle, in obedience to his father's orders (see above). Pursued by the Furies, he came to Arcadia, where he married the daughter of King Phegeus, to whom he gave the necklace of Harmonia. As a matricide he was a pollution on the land and was driven out. He came to western Greece and there married Callirhoë, daughter of the river-god Acheloüs, to whom he gave the necklace of Harmonia, having recovered it in Arcadia. His sons became the founders of the Greek district of Acarnania.

TIRESIAS

Tiresias, the blind prophet, was son of the nymph Chariclo. He was blinded by Hera for taking Zeus' side in a quarrel about which sex derived more pleasure from the sexual act, for he had been both man and woman. As a recompense, Zeus gave him the gift of prophecy.

Tiresias was consulted by Odysseus at the entrance to the Underworld and revealed his future wanderings (see Chapter 18). He accepted the worship of Dionysus at Thebes and warned Pentheus in vain of his mistake (see Chapter 11). He revealed the truth to Oedipus in Sophocles' Oedipus the King, and in Sophocles' Antigone he warned Creon of his errors.

Tiresias died during the Theban exodus after the attack of the Epigoni.

COMPACT DISCS

2. Albert, Stephen, Into Eclipse. Song cycle based on Seneca's Oedipus.
8. Bach, P. D. Q. (Peter Schickele), Oedipus Tex. Dramatic Oratorio for soloists, chorus, and orchestra. Very funny parody with the Oedipus legend set in the Old West.
71. "The End." An Oedipal song by Jim Morrison and his rock group The Doors.
72. Enesco, Georges, Oedipe. An operatic masterpiece (well worth investigating), which begins with the birth of Oedipus and ends at Colonus.
124. Honegger, Arthur, Antigone. Musical tragedy with text by Cocteau, adapted from Sophocles.
147. Lehrer, Tom, "Oedipus Rex." Humorous song about the Oedipus complex.
149. Leoncavallo, Ruggiero, Edipo Re. If you enjoy Pagliacci, you will be interested in this operatic condensation of Sophocles.
170 and **171.** Mendelssohn, Felix, Antigone and Ödipus. Incidental music for adaptations of Sophocles, for speakers, solo bass, two male choruses, and orchestra.
176. Milhaud, Darius, Trois Opéras-Minute: L'enlèvement d'Europe, L'abandon d'Ariane, and La délivrance de Thésée. The first of these very short operas is about Jupiter's abduction of Europa.
194. Naumann, J. G., Amphion. Opera.
201. Orff, Carl, Antigonae. Operatic setting of Hölderlin's German translation of Sophocles (M/L 604).
206. Paine, John Knowles, Oedipus Tyrannus-Prelude. Lovely work by the father of American classical music.
225. Raitio, Väinö, Antigone. Tone-Poem for Orchestra.
240. Rossini, Gioacchino, Edipo a Colono. Cantata.
250 and **251.** Schubert, Franz, "Amphiaraos." Song about Amphiaraus against Thebes and his death. "Antigone und Oedip." Duet. Antigone appeals to Oedipus, who is resigned to dying.
252. Schuman, William, Night Journey. Ballet. See Videos.
272. Stravinsky, Igor, Oedipus Rex. Opera-Oratorio. Text, after Sophocles, by Cocteau, translated into Latin by Jean Danielou. See Videos.
279. Telson, Bob, Gospel at Colonus. Musical. See Videos.
288. Wakeman, Rick, and Ramon Remedios, A Suite of the Gods. Classical new age songs for tenor, keyboards, and percussion, which include "The Oracle," about Oedipus.

VIDEOS

Night Journey. Martha Graham, choreographer. Music by William Schuman. Home video Exclusives, The Library of Master Performers 101V. <u>Martha Graham, an American Original in Performance</u>. Kultur 1177; this video includes both <u>Night Journey</u> and <u>A Dancer's World</u>, in which Graham talks about her philosophy, as she prepares for her role as Jocasta in a rehearsal of <u>Night Journey</u>.

Graham notes: "... it is not Oedipus who is the protagonist. The action turns upon that instant of Jocasta's death when she relives her destiny, sees with double insight the triumphal entry of Oedipus, their meeting, courtship, marriage, their years of intimacy which were darkly crossed by the blind seer, Tiresias, until at last the truth burst from him."

A Graham dance inspired by mythology elucidates the myth from the point of view of the heroine; it is an exploration of the inner world of the feminine soul, or better, psyche, with all of the Freudian implications that this word evokes. Another vital element in her art is its sublime eroticism: "I know my dances and technique are considered deeply sexual, but I pride myself in placing onstage what most people hide in their deepest thoughts."

To enhance appreciation of Martha Graham's genius one should read her own lengthy analysis of her "highly erotic dance" between Jocasta and Oedipus (Martha Graham, <u>Blood Memory</u>, New York: Doubleday, 1991, pp. 212-217)

If one is unfamiliar with Graham's art, <u>Night Journey</u> provides the very best introduction. It is concise, taut, and concentrated (about a half hour in length) and its stylized and simple sets by Isamu Noguchi enhance the intensity of the action: a bed, where Jocasta conceived and gave birth to Oedipus, their marriage-bed, and the setting for her suicide; and a rope, which in the episodes of the dance becomes the binding umbilical cord, the entangling thread of fate, and the noose of death.

<u>Antigone</u>. Cinematic version of Sophocles' play, written and directed by George Tzavellas and starring the great Irene Papas. In Greek with English subtitles. Ivy Classics Video. Also Video Yesteryear 2310.

<u>Antigone</u>. Produced and directed by Arlena Nys and starring Carrie O'Brien and Chris Bearne. Insight Media. AO422

<u>Oedipus at Colonus</u>. Music by Bob Telson and lyrics by Lee Breuer and Bob Telson. Warner Reprise Video. 38123-3. An original, moving, and faithful setting of Sophocles' play in the context of a black gospel service (M/L 607). An enlightening and moving comparison may be made between the sermon of the preacher (played by Morgan Freeman), describing the miracle of Oedipus' passing, with the messenger speech from Sophocles, upon which it is based.

<u>Oedipus Rex</u>. A brilliant film written and directed by Pier Paolo Pasolini (M/L 610). Original uncut version with English subtitles. Waterbearer Films WBF8013. To be preferred to the version offered by Corinth Video CV-037.

<u>Oedipus Rex</u>. Opera/Oratorio, by Igor Stravinsky, directed by Hans Hulscher and conducted by Bernard Haitink. Home Vision OED01. A highly esteemed work of the twentieth century. Do not miss Stravinsky's manipulation of themes from Verdi's <u>Aida</u> (M/L 603)!

<u>Oedipus Rex</u>. Insight Media. AO36. Film directed by Tyrone Guthrie, using masks and W. B. Yeats's translation of Sophocles (M/L 610).

<u>Oedipus Wrecks</u>. One of three short films (included in the movie <u>New York Stories</u>) directed by and

starring Woody Allen. Touchstone Home Video 952. About a fifty-year-old neurotic lawyer, tormented by the specter of his nagging mother.

There are some movies that are peripheral but nevertheless valuable for the enhancement of mythological study (cf. M/L 612-13). Woody Allen's <u>Mighty Aphrodite</u> not only testifies to the power of love but also provides a parody of Greek tragedy which some may find amusing. More important is <u>Voyager</u>, a movie based on the novel <u>Homo Faber</u> by Max Frisch, which is profoundly Greek in its mood and intensity because of its themes of family, incest, and fate. The excellent <u>Jean de Florette</u>, based on Marcel Pagnol's novel, is also steeped in the atmosphere and movement of Greek tragedy, as is made overtly clear in the dialogue of its equally fine sequel, <u>Manon of the Springs</u>.

In another vein, a study of <u>Star Wars</u> as an archetype of the genre of science fiction reveals that once again here is the mellow wine of classical mythology in attractive new bottles. The fantasy and excitement of Greek and Roman mythology and legend have been transported to outer space, along with all the familiar, universal motifs (which are not too difficult to identify).

INTERPRETATION

Europa and Zeus. The legend of Europa and Zeus is narrated by Ovid in <u>Metamorphoses</u> 2. 846-3 .2. Of many artistic representations, a relief sculpture from the Sicilian city of Selinus (ca. 540 B.C.) and the painting (now in Boston) by Titian (ca. 1560) are especially powerful.

Cadmus and Amphion and Zethus. The legend of Cadmus' teaching his subjects to write may be related to the introduction of the Phoenician alphabet in the eighth century B.C. and the invention of the Greek alphabet and the revival of writing in Greece.

The building of the walls of Cadmeia by Amphion and Zethus is a doublet of the original building of the city by Cadmus. The moving of the stones by Amphion's music demonstrated the power of harmony to bring order out of disorder, just as Cadmus and Harmonia had established civilized order in their city.

Dirce. The killing of Dirce is the subject of the so-called Farnese Bull (ca. A.D. 210, now in Naples), a marble group made for the Baths of Caracalla in Rome and discovered there in 1545.

Oedipus. The version of the saga of Oedipus given here follows Sophocles' tragedies <u>Oedipus the King</u> (428 B.C.) and <u>Oedipus at Colonus</u> (406 B.C.). There were other versions of the myth, including an early epic (now lost) called <u>Oedipodea</u>. In the <u>Odyssey</u>, Homer says that "Epicasta" hanged herself when the truth about her marriage became known, while Oedipus continued his unhappy reign. In the <u>Iliad</u>, Oedipus is said to have died in battle. Other authors give different names to the mother of his children.

The version of Sophocles has become the most authoritative and was used as the prime example of tragedy by Aristotle in his Poetics. In 1910 Freud identified the Oedipus complex (the word "complex" was first used by Jung, however), using Oedipus as the pattern of the son "directing his infantile sexual impulses toward [his] mother" and his "first impulses of hatred and resistance toward [his] father." Freud's discovery has been seminal, and it has led to many modern interpretations in literature, drama, music, ballet, and art. Many are surveyed by Lowell Edmunds in <u>Oedipus: The Ancient Legend and Its Later Analogues</u> (Baltimore: Johns Hopkins University Press, 1985).

Important representations of <u>Oedipus and the Sphinx</u> were painted by Ingres (1808, now in Paris) and Moreau (1864, now in New York). Very different is the painting <u>Oedipus Rex</u> (1922) by the surrealist painter Max Ernst, in which Freudian motifs are combined with motifs from Shakespeare's <u>Hamlet</u>, creating a dense web of associations with the infancy, fears, and hopes of the young king.

There was once available a valuable collection of major plays about Oedipus with related essays (<u>Oedipus, Myth and Dramatic Form</u>, edited by James L. Sanderson and Everett Zimmerman, Boston: Houghton Mifflin, 1968): The <u>Oedipus</u> of Sophocles, Seneca (ca. A.D. 45), Voltaire (ca. 1718), André Gide (1930), and Jean Cocteau's <u>The Infernal Machine</u> (ca. 1934), a particularly clever and stimulating retelling of the legend.

The Seven against Thebes. The saga of the Seven against Thebes was the subject of several tragedies and epics. <u>The Seven against Thebes</u> of Aeschylus (467 B.C.) focuses on the curse on the Theban royal family; it describes the attack on Thebes itself and the death of Menoeceus, and it ends with the report of the single combat and deaths of Polynices and Eteocles, a further working out of the curse. In his drama <u>The Phoenician Women</u> (412 B.C.), Euripides is sympathetic to Polynices. This play describes the attack on Thebes and the deaths of Menoeceus, Eteocles, Polynices, and Jocasta, who kills herself over the corpses of her sons. At its end, Creon sends Oedipus into exile, and Antigone refuses to obey the decree forbidding burial of Polynices. In the <u>Phoenissae</u> of Seneca (mid-first century A.D.), Oedipus, wandering in exile, curses his sons: at Thebes Jocasta fails to mediate between the brothers as the attack begins. The play breaks off at this point. The epic <u>Thebaid</u> of Statius (ca. A.D. 90) narrates the saga of the Seven from the preparations at Argos, through the expedition to Thebes, the failure of the attack, and the mutual killing and cremation of the brothers. Statius adds the episodes of Antigone's defiance and Theseus' expedition.

Antigone. Antigone is the heroine of Sophocles' tragedy <u>Antigone</u> (442 B.C.), which focuses primarily on the overriding importance of family relationships. When the law of Zeus conflicts with the law of the state, Antigone chooses execution rather than disobedience to divine law. Since the time of Sophocles, Antigone has been the symbol of individual conscience against unjust laws. There have been many reinterpretations of her legend, which have been discussed by George Steiner in <u>Antigones</u> (New York: Oxford University Press, 1984).

The Epigoni. The saga of the Epigoni is the subject of Euripides' drama <u>The Suppliant Women</u> (424 B.C.), which portrays Athens and its king, Theseus, in a very favorable light.

Tiresias. Tiresias has often been used as an archetypal seer, for example, in Seneca's <u>Oedipus</u> (mid-first century A.D.) and by Dante in <u>Inferno</u>, Canto 20. The avant-garde poet Guillaume Apollinaire wrote <u>Les Mamelles de Tirésias</u> (1903), which he called "a Surrealist drama". It was first performed in 1917 and was published, with illustrations by Picasso, in 1918. It was the libretto of a light opera with the same title by Francis Poulenc (1944), which is not yet available on CD. He appears at line 218 of T. S. Eliot's <u>The Waste Land</u> (1922). Eliot says of him: "Tiresias, although a mere spectator. . . is yet the most important personage in the poem, uniting all the rest. . . The two sexes meet in Tiresias."

CHAPTER 16

The Mycenaean Saga

TANTALUS AND PELOPS

The Banquet of Tantalus. TANTALUS [tan'ta-lus], or TANTALOS, an Asian prince and a son of Zeus, cut up his son PELOPS [pe'lops], boiled the pieces, and served them to the gods at a banquet. For this he was excluded from the companionship of the gods and condemned to suffer everlasting thirst and hunger in the Underworld (see Chapter 13). At the banquet the gods refused to eat, except for Demeter, who, distracted by grief for the loss of her daughter (see Chapter 12), ate part of Pelops' shoulder. The gods restored him to life, giving him an ivory shoulder to replace the part eaten by Demeter.

Pindar was doubtful about the myth of the banquet of Tantalus and explained Pelops' disappearance by saying that Poseidon took Pelops up to Olympus and that the other gods sent him back.

Pelops Wins Hippodamia. Pelops left Asia and came to Greece as a suitor for the hand of HIPPO-DAMIA [hip-po-da-me'a], or HIPPODAMEIA, daughter of OENOMAÜS [e-no-ma'us], or OINO-MAOS, king of Pisa. To win the bride, a suitor had to defeat Oenomaüs in a chariot race from Pisa to the Isthmus of Corinth, taking Hippodamia in his chariot and starting ahead of Oenomaüs. If Oenomaüs caught up with him, he would kill the suitor and take Hippodamia back. Thirteen suitors had failed before Pelops. Pelops prayed to Poseidon for success and won the race with the god's help. The scene before the start of the chariot race is the subject of the sculptures of the east pediment of the Temple of Zeus at Olympia (ca. 460 B.C., see Chapter 3).

In the best-known version, Pelops won by bribing MYRTILUS [mir'ti-lus], or MYRTILOS, the king's charioteer, to remove the linchpins from his chariot, causing the king to crash. His reward would be to spend the first night with the bride.

The Curse of Myrtilus. After winning the race in this way, Pelops did not honor the agreement and threw Myrtilus into the sea. As he fell, Myrtilus cursed Pelops and his descendants.

Pelops, King and Hero. Pelops returned to Pisa as king. After his death he was honored with a hero-cult at Olympia (in the territory of Pisa), and together with his grandfather, Zeus, he received sacrifices at the Olympic festival. He gave his name to the southern part of the Greek mainland, Peloponnese ("Island of Pelops").

THE HOUSE OF ATREUS

The Quarrel between Atreus and Thyestes. The sons of Pelops were ATREUS [a'tre-us] and THYESTES [thi-es'tez]. They quarreled over the kingship of Mycenae, which had been offered to "a son of Pelops." Atreus, as the possessor of a golden-fleeced ram, claimed the throne.

While Atreus was celebrating his coronation, his wife, AËROPE [a-er'o-pe], took Thyestes as her lover and gave him the ram. The story of Aërope's adultery is told by Euripides in his <u>Electra</u> (lines 698-725). Thyestes replaced Atreus as king and drove him into exile.

The Banquet of Atreus and the Curse of Thyestes. Atreus returned from exile and drove out Thyestes. Later he tricked him into returning, by pretending to be reconciled, and invited him to a banquet. He killed Thyestes' sons and served them up to their father, who ate them. At the sight of this crime, the sun hid and the heavens darkened. Thyestes cursed Atreus and left Mycenae.

THE FAMILY OF AGAMEMNON

Aegisthus. In his second exile Thyestes lay with his daughter, Pelopia, and became father of AEGISTHUS [e-jis'thus], or AIGISTHOS, who continued the vendetta against the family of Atreus.

Agamemnon and Clytemnestra: The Sacrifice of Iphigenia. AGAMEMNON [ag-a-mem'non] succeeded his father, Atreus, and ruled Mycenae with CLYTEMNESTRA [cli-tem-nes'tra], or KLYTAIMNESTRA, as his queen. To obtain a favorable wind for the Greek fleet to sail to Troy (see Chapter 17), he sacrificed his daughter IPHIGENIA [if-i-je-ni'a], or IPHIGENEIA, to Artemis.

Clytemnestra and Aegisthus: The Murder of Agamemnon and Cassandra. To avenge her daughter's murder, Clytemnestra took Aegisthus as her lover while she ruled Mycenae in the ten-year absence of Agamemnon at Troy. Together they murdered Agamemnon in the palace when he returned after the sack of Troy.

CASSANDRA [kas-san'dra], or KASSANDRA, a Trojan princess and seer (see Chapters 9 and 17), accompanied Agamemnon and was murdered with him. She described the coming murders before entering the palace.

In this and the following generation, Myrtilus' curse on the descendants of Pelops and the curse of Thyestes against Atreus afflicted only the family of Agamemnon. The troubles of his brother, MENELAÜS [men-e-la'us], or MENELAOS (king of Sparta: see Chapter 17), were not part of the working out of the curse.

ORESTES AND ELECTRA

The son of Agamemnon, ORESTES [o-res'tez], was away from Mycenae when his father was murdered, living with Strophius, king of Phocis. Apollo ordered him to fulfill his filial duty to avenge Agamemnon's death.

Orestes' Murder of His Mother Clytemnestra. Orestes returned to Mycenae in disguise and was recognized by his sister, ELECTRA [e-lek'tra], or ELEKTRA. With her support he entered the palace and there killed Clytemnestra and Aegisthus.

The Furies Pursue Orestes. Orestes, guilty of killing his mother, was pursued by the ERINYES [e-rin'i-ez], the FURIES (see Chapters 1 and 13), who drove him mad. He came to Delphi, where Apollo promised to protect him and ordered him to go to Athens.

Orestes Acquitted by the Areopagus. At Athens Orestes was tried for murder before the court of the AREOPAGUS [a-re-o'pa-gus], or AREIOPAGOS. Athena presided over the court, while the Erinyes prosecuted Orestes and Apollo defended him. The verdict of the jury of Athenian citizens was split, and Athena gave her casting vote for acquittal.

The Eumenides. The verdict broke the power of the Erinyes, to whom Athena gave a new home on the Acropolis at Athens and a new name, EUMENIDES [u-men'i-dez], "the kindly ones." The curse on the descendants of Pelops had worked itself out.

Orestes and Hermione. Orestes returned to Mycenae as king and ruled with HERMIONE [her-mi'o-ne], daughter of Menelaüs and Helen, whom he married after arranging the killing at Delphi of her husband, NEOPTOLEMUS [ne-op-tol'e-mus], or NEOPTOLEMOS, son of Achilles. Later Orestes ruled over Argos and Sparta as well. His son, Tisamenus, died defending the Peloponnese against the Heraclidae (see Chapter 20).

Orestes was buried at Tegea, a neighboring city and rival of Sparta. The Spartans, advised by the Delphic oracle, recovered his bones, which brought them victory over the Tegeans.

Iphigenia among the Taurians. In another version Orestes was purified at Delphi. In yet another Apollo ordered him to go to the land of the Tauri (i.e., the Crimea) and fetch a wooden statue of Artemis from the temple where Iphigenia (rescued from sacrifice by Artemis: see Chapter 17) was priestess of the goddess. She saved Orestes from being sacrificed to Artemis, and together they returned with the statue to Greece. Iphigenia became priestess of Artemis at Brauron in Attica.

Electra and Pylades. Electra lived on at Mycenae after Agamemnon's murder. She helped Orestes kill her father's murderers and married his companion, PYLADES [pi'la-dez], bearing him two sons, Strophius and Medon.

COMPACT DISCS

65. Diepenbrock, Alphons, Elektra. Symphonic Suite.

87 and **88.** Gluck, Christoph Willibald, Iphigenia in Aulis and Iphigenia in Tauris. Operas of great beauty and passion (M/L 599).

96. Haeffner, Johann Christian Friedrich, Electra. Opera.

177. Milhaud, Darius, L'Orestie d'Eschyle: Agamemnon; Les Choéphores; Les Euménides. Three short operatic treatments to a libretto by Paul Claudel.

192 and **193.** Music of Ancient Greece. First chorus from Euripides' Orestes.

220. Piccinni, Niccolò, Iphigénie en Tauride. Opera.

250 and **251.** Schubert, Franz, "Fragment aus dem Aeschylus" (song from a chorus from the Eumenides), "Der entsühnte Orest" and "Orest auf Tauris" (Orestes' song of purification and his address to the land of the Taurians).

269. Strauss, Richard, Elektra. Operatic masterpiece, with text brilliantly adapted from Sophocles by Hugo von Hofmannsthal (M/L 601).

278. Taneiev, Sergei, The Oresteia. Theatrical modern opera, after Aeschylus.

94. Traetta, Tommaso, Iphigénie en Tauride. Opera.

294. Xenakis, Iannis, Oresteia. Suite for chorus and orchestra drawn from music composed for a production of Aeschylus' trilogy, with the addition of a section entitled "Kassandra," with baritone and percussion solo (M/L 604).

VIDEOS

Agamemnon. Modernized production of Aeschylus by the London Small Theater Company. Insight Media. DP605.

Crete and Mycenae (Museum without Walls). An informative tour of these sites, providing invaluable archaeological background for this chapter as well as Chapter 21 (Theseus).

Electra. Sophocles' version performed in modern dress. The star and director is Arlena Nys. Overall an amateurish effort, perhaps of some interest, particularly for the interview with Nys, who perceptively identifies the universality of the play. Luxemburg Dionysus Theatricals. Insight Media.

Elektra. The three performances of Richard Strauss's opera on video are listed in order of preference; all have English subtitles.

1.   London 071 500-3 LH. Wiener Philharmoniker, cond. Karl Böhm, directed by Götz Friedrich and filmed on the outskirts of Vienna amidst filth and rain. The renowned Leonie Rysanek as Elektra and Dietrich Fischer-Dieskau as Orest make this cinematically and musically the most credible performance, despite other drawbacks, the worst of which is a break in the crucial moment of the recognition scene because of injudicious editing.
2.   Bel Canto Paramount Home Video. 12611. Metropolitan Opera Orchestra, cond. James Levine. Birgit Nilsson can no longer sing the role as radiantly as she once did (see CD above), and the camera is not flattering to this great Elektra. Rysanek as Chrysothemis lends splendid support.
3.   Home Vision ELE 02. Chorus and Orchestra of the Vienna State opera, cond. Abbado, with Eva Marton as Elektra.

Iphigenia. An adaptation of Euripides' Iphigenia in Aulis that is a cinematic masterpiece. Directed by Michael Cacoyannis, with a superb Greek cast, including the incomparable Irene Papas as Clytemnestra. Columbia Pictures Home Entertainment VCF31158.

Oresteia. Films for the Humanities & Sciences (see Introduction) offers a series of four videos on Classical Civilization: The Greeks (AGU702), originally produced for television: The Greek Beginning; The Classical Age; Heroes and Men; The Minds of Men. Part 3, Heroes and Men (AGU707), which may be purchased individually at greater expense, contains crucial scenes from the Oresteia, which are worth investigating, especially for the portrayal of Clytemnestra.

Oresteia. Films for the Humanities ADS900. Each of the plays (*Agamemnon, Choephori and Eumenides*) may be purchased individually at greater expense. The National Theater of Great Britain Production directed by Peter Hall, using masks (M/L 611).

INTERPRETATION

Many enriching and enjoyable pursuits may be followed in connection with the study of Mycenaean saga.

A reading of Euripides' Iphigenia at Aulis is greatly enhanced by a viewing of the great movie adaptation by Cacoyannis. And Gluck's operatic version (admired and revised by Richard Wagner) is one of his best works.

Perhaps most rewarding of all is a study of the three versions of the Electra story in Aeschylus' The Libation-Bearers and the Electra of Sophocles and of Euripides. We are fortunate to have this singular opportunity to compare the individual and unique treatments of the same legend by these three master playwrights. Through the manipulation of plot and with divergent purposes in the delineation of the human characters and the divine action, these three Electras could not be more different from one another (M/L 347).

Among many musical compositions, pride of place belongs to the opera Elektra by Richard Strauss (1909), with libretto by Hugo von Hofmannsthal, adapted from Sophocles' version. Both Hofmannsthal and Strauss were fascinated by the new and startling revelations made by Sigmund Freud, particularly in his writings about hysteria. Hofmannsthal, seeing in Electra a classic study of neurosis, brilliantly adapted Sophocles' play to highlight its insights for twentieth-century psychology. Sophocles' superb recognition scene between Electra and Orestes becomes even more overpowering when enhanced by Strauss's music which evokes the passion of a love duet. In this scene in Sophocles, Orestes expresses his concern that Electra's intense emotions might overwhelm her. In the opera, after the murder of Clytemnestra and Aegisthus and amidst the triumph of Orestes, Electra actually dies after an ecstatic dance of joy, succumbing to physical exhaustion and psychological devastation, wrought by cruel injustice, ingrained hatred, and the engulfing fulfillment of brutal vengeance.

These are brilliant examples of a phenomenon that we witness again and again: the eternal rejuvenation of Greek and Roman myth and legend to delight and instruct anew each generation. The Frenchman Jean-Paul Sartre in his play The Flies transforms Orestes into a paradigm of existentialism; in the ingenious novel Angel of Light by the American Joyce Carol Oates, Orestes and Electra have become students in Washington, D.C., descendants of the abolitionist martyr John Brown, who are convinced that their father, a director in the Ministry of Justice, has been murdered by their mother. More of these inspired and inspiring transformations are discussed below. What a shame that Cacoyannis' film of Euripides' Electra (with Irene Papas in the title role) has not yet appeared on video tape! There is more hope that the movie version of Eugene O'Neill's Mourning Becomes Electra (M/L 611, and below) will be released on video; it was once on Laser Disc.

The Banquet of Thyestes. Aeschylus twice refers to the banquet of Thyestes in the Agamemnon, first when Cassandra sees the murdered children in her vision before entering the palace and later when Aegisthus justifies the murder. Seneca, in his tragedy Thyestes, portrays Atreus as a cruel tyrant, gloating as he watches Thyestes' meal.

Iphigenia in Aulis and among the Taurians. The sacrifice of Iphigenia was narrated in the lost early epic Cypria. In the opening chorus of his tragedy Agamemnon (458 B.C.), lines 192-249, Aeschylus shows Agamemnon caught between two intolerable alternatives (to sacrifice a daughter or incur the wrath of Artemis and abandon the expedition) and choosing the one that breaks the most sacred laws of the family. The hubris (arrogance) of Agamemnon is further shown by his destruction of the temples of the gods at Troy and his entrance into the palace treading on purple carpets. Iphigenia's sacrifice was also narrated by Lucretius (ca. 55 B.C.), as an example of the evils that religion can bring (De Rerum Natura 1. 84-101). In Euripides' last tragedy, Iphigenia in Aulis (406 B.C.), Iphigenia, brought to Aulis on the pretext of marrying Achilles, first tries to avoid her fate but finally goes to her death willingly for the sake of the Greeks. Euripides' drama was adapted by Michael Cacoyannis in his film Iphigenia (1977, see above), portraying Iphigenia as both tragic victim and patriotic heroine. The sacrifice was the subject of a famous painting (now lost) by the Greek artist Timanthes (ca. 425 B.C.) showing Agamemnon veiled, because the artist could not portray the father's emotions. "The veil of Timanthes" became proverbial for emotional restraint. Of the many interpretations of the myth of Iphigenia, one of the most important was created in the late eighteenth century: Iphigenie in Aulis, Schiller's adaptation of Euripides' play (1790). The escape of Orestes and Iphigenia from the land of the Tauri is the subject of Euripides' drama Iphigenia in Tauris (414 B.C.) and was the inspiration for another work of the late eighteenth century, the drama Iphigenia auf Tauris by Goethe (1779, revised by Goethe in 1788 and by Schiller in 1802). A little later is J-L. David's painting The Wrath of Achilles at the Sacrifice of Iphigenia (1819). The American painter Mark Rothko was inspired by Aeschylus' lines preceding the sacrifice of Iphigenia (Agamemnon 104-21) in his painting The Omen of the Eagle (1942). The versions of Aeschylus and Euripides are the essential foundation of all subsequent interpretations.

The Legend of the Oresteia in Literature and Art. The narrative of the deaths of Agamemnon and Cassandra, and of Clytemnestra and Aegisthus, is based on the first two plays (Agamemnon and Libation-Bearers) of Aeschylus' trilogy Oresteia (458 B.C.). The pursuit of Orestes by the Erinyes and his trial and acquittal at Athens are the subjects of the third play in the trilogy, Eumenides. Again, Aeschylus has influenced all subsequent interpretations. A striking non-representational meditation on Clytemnestra is the pair of neon-tube sculptures by the Greek-American sculptress Chryssa—the preparatory one (1967) now in Washington, D.C., and the final version (1968) in Berlin.

Orestes and Electra were also the central characters in tragedies by Sophocles (Electra) and Euripides (Electra and Orestes). The three tragedians portray Electra as variously motivated by love for her father and brother, hatred of her mother and Aegisthus, and jealousy, as well as by love and justice. Homer in the Odyssey has Zeus praise Orestes for his piety (in avenging his father's death), while Sophocles focuses less on the horror of matricide than do the other tragedians. The saga of Orestes and Electra has given rise to innumerable interpretations. In the twentieth century especially memorable are Eugene O'Neill's trilogy Mourning Becomes Electra (1931), where the saga is set in nineteenth-century New England, and T. S. Eliot's The Family Reunion (1939), where the setting is the house of an English family. A collection of plays with related essays, Orestes and Electra, Myth and Dramatic Form, edited by William M. Force (Boston: Houghton Mifflin, 1968), includes the versions of the three Greek dramatists plus Jean Giraudoux's Electra (1937) and The Prodigal (1960) by an American playwright, Jack Richardson.

In Euripides' drama Orestes (408 B.C.), Orestes is condemned at Argos for the murder of his mother but saves himself by taking Hermione hostage. Apollo orders Orestes to marry Hermione and foretells his acquittal at Athens. The death of Neoptolemus and Orestes' marriage to Hermione are themes in Euripides' drama Andromache (ca. 430 B.C.).

CHAPTER 17
The Trojan Saga

THE CHILDREN OF LEDA

LEDA [le'da], wife of TYNDAREUS [tin-dar'e-us], king of Sparta, bore four children to Zeus, who appeared to her in the form of a swan. Polydeuces and Helen (who were immortal) were born from one egg, Castor and Clytemnestra (who were mortal) from the other.

Castor and Polydeuces. CASTOR [kas'tor], or KASTOR, and POLYDEUCES [pol-i-du'sez], or POLYDEUKES, whose Roman name is POLLUX [pol'luks], were not part of the Trojan saga. They are known as the DIOSCURI [di-os'ku-ri], or DIOSKUROI ("sons of Zeus"), and Tyndaridae ("sons of Tyndareus"). Castor died in a quarrel with the sons of Aphareus, IDAS [i'das] and LYNCEUS [lyn'se-us], but Zeus allowed Polydeuces to share his immortality, so that each brother was on Olympus or in Hades on alternate days. Castor was a horseman, Polydeuces a boxer. As gods they helped sailors, and they were especially honored at Sparta and at Rome.

Helen and Paris. The most beautiful of women, HELEN had many suitors. She chose MENELAÜS [men-e-la'us], or MENELAOS, as her husband and bore HERMIONE [her-mi'o-ne] to him. The other suitors swore to help Menelaüs in time of need.

PARIS (also called ALEXANDER or ALEXANDROS), son of Priam and Hecabe (Hecuba), rulers of Troy, seduced Helen and took her to Troy. To recover her and vindicate Menelaüs, the Achaeans (Mycenaean Greeks) raised an expedition, led by Agamemnon.

Another version, by Stesichorus (seventh century B.C.), says that Helen went to Egypt and spent the ten years of the Trojan war there, while her phantom went to Troy.

The Judgment of Paris. Paris took Helen as a reward for judging Aphrodite to be more beautiful than Hera and Athena. All the Olympian gods except ERIS [er'is], "discord," were invited to the wedding of Peleus and Thetis (see Chapter 23). Eris appeared and threw on the table an apple inscribed with "For the most beautiful," which was claimed by each of the three goddesses. They were brought by Hermes to Paris on Mt. Ida, where each promised him a reward if he judged her to be the most beautiful.

The Judgment of Paris is not narrated by Homer, who says that Paris insulted Hera and Athena when they visited him but praised Aphrodite, who made him irresistible to women.

TROY AND ITS LEADERS AND ALLIES

Apollo and Poseidon built the walls of Troy for King LAOMEDON [la-om'e-don], who cheated them of their reward. To punish him, Apollo sent a plague, and Poseidon a sea-monster. Laomedon, obeying an oracle, exposed his daughter HESIONE [he-si'on-e] to the monster, but she was saved by Heracles (see Chapter 20), whom Laomedon also cheated of his reward. Heracles attacked Troy with an army: he killed Laomedon and gave Hesione as wife to Teucer.

Priam and Hecuba. Laomedon's son Podarces became king of Troy, changing his name to PRIAM [pri'am]. He had fifty sons and twelve daughters, nineteen of the children by his wife and queen, HECABE [he'ka-be], whose Roman name is HECUBA [he'ku-ba]. Of these Paris and Hector were most important.

Paris and Oenone. Before the birth of Paris, Hecabe dreamed that she had given birth to a fire-brand that consumed Troy. She exposed Paris on Mt. Ida, but he survived and became a shepherd. There he was loved by the nymph OENONE [e-no'ne], who had the gift of healing. When Paris was mortally wounded, she refused to heal him, and after his death she killed herself in remorse. Paris had returned to Troy and was recognized by Priam as his son. In the Trojan War he was saved by Aphrodite from death in single combat with Menelaüs, and he killed Achilles by shooting him in the heel with an arrow.

Hector, Andromache, and Astyanax. HECTOR [hek'tor], or HEKTOR, was the leading Trojan warrior, inferior only to Achilles, who killed him in single combat. His wife was ANDROMACHE [an-drom'a-ke], who bore him a son, ASTYANAX [as-ti'a-naks].

Helenus and Deïphobus. Two other sons of Priam were HELENUS [hel'e-nus], or HELENOS, and DEÏPHOBUS [de-if'o-bus], or DEÏPHOBOS. Helenus was a seer, who was captured by the Greeks and spared by them. He married Andromache after Hector's death and went with her to Epirus. Deïphobus married Helen after the death of Paris and was killed in the sack of Troy.

Cassandra and Polyxena. Two of Priam's daughters were CASSANDRA [kas-sand'ra], or KAS-SANDRA, and POLYXENA [po-lik'se-na]. Cassandra was given the gift of prophecy by Apollo (see Chapter 9), who punished her for her refusal of his love with the fate that her prophecies should never be believed. She warned the Trojans in vain of the city's fall and of the deception of the Trojan horse. She went to Mycenae as part of Agamemnon's spoils and there was killed by Clytemnestra (see Chapter 16).

Polyxena was sacrificed at the tomb of Achilles after the fall of Troy.

Aeneas and Antenor. Other Trojan leaders, who were not sons of Priam, were AENEAS [e-ne'as], or AINEIAS, and ANTENOR [an-ten'or]. Aeneas was the son of Aphrodite and Anchises (see Chapter 7) and was saved by Poseidon from death in single combat with Achilles. He survived the war and led a band of survivors to Italy (for his saga see Chapter 24). Antenor, brother of Hecabe, advised the Trojans to give Helen back to the Greeks. He and his wife, Theano, were spared at the sack and eventually came to Italy.

Leading Allies of the Trojans. These were the Lycian princes, GLAUCUS [glaw'kus], or GLAU-KOS, and SARPEDON [sar-pe'don]. Glaucus, son of Hippolochus, exchanged his golden armor for the bronze armor of Diomedes and was eventually killed by Ajax. Sarpedon was the son of Zeus, who could not save him from death at the hands of Patroclus. Zeus honored him by raining drops of blood and ordering Sleep and Death to transport his corpse back to Lycia.

Late in the war the Ethiopians, led by MEMNON [mem'non], son of Eos and Tithonus, came to assist the Trojans, as did the Thracians, led by RHESUS [re'sus], or RHESOS, and the Amazons, led by PENTHESILEA [pen-thes-i-le'a], or PENTHESILEIA.

THE ACHAEAN LEADERS

Agamemnon and Menelaüs. AGAMEMNON [ag-a-mem'non], "lord of men," was the leader of the expedition. He is described first by Helen when Priam points out to her from the wall the leading Greek warriors. He was a lesser warrior than Achilles and less good in council than Odysseus, but he was greater than both in prestige. His brother, MENELAÜS [men-e-la'us], or MENELAOS, had less prestige and prowess, although he would have killed Paris in single combat if Aphrodite had not saved Paris.

Diomedes. Greater than Agamemnon and Menelaus as a warrior was DIOMEDES [di-o-me'dez], son of Tydeus and king of Argos. Diomedes was favored by Athena, who enabled him to wound even Ares and Aphrodite in battle. With Odysseus he fetched Achilles from Scyros, before the expedition, and Philoctetes from Lemnos toward the end of the war. He accompanied Odysseus in the night raid that led to the deaths of Dolon and Rhesus and the theft from Troy of the Palladium (a statue of Athena that Zeus had cast down from Olympus: it was the guarantee of the city's survival).

Ajax the Great or Greater. AJAX [a'jaks], or AIAS, son of TELAMON [tel'a-mon], was prince of Salamis and the most stalwart warrior after Achilles. He was the bravest defender of the ships against Hector's onslaught, and he defended the corpse of Patroclus. He accompanied Odysseus and Phoenix on the embassy to Achilles and competed with Odysseus in the funeral games for Patroclus and in the claim to the armor of Achilles.

Ajax the Less or Lesser. AJAX [a'jaks], or AIAS, son of OILEUS [oi'le-us], was prince of Locris and a leading warrior whose chief roles in the saga occurred in the sack of Troy, when he violated Cassandra, who had taken refuge at the altar of Athena, and during the return home.

Idomeneus, King of Crete. IDOMENEUS [i-dom'-e-nus] was a friend of Menelaüs and was a leading warrior and counselor. His principal legend also occurs after the fall of Troy.

Nestor, King of Pylos. Two leaders were especially prominent in the councils of war, Odysseus and NESTOR [nes'tor], son of Neleus and king of Pylos, who had become king after Heracles had sacked Pylos (see Chapter 20). He appears in the Iliad as an old and very experienced warrior whose advice, usually given at some length, was greatly valued by the younger leaders. His son, Antilochus, was killed by Memnon, but Nestor himself survived the war.

Odysseus, King of Ithaca. The second great counselor was ODYSSEUS [o-dis'se-us] (ULYSSES), son of LAERTES [la-er'tez]. In the *teichoskopia* (the viewing from the wall referred to above), Helen describes to Priam the power of Odysseus' oratory. When the expedition was being gathered, he tried to avoid service by pretending to be mad, a ruse which was uncovered by PALAMEDES [pal-a-me'dez]. He rallied the Achaeans in Book 2 of the Iliad to stay and finish the war, and he asserted the status of the Achaean leaders by beating the sardonic THERSITES [ther-si'tez], who had spoken bluntly but inappropriately in the council of war. He led the embassy to Achilles, and he undertook the night expedition with Diomedes to take the Palladium from the Trojans. Important as he is in council and in fighting, his major legends concern the fall of Troy and his return home.

Achilles. Greatest of all the heroes on either side was ACHILLES [a-kil′lez], or ACHILLEUS, son of Peleus and Thetis and leader of the Myrmidons. He was the swiftest and most handsome of the warriors, invincible in battle and eloquent in council. His passionate nature caused him to withdraw, which did great harm to the Achaeans, and when he returned he turned the tide of the war in the Greeks' favor. His mother had dipped him in the waters of the river Styx to make him invulnerable, so that only his heel (by which she held him) was vulnerable. The centaur CHIRON [ki′ron] educated Achilles. Thetis tried to keep her son from going to a war, in which she knew he would die young, by hiding him, disguised as a girl, among the daughters of LYCOMEDES [li-ko-me′dez], or LYKOMEDES, king of the island of Scyros. His disguise was revealed by Odysseus and Diomedes, and he joined the expedition. On Scyros he loved DEIDAMIA [de-i-da-me′a], or DEIDAMEIA, by whom he was the father of Neoptolemus.

Phoenix and Patroclus. Achilles had as friend and tutor PHOENIX [fi′niks], or PHOINIX (one of the envoys sent by Agamemnon to persuade Achilles to relent), and his closest friend was PATRO-CLUS [pa-tro′klus] or PATROKLOS, son of Menoiteus, who had been his companion as a boy. The death of Patroclus in single combat with Hector was the turning point in the events of the Iliad.

Neoptolemus. Achilles' son NEOPTOLEMUS [ne-op-tol′e-mus], or NEOPTOLEMOS (known also as PYRRHUS [pir′rhus], or PYRRHOS), joined the Achaeans at Troy after the death of Achilles and played an important and brutal role in the sack of Troy.

THE GATHERING AT AULIS AND THE ARRIVAL AT TROY

The Achaeans gathered at AULIS [aw′lis], where contrary winds kept them from sailing. The prophet CALCHAS [kal′kas], or KALCHAS ,said that Artemis had caused the unfavorable weather and could be appeased only by the sacrifice of IPHIGENIA [if-je-ni′a], or IPHIGENEIA. Agamemnon sacrificed her, favorable winds blew, and the fleet set sail (see Chapter 16).

At Aulis Calchas interpreted two omens: an eagle devouring a pregnant hare — an omen symbolic of Agamemnon's violence — and a snake devouring a bird and her eight fledglings — an omen meaning that the Achaeans would fight for nine years before capturing Troy in the tenth year.

Philoctetes. At the island of Chryse, during the voyage, PHILOCTETES [fi-lok-te′tez], or PHILOK-TETES, was bitten in the foot by a snake. The wound festered, and the Achaeans abandoned him on Lemnos. Philoctetes was son of Poeas, who had inherited the bow of Heracles, which was necessary (so the Trojan prisoner Helenus told the Greeks) for the capture of Troy. In the last year of the war Odysseus and Diomedes fetched Philoctetes and his wound was healed by the sons of Asclepius, Podalirius and Machaon. With the bow, Philoctetes shot and killed Paris.

Telephus. The Greeks also landed in Mysia (an area of Asia Minor), where Achilles wounded the king, TELEPHUS [tel′e-fus], or TELEPHOS, son of Heracles. Advised by the Delphic oracle, Telephus went in disguise to the Greek camp at Troy, and there the wound was healed by scrapings from the spear of Achilles, for, said the oracle, "he that wounded shall heal."

Protesilaüs and Laodamia. The first Greek to leap ashore at Troy was PROTESILAÜS [pro-te-si-la′us], or PROTESILAOS, who was killed by Hector. Hermes brought back Protesilaüs from the Underworld to his wife, LAODAMIA [la-o-da-mi′a], or LAODAMEIA, and when he had to return, she killed herself.

THE <u>ILIAD</u>

The events of the first nine years of the war were narrated in epic poems that are no longer extant. The <u>Iliad</u> is concerned with part of the tenth year. Its theme is "The Wrath of Achilles" (the first words in the poem), and its events start with the quarrel between Agamemnon and Achilles in the first book and end with the ransoming of Hector's corpse by Priam and his burial in the twenty-fourth book.

The Quarrel between Achilles and Agamemnon. The quarrel broke out over division of the spoils from raids on cities in Asia Minor. When Agamemnon had to give back his prisoner CHRYSEÏS [kri-se'is], because of the anger of Apollo (whose priest was the father of Chryseïs), he took BRISEÏS [bri-se'is], the prisoner of Achilles, in her place, thus insulting and devaluing Achilles in the eyes of the Achaeans. Achilles withdrew from the fighting, and his mother, Thetis, persuaded Zeus to honor Achilles by allowing the Trojans to be victorious in his absence.

The Role of the Gods. The gods have a prominent role in the <u>Iliad</u>. Apollo (the first to appear) favors the Trojans; he helps Hector kill Patroclus and later refreshes the corpse of Hector after it has been dragged behind the chariot of Achilles. Athena and Hera support the Greeks, and Athena assists Achilles in his final combat with Hector. Aphrodite protects Paris and compels Helen to make love to him after Aphrodite had saved him from death at the hands of Menelaüs. Thetis comforts Achilles after his humiliation by Agamemnon and again after the death of Patroclus, when she obtains new armor for her son from Hephaestus. She brings the order from Zeus to Achilles to desist from desecrating Hector's corpse and to give it back to Priam. Hermes escorts Priam through the Achaean camp. On two occasions the gods fight on the battlefield among themselves, and even are wounded (see above under Diomedes).

The Role of Zeus. Supreme among the gods is Zeus. While he is constantly opposed by Hera (who deceives him into making love at one point, so that while he is asleep the Greeks may be successful), his will is supreme. He honors Achilles in response to the complaint of Thetis, and he resists the importuning of Athena and Hera, who are impatient at the continued success of the Trojans.

Hector and Andromache. In Book 6 Hector returns to Troy from the battlefield and there meets with Hecabe, with Helen and Paris, and finally with Andromache and their son, Astyanax. His parting from Andromache brings into sharp focus the loss that the survivors in the defeated city must bear, and it foreshadows his death and the mourning of Andromache in the last books of the poem.

The Embassy to Achilles. In despair at the Trojan successes, Agamemnon sends Odysseus, Ajax (son of Telamon), and Phoenix to offer gifts and honor to Achilles in restitution for the dishonor done to him, if he will return to the fighting. But Achilles refuses.

The Death of Patroclus. The friend of Achilles, Patroclus, persuades Achilles to let him fight in Achilles' armor as the Trojans reach the Greek ships. He is victorious at first, killing SARPEDON [sar-pe'don], son of Zeus, but eventually is killed by Hector, with the help of Apollo. Hector strips the corpse of the armor of Achilles and puts it on.

The Return of Achilles to Battle. The death of Patroclus drives Achilles to relent; Thetis brings him new armor made by Hephaestus, including a splendidly decorated shield. He ends the quarrel with Agamemnon and returns to battle.

Achilles kills countless Trojans and even fights the river-god Scamander, whose flooding waters are quenched by Hephaestus. Eventually the Trojans are penned into the city.

Achilles and Hector. The two heroes are left to fight in single combat. Zeus weighs the fate of each in his golden scales, and Hector is doomed. Achilles kills him with a spear-thrust in his throat.

Each day for twelve days Achilles dragged Hector's corpse behind his chariot round the tomb of Patroclus. He celebrated funeral games in honor of his dead friend and only relented when Zeus ordered him, through Thetis, to give up his wrath against Hector and to ransom his body.

Priam and Achilles. Escorted by Hermes, Priam makes his way to the hut of Achilles and there ransoms Hector. The mutilation of Hector's corpse is perhaps the most extreme example of the passionate and violent nature of Achilles. Yet Achilles relents with magnanimity in relinquishing the corpse to Priam, who returns to Troy, and the Iliad ends with the lamentations of Andromache and Helen and the burial of Hector.

THE FALL OF TROY

Events after the end of the Iliad were narrated in epics (now lost) whose summaries survive in tragedies and in vase-paintings. Book 2 of Vergil's Aeneid is the major source for the sack of Troy itself.

Achilles against Penthesilea and Memnon. Achilles killed the leaders of the contingents that came to assist the Trojans—the Amazons, led by Penthesilea, and the Ethiopians, led by Memnon, son of Eos (Aurora, "dawn").

The Death of Achilles. Achilles himself was fatally wounded in the heel by Paris. His corpse was recovered by Ajax (son of Telamon), and Thetis and her nymphs attended the funeral on the promontory of Sigeum. The ghost of Achilles conversed with Odysseus when he visited the Underworld. Achilles' ghost demanded the sacrifice of Polyxena, daughter of Priam, at the tomb. Achilles (so some say) had loved her and was killed when meeting with her.

The Contest for the Armor of Achilles. Odysseus and Ajax each claimed the armor of Achilles, speaking to an assembly of Achaeans presided over by Athena. Trojan prisoners said that Odysseus had done them more harm, and he was awarded the armor. In shame, Ajax killed himself, and from his blood sprang a flower with AI on its petals (his name in Greek is Aias). See also Hyacinthus, Chapter 9.

The Arrival of Neoptolemus and Philoctetes. Odysseus captured Helenus (the seer and son of Priam), who advised the Achaeans to summon Neoptolemus and Philoctetes (see above).

The Wooden Horse. The Achaeans left a wooden horse, built by Epeus, outside the walls of Troy and sailed away to Tenedos. Inside the horse were the leading warriors. Deceived by the Greek SINON [si'non], the Trojans pulled down part of the city wall to admit the horse, and then at night Sinon let the Achaean warriors out. Meanwhile the other Greeks sailed back and entered the city.

Cassandra warned against admitting the horse and was not believed. The priest of Apollo, LAOCOÖN [la-o'ko-on], LAOKOÖN, or son of Antenor, hurled his spear at the horse and said it should be destroyed. The Trojans ignored his warning also, and watched as two serpents came from the sea and throttled Laocoön and his two sons.

The Fall of Troy. The Greeks sacked the city and killed its male inhabitants. Of the Trojan leaders, Antenor was spared, and Aeneas escaped. Priam was butchered by Neoptolemus, and Hector's infant son, Astyanax, was thrown from the walls. Andromache became the slave of Neoptolemus (see above, and Chapter 16). Cassandra was raped by Ajax (son of Oileus) in the temple of Athena, where she had sought the protection of the goddess, and was given as a slave to Agamemnon, who took her back to Mycenae, where she was killed by Clytemnestra (see Chapter 16).

The Fate of Hecabe (Hecuba). Hecabe began the voyage back to Greece as the slave of Odysseus. On the way she landed in Thrace and found the corpse of her son, POLYDORUS [pol-i-dor′us], or POLYDOROS, murdered by the local king, POLYMESTOR [pol-i-mes′tor]. She revenged herself by luring Polymestor and his children into her tent, where she murdered his children and blinded him. She turned into a bitch and her burial place (in Thrace) was called Cynossema, "the dog's tomb."

The Flight of Aeneas. Aeneas, protected by his mother, Aphrodite, escaped, taking with him his son, ASCANIUS [as-kan′i-us], or ASKANIOS (Iulus), and his father, ANCHISES [an-ki′sez]. His wife, CREUSA [kre-u′sa] or KREOUSA, disappeared in the escape. He led a group of survivors, men and women, on the voyage away from Asia, eventually reaching Italy, where he established himself and made possible the eventual founding of Rome (see Chapter 24).

COMPACT DISCS

1. "Achilles Last Stand." Rock song.
9. Barber, Samuel, Andromache's Farewell, for soprano and orchestra. Powerful rendition of the English text, translated from Euripides' The Trojan Women (M/L 602-3).
18. Berlioz, Hector, Les Troyens. Major operatic masterpiece based on Vergil, Aeneid, Book 4 (The Fall of Troy) and Book 6 (Dido and Aeneas). M/L 600.
21. Bliss, Arthur, Morning Heroes. Symphonic work for orator and chorus, which includes a stirring reading of Hector's farewell to Andromache from the Iliad, Book 6 (M/L 603).
36. Campra, André, Achille Oisif. Cantata for soprano, violin, and continuo, about Achilles disguised as a girl on Scyros.
43. "Cassandra." Rock song.
90. Gluck, Christoph Willibald, Paris and Helen. Lovely opera (M/L 599).
92. Goldmark, Karl, Penthesilea. Overture, inspired by Heinrich von Kleist's tragedy.
163. Manfroce. Nicola, Ecuba. Opera, not based on Euripides, about the love of Polyxena and Achilles, his murder, and her sacrifice at his tomb.
185. Moross, Jerome, The Golden Apple. Text by John Latouche. Classic American musical version of the Trojan saga, which incorporates both the Iliad and the Odyssey (M/L 606-7).
193. Music of Ancient Greece. Fragment from the Iliad.
199. Offenbach, Jacques, La Belle Hélène. Most delightful comic operetta about Paris' wooing of Helen.
211. Partch, Harry, Castor and Pollux, A Dance for the Twin Rhythms of Gemini. Partch explains: "It begins with the encounter of Zeus, the male swan, with the beautiful Leda, and ends with the

hatching of the fertilized eggs—first Castor, then Pollux. From the moment of insemination, each egg uses exactly 234 beats in cracking."

227. Rameau, Jean-Philippe, <u>Castor et Pollux</u>. Opera.

248. Schoeck, Othmar, <u>Penthesilea</u>. Harrowing operatic masterpiece (based on Kleist's tragedy) that rivals Strauss's <u>Electra</u>.

250 and **251.** Schubert, Franz, Songs: "Hektors Abschied" (Hector's farewell to Andromache), "Lied eines Schiffers an die Dioskuren" (A Sailor's song to the Dioscuri); "Memnon" (Memnon sings, as he is dying, to be united with his mother, the Dawn); and "Philoktet" (Philoctetes appeals to Ulysses for the return of his bow).

266. Strauss, Richard, <u>Die ägyptische Helena</u>. Philosophically complicated but musically rewarding opera about Helen in Egypt (M/L 601).

281. Tippett, Michael, <u>King Priam</u>. Opera on the Trojan War, beginning with the birth of Paris and ending with the death of Priam (M/L 603-604). See Videos

282. Uttini, F. A., <u>Thétis and Pelée</u>. Opera.

289. Walton, William, <u>Troilus and Cressida</u>. Significant twentieth-century opera. (M/L 602).

292. Wolf, Hugo, <u>Penthesilea</u>. Symphonic poem, inspired by a drama by Kleist, in three parts: Departure of the Amazons for Troy; Penthesilea's Dream of the Festival of the Roses, and Combats, Passions, Madness, Annihilation.

VIDEOS

<u>Excavations at Troy</u>. The University of Cincinnati offers a series of video tapes documenting the history of the excavations of Troy with an annual record of the results of the ongoing excavations. These invaluable videos are available through the Institute for Mediterranean Studies. David A. Traill's controversial book denigrating the work of Heinrich Schliemann (<u>Schliemann of Troy, Treasure and Deceit</u>. New York: St. Martin's Press, 1995) will, needless to say, receive serious attention from the new team of excavators. See M/L Introduction.

<u>Heinrich Schliemann: The Rediscovery of Troy</u>. Films for the Humanities ADS2413.

<u>In Search of the Trojan War</u>. This excellent series, made for TV and narrated by Michael Wood, is available from Insight Video. It provides an excellent survey of Minoan-Mycenaean archaeology as well as a discussion of Homer and the oral tradition that includes recitations by modern bards.

<u>Judgement of Paris</u>. A tribute to the famous choreographer Tudor, entitled <u>Antony Tudor</u> (Dance Horizons Video) includes a snippet about his comic ballet <u>Judgment of Paris</u>, in which Paris is transformed into a drunken Englishman who must chose among three Parisian prostitutes; and Agnes de Mille tells how she was delighted to dance Venus.

<u>King Priam</u>. Opera by Tippett. Macann et al. Kent Opera, cond. Norrington. Home Vision. The Compleat Operagoer 61. Fascinating modern work, marred by miscalculations in this production.

<u>Lost Treasure of Troy</u>. Films for the Humanities. AGU5010. A documentary about the fate of Schliemann's Treasure of Priam, which needs to be brought up to date. In April 1996 the Troy treasure was unveiled in Moscow.

The Odyssey of Troy (Ancient Mysteries). A&E Home Video. AAE-12307. Despite minor flaws, this is an excellent introduction, especially to the history of the excavations of Troy. We only wish visuals would always accurately depict what is described in the script and that someone (perhaps one of the professors involved) could have told the narrator Kathleen Turner how to pronounce Menelaüs.

The Trojan Women. Another cinematic treatment (this time in English) of Euripides by the director Michael Cacoyannis. U.S.A. Home Video 215-170. A great cast, Katherine Hepburn as Hecuba, Vanessa Redgrave as Andromache, Genevieve Bujold as Cassandra, and Irene Papas as Helen, makes this movie a treasure.

Les Troyens. Opera by Berlioz. The Metropolitan Opera, cond. Levine. Particularly commendable for the heroic Aeneas of Placido Domingo and the fervent Cassandra of Jessye Norman. Bel Canto Paramount Video 12509.

INTERPRETATION

Leda and the Swan. This is the subject of innumerable paintings, of which that by Leonardo da Vinci (ca. 1510), now lost, is best known from several copies. The union of human and bird has fascinated artists in all ages, and recently (1959-1963) Reuben Nakian explored the psychological potentialities of the legend in several media.

The Dioscuri. The quarrel of Idas and Lynceus with the Dioscuri has attracted artists, for example, Peter Paul Rubens, The Rape of the Daughters of Leucippus (ca. 1616, now in Munich).

Helen. Worshiped as a goddess at Sparta, Helen is usually thought of as the most beautiful of women. In the Iliad she is a lonely figure, bored with Paris and despised by the Trojans, except for Priam and Hector, over whose corpse she makes the final lamentation in the poem. In the Odyssey she entertains Telemachus at Sparta, where she is living peacefully with Menelaüs. Her beauty has inspired countless poems: Christopher Marlowe made her an object of sensual desire in Dr. Faustus (1604, revised 1616), with the lines beginning "Was this the face that launched a thousand ships / and burn't the topless towers of Ilium?" For Goethe, in Faust (Part 2: 1832), she symbolized all that is beautiful in classical antiquity. The tradition hostile to her is represented in the Agamemnon of Aeschylus (458 b.c.: lines 681-749) and in Vergil's Aeneid (2. 567-88), lines that Vergil himself may have wished to excise. The poem of Stesichorus is called the "Palinode" (i.e., a reversal of a previous tale), and the tale that Helen was protected in Egypt by Proteus is the basis of Euripides' drama, Helen (412 b.c.). A feminist study reveals just how controversial Helen continues to be: Helen, Myth, and the Culture of Misogyny, by Robert Emmet Meagher (New York: Continuum, 1995). We add to the observation on the dust jacket: "This is a book that will fascinate all feminists and infuriate most men" and enrage many scholars of both sexes.

The Judgment of Paris and Oenone. The Judgment of Paris has also fascinated artists, drawn to it by the possibilities of three nude female figures posing in a pastoral landscape before a judge. Exceptional versions are those by Lucas Cranach the Elder (1530, and repeated many times), who interprets the story satirically (as did Lucian in his Dialogues of the Gods 20 (mid-second century

A.D.), and by Peter Paul Rubens (1600 and 1607), who uniquely unites the beauty of the goddesses with the drama of the judgment and the consequences of the choice made by Paris.

Oenone. Ovid (Heroides 5) makes Oenone the wife of Paris and portrays her loneliness at his desertion of her for Helen. So also does Tennyson in his poem Oenone (1832), and the sculptress Harriet Hosmer in her marble Oenone (1855).

Achilles. In all ages Achilles has been the paradigm of physical excellence, courage, and intense passions, a hero necessary to his community yet impossible for it to contain. His life is portrayed in a cycle of eight tapestries and their preparatory oil sketches (now in Rotterdam) by Peter Paul Rubens (ca. 1632). His discovery on Scyros was narrated by Statius (ca. A.D. 90) in his unfinished epic Achilleis, and he has been the subject of many paintings, for example, Achilles and the Daughters of Lycomedes by Poussin (1650, now in Boston). His anger at the use of his name to entice Iphigenia to come to Aulis is the subject of J-L. David's The Wrath of Achilles (1819), and J. A. D. Ingres painted The Envoys of Agamemnon Sent to Achilles to Urge Him to Fight (1801). See the Iliad, below.

Philoctetes. Sophocles, in his tragedy Philoctetes (409 B.C.), portrays the suffering of Philoctetes and his departure from Lemnos. He makes Odysseus cynical and deceptive, and Neoptolemus honorable. The theme of the hero whose skills are essential to the community, while he himself is intolerable, is the subject of the essay by Edmund Wilson, The Wound and the Bow (1941).

Telephus. Telephus was the subject of lost tragedies by Sophocles and Euripides, whose play (ca. 440 B.C.) scandalized the Athenians by its sordid realism. As founding ancestor of the Mysians and their chief city, Pergamum, Telephus was honored in the reliefs of the Altar of Zeus at Pergamum (ca. 185 B.C., now in Berlin).

The Iliad. The Iliad is unique as the fundamental literary work of all Greek and Roman literature, and it is impossible to summarize the infinite number of works of literature, art, and music that interpret its episodes. Its portrayal of the all-too-human weaknesses of the Olympian gods and its presentation of passionate emotions (especially anger and grief) led Plato to exclude it from the educational curriculum of his ideal state. In recent years its primary role in Western literature has been the target of social and political criticism, a sign of the continuing significance of the poem (for supporters and critics alike) in education.

The universality of the Iliad and the devastating truth of Homer's depiction of war and its hero Achilles find powerful confirmation in a brilliant book illuminating the experiences and sufferings of Vietnam veterans through a study of the Iliad, and in particular the character and emotions of Achilles: Jonathon Shay, Achilles in Vietnam (New York: Atheneum, 1994). Dr. Shay, a psychiatrist, who appreciates Homer's contemporary value, finds parallel themes such as these: betrayal of "what's right" by a commander; the shrinkage of social and moral horizons; intense comradeship reduced to a few friends; the death of one of these special comrades followed by feelings of grief and guilt, culminating in a berserk rage.

While the Iliad refers to events (especially the fall of Troy) outside the frame of its narrative, most of the Trojan War was narrated in a series of epics, now lost, known from summaries given by Proclus (of uncertain date, perhaps fifth century A.D.). The Iliad, despite its concentration on a very short period in the ten-year war, became the dominant survivor of the epic tradition because of its unmatched poetical power, its portrayal of the Olympian gods and their interaction with mortals, and above all, its representation of the full range of human nobility and meanness, seen in the words and actions of the Greek and Trojan heroes, of whom Achilles is supreme.

The interaction of the Olympian gods with each other and with mortals in the Iliad is the canonical and fundamental version, important in that it is the one that was accepted in all of Greece, as opposed to local legends and cults or works concerned with a particular legend (e.g., tragedies). The scene, for example, between Zeus and Thetis is most memorably portrayed by J. A. D. Ingres in his huge work Jupiter and Thetis (1811, now in Aix-en-Provence). The gods of later epic are variations on the Homeric gods, even where there are fundamental changes, as with Jupiter in the Aeneid of Vergil (see Chapter 24). In art and music, similarly, the Homeric gods are the foundation of subsequent interpretations.

The meeting of Hector and Andromache focuses the narrative on the city and its families that must suffer if Hector fails. It was a popular subject for illustrations of the Iliad in the eighteenth century (especially in Pope's translation), which were used as models for amateur artists to copy in America and elsewhere. Among modern representations, the painting by G. de Chirico (1917, now in Milan) is austere and disturbing.

The decorations on the shield of Achilles portray the life of human communities away from the battlefield (although it includes some scenes of ambush and siege). Efforts have been made to recreate the shield (the most successful by John Flaxman, 1817), but the description is poetic, and its details cannot be translated satisfactorily into another medium.

The Works of Dictys Cretensis and Dares Phrygius. In the ages when Greek literature was lost to the West, the narrative of the Trojan War was known through two Latin prose works, both forgeries. Dictys Cretensis is the purported author of an eyewitness diary of the war and the heroes' return from the Greek point of view: the Latin version (the Greek original does not exist) probably dates from the second or third century A.D.

The work of Dares Phrygius (mentioned as a priest of Hephaestus at Iliad 5. 9), De Excidio Troiae, purports to be a diary of the war from the Trojan point of view (the Latin dates from perhaps the sixth century A.D.). These works were the sources for the Roman de Troie, the huge (30,000 lines) French romance by Benoît de St. Maure (ca. 1160). Benoît first developed the legend of Troilus and Cressida, which found its way through Latin and French paraphrases to William Caxton's Recuyell of the Historye of Troye (1471) and Chaucer's Troilus and Criseyde (ca. 1380), and eventually to Shakespeare's Troilus and Cressida. Although the ambush of Troilus by Achilles appears on the François Vase (ca. 575 B.C.), the literary form of the legend was developed in the late Middle Ages as a romance, and it is not classical. A dull summary of the Iliad is the Latin hexameter poem called the Ilias Latina, dating from about A.D. 60.

The Fall of Troy. This was the subject of a lost epic, Iliou Persis ("The Sack of Ilium"), and episodes were the subjects of several tragedies. Of these the Trojan Women of Euripides (415 B.C.) is especially moving. It focuses on the sufferings of Hecabe and Andromache, as well as the fates of Cassandra, Polyxena, and Astyanax. It looks forward to the sufferings also of the victors during and after their return home, and ends as the survivors leave Troy to go into slavery. The Troades of Seneca (mid-first century A.D.) conflates elements from the Trojan Women with the Hecuba of Euripides. By far the most detailed surviving account of the fall is the narrative of Aeneas in Book 2 of Vergil's Aeneid (see Chapter 24). The lost epic Aethiopis (possibly eighth century B.C.) included the deaths of Penthesilea, Memnon, and Achilles.

The Ajax of Sophocles. This play (written ca. 455 B.C.) focuses on the shame, death, and posthumous honors of Ajax. Rhetorically brilliant is the debate between Odysseus and Ajax over the armor of Achilles in Ovid's Metamorphoses (13. 1-398).

The Trojan Horse and Laocoön. The Trojan horse is proverbial for treachery by an insider, and it has frequently been portrayed in art, e.g., by G. D. Tiepolo (the younger) in two paintings of its building and its entry into the city (1773).

The episode of Laocoön is told by Vergil in the Aeneid (2. 199-231). It is the subject of one of the most famous of all ancient marble statues, made perhaps in the mid-first century A.D. as a copy of an original made two centuries earlier at Pergamum. It was rediscovered at Rome in 1506 and is now in the Vatican. It was also the origin of the immensely influential essay by G. E. Lessing, Laokoön (1766), whose subtitle was "On the Limits of Painting and Poetry." In contrast to the statue's portrayal of the dramatic torments of Laocoön and his sons, entwined by the huge serpents, the painting by El Greco (ca. 1610, now in Washington, D.C.) focuses less on the serpents and sets the heroic victims against the landscape of the city (in this case, Toledo).

Hecuba. The Hecuba of Euripides (424 B.C.) focuses on the deaths of Polydorus and Polyxena (the sacrifice of Polyxena is a central motif) and the revenge of Hecuba, which she justifies to the Greek victors.

Aeneas. The escape of Aeneas carrying his father (holding the household gods of Troy) and leading his son is symbolic of the present bearing the burden of the past and making possible the renewal of the future. It appears as an episode in Raphael's fresco The Fire in the Borgo (in the Raphael Stanze in the Vatican, 1514), and is the subject of the marble group Aeneas, Anchises, and Ascanius, by G. L. Bernini (1618, in the Borghese Palace at Rome).

CHAPTER 18

The Returns

The returns from Troy of the Achaean heroes, other than Odysseus, were narrated in a lost epic called <u>Nostoi</u> [nos'toy], "Returns." The return of Odysseus is the subject of Homer's <u>Odyssey</u>.

THE NOSTOI (RETURNS)

Ajax the Less or Lesser (Son of Oileus) and Agamemnon. Athena raised a storm in the Aegean in anger at the sacrilege of Ajax, son of Oileus, during the sack of Troy (see Chapter 17). The storm wrecked much of Agamemnon's fleet (with which Ajax was sailing), and Ajax, who boasted of his escape from drowning, was killed by Poseidon with his trident. A second storm struck the fleet, wrecking many more ships on the coast of Euboea. Agamemnon finally reached Mycenae, where he was murdered by Clytemnestra and Aegisthus (see Chapter 16).

Menelaüs. Menelaüs reached Egypt after losing five ships in another storm. The sea-god Proteus told him how to appease the gods and sail back safely to Greece. Menelaüs tells the story of his visit to Proteus in Book 4 of the <u>Odyssey</u> (see Chapter 5). The visit of Menelaüs to Egypt fits with the legend (see Chapter 17) that Helen spent the years of the war in Egypt, while her phantom went to Troy. Seven years after the fall of Troy, Menelaüs and Helen reached Sparta safely and resumed their former life together. At his death Menelaüs was transported to Elysium (rather than Hades), because, as the immortal Helen's husband, he was the son-in-law of Zeus.

Nestor, Diomedes, and Philoctetes. Of the other Peloponnesian leaders, Nestor returned to Pylos safely. Diomedes, who had wounded Aphrodite at Troy, returned to Argos to find that the goddess had caused his wife, Aegialia, to be unfaithful. He left Argos and came to Italy, where he founded several cities. Philoctetes returned to Thessaly and also was driven out by his people. He too went to Italy and founded several cities. The stories of Diomedes, Idomeneus, and Philoctetes seem to be connected with the foundation of Greek colonies in Italy (the first at Cumae in 732 B.C.).

Idomeneus. Idomeneus returned to Crete to find that his wife, Meda, had been unfaithful with Leucus, who then murdered her and her daughter and made himself king over ten cities. Leucus drove out Idomeneus, who went to Italy. Another story of the exile of Idomeneus is that he vowed to Poseidon that he would sacrifice the first living thing that came to meet him if he returned home safely. His son was the first to meet him, and Idomeneus sacrificed him. In punishment for the killing, the gods sent a plague on the Cretans, who drove Idomeneus out.

Neoptolemus. Neoptolemus went by land back to Phthia with Helenus and Andromache (see above, Chapters 16 and 17). With them and his wife, Hermione, he went to Epirus as king of the Molossi. He was killed at Delphi and was honored there with a hero-cult.

THE RETURN OF ODYSSEUS (THE <u>ODYSSEY</u>, BOOKS 1-12)

The return of Odysseus (Ulysses) is a separate saga, narrated in the Odyssey. It was delayed for ten years by the anger of Poseidon. When, after many adventures, he reached his home, he found his wife, PENELOPE [pe-nel′o-pe], hard-pressed by many suitors, who were ruining his property and plotting to kill his son, TELEMACHUS [te-lem′a-kus], or TELEMACHOS. Odysseus killed them all and was reunited with Penelope, resuming his rule over Ithaca.

The Mini-Odyssey of Telemachus. In the first four books of the <u>Odyssey</u>, Telemachus, helped by Athena, went to Pylos and Sparta to find out news of Odysseus from Nestor, Menelaüs, and Helen. On his return he avoided an ambush set by the suitors.

Calypso. Odysseus, meanwhile, had been living for seven years on the island of Ogygia with the nymph CALYPSO [ka-lip′so], or KALYPSO, daughter of Atlas. He refused her offer to make him immortal and she was ordered by Zeus, through his messenger Hermes, to release him. She helped him build a raft and he sailed away toward Ithaca.

The Phaeacians and Princess Nausicaä. His raft was wrecked by Poseidon near the island of Scheria, home of the PHAEACIANS (fe-a′shi-anz], or PHAIAKIANS. Helped by Leucothea (a sea-goddess, once the Theban princess Ino), he reached land, where he was helped by the princess NAUSICAÄ [naw-sik′a-a], daughter of King ALCINOÜS [al-sin′o-us], or ALKINOÖS, and Queen ARETE [a′re-te]. The Phaeacians were seafarers living a peaceful and prosperous life, and the splendid palace of Alcinoüs was equipped with gold and silver guard-dogs (made by Hephaestus) and with fifty golden torch-bearers in human form. The women were skilled weavers, and outside the palace were beautiful gardens and orchards. Odysseus appealed to ARETE for help, and Alcinoüs honored him with a banquet at which the bard DEMODOCUS [de-mod′o-kus], or DEMODOKOS, sang of the love of Ares and Aphrodite and the revenge of Hephaestus (see above, Chapter 3). Then he sang of the wooden horse and the sack of Troy, at which Odysseus wept. Invited by Alcinoüs, he told his story.

Maron of Ismarus. When he and his companions left Troy, they sacked the Thracian city of ISMARUS [is-mar′us], or ISMAROS, sparing the priest of Apollo, MARON [mar′on], who gave them twelve jars of wine.

The Lotus-Eaters. Then they sailed to the land of the lotus-eaters, where whoever ate of the fruit of the lotus forgot everything else and only wished to stay, eating lotus-fruit. Yet Odysseus managed to leave with his men.

The Cyclopes and Polyphemus. They sailed to the island of the CYCLOPES [si-klo′pez], or KYKLOPES, one-eyed giant herdsmen living in caves. Odysseus and twelve companions waited in the cave of the Cyclops [si′klopz], or KYKLOPS, POLYPHEMUS [po-li-fe′mus], or POLYPHEMOS, son of Poseidon, who returned from his herding in the evening and ate two of Odysseus' men; he ate four more the next day. Odysseus gave Polyphemus some of Maron's wine and told him that his name was Nobody (in Greek, *Outis*). Then, while Polyphemus lay in a drunken sleep, Odysseus and his companions drove a heated wooden pole into his eye. When the other Cyclopes, hearing the cries of Polyphemus, came to the cave (which was closed by a huge rock) to ask what was wrong, he cried out, "Nobody is killing me," and they left. Next morning Odysseus tied each man to the undersides of three sheep and himself clung to the belly of the biggest ram. Thus, as the blinded Cyclops felt the sheep when he let them out of the cave (having removed the rock), he could not discover the men, and so they escaped and went back to their ship. As they sailed away, Odysseus shouted out his real name, and Polyphemus tore off part of a mountain and nearly wrecked the ship when he threw it. He prayed to Poseidon for vengeance on Odysseus, asking that if he did return home it would be after many years, alone, in distress, and upon another's ship, and that he would find trouble at home. This was the source of the anger of Poseidon, who granted his son's prayer.

Aeolus. Odysseus sailed to the island of AEOLUS [e'o-lus], or AIOLOS, who gave him a bag holding all the winds and showed him how to release the wind favorable for his return. But just as he was in sight of Ithaca, he fell asleep and his men opened the bag. All the winds rushed out and blew them back to Aeolus, who refused to help them anymore.

The Laestrygonians. Next they came to the land of the LAESTRYGONIANS [les-tri-gon'i-anz], or LAISTRYGONIANS, who sank all the ships except one and ate the crews.

Circe. With the surviving ship Odysseus sailed to Aeaea, home of CIRCE [sir'se], or KIRKE, daughter of Helius, the Sun. She transformed Odysseus' crew into pigs, but Odysseus himself, warned by Hermes, used the herb *moly* as an antidote to Circe's charms and forced her to change his men into human form once more. He lived with Circe for one year, and she bore him a son, TELEGONUS [te-leg'o-nus], or TELEGONOS. Circe eventually let him go, and he sailed to the Underworld, to consult Tiresias.

The Book of the Dead. In the <u>Nekuia</u> ("The Book of the Dead," Book 11 of the <u>Odyssey</u>), Odysseus went to the entrance to the Underworld and there talked with many spirits of the dead. His primary purpose was to consult Tiresias, who foretold the difficulties yet remaining on his journey and at his return, and foretold also the events of the rest of his life and the manner of his death. Odysseus spoke with Agamemnon, Achilles, Ajax (son of Telamon), and his mother, ANTICLEA [an-ti-kle'a], or ANTIKLEIA, and he saw many other heroines.

The Sirens. Having returned to Aeaea, Odysseus sailed to meet the dangers of which Circe warned him. First were the Sirens, winged monsters with women's heads, who by their song lured sailors onto the rocks. Odysseus sailed past them by stuffing his men's ears with wax and having himself lashed to the mast.

The Planctae and Scylla and Charybdis. Then he avoided the PLANCTAE [plank'te], or PLANKTAI ("wandering rocks"), by sailing close to CHARYBDIS [ka-rib'dis], who sucked in the water of the strait three times daily and spouted it up again, and to SCYLLA [sil'la], or SKYLLA (daughter of Phorcys), who snatched six sailors and ate them. Scylla had been changed into a monster through the jealousy of Poseidon's wife, Amphitrite (see Chapter 5).

The Cattle of Helius. Odysseus next sailed to Thrinacia, where Helius pastured his cattle. Again he fell asleep, and his men disobeyed his orders not to touch the cattle and killed some of them for food. In response to Helius' complaint, Zeus raised a storm, which sank the ship, leaving Odysseus as the sole survivor. Once again escaping the dangers of Charybdis, Odysseus drifted to Ogygia.

The Phaeacians Bring Odysseus to Ithaca. After he had related his adventures to the Phaeacians, Odysseus was conveyed by them to Ithaca, where they put him on shore asleep, with the gifts they had given him. To punish the Phaeacians for helping Odysseus, Poseidon turned their ship into stone as it entered the harbor at Scheria.

THE HOMECOMING OF ODYSSEUS (THE <u>ODYSSEY</u>, BOOKS 13-24)

The second half of the <u>Odyssey</u> (Books 13-24) narrates how Odysseus returned to his palace, killed the suitors, and was recognized and reunited with Penelope, and how he resumed his rule over Ithaca.

Eumaeus, Telemachus, and Irus. Athena helped Odysseus when he woke up after being put ashore. He was recognized by the swineherd EUMAEUS [u-me'us], or EUMAIOS, and by Telemachus. Together they devised the plan for his entry, disguised as a beggar, into the palace, where he was insulted by the suitors and challenged to a fight (which he won) by the beggar IRUS [i'rus], or IROS.

Penelope's Web. Penelope was on the verge of having to choose a suitor as husband, for the suitors had discovered the ruse by which she had put off her choice. By day she would work on weaving a cloak to be a burial shroud for Laertes, father of Odysseus, and by night she would unravel her work.

Penelope and the Beggar Odysseus. After the fight with Irus, she spoke with Odysseus (still in disguise), who gave an exact description of himself. Encouraged by this, Penelope told him of her plan to give herself next day to the man who could string the bow of Odysseus and shoot it through twelve ax heads.

Euryclea. Odysseus was bathed by his nurse, EURYCLEA [u-ri-kle'a], or EURYKLEIA, who recognized him from a scar caused by a boar's tusk, but he prevented her from revealing his identity to Penelope.

The Contest of the Bow and the Battle in the Hall. Next day, when the suitors had failed even to string the bow, Odysseus did it effortlessly and shot the arrow through the ax heads. Then, helped by Telemachus and Eumaeus, he killed all the suitors after a battle in the hall, and he hanged the twelve maidservants who had been the suitors' lovers.

Penelope and Odysseus Reunited. Still Penelope would not admit to recognizing him until he revealed the secret of the construction of their bed, known only to him and Penelope. Then they were reunited in love and told each other of their patience and adventures over the twenty years of his absence.

The Triumph of Odysseus. Next day Odysseus made himself known to Laertes, and Athena, sent by Zeus, brought peace between him and the families of the dead suitors, whose spirits went to the Underworld and there talked with Agamemnon's ghost.

ODYSSEUS' FURTHER TRAVELS AND DEATH

Tiresias foretold the rest of Odysseus' life. He had to leave Ithaca once more, carrying an oar, and traveling until he came to a people who did not know of the sea or ships. When a man would say that he had a winnowing-fan on his shoulder, he was to plant the oar in the ground and offer a sacrifice to Poseidon and all the gods. Then he would return to Ithaca, and death would come to him easily from the sea in his old age.

All this came to pass. Odysseus appeased Poseidon and lived out his life in Ithaca. Years later he was accidentally killed by Telegonus, who had come to Ithaca in search of his father.

COMPACT DISCS

3. Anfossi, Pasquale, <u>La Maga Circe (The Enchantress Circe)</u>. Two travelers, a Frenchman and a Neapolitan baron, encounter Circe and her two servants in this comic opera by a contemporary of Mozart, who wrote arias that were to be inserted into some of Anfossi's works.

7. Bach, Johann Sebastian, Cantata 295, "Aeolus Propitiated." Zephyr, Pomona, and Pallas propitiate an angry Aeolus.

13. Bedford, David. <u>The Odyssey</u>. Popular musical setting of scenes from the poem.

35. "Calypso." Popular song.

39. Campra, André, <u>Idoménée</u>. Opera with a libretto that was adapted for Mozart, who changed Campra's ending from tragic to happy.

60. Debussy, Claude, <u>Nocturnes</u>, for orchestra and chorus. Part 3: <u>Sirènes</u>. Enchanting recreation of the Sirens' song.

73. Fauré, Gabriel, <u>Pénélope</u>. Opera focusing on Penelope's plight and Odysseus' homecoming.

77. Franck, César, <u>Les Eolides (The Breezes, or The Daughters of Aeolus)</u>. Inspired by a poem by Charles-Marie Leconte de Lisle.

84. Gliere, Reinhold, <u>The Sirens</u>. Symphonic Poem.

110. Harbison, John, <u>Ulysses' Bow</u>. The second part of an evening-length ballet.

128. Hovhaness, Alan, <u>Symphony No. 25 (Odysseus)</u>. Odysseus' spiritual journey and triumphant homecoming to Penelope, with three musical love themes dominant.

137. Kocáb, Michael, <u>Odysseus</u>. Kocab, a Czech pop/rock musician wrote this music for the Laterna Magika performance, a multimedia theatrical version. It is entitled "A Mysterium on the Motifs of Homer's *Odyssey*" and incorporates text in ancient Greek.

151. Lidholm, Ingvar, <u>Nausicaa Alone</u>. Setting for soprano and orchestra of a poetic monologue by Eyvind Johnson, who had written in the 1940s a Swedish novel <u>Strändernas svall</u>, an allegorical paraphrase of the <u>Odyssey</u>.

152. Liebermann, Rolf, <u>Penelope</u>. Opera based on the *Odyssey* which incorporates a parallel present-day tragedy.

168. Maw, Nicholas, <u>Odyssey</u>. Lengthy symphonic non-programmatic work depicting a spiritual journey or quest.

184. Monteverdi, Claudio, <u>Il Ritorno d'Ulisse in Patria (The Return of Ulysses)</u>. Opera. See Videos.

189. Mozart, Wolfgang Amadeus, <u>Idomeneo, Rè di Creta</u>. Opera. See Videos.

192 and **193.** <u>Music of Ancient Greece</u>. <u>Fragment from the tragedy Aias (Tecmessa's lament)</u>.

209. Parry, Hubert, "Blest Pair of Sirens." Choral setting of Milton's poem "At a Solemn Music." The sirens are Voice and Verse.

210. _____. <u>The Lotus Eaters</u>. Setting of Tennyson's poem for soprano, chorus, and orchestra.

241. Rossini, Gioacchino, <u>Ermione</u>. Opera based on Racine's <u>Andromaque</u>.

258. <u>Sirens</u>. Popular. Sections are: "Crash and the Call," "The Dance," "The Singing Contest," and "Farewell."

259. Skalkottas, Nikos, <u>The Return of Odysseus, Symphony in one movement</u>.

260. Smith, John Stafford, "Blest Pair of Sirens." Setting of Milton for 5 voices, piano, and harp. See Parry.

277. "Tales of Brave Ulysses." Rock song.

288. Wakeman, Rick, and Ramon Remedios, <u>A Suite of Gods</u>. New age songs for tenor, keyboards, and percussion, which include "The Voyage of Ulysses."

An important opera not in the Discography is by Peggy Glanville-Hicks (1912-1990), <u>Nausicaa</u>. The libretto by Robert Graves and A. Reid is derived from Graves' novel <u>Homer's Daughter</u>, a work influenced by Samuel Butler's <u>The Authoress of the Odyssey</u>, whose thesis is that Nausicaä (not Homer) is responsible for the composition of the <u>Odyssey</u>. Solo roles are sung in English, choral episodes in Greek, and the score reflects Greek folk music. Scenes from the opera, Teresa Stratas, et al., Athens Symphony Orchestra and Chorus, cond. Surinach. Composers Recordings Inc. CRI 695.

VIDEOS

<u>Greek Epic</u>. Films for the Humanities ADS766. An exploration of Homer's two epics in forty minutes!

<u>The Perilous Journey, Homer's Odyssey</u>. ADS2041. A series of six videos offered by Films for the Humanities: <u>The One-Eyed Cyclopes, Circe the Sorceress, Scylla and Charybdis, The Country of the Dead, The Homecoming</u>, and <u>The Slaying of the Suitors</u>. Films may be purchased individually at greater expense. Very basic and elementary.
The legend of the vow of Idomeneus is similar to the biblical story of Jephtha, Judges 11. 30-40. It is the material for Mozart's opera <u>Idomeneo</u> (1781), which ends, however, with Poseidon relenting at the moment of the sacrifice and the prophecy that the son of Idomeneus will live and reign over Crete.

<u>The Return of Ulysses</u>. Important and moving early opera by Monteverdi. Baker et al. Glynbourne Festival Opera. VAI Video Art International VAI-11.

<u>Ulysses</u>. A surprisingly good movie, starring Kirk Douglas and directed by Mario Camerini, which flounders, however, whenever it strays too far from Homer's masterpiece. Warner Home Video 11470 (M/L 609).

INTERPRETATION

Many people have tried to trace the wanderings of Odysseus, but his saga includes many folktales and romantic legends that are set in imaginary places. In fact the <u>Odyssey</u> is a splendid intermingling of true myth (tales about the gods), legend (stories ultimately reflecting the history of real heroes and heroines), and folktales, fairy tales, and the like, which both amuse and edify.
Homer's great epic has a unique, universal appeal to both young and old, and to the child and philosopher in us all. It can be read solely as a most entertaining story of travel and adventure, full of exciting episodes of delightful variety, a tale of abiding love that ends happily with the just triumph of good over evil; or it can reveal to the artist and the sage the most profound insights about men and women, the gods and fate, and the meaning of human existence—which should be only too evident even from our brief selection of interpretations.
As stated below, Odysseus more than any other is *the* archetypal hero, just as Penelope is par excellence *the* archetypal heroine, each illustrating beautifully aspects of a human and heroic arete which is exemplary. The word *odyssey* itself has come into our language as synonymous with a journey and a quest, and never has the universal concept of the word *homecoming* found a more joyous resonance or deeper meaning than in the final books of the poem.

The Return of Odysseus

The Character of Odysseus. Odysseus himself has been rightly seen as the archetypal hero, whose quest brings him back to his home, his kingdom, and his wife. He has been seen as a kind of Everyman, for example, in the most famous modern interpretation of his saga, James Joyce's <u>Ulysses</u> (1922), and in the huge epic by Nikos Kazantzakis, <u>The Odyssey, A Modern Sequel</u> (in Greek, 1938; translated into English, 1958). Jorge Luis Borges ends his story "The Immortal" (from <u>Labyrinths</u>, in Spanish, 1953, translated into English, 1962): "shortly I shall be No One, like Ulysses; shortly I shall be all men; I shall be dead." An ironic variation adapting motifs from the saga of Odysseus is John Cheever's story "The Swimmer" (about 1970). To the Romans, Odysseus (Ulysses) was a symbol of virtuous patience, and his endurance of adversity made him an example especially for the Stoics. Plato, in the Myth of Er that ends his <u>Republic</u>, shows Odysseus in the Underworld choosing for his next life an inconspicuous one because of his memory of adversity.

Telemachus. Telemachus has been interpreted as the quintessential son, weak at first in the absence of his father, but eventually gaining wisdom and courage. He is the hero of the romance by François Fénelon <u>Les Avantures de Télémaque</u> (1699). In James Joyce's <u>Ulysses</u> (1922), he becomes Stephen Dedalus. The return of Telemachus from his journey (Books 1-4 of the <u>Odyssey</u>) has often been painted, e.g., by Pintoricchio (Bernardo Betti, 1509) in his painting <u>The Return of Odysseus</u> (1509), in which, despite the title, Telemachus is the central figure.

Calypso. Odysseus on the island of Calypso has been frequently painted, for example, by Jan Brueghel the Elder (with Hendrik van Balen), <u>The Feast of the Nymph Calypso for Odysseus</u> (1616), and Gérard de Lairesse, <u>Hermes Ordering Calypso to Release Odysseus</u> (1670, now in Cleveland): both paintings show the couple as lovers surrounded by an ideal landscape and about to enjoy the pleasure of a feast. Homer is more ambiguous: Odysseus stays as Calypso's lover for seven years, yet he longs for Penelope and Ithaca and refuses the immortality that Calypso offers him if he stays. Was Odysseus, then, faithful to Penelope? Many people deny this, but others (including prominent feminist scholars) say that he was and that his liaison with Calypso was acceptable and in keeping with the conventions of Homeric society.

Nausicaä. She is the marriageable princess who does not marry the attractive stranger, a paradoxical variation of the usual pattern of the hero's quest, but an appropriate one for Odysseus, who never forgets Penelope. Nausicaä, like Calypso and Circe, cannot keep him permanently, but her case is more poignant because she does not have the powers of the divine figures. She has attracted many artists—for example, Jacob Jordaens in his cartoon (painting; ca. 1635) <u>Odysseus and Nausicaä</u>, for the tapestry series <u>The Story of Odysseus</u> (woven in 1665). In the twentieth century the lame girl Gertie is an especially sympathetic evocation of Nausicaä in James Joyce's <u>Ulysses</u> (1922). The Phaeacians were proverbial as skilled seafarers (the Greek word *naus*, for a ship, is part of the name of Nausicaä and of the Phaeacians' founder, Nausithoös, who was a son of Poseidon), and the honor accorded by Alcinoüs to Arete (who was his niece as well as wife) was, says Homer, unique. Exceptional, too, was the comfortable life and prosperity of the Phaeacians, while the Gardens of Alcinoüs were proverbial for their order, beauty, and fruitfulness.

The Lotus Eaters. Tennyson's poem "The Lotus-Eaters" (1832) is the best-known evocation of the land whose food, once eaten, makes the eater want to stay forever.

Polyphemus. The cannibal giant, living alone and apart from the life of the civilized community, is a common folktale figure. Among the many ancient representations of Polyphemus is an early Attic vase (ca. 650 B.C.) showing Odysseus and his men driving a long pole into his eye. Among many later representations is the painting by Poussin (ca. 1660, now in St. Petersburg) Landscape with Ulysses Deriding Polyphemus.

The Laestrygonians. The episode of the Laestrygonians is the subject of two frescoes (ca. 50 B.C.) that were painted for a house on the Esquiline Hill at Rome.

Circe. She is another folktale figure, the powerful woman who can turn men by magic into beasts. The transformation of Odysseus' men was often painted on Greek vases (as in a black-figure cup, ca. 550 B.C., now in Boston). A Theban cup (ca. 400 B.C., now in Oxford) has a burlesque version of Odysseus rushing at Circe with his sword. The painting by Dosso Dossi (ca. 1525, now in Washington, D.C.) shows Circe using written spells to perform her magic, whereas Homer's Circe uses drugs and a wand. Especially powerful is the interpretation of Circe in the Nighttown episode of James Joyce's Ulysses (1922), where the Circe-figure, Bella Cohen (the madam of the brothel), turns Bloom into a bestial figure. The name of Circe survives in the promontory of Monte Circeo on the western coast of Italy.

The Book of the Dead. While the Nekuia is the equivalent of the hero's conquest of death, Odysseus does not himself enter the Underworld. His purpose is to obtain knowledge of the future from Tiresias, rather than to perform a death-defeating task. Vergil combines the two types in Book 6 of the Aeneid, where Aeneas both journeys through the Underworld and obtains a vision of the future from Anchises. In Book 24 of the Odyssey there is another view of the Underworld, when the souls of the dead suitors are escorted there by Hermes.

The Sirens. The Sirens have been interpreted as death spirits, and they are shown graphically in a red-figure vase (ca. 450 B.C., now in the British Museum) looming over Odysseus (lashed to the mast) and his ship, as one Siren plunges into the sea. More often they are taken as allegories of the seductive power of sensual pleasures, as, for example, in the temptation of Guyon in Book 2 of Spenser's Faerie Queen (1590).

The Homecoming of Odysseus

Almost every episode in the return of Odysseus has been the subject of many interpretations in literature, music, and painting. Once again, James Joyce has been preeminent in his understanding of the saga of Odysseus: Ulysses ends, not with the figure of Bloom (who is Everyman as well as Odysseus), but with the soliloquy of his Penelope, Molly Bloom, recalling their youthful love and her joy, a far more optimistic ending than Homer's (which looks forward to further travels for the hero) or, for example, Tennyson's (see below). The return of the warrior from a long and distant war, or of the husband from long travel to a domestic scene, is an experience shared by millions who have found their archetypes in Odysseus and Penelope. Recently more attention has been given to the character and motives of Penelope, a development foreshadowed both by Monteverdi (see below) and James Joyce. She has been seen as the peer of Odysseus in intelligence and in patience, qualities shown in her resistance to the long siege by the suitors and in her restraint in declaring her recognition of Odysseus. Penelope's reluctance to recognize Odysseus has increasingly been seen as a manifestation of her wisdom and self-control, leading attributes of her husband. The final reunion of husband and wife is accomplished through the incident concerning their bed, a powerful symbol of the strength and constancy of their love. The construction of the bed, with the olive-tree forming one leg, is susceptible to Freudian interpretations. One of the most sustained and profound interpretations of the Return of Odysseus is Claudio Monteverdi's opera Il Ritorno d'Ulisse in Patria, produced at Venice in 1640 (see Compact Discs and Videos). The secret token of the bed is changed into its embroidered cover, but otherwise Monteverdi faithfully portrays the hesitation and patience of Penelope and the joy of her final recognition and reunion.

Other Scenes from the Odyssey in Art and Literature.   The scene between Odysseus and Athena, when he first wakes up after being left on Ithaca by the Phaeacians, was painted by Pieter Lastman, Odysseus and Athena (1633, now in The Hague).

The recognition by Eurycleia appears on a red-figure vase (ca. 440 B.C., now in Chiusi, Italy): Odysseus wears his conical hat (called the pilos), symbolic of a traveler. (On the other side of this vase Penelope sits dejectedly by her loom as Telemachus talks with her.)

The battle in the hall, shown in a red-figure vase (ca. 440 B.C., now in Berlin), was twice imitated by Ovid in his Metamorphoses, Books 5 (Perseus) and 12 (the Centaurs and Lapiths).

Odysseus' Further Travels

Of the many poets who have imagined the substance of Odysseus' further travels, Tennyson has been most successful in Ulysses (1833), a monologue in which Odysseus rejects staying at home to grow old with Penelope and resolves to set out once again "to strive, to seek, to find, and not to yield."

CHAPTER 19

Perseus and the Legends of Argos

Argos, Mycenae, and Tiryns are close geographically and in the sagas confused. Argos itself was associated with Thebes and Corinth, and its myths reflect its contacts with the Levant and Egypt.

HERA, POSEIDON, AND PHORONEUS

Argos was the most important center on the Greek mainland for the worship of Hera. Its founder, PHORONEUS [for-ro′ne-us], decided in favor of Hera in her contest with Poseidon for divine patronage of Argos. In anger Poseidon dried up the Argive rivers, including INACHUS [in′ak-us], or INACHOS, father of Phoroneus. Argive rivers since then have always been short of water.

PERSEUS

Abas had twin sons, Proetus (who became king of Tiryns) and ACRISIUS [a-kris′i-us], or AKRISIOS (who ruled Argos). An oracle foretold that the son of DANAË [da′na-e], the only child of Acrisius, would kill her father. Acrisius shut her up in an underground chamber, but Zeus lay with her, entering in the form of a shower of gold. Their child was PERSEUS [pers′e-us], whom Acrisius discovered after four years from the noise the child made by playing. He put Danaë and Perseus into a chest which he put into the sea. It floated to Seriphos, where it was found by DICTYS [dik′tis], or DIKTYS (brother of POLYDECTES [pol-i-dek′tez], or POLYDEKTES, king of Seriphos), who rescued Danaë and her son and gave them shelter in his home.

Meanwhile Polydectes loved Danaë, who refused him. He ordered the men of Seriphos (including Perseus, now grown) each to give him a horse. When Perseus said, "I can as easily give you the Gorgon's head," Polydectes ordered him to perform this task.

The Graeae and the Nymphs. Hermes and Athena advised Perseus how to perform the task, telling him first to go to the three GRAEAE [gri′i] or [gre′e], or GRAIAI (daughters of Phorcys and Ceto, children of Pontus and Ge and sisters of the Gorgons), who between them had but one eye and one tooth. Perseus got hold of the eye and tooth and gave them back only when they told him the way to certain (unnamed) Nymphs who possessed three magic objects. From the Nymphs Perseus obtained a Cap of Invisibility, a pair of winged sandals, and a bag (kibisis [ki′bi-sis]). Hermes gave him a scimitar.

The Gorgons and the Beheading of Medusa. Thus equipped he flew to the GORGONS [gor′-gonz], who lived on the edge of the world (usually located in North Africa or in the far north, in the land of the Hyperboreans). Two of the Gorgons (STHENO [sthen′o] and EURYALE [u-ri′a-le]) were immortal; the third, MEDUSA [me-du′sa], or MEDOUSA, was mortal. Those who looked on their faces were turned to stone. Guided by Athena, Perseus, looking at the Gorgon's reflection in his shield, beheaded Medusa and put her head in the kibisis.

Medusa had been loved by Poseidon, and from her body sprang their children, CHRYSAOR [kris-sa′or], "golden sword," and the winged horse PEGASUS [peg′a-sus], or PEGASOS. Chrysaor became father of Geryon (see Chapter 20), and Pegasus played an important role in the saga of Bellerophon (see Chapter 23). When the hoof of Pegasus struck Mt. Helicon (in Boeotia), the fountain HIPPOCRENE [hip-po-kre′ne], or HIPPOKRENE, "Horse's Fountain," gushed forth: it was sacred to the Muses and associated with poetic inspiration.

Imitating the lament of the two surviving Gorgons, Stheno and Euryale, for Medusa, Athena invented the flute.

Atlas. Perseus, wearing the Cap of Invisibility, escaped from the Gorgons and began his flight back to Seriphos. Medusa's blood dripped through the *kibisis* as he flew over Libya and from it sprang the poisonous snakes that were said to infest Libya. The Titan Atlas, who supported the heavens (see Chapter 2), refused hospitality to Perseus, who turned him into stone, now the Atlas range of mountains. When Perseus came down to the seashore to bathe his hands in the sea, the seaweed upon which he placed the *kibisis* hardened into coral.

Andromeda. Flying past the coast of the Levant (or, some say, Ethiopia, that is, the part of Africa lying to the south of Egypt), Perseus saw a young woman chained to a rock, threatened by a sea-monster. She was ANDROMEDA [an-drom'e-da], daughter of King CEPHEUS [sef'e-us], or KEPHEUS, and Queen CASSIEPEA [kas-si-e-pe'a], or KASSIEPEIA. Cassiepea had boasted that she was more beautiful than the Nereids, and Poseidon punished her pride by flooding the kingdom of Cepheus and sending the sea-monster to ravage it. The oracle of Zeus Ammon told Cepheus that he could appease the monster only by chaining his daughter to the rock. Perseus killed the monster with the scimitar of Hermes and was rewarded with Andromeda as his wife.

Phineus Since Andromeda was already betrothed to PHINEUS [fin'e-es], her uncle, Perseus had to assert his claim by fighting Phineus and his followers, all of whom he turned to stone with the Gorgon's head. The fight between Perseus and Phineus was described by Ovid as a full-scale battle in the dining-hall (like that of Odysseus), in <u>Metamorphoses</u> 5. 1-209, narrated at great length and with much ingenuity.

The Return. Perseus and Andromeda flew back to Seriphos, leaving a son, Perses, to inherit the kingdom of Cepheus.

At Seriphos Perseus found Danaë and Dictys being threatened by Polydectes, whom he turned to stone. Leaving Dictys as king, he returned to Argos with Andromeda and Danaë (whom he had released), and gave the winged sandals, the *kibisis*, and the Cap of Invisibility to Hermes (who returned them to the nymphs), along with the scimitar. To Athena he gave the Gorgon's head, which she placed in the middle of her *aegis*, or shield.

The Killing of Acrisius. Acrisius fled from Argos to Larissa (a city in Thessaly) to avoid Perseus. Perseus followed him there and took part in funeral games being celebrated for Abas, father of Acrisius. In the discus-throw his discus accidentally killed Acrisius, and so the prophecy of the oracle was fulfilled.

Perseus, as the killer of his grandfather, could not return to Argos and went to Tiryns, where he became king, exchanging his kingdom with the king of Tiryns, Megapenthes. He founded Mycenae, and from him and Andromeda descended the kings of Mycenae in the generations before the family of Atreus. From them also descended Heracles and Eurystheus (see Chapter 20).

THE FAMILY OF INACHUS

Inachus, Io, and Epaphus. Inachus, father of Phoroneus (see above), was son of Oceanus and Tethys and is sometimes said to be the founder of Argos. He gave his name also to the river Inachus.

His daughter was IO [i'o] (see Chapter 2), who was loved by Zeus and changed into a cow, resuming her human form when she came in her wanderings to Egypt, where she gave birth to Epaphus. Hera persuaded the Curetes to kidnap EPAPHUS [ep'a-fus], or EPAPHOS, and Io, after searching through many lands, found him in Syria. After her return to Egypt she was worshiped as the goddess Isis (see Chapter 14).

Epaphus and His Descendants. Epaphus was identified by the Egyptians with the sacred bull, Apis. In the mythology of Argos, a son of Phoroneus was also called Apis, from whom came the ancient name for the Peloponnese, Apia.

The daughter of Epaphus was Libya (from whom the geographical Libya is named), whose twin sons were Agenor and Belus. Agenor, who became the ruler of Phoenicia, was father of Cadmus and Europa (see Chapter 15), while Belus ruled in Egypt.

Aegyptus and Danaüs and the Danaïds. The sons of Belus were AEGYPTUS [e-jip'tus], or AIGYPTOS, and DANAÜS [dan'a-us], or DANAOS, who quarreled. Danaüs left Egypt and came to Argos, where he became king: his subjects were called Danaï, which is one of the names that Homer uses for the Greeks. The fifty sons of Aegyptus demanded the fifty daughters of Danaüs (DANAÏDS [dan'a-idz]) in marriage; on their wedding night forty-nine Danaïds stabbed their husbands with daggers given them for the purpose by Danaüs, and for this were punished in the Underworld by having to fill perforated water-jars. The fiftieth, HYPERMNESTRA [hi-perm-nes'tra], spared her husband LYNCEUS [lins'e-us], and from them descended Abas, great-grandfather of Perseus.

Amymone and Poseidon. The Danaïd AMYMONE [a-mi'mo-ne] was loved by Poseidon, who with his trident caused water to gush from a rock; this is the spring Amymone. Their son was Nauplius, founder of Nauplia and father of Palamedes. Nauplius, to avenge his son's death at the hands of Odysseus, caused many ships of the Greek fleet to be wrecked on the rocks of Euboea during the return voyage from Troy (see Chapter 18).

Other Argive heroes were Melampus (see Chapter 23) and the five Argives among the Seven against Thebes—Adrastus, Amphiaraus, Capaneus, Hippomedon, and Tydeus (see Chapter 15). The son of Tydeus was Diomedes, a leading Greek hero in the Trojan War (see Chapter 17).

COMPACT DISCS

66. Dittersdorf, Carl Ditters von, Symphony in F Major, "The Rescuing of Andromeda by Perseus," and Symphony in D Major, "The Petrification of Phineus and His Friends."
148. Lekeu, Guillaume, Andromede. Cantata. Lyric poem for soloists, chorus, and orchestra about Perseus' rescue of Andromeda.
246. Salieri, Antonio, Les Danaïdes. Opera about Danaüs, Hypermnesta, and Lynceus, by Mozart's rival.
270. Strauss, Richard, Die Liebe der Danae. Operatic amalgamation of the wooing of Danaë by Jupiter as a shower of gold and Midas with his golden touch (M/L 601).
283. Vaccaj (Vaccai), Nicola, Andromeda. Cantata for soprano and orchestra.

VIDEOS

Clash of the Titans. A stellar cast (including Laurence Olivier as Zeus) directed by Desmond Davis makes this an entertaining adventure. MGM/UA Entertainment Co. MV 700074. Worth seeing, if only for the imagination and suspense of the encounter between Perseus and Medusa, ending with Perseus (Harry Hamlin) triumphantly holding up the head of the monster in the stance of Bernini's masterpiece (M/L 611-12).

The Gorgon. A modern-day gorgon terrorizes a village in this horror movie starring Peter Cushing and Christopher Lee. Directed by Terence Fischer. RCA/Columbia Pictures Home Video.

The Seven Faces of Dr. Lao. This fantasy, starring Tony Randall and directed by George Pal, includes a vision of Medusa (as well as Pan). MGM/UA M600667V

INTERPRETATION

The saga of Perseus contains an unusual number of genuine folktale motifs, indicating that the tale of the local hero (Perseus) has been combined with motifs that are widespread (if not universal) in folktales. Such motifs are:

- The magic conception of the hero.
- Discovery of the infant hero through the noise of his playing.
- The shutting up of the hero and his mother in a chest.
- The villainous king and his good and humble brother.
- The hero's rash promise.
- The help of supernatural helpers and magic objects in completing the hero's task.
- The three wise women.
- The ferocious and ugly monsters.
- The vindication of the hero and the punishment of the villain.

Although the conception of the hero is indeed magical, the golden shower represents a variation of the archetypal holy marriage in which the rain of the god of the sky fertilizes mother earth.

Unusual in Greek saga is the help of two gods (Hermes and Athena) and the gift by one god of a magic object (the scimitar of Hermes).

The saga of Perseus ("The Gorgon's Head") was the first tale in Nathaniel Hawthorne's A Wonder Book (1851), in which the hero is presented consistently with Hawthorne's view that Greek myths were "legitimate subjects for every age. . . to imbue with its own morality." Hawthorne mentions the legend of Andromeda only incidentally.

Zeus and Danaë. The tale of Zeus appearing to Danaë in the form of a golden shower is easily interpreted as an allegory of the power of gold to corrupt. It has been popular with painters, especially in the Renaissance; some well-known interpretations are the paintings by Correggio (1530, in the Borghese Gallery at Rome) and Titian (1545, different versions in Naples, Madrid, and Vienna).

The Gorgons and the Gorgon's Head. The location of the Gorgons (like that of the kingdom of Cepheus in the legend of Andromeda) is somewhere on the edge of the world, sometimes in the far west of Africa, or in the far north, the land of the Hyperboreans (described by Pindar), an imaginary land which, says Pindar, "you would not find either with ships or on foot."

The terrifying head of a monster is a universal motif in art and poetry. The Greeks, exceptionally, incorporated the Gorgon's head into their ordered world as a symbol of the disorder or punishment awaiting those who transgressed or opposed their laws. Appropriately, it is placed in the shield of Athena, the goddess of civic excellence, above all on the statue of Athena Parthenos in her temple on the Acropolis of Athens. Homer places it on the aegis of Athena when she arms for battle (Iliad 5. 741), along with personifications of the terror of battle, and again Agamemnon's shield (Iliad 11. 36) has the Gorgon's head at its center with Fear and Terror around it. Yet Ovid dwells on the beauty of Medusa, as did the sculptress Harriet Hosmer, moved by the pathos of her tragedy, in Medusa (1854, now in Detroit). The Gorgon's head is very common on Greek vases and in sculpture, sometimes as an architectural filler or ornament, often by itself or in a decorative scheme. There is a fine limestone relief panel from Selinus (in Sicily, ca. 540 B.C.) showing the death of Medusa and the birth of Pegasus, with Athena standing beside Perseus. Of later works, preeminent are the statue of Perseus by Benvenuto Cellini (ca. 1550, in the Loggia dei Lanzi in Florence) and the painting by Caravaggio (1592, in the Uffizi at Florence). A cycle of paintings of the saga of Perseus was painted by Edward Burne-Jones (between 1877 and 1897, now in Stuttgart), in which the final painting, The Baleful Head, shows love (in the persons of Perseus and Andromeda) victorious over death (i.e., the Gorgon's head).

Perseus and Andromeda.   In the original story, Perseus would have gone straight back to Seriphos. The legend of Andromeda (a variant of the universal folktale of Beauty and the Beast) is an addition, popular because of its romantic and visual elements. The maiden chained to a rock, threatened by a monster and saved by a chivalrous hero, has been popular with artists; in the Renaissance and Baroque periods alone, the legend of Perseus and Andromeda was painted by Annibale Caracci (1603, in the Farnese Palace at Rome), Rubens (1622, now in Berlin, and several times later), and Rembrandt (ca. 1635, now in The Hague), and by many others. The story has also been popular with Freudian and post-Freudian artists, beginning with Odilon Redon (1908, five paintings and a drawing) and including Salvador Dali (drawings, 1930-1931) and André Masson (1943, in New York). Both Andromeda and Cassiepeia became constellations (in the Catasterisms of pseudo-Eratosthenes at Alexandria, ca. 225 B.C.), and the Gorgon's head became the Arabic monster Algol, part of the constellation of Perseus; Algol returned to its classical form of Medusa's head in Dürer's Sky-Map of the Northern Hemisphere in 1503.

Io and the Danaïds.   The connection between the Greek Io and Egyptian religion is confusing and does not seem to have a genuinely religious or mythological basis. Io was originally a priestess of Hera, and her identification with Isis derives in part from the fact that in her statues her head was horned, like that of Isis.

Aeschylus wrote a trilogy (perhaps 463 B.C.) on the Danaïds, of which the first play, Suppliants, survives. The story of Io is told in this play, and Io herself has a major role in Aeschylus' tragedy Prometheus Bound.

CHAPTER 20

Heracles

HERACLES [her′a-kles], or HERAKLES (HERCULES), the most popular of Greek heroes, is associated especially with the area around Argos and with Thebes, where he was born.

AMPHITRYON AND ALCMENA

ELECTRYON [e-lek′tri-on], or ELEKTRYON, son of Perseus and king of Mycenae, fought with Pterelaüs, king of the Teleboans. Electryon planned to attack the Teleboans, who had retreated to their land in western Greece taking his cattle. He planned to leave his nephew AMPHITRYON [am-fi′tri-on] as king in his place, and he betrothed his daughter ALCMENA [alk-me′na], or ALKMENE, to him.

Amphitryon accidentally killed Electryon and left Mycenae to go into exile at Thebes, taking Alcmena with him. She would not lie with him until he had attacked the Teleboans and avenged her brothers, whom they had killed in the earlier war.

Amphitryon returned victorious to find that Alcmena had already lain with Zeus in the same night. She conceived twins, Heracles, son of Zeus, and IPHICLES [if′i-klez], or IPHIKLES, son of Amphitryon.

THE BIRTH AND YOUTH OF HERACLES

Hera, angry with Zeus, sent Eileithyia to delay the birth of Alcmena's twins and hasten the birth of EURYSTHEUS [u-ris′the-us], child of Sthenelus, grandson of Zeus and king of Mycenae. The prophecy of Zeus that the child of his blood to be born that day would rule over those that lived around him was fulfilled by Eurystheus, for whom Heracles performed his labors.

After the birth of Heracles, which took place when a servant of Alcmena tricked Eileithyia into relaxing her guard, Hera sent a pair of snakes to kill the twins. Heracles strangled them, and Tiresias, summoned by Amphitryon, foretold how Heracles would go on to perform great labors for humankind and finally join the gods on Olympus.

Heracles was taught chariot driving, wrestling, archery, and music by various heroes. He killed LINUS [li′nus], or LINOS, his music teacher, by striking him with his lyre.

For this murder he was exiled to Mt. Cithaeron on the borders of Boeotia, where he saved the town of Thespiae from the ravages of a lion and freed the Thebans from paying tribute to the people of Orchomenus. Creon, king of Thebes, gave him his daughter MEGARA [meg′a-ra] as wife.

THE MADNESS OF HERACLES

After Megara had borne several children to Heracles, he killed her and the children in a fit of madness caused by Hera. He inquired at Delphi how he might expiate his crime; the Pythia first called him Heracles ("Glory of Hera") rather than by his usual name, ALCIDES [al-si′dez], or ALKIDES, "Grandson of Alcaeus," and told him to serve Eurystheus, king of Tiryns, for twelve years, performing the labors that he would impose.

THE TWELVE LABORS (ATHLOI)

The Greek word for the labors is *athloi*, i.e., contests for a prize, which for Heracles was immortality. The first six of the labors were undertaken in the Peloponnese, and the other six elsewhere. Associated with them are incidental or subsequent exploits, known as *parerga*, "incidental deeds" (*parergon* in the singular).

1. The Nemean Lion. Heracles killed a lion at NEMEA [nem'e-a] by means of a club, skinning it by using the animal's own claws. Henceforth he carried the club and wore the lionskin, his two most prominent attributes in art.

2. The Lernaean Hydra. A nine-headed serpent, or HYDRA [hi'dra], lived in the marshes of LERNA [ler'na]. Each time Heracles clubbed a head two more grew in its place, while Hera sent a crab to make things even more difficult. Helped by his nephew IOLAÜS [i-o-la'us], or IOLAOS, Heracles killed both monsters and dipped his arrows in the Hydra's poison. The crab became the constellation Cancer.

3. The Cerynean Hind. A hind with golden horns, sacred to Artemis, lived on Mt. CERYNEA [se-ri-ne'a], or KERYNEA. After pursuing it for a year Heracles caught it and carried it back alive to Eurystheus and then released it. Pindar says that Heracles went to the land of the Hyperboreans to find the animal.

4. The Erymanthian Boar. Heracles brought back to Eurystheus the monstrous boar that lived on Mt. ERYMANTHUS [er-i-man'thus], or ERYMANTHOS.

5. The Augean Stables. Heracles cleaned the stables of AUGEAS [aw-je'as] or [aw'je-as], son of Helius and king of Elis, who kept vast herds of cattle. Helped by Athena, he diverted the rivers Alpheus and Peneus so that they flowed through the stables.

6. The Stymphalian Birds. Heracles shot the birds that lived beside Lake STYMPHALUS [stim'-fal-us], or STYMPHALOS, in Arcadia.

7. The Cretan Bull. Heracles caught the bull that the Cretan king, MINOS [mi'nos], had failed to sacrifice to Poseidon. After bringing it back from Crete alive, he released it, and it came to Marathon, where Theseus caught it (see Chapter 21).

8. The Mares of Diomedes. The Thracian king DIOMEDES [di-o-me'dez], son of Ares, owned a herd of mares that ate human flesh. He brought them back to Eurystheus, who released them and dedicated them to Hera.

9. The Girdle of Hippolyta. Heracles killed HIPPOLYTA [hip-pol'i-ta], queen of the Amazons, in battle and brought her girdle back to Eurystheus.

10. The Cattle of Geryon. Heracles brought back the cattle of GERYON [jer'i-on] from Erythia, a land far away in the west. He sailed there in a cup given him by Helius and killed Geryon (who had three bodies) and his herdsman, EURYTION [u-rit'i-on], and hound (Orthrus) and drove the cattle back to Greece.

11. The Apples of the Hesperides. Heracles needed the help of Athena and Atlas to get the apples of the HESPERIDES [hes-per'i-dez], "daughters of night," which they guarded in a garden far to the west; around the apple tree was coiled the serpent LADON [la'don]. The many-formed sea-god Nereus first had to be held by Heracles before he would divulge the location of the garden. While Euripides says that Heracles killed Ladon and took the apples himself, usually he is said to have held up the heavens, with the aid of Athena, while the Titan Atlas fetched the apples. After shifting the heavens back to the shoulders of Atlas, he brought the apples back to Eurystheus. Later Athena took them back to the garden of the Hesperides.

12. Cerberus. The final labor was to go to the Underworld and bring back the three-headed hound of Hades, CERBERUS [ser'ber-us], or KERBEROS. Heracles himself said (in the <u>Odyssey</u>) that this was the hardest labor. He brought Cerberus back to Eurystheus and then returned him to Hades.

PARERGA (INCIDENTAL DEEDS)

The Centaurs. As a <u>parergon</u> to the fourth labor, Heracles was attacked by the centaurs while he was drinking wine with the centaur PHOLUS [fo'lus], or PHOLOS. He defeated them, but the immortal centaur CHIRON [ki'ron] was wounded by one of the poisoned arrows and only ended his suffering by exchanging his immortality with Prometheus (see Chapter 2). Pholus died when he dropped one of the poisoned arrows on his hoof.

The Olympic Games. After cleaning the Augean stables, Heracles, cheated of his promised reward (one tenth of the cattle) by Augeas, returned with an army and killed Augeas. After this victory he instituted the Olympic Games in the territory of Elis (they were actually founded several centuries after the supposed time of Heracles).

Admetus and Alcestis. On his way to Thrace for his eighth labor, Heracles was entertained by ADMETUS [ad-me'tus], or ADMETOS, king of Pherae, who was mourning the death of his wife, ALCESTIS [al-ses'tis], or ALKESTIS. Heracles wrestled with Death (Thanatos) and recovered Alcestis for her husband (see Chapter 9).

Hesione. Coming back from his ninth labor, Heracles rescued HESIONE [he-si'o-ne] from the sea-monster at Troy (see Chapter 17). When the king, LAOMEDON [la-o'me-don], cheated him of his reward, he returned with an army, sacked Troy, and replaced Laomedon with PRIAM [pri'am], who had been called Podarces.

Pillars of Heracles. As a monument of his journey to Geryon's island, Heracles set up the Pillars of Heracles at the straits where the Mediterranean Sea meets the Atlantic Ocean.

Cacus. On his overland journey back he was attacked by the Ligurians (in southern France) and was helped by Zeus to drive them off. At Pallanteum (on the site of Rome, see Chapter 24) he was entertained by king Evander and killed the fire-breathing monster, CACUS [ka'kus] or KAKOS, "evil one."

Eryx. Crossing the straits to Sicily he wrestled with ERYX [er'iks], king of the western tip of the island, and killed him.

Alcyoneus. Lastly, at the Isthmus of Corinth he killed the giant ALCYONEUS [al-si-on'e-us], or ALKYONEUS.

Echidna and Scythes. According to Herodotus, Geryon lived in the far north, where Heracles lay with ECHIDNA [e-kid'na], "snake-woman," who bore him SCYTHES [si'thez], or SKYTHES, and two other sons. As a young man Scythes, alone of the three, could string a bow left behind by Heracles, and he became king and ancestor of the Scythians.

Busiris. Journeying to the Garden of the Hesperides, Heracles killed the murderous king of Egypt, BUSIRIS [bu-si'ris].

Antaeus. In Libya he wrestled with ANTAEUS [an-te'us], or ANTAIOS, son of Ge and Poseidon, who could not be beaten so long as he kept contact with the earth, his mother. Heracles held him aloft until he had crushed him to death.

Prometheus. On this journey also it was said that he came to the Caucasus and there released PROMETHEUS [pro-me'the-us]. See Centaurs, above, and Chapter 2.

Theseus, Pirithoüs, and Meleager. In Hades Heracles saw THESEUS [the'se-us] and PIRITHOÜS [pir-ith'o-us], or PIRITHOÖS, chained fast to stone seats, and released Theseus. He saw the ghost of MELEAGER [me-le-a'jer] (see Chapter 23), whose sister DEIANIRA [de-ya-ni'ra], or DEIANEIRA, he offered to marry.

OTHER DEEDS OF HERACLES

The Robbers Cycnus and Syleus. Helped by Athena and Iolaüs, Heracles killed the Thessalian robber CYCNUS [sik'nus], or KYKNOS, son of Ares, and near the Straits of Euboea he killed another robber, SYLEUS [sil'e-us].

The Cercopes. This pair of mischievous dwarfs, the CERCOPES [ser-ko'pez], or KERKOPES, tried to steal the weapons of Heracles, who caught them and slung them upside down from a pole across his shoulders. They laughed so much at the sight of his buttocks, burned black by the sun, that he let them go. Later they were turned by Zeus into apes (or stones).

The Argonautic Expedition and Hylas. Heracles was one of the Argonauts who sailed with Jason (see Chapter 22), but at Cios he left the ship to search for his companion HYLAS [hi'las], who had been abducted by the water-nymphs. The Argo sailed on without him, and he instituted a cult of Hylas at Cios.

Expedition against Pylos. Besides the expeditions against Augeas and Laomedon, Heracles led an army against NELEUS [nel'e-us], king of Pylos, whom he killed along with eleven of his twelve sons. He left as king the survivor, NESTOR [nes'tor], who was a prominent Greek hero in the Trojan War (see Chapter 17). In the battle at Pylos, Heracles is said to have wounded the gods Hades and Hera, and Apollo and Poseidon are said to have driven him back from the city. He attacked Hippocoön, king of Sparta, who had helped Neleus.

Auge and Telephus. During his journey back to Tiryns he lay with AUGE [aw′je] at Tegea. Their son, TELEPHUS [tel′e-fus], or TELEPHOS, was put in a chest by her father and floated over the Aegean to Asia Minor. There Telephus became king and ancestor of the Mysians (see Chapter 17).

DEIANIRA AND IOLE

In Hades during his last Labor, Heracles had promised Meleager that he would marry his sister, DEIANIRA [de-ya-ni′ra], or DEIANEIRA (sometimes spelled in English Dejanira). To win her he wrestled with the river-god ACHELOÜS (ak-e-lo′us], or ACHELOÖS, who also wished to marry her. As a river-god, Acheloüs could turn himself into different creatures. He had bull's horns on his head, one of which was broken off in the fight and became (or was exchanged with) the miraculous *cornucopia* (in Latin, *cornu copiae*, "horn of plenty"), said also to have been the horn of Amalthea, the goat who suckled the infant Zeus on Crete (see Chapter 1).

Nessus. On the way back to Tiryns with Deïanira, Heracles came to the river Evenus, which was in spate. The centaur NESSUS [nes′sus], or NESSOS, carried Deïanira over and, before Heracles could cross, attempted to violate her. Heracles shot him with his bow, and as Nessus lay dying, he told Deïanira to collect some of his blood and keep it, for, he said, it would prevent Heracles from loving any other woman more than Deïanira. She collected the blood and kept it out of the sunlight. She did not know that the arrow that killed Nessus had been dipped in the poison of the Hydra.

Iole. Deïanira bore Heracles a son, HYLLUS [hil′lus], or HYLLOS, and a daughter, MACARIA [ma-kar′i-a], or MAKARIA. Later he fell in love with IOLE [i′o-le], daughter of EURYTUS [ur′i-tus], or EYRYTOS, king of Oechalia (a city on the island of Euboea), who had taught Heracles archery. Eurytus would not give her to Heracles, even though he won an archery contest to decide who should have her as wife or concubine. Later the brother of Iole, IPHITUS [if′i-tus], or IPHITOS, came to Tiryns, and there Heracles threw him from the acropolis and killed him.

Heracles and Apollo. Heracles asked the Delphic oracle how he might be cured of his fits of murderous madness. When the Pythia refused to answer him, he began to carry off the tripod, so as to set up his own oracle. Apollo prevented him, and their fight was ended by Zeus. Finally the Pythia told him that he must serve as a slave for one year.

Omphale. Heracles was sold to OMPHALE [[om′fa-le], queen of Lydia, and served as her slave, even dressing as a woman and spinning wool for her.

Heracles and Deïanira in Trachis. Because of the murder of Iphitus, Heracles no longer could live at Tiryns, and he and Deïanira were received by Ceyx, king of TRACHIS [tra′kis]. On the way back to Trachis from Lydia, Heracles attacked Oechalia: he sacked the city, killed Eurytus, and took Iole prisoner, sending her back to Deïanira with his herald, LICHAS [li′kas].

THE DEATH OF HERACLES

Deïanira learned from Lichas that Heracles loved Iole. Remembering the advice of Nessus, she smeared a robe (or shirt) with the centaur's blood and sent Lichas to give it to Heracles to wear at the sacrifice to Zeus, which Heracles was performing in thanksgiving for his victory. The flames of the sacrificial fire warmed the blood and the robe clung to the flesh of Heracles, burning him with intolerable pain. In agony he hurled Lichas into the sea and had himself carried back to Mt. Oeta in Trachis, where he was placed on a huge funeral pyre. In the end, the mighty Heracles was killed unwittingly by a woman, his loving wife.

When Deïanira heard what had happened, she killed herself. Hyllus went with his father to Mt. Oeta, where Heracles ordered him to marry Iole.

The Apotheosis of Heracles. Heracles gave his bow to POEAS [pe'as], or POIAS, father of PHILOCTETES [fi-lok-te'tez], or PHILOKTETES (see Chapter 17), as a reward for lighting the pyre. The mortal part of Heracles perished in the flames, while his immortal part ascended to Olympus in a chariot sent by Zeus. There Heracles became one of the immortal gods; he was reconciled with Hera and was given Hebe as his wife.

ALCMENA AND EURYSTHEUS

Alcmena and the children of Heracles were persecuted by Eurystheus despite the protection of King Ceyx. They fled from Trachis to Athens and were received by King Demophon, son of Theseus. The Athenians killed Eurystheus with his five sons in battle. Alcmena revenged herself by mutilating his severed head.

Euripides said that the Athenian victory was assured by the voluntary sacrifice of Macaria (daughter of Heracles) to Persephone, and that the nephew of Heracles, Ioläus, was miraculously rejuvenated and captured Eurystheus, who was later executed. Pindar says that Ioläus himself killed Eurystheus, whose body was buried in the tomb of Amphitryon at Thebes.

Alcmena died at Thebes and went to the Elysian Fields, where she became the consort of Rhadamanthys. In another version she married Rhadamanthys in Thebes (after the death of Amphitryon). After her death, Hermes substituted a large stone for her body in the coffin, and her grandchildren set up a shrine to her with a cult.

THE HERACLIDAE

Hyllus married Iole and led an expedition in an attempt to return to the Peloponnese. He was killed by Echemus, king of Tegea.

After 100 years his descendant, Temenus, invaded the Peloponnese and defeated its defenders, who were led by Tisamenus, son of Orestes.

Thus the HERACLIDAE [her-a-kli'de], or HERAKLIDAI, "descendants of Heracles," returned to the Peloponnese, where the three principal areas were divided among them: Procles and Eurysthenes ruled Sparta, Temenus ruled Argos, and Cresphontes held Messene. These were the principal Dorian kingdoms in the Peloponnese, and Sparta, which subjugated Messene, and Argos flourished for centuries.

COMPACT DISCS

91. Goebbels, Heiner, <u>Herakles 2</u>, for five brass players, drums, and sampler. The composer explains that "the title was taken from a prose text in Heiner Müller's play <u>Zement</u> which describes Hercules' second task, his struggle with the Hydra, and the fighter's gradual transformation into his adversary, a fighting machine."

102. Handel, George Frideric, <u>The Choice of Hercules</u>. Cantata about Hercules' choice between Pleasure and Virtue. Bach's Cantata 213, <u>Hercules auf dem Scheidenwege</u> (not yet on CD) is on this same subject.

103. _____. <u>Hercules</u>. Significant among Handel's operas, about Heracles, Deïanira, and Iole, based upon Sophocles' <u>Trachiniae</u>.

129. Mercadante, <u>L'Apoteosi d'Ercole</u>. Opera on the same theme as that of Handel, above. Verdi's early operas are very much influenced by Mercadante.

221. Porter, Cole, <u>Out of This World</u>. Splendid musical loosely based on the Amphitryon legend, telling of Jupiter's infatuation with a lovely American mortal (M/L 606).

236. Rodgers, Richard, <u>The Boys from Syracuse</u>. Lyrics by Hart. Musical based on Shakespeare's <u>The Comedy of Errors</u>, which is reminiscent of Plautus' <u>Amphitruo</u> and <u>Menaechmi</u>.

237. _____. <u>By Jupiter</u>. Lyrics by Hart. Fine musical inspired by Heracles' ninth labor, the Girdle of Hippolyta (M/L 606).

244 and **245.** Saint-Saëns, Camille, <u>La Jeunesse d'Hercule</u> and <u>Le Rouet d'Omphale</u>. Interesting symphonic poems. The latter incorporates the sound of Omphale's spinning wheel.

261. Sondheim, Stephen, <u>A Funny Thing Happened on the Way to the Forum</u>. See Videos.

280. Terrace, Claude, <u>Les Travaux d'Hercule</u>. Comic operetta in the manner of Offenbach about the exploits of Heracles.

288. Wakeman, Rick, and Ramon Remedios, <u>A Suite of Gods</u>. Classical new age songs for tenor, keyboards, and percussion which include the lengthy "Hercules."

VIDEOS

<u>A Funny Thing Happened on the Way to the Forum</u>. Outstanding musical with music and lyrics by Stephen Sondheim and starring Zero Mostel and Phil Silvers; directed by Richard Lester. MGM/UA. CBS/FOX Video 4618. Since this musical is based on several plays of Plautus to create an archetypal new comedy, it can be enjoyed in conjunction with a reading of <u>Amphitruo</u> (see also CD version). In connection with a study of Plautus, one can also savor Rodgers and Hart's delightful <u>The Boys from Syracuse</u> on CD (listed above).

The number of movies about Heracles is legion; those starring bodybuilder Steve Reeves are perhaps the most well known (M/L 609). Many of these B movies are readily available on video; the more difficult to find may be purchased from dealers such as Sinister Cinema (where other movies on classical themes may be found). In the world of Heraclean films, the TV series <u>Hercules: The Legendary Journeys</u>, starring Kevin Sorbo (with Anthony Quinn as a bumbling Zeus), however juvenile, deserves credit for some clever reworking of material that is still recognizably classical and employment of certain wonderful special effects. One would expect a release on video tape.

INTERPRETATION

Characteristics of Heracles and his Legend

Mortal Prince, Hero, and God. The name _Heracles_ means "glory of Hera," indicating that Heracles was originally mortal (gods do not have names compounded from the names of other gods). He may have been a prince of Tiryns, vassal to the king of Mycenae.

Herodotus thought that Heracles the god was separate from Heracles the man, and that he was one of the twelve ancient gods of Egypt. At Tyre (in Phoenicia) he was identified with the god Melkart.

Heracles was a Greek hero who became a Greek god. He performed labors and conquered animals and monsters like many other heroes (e.g., the biblical Samson or the Indian Indra), but his myths are Greek traditional tales. His primitive origins are shown by his violence, his clothing of an animal's skin, and his club. He fights animals like the hunter who provides food for the primitive community. The Greek myths transformed him into the son of Zeus and exemplar of strength and patience.

His legends may have spread from the Peloponnese all over Greece, or he may have been a hero brought into Greece by invaders from the north at the end of the Mycenaean age. Eventually his legends and his cults spread all over the Greek world, and in Italy he became prominent in the religion of the Roman state.

The Comic and Philosophic Heracles. We should remember that there is a humorous side to Heracles and his legend. The story of Amphitryon, Zeus, and Alcmena (with its theme of mistaken identity) provides a recurrent comic theme from ancient to modern times, and Heracles himself can appear as a hero of more brawn than brains, a drunkard, glutton, and womanizer.

Yet the persevering and philosophical Heracles has become a more influential and inspiring archetype. Because of his Labors, Heracles became a model of virtue, who through patience transcended human limitations and became immortal. Many of the Labors have folktale elements, and three—Geryon, the Hesperides, and Cerberus are certainly conquests of death.

Heracles became an ideal for moralists and philosophers. Prodicus (ca. 400 B.C.), a sophist (teacher of philosophy), told the parable of the Choice of Heracles. As a young man he was invited by two young women, representing Pleasure and Virtue, respectively, to choose between the easy path of pleasure and the rocky uphill path of virtue. He chose the path of virtue.

Heracles (like Odysseus) became an example of patience in adversity for the Stoics, especially in Roman Stoicism, which focused on subduing the emotions, on self-reliance, and on fortitude. Even in some Christian writings he is a model of Christ-like patience.

Hercules in Roman Religion. As Hercules, Heracles was important in Roman religion, and his was the only cult of a non-Italian god accepted by Romulus at the founding of Rome (according to Livy). He himself (or the Greek king of Pallanteum, Evander) established the cult on the site of the future Forum Boarium (cattle market) to commemorate his victory over Cacus and the recovery of his cattle. Its altar was called the Ara Maxima (the Greatest Altar), and there were at least twelve other shrines to Hercules in Rome.

Hercules (like the god Mercury) became the patron of traders, the bringer of profit and good luck in business.

Heracles in Literature
Greek Literature. No epic or tragedy could encompass his saga. Of extant Greek tragedies, Sophocles' Trachiniae (ca. 440 B.C.) deals with Deïanira and the agony of Heracles before his death; of the two surviving Heracles plays of Euripides, the Heracles Furens (ca. 420 B.C.) deals with his madness, and the Alcestis (438 B.C.) with his role in the return of Alcestis from the dead. Euripides also wrote an Alkmene (now lost), in which Alcmena was accused by Amphitryon of unfaithfulness and was saved from death by Zeus. Heracles appears in the Frogs of Aristophanes (405 B.C.) as a comic glutton. Of the Alexandrian poets, Apollonius of Rhodes (ca. 260 B.C.) includes Heracles in the crew of the Argo, and narrates the loss of Hylas and Heracles' vain search for him in the first book of his epic Argonautica (1153-1357). Theocritus (ca. 275 B.C.) also focuses on Heracles' love for Hylas

in his thirteenth <u>Idyll</u>, and in the twenty-fourth <u>Idyll</u> he tells the story of the infant Heracles and the serpents.

Roman Literature. In Rome, Plautus emphasized the divine birth of Heracles in his <u>Amphitruo</u> (ca. 200 B.C.: his only mythological comedy) and portrays Alcmena sympathetically as the object of the lust of Zeus (Jupiter) and Amphitryon.

In Roman epic Heracles is important in Vergil's <u>Aeneid</u>, where in Book 8 (184-305) Evander describes his victory over Cacus. Aeneas has many similarities to Heracles—the hostility of Juno, for example, and the theme of virtue achieved through labor. This is expressed by Jupiter in consoling Hercules, to whom the doomed Pallas has vainly prayed for victory (10. 460-72). Ovid describes the apotheosis of Hercules in the <u>Metamorphoses</u> (9. 134-272). Lucan (d. A.D. 65), in his <u>Bellum Civile</u> (4. 593-655), tells the story of Hercules and Antaeus. Hercules is the pattern of virtue for Scipio Africanus, the hero of the historical epic <u>Punica</u> of Silius Italicus (A.D. 26-101), and he has a bigger part in the <u>Argonautica</u> of Valerius Flaccus (ca. A.D. 90) than in the epic of Apollonius.

Seneca (d. A.D. 65) wrote a tragedy on the madness of Heracles (<u>Hercules Furens</u>), and he may have been the author of a second extant tragedy (<u>Hercules Oetaeus</u>) that deals with his suffering and death. There are innumerable references to Heracles throughout Greek and Roman literature.

Western Literature. Heracles was popular throughout the Middle Ages in the West, and he even appears in Persian astronomical manuscripts with a turban and scimitar. He resumed his classical form in Renaissance art and iconography. In sixteenth-century France he represented eloquence and is sometimes shown drawing people to himself by a chain coming out of his mouth. The French poet Ronsard (1524-1585) likened him to Christ, as did John Milton (1671) in England, who used the legend of Antaeus as a simile for Christ's victory over the Tempter (<u>Paradise Regained</u> 4. 562-71). Edmund Spenser (1552-1599) frequently used Heracles in the <u>Faerie Queene</u> as an example of justice and virtue, most of all in the first and tenth cantos of Book 5.

Heracles appears frequently in German poetry, notably in the poems of Friedrich Hölderlin (1770-1843), who saw in Heracles the symbol of the human struggle against adversity. Later, in the nineteenth century, Robert Browning used the Alcestis myth in <u>Balaustion's Adventure</u> (1871). Heracles continues to be used in twentieth-century poetry and drama: as "Harcourt-Reilly" he is a Christ-like figure in T. S. Eliot's <u>The Cocktail Party</u> (1939), while a fine adaptation of Sophocles' <u>Trachiniae</u> is Ezra Pound's <u>The Women of Trachis</u> (1954).

Plautus' <u>Amphitruo</u> has been an endless source for inspiration. In 1929 the French playwright Jean Giraudoux wrote <u>Amphitryon 38</u>, which he claims is the thirty-eighth comedy on this theme; and there have been more since.

Heracles in Art
In Greek Art. Heracles is the most popular hero in Greek art, appearing on many vases and in many architectural contexts. He kills Nessus on one of the earliest Athenian vases with a mythological narrative (the Nessus vase in Athens, ca. 620 B.C.), and there are representations of all his Labors and parerga. Especially popular was the Nemean lion. An Attic vase, now in Boston, by the Andocides painter (ca. 530 B.C.) shows Heracles driving a bull to sacrifice, on one side in black-figure technique and on the other in red-figure. From the same period is an Etruscan vase showing Eurystheus jumping into a huge pot to hide from Cerberus, whom Heracles is bringing to him. The struggle with Apollo for the Pythian tripod is shown on several vases, for example, an Attic red-figure vase (ca. 480 B.C., now in Malibu) by the Geras painter.

The canonical representation of the twelve Labors is the twelve metopes in the Temple of Zeus at Olympia (ca. 460 B.C.), in which the local legend of the Augean stables was given pride of place as the final Labor. Heracles appeared on the metopes of the temples at Selinus in Sicily: in one metope (ca. 540) he is carrying the Cercopes slung from his shoulders upside down. His Labors were portrayed in the metopes of the Athenian treasury at Delphi (ca. 490). On the pediment of the temple of Aphaea on the island of Aegina (ca. 500), he appeared as an archer, probably during his expedition against Troy.

The most famous statue of Heracles from the Roman world is the so-called Farnese Hercules (now in Naples), a marble copy by Glycon of a statue by Lysippus (ca. 350 B.C.). Glycon made it specially for the Baths of Caracalla, built at Rome in the early third century A.D. The vast hero leans on his club (draped with the lionskin), weary from his Labors and holding the apples of the Hesperides. A bust of the emperor Commodus (180-192) portrayed him as Hercules, holding the Apples of the Hesperides in his left hand, and the club in his right hand, while the lionskin is fitted over his head. Like the emperor Nero (A.D. 54-68), Commodus wished to be identified with the greatest of Greek heroes, and was only prevented from wrestling with a specially prepared lion in the Circus Maximus by his assassination.

In Western Art. Hercules has been equally popular in art since Greek and Roman times, and from the great number of artists who painted the Labors and his other deeds two seventeenth-century painters have been chosen here. Peter Paul Rubens (1577-1640) painted oil-sketches of several scenes from the life of Heracles for the decorations of the Torre della Parada in 1636-1638, some of which were executed by his assistants as oil-paintings after his death. Outstanding is the Apotheosis of Hercules (now in Brussels), which follows the narrative of Ovid. Rubens used Heracles as an allegory of virtue, for example, in the decorations for the ceiling of the Banqueting House in Whitehall, London, where Heracles represents Heroic Virtue Overcoming Discord (the oil-sketch is in Boston), portrayed as the muscular hero violently clubbing the female figure of Discord. Rubens used the allegory of the Choice of Heracles by representing the governor of the Spanish Netherlands, the Cardinal Infante Ferdinand, as Heracles choosing Virtue (representing the Catholic church) over Pleasure: this scene was part of the decorations for Ferdinand's entry into Antwerp in 1635. Thus Heracles was represented by Rubens in mythological narrative, and for the purpose of moral or political allegory. Rubens also painted him as a giant drunkard in The Drunken Heracles (1614, now in Dresden).

The second seventeenth-century painter selected is Francisco Zurbarán (1598-1664), who painted ten Labors of Hercules for the decoration of the Hall of Realms in the Palace of the Buen Retiro in Madrid (1634, now in the Prado). Heracles was especially important in Spain, as the mythical founder of cities and ancestor of many Spanish noble families. Zurbarán chose seven of the Labors and three other scenes from the life of Hercules, including the creation of the Pillars of Heracles and his agony in the flames of Nessus' robe.

CHAPTER 21

Theseus and the Legends of Attica

The legends of Attica fall into three groups:

- Foundation myths and legends of the early kings of Athens.
- The saga of Theseus.
- Legends involving Minos, king of Crete.

FOUNDATION MYTHS AND LEGENDS OF THE EARLY KINGS OF ATHENS

Cecrops. The Athenians said that they were autochthonous ("sprung from the earth"). The first king was CECROPS [se'kropz], or KEKROPS, who was autochthonous and half-serpentine. Attica was called Cecropia after him. The contest between Poseidon and Athena for control of Attica took place in Cecrops' time (see Chapter 6). For Cecrops' daughters, see Erichthonius.

Erichthonius. The second king, ERICHTHONIUS [er-ik-thon'i-us], or ERICHTHONIOS, was also autochthonous and half-serpentine, sprung from the semen of Hephaestus that fell to the ground when Hephaestus tried to violate Athena. Erichthonius was put in a basket and given to the daughters of Cecrops, who ignored the taboo against looking inside the basket. Driven mad, they killed themselves, and Erichthonius was brought up by Athena. He founded the festival of the Panathenaea and set up the wooden statue of Athena on the Acropolis (see Chapter 6).

In another version, the daughters of Cecrops (Aglauros, Herse, and Pandrosos) did not kill themselves. Herse became mother of Cephalus by Hermes. Aglauros, because of her earlier disobedience and because she asked Hermes for gold as a reward for her help in bringing him to Herse, was punished by Athena with insatiable envy. Hermes turned her into a rock.

Erechtheus. The third king was ERECHTHEUS [e-rek'the-us]. He was later worshiped at Athens and was closely associated with Poseidon. The ERECHTHEUM [e-rek-the'um], or ERECHTHEION, was a temple on the Acropolis dedicated to him and to Athena Polias (i.e., Athena as guardian of the city). It contained the wooden statue of Athena set up by Erichthonius and the olive tree and salt sea produced in the contest of Poseidon and Athena. It also housed the tomb of Erechtheus.

Erechtheus defended Athens against Eumolpus, son of Poseidon and king of Eleusis. To secure the victory he sacrificed his daughter (sometimes called Chthonia). Erechtheus killed Eumolpus and was himself killed by a blow from Poseidon's trident.

Creusa and Ion. In his drama Ion, Euripides made CREUSA [kre-u'sa], or KREOUSA, a daughter of Erechtheus who survives after all her sisters have been sacrificed to Earth to win the victory. By Apollo she became the mother of ION [i'on], who was rescued from exposure by Hermes and brought up at Delphi. Later he was recognized by Creusa and returned to Athens. He became the ancestor of the Ionic tribes of Athens and the Greek colonies in Ionia. Ion is the eponym of the four Ionic tribes of the early Athenian political organization. Euripides is critical of Apollo's violation of Creusa in his drama Ion.

Cephalus and Procris. CEPHALUS [se'fa-lus], or KEPHALOS, the son of Hermes and Herse (Cecrops' daughter), married PROCRIS [pro'kris], or PROKRIS, a daughter of Erechtheus. He was a hunter loved by Eos, goddess of the dawn. In disguise he seduced his wife, and she fled, becoming a follower of Artemis. When she returned to Cephalus, Artemis gave her a hound, Laelaps, that always caught its prey, and a javelin that never missed its mark. (The hound chased a fox that could not be caught and finally both were turned into stone.) Later Procris secretly watched Cephalus as he rested in the forest from hunting. When he called on the breeze (Latin <u>aura</u>) to cool him, she thought he was calling on the Dawn (<u>Aurora</u> in Latin) and moved. Cephalus threw the javelin into the bushes where he had seen the movement and killed his wife.

Orithyia and Boreas and Their Children. Another daughter of Erechtheus was ORITHYIA [or-i-thi'ya], or OREITHYIA. By BOREAS [bor'e-as], the North Wind, she was the mother of ZETES [ze'tez] and CALAÏS [ka'la-is], or KALAÏS, (who were winged), and of Cleopatra and Chione. Cleopatra married Phineus, king of Thrace (see Chapter 22), and Chione, her daughter by Poseidon, was the mother of Eumolpus, the king of Eleusis against whom Erechtheus fought (see above).

Pandion. The fourth king was PANDION [pan-di'on]. Pandion was driven out of Athens by Metion. His four sons recovered the throne, and eventually Aegeus ruled as the fifth king of Athens, while his brother Nisus ruled at Megara.

Philomela and Procne. Pandion was the father of PHILOMELA [fil-o-me'la] and PROCNE [prok'ne], or PROKNE. Procne went to Thrace as wife of TEREUS [ter'e-us], and her son was ITYS [it'is]. When Philomela visited her sister, Tereus raped her, cut out her tongue, and shut her up in a hut in the forest. Procne discovered the truth and revenged herself on Tereus by killing Itys and serving him to his father to eat. She was turned into a swallow, Philomela into a nightingale, and Tereus into a hoopoe. (For the Greeks, Procne became the nightingale and Philomela the swallow.)

THE SAGA OF THESEUS

AEGEUS [e'je-us], or AIGEUS, son of Pandion and king of Athens, was father of Theseus by AETHRA [e'thra], or AITHRA, daughter of Pittheus, king of TROEZEN [tre'son], or TROIZEN, where Theseus spent his childhood. Aegeus left a sword and pair of sandals under a rock as tokens by which he could recognize his son. When he was strong enough to lift the rock, Theseus recovered the tokens and set out for Athens.

The Labors of Theseus. On his journey from Troezen to Athens, Theseus performed six labors.

1. He killed a son of Hephaestus, PERIPHETES [per-i-fe'tez], also called Corynetes ("CLUB-MAN") from the club that was his weapon.
2. He killed SINIS [si'nis], also called Pityocamptes ("PINEBENDER"), by tying him to two bent trees which he then released; this had been the way in which Sinis killed his victims.
3. He killed the monstrous SOW of Crommyon.
4. He killed SCIRON [ski'ron], or SKIRON, who kicked travelers on the narrow path on the sea-cliffs into the sea, where a huge turtle devoured them. Theseus killed him in the same way.
5. He wrestled to the death with CERCYON [ser'si-on], or KERKYON, at Eleusis.
6. He killed PROCRUSTES [pro-krus'tez], or PROKRUSTES ("the STRETCHER"), who would kill travelers by making them lie on a bed. He would hammer out those who were too short, until they fit the bed, and he would shorten with a saw those who were too long. Theseus killed him by his own methods.

Theseus and Aegeus. Theseus arrived at Athens and was almost poisoned by Aegeus on the advice of Medea (see Chapter 22). Aegeus recognized him in time by the sword that he had left in Troezen and made him his successor. Pallas (brother of Aegeus) and his sons disputed Theseus' claim to the throne, and many of them were killed by Theseus.

The Bull of Marathon. Theseus caught the bull of Marathon and sacrificed it at Athens to Apollo. On his way to Marathon he was entertained by HECALE [hek'a-le], or HEKALE, and after her death, on his orders, she was honored at the annual festival of Zeus Hecalus.

Theseus Kills the Minotaur. Theseus' most important myth is the killing of the MINOTAUR [min'o-tawr], the monstrous son of MINOS [mi'nos] and PASIPHAE [pa-sif'a-e], which was shut up in the Labyrinth in the palace of Minos at CNOSSUS [knos'sus], or KNOSSOS. While visiting Athens, Androgeos, son of Minos, was killed by the Athenians, and Minos attacked Athens and her ally Megara, in a war of revenge. As a result the Athenians agreed to send fourteen girls and boys every seven years to be devoured by the Minotaur, and Theseus volunteered to go. On the voyage to Crete, Minos challenged Theseus to prove that he was the son of Poseidon by recovering a ring that he threw into the sea. Theseus jumped into the sea and came to the palace of Amphitrite, the wife of Poseidon, who gave him a robe and a wreath (and, presumably, the ring).

Theseus and Ariadne. At Cnossus Theseus was helped by ARIADNE [ar-i-ad'ne], who some say gave Theseus the wreath to illuminate the Labyrinth, but others say gave him a thread by which to find his way out of the Labyrinth. Thus Theseus slew the Minotaur and emerged from the Labyrinth. He sailed from Crete with Ariadne, whom he deserted on the island of NAXOS [nak'sos], also called Dia. She was rescued by Dionysus, who took her wreath and set it in the heavens as the constellation Corona, making Ariadne his wife (see Chapter 11).

Theseus, King of Athens. Theseus sailed from Naxos to Delos, where he danced the Crane dance (a traditional dance at Delos with labyrinthine movements). From Delos he sailed to Athens, forgetting to change his sails from black to white, the signal to Aegeus that he had been successful. When Aegeus saw the black sails, he threw himself into the sea, which was thenceforth called the Aegean Sea, and Theseus became king of Athens.

Theseus and the Amazons. Theseus joined Heracles in his ninth labor (see Chapter 20) and fought the Amazons, bringing back with him the Amazon queen HIPPOLYTA [hip-pol'i-ta] (or, others say, ANTIOPE [an-ti'o-pe]), by whom he became the father of Hippolytus (see Chapter 8). He defended Athens from an attack by the Amazons during which Hippolyta (or Antiope) died.

Other Adventures. Theseus took part in the Argonauts' expedition (see Chapter 22) and the Calydonian boar-hunt (see Chapter 23).

Theseus and Phaedra. At some time after his encounter with the Amazons and the birth of Hippolytus, Theseus married PHAEDRA [fe'dra], or PHAIDRA, daughter of Minos and sister of Ariadne (see Chapter 8).

Theseus' Friendship with Pirithoüs. PIRITHOÜS [pi-rith'os], or PIRITHOÖS, son of Ixion and king of the Thessalian Lapiths, was Theseus' friend. Theseus attended the marriage feast of

Pirithoüs and Hippodamia and fought against the drunken centaurs (see Chapter 23). They later decided each to take a wife worthy of their divine ancestry. Together they seized Helen for Theseus.

Theseus and Helen.   While Theseus was away in the Underworld, he left Helen with his mother, Aethra, in the Attic village of Aphidnae. The Dioscuri, Helen's brothers, rescued her and took Aethra back to Sparta as Helen's slave. She went with Helen to Troy.

Theseus and Pirithoüs in the Underworld.   After seizing Helen, the two friends descended to the Underworld to seize Persephone for Pirithoüs. There Hades imprisoned them on magic chairs; Heracles set Theseus free during his twelfth labor, but Pirithoüs was left in the house of Hades forever.

Theseus the Protector.   Theseus protected Oedipus in his old age and was present at his "translation" at Colonus. He championed the mothers and widows of the Seven against Thebes (see Chapter 15), and he offered a refuge at Athens to Heracles after he had murdered his wife and children (see Chapter 20).

Theseus' Death and Successors.   He was driven out of Athens by the usurper Menestheus and went to the island of Scyros, where King Lycomedes probably killed him. Demophon, son of Theseus, succeeded Menestheus as king and rescued his grandmother, Aethra, at the fall of Troy. He gave refuge to Alcmena, mother of Heracles, and helped the Heraclidae (see Chapter 20).

The last king of Athens was Codrus, who gave up his life to bring victory to Athens.

THE LEGENDS OF MINOS

Minos was the son of Europa and Zeus (see Chapter 15), and much of his legend has been told above.

Minos and Scylla.   In his war against Athens and Megara because of the murder of his son Androgeos, he attacked Megara. SCYLLA [sil'la], or SKYLLA, daughter of Nisus, king of Megara, betrayed her father out of love for Minos, by cutting off a magic purple lock from his head. Rejected by Minos, she clung to his ship as he sailed away and was turned into a seabird, the <u>ciris</u>.

Daedalus, Pasiphaë, and the Minotaur.   The Athenian craftsman and inventor DAEDALUS [de'da-lus], or DAIDALOS, fled from Athens to Crete after he had hurled PERDIX [per'diks], the inventor of the saw, off the Acropolis. Perdix was turned into a partridge.

Minos had kept a bull, sent from the sea by Poseidon, for himself instead of sacrificing it to the god as he had vowed. Poseidon caused PASIPHAË [pa-sif'a-e] to fall in love with the bull, and Daedalus built a hollow wooden cow, into which Pasiphaë climbed to mate with the bull. From this union came the MINOTAUR [min'o-tawr], which was shut up in the Labyrinth, built by Daedalus.

Daedalus and Icarus.   Daedalus escaped from Crete by flying with the aid of wings that he invented for himself and his son, ICARUS [ik'a-rus], or IKAROS. Icarus, flying too near the sun, fell into the sea, but Daedalus came to Sicily, where he was protected by King Cocalus. The story of Daedalus and Icarus is similar in its motifs to that of Phaëthon (Chapter 1).

The Death of Minos.   Minos followed him to Sicily and there was killed by the daughters of Cocalus. As son of Zeus he became a judge in the Underworld.

The Children of Minos. Of the children of Minos, Ariadne and Phaedra have been mentioned. His son Catreus was associated with Rhodes, where he was worshiped as a hero. Another son, Deucalion, was the father of the Trojan war hero Idomeneus (see Chapters 17 and 18). A third son, GLAUCUS [glaw'kus], or GLAUKOS, was miraculously brought back to life (after falling into a vat of honey) by the seer Polyidus. The death of the fourth son, Androgeos, has already been mentioned.

COMPACT DISCS

4. Babbitt, Milton, <u>Philomel</u>, for soprano, recorded soprano, and synthesized sound. Text by John Hollander. Philomel flees through the woods, is transformed into a nightingale, and sings an "Echo Song."

41. Carter, Elliott, The <u>Minotaur</u>. Score for a ballet, choreographed by Balanchine, which tells the story of Pasiphaë and Theseus and Ariadne.

74. "Flight of Icarus." Rock song.

107. Handel, George Frideric, <u>Teseo</u>. Opera about Theseus, Medea, and Aegeus.

111. Harrison, Lou, <u>Ariadne</u>. The score, for flute and percussion, is in two sections: "Ariadne Abandoned" and "The Triumph of Ariadne and Dionysos."

116. Haydn, Franz Joseph, <u>Arianna a Naxos</u>. Cantata for soprano and keyboard.

121. Hoffmann, E. T. A. <u>Aurora</u>. Opera based on the legend of Cephalus and Procris.

131. "Icarus." New Age music that has become the theme of the Consort of Paul Winter, whose concerns are with nature and ecology. Cf. his <u>Missa Gaia</u>. See Chapter 1, Compact Discs.

132. "Icarus Ascending." Rock song.

133. "Icarus—Borne on the Wings of Steel." Rock song.

145. Lazarof, Henri, <u>Icarus (Second Concerto for Orchestra)</u>. Inspired by Houston's NASA program and parallels between the modern quest to conquer space and the classical legend.

165. Martinu, Bohuslav, <u>Ariane</u>. Based on the play <u>Le Voyage de Thésée</u>, by Neveux, comprising the entire Theseus and Ariadne episode.

172. Menotti, Gian Carlo, <u>Errand into the Maze</u>. Music for the ballet. See Video, Graham, below.

176. Milhaud, Darius, <u>Trois Opéras-Minute: L'Enlèvement d'Europe</u>, <u>L'Abandon d'Ariane</u>, <u>La Délivrance de Thésée</u>. The second of these very short operas is about Dionysus' rescue of Ariadne, abandoned by Theseus.

181 and **140.** Monteverdi, Claudio, "Lamento d'Arianna." There is more than one version of this aria by Monteverdi himself (M/L 596). Other treatments of Ariadne's lament are by Severo Bonini, Francesco Antonio Costa, Claudio Pari, Francesco Maria Rascarini, and Antonio il Verso.

226. Rameau, Jean-Philippe, <u>Les Boréades</u>. Opera about Alphisa, Queen of Bactria, in love with Abaris, son of Apollo and descendant of Boreas, who plays a significant role.

242. Roussel, Albert, <u>Bacchus et Ariane</u>. Music for a ballet about Theseus, Ariadne, and Bacchus, which ends with a bacchanale.

267. Strauss, Richard, <u>Ariadne auf Naxos</u>. Operatic masterpiece that depicts the abandoned Ariadne redeemed by Bacchus (M/L 601). See Videos.

VIDEOS

<u>Ariadne auf Naxos</u>. Opera by Richard Strauss, starring Jessye Norman. Metropolitan Opera Orchestra, cond. James Levine. Bel Canto Paramount Home Video.

Errand into the Maze. Ballet, Martha Graham, choreographer. Graham describes the work: "There is an errand into the maze of the heart's darkness in order to do battle with the Creature of Fear. There is the accomplishment of the errand, the instant of triumph, and the emergence from the dark." Martha Graham: Three Contemporary Classics (includes both Errand into the Maze and Cave of the Heart). Martha Graham Dance Company. VAI Video Arts International 69030. Dance Horizons Video.

Minoan Civilization. Films for the Humanities. AGU3289. Historical and archaeological survey that may be brought to bear upon the legend of Theseus and the Minotaur. Lost City of the Aegean (AGU5012) presents a closer look at Thera (Santorini).

INTERPRETATION

History and Legend. Theseus of all the legendary heroes has the strongest claim to being a real person. He very likely was a king of Athens in the eighth century B.C. But profound historical and chronological problems arise when we try to understand how he also appears as the great conqueror of the Minotaur in the much earlier Mycenaean Age, and a king of Athens who also has serious claims to reality. Were there two Theseuses or only one, around whom all the stories clustered? Some scholars question the traditional dates established for the dark age that descended upon Greece after the fall of the Mycenaean kingdoms, ca. 1100 to ca. 800 B.C.; on the basis of comparative studies, they would eliminate this dark age altogether or at least place the chronology of the Mycenaean kings of Athens much closer in time to the chronology of the later historical monarchy, thus making one historical Theseus more comprehensible.

The excavations of Sir Arthur Evans at Cnossus in Crete seem to confirm details of the saga in Minoan Mycenaean times. For one thing, the elaborate palace and its complexity of levels and rooms suggest a labyrinth (for the history and the archaeology of the Minoan and Mycenaean period, see M/L Introduction).

An entertaining novel retelling the life of Theseus in a very compelling fashion is The King Must Die, by Mary Renault, who is exceptional in her ability to make classical mythology and legend come alive (Robert Graves is another so gifted, with his novel Hercules My Shipmate). Renault has a firm grasp of both the ancient sources and modern archaeology, and by her sensitive art she is able to recreate the civilization and the characters in a most exciting and convincing manner. Dominant is the overriding motif of Theseus caught in the archetypal battle between matriarchy and patriarchy. This young and inspiring hero could never be the victim of the archaic and horrifying ritual by which the king must die to insure the fertility and dominance of the earth mother.

Thematic Motifs. In the saga of Theseus we meet many familiar themes and motifs, which we need not repeat again. We must, however, identify characteristics of this Athenian legend which have not yet been identified.

- Since many (certainly not all) of its elements are late and deliberately modeled on the adventures of other heroes, such as Heracles, one can sometimes detect an undercurrent of tongue-in-cheek, sophisticated amusement, e.g., in the whole aura of the telling of Theseus' own labors.

- Heroes do not always finish in a blaze of glory. Theseus ends his life miserably as an exile, and the accounts of his death seem uncertain, suggesting that he slipped and fell off the highest cliff in Scyros or was pushed by Lycomedes.

Since Jason (the hero of the next chapter) illustrates this gloomy motif even more clearly, we need to anticipate some of the details of his life. Jason's heroism is far too dependant on Medea, who overcomes the dragon and wins for him the golden fleece. He fails to regain his rightful kingdom upon his return, and it is as a has-been that he tries to win power and success through marriage into the royal family of Corinth. Jason's death is most unheroic and ignoble. As the scorned Medea triumphantly predicts, he will die struck by a piece from the Argo, the ship of his former glory.

- In the case of Jason particularly, whose achievements are sometimes extremely dubious, we must add to the list the motif of the hero with feet of clay.

- Medea is a powerful example of the abandoned heroine who was once vital for the hero's success, but Ariadne, deserted by Theseus after she has saved him, also illustrates this important theme. A hero does not always live happily ever after with his princess; see below.

The Early Kings of Athens. Snakes symbolize chthonic cults. Therefore the autochthonous kings are partly in the form of snakes. Rubens shows Erichthonius with snakes for legs in his painting The Discovery of the Infant Erichthonius (1616, now in Vaduz). An Athenian red-figure vase (ca. 400 B.C., now in Richmond, Va.) shows Gaia giving the baby to Athena. In this painting, Hermes, Hephaestus, Zeus, and Hera look on, and Athena's owl and the figure of Nike hover above.

The legends of the early kings attempt to give a rational account of the early stages of the community of Athens, before the *synoecism* (see below) of Theseus. They also explain the succession of Athena to Poseidon as divine protector of Athens.

The kings Erichthonius, Erechtheus, and Aegeus are all forms of Poseidon who were eventually subordinated to Athena. The struggle between Athena and Poseidon was the subject of the sculptures of the west pediment of the Parthenon (see Chapter 6). The sacrifice of the daughter of Erechtheus was the central event in Euripides' tragedy Erechtheus (of which only fragments survive).

The Daughters of Cecrops. The names of the daughters of Cecrops mean "Bright" (Aglauros), "Dew" (Herse), and "All-dewy" (Pandrosos), showing that they were fertility divinities originally. The Cave of Aglauros was a large fissure deep in the north side of the Acropolis, and at its bottom was a spring of water. The young girls who were Athena's servants and carried sacred objects to the sanctuary of Aphrodite below the Acropolis, as part of the ritual of the Arrephoria, went by way of an ancient stairway cut into the cave.

Cephalus and Procris. Ovid's narrative in Book 8 of the Metamorphoses is a romantic tale of the love of Cephalus and Procris and her tragic death. It has many folktale motifs: a mortal loved by a goddess; the magic hound and javelin; mistaken identities; tragic death. Poussin's beautiful painting of Aurora and Cephalus (ca. 1630, now in London) shows the young mortal rejecting the advances of Aurora (Eos) as he gazes at a portrait of Procris.

Philomela and Procne. Ovid narrates the myth of Procne in Book 6 of the Metamorphoses. Rubens's painting The Banquet of Tereus (1638, now in Madrid) dramatically portrays the moment when Procne shows Tereus the head of Itys. Many poets have focused on the tragedy of Philomela and have used the nightingale's song as a symbol of grief. T. S. Eliot includes a painting of the metamorphosis of Philomela in his satirical description of the room in "A Game of Chess," in Part 2 of The Waste Land (1922).

Theseus. Theseus is like Heracles in the range of his deeds, but he is the local hero of Athens and Attica, not the hero of all Greece. He is closely connected with the Athenian community and its city, whereas Heracles could not fit easily into any community. They were honored together in the sculptures of the Hephaesteum (formerly called the Theseum, ca. 445 B.C.), which is still well preserved and overlooks the Agora in Athens. Eight of the eighteen metopes showed the deeds of Theseus, the frieze showed his battles (precisely which ones is not certain), and the west pediment showed the battle between the Lapiths and the Centaurs on the mountain (not the battle at the wedding-feast).

Theseus was credited with the political organization of Attica (the so-called *synoecism*, or "living together"), a historical event whose date is unknown. Theseus became an important political symbol at Athens in the early fifth century B.C., the time when the poet Bacchylides wrote two dithyrambs in his honor (ca. 475 B.C.) and the political leader Cimon claimed to have discovered the hero's bones on Scyros and brought them back to Athens, to be reburied in a shrine in the center of the city. An important source for the legends of Theseus is the Life of Theseus by Plutarch (ca. A.D. 100), in which myth is presented as history. Since Plutarch was interested in the moral excellence (or defects) of the people whose biographies he wrote, the relationship between myth and historical fact is not as distant as it would be for a modern biographer.

From ca. 470 B.C. is a red-figure vase painting by the Sabouroff painter of Theseus lifting the rock to find the objects left by Aegeus. Around this time also, the cycle of the deeds of Theseus (that is, the six labors he performed on his journey from Troezen to Athens) was often represented on circular cups (*kylikes*) and vases. More than twenty survive of this type, which is well represented by one in the British Museum (ca. 475 B.C.). In the center Theseus drags the dead Minotaur out of the Labyrinth; around are the six deeds, which are also painted on the outside of the kylix. The Sow of Crommyon is shown rather than Periphetes, who does not enter the cycle until after 475. A beautiful red-figure painting by Onesimus (ca. 500 B.C.) shows the boyish Theseus under the sea (he is supported by the hands of a tiny Triton) being given Amphitrite's wreath, just as Bacchylides relates the story. Between the boy and the goddess stands Athena.

The Slaying of the Minotaur. The slaying of the Minotaur is shown on the circular vase paintings, mentioned above, of the labors. On a black-figure vase (about 540 B.C., now in London) Theseus is shown as an older and bearded man plunging his sword into the Minotaur as two women and two men look on. Theseus has not had the popularity of Heracles in post-classical art, but the Minotaur of G. F. Watts (1885, now in London) evokes both the pathos and the grotesqueness of the monster. Picasso was fascinated by the Minotaur, which occurs repeatedly in his work. Representative is the drawing of Death of a Monster (in a private collection in London), done in 1937, eight months after the atrocity of the bombing of Guernica in the Spanish Civil War. As the monster dies, pierced by an arrow, he sees himself in a mirror held up by a sea-goddess, perhaps Amphitrite. Most persistent has been the psychological archetype of the labyrinth, or maze, with the terrifying monster within (see Errand into the Maze, Videos, above).

Theseus, Ariadne, and Dionysus. On the François Vase (ca. 575 B.C.), Theseus and the fourteen Athenian girls and boys whom he had rescued perform the Crane Dance at Delos in front of Ariadne. In other versions he leaves her on Naxos before going to Delos. The desertion of Ariadne on Naxos is the subject of a huge number of works. For the red-figure vase by the Syleus painter (ca.

470 B.C.) and for Titian's painting of <u>Bacchus and Ariadne</u>, see Chapter 11. Roman poets focused on the emotions of Ariadne before the coming of Dionysus: Catullus tells the story in Poem 64, and Ovid narrated it three times (in the <u>Heroides</u>, <u>Ars Amatoria</u>, and <u>Metamorphoses</u>). A fine painting is that by John Vanderlyn, <u>Ariadne Asleep on the Island of Naxos</u> (1814, now in Philadelphia), in which the sleeping Ariadne dominates the foreground and Theseus is setting sail in the background. For the allegorical importance of the waking of Ariadne to the coming of Dionysus, see Chapter 11.

The theme of the abandoned Ariadne has become an important motif in music (see Compact Discs and Videos above). The early treatment by Monteverdi became very popular and still is to this day; his "Lamento d'Arianna" is all that survives from his complete opera <u>Arianna</u>; and many are the laments that have followed through the ages. A particularly moving variation appears in Richard Strauss's opera <u>Ariadne auf Naxos</u> (libretto by Hugo von Hofmannsthal). In her aria of desolation, "Es gibt ein Reich," Ariadne longs for death and awaits the arrival of the beautiful god Hermes, who will free her from her pain and bring her to the serene and pure kingdom of death. It is Bacchus, however, and not Hermes, who will save her as he declares his love in a thrilling final duet.

Battle between the Greeks and the Amazons. Battles between Greeks and Amazons are very common in Greek and in post-classical art, but it is not always clear whether the battles of Heracles or Theseus are being portrayed. From the west pediment of the temple of Apollo at Eretria, in Euboea, a group survives of Theseus carrying Antiope into his chariot (ca. 500 B.C., now in Chalkis, Euboea), and battles with the Amazons (Amazonomachies) were shown on the shield of Athena in the Parthenon (see Chapter 6), on the throne of the statue of Zeus at Olympia (see Chapter 3), on paintings (now lost) in the Stoa Poikile and in the sanctuary of Theseus at Athens, and (possibly) on the frieze of the temple of Hephaestus at Athens. Battles with Amazons were still being carved on sarcophagus-reliefs under the Roman Empire, for example, showing Trojan War heroes fighting the Amazons (ca. A.D. 180, now in Paris). From post-classical art the painting by Rubens <u>Battle of the Amazons</u> (1615, now in Munich) continues the tradition: here the battle is being fought on a bridge, and Theseus is prominent at the center.

Theseus and Pirithoüs. Theseus is a central figure in the battle with the centaurs at the wedding feast of Pirithoüs. The battle was painted on the François Vase (ca. 575 B.C.), on which Theseus is named. He wields an ax on a red-figure vase (ca. 450, now in New York), and the battle was the subject of the metopes on the Parthenon and of the reliefs on the sandals of the statue of Athena Parthenos (see Chapter 6), and on the west pediment of the temple of Zeus at Olympia (see Chapters 3 and 9). Ovid's narrative in Book 12 of the <u>Metamorphoses</u> is the most complete (and ingenious), and it was illustrated in a vigorous oil-sketch by Rubens of <u>The Abduction of Hippodamia</u> (1636, now in Brussels). The abduction of Helen is (probably) the subject of a red-figure vase painting by Euthymides (ca. 510 B.C., now in Munich), and Theseus' grandsons, Demophon and Acamas, are shown rescuing their grandmother, Aethra, from Troy in a red-figure vase painting by Myson (ca. 500 B.C., now in London). The imprisonment of Pirithoüs by Hades is shown in a number of Underworld scenes (see Chapter 13), and it is used as an image of inexorable death in Horace's poem celebrating the coming of spring (<u>Odes</u> 4. 7), with its sensitive adaptation by A. E. Housman, <u>Diffugere Nives</u> (published in <u>More Poems</u>, 1936).

Theseus in Literature. Toward the end of the fifth century B.C., several dramas show Theseus (and therefore the Athenians) in the favorable role of protector and champion of the helpless. The masterpiece of this portrayal is Sophocles' last tragedy, <u>Oedipus at Colonus</u> (produced in 401 B.C., five years after the death of Sophocles). He offers refuge to Heracles in the <u>Heracles Furens</u> of Euripides (ca. 423 B.C.) and intervenes to protect the survivors of the Seven against Thebes in the <u>Suppliant Women</u> (ca. 424 B.C.). The portrait of the humane Theseus was further developed in the later Middle Ages and the Renaissance. This Theseus is the hero of Boccaccio's epic in Italian <u>Teseïda</u> (ca. 1340), from which Chaucer developed his character of Theseus in <u>The Knight's Tale</u> (the first of the <u>Canterbury Tales</u>, 1395). Theseus is Duke of Athens, with Hippolyta as his consort, in Shakespeare's <u>Midsummer Night's Dream</u> (1595).

Daedalus and Icarus.   The Cretan myths were summarized by Vergil in Book 6 of the <u>Aeneid</u> (6. 14-33), in a passage describing how Daedalus decorated the doors of the temple of Apollo at Cumae. The Minotaur has been discussed above, and the myth of Phaedra was discussed in Chapter 8. The fall of Icarus was shown on a red-figure vase (ca. 470 B.C., now in New York), and Daedalus is shown making the wings and fitting them on Icarus in Roman marble reliefs of the second century A.D. (now in Rome). The fall of Icarus appears in two extant paintings from Pompeii (mid-first century A.D.), and it was narrated in Book 8 of Ovid's <u>Metamorphoses</u>. Derived from Ovid's narrative is by far the most impressive representation of the myth, the painting by Pieter Brueghel the Elder of <u>The Fall of Icarus</u> (1569, now in Brussels), which is the subject of W. H. Auden's poem <u>Musée des Beaux Arts</u> (1944). Vergil evokes the tragedy of the loss of a son when he describes how Daedalus was unable to finish this part of his story on the doors of the temple of Apollo at Cumae (see above).

CHAPTER 22
The Argonauts

SAGA AND FOLKTALE

The saga of the ARGONAUTS [ar'go-nots] concerns the quest for the Golden Fleece by Jason and the crew of the ARGO, who included many of the leading Greek heroes from the age before the Trojan War. As a group they are sometimes called Minyae, and two cities that claimed to be Minyan were Iolcus (in Thessaly) and Miletus (in Ionia), which was especially active in founding colonies in the Euxine (Black Sea) area, the setting for the quest. Themes in the saga also common to folktale are as follows:

- The mysterious land, Aea (a Greek word for land), at the edge of the world, and its king, Aeëtes ("land-man").
- The hero and his quest for a prize; the series of impossible tasks performed with magic or supernatural help.
- The winning by the hero of a princess as his bride.

THE GOLDEN FLEECE

ATHAMAS [ath'a-mas] of Thebes married NEPHELE [nef'e-le] ("Cloud"), who bore him PHRIXUS [frik'sus], or PHRIXOS, and HELLE [hel'le] and then returned to the sky. Athamas then married INO [i'no], daughter of Cadmus (see Chapter 15), who out of jealousy of her stepchildren caused a famine and, after Delphi had been consulted, plotted to have Athamas sacrifice Phrixus to end the famine. At the moment of sacrifice, Nephele caught up Phrixus and Helle and set them on a ram with a golden fleece, the gift of Hermes, which carried them eastward through the heavens. Helle fell off into the straits between Europe and Asia, thenceforth called Hellespont ("Helle's Sea"), while Phrixus continued to Colchis, at the eastern end of the Black Sea. Here he was received by King AEËTES [e-e'tez], son of Helius and brother of Circe and Pasiphaë, who give him his daughter Chalciope as wife.

Phrixus sacrificed the ram to Zeus Phyxius (Zeus, god of escape) and gave the golden fleece to Aeëtes. It was hung in a grove sacred to Ares and guarded by a serpent.

JASON AND PELIAS

Cretheus (brother of Athamas) was king of Iolcus. His son and successor, AESON [e'son], or AISON, was deposed by his stepson PELIAS [pel'i'as], son of Poseidon and Tyro. Aeson's son, JASON [ja'-son], or IASON, was sent to the hills to be educated by the centaur CHIRON [ki'ron], and after twenty years returned to Iolcus to reclaim his family's throne.

On his journey back Jason carried an old woman across the river Anaurus, losing a shoe during the crossing. She was the goddess Hera, who thereafter favored Jason.

Pelias was warned by the Delphic oracle to beware of a man with one shoe. As the price for giving up the throne he ordered Jason to fetch him the Golden Fleece, an impossible task that he thought would get rid of Jason.

THE VOYAGE OF THE ARGONAUTS TO COLCHIS

The <u>Argo</u> [ar′go] was the first ship, built by ARGUS [ar′gus], or ARGOS (son of Arestor), with the help of Athena. In its bow was a piece of wood from the sacred grove of Zeus at Dodona that had the power of speech.

Its crew (usually fifty in number) included the best Greek heroes: Jason, the leader, Augeas, Theseus, Meleager, Peleus, Telamon, Nauplius, Orpheus, and Heracles. Many were fathers of Trojan War heroes, while others had special skills: Idmon and Mopsus were seers; Castor and Polydeuces were, respectively, a horseman and a boxer; Lynceus had special powers of sight; Zetes and Calaïs (sons of Boreas) were winged; Argus was the shipwright, and Tiphys the helmsman.

Hypsipyle and the Lemnian Women. They sailed to Lemnos, where the women, under Queen HYPSIPYLE [hip-sip′i-le], had killed every male except for THOAS [tho′as], father of Hypsipyle. She put him in a chest, in which he floated to the land of the Tauri (i.e., southern Russia). The Argonauts stayed for a year and fathered many children. After their departure Hypsipyle was driven by the other women from the island, because of her deception in saving Thoas, and she came eventually to Nemea, where she had a role in the saga of the Seven against Thebes (see Chapter 15).

Heracles and the Argonauts. The Argonauts sailed to CYZICUS [siz′i-kus], or KYZIKOS, where Heracles killed the earthborn giants (Gegeneis) who lived nearby. In a night-battle they mistakenly killed King Cyzicus (after whom the city was named). At their next landfall, Cios, Heracles left in search of his companion HYLAS [hi′las] and the <u>Argo</u> sailed on without him (see Chapter 20).

Polydeuces and Amycus. Coming to the Bebryces (on the Euxine coast), POLYDEUCES, or POLYDEUKES (POLLUX), boxed against their king, AMYCUS [am′i-kus], or AMYKOS, and killed him.

Phineus and the Harpies. At Salmydessus they were received by the blind king PHINEUS [fin′e-us], who was tormented by the Harpies ("snatchers"), winged monsters who snatched away his food and fouled what was left. ZETES [ze′tez] and CALAÏS [ka′la-is], or KALAÏS, pursued them to the Strophades ("turn-around") Islands, where the Harpies swore never to harass Phineus again.

The Clashing Rocks. Next were the SYMPLEGADES [sim-pleg′a-dez], "clashing rocks," between which nothing had ever passed. Forewarned by Phineus, Jason sent a dove between the rocks: as they parted after trying to crush the dove, the Argonauts rowed furiously through the gap, and the rocks were fixed ever after.

Further along the Euxine coast Idmon was killed by a boar, and Tiphys, the helmsman, died. His place was taken by Ancaeus. The Argo sailed past the land of the Amazons and the land of the Chalybes ("iron-workers") to the Island of Ares.

The Stymphalian Birds. They frightened away the STYMPHALIAN [stim-fa′li-an] Birds, which had settled on the Island of Ares after being driven out of Greece by Heracles in his sixth Labor. Here they took on board the four sons of Phrixus (who had been shipwrecked) and sailed on to the river Phasis, on whose banks was Colchis.

JASON AT COLCHIS

Aeëtes set Jason a series of impossible tasks before he would let him take the Golden Fleece. He was to yoke a pair of brazen-footed, fire-breathing bulls (the gift of Hephaestus to Aeëtes) and plow a field. In the furrows he was to sow dragon's teeth and kill the armed men who would spring up from the teeth. Helped by Medea, daughter of Aeëtes, Jason performed these tasks and took the fleece.

Medea. A priestess of Hecate, MEDEA [me-de'a], or MEDEIA, was as skilled in magic as her aunt, Circe. Hera and Aphrodite made her fall in love with Jason, to whom she gave a magic ointment to protect him from fire and iron, and drugs to tranquilize the serpent that guarded the fleece.

Euripides makes Medea kill the dragon, so that she may claim that she, not Jason, is the dragon-slayer; on a vase by Douris (ca. 470 B.C.), Jason is swallowed by the dragon and disgorged, while Athena looks on.

THE RETURN OF THE ARGONAUTS

The Argonauts set sail with the fleece and the princess, pursued by the Colchians. Their leader, APSYRTUS [ap-sir'tus], or APSYRTOS, brother of Medea, was killed on land by Jason: some say that Medea killed him on the Argo and threw him piecemeal into the sea to delay the pursuers.

The Return Route. Pindar has the Argonauts sail by the River of Ocean (i.e., at the edge of the world) to the "Red Sea," then to Lemnos, and so home.

In the Argonautica of Apollonius, the Argonauts sail from the Euxine up the Danube, across to the Adriatic, up the Eridanus (a mythical river sometimes identified with the Po), and across to the Rhone, down which they sailed to the Mediterranean.

The Phaeacians. In this version, they confronted many of the dangers later faced by Odysseus (see Chapter 18) and came to the land of the PHAEACIANS [fe-a'shi-anz], or PHAIAKIANS. Here they appealed to Queen Arete for protection from the Colchians, and the king, Alcinoüs, promised not to give Medea up if she and Jason were already married. There they celebrated the marriage and the Colchians gave up the pursuit.

The Argonauts sailed to Libya and were stranded on the Syrtes (shoals off the Libyan coast). They carried the Argo on their shoulders for twelve days to Lake Tritonis (Mopsus died in the desert) and from there made their way back to the sea.

Talus. Continuing their voyage, they killed the bronze giant TALUS [ta'lus], or TALOS, who guarded the island of Crete, by opening a vein above one of his ankles, through which his life-supporting ichor (the divine equivalent of blood) leaked out.

Jason and Pelias. Finally they sailed back to Iolcus. Jason handed over the fleece to Pelias and dedicated the Argo to Poseidon at the Isthmus of Corinth. But Pelias refused to give up his throne to Aeson, Jason's father, as he had promised.

Medea and the Daughters of Pelias. Medea tricked the daughters of Pelias into trying to rejuvenate him by cutting him up and boiling him in a cauldron. They only succeeded in killing him. For this murder Medea and Jason were driven out of Iolcus and went to Corinth.

JASON AND MEDEA IN CORINTH

Aeëtes had originally been king of Ephyra (an early name of Corinth), which he left to go to Colchis. In the original version of the saga, the Corinthians sent for his daughter Medea to be their queen, and through her Jason became king of Corinth. She was favored by Hera, in whose sanctuary her children (by Jason) died and were honored with a cult.

In another version, the king of Corinth was CREON [kre'on], or KREON. He was killed by Medea, who left her children in the sanctuary of Hera, where they were murdered by Creon's family, after Medea had fled to Athens.

Euripides' Medea. In Euripides' tragedy Medea, Jason divorces Medea so that he can marry Creon's daughter GLAUCE [Glaw'se], or GLAUKE (also called CREUSA [kre-u'sa], or KREOUSA), and Creon orders Medea to leave Corinth. Medea sent her children with gifts for Glauce — a robe and a crown smeared with magic ointment that burned Glauce and Creon to death. Medea then killed the children as a final revenge on Jason. She escaped to Athens (where King AEGEUS [e'je-us], or AIGEUS, had promised to receive her) in a chariot drawn by winged dragons and sent by her grandfather, Helius. Jason lived on in Corinth, where he died, struck by a piece of wood that fell from the Argo.

Medea in Athens. At Athens Medea failed to trick Aegeus into poisoning his son Theseus (who had been one of the Argonauts), and she fled to Persia. There Medus, her son by Aegeus, founded the kingdom of Media. Medea herself returned to Colchis.

COMPACT DISCS

11. Barber, Samuel, Medea and Medea's Meditation and Dance of Vengeance. Orchestral suites from the original score for the ballet Cave of the Heart. See Videos.
23. Blitzstein, Marc, The Harpies. An operatic treatment of the Argonauts' encounter with Phineus and the Harpies that satirizes opera, employs pop music, and allegorizes criticism of the Great Depression.
34. Caldara, Antonio, Medea in Corinto. Cantata for alto solo and orchestra.
47. Cavalli, Francesco, Giasone. Opera.
51. Charpentier, Marc-Antoine, Médée. Opera.
53. Cherubini, Luigi, Medea. A superb operatic treatment and a wonderful vehicle for great singing-actresses such as Maria Callas and Magda Olivero.
57. Clerambault, Louis-Nicolas, Médée. Cantata for voice and orchestra.
169. Mayr, Giovanni Simone, Medea in Corinto. Opera.

VIDEOS

Cave of the Heart. Ballet. Martha Graham, choreographer, music by Samuel Barber, with designs by Isamu Noguchi. Original title, Serpent Heart. Barber notes that both he and Graham did not wish to make a literal use of the legend; the mythical Medea and Jason "served rather to project psychological states of jealousy and vengeance which are timeless." Martha Graham: <u>Three Contemporary Classics</u> (includes both <u>Cave of the Heart</u> and <u>Errand into the Maze</u>). Martha Graham Dance Company. VAI Video Arts International. 69030.

<u>A Dream of Passion</u>. A harrowing modern version of Medea, which includes scenes from Euripides. Starring Melina Mercouri and Ellen Burstyn and written and directed by Jules Dassin (M/L 610). Avco Embassy Pictures Release. Charter Entertainment 90179.

<u>Jason and the Argonauts</u>. Justly admired movie, particularly for its special effects by Ray Harryhausen, but marred by the performance of a Medea weakened by the screenplay. Starring Todd Armstrong and directed by Don Chaffey. RCA/Columbia Pictures Home Video 60025.

<u>The Jason Voyage: The Quest for the Golden Fleece</u>. Films for the Humanities AGU4293. A contemporary retracing of the voyage of the Argo in a replica of a Bronze Age twenty-oar galley.

<u>Medea</u>. A powerful film by Pier Paolo Pasolini, not to be missed for the dramatic (non-singing) performance of the renowned Maria Callas. In Italian with English subtitles (M/L 609-10). Video Arts International VAI-17.

<u>Medea</u>. Euripides' play performed in ancient Greek with English subtitles. The New York Greek Drama Company, Box 3113, Hartford, N.Y. 12838. A provocative experiment not for everyone (M/L 610).

<u>Medea</u>. A splendid, free adaptation of Euripides' play by the American poet Robinson Jeffers, except for the ending, which disappointingly and needlessly strives for realism by eliminating the chariot sent by Helius, so essential for the plot and its meaning. Starring Judith Anderson (for whom Jeffers wrote the play). Ivy Classics Video, also Insight Media DP421; starring Zoe Caldwell, with Judith Anderson as the nurse. Films for the Humanities ADS 748. The most recent London stage presentation with Diana Rigg as a superb Medea is perhaps best of all; it does not seem to be on film (M/L 610).

<u>Medea</u>. Ballet. Georgiy Aleksidze, choreographer, music by Gabichvadze. Russian cast. Kultur 1114.

INTERPRETATION

The Development of the Saga. The original saga (which included many folktale elements) was Jason's quest for the Golden Fleece, his success in performing impossible tasks, his winning of the prize and of a princess for his wife, and finally, his return home.

The hero's bride, Medea, was unusual in that she was powerful because she was the granddaughter of the Sun (Helius) and knew magic. She takes the role of the divine helper found in other sagas and folktales. Only the fifth century (B.C.) vase-painting by Douris (mentioned above) shows a divine helper, Athena, rather than Medea.

Medea's love for Jason is an addition to the original saga. The theme of her hatred for Jason and her revenge was developed by Euripides. Yet he retained her original character as the granddaughter of the Sun by introducing the dragon-drawn flying chariot.

The original locations of the saga were Thessaly and the Euxine. Many geographical features cannot be identified, for they are for the most part mysterious places on the far edges of the world, as in the typical quest stories. As Greek cities were founded in the Euxine, and as Greek traders sailed ever further from Greece, the Argonauts were said to have journeyed to many more places known to the Greeks than in the original saga.

Corinth became involved in the saga because of Aeëtes' connection with Ephyra (the archaic name for Corinth). Its connection with Medea was made by the epic poet Eumelos (eighth century B.C.). The cult of the dead children predated the legend that they were killed by Creon's family. Euripides made Medea their killer, and he also brought Aegeus into the saga so as to provide Medea with a place of refuge in Athens after the murder.

The Legend in Literature. The <u>Argo</u> was known to Homer, who calls it "all men's concern," and the gathering of the Argonauts was prominent in the fourth <u>Pythian Ode</u> of Pindar (462 B.C.), who focuses on the *arete* (excellence) of the heroes. Euripides' tragedy <u>Medea</u> (431 B.C.) powerfully explores the tension between Jason and Medea and creates an unforgettable psychological portrait of Medea. Euripides' drama has decisively influenced subsequent interpretations of Medea's part in the saga, for example, in the work of Ovid (43 B.C.-A.D. 17), whose <u>Medea</u> was much admired in antiquity but is not extant; Seneca (d. A.D. 65), whose <u>Medea</u> does survive; and the American poet Robinson Jeffers (1946), whose <u>Medea</u> is an adaptation of Euripides' play (see Videos). The Medea theme also appears in Jeffers's poetic narrative <u>Solstice</u>. Ovid also composed a letter from Hypsipyle to Jason (No. 6) and from Medea to Jason (No. 12) in his <u>Heroides</u>. He focused on Medea's magic powers in Book 7 of his <u>Metamorphoses</u> 2. 2. The saga has been the subject of several epic poems. In the eighth century B.C. the Corinthian poet Eumelos told of the connection between Corinth (which he calls Ephyra) and the family of Medea. Apollonius of Rhodes (ca. 260 B.C.), who worked at Alexandria, revived Greek epic with his <u>Argonautica</u>, written in Homeric meter and with many features of Homeric epic style. His epic is the single most important source for the saga, although his focus on the romantic relationship of Jason and Medea is extraneous to the original legend. In the first century B.C., the Roman poet Varro of Atax translated Apollonius' epic. In the last part of the first century A.D., Valerius Flaccus also adapted Apollonius in his <u>Argonautica</u>, which is an important example of Roman epic, although it is unfinished, and the extant poem ends with the early part of the voyage from Colchis.

In the nineteenth century, Jason enjoyed a revival in England and the United States. Episodes from his saga were brilliantly narrated by Nathaniel Hawthorne in <u>Tanglewood Tales</u> (1853) and by Charles Kingsley in <u>The Heroes</u> (1855). In these tales the authors focused on Jason's courage and boldness, moral virtues to be emulated by their young readers. In 1867 William Morris published his seventeen-book epic <u>The Life and Death of Jason</u>. Morris was influenced by his ideas of medieval chivalry, and his Jason is a less ambiguous hero than the Jason of Apollonius and Euripides. In other countries also, most notably France and Germany, there were several authors who wrote dramas based on the saga.

It is unfortunate that a collection of plays about Medea with related essays is out of print: <u>Medea, Myth, and Dramatic Form</u>, edited by James L. Sanderson and Everett Zimmerman (Boston: Houghton Mifflin, 1967). It contains the works of Euripides, Seneca, and Jeffers noted above, as well as Jean Anouilh's <u>Medea</u> (1946) and Maxwell Anderson's <u>The Wingless Victory</u> (1936), a muted version of the myth.

The Legend in Art. Episodes from the saga appear fairly frequently on Greek vases, and mention has already been made of the vase by Douris (ca. 470 B.C., now in Rome), which is the only source for Jason's being swallowed by the dragon. At the end of the fifth century B.C., a vase (now in Cleveland) by the Policoro painter depicted the final scene of Euripides' Medea, showing Medea leaving Corinth in her chariot, which is framed in the rays of the sun; Jason remonstrates below, while the dead children lie on an altar. The Etruscan bronze urn known as the Ficoroni Cista (late fourth century B.C., now in Rome) is incised with the scene of the defeat of Amycus in boxing by Polydeuces.

Among the many representations of Jason's deeds, the oil-sketch by Peter Paul Rubens (ca. 1636, now in Brussels) of Jason Taking the Golden Fleece is remarkable. A century later (1746) the French artist J. F. de Troy designed a series of tapestries on The History of Jason; the scene of Jason Swearing Eternal Fidelity to Medea (now in London) is a distinguished example of the many works that are based on the romantic embellishments of Apollonius. In recent times, Euripides' Medea has especially fascinated artists. The threatening power of the foreign princess is conveyed in Eduardo Paolozzi's Medea (1964; now in Otterlo), an abstract metal sculpture of machinelike aluminum parts welded together.

CHAPTER 23
Myths of Local Heros and Heroines

Many legends are associated with local heroes and heroines, often in conjunction with a local hero-cult. Some legends attracted folktale elements and spread beyond their original region. Others owe their fame to the quality of a literary narrative, for example, Ovid's story of Pyramus and Thisbe. The myths in this chapter are arranged by region.

CENTRAL GREECE: THESSALY, PHTHIA, AND TRACHIS

Ixion and Centaurus. IXION [ik-si'on], king of the Thessalian Lapiths, was the first mortal to murder a relative when he lured his wife's father, EIONEUS [i-yo'ne-us], to his death. Only Zeus could purify him for this unprecedented crime, yet after his purification Ixion attempted to lie with Hera. In her place Zeus put a cloud (Nephele), whose child was the monster Centaurus, from whom descended the race of CENTAURS [sen'tawrs], half-human and half-equine. Ixion was punished in the Underworld (or, in an earlier version, in the sky) bound to the spokes of an ever-revolving wheel (see Chapter 13).

Chiron. Of the Centaurs the most important was CHIRON [ki'ron], whose mother was PHILYRA [fil'i-ra]. He was wise and gentle, skilled in medicine and music, and he taught these arts and others to a number of heroes, including Achilles and Jason. Chiron was immortal and could not end by death the intolerable pain of the wound he received from the arrow of Heracles (see Chapter 20). He exchanged his immortality with Prometheus, dying in place of Prometheus when he was released by Heracles (see Chapter 2).

The Wedding of Pirithoüs and Hippodamia. The other Centaurs were more violent. At the wedding feast of the Lapith prince PIRITHOÜS [pi-rith'o-us], or PIRITHOÖS and HIPPODAMIA [hippo-da-me'a] or [hip-po-da-mi'a], or HIPPODAMEIA, they attempted to carry off the bride and the other Lapith women. They were prevented after a brutal battle with the Lapiths and their human guests (including the Athenian hero Theseus).

Caeneus. During this battle the Centaurs killed the Lapith CAENEUS [SE'NE-US], or KAINEUS, burying him under a pile of tree-trunks. He had originally been a girl, CAENIS, who had been seduced by Poseidon and had been turned by him (at her request) into a man, invulnerable to weapons or to seduction and rape.

Peleus and His Wedding with Thetis. The leading hero of Phthia (a region to the south of Thessaly) was PELEUS [pe'le-us], son of Aeacus (king of Aegina) and brother of Telamon (father of Ajax). He left Aegina because he had killed a half brother and was purified by Eurytion, king of Phthia, whom he later killed accidentally during the Calydonian boar-hunt (see below). Driven out once more for murder, he came to Iolcus, where he was purified by King ACASTUS [a-kas'tus], or AKASTOS, whose queen, ASTYDAMIA [as-ti-da-me'a] or [as-ti-da-mi'a], or ASTYDAMEIA, fell in love with him. When he refused her, she accused him before Acastus of trying to seduce her. Acastus took him hunting on Mt. Pelion and abandoned him there asleep, after hiding his sword in a pile of dung. When he awoke, Chiron saved him from the attacks of wild animals and Centaurs and returned the sword to him.

Zeus gave the sea-goddess THETIS [the'tis] to Peleus as wife (see Chapter 5), and all the Olympian gods and goddesses came to the wedding feast on Mt. Pelion. Not invited was Eris (Discord), who still came, bringing the apple that led to the judgment of Paris and eventually to the Trojan War (see Chapter 17). Peleus and Thetis returned to Phthia, where their son, Achilles, was born. Soon afterward Thetis returned to the sea.

In the Iliad Peleus is mentioned as a lonely old man back in Phthia, but in Euripides' play Andromache he appears at Delphi after the Trojan War, defending Andromache from Orestes and Hermione (see Chapter 16). At the end of the Andromache, Thetis appears and prophesies that Peleus will be immortal and will be reunited with her.

Salmoneus. The Thessalian hero SALMONEUS [sal-mon'e-us], son of Aeolus, is associated with Elis, where he founded Salmone. He tried to imitate Zeus and demanded that he be honored as a god, for which Zeus killed him with his thunderbolt and hurled him into eternal punishment in the Underworld.

Ceyx and Alcyone. CEYX [SE'IKS], or KEYX, king of Trachis, and ALCYONE [al-si'on-e], or ALKYONE (daughter of Aeolus), called themselves Zeus and Hera and were punished by being turned into seabirds. Ovid is more romantic: in his story Ceyx was drowned during a sea-voyage and told Alcyone of his death in a dream. She found his corpse on the seashore and in grief changed into a seabird (the mythical *halcyon* is sometimes identified with a kingfisher), while Ceyx came to life also as a seabird (perhaps a tern). When the halcyon sits on her eggs afloat on the sea, her father, Aeolus, forbids the winds to blow.

Tyro. The daughter of Salmoneus was TYRO [ti'ro], who was seduced by Poseidon in the form of a river-god, Enipeus. Their twin sons were Neleus, founder of Pylos and father of Nestor (see chapter 20), and Pelias, king of Iolcus and father of Acastus.

Tyro later married Cretheus, founder of Iolcus. Their sons were Aeson, father of Jason (see Chapter 22), Pheres, father of Admetus and founder of Pherae, and Amythaon, father of Bias and Melampus. Admetus won Alcestis as wife by harnessing a lion and a boar to a chariot: for her loss and recovery from Death (Thanatos) by Heracles see Chapters 9 and 20.

Melampus and Bias. MELAMPUS [me-lam'pus], or MELAMPOS, was a seer, who also understood the language of animals. He helped his brother BIAS [bi'as] win PERO [pe'ro], daughter of Neleus, as bride by winning for him the cattle of PHYLACUS [fi'la-kus], or PHYLAKOS, a Phthian prince, as a reward for telling Phylacus how to cure the impotence of his son IPHICLUS [if'ik-lus] or IPHIKLOS. Before that he had been put in prison by Phylacus, whom he warned of the imminent collapse of the prison through hearing the conversation of two woodworms who were gnawing through the roof-beams.

Melampus introduced the worship of Dionysus to Greece, according to Herodotus. The daughters of King PROETUS [pro-e'tus], or PROETOS, of Tiryns were driven mad when they resisted Dionysus, killing their children and rushing around the countryside. Melampus cured them and was rewarded with half of Proetus' kingdom, ruling at Argos. His great-grandson was Amphiaraüs, one of the Seven against Thebes (see Chapter 15).

BOEOTIA

The principal myths of Boeotia are the Theban sagas (see Chapter 15).

The Daughters of Minyas. At Orchomenus the daughters of King MINYAS [min'i-as] refused to join in the worship of Dionysus, who drove them mad. They tore apart HIPPASUS [hip'pa-sus], or HIPPASOS, the son of Leucippe, and were turned into bats.

The Loves of Helius. Another daughter of Minyas, CLYMENE [kli'me-ne], had five husbands. By Helius (the sun) she was the mother of Phaëthon (see Chapter 1), by Pheres the mother of Admetus, and by Iasus the mother of Atalanta.

Besides the Boeotian Clymene, Helius loved the eastern princess LEUCOTHOË (lu-ko'tho-e], or LEUKOTHOE, whose father, Orchamus, buried her alive. Helius shed drops of nectar over her body, from which the frankincense tree grew. Orchamus' informer was CLYTIE [kli'ti-e] or [kli'shi-e], or KLYTIE, daughter of Oceanus and Tethys, who herself loved Helius. He would not forgive her for betraying Leucothoë, and with her eyes she followed his progress across the heavens until she turned into a sunflower, or heliotrope (Greek for "turning toward the sun").

Trophonius and Agamedes. At Lebadeia was the shrine and cult of the Boeotian hero TROPHO-NIUS [tro-fo'ni-us], or TROPHONIOS. He and his brother AGAMEDES [a-ga-me'dez] built trea-suries for the kings Augeas (in Elis) and Hyrieus (in Boeotia). In one of these they included a mov-able stone, which they used to enter the treasury and steal treasure. When Agamedes was caught in a trap inside, Trophonius cut off his head and escaped. He fled to Lebadeia and there was swallowed up by the earth. Pindar says that the brothers built the temple of Apollo at Delphi and were reward-ed by the god's gift of eternal sleep.

AETOLIA

Aetolia lies in the southwestern part of the Greek mainland, bordered on the west by the River Acheloüs and on the south by the Gulf of Corinth. Its principal city in mythology is Calydon, which lies on the River Evenus. For the struggle of Heracles with the river-god Acheloüs for Deïanira, which took place near Calydon, and for his killing of Nessus at the River Evenus, see Chapter 20.

The Calydonian Boar Hunt. The founder of Calydon was Oeneus, father of MELEAGER [mel-e-aj'er], Deïanira, and Tydeus and grandfather of the Trojan War hero Diomedes. He forgot to sacrifice to Artemis, who sent a huge boar to ravage the land at the time of a war between the CALYDO-NIANS [kal-i-do'ni-anz], or KALYDONIANS, and the CURETES [ku-re'tez], or KURETES.

According to Homer, Meleager's mother, ALTHAEA [al-the'a], or ALTHAIA, cursed her son because he had killed her brother, and in anger he withdrew from the war against the Curetes. He returned to fight because of the entreaties of his wife, CLEOPATRA [kle-o-pa'tra], or KLEOPATRA, and drove the Curetes back from the city, yet still was not given his promised reward by the Calydonians. Presumably he died because of Althaea's curse.

According to Bacchylides (ca. 475 B.C.), Meleager killed Althaea's brothers accidentally in battle, and she brought about his death by burning a log that contained his *Moira* (allotted portion of life), which the Moirai (Fates) had advised her to snatch from the fire at his birth and keep in a chest. As the log burned, Meleager's life ebbed away.

Many heroes took part in the Calydonian boar hunt, which was led by Meleager. According to Ovid, Meleager killed the boar and gave its skin to ATALANTA [at-a-lan'ta], daughter of Schoeneus, who had first wounded it with her spear. When Althaea's brothers protested, Meleager killed them. In anger, Althaea burned the log, and Meleager died. Later Althaea and Cleopatra hanged themselves, and the women who mourned for Meleager were turned into guinea-fowl (meleagrides).

Atalanta. Atalanta is shown on the François vase (ca. 575 B.C.), marching to the hunt beside Milanion, while Euripides, in his Phoenissae (411 B.C.), mentions her as an archer.

Another Atalanta is the daughter of the Arcadian hero Iasus. Nurtured by wild animals, she, too, was a huntress. Ovid says that the suitor who could win a foot-race against her would win her as wife. Those who lost were killed. After many suitors had failed, MILANION [mi-lan'i-on], also called HIPPOMENES [hip-po'me-nez], dropped three golden apples (the gift to him of Aphrodite) one by one during his race, which he won because Atalanta stopped to pick each one up.

CORINTH

The Corinthian poet Eumelos (eighth century B.C.) identified "Ephyra" with Corinth, which was originally a minor city subject to Argos. He named the two principal Corinthian heroes, Sisyphus and his grandson Bellerophon.

Sisyphus. SISYPHUS [sis'i-fus], or SISYPHOS, son of Aeolus, came from Thessaly. Either he founded Corinth or it was founded by Aeëtes, and Sisyphus became its king after Medea had left (see Chapter 22). He founded the Isthmian Games in honor of MELICERTES [mel-i-ser'tez], or MELIKERTES, son of his brother ATHAMAS [a'tha-mas] and INO [i'no]. The child's body had come to shore at the Isthmus after Ino had leaped into the sea with him in her arms (see Chapter 11). Mother and son became sea-gods, respectively, LEUCOTHEA [lu-ko-the'a], or LEUKOTHEA, and PALAEMON [pa-le'mon], or PALAIMON.

Sisyphus stole the cattle of the master-thief Autolycus, whose friend he became. In one version of his myth, he seduced the daughter of Autolycus, Anticlea, before she married Laertes, and was the father of Odysseus.

Sisyphus outwitted THANATOS [than'a-tos], "Death," whom Zeus had sent to carry him off because he had told the river-god Asopus that Zeus was seducing the river-god's daughter AEGINA [e-ji'na], or AIGINA. First Sisyphus chained Thanatos, so that no mortals could die. After Ares had freed Thanatos, Sisyphus had to go to the Underworld, but first he told his wife, Merope, not to offer sacrifices for the dead. Hades sent Sisyphus back to tell Merope to offer the sacrifices, but Sisyphus stayed on in Corinth until he died at an advanced age.

Sisyphus was punished in the Underworld for revealing the secret of Zeus' love for Aegina by having to push a huge rock uphill endlessly only to have it roll down again.

Bellerophon. BELLEROPHON [be-ler'o-fon] was the grandson of Sisyphus. He left Corinth to go to Tiryns, where STHENEBOEA [sthen-e-be'a], or STHENEBOIA (also called Antea), wife of King PROETUS [pro-e'tus] or PROETOS, fell in love with him. When he rejected her, she told Proetus that he had tried to seduce her. Proetus sent him to the king of Lycia, IOBATES [i-ob'a-tez], with a sealed letter instructing Iobates to kill him.

Iobates set Bellerophon various tasks: first to kill the CHIMAERA [ki-mi'ra] or CHIMAIRA, a fire-breathing monster that was part lion, part serpent, part goat. Then he had to fight the Solymi, a tribe of violent warriors, and then the Amazons. After this Iobates set an ambush for Bellerophon, who killed all his attackers. Iobates then gave Bellerophon his daughter as wife and half of his kingdom. He was the father of Hippolochus, whose son was the Trojan war hero Glaucus, and of Laodamia, who by Zeus became the mother of Sarpedon (see Chapter 17) and of a second son, Isandrus.

Bellerophon ended his days "hated by men" (says Homer) and wandering alone. Later authors (Pindar and Euripides) associate him with the winged horse Pegasus (for whose birth see Chapter 19), the gift of Poseidon. At Corinth Athena gave him a magic bridle with which to master Pegasus, with whose help he performed the tasks for Iobates.

Bellerophon then returned to Tiryns and punished Stheneboea by luring her onto Pegasus and throwing her off as they flew over the sea. Eventually he tried to fly up to Olympus itself and fell to his death in the sea.

Arion of Lesbos. ARION [a-ri'on] was honored at Corinth, where he was favored by the tyrant (i.e., ruler) Periander (ca. 600 B.C.). He was the inventor of several kinds of Greek music and poetry, among them the dithyramb [dith'i-ramb], the ritual choral song sung in honor of Dionysus. Arion may be historical, but his myth is not. The crew of a ship carrying him from Italy to Corinth threw him overboard after he had sung a final song for them. He was saved by a dolphin, which brought him safely to the sanctuary of Poseidon at Cape Taenarum, whence he made his way back to Corinth.

OTHER PELOPONNESIAN LEGENDS

Arethusa. The river-god ALPHEUS [al-fe'us], or ALPHEIOS (the chief river of the Peloponnese), pursued the nymph ARETHUSA [ar-e-thu'sa]. She prayed to Artemis to save her and was turned into a stream which flowed underground and under the sea, emerging at Syracuse (in Sicily) as the fountain Arethusa, where it is still called by that name.

Iamus. Evadne, daughter of Poseidon and Pitane, became by Apollo the mother of IAMUS [i-am'us], or IAMOS, whom she left on the bank of the Alpheus. He was fed on honey by two serpents and brought up by the Arcadian hero Aepytus. When he was grown, Poseidon and Apollo brought him to Olympia, where he received the gift of prophecy and established an oracle associated with the altar of Zeus. Iamus appears as a seer in the sculptures of the east pediment of the Temple of Zeus at Olympia (ca. 460 B.C.), and he was the mythical ancestor of the Iamids, the hereditary prophets at Olympia.

THE AEGEAN ISLANDS

Delos. This island was sacred to Apollo (see Chapter 9). A son of Apollo, Anius, ruled the island and had three daughters, Elaïs (olive-girl), Spermo (seed-girl), and Oeno (wine-girl), to whom

Dionysus gave the power of producing olive oil, grain, and wine. He turned them into doves when they tried to resist being forced by Agamemnon to go to Troy.

Samothrace. At Samothrace the CABIRI [ka-bi'ri], or KABIROI, were worshiped as <u>theoi megaloi</u> ("great gods") with an ancient and important mystery cult that was active as late as the fourth century A.D.

Ceos. On Ceos CYPARISSUS [si-par-is'sus], or KYPARISSOS, was loved by Apollo. Grieving for the death of a favorite stag (which he had accidentally killed), he was turned into a tree, the cypress, henceforth associated with mourning and burial.

Also on Ceos CYDIPPE [si-dip'e], or KYDIPPE, was loved by ACONTIUS [a-kon'ti-us], or AKONTIOS, who left an apple for her to pick up inscribed with the words: "I swear before Artemis only to marry Acontius." She bound herself by reading the words out loud and eventually married Acontius.

Rhodes. This island was sacred to HELIUS [he'li-us], or HELIOS, the Sun. Zeus loved the eponymous nymph of the island, RHODE [ro'de], whose three grandsons were the founding eponymous heroes of the island's three principal cities, Camirus, Ialysus, and Lindos. Each October the Rhodians threw a chariot and four horses into the sea as a replacement for Helius' team, worn out by the labors of the summer.

Lindos. The temple of Athena at Lindos was founded by the Egyptian hero, Danaüs (see Chapter 19). The Rhodian contingent in the Trojan War was led by a son of Heracles, Tlepolemus, who wounded Sarpedon. The TELCHINES [tel' kin-ez], skilled metalworkers, lived at Rhodes and were drowned by Zeus because (says Ovid) they could ruin everything by their evil eye. But they were originally pre-Olympian beings associated with the sea who nurtured the infant Poseidon.

Lesbos. The founder of the kingdom of Lesbos was MACAREUS [ma-kar'e-us], or MAKAREUS, son of Aeolus, who committed incest with his sister Canace. Aeolus killed their baby and forced CANACE (kan'a-se], or KANAKE, to kill herself. Macareus also killed himself.

Cyprus. Aphrodite was worshiped especially at Paphos on the island of Cyprus, founded by its eponymous hero Paphos. (For the myth of his father, Pygmalion, see Chapter 7.) In Cyprian Salamis lived ANAXARETE [a-na-xar'e-te], who scorned her lover, IPHIS [i'fis], and showed no pity even when he hanged himself before the door of her house. As she watched his funeral procession pass she was turned into stone and became the cult-statue of Aphrodite at Salamis, called in Latin <u>Venus Prospiciens</u> (Venus the Watcher).

Crete. On Crete lived another IPHIS, daughter of Ligdus and Telethusa. Her mother disobeyed the order of Ligdus to expose the baby girl and deceived him by dressing Iphis as a boy, whom Ligdus betrothed to IANTHE [i-an'the]. Telethusa prayed to Isis to pity the lovers, and the goddess turned Iphis into a boy, and he and Ianthe were married.

ASIA MINOR

The Greek cities on the Aegean and Black Sea coasts of Asia Minor absorbed many non-Greek legends, several of which have been included in classical mythology because they were narrated by Ovid.

The Troad. DARDANUS [dar'da-nus], or DARDANOS, was the son of Zeus and Electra (daughter of Atlas). He came to the Troad and there married the daughter of King TEUCER [tu'ser], or TEUK-ER (son of the river-god Scamander). He ruled over the land, which he called Dardania, and was the ancestor of the Trojan royal family. In the Trojan saga the Trojans are called both Dardani and Teucri.

Sestos (European) and Abydos (Asiatic). These are two cities on the shores of the Hellespont. LEANDER [le-an'der] of Abydos loved HERO [he'ro], priestess of Aphrodite at Sestos, swimming the straits each night to visit her. One night a storm put out the light that she placed in a tower to guide him. He drowned, and when Hero discovered his body washed up on the shore, she fell to her death from the tower.

Phrygia. BAUCIS [baw'kis], or BAUKIS, and his wife PHILEMON [fi-le'mon] were a pious Phrygian couple who unwittingly entertained Zeus and Hermes in their cottage. The gods rewarded them by saving them from the flood with which they punished the other Phrygians for their lack of hospitality. Their cottage became a temple, of which they were the priests, and their prayer that they be allowed to die together was answered when they simultaneously were turned into trees, an oak and a linden.

Miletus. BYBLIS [bib'lis], daughter of Miletus (eponymous founder of the city of Miletus), revealed her love for her brother CAUNUS [Kaw'nus], or KAUNOS. He fled, followed by Byblis, who out of exhaustion melted into a fountain. Byblis and Thisbe are both the names of fountains in Asia Minor.

Pyramus and Thisbe. THISBE [thiz'be], like Byblis, is the name of a fountain in Asia Minor, and PYRAMUS [pi'ra-mus], or PYRAMOS, is one of the major rivers of Cilicia, although Ovid sets the legend in Babylon. Pyramus and Thisbe were lovers who lived next door to each other but were forbidden by their parents to meet or to marry. They talked through a crack in the party-wall and arranged to meet at the tomb of Ninus outside the city. Thisbe came first and fled when a lioness, her jaws bloody from a recent kill, came to drink at the nearby fountain. She dropped her veil, which the lioness mangled. Later Pyramus recognized the veil lying there and assumed that Thisbe had been killed. He killed himself, just as Thisbe returned to find him dying. She in turn killed herself, and the fruit of the mulberry tree, under which the tragic deaths took place, turned from white to black as a memorial of their deaths.

COMPACT DISCS

28. Britten, Benjamin, "Arethusa," for solo oboe, from <u>Metamorphoses after Ovid</u>. Britten also has an operatic version of Shakespeare's <u>A Midsummer Night's Dream</u> (with the Pyramus and Thisbe scene) which should be added. Several recordings are available.
36. Campra, André, <u>Arion</u>. Cantata for soprano and chamber orchestra.
115. Hasse, Johann Adolf, <u>Piramo e Tisbe</u>. Opera.
141. Lampe, John Frederick, <u>Pyramus and Thisbe</u>. A Mock Opera. The text is taken from Shakespeare.

164. Marais, Marin, <u>Alcyone</u>. Opera inspired by the legend of Alcyone and Ceyx.
228. Rameau, Jean-Philippe, <u>Dardanus</u>. Opera about Dardanus' marriage to the daughter of King Teucer.
234. Ravel, Maurice, <u>Alcyone</u>. Cantata.
282. Uttini, Francesco Antonio, <u>Thétis and Pelée</u>. Opera.

VIDEO

<u>A Midsummer Night's Dream</u>. The movie of Max Reinhardt's production of Shakespeare's play with James Cagney as Pyramus and Joe E. Brown as Thisbe is worth searching out on video. MGM/UA Home Video M202543.

INTERPRETATION

Ixion. Like Tantalus and Bellerophon, Ixion abused his friendship with the gods. His legend has been interpreted as a solar myth (the wheel of fire circling through the heavens), not very convincingly. In art he is usually shown bound to the wheel, and in literature (for example, Book 6 of Vergil's <u>Aeneid</u>) he is one of the sinners who are punished in the Underworld.

Centaurs. Centaurs are very common in Greek art as symbols of uncivilized barbarism. The battle between Centaurs and Lapiths was shown in the west pediment of the Temple of Zeus at Olympia (ca. 460 B.C.) and in the metopes on the south side of the Parthenon at Athens (ca. 440 B.C.). Both sculptural programs celebrated the triumph of Greek civilization over the (supposedly) barbarian Persian empire. They appear in funerary reliefs in Roman times as part of the procession accompanying Dionysus, and they are often introduced in European art as part of a classical landscape. The death of Nessus is shown in one of the earliest of Greek narrative vase paintings on the neck of an Attic amphora (ca. 620 B.C., now in Athens); over two thousand years later the same scene was painted by Guido Reni in his Hercules cycle (1621, originally in Mantua, now in Paris). Chiron, however, is usually shown as a contemplative and peaceful figure, typically in scenes where he receives the young Achilles as his pupil. In the Renaissance, Chiron was used as a symbol of the wise adviser to inexperienced princes; he is so shown in Alciati's <u>Emblemata</u> (first published in 1521) and in the Education of Achilles by Rubens (oil-sketch for a tapestry, 1632, now in Rotterdam). The centaurs, including Chiron, Nessus and Pholus, guard the violent criminals in the twelfth canto of Dante's <u>Inferno</u>.

The Battle of the Centaurs and Lapiths. This battle was narrated by Ovid in Book 12 of the <u>Metamorphoses</u> with great ingenuity and violence; his literary model was the battle in the hall of Odysseus' palace in Book 22 of the <u>Odyssey</u>. Odysseus' great leap at the beginning of that book may have been the source for Peter Paul Rubens' figure of Theseus in his oil-sketch (1636, now in Brussels) and painting (now in Madrid) of the battle of the Centaurs. There is a marble relief by Michelangelo of the <u>Battle of the Centaurs</u> (ca. 1492, still in the artist's house in Florence). Of recent artists, Picasso especially has been attracted by Centaurs, most likely as symbols of lust and animal power.

Peleus and Thetis. The struggle of Peleus and Thetis, in which she changed herself into many different shapes (a snake, a flame, and so on), was popular on Attic vase paintings in the late sixth and early fifth centuries B.C. The wedding procession also was frequently painted, for example, on the François Vase (painted by Kleitias, ca. 575 B.C., now in Florence). The wedding feast is frequently shown by painters of all periods, and it is closely related to scenes of the Banquet of the Gods. The wedding feast is the main theme of Catullus' sixty-fourth poem (ca. 55 B.C.).

Melampus. Among the folklore motifs in the myth of Melampus is his understanding of the language of animals. Like Heracles in his tenth labor (see Chapter 20), he must bring back cattle from a distant place guarded by a dog; his place of imprisonment, Phylace (the Greek word for prison), can be interpreted as a symbol of Hades, so that Melampus also conquers death.

Trophonius and Agamedes. The legend of the clever builder-thieves is also told in Book 2 of Herodotus' Histories, where the king is the Egyptian pharaoh Rhampsinitus (i.e., Rameses). The element *troph-* (the Greek root of words for "growing") in the name Trophonius indicates that he was a chthonic hero, concerned with the growth of crops. The awesome ritual at his oracle included a symbolic descent (*katabasis*) into the Underworld. His cult continued unbroken into the fourth century A.D. The reward of falling asleep in the god's temple at Delphi is similar to the myth of Cleobis and Biton at Argos, related by Herodotus in his first book (see Chapter 4).

Meleager and the Calydonian Boar Hunt. The myth of Meleager is told to Achilles by Phoenix in Book 9 of the Iliad as a parable of relenting from one's anger. Homer mentions the boar, but not the hunt, which is narrated by Ovid in Book 8 of the Metamorphoses. The hunt is shown on the François Vase (ca. 575 B.C.), where many heroes are named (Meleager and Peleus together in the front rank), along with Atalanta. The Calydonian Boar Hunt became an adventure that included the noblest Greek heroes, as with the Trojan Horse and the Argonauts. The theme of the monstrous boar appears also in Book 1 of Herodotus in his narrative of the destiny of Croesus, king of Lydia (see Chapter 4).

Atalanta. Atalanta and Meleager are shown in many paintings of hunting scenes (e.g., Rubens, ca. 1618, now in Vienna). The race between Atalanta and Milanion (Hippomenes) has been even more popular, especially in the nineteenth century (e.g., the poem "Atalanta's Race," by William Morris, 1864, illustrated by Edward Burne-Jones). The race and the metamorphosis of the lovers into lions is narrated in Book 10 of Ovid's Metamorphoses. But they are also said to be the parents of the Argive hero Parthenopaeus, one of the Seven against Thebes (see Chapter 15); hence the device of a boar on his shield in Euripides' Phoenissae (411 B.C.). Euripides also wrote a tragedy Meleager (416 B.C.), which dealt with Meleager's love for Atalanta and his death.

Sisyphus. There are two aspects of the mythical Sisyphus. He is the founder of a city and its religious cults, but he is also a well-known folklore figure, the trickster-thief. In this aspect he outwits Death itself, and he is associated with another trickster-thief, Autolycus, grandfather of the wily Odysseus. Like Ixion, he abused the friendship of the gods by betraying Zeus' secret love for Aegina to her father, and for this he suffered exemplary punishment in the Underworld. The futility of rolling a rock endlessly uphill is the theme of Albert Camus, Le Mythe de Sisyphe: Essai sur L'Absurde (1942; English translation, New York, 1955), in which the mythical hero deliberately takes upon himself the absurdity of life.

Bellerophon. Originally Bellerophon was a hero who had to undertake a journey and complete various tasks in order to win the prize of a wife and a kingdom. The myth has acquired elements common to folktale and other legends; the theme of a false accusation to her husband by a wife, rejected as a lover by the hero, is familiar from the biblical tale of Joseph and Potiphar's wife (Genesis 39) and from the myth of Phaedra and Hippolytus (see chapter 21). The Chimaera is like oriental monsters (and perhaps it was added to the myth of Bellerophon because of his association with Lycia, a district of Asia Minor). It has passed into the English language (along with its adjective, *chimerical*) as something fantastic and unrealizable. Nathaniel Hawthorne tells the story of Bellerophon's taming of Pegasus and their battle with the Chimaera in his <u>Tanglewood Tales</u> (1851); he includes the magic bridle but omits the rest of the myth so as to focus on the youthful courage of the hero.

The story of Bellerophon is narrated by his grandson, Glaucus, to Diomedes in Book 6 of the <u>Iliad</u>; Homer does not mention Pegasus, but he does describe the unhappy ending to the hero's life, and he does narrate the story of Stheneboea, whom he calls Antea. Pindar (ca. 470 B.C.) included Pegasus in his version, along with a divine helper, Athena, and the magic bridle. Like Homer, Pindar alludes to Bellerophon's unhappy end; by trying to enter Olympus he aimed to pass the limits allowed to mortals and suffered the fate of those who aim too high.

The Chimaera is a popular figure in Greek vase-painting, with representations on Corinthian vases from as early as ca. 650 B.C., some of which also show Bellerophon on Pegasus. There is a famous Etruscan bronze Chimaera from Arezzo (perhaps of the fifth century B.C., now in Florence). Other scenes from the myth, notably those involving Stheneboea, appear on later vases, perhaps derived from Euripides' lost tragedy <u>Stheneboea</u>, which included the punishment of Stheneboea. Euripides' <u>Bellerophon</u> (also lost) portrayed the hero trying to enter the heavens.

In later art Pegasus is often (and erroneously) associated with Perseus, particularly in his rescue of Andromeda. Representations of St. George killing the dragon (e.g., by Sodoma, 1518, now in Washington) have a lot in common with the myth of Bellerophon and the Chimaera.

Arion. Arion is both historical and mythological. The historical Arion was a lyric poet from Methymna (in Lesbos), who around 600 B.C. was at the court of Periander of Corinth. He elaborated the *dithyramb* and was also said to have presented the first tragic drama and to have been the first to train a tragic chorus, which he dressed as satyrs to perform his dithyrambs. Thus he is an important figure in the development of Greek tragedy at Corinth. On the other hand, the myth of the dolphin (first told by Herodotus) appears many times in classical literature. Herodotus explains it by referring to a bronze statue of Arion and the dolphin at Cape Taenarum (the southernmost point of the Peloponnese). A more likely explanation, however, is that Arion was protected by the gods, for in the <u>Homeric Hymn to Apollo</u>, Apollo (protector of musicians) appeared in the form of a dolphin, and one of his titles was Apollo Delphinius (see Chapter 9). Arion has inspired comparatively few post-classical works of art: exceptional is François Boucher's painting representing the element of water, <u>Arion Rescued by the Dolphin (Water)</u> (1748, now in Princeton, N. J.).

The Cabiri. Although they do not have a myth, the mystery cult of the Cabiri was one of the oldest and most enduring in the Greek world. The Argonauts were said to have been initiated at Samothrace, and many figures from Greek and Roman history (including Herodotus) followed them. They were also worshiped at Thebes and on Lemnos, and they were associated with the sea and with salvation (both from the sea and in the moral sense). Even the names of the Cabiri (the "Great Gods") are not known, and there were non-Greek elements in the cult and its ritual language. From Samothrace comes one of the most famous of classical Greek statues, the Winged Victory (<u>Nike</u>, ca. 200 B.C., now in Paris), which commemorates a victory by sea, won (one may infer) under the protection of the Cabiri. From the Theban sanctuary of the Cabiri come so-called Cabiric vases of the fourth century B.C., on which burlesques of mythological figures are painted in black: on one vase (now in Oxford), a potbellied Odysseus with a huge phallus propels his raft, which is made of two wineskins, by means of a trident; on the other side of the vase he threatens Circe at her loom.

Hero and Leander. The stories of Cyparissus, Anaxarete, and Iphis (child of Telethusa) are related in Ovid's <u>Metamorphoses,</u> while those of Cydippe, Canace, and Hero are told in his <u>Heroides.</u> Of these, the legend of Hero and Leander has been especially popular with poets and artists in all ages; the story was told by the late Greek poet Musaeus (ca. A.D. 500), and his poem was imitated by Bernardo Tasso (1537) and Christopher Marlowe (1593), whose version was completed by George Chapman (1616). Of many paintings of the myth, that of Peter Paul Rubens is notable (1605, now in New Haven). The legend inspired a large number of musical works and poems in the nineteenth century, while Byron was moved by it to swim from Sestos to Abydos in 1810 and to write a poem on his feat.

Baucis and Philemon. One of Ovid's most famous stories in the <u>Metamorphoses</u> is that of Baucis and Philemon (Book 8). Ovid uses the poor couple as an example of piety rewarded, and their story was especially popular with Dutch and Flemish artists in the seventeenth century: for example, there are paintings by Adam Elsheimer (1609, now in Dresden), Peter Paul Rubens (1625, now in Vienna), and Jacob Jordaens (ca. 1645, versions now in Helsinki and Raleigh, N.C.). There is a beautiful <u>Landscape for Philemon and Baucis</u> by the American painter David Ligare (1984) in Hartford, which is remarkable for its evocation of the legend without the use of human or divine figures. The story was given a strong moral bias by Nathaniel Hawthorne in "The Miraculous Pitcher," one of the tales in <u>A Wonder-Book</u> (1851). A sour interpretation is given by Graham Hough in his poem "The Heavenly Visitors" (1961), in which the gods, "aglow with high Olympian charity," by selfish munificence turn the pious couple's simple life upside down.

Pyramus and Thisbe. Ovid says that his tale of Pyramus and Thisbe is "not well known," but thanks to him it has become one of the best known of all his tales (Book 4 of the <u>Metamorphoses</u>). Among the many poets who have narrated it are Petrarch (1340), Boccaccio (1343), and Chaucer (1386, in <u>The Legende of Goode Women</u>). Best known of all is Shakespeare's double use of it in <u>A Midsummer Night's Dream</u> (1596), where the main plot follows the legend with its lovers' errors and meetings outside the city, while the "Rude Mechanicals" of Act 5 have endeared their hilarious version to audiences in all ages.

The legend has been equally popular in art: a woodcut by the German artist Hans Wechtlin (ca. 1515, now in Cleveland) focuses on both the power and the blindness of love. Among many paintings, those by Lucas Cranach (1525, now in Bamberg) and Edward Burne-Jones (<u>Thisbe</u>, 1861, now in London, and <u>Pyramus and Thisbe</u>, 1876, now in Birkenhead) are representative of different interpretations.

CHAPTER 24

The Nature of Roman Mythology

Roman religion and mythology had their roots among pre-Roman Italian peoples, for example, the Sabines and Etruscans.

Italian gods were not originally anthropomorphic like Greek gods, with whom they became identified: Saturnus (Cronus); Jupiter (Zeus); Juno (Hera); Vesta (Hestia); Minerva (Athena); Ceres (Demeter); Diana (Artemis); Venus (Aphrodite); Mars (Ares); Mercurius (Hermes); Neptunus (Poseidon); Vulcanus (Hephaestus); Liber (Dionysus); Dis Pater (Hades or Pluto). Non-Italian gods whose names changed from the Greek included Hercules (Heracles); Castor and Pollux (Castor and Polydeuces); Aesculapius (Asclepius); Apollo kept the same name at Rome.

ITALIAN GODS

Janus. The god JANUS [ja'nus] was the god of beginnings, associated originally with water and bridges. The doors of his temple were closed only in time of peace. He was also the god of doors, entrances, and archways, and was identified with Portunus, god of harbors. He was portrayed with two faces, one looking forward and one looking backward.

Mars. Originally an agricultural god, MARS [marz] gave his name to March, the first month of the year in the pre-Julian calendar. His consort was Nerio, a Sabine fertility goddess. He became the Roman god of war, sometimes with the title of Gradivus ("the marcher"), and sometimes associated with the Sabine war god, Quirinus. Among other Roman deities of war was Bellona. Animals associated with Mars were the wolf and the woodpecker (*picus* in Latin), said once to have been a Latin king, Picus, who was turned into a bird by Circe, while his wife, Canens ("singer") wasted away into a voice.

Jupiter. The Italian sky-god was JUPITER [ju'pi-ter], whose principal temple was dedicated on the Capitoline Hill at Rome in 509 B.C. There he was worshiped as Jupiter Optimus Maximus (Jupiter, Best and Greatest), and he shared his temple with Minerva and Juno. The *triumphus*, the procession celebrating a Roman general's victories, had this temple as its terminus. Like Zeus, Jupiter had the thunderbolt as his special weapon, and the place where lightning had struck had to be purified by an expiatory ritual. Jupiter caused a shield (*ancile*) to fall from heaven into Rome as a talisman of Roman power. Along with eleven other *ancilia* (made so that there would be less chance of the genuine *ancile* being stolen), it was kept in the Regia, the official quarters of the Pontifex Maximus, the head of Roman state religion. As Jupiter Latiaris, Jupiter was chief god of the Latin tribes, and as the god associated with Fides (Good Faith), he was identified with the Sabine god Dius Fidius, who also was identified with a Latin deity, Semo Sancus. As Jupiter Indiges, Jupiter was worshiped beside the river Numicus, about twenty miles to the south of Rome. The Di Indigetes (the plural of *Indiges*) were a group of gods whose functions are not known, and Aeneas was deified as Indiges after his death beside the Numicus.

Juno. The goddess JUNO [ju'no] originally presided over all aspects of the life of women, particularly marriage (as Juno Pronuba) and childbirth (as Juno Lucina, whose annual festival was the Matronalia). As Juno Moneta ("adviser") she was worshiped on the Arx (part of the Capitoline Hill) with a temple next to the Roman Mint (which was called *ad Monetam*, hence the origin of the word *mint*). As Juno Regina (Queen) she was escorted to Rome from the Etruscan city of Veii on its defeat by the Romans in 396 B.C. Like Hera with Zeus, Juno became the wife and sister of Jupiter in Roman literature, sometimes opposing the will of Jupiter, as in her efforts to prevent the fated success of Aeneas.

Minerva. Also a pre-Roman goddess, MINERVA [mi-ner'va] was brought to Rome by the Etruscans and identified with Athena in her attributes and functions, especially as goddess of activities requiring intelligence. She was patroness of craftspeople and of schoolchildren; her festival was the Quinquatrus.

Vesta. The Italian fire-gods were Vesta, Cacus, and Vulcan. VESTA [ves'ta], the Greek Hestia, was the goddess of the hearth, the center of family life and of the state's life as a community, symbolized by the ever-burning fire in her temple in the Forum of Rome. Her cult was tended by six Vestal Virgins, high officials in the hierarchy of state religion. Other household divinities, along with Vesta, were the PENATES [pe-na'tez], defined as "the gods who are worshiped in the home." The Penates were identified with the household gods of Troy entrusted by Hector's ghost to Aeneas and brought by him to Italy. The Trojan Palladium (see Chapters 6 and 17) was kept in the temple of Vesta; it was said to have been given by Diomedes to the embassy of Aeneas that had sought his help.

Cacus. In Book 8 of the <u>Aeneid</u>, the Italian fire-god CACUS [ka'kus] is made out to be a fire-breathing monster, who stole the Cattle of Geryon from Hercules and was killed by him. The myth identifies his home with a cave on the Aventine Hill, and an ancient pathway leading up to the southwest part of the Palatine Hill was called the *Scalae Caci* ("Ladder of Cacus").

Vulcan. The chief Italian fire-god was VULCAN [vul'can] (Volcanus), originally the god of destructive fire but (through his identification with Hephaestus) also of creative fire. He was more important in the pantheon than Hephaestus was among the Olympians. His forge was beneath Mt. Etna, and his associates (the Cyclopes) and myths are all taken over from the Greek legends of Hephaestus.

Saturn. The leading Italian agricultural gods were Saturn, Mars (discussed above), and Ceres. SATURN [sat'urn] was identified with Cronus, and his consort, Ops, was identified with Rhea. In cult his partner was Lua, and the partner of Ops was Consus (at whose festival, the Consualia, the rape of the Sabine women took place: see below), who presided over grain when it was stored. Saturn was said to have ruled over a Golden Age in the early history of humankind. His festival, the Saturnalia, was a midwinter celebration, perhaps originally connected with the sowing of grain.

Ceres. The Italian goddess of grain, CERES [se'rez], was identified with Demeter. A temple was dedicated to her at Rome in 493 B.C. She was associated with Liber (identified with Dionysus) and Libera (identified with Kore-Persephone), so that the Roman triad of Ceres-Liber-Libera repeated the Eleusinian triad of Demeter-Iacchus/Bacchus-Kore. When the grain was sown in the earth, it was protected by another Italian earth-goddess, Tellus Mater (Earth Mother).

Flora and Pomona. Minor fertility-deities were FLORA [flo'ra] and POMONA [po-mo'na]. Flora was the goddess of the flowering of plants (including grain and the vine), and was said to be the consort of Zephyrus, the West Wind, who gave her a garden filled with flowers and tended by the Horae (the Seasons) and Graces (Greek *Charites*).

Pomona was the goddess of fruit that can be picked from trees, and she kept a garden from which she excluded would-be suitors. The Etruscan god Vertumnus (perhaps "Changer" or "Turner") turned himself into an old woman who advised Pomona to marry Vertumnus. When he resumed his usual form as a young male god, she accepted him.

Pales. The deities (originally two) who protected the farmers' livestock were called PALES [pal'ez], whose name later was used for one deity, male or female. Their festival, the Parilia (or Palilia), was considered to be the anniversary of the founding of Rome.

Silvanus and Faunus. Two divinities of the woods were SILVANUS [sil-va'nus], "Forester," and FAUNUS [faw'nus], "Favorer." In Vergil, Faunus is son of Picus and grandson of Saturn and father (by Marica) of Latinus. Both he and Silvanus were identified with Pan and were thought to be responsible for strange and sudden sounds in the woods. Faunus had oracular powers (both Latinus and the second Roman king, Numa, consulted him), and his consort, Fauna, was identified with the Bona Dea ("Good Goddess"), whose worship was open only to women.

Faunus (as the equivalent of the Arcadian god Pan) was worshiped by King Evander, who came from Arcadia and founded Pallanteum, the first settlement on the Palatine Hill. His sanctuary was a cave on the Palatine, called the Lupercal, where the infant Romulus and Remus were later suckled by the wolf (*lupa*). In historical times young men ran around the boundaries of the Palatine nearly naked, and the barren women whom they struck with leather straps became fertile. They were naked because Faunus had tried to seduce Omphale (see Chapter 20) when she and Hercules were asleep in the Lupercal. He did not know that they had exchanged clothes and found himself attempting to seduce Hercules. After that his followers (the Luperci) went naked to prevent the repetition of such a painful error.

Venus. Originally VENUS [ve'nus] was an Italian fertility goddess, especially the protectress of gardens. Later she was identified with Aphrodite, whose myths she appropriated, and her consort was Mars (although her husband in myth was Vulcan). As mother of Aeneas she became much more important in Roman mythology, a process that culminated in the dedication (A.D. 121) of a temple to Venus Felix ("Bringer of Success") and Roma Aeterna ("Eternal Rome") by the emperor Hadrian. As Venus Cloacina she had a shrine in the Forum beside the drainage system of the area (called the Cloaca); Pompey dedicated a temple to her as Venus Victrix ("Conqueror") as part of his theater, the first permanent stone theater at Rome (55 B.C.). Julius Caesar (46 B.C.) dedicated a temple to her as Venus Genetrix ("Ancestress"), honoring her as the founder of his family, the *gens Iulia*. Her first temple at Rome (215 B.C.) was that of Venus Erycina (i.e., the Venus who was worshiped at Eryx in Sicily).

Priapus. The god PRIAPUS [pri-a'pus] (see Chapter 7) was the principal protector of gardens after the promotion of Venus to the ranks of the major divinities. He was represented by a statue painted red with an erect phallus. Ovid relates (Fasti 1. 415-440) that he tried to seduce the Naiad Lotis and was interrupted by the braying of the donkey of Silenus, which then became the animal sacrificed to Priapus.

Deities of Waters. Besides Janus (see above), the Italian water-gods were the river-gods, the nymphs of springs and fountains, NEPTUNE [nep'tune] (NEPTUNUS), and PORTUNUS [portu'nus]. The most important river-god was TIBERINUS [ti-ber-i'nus], who in Book 8 of the <u>Aeneid</u> appeared in a dream to Aeneas and smoothed his waters so that the Trojans could sail up to Pallanteum. Notable fountain-nymphs were JUTURNA [ju-tur'na] and the CAMENAE [ka-me'ne]. Juturna was the sister of the Rutulian hero Turnus and had been raped by Jupiter. Her shrine was in the Forum and her precinct included the headquarters of the water-administration of Rome. The Camenae (identified with the Muses) were worshiped outside the Porta Capena at Rome. Associated with them were the nymphs EGERIA [e-je'ri-a] and Carmentis [kar-men'tis], both water-divinities associated with childbirth. Egeria was said to have advised King Numa, and Carmentis was said to be the mother of Evander and to have prophetic powers.

Diana. Later identified with Artemis, DIANA [di-a'na] was worshiped at the Latin town of Aricia, near which is Lake Nemi, called "Diana's mirror." She was concerned with the life of women and was sometimes identified with Lucina, the birth-goddess more commonly identified with Juno. Through her identification with Artemis, she became goddess of the hunt and of the moon, and was further identified with Hecate as an Underworld goddess. At Aricia she was associated with a minor Italian deity, Virbius, who was identified with Hippolytus, brought to life again by Aesculapius.

Mercury (Mercurius). The temple of MERCURY [mer'ku-ri], originally a god of trade and profit, was in the commercial center of Rome. Through his identification with Hermes he acquired the attributes, functions, and myths of Hermes.

The Roman Underworld. ORCUS [or'kus] was the Roman Underworld, and its ruler was DIS PATER [dis pa'ter], the equivalent of the Greek Pluto, since *Dis* is a form of *dives*, "wealthy," and in Greek, "wealth" is *ploutos*. His cult was established in 249 B.C., and his consort was PROSERPINA [pro-ser'pi-na], the Greek Persephone. Roman poets inherited the mythology of the Underworld from Homer and other Greek poets and from the philosophers (most notably Plato), and also used the beliefs of the mystery religions, both Greek and oriental (see Chapters 13 and 14). These literary, philosophical, and religious beliefs achieved a majestic synthesis in Book 6 of Vergil's <u>Aeneid</u>. Native Italian ideas of the Underworld originated from the religious beliefs of early agricultural communities. Each person had his or her own *Manes* (spirits of the dead), and epitaphs began with "Sacred to the Manes of. . . ," <u>Dis Manibus Sacrum</u>, followed by the person's name. Spirits of ancestors were honored at the festival of the Parentalia (in February, the last month of the old Roman calendar); the *divi parentum* (gods of the ancestors) had no names and no mythology. Other spirits of the dead were the *Lemures* (identified by some poets with the Manes), who were propitiated in the family festival of the Lemuria in May. The burial goddess was Libitina, and undertakers were called *libitinarii*.

Lares. The LARES [lar'ez] were household spirits, often linked with the PENATES [pe-na'tez], for whom see Vesta, above. They could bring prosperity to the householder (in early times a farmer), and they were honored at the winter festival of the Compitalia, at which dolls were hung up in shrines, one for each member of the household. Each house had its *Lar Compitalis*, and each city had its *Lares praestites* (guardian Lares). The Lares also protected travelers by land and sea.

Genius and Juno. The creative power of a man was symbolized by his *GENIUS* [jen'i-us], and of a woman by her *Juno*. The marriage-bed, symbol of the continuing life of the family, was the *lectus genialis*.

NON-ITALIAN GODS

Hercules (Heracles). The earliest newcomer was HERCULES [her'ku-lez], and his was the only foreign cult that Romulus was said to have accepted at the founding of Rome (see Cacus, above). His precinct was in the busy commercial area of the cattle market (Forum Boarium) and his altar there was the Ara Maxima (Greatest Altar). Like Mercury, he was the patron of traders, to whom they dedicated a tithe of their profits.

The Dioscuri. CASTOR [kas'tor] and POLLUX [pol'luks] (the Latin form of Polydeuces), the DIOSKURI [di-os-ku'ri] appeared on white horses at the battle of Lake Regillus in 496 B.C. and led the Romans to victory, which they announced in the Forum after watering their horses at the fountain of Juturna. Their temple was dedicated in the Forum soon after.

The Sibylline Books. The collection of oracles, written in Greek, known as the SIBYLLINE [si'bi-lin] books were bought, it was said, by the last Roman king, Tarquinius Superbus, from the Cumaean Sibyl herself (see Chapter 9). She burned three of the nine books each time Tarquin refused to pay her price, and he finally bought the last three at the price originally asked for all nine. The Sibylline oracles were kept in the Temple of Jupiter on the Capitoline Hill and were consulted in times of public difficulty. After the original three were burned in a fire in 83 B.C., a new collection was made, which was put in the base of the statue of Apollo in his temple on the Palatine Hill.

Apollo. The first temple of APOLLO [a-pol'lo] at Rome was dedicated in 431 B.C. on the advice of the Sibylline books at a time of pestilence, and he was originally worshiped as Apollo Medicus (the Healer). His other functions were introduced over the next two centuries, and he was especially worshiped by Augustus, the first Roman emperor, who dedicated a temple to him on the Palatine Hill. His functions, name, and mythology were taken over from the Greek Apollo, except that the oracle at Delphi no longer had the importance that it had had in the Greek world, although it continued to exist until the fourth century A.D. Apollo's oracles at Claros and Didyma (both in Asia Minor) were more active under the Roman empire, while the oracle of Apollo's father, Zeus, at Dodona ceased to function early in the period of Roman rule.

Asclepius. The Sibylline books also advised the bringing of ASCLEPIUS [as-kle'pi-us] (in Latin, Aesculapius) to Rome in 293 B.C. He came in the form of a snake, slipping from the ship that brought him from Epidaurus (see Chapter 9) onto the island in the middle of the river Tiber in Rome, where his temple was built.

Cybele and Mystery Religions. The goddess CYBELE [syb'e-le] also came to Rome (where she was called the Magna Mater, Great Mother) on the advice of the Sibylline books. She came in 205 B.C. in the form of a black stone from the Phrygian city of Pessinus, after the Delphic oracle had been consulted. Her temple was dedicated on the Palatine Hill and her festival was the Megalensia. Her priests, called Galli, performed ecstatic and colorful rituals, including self-mutilation, in their public processions (see Chapter 7).

    The Greek, Egyptian, and Asiatic mystery religions were strong in the Roman empire (see Chapter 14). Besides Dionysus and Demeter, Isis, Ma (Dea Syria, the Syrian Goddess), Baal (identified with Jupiter Dolichenus), and Mithras were widely worshiped.

LEGENDS OF THE FOUNDING OF ROME

There were two Roman foundation myths: the earlier (in time) went back to Aeneas, the Trojan prince and survivor of the sack of Troy (see Chapter 17), whose son Iulus founded Alba Longa. The second, precisely dated by the Romans to the equivalent of 753 B.C. (some 475 years after the sack of Troy), was the foundation of Rome itself by Romulus.

Aeneas and the Aeneid. Vergil's epic, Aeneid, narrates the wanderings of its hero AENEAS [e-ne'as], his arrival in Italy, and his battles with the native Italians led by the Rutulian prince TURNUS [tur'nus], whose death in single combat with Aeneas is the end of the epic. The survival of Aeneas was foretold by Poseidon in the Iliad (20. 300-308), and his adventures were part of the tradition among the Etruscans and Romans long before Vergil's time. Constant elements in his myth are the following: his escape from Troy with his father ANCHISES [an-ki'sez] and his son IULUS [jul'us] (ascanius), his wanderings, his arrival in Italy (first narrated by Cato the Elder around 150 B.C.), his battles with the native Italians (called Aborigines), his marriage with the Latin princess LAVINIA [la-vin'i-a] and the founding of Lavinium, his death soon after his victory over the Aborigines, and his deification. Vergil combines the traditional elements of the myth with political, historical, and philosophical insights so as to link the myth to the renewal of Rome by Augustus in his own time (Vergil died in 19 B.C.).

The first part of the Aeneid is set in Carthage, recently founded by DIDO [di'do], where Aeneas was driven by a storm. Aeneas relates the fall of Troy and his wanderings to Thrace, Delos, Crete, Epirus (where he meets Andromache and Helenus), and Sicily (where Anchises dies), before his arrival in Africa. Dido fell deeply in love with Aeneas and killed herself when he left on the orders of Jupiter, transmitted to him by Mercury. Arriving in Italy, Aeneas, guided by the Cumaean Sibyl, visited the Underworld and there consulted with his dead father, Anchises, and saw a vision of the future leaders of Rome (see Chapter 13). After returning from the Underworld, he sailed to the Tiber and there realized that he had reached the end of his wanderings. Here king Latinus betrothed his daughter Lavinia to him on the advice of the oracle of Faunus, even though she was already betrothed to Turnus. With the help of PALLAS [pal'las], son of EVANDER [e-van'der], king of Pallanteum (founded on the future site of Rome), and his followers, Aeneas fought against Turnus and his allies, prominent among whom were the Etruscan king, MEZENTIUS [me-zen'shi-us], and CAMILLA [ka-mil'la], a follower of Diana. The eventual victory of Aeneas is prophesied by Jupiter but is only implied in the poem by the death of Turnus.

Vergil incorporated many features of the Homeric epics and adapted others. His most original contributions to the myth are the development of the character and tragedy of Dido (originally the Phoenician queen Elissa) and his description of the Underworld (see Chapter 13). The deaths of several warriors are also significant—the young NISUS [ni'sus] and his older friend, EURYALUS [u-ri'a-lus], on a night patrol; the deaths of Pallas, killed by Turnus, of Mezentius and his son LAUSUS [law'sus], killed by Aeneas, and of Camilla, killed by ARRUNS [ar'runz]. The Olympian gods played a prominent role, as they had in Homer: Jupiter announces his will and achieves his fated purposes despite the hostility of Juno to Aeneas; Venus helps her son much as Thetis helped Achilles in the Iliad; Hercules (whose conquest of Cacus is told in Book 8) and Apollo also play lesser but significant roles. The narrative of the sack of Troy in Book 2 is the fullest one that survives.

Aeneas lived only a short time after his victory and died fighting near the River Numicus. He became a god, worshiped as *Indiges* (see Jupiter, above).

Dido. Dido had left Tyre because of the cruelty of her brother, PYGMALION [pig-ma'li-on], who had killed her husband, SYCHAEUS [si-ke'us]. She sailed to Africa and there founded Carthage, whose patron goddess was Juno. She rejected the love of IARBAS [i-ar'bas], an African prince whose mother had been seduced by Jupiter, and he eventually prayed to Jupiter to break the romance between Dido and Aeneas. The sister of Dido was ANNA [an'na], who was identified by Ovid (in Book 3 of his <u>Fasti</u>) with the Italian goddess of the new year, Anna Perenna. After Dido's death she left Carthage and came to Melita (Malta) and eventually fled to the coast of Latium, where Aeneas protected her but Lavinia plotted to kill her. Warned by Dido in a dream, she came to the river Numicus and there was transformed into a water-nymph.

LEGENDS OF THE EARLY HISTORY OF ROME

Romulus and Remus. The last king of ALBA [al'ba] LONGA [lon'ga] (founded by Iulus) was Amulius, who had driven out the rightful king, his brother Numitor. Numitor's daughter, RHEA [re'a] SILVIA [sil'vi-a] (or Ilia), although she was a Vestal Virgin, conceived twin boys by Mars, whom the servants of Amulius exposed on the bank of the Tiber. A she-wolf suckled them near the cave of the Lupercal, below the Palatine Hill. They were found by a shepherd, Faustulus, who, with his wife, Acca Larentia, brought them up, naming them ROMULUS [rom'u-lus] and REMUS [re'-mus]. When they were grown, the young men were recognized by their grandfather, whom they restored to his throne at Alba.

The Founding of Rome. Romulus and Remus left Alba and founded their own city at the site of their miraculous rescue from the river. The omens seen by Romulus through augury (divination by means of the flight of birds) were more favorable than those seen by Remus, and the city was called Roma after Romulus. During its building, Remus offended Romulus by jumping over his walls while they were being built and was killed by his brother.

Romulus established his city and gave it laws. He enlarged the number of citizens by declaring the area between the two parts of the Capitoline Hill to be an *asylum*, that is, a sanctuary where anyone could come without fear of violence or prosecution. To provide women, Romulus and his men seized the women of the Sabine tribes, who were spectators at the festival of the Consualia (see Saturn, above). This act led to war with the SABINES [sa'binz], which was ended by the Sabine women themselves (now the wives and mothers of Romans), and the Sabines and Romans agreed to live together under the joint rule of the Sabine king Titus Tatius, and Romulus. The Romans were called by the Sabine title *Quirites*.

During the war with the Sabines, Romulus killed a Sabine leader and dedicated the *spolia opima* (i.e., spoils taken from an enemy commander killed by the Roman commander in person) to Jupiter Feretrius. After a second battle, the wife of Romulus, Hersilia, persuaded him to accept the Sabines as Roman citizens. Later TARPEIA [tar-pe'a] betrayed the Capitoline Hill to the Sabines, who crushed her to death under their shields, and the Tarpeian Rock (from which criminals were thrown to their death) was called after her. The god Janus saved the Forum from capture by causing jets of boiling water to burst forth, and Romulus eventually won the battle there by vowing a temple to Jupiter Stator (the Stayer). During this battle also, a Sabine warrior, METTUS [met'tus] CURTIUS [kur'shi-us], rode his horse through a marshy depression in the Forum, thereafter called the Lacus Curtius. The Romans later said that it took its name from a Roman, Marcus Curtius, who sacrificed himself in 362 B.C. by riding his horse into a chasm, since the soothsayers had advised that it would be closed only when "that which was most valuable to Rome" was put into it.

Romulus disappeared from the earth miraculously and was deified as Quirinus, a Sabine god associated with Mars. Hersilia became Hora Quirini ("the power" or "the will" of Quirinus).

The Successors of Romulus. Under the third king, TULLUS [tul′lus] HOSTILIUS [hos-til′i-us], a war between Rome and Alba Longa was settled by combat between three brothers on each side: the Alban champions were the CURIATII [kur-i-a′shi-i], and the Romans were the HORATII [ho-ra′shi-i]. The victor (and only survivor) was HORATIUS [ho-ra′shi-us], who killed his sister because she mourned the death of the CURIATIUS [ku-i-a′shi-us] to whom she was betrothed. As part of the ritual of purification for his crime he passed under a kind of crossbar, the *tigillum sororium*, beside which were altars dedicated to Janus Curiatius and Juno Sororia.

The sixth king, SERVIUS [ser′vi-us] TULLIUS [tul′li-us], was said to be a grandson of Vulcan, who showed his favor by various portents. Servius carried out many political reforms and introduced the worship of Diana. He was murdered by the plotting of his daughter TULLIA [tul′li-a] and her husband, TARQUINIUS [tar-kwin′i-us] SUPERBUS [su-per′bus] (the Proud). Tullia drove her coach over the body of her father, which lay in the street, thereafter called Vicus Sceleratus (Crime Street).

Tarquinius Superbus was the last king of Rome. His son, SEXTUS [sex′tus] Tarquinius, raped LUCRETIA [lu-kre′she-a], the wife of Tarquinius COLLATINUS [col-la-ti′nus], who had been found to be the most virtuous of all the Roman wives while their husbands were away on military service. She told her husband and father of the crime and then stabbed herself. Tarquinius Superbus and his sons went into exile, and the Roman monarchy came to an end.

COMPACT DISCS

30. Britten, Benjamin, The Rape of Lucretia. Opera (M/L 602).

36. and **37.** Campra, André, Didon and Énée & Didon. Cantatas.

46. Cavalli, Francesco, Didone. Opera.

56. Cimarosa, Domenico, Gli Orazii e Curiazi. Opera based on Corneille's play about this Roman legend from Livy.

63. De Paul, Gene, Seven Brides for Seven Brothers. Lyrics by Johnny Mercer. Original London cast. See Videos.

112. Harrison, Lou, Suite from the Ballet "Solstice." The ballet, conceived by Jean Erdman, concerns Earth, the seasons, and the conflict between the "sun-lion" and the "moon-bull" and includes an orgiastic saturnalia.

135. Jommelli, Nicolò, Didone Abbandonata. Opera.

173. Mercadante, Saverio. Orazi e Curiazi. Opera.

180. Montéclair, Michel Pignolet de, La Mort de Didon. Cantata for voice and orchestra.

186. Mozart, Wolfgang Amadeus, Ascanio in Alba. Opera about Ascanius' marriage to Silvia in Alba Longa (M/L 599).

219. Piccinni, Niccolò, Didon. Opera.

224. Purcell, Henry, Dido and Aeneas. Opera.

235. Respighi, Ottorino, Lucrezia. Opera after Shakespeare.

287. Vinci, Leonardo, Didone Abbandonata. Opera.

Here are some other works on both Greek and Roman history in general, which certainly can be called mythical and legendary in nature.

10. Barber, Samuel, <u>Antony and Cleopatra</u>. Opera based on Shakespeare's play.

15. Bellini, Vincenzo, <u>Norma</u>. Opera (M/L 600).

16. Berlioz, Hector. <u>La Mort de Cléopâtre</u>. Cantata.

18. _____, <u>Les Troyens</u>. Major operatic masterpiece based on Vergil, <u>Aeneid</u>, Book 4 (The Fall of Troy) and Book 6 (Dido and Aeneas). M/L 600.

25. Boito, Arrigo, <u>Nerone</u>. Opera.

44. Catalani, Alfredo, <u>Dejanice</u>. The setting of this opera is in Syracuse in 400 B.C.

48. Chabrier, Emmanuel. <u>Briséïs</u>. Act 1 of an unfinished opera set in Corinth in the time of Hadrian, derived from Goethe's ballad "The Bride of Corinth." Two lovers are caught in the conflict between paganism and Christianity.

64. Dessau, Paul, <u>The Condemnation of Lucullus</u>. Opera about the notorious Roman Lucullus, general, politician, patron, and gourmet, who is depicted as an archetypal war criminal, judged by a court of souls in Hades.

67. Donizetti, Gaetano, <u>L'Esule di Roma</u> (The Exile of Rome). Opera about a senator who unjustly condemns his daughter's fiance in the time of Tiberius.

69. _____. <u>Poliuto</u>. Opera, set in reign of the emperor Decius, concerning the pagan Paolina who converts to the Christianity of her husband Poliuto and is martyred with him.

70. Elgar, Sir Edward, <u>Caractacus</u>. Cantata about Caractacus against the Romans in Britain, with Druid elements and a love interest.

81. Gade, Niels W., <u>Kalanus</u>. Oratorio about the relationship between Alexander the Great and the Indian sage Kalanus.

99. Handel, George Frideric, <u>Agrippina</u>. Opera about Agrippina, Nero, and Poppea.

100. _____. <u>Alessandro</u>. Opera about Alexander the Great.

104. _____. <u>Julius Caesar (Giulio Cesare in Egitto)</u>. Opera about Caesar and Cleopatra.

105. _____. <u>Scipione</u>. Opera about how Scipio yielded the hand of Berenice to his rival.

114. Hasse, Johann Adolf, <u>Cleofide</u>. Opera about Alexander the Great and King Poros of India and his wife Cleofide (Cleophis).

174. _____. <u>La Clemenza di Tito</u>. Opera on the same theme as that of Mozart.

94. _____. <u>Il Trionfo di Clelia</u>. Opera about Titus Tarquinius, Porsenna, and Horatius, who marries Clelia.

174. Jommelli, Niccolò, <u>Temistocle</u>. Opera.

162. Mancinelli, Luigi, <u>Cleopatra</u>. Orchestral suite of music for the play by Pietro Cossa.

166. Mascagni, Pietro, <u>Nerone</u>. Opera focusing upon Nero as artist and lover, with a dramatic death scene.

167. Massenet, Jules, <u>Cléopâtre</u>. Opera about Antony and Cleopatra.

180. Montéclair, Michel Pignolet de. <u>La Mort de Didon</u>. Cantata.

182. Monteverdi, Claudio, <u>L'Incoronazione di Poppea</u>. Important early operatic treatment of Nero and his relationship with Poppea.

188. Mozart, Wolfgang Amadeus, <u>La Clemenza di Tito</u>. Opera about intrigue and the magnanimity of the emperor Titus.

190. _____. <u>Mitridate, Rè di Ponto</u>. Opera about the final days of Mithridates, the great opponent of Sulla and Pompey. (M/L 599).

94. Piccinni, Niccolo, <u>Tigrane</u>. Opera about the conflict between the Armenian King Tigranes and Mithridates.

129. Pucitta, Vincenzo, <u>La Vestale</u>. Opera on the same theme as that of Spontini, below.

129. Rossini, Gioacchino, <u>Il Trionfo di Quinto Fabio</u>. Rossini contributed a duet to this opera (written by another composer), inspired by Livy, Book 8.

243. Rózsa, Miklós, <u>Quo Vadis</u>. Music from the epic film about pagans and Christians in the time of Nero and Galba.
264. Spontini, Gaspare, <u>Olimpia</u>. Opera about the struggle for power among Olympia, Cassander, and Antigonus after the death of Alexander the Great.
265. _____. <u>La Vestale</u>. Opera about a Druid priestess and a Roman general, which unlike Bellini's <u>Norma</u>, ends happily.
287. Vinci, Leonardo, <u>Catone in Utica</u>. Opera.

VIDEOS

The number of movies about the ancient world, particularly in the early years of Christianity, is legion. We list here only operas and musicals. In addition to the Hollywood grand epics, countless movies of lesser stature dealing with early legendary Rome are available, e.g., Roger Moore in <u>The Rape of the Sabines</u> (Unicorn Video). Similar titles are available from Sinister Video, e.g., <u>Romulus and Remus</u> or Steve Reeves as Aeneas in <u>The Avenger</u>, also titled <u>Last Glory of Troy</u> or <u>The Wooden Horse</u>. The one educational video that perhaps should be listed, <u>Greek and Roman Legends</u>, examines the difference between Greek and Roman legends in 35 minutes! Films for the Humanities ADS848.

<u>Agrippina</u>. Opera by Handel. Daniels et al. The Schwetzingen Festival, cond. Östman. Home Vision The Compleat Operagoer 60.

<u>La Clemenza di Tito</u>. Opera by Mozart. Langridge et al. Glyndbourne Festival Opera, cond. Davis. Home Vision CLE 020.

<u>Giulio Cesare (Julius Caesar)</u>. Opera by Handel. Gall et al. Sächsische Staatskapelle Dresden, cond. Craig Smith. London Polygram Video 440 071 508-3. Directed by the controversial Peter Sellars.

<u>L'Incoronazione di Poppea</u>. Opera by Monteverdi. Ewing et al. Glyndebourne Festival Opera, cond. Leppard. HBO Video TVE 3398.

<u>Jupiter's Darling</u>, starring Esther Williams and Howard Keel and directed by George Sidney. Amusing musical about Hannibal, based on Robert E. Sherwood's play <u>Road to Rome</u>. MGM Home Video M202583.

<u>Roman Scandals</u>. A fellow from Oklahoma (Eddie Cantor) dreams his way back to an ancient Rome that enjoys Busby Berkeley musical numbers. Embassy Home Entertainment VHS 3060.

<u>Seven Brides for Seven Brothers</u>. Classic musical (based on Stephen Vincent Benet's <u>The Sobbin' Women</u>) transforming the legend of the rape of the Sabine women and starring Jane Powell and Howard Keel. Directed by Stanley Donen. MGM/UA Home Video MV700091.

<u>Les Troyens</u>. Opera by Berlioz. The Metropolitan Opera, cond. Levine. Placido Domingo and Tatiana Troyanos are commendable as Dido and Aeneas. Bel Canto Paramount Video 12509.

The popular <u>Masterpiece Theatre</u> series <u>I Claudius</u> (based on the novels by Robert Graves) has now been re-released on video in the original, uncut British version, with the addition of a program, "The

Epic That Never Was," about the filming of an earlier production. The Warner Brothers spectacular <u>Helen of Troy</u>, starring Brigitte Bardot, has at last been released on video (M/L 609) and should be added to Chapter 17. Both are available generally.

INTERPRETATION

Few Roman mythological narratives are independent of Greek mythology: the names change and the narrative may have a different purpose (for example, political or moral allegory). Roman uses of Greek gods and their myths and Roman adaptations of epic and mythological themes are generally the most original aspects of Roman mythology, which find their most complex and influential expression in Vergil's <u>Aeneid</u>. There are few Roman or Italian myths that are independent of the Greek tradition (for example, Vertumnus and Pomona), while some of the best-known Roman myths concern the early history of Rome. Their most important narrator, Livy, recognized that the "historical" narratives in his first book were more like poetry and myth than history, and that their purpose was more moral than historical.

Ovid's <u>Metamorphoses</u>. By far the most important source for the Roman narrative of Greek myths is Ovid's epic poem <u>Metamorphoses</u> (completed probably in A.D. 8), which begins with the myth of creation and ends with the deification of Julius Caesar in 44 B.C. The last two books of the poem (14-15) make the transition from the Trojan war to early Roman history, and they include some myths (for example, Picus, Vertumnus) that are not part of the Roman historical tradition. Ovid's poem is by far the richest source for mythological narrative paintings and other works of art (especially in the seventeenth and eighteenth centuries) and for operas and other musical works (especially in the eighteenth century).

Vergil's <u>Aeneid</u>. Ovid's poem in its way emulated Vergil's <u>Aeneid</u> (left incomplete at the poet's death in 19 B.C.), the greatest of all Roman literary works. Vergil adapted Homeric conventions and the Homeric gods to his purposes, which were to show how the deeds of Aeneas led in time to the destined founding of Rome and the growth of the Roman Empire. Thus the gods play the conventional Homeric roles of favoring a particular cause or hero, but they never descend to the theomachies of the <u>Iliad</u> or the lusts of Ares and Aphrodite in Book 8 of the <u>Odyssey</u>. Jupiter, above all, is the embodiment of Fate, who prophesies what is destined to happen in Book 1 and definitively announces his purposes in the Council of the Gods at the beginning of Book 10. Vergil's Underworld is more complex than Homer's (see Chapter 13) and embodies philosophical and religious doctrines which are linked to the historical destiny of Rome. The hero, Aeneas, incorporates the characteristics of the Homeric bronze-age warrior (ferocity in single combat, for example), but he also has moral attributes quite unlike those of any Homeric hero. Above all, he is driven by a sense of duty (in Latin, *pietas*) to achieve a goal that he does not even begin to understand until his *katabasis* in Book 6, that is, the founding of a new people (eventually to be the Romans) in Italy. The mythological figure of Elissa (known before Vergil in early Latin epic) became in the <u>Aeneid</u> the founding queen of Carthage, Dido, whose passion and destruction outweigh for modern readers her importance as the symbol of Carthage, Rome's historical enemy, which was Vergil's primary purpose in combining her saga with Roman history. St. Augustine, indeed, confessed that he shed tears for Dido before he did for Christ.

Other Latin Sources. While mythology is part of the fabric of much of Roman poetry, the prose writer Cicero (106-43 B.C.) is an important source for Roman religion and the stories of its gods, especially in his work <u>De Natura Deorum</u> (On the Nature of the Gods), as is the antiquarian Marcus Terentius Varro (died 27 B.C.). Ovid's poem <u>Fasti</u> (Calendar) is an important source for the myths and cults of the Roman gods; for each of the first six months of the year (the poem is half-finished) Ovid describes the religious institutions and the myths associated with them for the appropriate days. Propertius (died 16 B.C.) is important for certain myths (for example, Hercules, Vertumnus) which he narrated in Book 4 of his poems. After the time of Augustus (died A.D. 14), Roman mythological narratives became less creative (at least when compared to Vergil and Ovid), but important poems were still written on mythological themes. By far the most influential was the <u>Thebaid</u> of Statius (died A.D. 96), which was widely read in the later Middle Ages, so much so that Dante gave Statius a place in his poem second only to Vergil. Even in late antiquity the myths still were narrated in Roman poetry: the Greek-speaking Alexandrian poet Claudian left an unfinished Latin epic <u>De Raptu Proserpinae</u> (On the Rape of Proserpina) unfinished at his death in about A.D. 400 (see Chapter 12).

Several of the Olympian gods (other than Jupiter) had important roles in Roman epic and political allegory. Juno is the leading force resisting Roman destiny and favoring Carthage in the <u>Aeneid</u>. Mars is important in the myths of Roman origins, and his temple (as Mars Ultor, the Avenger), dedicated by Augustus in 2 B.C., was one of the most conspicuous buildings in Augustan Rome. The family of Julius Caesar and Augustus (the *gens Iulia*) traced its ancestry back to Venus and Anchises (see Venus, above and Chapter 7), and Venus was important in the promotion of the family's public image. Augustus was especially devoted to Apollo, to whose favor he attributed his victory at the battle of Actium (31 B.C.), and he dedicated a splendid temple to him on the Palatine Hill.

Once Roman emperors, following the example of Julius Caesar, began to be deified (an honor accorded by vote of the Senate to selected emperors), the majesty of the Olympian gods was in a way compromised. Thus the identification of Nero (died A.D. 68) with Apollo (as patron of the arts) was manifestly inappropriate, as was the identification (still to be seen in a bust now in the Capitoline Museum at Rome) of Commodus (died A.D. 193) with Hercules. The Olympian gods continued to be used for political allegory throughout the first centuries of the Roman Empire; a successful example is the relief on the Arch of Trajan at Benevento (ca. A.D. 112) in which Jupiter, flanked by Minerva and Juno, hands his thunderbolt to Trajan as a symbol of the divine source of Trajan's power.

The Italian Gods. Of the Italian gods who were not absorbed into the Greek pantheon, Janus was important as the god of crossing places over water, and his herms can still be seen on the Pons Fabricius (built in 62 B.C. and still in use) over the Tiber in the center of Rome, each with four faces. His most visible function at Rome was in the opening of the gates of his temple in time of war and their closing (a rare event) in time of peace. Cacus, on the other hand, lost his importance as a fire-god to Volcanus, who was identified with Hephaestus, and became a fire-breathing monster, the grotesque opponent and victim of Hercules in Book 8 of the <u>Aeneid</u>.

Flora's festival, the Floralia, introduced in 238 (or 173) B.C., was a spring celebration marked by licentiousness and the nudity of actresses. More sober is Poussin's painting (inspired by a passage in Book 5 of Ovid's <u>Fasti</u>) of <u>The Realm of Flora</u> (1631, now in Dresden) in which the garden of Flora is populated with mythological characters (Ajax, Clytie, Narcissus, Hyacinthus, Crocus, and Smilax) who were changed into flowers. The legend of Vertumnus and Pomona has been one of the most popular of all Roman myths with poets, artists, and composers. Propertius makes Vertumnus the speaker in one poem (4.9), and Ovid, in Book 14 of the <u>Metamorphoses</u>, tells the story at length. It was especially important in the seventeenth and eighteenth centuries, with paintings by Goltzius (1613) and Rubens (completed by Jordaens, 1638) and many others, and an opera, <u>Pomone</u>, by

Robert Cambert (1671). François Boucher designed a series of tapestries inspired by operas and court-ballets on the legend in 1763 (examples are in New York and San Francisco) and in 1749 he painted a series on the four elements, of which Earth is represented by Pomona and Vertumnus (now in Columbus, Ohio).

Of the water-nymphs, the Camenae (as the Italian equivalent of the Muses) were addressed by poets as the source of their inspiration. Juturna, with her precinct next to the Temple of Vesta, was a presence in the center of Rome, and she is given a major role by Vergil in the final combat between Turnus (her brother) and Aeneas in the last book of the Aeneid.

The cult of Diana at Aricia was the starting point for Sir James Frazer's The Golden Bough, first published in 1890, whose first sentence invokes the mystery of the Lake of Nemi. Ovid (in Book 15 of the Metamorphoses) identifies Hippolytus with Virbius and so continues the association of Hippolytus and Artemis in an Italian setting. The same story is told by Vergil in Book 7 of the Aeneid.

The Non-Italian Gods. Of the non-Italian gods, Apollo and Hercules were especially important, but their myths (other than the myth of Cacus) were substantially the same as the Greek legends. The appearance of the Dioscuri at the battle of Lake Regillus is a Roman addition to their myths.

Cybele, with her festival, the Megalensia, was more prominent in Roman ritual than in Greece. The self-castration of her priests, the Galli, both repelled and attracted the Romans, and it inspired one of the greatest of all Latin shorter poems, the "Attis" (no. 63) of Catullus. The Galli are vividly described by Lucretius (in Book 2 of the De Rerum Natura) and Ovid (in Book 4 of the Fasti).

Dionysus, as Bacchus, was widely worshiped in Roman Italy, and his rituals were so bizarre that in 186 B.C. they were considered to be a threat to public order and were suppressed by the Senate. Although Dionysus was believed to inspire poets, he generally did not have the power and popularity (except through his Mysteries) that he had in Greece. There are many paintings with Dionysiac symbols and themes from Pompeii, and especially famous and inexplicable is the fresco, still in place, in the Villa of the Mysteries at Pompeii (ca. 50 B.C.), which appears to represent an initiation-ritual presided over by Dionysus and Ariadne.

Other mystery religions, with their myths and cults, were widely practiced in the Roman world (see Chapter 14). Unique among literary descriptions of a religious conversion is the final book of the Metamorphoses of Apuleius (mid-second century A.D.), in which the hero, Lucius, prays to Isis and with her help resumes his human form and becomes her devotee. Apuleius shows how Isis had become a goddess who subsumed the powers and attributes of Olympian and pre-Olympian female divinities, a perfect example of syncretism.

Dido and Aeneas. Of all Roman mythological figures, Aeneas is preeminent and has inspired countless literary, musical, and artistic works. Here we will mention a few examples from the episode of Dido. Her passion inspired the opera Dido and Aeneas by Henry Purcell (1689) and the second part (Troyens à Carthage) of the monumental opera Les Troyens by Hector Berlioz (1856-1858). See above. Among paintings we select Rubens's The Death of Dido (1638, now in Paris) and Washington Allston's Dido and Anna (1809, now in Miami, Fla.), in which Anna comforts Dido while a furtive Aeneas escapes in the background.

The Legends of Early Rome. The legends of early Rome, particularly as narrated in Livy's first book, have been a frequent source of inspiration for artists. Rubens has a splendid oil-sketch (a design for a tapestry) of Mars and Rhea Silvia (1616-1617, now in Vaduz), and he also painted The

Discovery of Romulus and Remus (1617, now in Rome). Quite different is the large and witty wire sculpture by Alexander Calder (1928, now in New York), a satirical reinterpretation of the Capitoline Wolf, an Etruscan bronze sculpture of ca. 500 B.C. A painting by Jacques-Louis David, The Oath of the Horatii (1787, in Paris), represents the courage and dedication of the Roman heroes before their battle with the Curatii.

Both Rubens (ca. 1635, now in London) and Poussin (1631, now in Paris, and 1635, now in New York) painted The Abduction of the Sabine Women. The tragedy of Lucretia has frequently been represented, for example, by Titian in Lucretia and Tarquinius (1570, now in Cambridge; another version is in Vienna). Yet more violent and menacing is the steel sculpture Rape of Lucrece by Reuben Nakian (1953-1958), to be seen in the garden of the Hirshhorn Museum in Washington, D.C. Its disjointed forms, steel plates, and pipes reflect the breakdown of the moral and social order that in Livy's narrative led to the replacement of the Roman monarchy by the Republic.

Appendix: Using Perseus

A computer disk has been developed to link the chapters of both this *Companion to Classical Mythology* and the textbook *Classical Mythology*, by Mark P. O. Morford and Robert Lenardon (Longman, 1995), to Perseus 2.0, an electronic archive of data on ancient Greek culture available from Yale University Press. This linking disk is available on request by professors when they adopt this *Companion* for their classes. Once the disk has been installed to the Path file of Perseus 2.0, you will be able to access all the material relevant to each chapter in the *Companion*. The following pages explain, step by step, how two such paths work.

If your professor has not requested a copy of the disk, he or she may do so by calling the Addison Wesley Longman Customer Service number, 1-800-552-2499, and using the following numbers: ISBN 0-8013-1992-7 or title code 77857.

A Guided Tour of Chapters 3A and 3B: The Olympians

The Perseus project (now updated to Perseus 2.0) is a growing computer database of ancient Greek culture. It offers access to major classical authors, modern histories and essays, topographical maps of archaeological sites, and a vast reservoir of up to 27,000 images of architecture, vases, sculpture, and coins. Incorporated into its program is a host of sophisticated searching tools to facilitate use. The Perseus project is a remarkable stimulus for independent research by both the beginning student and the advanced scholar and it is an invaluable asset for instructor-directed education.

Perseus uses **Paths** to guide the user through what can initially seem a confusing and discouraging amount of material. These Paths facilitate the organization of selected information pertinent to a particular topic. Within each Path, **Stops** are created, wherein related data from various categories are collected. It is as if one were to organize a tour (Path) around a specific theme and then, for the itinerary, to isolate and identify along the way special points of interests (the Stops), essential for elucidation. This is not to say that one may not at any time leave temporarily the organized tour to explore individual interests that have been aroused.

On the computer disk accompanying this <u>Companion</u>, we have culled from the vast database of Perseus 2.0 information related to the study of classical myth and legend. We have organized this copious and varied material into Paths designed to follow as closely as possible the subject-matter as treated in Chapters 1-23 of Morford and Lenardon's <u>Classical Mythology</u>.

The amount and nature of this material inevitably differs from chapter to chapter for two major reasons: 1. Abundant illustrations (of any sort) for the subject of the first Chapter, Myths of Creation, simply do not exist, whereas for other chapters (e.g., dealing with Trojan War and with Heracles) the amount of resources from the ancient world is voluminous. 2. We are limited by the material that has actually been incorporated into the Perseus program. Although the database is large, it does not always accommodate a mythological topic as one would wish, since it was designed to embrace Greek culture as a whole. One is continually so delighted by the abundance of mythological resources made available by Perseus that it would be ungrateful to complain about any omissions.

It is important to gain an easy familiarity with the Greek and Roman spellings, since Perseus uses either one interchangeably. For this reason we have included in the text of this <u>Companion</u> both Greek and Roman spellings of at least the important names. A helpful glossary on "The Greek Spelling of Names" may be found in <u>Classical Mythology</u>, pp. 651-654.

We have chosen to offer here a printed version of the Paths for Chapters 3A and 3B (The Olympians), as they appear on the accompanying computer disk. By means of this text we guide the user, step by step, through the Paths to illustrate the use and manipulation of the Perseus Program. Details explaining how the Stops were created will encourage and facilitate individual research. By the time users have worked through both the printed material and the disk, they will have acquired the requisite expertise to explore their own projects.

Preliminaries

It is assumed that one will have acquired familiarity with the basic operation of the Macintosh computer and that Perseus has already been installed with the proper configuration, according to the specifications in the Perseus *User's Guide.* It is recommended that one also become acquainted with the basic terminology of Perseus.

A backup copy should be made of the Hypercard stacks that come with this disk.

Whenever you start up Perseus, you will see the following:

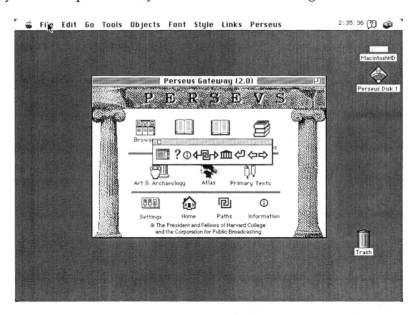

The **Perseus Gateway** appears on the screen with a small floating window, which is the **Navigator,** and a series of pop-menus along the very top of the screen.

>Reposition the Navigator by clicking and holding the mouse on the top shaded bar of the Navigator window and dragging it off to one side.

You will notice that the Navigator has a tiny white box in its upper left hand corner. Any window which includes this tiny white box can be closed simply by clicking within it. It is a good practice never to leave too many of these collapsable windows open at any one time. Make it a habit to close these windows, whenever you are done with them.

The Navigator has a number of Icons. Those most important for you are:

The **Path** Icon, which can take you backward and forward within a path by clicking on the appropriate arrow or can create a new stop by clicking on the center or meander.

The **Gateway** Icon returns you to the Perseus Gateway.

The **Go Back** Icon returns you to the previous location, no matter what Perseus stack (or resource) you were in.

The **Go To Previous Card** Icon takes you back to the previous card within the stack you are using. It can not, unlike the Go Back Icon, jump from one stack to another. If you are reading Homer's *Iliad* Book 1, lines 200-225, clicking this arrow will take you to the passage which precedes it.

The **Go To Next Card** Icon takes you forward to the next card within the stack you are using. It, too, cannot jump from one stack to another.

The Gateway (as well as the Navigator) contains a number of Icons. It links you to all the resources in Perseus by clicking the Icon of your choice. Another way of accessing the resources, and the one which you will employ most often, is to use the pop-up menu bar at the very top of the screen. The two most important menu items are **Links** and **Perseus**.

>Click and hold the **Links** menu. The resources listed can be selected by dragging the mouse, highlighting the resource you want, and then letting go. The **Perseus** menu next to the Links Menu operates in the same way. It, too, is a pop-up menu.

Along the bottom of the Gateway are two important Icons: the **Settings** Icon and the **Paths** Icon. You need to make sure the right path and notebook settings are in place, therefore click the Settings Icon. You will see the following:

Perseus Settings Card

Click on these fields and buttons to customize your version of Perseus.

Select Player Type: [None] ☐ Use Video Images ☒ Use Digital Images ☒ Indexed Color

Path Stack: [MacintoshHD:Perseus 2.0:Local]

Notebook Stack: [MacintoshHD:Perseus 2.0:Local]

CD Swapper: [MacintoshHD:Perseus 2.0:Local Stacks:Perseus]

Window Control: ○ Go to cards in new window ● Go to cards in same window

(Remember, holding down the shift key temporarily reverses the choice.)

On the Settings Card you are given the option of selecting the **Path** and **Notebook Stack** that you wish to use. If you click on the rectangular box to the right of Path Stack above, the computer will ask you to locate on the hard drive or disk the stack you want. The same is true for the Notebook Stack. [Remember both your Mythology Path Stack and Mythology Notebook Stack should already be in the Local Stacks Folder.]

>Click the **Settings** button.

>Select the **Mythology Path** and **Mythology Notebook** Stacks from the **Local Stacks** folder. Then return via the Navigator to the Gateway.

>Click the **Paths** button on the **Perseus Gateway** to call up the complete **Path Index** located in the Mythology Stack. You will see the following:

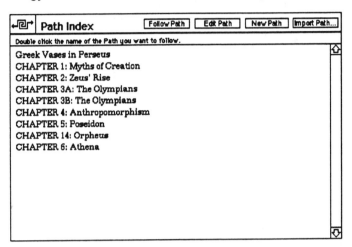

You need to select the sample path to be followed.

>Click on **CHAPTER 3A: The Olympians**. [Note: If you were now to click on the **Follow Path** button, you would be taken to the first stop in the path, bypassing the Path Card itself, which gives an overall view of the stops in this path. You do not want to do this because your purpose is to learn about the construction of paths.]

>Click on the **Edit Path** button. You will see the following:

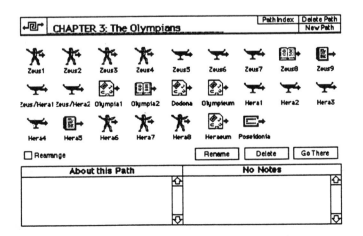

There are 25 stops on this Path Card. The order of stops is from left to right, beginning with **Zeus1** and ending with **Poseidonia**. This particular chapter, however, contains a second Path Card.
>Follow the same procedure and call up the Path Card entitled **CHAPTER 3B:The Olympians.** [Remember the complete list of Path Cards is located in the Path Index.] You will find the following:

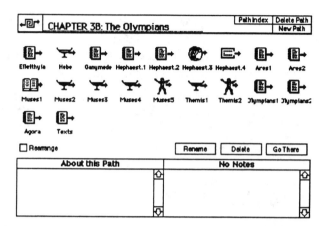

>Recall Path Card **Chapter 3A: The Olympians** in preparation for your guided tour.

The Path Card is divided into three sections: an upper title bar, a middle area with icons designating the stops, and at the bottom, two scroll windows for notes. You will see a number of buttons. At the top right corner of the title bar there are three: **Path Index** (with which you should be familiar), **Delete Path**, and **New Path**. The functions of the last two are self-evident. Below the stops in the middle area you will notice four more buttons: **Rearrange** (by clicking this you can change the order of the stops), **Rename** (which allows you to rename individual stops), **Delete** (which deletes individual stops), and **Go There** (which takes you to any stop you select). At the bottom are included two areas for notes.
> Click once on the first stop, **Zeus1.** The notes for this stop should now be visible. If you wish to add your own comments, all you need do is select the stop you wish to annotate, click in the **Notes** field, and begin typing. After you have finished, clicking once outside of the Notes field will store your remarks.

Each stop uses a special icon descriptive of its content:

 Sculpture   Coins   Primary Texts.

 Vases   Architecture   Notebook

 Secondary Sources   Sites   Atlas

these preliminaries dispensed with, you are ready to begin the tour.

Under normal circumstances you would move through a path using the Path Icon, which takes you directly from stop to stop, forward or backward, without explanatory information. Since the object of this guided tour is to learn how the stops were created, you should not use the Path Icon to navigate through the path, but instead follow the directions given below.

A Guided Tour of Chapter 3A: The Olympians

Stop 1

>If you haven't done so already, click the first stop, **Zeus 1** on the Path Card. >Click the **Go There** button. You should see the following Catalog Card with the individual notes for this stop included in a separate window. This note window can be removed simply by clicking the tiny box in the upper left hand corner of the window. **It is a good idea to keep pen and paper handy to jot down items or directions that you may need to refer to later.**

This card is located in the Sculpture Catalog and there are a number of ways of getting to it, as is true with most of the material in Perseus. But first look at the card itself. It is much like other cards in the Sculpture, Vase, Site, Coin, or Architecture Catalogs. At the top is a title bar with a sculpture icon to the left, helpful if you have forgotten where you are. The title bar includes a number of buttons to the right: **Thumbs** (used to call up thumbnail pictures of all the views of a particular item), **Description** (which gives a material and contextual description of the item), and **Index** (which will take you to the Sculpture Index where all sculpture in Perseus is classified). Below the title bar is specific information which is used to classify the object, including the catalog number, the collection in which it is housed, the subject, material, date, etc. Below this middle section is a scroll window, which gives access each drawing or photograph of the item.

>Click on some of the views of Artemision Zeus then jot down some of the information, especially the name and catalog number.

>Click the **Description** button for some background information.

There are a number of ways to access this card, as follows:

>Click on **Index**. This will take you to the **Sculpture Index,** which classifies material by certain categories.
>Click and hold the **Index Type** button, you will notice the range of parameters for narrowing a search. The statue of Artemesion Zeus, for example, can be isolated with others of its type, whether you classify it by **Material, Type, Period,** etc.
>Click **Index Type** and drag the mouse and highlight **Material.** You will see a selection of materials in the left hand column of the **Index.**
>Click Bronze, the material out of which the sculpture of Artemesion Zeus is made, you will notice the right hand column fill with a selection of bronze sculptures in Perseus. As you can see Artemision Zeus is included in this listing.
>Click **Index Type** again, highlight **Type.** And select **Free-standing** from the left column. Again Artemision Zeus can be selected

Another way of locating an item is to use the **Lookup** command located under the **Links Menu.** This is especially helpful if you know the catalog number.
>Click **Links** and highlight **Lookup.** A small window will appear. Type in **Athens, NM Br. 15161.**
>Click **Links** again and highlight **Sculpture.** The card for Artemision Zeus will be called up.

Yet another way to access cards in any catalog is to use the **Browser.** This is particularly handy when you lack specific information about a piece.
>Click **Links** and highlight **Browser.**
>Select **Sculpture** from the top left column.
>Select **Keywords** by clicking the pop-up menu just to the right. A second pop-up menu will appear next to **Keywords.**
>Click and select **Divinities.**
>Scroll down and select **Zeus.** The three columns below will list the eight sculptures that satisfy the parameters chosen. These three columns each have a pop-up menu at the top. Make sure one of these columns is selected for **Title.** Just click and hold the button to view your options. You will see Artemision Zeus.
>Select it by clicking on the entry in the first column. (Clicking in the second or third column will not work.)

Stop 2   Location 2 of 25: Herm of the Dresden Zeus Type, Munich GL 294.

>From the **Links** menu select **Sculpture**.
>From the **Index Type** select **Collection**.
>Scroll down and select **Munich, Glyptothek** from the left hand column.
>Scroll down the right column, select **Herm of Dresden Zeus Type**.
>Select some **Views** and then click **Description** in the upper right h a n d corner.

Stop 3   Location 3 of 25: Cave of Pan relief, Athens, Agora, I 7154

>From the **Links** menu select **Sculpture**.
>From the **Index Type** select **Material**.
>Select **Marble** from the left hand colum.
>Scroll down the right column (about halfway) and select **Cave of Pan Relief.**
>Select **Views** and click **Description**.

Stop 4   Location 4 of 25: East Pediment of Siphnian Treasury

>From the **Links** menu select **Sculpture**.
>From the **Index Type** select **Context**.
>Scroll down and select **Delphi** from the left hand column.
>Scroll down the right column and select **Delphi, Siphnian Treasury East Pediment.**
>Select **Views** and read **Description**.

Stop 5   Location 5 of 25: London E 313, attributed to the Berlin Painter.

>From the **Links** menu select **Vases**. You will notice that, much like the **Sculpture Index**, the **Vase Index** has an **Index Type** button in the upper right hand corner.
>From the **Index Type** select **Painter**.
>Scroll down and select **Berlin Painter** from the left hand column.
>Scroll down the right hand column and select **London E 313**.
>Select **Views** and read **Description**.

Stop 6   Location 6 of 25: Harvard 1925.30.124, Attic Black Figure.

>From the **Links** menu select **Vases**.
>From the **Index Type** select **Ware**.
>Select **Attic Black Figure** from the left hand column.
>Scroll down the right column and select **Harvard 1925.30.124**.
>View **Side A: miniature Zeus on top of right colonnette** and the two boxers on **Side B**. Read **Description**.

Stop 7   Location 7 of 25:Birmingham 57.263, Attic Red Figure, Amphora.

>From the **Links** menu select **Vases**.
>From the **Index Type** select **Shape**.
>Select **Amphora** from the left hand column.
>Select **Birmingham 57.263**.
>View **Side A: Zeus pursuing a woman** and read **Description**.

Stop 8   Location 8 of 25: Caskey and Beazley: *Attic Vase Paintings in the Museum of Fine Arts Boston*, No. 110, Boston 00.346, Bell-Krater.

>In this stop you will investigate the **Essays and Catalogs**, which are devoted to vase painters, sculpture, history, biography, music, and the regions of Greece. Some of the articles will take you to the **Encyclopedia**, the stack in which they are stored. Others are separate stacks of their own, which are linked to Perseus' other resources.
>From the **Links** menu select **Essays and Catalogs**.
>Scroll down the list and select under vase catalogs *Attic Vase Paintings in the Museum of Fine Arts, Boston* by L. D. Caskey and J. D. Beazley.
>The first card shows the vases which are described in individual essays. You are looking for item **No. 110**, a Bell-Krater, catalogued as **Boston 00.346** and depicting Zeus and Lyssa. Select this item. You will see the following:

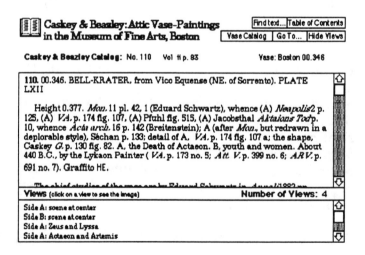

This card is divided into 3 main areas: title bar, the body of the window containing a description of the vase, and the bottom bar with a number of views. The title bar includes the index number we used (No. 110), as well as the reference to the text from which the material has been drawn (vol ii p. 83). You will also note the catalog number: Boston 00.346. In the top right corner there are five buttons:

>Click **Find Text**. A search window will appear. Enter the word **Zeus**

and click **Search**. The first instance of the word in the essay will be boxed.

>Click the **Table of Contents**. The introductory card will again be called up. Select **No. 110** to return to it.
>The **Vase Catalog** button allows you to select a catalog reference and search for it in the Vase collection, but the procedure is a bit tricky. Locate in the top bar the catalog reference for the vase (**Boston 00.346**). You will notice that the cursor changes from pointer to insertion mode around the catalog number. You need to click and drag the cursor across **Boston 00.346**, but it is difficult to do so from the beginning of the entry (from left to right).
>Click and drag the cursor backward (from right to left) across **Boston 00.346** and then click the **Vase Catalog**. You will be taken to the card for this vase in the Vase collection.

You will notice that the **Views** of this vase are identical to those found in Caskey & Beazley. Sometimes, however, the descriptions of the vase differ in length, so it might be useful to check both sources. Return to Caskey & Beazley. To do so, click the Back arrow in the navigator or try the following.

>Click the **Description**. You will note that the **Description Card** begins with the reference to Caskey & Beazley, the source from which description is drawn.
>Click and drag the cursor across the second reference to **Caskey-Beazley, No. 110.** (The computer will not call up the first reference, Caskey & Beazley.
>From the **Links** menu select **Essays and Catalogs**.

>Click the **Go To** button. Another window will appear. Enter **No. 120** and click **OK**. You will be taken to another entry in Caskey-Beazley. From that entry click **Go To** (as before) to return to No. 110.

The fifth button simply shortens the window and hides the choice of views.

>View **Zeus and Lyssa** and read **Essay**.

Stop 9   Location 9 of 25: Notebook: Chapter 3: Zeus/Coins.

>This location groups together in one Notebook stop a number of coins depicting Zeus. From the menu select **Notebook**. Perseus will usually return to the last notebook card consulted, which may not be the Index.
>Click on **Notebook Index**.

>Scroll down the list and select **Chapter 3: Zeus/Coins** and then click the **Go To Note** button.
>The access a coin entry in this note, first click and drag the cursor across the **collection name and number**, leaving out anything in parentheses.
>From the **Links** menu select **Coins**.
>View a selection of coins and read their description. Each coin card is much the same as a vase card. If you need to return to the Notebook, go to the the **Perseus** menu select **Notebook** or click the **Go Back** Icon in the Navigator.

Stop 10   Location 10 of 25: Louvre CA 616, Black Figure, Tripod Kothon, Archaic.

> From the **Links** menu select **Vases**.
>From the **Index** select **Period**.
>Select **Archaic** from the left column.
>Scroll down the right column and select **Louvre CA 616**.
>View **Side C: Wedding of Zeus and Hera** and read **Description**.

Stop 11   Location 11 of 25: Villa Giulia 2382.

> From the **Links** menu select **Vases**.
>From the **Index** select **Collection**.
>Scroll down and select **Rome, Museo Nazionale di Villa Giulia** from the left column.
>Scroll down the right column and select **Villa Giulia 2382**.
>Select **Views** and read **Description**.

Stop 12   Location 12 of 25: Olympia.

>This stop takes you to the **Site Catalog**. From the **Links** menu select **Sites**. You will see the entire list of sites in Perseus.
>From the **Index Type** select **Type**. This narrows your search a bit.
>Select **Sanctuary** from the left column.
>Scroll down the right column and select **Olympia**. At first glance this card resembles in its layout ones you have seen so far. The **Plans** and **Views** at the bottom, however, open up a new feature, the **Composite Site Plan**. First read the **Description** of the Site and then return to the **Site Card** by clicking the **Summary** button.
>Scroll down the list and view some photographs, which are listed after **Drawings**.
>Under **Drawings** select **Central Sanctuary Area (sm.).** This will call up the **Site Plans, Olympia, Sanctuary Composite**. This card contains a **Construction Phases** button. Click and highlight **Sanctuary Early Bronze Age**. Not much to look at. Click and highlight other periods to see how the site developed. When you have finished, click once more **Construction Phases** and highlight **Sanctuary Composite**. This is where

we started. You will notice that along the **Menu** bar another item has been added to the right of the **Perseus** menu, labelled **Plan**. The **Plan** menu will come in handy if you need to return to the **Site Plan**.

>Click once anywhere on the Site Plan itself. You will see the following:

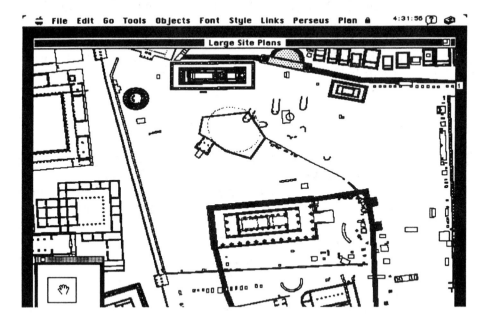

You are now in the **Large Site Plan** of the sanctuary. If you move the pointer around the site, you will notice that certain buildings become highlighted.

>Highlight the large temple at the bottom of the screen and click once. A window will tell you that this is the **Temple of Zeus at Olympia**. You are also given a selection of **Plan, Catalog,** or **Cancel**.

>Click **Plan** and access the layout of the temple. Click **Cancel** to close the plan.

>Highlight and click the **Temple of Zeus** again. Click **Catalog**. One of the most useful features of the Site Catalog is its capacity to be used in conjunction with the Architecture Catalog. You should now see the card for the **Sanctuary of Zeus at Olympia** in the **Architecture Catalog**. Select some **Views**, especially the **Reconstruction elevation of the Statue of Zeus by Phidias**. After you have finished, close all the pictures.

>Read the **Description** and return to the main **Summary** card. In the top right hand corner, you will notice a button you have not seen before.

>Click **Locate Bldg**. This returns you to the **Large Site Plan** and the temple flashes briefly to show its location.

>In the bottom left corner of the screen there is a small scroll window with a smaller box inside. If you place the cursor along the edge of this smaller box, the cursor will change into a two-directional arrow. This allows you to increase or decrease the size of the large Site Plan on the

screen.

>Click and resize the inner box to change the size of the **Large Site Plan**.

>If you place the cursor within the smaller box, it becomes a hand. By clicking and dragging the hand you can now move around the site.

>Locate the **Temple of Hera** and the **Naiskos of Eileithyia and Sosipolis**. You can, if you choose, move back and forth from the Architecture Catalog to see pictures of each of these structures, as we did for the Temple of Zeus. (Note: In the picture of the screen above, the Naiskos is a small building to the right of the semi-circle, which is to the right of the Temple of Hera.)

Stop 13   Location 13 of 25: Thomas R. Martin, Historical Overview.

>This stop gives some historical background about the Olympic games.

>From the **Links** menu select **Historical Overview**.

>From the **Table of Contents (toc)** select 4.10. **The Olympic Games of Zeus and Hera**. This card contains a **Table of Contents** button, as well as a toggle switch, which when clicked alternates between **See Links/Lock Text** and **Hide Links/Unlock Text**.

>Click **See Links/Lock Text**. Several words are now underlined in the text.. If you click on a word, you will be given the option of searching a ready-made link in Perseus.

>Click and hold the word <u>wrestling</u>. A box appears with two choices.

>Highlight **Example of Wrestling [Text]**. You will be taken to the **Primary Texts** collection, specifically **Pindar's Ninth Olympian Ode**, written in commemoration of the victory by Ephormostus in the wrestling contest. You can read the sections before or after this passage by clicking the **Go To Previous Card** Icon or the **Go To Next Card** Icon in the Navigator, which takes you from card to card within a single stack.

>To return to the **Historical Overview** click the **Go Back** Icon, or select **Historical Overview** from the **Links** menu.

>Read the pertinent sections through **4.11. Competition and Community**. You can advance the Overview in the same way you would a Primary Text, by clicking the appropriate arrow on the right side of the navigator.

Stop 14   Location 14 of 25: Dodona.

>From the **Links** menu select **Sites**.

>Scroll down and select **Dodona**.

>Unlike Olympia, this site does not have a Large Site Plan to scroll around. View photographs and read the **Description** of this sanctuary.

Stop 15   Location 15 of 25: the Olympieion in Athens.

>From the **Links** menu select **Sites**.

>From the **Site Index (All)** select **Athens.**
>Your objective here is to view the major temple of Zeus and not take a tour of Athens. Scroll down and view **Athens, Olympieion.**

Stop 16   Location 16 of 25: RISD 25.078, Attic Red Figure, Lekythos.

>From the **Links** menu select **Vases.**
>From the **Index Type** select **Collection.**
>Scroll down and select **Museum of Art, Rhode Island School of Design (RISD)** from the left column.
>Select **RISD 25.078** from the right column.
>View **Hera seated** and read **Description.**

Stop 17   Location 17 of 25: London E 65, Attic Red Figure, Kylix.

>From the **Links** menu select **Vases.**
>From the **Index Type** select **Shape.**
>Scroll down and select **Kylix** from the left column.
>Scroll down the right column and select **London E 65.**
>Select **Views** and read **Description.**

Stop 18   Location 18 of 25: RISD 35.707, Attic Red Figure, Lekythos.

>From the **Links** menu select **Vases.**
>From the **Index Type** select **Shape.**
>Scroll down and select **Lekythos** from the left column.
>Scroll down the right column and select **RISD 35.707.**
>View **Hera and Nike** and read **Description.**

Stop 19   Location 19 of 25: Toledo 1982.88, Attic Red Figure, Skyphos.

>From the **Links** menu select **Vases.**
>From the **Index Type** select **Shape.**
>Scroll down and select **Skyphos** from the left column.
>Scroll down the right column and select **Toledo 1982.88.**
>View **Hera and attendant** and read **Description.**

Stop 20   Location 20 of 25: Notebook: Chapter 3: Hera/Coins.

>From the **Perseus** menu select **Notebook.**
>Perseus will return to the last card consulted, which may still be Chapter 3: Zeus/Coins.
>Click **Notebook Index.**
>Scroll down and select **Chapter 3: Hera/Coins.** Then click the **Go To Note** button.

>Click and drag cursor across a coin entry and highlight it.
>From the **Links** menu select **Coins**.
>Look at a selection of coins.

Stop 21   Location 21 of 25: Hera of Cheramyes, Louvre Ma 686.

>From the **Links** menu select **Sculpture**.
>From the **Index Type** select **Collection**.
>Scroll down and select **Paris, Musée du Louvre** from the left column.
>Scroll down the right column and select **Hera of Cheramyes.**
>Select **Views** and read **Description**.

Stop 22   Location 22 of 25: Athenian Decree Honoring the Samians, Athens, Acropolis 1333.

>From the **Links** menu select **Sculpture.**
>From the **Index Type** select **Context.**
>Scroll down and select **Athens, Acropolis** from the left column.
>Scroll down the right column and select **Athens, Acropolis 1333.**
>There are no pictures for this item, but it would be worthwhile to read the **Description** of the stele, which depicts Hera and Athena.

Stop 23   Location 23 of 25: Head of Hera (?), Athens, National Archaeological Museum.

>From the **Links** menu select **Sculpture.**
>From the **Index Type** select **Collection.**
>Select **Athens, National Archaeological Museum** from the left column.
>From the right column select the Head of Hera (?).
>Read **Description.**

Stop 24   Location 24 of 25: Samos, Heraion.

>From the **Links** menu select **Sites.**
>From the **Site Indes (All)** select **Samos, Heraion.**
>View photographs of Samos and read **Description.**
>Select **Composite Plan (lg.).** Scroll around the site and identify various structures. Remember that you can investigate specific buildings in the **Architecture Catalog** by highlighting a building, clicking once, and then clicking **Catalog.** Investigate especially **Samos, Great Hera Temple.**

Stop 25   Location 25 of 25: Poseidonia, "Temple of Poseidon".

> From the **Links** menu select **Architecture.**
>From the **Index Type** select **Site.**
>Scroll down and select **Poseidonia** from the left column.

>Scroll down the right column and select **Poseidonia, "Temple of Poseidon".**
>Select **Views** and read **Description** of what is actually a temple of Hera.

You have come to the end of the first guided tour.

You cannot move from stop 25 of the first guided tour to the first stop of the seond guided tour by clicking the Path Icon.

A Guided Tour of Chapter 3B: The Olympians

Stop 1 >From the **Perseus** menus select **Path Index**.

>Scroll down the list and highlight **Chapter3B: The Olympians**.
>Click the **Edit Path** button. You will see the Path Card for Chapter 3B: The Olympians.
>Select the first stop, **Eileithyia**.
>Click **Go There**. This is a Notebook stop, which groups together vases depicting Eileithyia. Since she is a goddess of childbirth, she is often placed at the birth of Athena. As with the other notebook cards you have seen, access the individual entries by clicking and dragging the cursor across them to highlight the catalog name and number.
>Highlight **Boston 00.330**.
>From the **Links** menu select **Vases**.
>View **Side A: Birth of Athena** and read **Description**. Take note of Ares as well. At this stop it is worthwhile to illustrate another powerful function of Perseus.

>From the **Links** menu select **English Index**.
>At the **Look For** window you can enter any string or combination of letters (or numbers) you wish to search. Enter **Eileithyia**.
>The **Show List at** button is pop-up menu. Click button and select **Top of List.**
>Click the **Postion** pop-up menu and select **Exact Match**.
>Click **Do Search**. You will see the following:

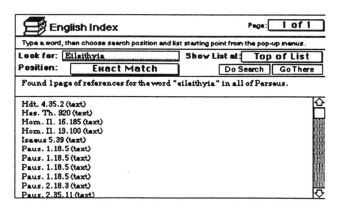

The scroll window contains a list of all the occurrences of "eileithyia" in Perseus. This is a handy tool, if you want an exhaustive search. [The Browser enables you to limit your search to Vases, Sculpture, etc.]

> Click the **Show List at** pop-up menu and select **Vases**. Perseus will take you to that part of the list where the vase references begin. This is a useful feature, if you are searching a string with more that one page of references.

>For example, type in **Zeus** at the **Look For** window.

>Click **Do Search**. You will notice that there are 34 pages of references for Zeus.

>At **Show List at** select **Sculpture** to isolate the sculpture portion of the list. Perseus will automatically scroll down to page 26 of 34, where the sculpture references begin. You will now see the entry for **Artemision Zeus (sculpture description)**. This entry tells you that on the Description Card for Artemison Zeus in the Sculpture Catalog there is, not surprisingly, a reference to Zeus.

>Scroll down and locate **Olympia Amazon Metope (sculpture description)**. On this Sculpture Description Card there are three references to Zeus.

>Highlight the first entry for **Olympia Amazon Metope (sculpture description)** and click **Go There**. The first reference to Zeus on this card will be enclosed in a box.

>Click the **Go Back** Icon in the Navigator.

>Look up a text reference. At **Show List at** select **Homer**.

>Highlight **Hom. Il.1.500** and click **Go There**. In this passage the Olympians are returning to their home on Mt Olympus and Thetis, the mother of Achilles, is about to make a request of Zeus that will temporarily change the course of the Trojan War.

Stop 2   Location 2 of 20: Philadelphia MS 5462, Attic Red Figure.

>From the **Links** menu select **Vases**.

>From the **Index Type** select **Collection**.

>Scroll down and select **University Museum, Unversity of Pennsylvania** from the left column.

>Scroll down the right column and select **MS 5462**.

>View **Lid: Marriage of Herakles and Hebe**.

Stop 3   Location 3 of 20: Notebook stop with a collection of vases depicting Ganymede.

>From the **Perseus** menu select **Notebook**.

>Click **Notebook Index** and select **Chapter 3B: Ganymede/Vases**.

>Highlight only the catalog name and number and select **Vases** from the **Links** menu.

Stop 4   Location 4 of 20: Notebook stop with a collection of vases depicting Hephaestus and Thetis.

>From the **Perseus** menu select **Notebook**.
>Click **Notebook Index**.
>Select **Chapter 3B: Hephaestus/Thetis** and follow the same procedure as above.

Stop 5   Location 5 of 20: Notebook stop with collection of vase depicting Hephaestus' Return.

>From the **Perseus** menu select **Notebook**
>click **Notebook Index**.
>Select **Chapter 3B: Hephaestus' Return** and follow the same procedure.

Stop 6   Location 6 of 20: Dewing 968, Bronze, Mint: Lipara.

>From the **Links** menu select **Coins**.
>From the **Index Type** select **Mint**.
>Scroll down and select **Lipara** from the left column.
>Select **Dewing 968** from the right column.
>View **Obverse: Hephaistos, seated r., with Kantharos and hammer.**
But what is a Kantharos?
>Click and drag cursor across the word **Kantharos** on the card to highlight it.
>From the **Links** menu select **Encyclopedia**. You will see an article describing a Kantharos. In the lower right corner of the card is a small scroll window that lists related articles.
>Select **Skyphos**. You have seen one of these before.
>Click **Skyphos** under **Views** at the bottom of the card.
What is a Kylix?
>Click **Index** button at the top.
>From the the alphabet at the bottom select K.
>Scroll down the list and select **Kylix**. Read **Description** and select the drawing under **Views**.

Stop 7   Location 7 of 20: Athens, Peripteral temple; on the west side of Agora, on the Kolonos Agoraios.

>From the **Links** menu select **Architecture**.
>From the **Index Type** select **Type**.
>Scroll down and select **Temple** from the left column.
>Scroll down the right column and select **Athens, Temple of Hephaestus**.
>View photographs, read **Description**, and return to the **Summary** Card.
>Click **Locate Bldg.** in the top right corner.

>From the **Plan** menu (now visible next to the Perseus menu) select **Small Site Plan** to get an overview of the Agora.

Stop 8   Location 8 of 20: Notebook stop with a selection of sculpture depicting Ares.

>From the **Perseus** menu select **Notebook**.
>Click **Notebook Index** and select **Chapter 3B: Ares/Sculpture**.
>To view images highlight catalog name and number and select **Sculpture** from the **Links** menu.

Stop 9   Location 9 of 20: Notebook stop with a selection of vases depicting Ares.

>From the **Perseus** menu select **Notebook** and then click **Notebook Index**.
>Select **Chapter 3B: Ares/Vases** and call up vases depicting Ares and Heracles' combat with Cycnus, a son of Ares.

Stop 10   Location 10 of 20: Caskey-Beazley, Boston 98.887.

>From the **Links** menu select **Lookup**.
>Type **Caskey-Beazley, No. 37** in the small window that appears.
>From the **Links** menu select **Essays and Catalogs**.
>View **Main Panel: Cowherd and six Muses**.
>In the upper right corner highlight, from back to front, **Boston 98.887**.
>Click **Vase Catalog**.
>Read **Description** card for this vase, which contains a fuller entry than the Caskey-Beazley article.

Stop 11   Location 11 of 20: London E 271, Side A: Terpsichore with Mousaios and Melousa.

>From the **Links** menu select **Browser**.
>Select **Vases** from the **Browser** window.
>From the pop-up menu select **Keywords: Divinities**.
>Scroll down and select **Muse**.
>From the far left column at the bottom select **London E 271**.
>View **Side A: Terpsichore with Mousaios and Melousa** and read **Description**.

Stop 12   Location 12 of 20: Munich Shoen 80, Achilles Painter.

>From the **Links** menu select **Vases**.
>From the **Index Type** select **Painter**.
>Select **Achilles Painter** from the left column.
>From the right column select **Munich Shoen 80**.

>View **Main Panel** and read **Description**.

Stop 13   Location 13 of 20: Munich 2362, Pelike.

>From the **Links** menu select **Vases**.
>From the **Index Type** select **Shape**.
>Scroll down and select **Pelike** from the left column.
>Scroll down the right colum and select **Munich 2362**.
>View **Side A: Apollo and Muse** and read **Description**.

Stop 14   Location 14 of 20: Athens, NM 216, Context: Mantinea.

>From the **Links** menu select **Sculpture**.
> From the **Index Type** select **Context**.
>Scroll down and select **Mantinea** from the left column.
>Select **Athens, NM 216** from the right column.
>Unfortunately there are no illustrations for this relief, but read its
Description. You will notice the reference **Primary Texts: <u>Paus. 8.9.1</u>**.
Take a look at it.
>Click and drag cursor across <u>**Paus. 8.9.1**</u> to highlight it.
>From the **Links** menu select **Primary Texts**.
>Read Pausanias' description of a temple in Mantinea composed of two
parts, one side dedicated to Asclepius, the other to Leto and her children,
Apollo and Artemis. It is Apollo's connection with the Muses that is
significant.

Stop 15   Location 15 of 20: St. Petersburgh St. 1793, Eleusinian Painter.

>From the **Links** menu select **Vases**.
>From the **Index Type** select **Painter**.
>Scroll down and select **Eleusinian Painter** from the left column.
>Select **St. Petersburg St. 1793** from the right column.
>View **Side A: Zeus consulting Themis before the Trojan War** and read
Description. You will notice that the **Path Note** contains a reference to
another vase, **Berlin F 2538**.
>From the **Links** menu select **Lookup**.
>Type in **Berlin F 2538** in the small window that appears.
>From the **Links** menu select **Vases**.
>View **Drawing of Tondo: Themis and Augeus**.

Stop 16   Location 16 of 20: Themis or Demokratia, Athens, Agora S 2370.

>From the **Links** menu select **Sculpture**.
>From the **Index Type** select **Context**.
>Select **Athens, Agora** from the left column.
>From the right column select **Athens, Agora S 2370**.

>View **Themis (?)** and read **Description**.

Stop 17   Location 17 of 20: Notebook stop with a collection of vase depicting various deities.

>From the **Perseus** menu select **Notebook**.
>Click **Notebook Index** and select **Chapter 3B: Deities/Vases**.
>Call up vases of various deities discussed in this and the previous path from the **Links** menu.

Stop 18   Location 18 of 20: Notebook stop with a collection of sculpture depicting varous deities.

>From the **Perseus** menu select **Notebook**.
>Click **Notebook Index** and select **Chapter 3B: Deities/Friezes**.
>Call up sculpture references to **Siphnian Treasury, Delphi** from the **Links** menu.

Stop 19   Location 19 of 20: Notebook stop of three buildings in the Athenian Agora.

>Locate the **Note** entitled **Chapter 3B: Agora** in the **Notebook**.
>Call up each building from the **Architecture Catalog**.
>From the **Architecture card** you can pinpoint each building in the Agora by clicking **Locate Bldg**. This will take you to the **Site Plan** in the **Site Catalog** and the building will flash for you.

Stop 20   Location 20 of 20: Notebook stop with a collection of Primary Texts.

>This Notebook stop collects in one convenient location important textual references to the material in this chapter. You can access any passage by highlighting the reference, going to the **Links** menu, and selecting **Primary Texts**. If you wish, you can reorganize this material for your own needs. For example, you can put all the references to Ares in a Path Note of a stop that deals with Ares by using the **Cut** and **Paste** command from the **Edit** menu.

You have now completed the second of your tours. What follows is an exercise, which teaches you how to create an additional stop.

Stop 21   Location 21 of 21: Atlas.

A number of places have been referred to in the tours you have taken. Some of them may have been familiar to you, others perhaps not. With Perseus you can locate a particular place or region by using the Atlas feature.

>From the **Links** menu select **Atlas**. You will notice an **Altas** menu open up next to the **Perseus** menu. Like the Site plans, the Atlas contains a small scroll window to move around the maps. The first map you see is the Outline Map. On the rectangular box in the center of the screen there are some buttons or "hot spots".

>Click on the Magnifying Glass Icon to the right in the rectangular box. This will take you in for a closer look of the map.
>Click on the **Graphic Index of Maps**. This returns you to the previous **Outline Map**, which now designates those regions to which specific individual maps are devoted.
>Click back on **Outline Map** to return to the map, as it was originally, without the regions highlighted.
>Click on the **small flag** next to **Show Tools**. The rectangular box opens up. You can select a site from the new scroll window in the left column and plot it on the map.
>Scroll down and select **Mt. Olympus**.
>Click **Plot Selected Sites**.
>Relocate the rectangular bar, which is in the center of the map. Click and hold on the top shaded bar and drag it off to one side. You will see that Mt. Olympus has been plotted on the Outline Map.
>Individually select and plot the following: **Athens**; **Delphi**; **Dodona**; **Lemnos**; **Mt. Helicon**; **Olympia**; **Samos, Heraion**; and **Troy**.
>Click the center of the **Path Icon** in the Navigator to create a new stop. Perseus will ask into which path you want the stop placed.
>Select **CHAPTER 3B: The Olympians** and click **OK**. Now you will be asked to name the stop.
>Type in **Atlas** and click **OK**. The Path card will flash by and then the Atlas will replot each of the sites you selected, one by one, and store them.
>From the **Perseus** menu select **Current Path Card**. You will now see a new stop with the **Atlas Icon**, which will be location 21 of 21.
>Select this last stop and type into the **Notes** field in the bottom right corner any comments you wish. You might list the sites plotted in this Atlas stop. When you are done typing, click once outside of the note field to store it.
>Highlight again the **Atlas** Icon and click **Go There**. The stop will be displayed with the path note you have just created.
>From the **Atlas** menu select **Save Plotted Sites to Notebook**. A Notebook Card will be created containing the previous list of sites. Whenever you want to call up a site simply go to the note card, now entitled **Atlas Sites**, highlight the site you want plotted, and then select **Atlas** from the **Links** menu. This will work like any of the Notebook Cards we have used throughout these two guided tours.
>From the **Perseus** menu select **Notebook**.

>Click **Notebook Index**. You will see a new entry: Note (followed by the time and date it was created).

>Highlight this new note and click **Rename Note**.

>Type in **Atlas Sites** and click **OK**. Unlike the stop you just created, you can call up this note in any path you choose.

There are a number of other features in the Atlas that you can explore on your own. To access the color maps listed in the Map Index under the Atlas menu you will need Hypercard 2.2.

Test Questions

CHAPTER 1

A. Multiple Choice

1. Which of the following did not arise from Chaos?
   - a. Tartarus
   - b. Erebus
   - c. Uranus
   - d. Eros

2. The Greek term *hieros gamos* means:
   - a. an epiphany of the god
   - b. the birth from Chaos
   - c. a yawning void
   - d. a holy marriage

3. The Titans are the offspring of:
   - a. Gaia and Eros
   - b. Gaia and Uranus
   - c. Gaia and Cronus
   - d. Gaia alone

4. Greek mythology imagines the earth as a flat disc encircled by:
   - a. Oceanus
   - b. Chaos
   - c. Erebus
   - d. Uranus

5. Which of the following drove the chariot of the sun disastrously?
   - a. Helius
   - b. Hyperion
   - c. Apollo
   - d. Phaëthon

6. Selene, goddess of the moon, fell in love with the handsome shepherd:
   - a. Tithonus
   - b. Endymion
   - c. Adonis
   - d. Eros

7. Eos is the goddess of the:
   - a. night
   - b. rainbow
   - c. dawn
   - d. sun

8. Aphrodite was born as a result of the castration of:
   - a. Cronus
   - b. Zeus
   - c. Uranus
   - d. Oceanus

9. Cronus devoured all his children except:
   - a. Hera
   - b. Hades
   - c. Poseidon
   - d. Zeus

10. The mother-earth goddess, Rhea, was the consort of:
    - a. Cronus
    - b. Zeus
    - c. Uranus
    - d. Tithonus

B. Fill in the Blanks

1. Hesiod gives an account of genesis in his poem _____.
2. Tithonus was finally turned into a _____.
3. The name *Hecatonchires* literally means _____.

4. The father of Helius was _____.
5. The daughters of Oceanus are called _____.

C. Short Essays

1. How does Aphrodite's birth relate to her essentially sexual nature?
2. What is a *hieros gamos* and how is it continually employed in the myths thus far?
3. How might the story of Cronus' usurpation of Uranus' place be understood in a psychological interpretation?
4. What is the place and role of the mother-goddess in Greek mythology?
5. What is the place and role of the father-god in Greek mythology?

CHAPTER 2

A. Multiple Choice

1. In Zeus' bid for power, from which of the following did he not receive aid?
    a. Hecatonchires
    b. Cyclopes
    c. Titans
    d. Prometheus

2. In another struggle Zeus fought against the Gegeneis, whose name means:
    a. the One-hundred Handers
    b. the Earthborn
    c. the Powerful One
    d. the One-eyed Ones

3. One of the most difficult opponents for Zeus to overcome was the dragon named:
    a. Typhoeus
    b. Themis
    c. Enceladus
    d. Ephialtes

4. In the traditional version of the creation of man, who is depicted as the creator?
    a. Epimetheus
    b. Athena
    c. Deucalion
    d. Prometheus

5. Zeus punished Prometheus for which of the following?
    a. for giving men hope
    b. for creating Pandora
    c. for the deception of the sacrifice
    d. for the creation of man

6. The offspring of Zeus and Io was:
    a. Epaphus
    b. Pyrrha
    c. Deucalion
    d. Epimetheus

7. Who was the slayer of Argus?
    a. Prometheus
    b. Hermes
    c. Zeus
    d. Epaphus

8. Which of the following was the final outrage that preceded the flood?
    a. Lycaon attempted to rape Hera.
    b. Lycaon attempted to kill Zeus.
    c. Lycaon attempted to overthrow Zeus.
    d. Lycaon attempted to feed Zeus human flesh.

9. Who survived the flood sent by Zeus?
   a. Prometheus and Pyrrha
   b. Deucalion and Hellen
   c. Deucalion and Pyrrha
   d. Noah

10. According to the tradition, mankind is recreated:
    a. from the bones of those killed in the flood
    b. from rocks
    c. by Zeus
    d. as the natural offspring of the surviving man and woman

B. Fill in the Blanks

1. What Titan is condemned to uphold the vault of the sky? _____
2. What two giants attempted to force a way to Olympus by piling Ossa on Pelion? _____
3. According to Hesiod, what are the Five Ages of Man? _____ _____
4. Who is the eponymous ancestor of the Greeks? _____
5. From what source did the peacock receive its distinctive pattern? _____

C. Short Essays

1. Explain the following statement: Prometheus is often viewed as a "culture god."
2. In the myth of Pandora, what is the nature of Hope?
3. In Hesiod the punishment of Prometheus, though seemingly cruel, is a necessary consequence of a righteous and majestic Zeus. In <u>Prometheus Bound</u> the focus has shifted. How does the playwright contrast the figures of Zeus and Prometheus? Does our view of Zeus suffer from the contrast? What role might Io's suffering play in our final understanding of Zeus?
4. Discuss the Five Ages of Man and the distinctive features of each according to Hesiod.
5. Discuss the striking parallels between Greek and Near Eastern myth.

CHAPTER 3

A. Multiple Choice

1. Who is the goddess of the hearth?
   a. Demeter
   b. Hera
   c. Hestia
   d. Rhea

2. Etymologically the name *Zeus* means:
   a. bright
   b. the thunderer
   c. the lightning-bringer
   d. the storm cloud

3. Zeus' chief sanctuary is at:
   a. Dodona
   b. Delphi
   c. Olympia
   d. Athens

4. Which of the following is not a child of Zeus and Hera?
   a. Eileithyia
   b. Hebe
   c. Hephaestus
   d. Ganymede

5. Which statement is not true of Hephaestus?
   a. He worked in a forge.
   b. He was cast down to earth.
   c. His wife was the goddess of love, Aphrodite.
   d. Samos, the island where he landed, was the site of an important sanctuary of Hephaestus.

6. Which bird is sacred to Hera?
   a. the eagle
   b. the peacock
   c. the dove
   d. the raven

7. Ares' cult partner was:
   a. Aphrodite
   b. Hera
   c. Athena
   d. Hebe

8. The Muses are the children of Zeus and Mnemosyne, whose name means:
   a. poetry
   b. necessity
   c. memory
   d. dance

9. Ares was known to the Romans as:
   a. Pluto
   b. Mercury
   c. Vulcan
   d. Mars

10. Another name for the Fates is:
    a. the Graeae
    b. the Moirai
    c. the Erinyes
    d. the Horae

B. Fill in the Blanks

1. The three children of Zeus and Themis are the three Fates, named_____, _____, and _____.
2. The Athenian sculptor _____ carved the famous chryselephantine statue of Zeus.
3. On the west pediment of the temple of Zeus at Olympia, the commanding, central figure of _____ is the one serene figure in the battle of the Lapiths and Centaurs.
4. Both _____ and _____ serve as official cupbearers to the gods.
5. Name four of the nine muses: _____, _____, _____, _____.

C. Short Essays

1. Discuss the different aspects of Zeus' character.
2. Compare and contrast the picture of Hephaestus as he shambles around as cupbearer (Iliad 1. 577ff.) and the story of his wife's affair with the god of war (Odyssey 8. 266ff.).
3. What do you make of the interpretations of the myth of Ganymede?
4. How did the sculptures of the temple of Zeus at Olympia celebrate the struggle between savagery and civilization, the ideal of Panhellenic unity, and the glory of Zeus?

5. Though surrounded by little mythology, Hestia's position is important to Greek religious, political, and social life. Why?

CHAPTER 4

A. Multiple Choice

1. What is the hallmark of the Greek conception of the Olympians?
    a. Animism
    b. Anthropomorphism
    c. Monotheism
    d. Deism

2. Which statement is not true of the supreme gods of the Greek pantheon?
    a. They usually have their homes on Mt. Olympus.
    b. They drink ambrosia and eat nectar.
    c. Ichor, not blood, flows in their veins.
    d. They are worshiped by sacrifice.

3. What is the most important difference that separates the gods from humans?
    a. They are of immense stature.
    b. They are more powerful than men.
    c. They are immortal.
    d. Their knowledge is superior to that of mortals.

4. Chthonian deities are deities who
    a. inhabit Olympus
    b. animate nature
    c. are long-lived but not immortal
    d. are associated with the earth and the Underworld

5. The Tanakh is
    a. the Greek New Testament
    b. the Hebraic Old Testament
    c. a Babylonian epic
    d. the title of Herodotus' work

6. Who is the writer who records the tale of Solon and Croesus?
    a. Herodotus
    b. Hesiod
    c. Plato
    d. Xenophanes

7. Which may not be said of the story of Solon and Croesus?
    a. Solon's lesson is that a man cannot be counted blessed until he has died well.
    b. Croesus' life illustrates the power of nemesis.
    c. A man should guard against overweening pride.
    d. The gods show their favor by lavishing mortals with power and riches.

8. Who was the instrument of fate and caused Croesus' son's death?
    a. Atys
    b. Adrastus
    c. the monstrous boar
    d. Cleobis and Biton

9. What mortal brought about the eventual downfall of Croesus?
    a. Cyrus the Great
    b. the oracle at Delphi
    c. Tellus the Athenian
    d. Solon

10. According to Herodotus, which god rescued Croesus from the pyre?
    - a. Zeus
    - b. Nemesis
    - c. Apollo
    - d. Athena

B. Fill in the Blanks

1. Croesus was the legendary king of _____.
2. What three individuals did Solon name in response to Croesus' question? _____, _____, _____.
3. What was the name of Croesus' son, who was killed while on a hunting expedition? _____.
4. What pre-Socratic poet-philosopher attacked the anthropomorphic conception of the gods? _____.
5. Cyrus the Great was the king of the _____.

C. Short Essays

1. Defend this statement using Greek mythology: Monotheism and polytheism are not mutually exclusive terms.
2. In the Greek tradition, anthropomorphism and humanism are bound together. Explain.
3. How might we describe the story of Croesus as a Greek tragedy?
4. Though the Greek gods are conceived in human terms, discuss the guif which separates mortals from immortals.
5. Write an essay explaining how Greek religion, myth, philosophy, and history are intertwined.

CHAPTER 5

A. Multiple Choice

1. The sea-nymph Thetis married the mortal:
    - a. Achilles
    - b. Nereus
    - c. Peleus
    - d. Chrysaor

2. Galatea, having spurned the advances of Polyphemus, fell in love with:
    - a. Acis
    - b. Erechtheus
    - c. Poseidon
    - d. Triton

3. Polyphemus, a cyclops, was the son of:
    - a. Zeus
    - b. Triton
    - c. Poseidon
    - d. Pontus

4. Which of the following is true?
    - a. Amphitrite, the daughter of Proteus, gave birth to Triton.
    - b. Thetis, the daughter of Nereus, was the consort of Poseidon.
    - c. Thetis, the daughter of Peleus, gave birth to Achilles.
    - d. Amphitrite, the daughter of Nereus, was the consort of Poseidon.

5. Triton is often depicted as:
    - a. a half-man/half-horse because his father is the tamer of horses
    - b. a half-man/half-fish blowing on the conch shell
    - c. a mortal, young man who can change shape
    - d. the old man of the sea

6. Poseidon is usually seen:
    a. bearing the thunderbolt
    b. holding a cornucopia of fish
    c. wearing a crown of sea-shells
    d. wielding the trident

7. With which of the following is Poseidon not associated?
    a. earthquakes
    b. horses
    c. bulls
    d. the Underworld

8. Iris was the goddess of:
    a. waters
    b. the rainbow
    c. childbirth
    d. storms

9. Aristaeus goes to his mother for help because:
    a. He was detained off the coast of Egypt.
    b. He was changed into a sea-monster.
    c. He has lost his bees.
    d. He has lost Galatea.

10. Eidothea was the daughter of:
    a. Poseidon
    b. the monster Scylla
    c. Nereus
    d. Proteus

B. Fill in the Blanks

1. The father of the sea-nymph Galatea was _____.
2. The nymph who was changed into a creature girded by dogs' heads is named _____.
3. The whirlpool which terrorized sailors in the straits between Sicily and Italy was known as _____.
4. _____ was the old man of the sea, who could change his shape at will and knew the future.
5. Whom must Aristaeus appease by his sacrifice and rituals? _____.

C. Short Essays

1. Discuss the appearance and character of Poseidon.
2. Explain how the figures of Nereus, Proteus, and Triton merge and become confused with one another.
3. Compare and contrast Homer's and Vergil's depiction of Proteus.
4. Discuss how Ovid treats the story of Galatea and Polyphemus.

CHAPTER 6

A. Multiple Choice

1. According to Hesiod, Zeus gave birth to Athena after having swallowed:
    a. Thetis
    b. Metis
    c. Galatea
    d. Tritogeneia

2. The Parthenon was dedicated to Athena Parthenos, which means:
    a. virgin
    b. strong in battle
    c. wisdom
    d. daughter of Zeus

3. The sculptures which adorn the Parthenon were crafted under the guidance of:
    a. Praxiteles
    b. Myron
    c. Pheidias
    d. Ictinus

4. Which name is not associated with Athena?
    a. Pallas
    c. Cythera
    b. Tritogeneia
    d. Parthenos

5. What object served as a talisman for the city of Troy?
    a. the aegis
    c. the head of Medusa
    b. the Palladium
    d. Athena's shield

6. In the contest with Arachne, Athena grew enraged because:
    a. Arachne was cheating.
    b. Arachne depicted an embarrassing incident in Athena's life.
    c. Arachne recorded the love affairs of the gods.
    d. Arachne kept talking while Athena was trying to work.

7. What is usually depicted on Athena's shield?
    a. the head of a gorgon
    c. the thunderbolt
    b. Nike, the goddess of victory
    d. the head of Athena herself

8. Which is not generally associated with Athena?
    a. the olive
    c. the snake
    b. the owl
    d. the eagle

9. What is the theme of the inner, continuous frieze of the Parthenon?
    a. the birth of Athena
    b. the contest between Athena and Poseidon
    c. the Panathenaic procession
    d. the Gigantomachy

10. Which of the following is not true of Athena?
    a. She is the goddess of handicrafts.
    c. She invented the flute.
    b. She is the goddess of battle.
    d. She has no close relationships with men.

B. Fill in the Blanks

1. Athena's childhood girlfriend, whom she accidently killed, was named _____.
2. Who is depicted on a Panathenaic amphora? _____.
3. What two mythological scenes are rendered on the east and west pediment of the Parthenon? (east)_____, (west)_____.
4. What was the name of the cult statue housed in the Parthenon? _____.
5. The god _____ split the head of Zeus to facilitate the birth of Athena.

C. Short Essays

1. Discuss the sculptural details of the Parthenon and how they celebrate the patron goddess of Athens.
2. Discuss the evidence which might support the claim that Athena was originally a fertility goddess.
3. How does the story of Athena's contest with Arachne illustrate the "severe, moral earnestness" of this goddess?
4. Discuss the masculine and feminine elements in the character and appearance of Athena.
5. Explain the close relationship between Zeus and his daughter.

CHAPTER 7

A. Multiple Choice

1. Which of the following are not usually seen in Venus' entourage?
   a. the Charites
   b. the Horae
   c. the Fates
   d. Cupid

2. Which place is not associated with Aphrodite?
   a. Paphos
   b. Cythera
   c. Cyprus
   d. Crete

3. Who is the ithyphallic son of Aphrodite who insures prosperity and guards against thieves?
   a. Cupid
   b. Priapus
   c. Phallus
   d. Pan

4. Which is not true of Adonis?
   a. He was Aphrodite's lover who was gored by a boar.
   b. He was the consort of Cybele who castrated himself.
   c. The anemone sprang from drops of his blood.
   d. He was compelled to remain in the Underworld with Persephone for a part of the year.

5. Who was the mortal by whom Aphrodite conceived the Trojan Aeneas?
   a. Anchises
   b. Attis
   c. Adonis
   d. Pygmalion

6. In what dialogue does Plato inquire into the nature of Eros?
   a. The Apology
   b. The Euthyphro
   c. The Symposium
   d. The Republic

7. Who, in Plato, narrates the story of the three original sexes?
   a. Socrates
   b. Aristophanes
   c. Pausanias
   d. Agathon

8. In the dialogue, Socrates claims to have learned about the true nature of Eros from:
   a. the goddess Aphrodite herself
   b. the god of love, Eros
   c. his own careful investigations
   d. a Mantinean woman named Diotima

9. In what work do we find the tale of Cupid and Psyche?
   a. Apuleius' Metamorphoses
   b. Ovid's Metamorphoses
   c. Plato's Symposium
   d. Hesiod's Theogony

10. Who was the famous poetess from Lesbos?
   a. Lesbia
   b. Sappho
   c. Polyhymnia
   d. Urania

B. Fill in the Blanks

1. What two epithets of Aphrodite suggest the dual nature of love? _____ and _____.
2. _____ was the mortal who fashioned an ivory statue of his ideal woman.

3. The male counterpart of Aphrodite is _____ or Cupid.
4. The name of the daughter of Cupid and Psyche was _____.
5. In the tale of Cupid and Psyche, what was Psyche's last task before she was reunited with her beloved? _____.

C. Short Essays

1. How does the story of Aphrodite and Adonis parallel that of Cybele and Attis?
2. How does the Platonic Socrates relate the initial attraction of physical love to the final purpose of love?
3. How might we say that the comic tale of the Platonic Aristophanes has an essentially serious purpose?
4. Discuss the nature and character of Aphrodite, with special attention to the dual tradition of her origin.
5. Relate the story of Cupid and Psyche and illustrate how it combines elements of myth, folktale, fairy tale, and romance.

CHAPTER 8

A. Multiple Choice

1. What is the function of Artemis that she shares with Hera and Eileithyia?
   a. goddess of the moon
   b. goddess of childbirth
   c. goddess of the hunt
   d. protectress of young animals

2. Who was the woman whose children were slain because of their mother's pride?
   a. Callisto
   b. Leto
   c. Niobe
   d. Hecuba

3. Actaeon was punished by Artemis because:
   a. He tried to seduce her.
   b. He insulted her mother, Leto.
   c. He bested Artemis in the hunt.
   d. He caught sight of her bathing.

4. With whom of the following does Artemis not share the quality of chastity?
   a. Athena
   b. Callisto
   c. Hestia
   d. Minerva

5. What was the fate of the young hunter Arcas?
   a. He became the constellation Arcturus.
   b. He was destined to roam the world as a bear.
   c. He was fated to kill his mother.
   d. He was turned into a stag and was ripped apart by his own dogs.

6. What was Orion punished for?
   a. He killed an animal sacred to Artemis.
   b. He unwittingly slew his own mother.
   c. He tried to rape Artemis.
   d. He saw Artemis bathing.

7. With what two deities is Artemis usually associated?
   a. Athena and Apollo
   b. Hecate and Selene
   c. Selene and Helius
   d. Poseidon and Leto

8. What deity is seen as a foil to Artemis in Euripides' <u>Hippolytus</u>?
    a. Aphrodite
    b. Poseidon
    c. Apollo
    d. Athena

9. What city in Asia Minor was home to one of the most famous cult centers of Artemis?
    a. Delos
    b. Troy
    c. Miletus
    d. Ephesus

10. Who was responsible for divulging Phaedra's secret to Hippolytus?
    a. Phaedra's nurse
    b. Phaedra herself
    c. Theseus
    d. no one; Hippolytus overheard his stepmother revealing her passion.

B. Fill in the Blanks

1. The twin brother of Artemis is _____.
2. Artemis became associated with childbirth because _____.
3. The mother and father of the twins are _____ and _____.
4. To Ovid, Artemis was known as _____.
5. The god who responds to Theseus' curse and kills Hippolytus is _____.

C. Short Essays

1. How do you interpret and assess the character of Hippolytus?
2. What do Artemis and Aphrodite represent for Euripides in the <u>Hippolytus</u>?
3. Artemis demands purity for herself and her female followers. Defend this statement using the mythology surrounding the goddess.
4. How do you interpret and assess the character of Phaedra?
5. What aspects of the virginal Artemis reveal the characteristics of a fertility goddess?

CHAPTER 9

A. Multiple Choice

1. What island is the site of Apollo's birth and site of a famous sanctuary?
    a. Samos
    b. Delphi
    c. Delos
    d. Lesbos

2. Why is Apollo called the Pythian?
    a. His priestess is known as the Pythia.
    b. His favorite shrine was the site of the Pythian games.
    c. The name of Delphi was originally Pytho.
    d. Apollo killed the dragon that guarded the site.

3. What was the fate of the Cumaean Sibyl?
    a. She spurned Apollo's advances and was doomed to live for generations until only her voice remained.
    b. She spurned Apollo's advances and was fated to give true oracles but never to be believed.
    c. She spurned Apollo's advances and was turned into a laurel tree.
    d. Apollo never tried to seduce her and she died old and unmarried.

4.   The one successful love affair was that which Apollo had with:
   a.   Cassandra   c.   Daphne
   b.   Cyrene   d.   Marpessa

5.   Who was the youth that Apollo loved but accidently killed with a discus?
   a.   Ganymede   c.   Narcissus
   b.   Marsyas   d.   Hyacinthus

6.   For what action did Zeus kill Apollo's son Asclepius?
   a.   He tried to seduce Hera.
   b.   He refused to sacrifice to the gods because he was the son of Apollo.
   c.   He brought Hippolytus back from the dead.
   d.   Trick question: Asclepius did not die; he is the immortal son of Apollo.

7.   Which musical opponent did Apollo flay alive for daring to challenge the god?
   a.   Marsyas   c.   Homer
   b.   Pan   d.   Midas

8.   The foolish music critic who decided against Apollo was:
   a.   Tmolus   c.   Midas
   b.   Marsyas   d.   Cassandra

9.   How did the laurel become sacred to Apollo?
   a.   On the spot where Apollo was born a laurel tree sprang up.
   b.   On the spot where Apollo killed Hyacinthus a laurel tree sprang up.
   c.   His sanctuary at Delphi was noted for the laurel trees which grew on Mt. Parnassus.
   d.   Daphne was turned into a laurel tree to escape Apollo's advances, and in his grief the laurel always had a special place in his heart.

10. What king was Apollo condemned to serve as punishment for killing the Cyclopes?
   a.   Midas   c.   Alcestus
   b.   Admetus   d.   Arthur

B. Fill in the Blanks

1.   The priestess of Apollo would deliver her oracles seated upon a _____.
2.   From what animal does Delphi receive its name? _____
3.   What is the Greek name for the navel stone which was located at Delphi? _____
4.   The mother of Asclepius was _____.
5.   In one of the famous contests, Mt. Tmolus judged in favor of Apollo and against _____.

C. Short Essays

1.   Compare and contrast Apollo's contest with Marsyas and Pan.
2.   Discuss the nature of the god Apollo. Why is he often seen as "the most characteristically Greek god in the whole pantheon"?
3.   Relate three stories which depict the god Apollo in love and tell how they color his character.
4.   Give a description of Delphi, the sanctuary, the oracle, and the competitions.
5.   How do you view Ovid's account of Apollo and Daphne?

CHAPTER 10

A. Multiple Choice

1. Which is not a function or epithet of Hermes?
   - a. Argeiphontes
   - b. Psychopompus
   - c. Messenger of the gods
   - d. God of Florists

2. What instrument did Hermes invent and give to Apollo?
   - a. the lyre
   - b. the caduceus
   - c. winged sandals
   - d. the tripod for the Pythia of Apollo

3. Who is the mother of Hermes?
   - a. Metis
   - b. Maia
   - c. one of the Muses
   - d. Hera

4. With which rustic region of Greece is Hermes most associated?
   - a. Athens
   - b. Delos
   - c. Olympia
   - d. Arcadia

5. What is the caduceus?
   - a. a staff topped with a pine cone and entwined with tendrils of ivy
   - b. the special winged sandals Hermes wears
   - c. the staff entwined with two snakes
   - d. the special hat Hermes wears as messenger

6. Why was Apollo upset with the infant Hermes?
   - a. Hermes insulted the oracle of Apollo.
   - b. Hermes tried to steal the lyre from him.
   - c. Apollo was jealous because Hermes played music better than he.
   - d. Hermes stole the cattle of Apollo.

7. Which of the following is not true of Hermes?
   - a. He is a mischievous god.
   - b. He is the god of undertakers.
   - c. He is a patron of teenage boys.
   - d. He protects thieves.

8. In his role as Psychopompus, Hermes:
   - a. delivers the divine commands of his father Zeus
   - b. watches over the prosperity of a household
   - c. brings fertility to one's land
   - d. guides the souls of the dead into the Underworld

9. What is the name of the numerous statues of the head of Hermes on a pillar, with male genitals?
   - a. petasus
   - b. herms
   - c. phalli
   - d. hermits

10. What is the name of the youth loved by Salmacis?
    - a. Hermaphroditus
    - b. Hyacinthus
    - c. Narcissus
    - d. Argus

B. Fill in the Blanks

1. The name of Hermes' traveling hat is the _____.
2. Hermes fashioned the lyre from a _____.
3. Hermes was a quick study. According to Homeric Hymn, he was born in the morning, by midday he had _____, and by evening he had _____.
4. What was the fate of Hermaphroditus? _____.
5. The Roman name for Hermes is _____.

C. Short Essays

1. Relate the story of Hermes' birth and his quarrel with his brother Apollo.
2. Discuss the multifaceted nature of Hermes and the apparent incongruity of some of the elements of his character.
3. Retell the story of Hermaphroditus and Salmacis. What does the story attempt to explain?
4. Contrast the character of Apollo with that of Hermes.
5. What are the characteristics of the lengthy Homeric Hymn to Hermes that make it so admired? What is your judgment of its artistry?

CHAPTER 11

A. Multiple Choice

1. What was the fate of Semele?
    a. She cheated on Zeus and he struck her with his thunderbolt.
    b. She was turned into a cow and Hera sent a gadfly to harass her.
    c. She asked to see Zeus in his true form and was blasted by his appearance.
    d. She killed herself when she learned she had conceived a child by Zeus.

2. Which is not true of Dionysus?
    a. He was sewn into the thigh of Zeus until he came to term.
    b. He is fundamentally a vegetation god.
    c. From the myths about him, it appears that he was native to Greece.
    d. He was cared for by the nymphs of Nysa and Semele's sister Ino.

3. In the Bacchae, what young king of Thebes rejects the worship of Dionysus?
    a. Lycurgus   c. Icarius
    b. Pentheus   d. Cadmus

4. What does the term *omophagy* mean?
    a. It refers to the sacred band that attend the god.
    b. It signifies the rending of the sacrificial animal.
    c. It is the magic wand that Dionysus and his attendant carry.
    d. It means the eating of the raw flesh of the sacrificial animal.

5. What is the name given to older satyrs?
    a. sileni   c. maenads
    b. bacchants   d. Galli

6. Who was given the gift of wine for welcoming the god?
   a. Erigone
   b. Icarius
   c. Lycurgus
   d. Midas

7. What happened to the pirates who abducted Dionysus?
   a. They were torn apart.
   b. They were drowned at sea.
   c. They were sacrificed to the god.
   d. They were turned into dolphins.

8. What nymph was changed into reeds, which were then used by Pan to fashion a pipe?
   a. Pitys
   b. Echo
   c. Syrinx
   d. Daphne

9. Which is not true of Echo?
   a. She delayed Juno in conversation and her punishment was that she could only repeat words spoken to her.
   b. She fell in love with Narcissus, who rejected her.
   c. She spurned the advances of Pan and was torn apart by shepherds.
   d. She spurned the advances of Pan and was transformed into a pine tree.

10. What is the name of the wand carried by Dionysus and his followers?
   a. the caduceus
   b. the thyrsus
   c. the *thiasus*
   d. the petassus

B. Fill in the Blanks

1. Zeus first mated with _____, who gave birth to Zagreus.
2. _____ received the gift of the golden touch for returning Silenus to Dionysus.
3. In Euripides' Bacchae, Dionysus is angry because Semele's sisters say that her lover was _____.
4. The daughter of Cadmus and mother of Pentheus was _____.
5. Another name for the *Bacchae* is _____.

C. Short Essays

1. Discuss the manifold nature of Dionysus and Dionysian worship.
2. Discuss the character of the two opponents Pentheus and Dionysus, in Euripides' Bacchae.
3. What role do women play in the worship of Dionysus and in the mythology that surrounds this god?
4. At the end of Euripides' Bacchae, the royal house of Thebes is devastated. Agave, returned to her senses after a madness that has driven her to kill her own son, must face her guilt and the power of the new god. How do you think she can reconcile herself to what has happened as she does not even want to remember Dionysus and leaves his worship to others?
5. In your reading you have been introduced to two seemingly diametrically opposed deities, Apollo and Dionysus. Compare and contrast the two forces in the world these gods represent, the Apollonian and the Dionysian.

CHAPTER 12

A. Multiple Choice

1. According to the Homeric Hymn, Demeter at Eleusis tried to immortalize:
   a. Celeus
   b. Demophoön
   c. Triptolemus
   d. Diocles

2. Which is not a name for the queen of the Underworld?
    a. Hecate
    b. Kore
    c. Proserpina
    d. Persephone

3. Where is the chief sanctuary for the performance of Demeter's mysteries?
    a. Dodona
    b. Olympia
    c. Delphi
    d. Eleusis

4. Why was Demeter's daughter required to spend a part of the year in the Underworld?
    a. She ate of the pomegranate.
    b. She had consummated her marriage with Hades.
    c. She had offended Zeus.
    d. She had to atone because Demeter had withheld fertility from the earth.

5. What does the term *hierophant* refer to?
    a. the sacred object
    b. the ritual sacrifice
    c. the high priest
    d. the ritual prayer

6. What is the *kykeon*?
    a. the pomegranate Persephone ate
    b. the altar of sacrifice
    c. the basket concealing the sacred objects
    d. the prescribed drink first mixed for Demeter

7. When Demeter first arrived at Eleusis, she stopped at
    a. the house of Celeus
    b. the Maiden Well
    c. her temple
    d. her altar

8. Whom did Demeter select to spread her arts of agriculture?
    a. Iacchus
    b. Iambe
    c. Celeus
    d. Triptolemus

9. Which is not another name for the god who rules the Underworld?
    a. Dis
    b. Pluto
    c. Plutus
    d. Hades

10. Who finally told Demeter that Hades had carried off her daughter?
    a. Helius
    b. Hecate
    c. Rhea
    d. Hermes

B. Fill in the Blanks

1. The one who first made Demeter laugh during her time of mourning was _____.
2. Demeter disguised herself as an old woman named _____.
3. _____ was sent by Zeus to bring back Demeter's daughter.
4. The sacred objects used during Demeter's mysteries were called _____.
5. _____ caught Demeter putting her infant son in fire and cried out.

C. Short Essays

1. Retell the myth of Demeter and Persephone.
2. Describe elements of the Eleusinian mysteries that relate to particulars in the <u>Homeric Hymn.</u>

3.   How are matriarchy and patriarchy dealt with in the <u>Homeric Hymn</u>?
4.   Describe the similarities between the myth of Demeter and Persephone and the stories of Aphrodite and Adonis, and Cybele and Attis.
5.   Along what main lines can mystery religions and public cult worship be distinguished?

CHAPTER 13

A. Multiple Choice

1.   What comrade did Odysseus find had not been properly buried?
    a.   Elpenor
    b.   Agamemnon
    c.   Achilles
    d.   Ajax

2.   Achilles in the Underworld tells Odysseus:
    a.   that he should beware the fickle heart of women and return home quickly
    b.   that he should find his body and bury it properly
    c.   that he should not have killed Hector
    d.   that he would rather be a slave among the living than a king in Hades

3.   With whom did Odysseus first speak in the Underworld?
    a.   the seer, Tiresias
    b.   his mother, Anticlea
    c.   his father, Laertes
    d.   his comrade, Agamemnon

4.   In what dialogue can Plato's <u>Myth of Er</u> be found?
    a.   the <u>Apology</u>
    b.   the <u>Phaedo</u>
    c.   the <u>Republic</u>
    d.   the <u>Symposium</u>

5.   Aeneas travels to the Underworld:
    a.   to see Dido
    b.   to find his way to Italy
    c.   to offer sacrifice for the dead
    d.   to speak with his father, Anchises

6.   What does Aeneas not bring with him when he enters the Underworld?
    a.   a sop for Cerberus
    b.   a coin for Charon
    c.   the golden bough
    d.   the Cumaean Sibyl

7.   In the *Myth of Er,* where do the virtuous go?
    a.   to Elysium
    b.   to the Islands of the Blessed
    c.   upward through an opening in the sky
    d.   to Olympus

8.   What region of the Underworld is Hell?
    a.   the Mourning Fields
    b.   the Fields of the Untimely Dead
    c.   Tartarus
    d.   Elysium

9.   What does the term *chthonian* mean?
    a.   It is another term for an Olympian deity.
    b.   It refers to a divinity who is *of the sky.*
    c.   It refers to a divinity who is *of the earth.*
    d.   It refers to one condemned to Tartarus.

10. In the Underworld, what is the River of Forgetfulness?
    a. Styx
    b. Acheron
    c. Cocytus
    d. Lethe

B. Fill in the Blanks

1. In Plato's <u>Myth of Er</u>, who chooses the pattern for one's next life? _____.
2. How is Sisyphus punished in the Underworld? _____,
3. Besides Sisyphus, who is another great mythological sinner? _____.
4. One of the three judges in the Underworld is _____.
5. The guide of Dante in Hell is _____.

C. Short Essays

1. Compare and contrast the Homeric and Vergilian Underworld.
2. Describe the fundamental differences between the quest of Aeneas and that of Odysseus, which leads them to the Underworld, and the lessons learned from their encounters.
3. How does Plato's philosophic view of the afterlife compare with the Homeric and Vergilian visions?
4. What from the Greco-Roman traditions of the Underworld persists in the Judeo-Christian conception of hell? How do they differ?
5. How do you value the depiction of the Afterlife by the Greeks and the Romans in terms of your religious or philosophical beliefs?

CHAPTER 14

A. Multiple Choice

1. According to Vergil, Eurydice's untimely death resulted from:
    a. a snakebite she suffered while attempting to flee the advances of Aristaeus
    b. the wrath of Hera, for her succumbing to the seduction of Zeus
    c. a pact she had made with Hades
    d. a jealous attack by maenads

2. Orpheus had his origins in:
    a. Asia Minor
    b. Thrace
    c. Sicily
    d. Egypt

3. Which of the following is said of Orpheus?
    a. He was torn apart by enraged maenads.
    b. He was killed because of Aristaeus.
    c. He was attacked by his Thracian countrymen.
    d. Having come for Eurydice, he was not allowed to leave Hades.

4. Which divinity is not associated with the stories of Orpheus?
    a. Apollo
    b. Artemis
    c. Dionysus
    d. Hades

5. According to Orphic theogony, the first principle was:
    a. Gaia
    b. Eros
    c. Chronos
    d. Uranus

6. Like Hesiod, the Orphic tradition introduces early on the procreative power of Eros, also called by the Orphics:

    a. Cupid
    b. Phanes
    c. Aphrodite
    d. Zeus

7. Which sea-god does Aristaeus consult to learn why his bees have died?

    a. Nereus
    b. Triton
    c. Pontus
    d. Proteus

8. Which is not a typical feature of mystery cults?

    a. secrecy
    b. initiation
    c. disbelief in an afterlife
    d. revelation

9. A full account of the initiation into the rites of Isis is given in:

    a. Ovid's <u>Metamorphoses</u>
    b. Hesiod's <u>Theogony</u>
    c. Vergil's <u>Georgics</u>
    d. Apuleius' <u>Metamorphoses</u>

10. Which god is a consort of Dea Syria?

    a. Tammuz
    b. Osiris
    c. Attis
    d. Adonis

B. Fill in the Blanks

1. In Cybele's worship, her eunuch priests are known as _____.
2. The _____ is a Bacchic rite by which the initiate was baptized by the blood of a slain bull.
3. The mysteries of the Persian sun god, _____, were widely practiced in the Roman Empire.
4. In the worship of the Egyptian Isis, her husband and brother is _____.
5. The hero of <u>The Golden Ass</u> is _____.

C. Short Essays

1. How might Plato's myth of Er and Vergil's Underworld indicate the influence of the Orphic tradition?
2.. What is a mystery cult? What are some of its typical features?
3. What are the elements in the myth of Orpheus and Eurydice which make it so influential and universal?
4. What does Christianity have in common with other mystery religions of antiquity (particularly that of Dionysus and Orpheus) in its teachings, ritual, and conception of deity?
5. Compare and contrast the myth of Orpheus and Eurydice as told by Vergil and Ovid. Which do you prefer and why?

CHAPTER 15

A. Multiple Choice

1. Greek saga concerns cities and regions that were important in what historical period?

    a. the Classical Period, from 480 to 404 B.C.
    b. the late Bronze Age, from 1600 to 1100 B.C.
    c. the Hellenistic Period, from 323 to 146 B.C.
    d. the Archaic Age, from 750 to 479 B.C.

2. Who was the legendary founder of Thebes?
   - a. Cadmus
   - b. Labdacus
   - c. Lycus
   - d. Laius

3. What woman was abducted by Zeus in the guise of a bull?
   - a. Io
   - b. Pasiphae
   - c. Phaedra
   - d. Europa

4. The noble houses of Thebes were descended from the "Spartoi," whose name means:
   - a. "men of battle"
   - b. "those who live purely"
   - c. "sown-men"
   - d. "armed men"

5. How did Laius bring a curse upon his house?
   - a. He killed Lycus, the legitimate king, and tied his wife to the horns of a bull.
   - b. He tried to seduce the goddess Hera.
   - c. He carried off the son of his host.
   - d. He married his mother and killed his father.

6. Who raised Oedipus but were not his true parents?
   - a. Laius and Jocasta
   - b. Laius and Merope
   - c. Polybus and Merope
   - d. Polybus and Jocasta

7. In what place was Oedipus promised a respite from his sorrows?
   - a. Thebes
   - b. Corinth
   - c. Mycenae
   - d. Colonus

8. What trinket would prove the undoing of Alcmaeon?
   - a. a chest
   - b. a ring
   - c. a brooch
   - d. a necklace

9. For what treasonous act was Antigone condemned?
   - a. She buried her brother Eteocles.
   - b. She refused to marry Creon's son Haemon.
   - c. She buried her brother Polynices.
   - d. She cursed the priest Tiresias.

10. Which of the following is not true of Tiresias?
   - a. After his death, he lost the gift of prophecy.
   - b. He was blinded by Juno for taking Zeus' side in a quarrel.
   - c. He was blinded by Athena after he saw her naked.
   - d. He is descended from one of the Spartoi.

B. Fill in the Blanks

1. The only two who escaped death by combat during the first expedition to Thebes were _____ and _____.
2. The sons of the Seven against Thebes were known as the _____.
3. _____ and _____ were the two sons of Antiope who avenged their mother.
4. The citadel of Thebes, named after its legendary founder, is called the _____.
5. The playwright _____ wrote the tragedy <u>Seven against Thebes</u>.

C. Short Essays

1. Using the elaboration of the nine motifs that frequently occur in Greek saga, discuss in what ways these motifs are manipulated in the story of Oedipus.
2. A major category of thought, whose moral dimensions Greek writers often explored, was the conflict between *nomos* and *physis*, or law and nature. How is this dilemma brought out in Sophocles' Antigone?
3. Discuss the roles of Tiresias and Jocasta in Sophocles' Oedipus.
4. What is the role of fate and free will in Sophocles' Oedipus?
5. Discuss the religion and philosophy of Sophocles' Oedipus at Colonus.

CHAPTER 16

A. Multiple Choice

1. Who was the charioteer bribed by Pelops?
    - a. Aegisthus
    - b. Myrtilus
    - c. Tantalus
    - d. Oenomaus

2. How did Atreus perpetuate the curse of his house?
    - a. He seduced the wife of Thyestes.
    - b. He tried to feed the gods human flesh.
    - c. He cast Myrtilus over a cliff.
    - d. He fed his brother his own children.

3. Agamemnon incurred the bitter hatred of his wife by:
    - a. bringing home a Trojan woman
    - b. insulting her sister Helen
    - c. sacrificing his daughter Iphigenia
    - d. leading the ten-year expedition against Troy

4. The father of Aegisthus was:
    - a. Pelops
    - b. Atreus
    - c. Tantalus
    - d. Thyestes

5. By which of the following is Orestes not given direct assistance?
    - a. Athena
    - b. Apollo
    - c. Electra
    - d. Zeus

6. Who wrote Iphigenia in Tauris, in which we find Iphigenia a priestess of Artemis?
    - a. Aeschylus
    - b. Ovid
    - c. Euripides
    - d. Sophocles

7. At the end of Aeschylus' Oresteia, the Furies are transformed into:
    - a. judge and jury
    - b. the Eumenides
    - c. the Erinyes
    - d. the Avenging Spirits

8. According to Homer, where did Agamemnon and Menelaus rule?
    - a. Agamemnon at Sparta and Menelaus at Mycenae
    - b. Agamemnon at Thebes and Menelaus at Corinth
    - c. Agamemnon at Mycenae and Menelaus at Corinth
    - d. Agamemnon at Mycenae and Menelaus at Sparta

9. Who served his son as food for the gods at a banquet?
   a. Ixion
   b. Sisyphus
   c. Tantalus
   d. Tityus

10. In what city is Orestes' guilt finally expunged?
   a. Athens
   b. Mycenae
   c. Thebes
   d. Corinth

B. Fill in the Blanks

1. _____ was the princess won in a chariot contest by Pelops.
2. The Trojan prisoner that Agamemnon brought home was _____.
3. Orestes returns to Mycenae to kill _____ and _____.
4. _____, the daughter of Helen and Menelaus, became the wife of Orestes.
5. What name, drawn from one of the forebears of the house of Atreus, was given to the southern part of the Greek mainland?

C. Short Essays

1. Discuss the movement from blood-vengeance to civil litigation to be found in Aeschylus' Oresteia.
2. Clytemnestra is one of the greatest creations of the tragic stage. Discuss her motives and her character in the legend or with specific reference to Aeschylus' Agamemnon or Sophocles' Electra.
3. In Orestes we see a young man torn between competing demands of justice. What are the demands placed upon him by his situation and by the gods? What is the strength of his character, and how is his dilemma resolved?
4. The figure of Electra has proved to be fertile ground for the creative imagination. Discuss her motives and her character in the legend, or compare and contrast her depiction in Aeschylus' Libation Bearers, Sophocles' Electra, and Euripides' Electra.
5. How do you judge the character and actions of Agamemnon? Is he the villain described by his wife Clytemnestra or the paragon envisioned by his daughter Electra?

CHAPTER 17

A. Multiple Choice

1. In what shape did Zeus visit Leda?
   a. in a shower of gold
   b. in the form of a swan
   c. in the shape of a bull
   d. in the guise of a bull

2. Which of the following is not true of Castor and Polydeuces?
   a. They are also known as the Dioscuri, twin sons of Zeus.
   b. They are patrons of sailors.
   c. Polydeuces shared his immortality with Castor.
   d. Castor was a tamer of horses, Polydeuces skilled in archery.

3. Which goddess was not involved in the judgment of Paris?
   a. Athena
   b. Aphrodite
   c. Hestia
   d. Hera

4. What king of Troy cheated Apollo and Poseidon of their pay?
   a. Priam
   b. Tros
   c. Laomedon
   d. Podarces

5. Who was the ill-fated son of Hector?
   a. Astyanax
   b. Paris
   c. Ascanius
   d. Aeneas

6. Agamemnon refused to give back to Apollo's priest his daughter named:
   a. Briseïs
   b. Chryseïs
   c. Helen
   d. Andromache

7. Which two heroes tried to dodge the Trojan expedition?
   a. Odysseus and Achilles
   b. Odysseus and Agamemnon
   c. Achilles and Menelaus
   d. Agamemnon and Menelaus

8. Who carried the bow of Heracles, without the aid of which Troy could not fall?
   a. Patroclus
   b. Achilles
   c. Telephus
   d. Philoctetes

9. Who was left behind by the Greeks to insure that the Wooden Horse was taken into the city?
   a. Sinon
   b. Odysseus
   c. Epeus
   d. Philoctetes

10. What priest of Apollo gave warning about the horse but was strangled by two serpents?
    a. Cassandra
    b. Chryses
    c. Laocoon
    d. Helenus

B. Fill in the Blanks

1. _____ was the Amazon warrior who was killed by Achilles.
2. The first Greek to be killed in the Trojan War was _____, who was subsequently given a few hours to spend with his grieving wife, Laodamia.
3. The wisest and oldest member of the Greek contingent was _____, the king of Pylos.
4. The two Greek Heroes who contested for the armor of Achilles were _____ and _____.
5. The principal ancient source for the fall of Troy is _____ by _____.

C. Short Essays

1. Compare and contrast the two principal warriors in Homer's Iliad, Achilles and Hector, in terms of their actions and their character.
2. Although the Judgment of Paris is not in Homer, how do you account for its popularity and importance? What do you make of Lucian's satiric treatment?
3. In Homer's Iliad, Achilles is called "godlike," and it has been said that he evinces this quality most in his rage. Explain this statement and the way in which Achilles begins to pull back from his anger, which has distanced him from his comrades, and to come to an understanding of his nature and his common humanity.
4. Compare and contrast the relationship of Paris and Helen with that of Hector and Andromache.
5. What is Homer's view of war in the Iliad? In your answer discuss the importance of the divinely crafted shield of Achilles.

6. Write a critical essay about the actions and character of Helen.

7. Discuss the heroic code (for both men and women) as depicted in the Iliad. What are its advantages to the society depicted in the work and its defects?

CHAPTER 18

A. Multiple Choice

1. Which character learns of Odysseus' identity through a scar?
   a. Telemachus
   b. Euryclea
   c. Argos
   d. Laertes

2. Who is the princess that takes Odysseus to her father's palace?
   a. Euryclea
   b. Nausicaä
   c. Calypso
   d. Scylla

3. How did Odysseus escape from the lair of the Cyclops?
   a. He tricked Polyphemus into divulging the secret exit.
   b. He got Polyphemus drunk, pried open the door, and fled.
   c. He clung to the underside of a black ram as it was going out to pasture.
   d. Polyphemus let him go because he proved too cunning an adversary.

4. Among what people were Odysseus' men almost lulled into staying, forgetting their own homeland?
   a. the Cicones
   b. the Laestrygonians
   c. the Phaeacians
   d. the Lotus Eaters

5. How did Odysseus and his men offend the god Helius?
   a. They blinded his son Polyphemus.
   b. They killed his cattle.
   c. They tried to trick the Sirens by stopping their ears with wax.
   d. They tried to carry off Calypso.

6. Which goddess especially protected Odysseus?
   a. Athena
   b. Circe
   c. Hera
   d. Aphrodite

7. How will Odysseus eventually die?
   a. Storm and shipwreck will finally take him.
   b. He will live to old age and die of natural causes.
   c. His own son will kill him.
   d. Athena will take him up to Mt. Olympus.

8. How does Aeolus try to help Odysseus?
   a. He tells him of the dangers he must still face.
   b. He instructs him to descend into the Underworld.
   c. He gives him a magic herb to counteract Circe's magic.
   d. He gives him a leather bag containing the winds.

9. Which of the following kings was detained in Egypt?
      a. Agamemnon   c. Idomeneus
      b. Menelaus   d. Diomedes

10. Which god is the special bane of Odysseus?
      a. Hermes   c. Poseidon
      b. Zeus   d. Oceanus

B. Fill in the Blanks

1. The witch _____ turned Odysseus' men into swine.
2. Book 11 of the <u>Odyssey</u>, in which Odysseus travels to the Underworld, is also known as the _____.
3. The son of Penelope and Odysseus was _____.
4. Upon returning home Odysseus was also recognized by the swineherd _____.
5. The name of Odysseus' son by Circe was _____.

C. Short Essays

1. Discuss the transformation that Odysseus undergoes as he tries to return home.
2. Discuss the character and role of Penelope in the <u>Odyssey</u>.
3. The <u>Iliad</u> has been sometimes called "high noon" and the <u>Odyssey</u> "eventide." One is seen as essentially tragic and the other as essentially romantic. Expand on these statements.
4. There are many fascinating characters in the <u>Odyssey</u>. Discuss at least two of the following: Telemachus, Nausicaä, Polyphemus, and Circe.
5. With your understanding of Odysseus, render an appreciation of these lines from Tennyson's <u>Ulysses</u>. What does Tennyson see in Odysseus?

> *I cannot rest from travel: I will drink*
> *Life to the lees: all times I have enjoy'd*
> *Greatly, have suffer'd greatly, both with those*
> *That loved me, and alone; on shore, and when*
> *Thro' scudding drifts the rainy Hyades*
> *vext the dim sea: I am become a name;*
> *For always roaming with a hungry heart*
> *Much have I seen and known; cities of men*
> *And manners, climates, councils, governments,*
> *Myself not least, but honour'd of them all;*
> *And drunk delight of battle with my peers,*
> *Far on the ringing plains of windy Troy.*
> *I am a part of all that I have met. . . .*
> *Yet all experience is an arch where thro'*
> *Gleams that untravell'd world, whose margin fades*
> *For ever and for ever when I move.*
> *How dull it is to pause, to make an end,*
> *To rust unburnish'd, not to shine in use!*
> *As tho' to breathe were life. Life piled on life*
> *Were all too little, and of one to me*
> *Little remains: but every hour is saved*

From that eternal silence, something more
A bringer of new things; and vile it were
For some three suns to store and hoard myself,
And this gray spirit yearning in desire
To follow knowledge, like a sinking star,
Beyond the utmost bound of human thought. . . .
Come, my friends,
'Tis not too late to seek a newer world.
Push off, and sitting well in order smite
The sounding furrows; for my purpose holds
To sail beyond the sunset, and the baths
Of all the western stars until I die.
It may be that the gulfs will wash us down:
It may be we shall touch the Happy Isles,
And see the Great Achilles, whom we knew.
Though much is taken, much abides; and tho'
We are not now that strength which in old days
Moved earth and heaven; that which we are, we are
One equal temper of heroic hearts,
Made weak by time and fate, but strong in will
To strive, to seek, to find, and not to yield.

CHAPTER 19

A. Multiple Choice

1. Who was the mother of Perseus?
    a. Europa
    b. Andromeda
    c. Danaë
    d. Hypermnestra

2. How did Zeus seduce her?
    a. He locked her in a chest and wouldn't let her out until she said yes.
    b. He came to her as a shower of gold.
    c. He promised that she would bear a heroic son.
    d. He said that he would turn her into a Gorgon.

3. Perseus, in his efforts to kill the Gorgon, was given aid by all but one of the following:
    a. the Graeae
    b. some nymphs
    c. Athena and Hermes
    d. Aphrodite and Poseidon

4. What object was Perseus not given for his quest?
    a. Bubo, Athena's owl
    b. the cap of invisibility
    c. a scimitar
    d. a bag, or *kibisis*

5. In order to get information from the three sisters of the Gorgons, Perseus:
    a. stole their magic wand
    b. stole their one eye and tooth
    c. threatened to do them bodily harm
    d. threatened to disclose the secret location of their lair

6. What creature sprang from the beheaded trunk of the Gorgon?
   - a. Scylla
   - b. the Chimaera
   - c. Pegasus
   - d. the Hydra

7. Whose hand did Perseus receive in marriage?
   - a. Andromeda
   - b. Cassiepea
   - c. Io
   - d. Danaë

8. What is the fate of Acrisius?
   - a. He is shown the head of Medusa and turned to stone.
   - b. He is killed by the sea-monster sent by Poseidon.
   - c. He escapes the prophecy by going into exile.
   - d. He is killed by a misthrown discus.

9. The brother of Danaüs was named:
   - a. Nauplius
   - b. Aegyptus
   - c. Argos
   - d. Abas

10. With which Egyptian goddess is Io identified?
   - a. Isis
   - b. Astarte
   - c. Demeter
   - d. Cybele

B. Fill in the Blanks

1. The women who killed their husband on their wedding night were _____.
2. The only one to refuse to do so was _____.
3. _____ was the girl who gave her name to the spring near Argos where she was seduced by Poseidon.
4. According to the Greeks, the poisonous snakes of Libya sprang from _____.
5. _____ was the name of the town or area important for the worship of Hera.

C. Short Essays

1. Discuss the number of folktale motifs included in the saga of Perseus.
2. Identify parallels to the folktale and fairy-tale themes of the saga of Perseus in other stories with which you are familiar.
3. Tell the story of Io, and explain how Io and her descendants are associated with Egypt?
4. What is the meaning and fascination of the archetypal concept of the Gorgon's head?
5. How would you characterize Danaë and Andromeda as heroines of saga?

CHAPTER 20

A. Multiple Choice

1. Where is Heracles' traditional birthplace?
   - a. Athens
   - b. Sparta
   - c. Crete
   - d. Thebes

2. Who were Heracles' real parents?
   - a. Alcmena and Amphitryon
   - b. Alcmena and Zeus
   - c. Hera and Iphicles
   - d. Hera and Zeus

3. Which tutor did Heracles kill?
   a. Linus, his music teacher
   b. Amphitryon, his chariot-driving instructor
   c. Autolycus, his wrestling coach
   d. Eurytus, his archery instructor

4. Heracles was to serve Eurystheus for twelve years, during which he performed his twelve labors for what offense?
   a. He had insulted Hera.
   b. He had tried to rob Eurystheus of his kingship.
   c. He had lied about his parentage.
   d. He had killed his wife and children in a mad rage.

5. Heracles spared the lives of the Cercopes, two mischievous dwarfs, because:
   a. He didn't have the heart to kill those ill-matched for him.
   b. They had made fun of his sunburnt behind and made him laugh.
   c. Zeus had commanded him to let them go.
   d. He found out that they were, in fact, his cousins.

6. Heracles missed the Argonaut expedition because:
   a. He fell asleep, and when he awoke Jason had already set sail.
   b. He was afraid of sea travel.
   c. He had eaten so much, he almost sank the ship.
   d. He lost track of time searching for his beloved Hylas.

7. By besting the river-god Achelous, Heracles won the hand of:
   a. Iole   c. Deïanira
   b. Omphale   d. Oechalia

8. Heracles experienced "death" by which of the following?
   a. He had wounded Hera, so she killed him.
   b. He had attempted to battle Apollo, and Zeus struck him with his thunderbolt.
   c. He was engulfed in flames from a blood-soaked robe and then burned on a pyre.
   d. He had tried to battle Hades himself and lost.

9. Which is not one of Heracles' twelve labors?
   a. the killing of the Nemean lion   c. the capture of Cerberus
   b. the cleaning of the Augean stables   d. the slaughter of the giant Antaeus

10. Who helped Heracles fetch the Apples of the Hesperides?
    a. Iolaus   c. Nessus
    b. Atlas   d. Chiron

B. Fill in the Blanks

1. The generic term given to Heracles' side adventures is _____.
2. Heracles' last wife was _____.
3. The descendants of Heracles were known as the _____, corresponding to the Dorian tribes which occupied the Peloponnese after the Mycenaean Age.
4. The twelve labors of Heracles can be geographically divided into those _____ and those _____.

5. _____ is the Greek word for labors.

C. Short Essays

1. Explain how the last three labors of Heracles can be seen as a conquest of death.
2. Discuss the development of Heracles from a rather primitive "master of animals," known more for his brute strength and endurance, to a more compassionate, unselfish hero, a paradigm of virtue and self-reliance with divine associations.
3. Compare and contrast the saga of Perseus with the saga of Heracles.
4. How many themes from saga and folktale can you identify in the legend of Heracles?
5. Discuss the nature and importance of goddesses and heroines in Heracles' life and death.

CHAPTER 21

A. Multiple Choice

1. What legendary figure was credited with instituting the Panathenaea and setting up the cult image of Athena on the Acropolis?
   - a. Cecrops
   - b. Erechtheus
   - c. Erichthonius
   - d. Theseus

2. Who was violated by Tereus and had her tongue cut out to silence her?
   - a. Procne
   - b. Philomela
   - c. Procris
   - d. Itys

3. The North Wind (Boreas) was the father of Zetes and Calaäs. Who was their mother?
   - a. Creusa
   - b. Procris
   - c. Cleopatra
   - d. Orithyia

4. How did Procrustes terrorize travelers?
   - a. He compelled them to engage in a wrestling match with him.
   - b. He compelled them to wash his feet, and when they had bent down he kicked them off the cliff.
   - c. He compelled them to lie on his bed. It they were too short, he would cut them down to size, if too long, hammer them to fit.
   - d. He compelled them to answer a riddle. If they couldn't answer correctly, he would have them for lunch.

5. What god is said to be the father of Theseus?
   - a. Poseidon
   - b. Apollo
   - c. Zeus
   - d. Hades

6. Who rescued Ariadne from the island of Naxos?
   - a. Theseus
   - b. Dionysus
   - c. Poseidon
   - d. Heracles

7. Theseus joined Heracles in his battle with:
   - a. the Lapiths
   - b. the Centaurs
   - c. the Giants
   - d. the Amazons

8. What was the fate of Perithoüs?
   a. He was chained to a rock and had his liver eaten by vultures.
   b. He was bound to a fiery wheel for eternity.
   c. He was fixed to a magic chair forever.
   d He was thrown in a pit and devoured by wild animals.

9. Who was the last king of Athens?
   a. Demophon
   b. Theseus
   c. Erechtheus
   d. Codrus

10. Why was Poseidon angry with Minos?
    a. Because he married Pasiphaë.
    b. Because he did not sacrifice the bull sent to him.
    c. Because he challenged Theseus.
    d. Because he hated the Minoans.

B. Fill in the Blanks

1. _____ constructed a hollow cow, by means of which Pasiphaë could mate with the bull of her dreams.
2. Disregarding his father's warning, _____ flew too close to the sun and perished.
3. _____ was restored to life after having fallen in a vat of honey.
4. The palace of Minos was at _____.
5. The _____ was a temple on the Acropolis, said to contain the wooden statue of Athena and the trident marks of Poseidon.

C. Short Essays

1. Relate the story of Philomela, Procne, and Tereus.
2. Identify archetypal motifs or themes in the saga of Theseus.
3. The bull image runs through tales of Athens as well as of Crete. Trace the use of this image in the stories you have read. What might be the significance of its ubiquitous presence?
4. Compare and contrast the legends of Icarus and Phaëthon.
5. What relationships do you detect between Minoan-Mycenaean excavations and the legend of Theseus?

CHAPTER 22

A. Multiple Choice

1. The name of the king of Colchis who was given care of the golden fleece was:
   a. Phrixus
   b. Aeëtes
   c. Argus
   d. Athamas

2. Who usurped the throne from Jason's father, the rightful heir?
   a. Aeson
   b. Athamas
   c. Iolcus
   d. Pelias

3. How was Jason recognized by the illegitimate king?
   a. He was wearing one sandal.
   b. He wore the family coat of arms.
   c. He resembled his father.
   d. He wore a ring left with him as a baby.

4. What deity helped Argus build the Argo?
   a. Hera
   b. Hermes
   c. Athena
   d. Apollo

5. On their return journey, the Argonauts encountered on Crete a bronze giant named:
   a. Thoas
   b. Talus
   c. Cyzicus
   d. Creon

6. The blind prophet Phineus was tormented by:
   a. the Gorgons
   b. the Furies
   c. the Chimaera
   d. the Harpies

7. What advice did Phineus give to Jason?
   a. to sail quickly past Scylla and Charybdis
   b. to release a dove and see if it passed through the Symplegades
   c. to visit the Graeae and receive divine armor
   d. to offer a sacrifice to Poseidon

8. Medea took vengeance on King Pelias by:
   a. cutting up his son and feeding him to the king
   b. giving him a poisoned cloak which consumed him in flames
   c. tricking his daughters into cutting him up and boiling him
   d. concealing a poisoned snake on his throne

9. Who wrote the Greek tragedy <u>Medea</u>?
   a. Sophocles
   b. Apollonius
   c. Aeschylus
   d. Euripides

10. In which city did Medea seek refuge after the murder of Glauce?
    a. Athens
    b. Iolcus
    c. Corinth
    d. Thebes

B. Fill in the Blanks

1. The crew of the Argo were called _____.
2. Symplegades means _____.
3. Medea was a priestess of _____.
4. Jason died as a result of _____.
5. Nephele was the mother of _____ and _____.

C. Short Essays

1. How does the legend of Jason exemplify the Hero's Quest on Propp's model?
2. Compare and contrast any two of the following heroes: Odysseus, Heracles, Theseus, and Jason.
3. How is the figure of Medea depicted as a quasi-divinity, a sorceress, and a romantic heroine?

4. How do you judge Jason for his betrayal of Medea and Medea for the killing of their children?
5. What are the elements of folktale in the legend of the Argonauts?

CHAPTER 23

A. Multiple Choice

1. How was Ixion punished in the Underworld?
   a. He had to roll a stone up a hill.
   b. He had to bring water in a sieve.
   c. He was bound to a revolving wheel.
   d. He was forever hungry and thirsty.

2. Who are the parents of the race of Centaurs?
   a. Centaurs and the mares of Magnesia
   b. Centaurs and Nephele
   c. a cloud Nephele and Ixion
   d. Philyra and Pegasus

3. What Lapith man was once a girl?
   a. Perithoüs
   b. Caeneus
   c. Chiron
   d. Eioneus

4. What was the fate of Alcyone?
   a. She drowned during a storm at sea.
   b. She was loved by Poseidon and bore twin sons.
   c. Centaurs attempted to carry her off at her wedding.
   d. She was transformed into a seabird that nests upon the waves.

5. Who was the prophet gifted with understanding the speech of animals?
   a. Bias
   b. Melampus
   c. Amphiaraus
   d. Trophonius

6. Which is not true of the hero Bellerophon?
   a. He killed the monstrous Chimaera.
   b. He succeeded in mounting Pegasus but died trying to reach heaven.
   c. He did battle with the Solymi and Amazons.
   d. He slew the race of Centaurs.

7. Who was the youth who was rescued from the sea by a dolphin?
   a. Meleager
   b. Arion
   c. Hippomenes
   d. Periander

8. Which Aegean island was home to the cult of the Cabiri?
   a. Delos
   b. Cyprus
   c. Samothrace
   d. Rhodes

9. From whom was the Trojan royal house descended?
   a. Iasion
   b. Leander
   c. Aeneas
   d. Dardanus

10. Which of the following is true of Baucis and Philemon?
    a.   Philemon would swim the Hellespont each night to visit his beloved Baucis.
    b.   They were an old couple rewarded for entertaining Zeus and Hermes unawares.
    c.   They were lovers forbidden to marry one another by their parents.
    d.   Baucis was tormented with forbidden love for her brother Philemon.

B. Fill in the Blanks

1.   The nymph _____ was transformed by Artemis into a spring in Sicily to escape the advances of the river-god Alpheus.
2.   The huntress _____ was eventually won in a race when her opponent dropped golden apples along the track to delay her progress.
3.   _____ was the hero whose life would be extinguished when a log was consumed in flames.
4.   A dithyramb is _____.
5.   _____ was the island sacred to the sun-god Helius.

C. Short Essays

1.   Relate the legend of the Calydonian Boar Hunt and its important variants.
2.   In this chapter we have learned of an important variant in the genealogy of Odysseus. What is this alternate tradition, and why is it important for an understanding of Odysseus' character?
3.   Discuss the story of Bellerophon and the quintessentially Greek lesson it conveys.
4.   What are the details in the story of Pyramus and Thisbe, and how do you account for its appeal?
5.   Write a biography of Peleus and identify recurring themes by identifying parallels elsewhere in myth and saga.

CHAPTER 24

A. Multiple Choice

1.   Who was the Italian god presiding over beginnings and depicted with two faces?
     a.   Jupiter   c.   Janus
     b.   Mars   d.   Bellona

2.   What was the original function of Mars?
     a.   He was a god of war.   c.   He was the god of crossroads.
     b   He was an agricultural deity.   d.   He was a god of the Underworld.

3.   In what capacity was the chief Italian sky-god worshiped on the Capitoline Hill?
     a.   Jupiter Latiaris   c.   Jupiter Optimus Maximus
     b.   Jupiter Dius Fidius   d.   Jupiter Indiges

4.   With what deities did Jupiter share his temple on the Capitoline to form a triad?
     a.   Jupiter, Juno, and Minerva   c.   Jupiter, Juno, and Venus
     b.   Jupiter, Juno, and Mars   d.   Jupiter, Minerva, and Venus

5.   Which of the following was not an Italian deity associated with fire?
     a.   Vesta   c.   Cacus
     b.   Vulcan   d.   Hestia

6. What major Italian festival was celebrated in midwinter?
   - a. the Liberalia
   - b. the Cerealia
   - c. the Saturnalia
   - d. the Lupercalia

7. Who was the mother of Aeneas?
   - a. Juno
   - b. Venus
   - c. Priapus
   - d. Roma

8. What Italian goddess was worshiped at Aricia near Lake Nemi?
   - a Diana
   - b. Artemis
   - c. Ceres
   - d. Fauna

9. Who had a temple that stood near the Circus Maximus, in the bustling commercial district?
   - a. Juno Moneta
   - b. Mercury
   - c. Plutus
   - d. Castor and Pollux

10. Who was the last king of Rome?
    - a. Romulus
    - b. Tarquinius Priscus
    - c. Numa Pompilius
    - d. Tarquinius Superbus

B. Fill in the Blanks

1. _____books were stored in the Capitoline temple of Jupiter and consulted by the Senate in times of crisis.
2. _____ was the only one of the gods who kept his original Greek name.
3. The rape of _____ was the event that precipitated the overthrow of the Roman kingship.
4. Aeneas in his wanderings falls in love with _____, the queen of Carthage.
5. The story of Aeneas and his journey to Italy was given canonical form by the poet _____ in his _____.

C. Short Essays

1. Discuss the fundamental differences between Greek and Roman conceptions of divinity.
2. Give an account of the legendary traditions of the foundation of Rome and of how the Trojan Aeneas became associated with Romulus and Remus and with Rome.
3. Compare and contrast the Homeric conception of the Hero, as exemplified by Achilles and Odysseus, and the Vergilian, as exemplified by Aeneas. What are the fundamental differences between how they view themselves, their people, and their quest?
4. Compare and contrast the first six books of Vergil's Aeneid with Homer's Odyssey.
5. Compare and contrast the last six books of Vergil's Aeneid with Homer's Iliad.
6. One of the greatest obstacles to Aeneas' destiny is his encounter with Dido, queen of Carthage. Discuss Vergil's characterizations of Dido and Aeneas. How do you judge their actions and behavior? Was Aeneas justified in leaving Dido?
7. What characteristics does Aeneas share with Hector?

Test Answers

Chapter 1
A. 1. c 2. d 3. b 4. a 5. d 6. b 7. c 8. c 9. d 10. a
B. 1. Theogony 2. grasshopper 3. hundred-handed 4. Hyperion 5. Oceanids

Chapter 2
A. 1. c 2. b 3. a 4. d 5. c 6. a 7. b 8. d 9. c 10. b
B. 1. Atlas 2. Otus and Ephialtes 3. Gold, Silver, Bronze, Heroes, Iron 4. Hellen 5. From the eyes of Argus

Chapter 3
A. 1. c 2. a 3. c 4. d 5. d 6. b 7. a 8. c 9. d 10. b
B. 1. Clotho, Lachesis, and Atropos 2. Pheidias 3. Apollo 4. Hebe and Ganymede 5. Any four of Calliope, Clio, Erato, Euterpe, Melpomene, Polyhymnia, Terpsichore, Thalia, Urania

Chapter 4
A. 1. b 2. b 3. c 4. d 5. b 6. a 7. d 8. b 9. a 10. c
B. 1. Lydia 2. Tellus, Cleobis, and Biton 3. Atys 4. Xenophanes 5. Persians

Chapter 5
A. 1. c 2. a 3. c 4. d 5. b 6. d 7. d 8. b 9. c 10. d
B. 1. Nereus 2. Scylla 3. Charybdis 4. Nereus or Proteus 5. the nymphs with whom Euridice used to dance (the companions of Euridice)

Chapter 6
A. 1. b 2. a 3. c 4. c 5. b 6. c 7. a 8. d 9. c 10. d
B. 1. Pallas 2. Athena 3. (east) Birth of Athena; (west) Contest between Athena and Poseidon 4. Athena Parthenos 5. Hephaestus

Chapter 7
A. 1. c 2. d 3. b 4. b 5. a 6. c 7. b 8. d 9. a 10. b
B. 1. Urania and Pandemos 2. Pygmalion 3. Eros 4. Pleasure (Voluptas) 5. descent into the Underworld (to get Persephone's beauty)

Chapter 8
A. 1. b 2. c 3. d 4. b 5. a 6. c 7. b 8. a 9. d 10. a
B. 1. Apollo 2. she was born first and helped deliver her brother 3. Leto and Zeus 4. Diana 5. Poseidon

Chapter 9
A. 1. c 2. d 3. a 4. b 5. d 6. c 7. a 8. c 9. d 10. b
B. 1. tripod 2. dolphin 3. omphalos 4. Coronis 5. Pan

Chapter 10
A. 1. d 2. a 3. b 4. d 5. c 6. d 7. b 8. d 9. b 10. a
B. 1. petasus 2. tortoise 3. invented the lyre; stolen Apollo's cattle 4. He became a hermaphrodite 5. Mercury

Chapter 11
A. 1. c 2. c 3. b 4. d 5. a 6. b 7. d 8. c 9. d 10. b
B. 1. Persephone 2. Midas 3. a mortal 4. Agave 5. maenads

Chapter 12
A.   1. b 2. a 3. d 4. a 5. c 6. d 7. b 8. d 9. c 10. a
B.   1. Iambe 2. Doso 3. Hermes 4. hiera 5. Metaneira

Chapter 13
A.   1. a 2. d 3. a 4. d 5. d 6. b 7. c 8. c 9. c 10. d
B.   1. one chooses for oneself 2. he must continually attempt to roll a rock up a hill 3. Ixion or Tantalus or Tityus or a Danaid (Danaids) 4. Minos or Rhadamanthys or Aeacus 5. Vergil

Chapter 14
A.   1. a 2. b 3. a 4. b 5. c 6. b 7. d 8. c 9. d 10. a
B.   1. Galli 2. taurobolium 3. Mithra(s) 4. Osiris 5. Lucius

Chapter 15
A.   1. b 2. a 3. d 4. c 5. c 6. c 7. d 8. d 9. c 10. b
B.   1. Amphiaraus and Adrastus 2. Epigoni 3. Amphion and Zethus 4. Cadmeia 5. Aeschylus

Chapter 16
A.   1. b 2. d 3. c 4. d 5. d 6. c 7. b 8. d 9. c 10. a
B.   1. Hippodamia 2. Cassandra 3. Clytemnestra and Aegisthus 4. Hermione 5. Pelops

Chapter 17
A.   1. b 2. d 3. c 4. c 5. a 6. b 7. a 8. d 9. a 10. c
B.   1. Penthesilea 2. Protesilaus 3. Nestor 4. Ajax (the great or greater, son of Telamon) and Odysseus 5. (Vergil's) <u>Aeneid</u> (Book 2)

Chapter 18
A.   1. b 2. b 3. c 4. d 5. b 6. a 7. c 8. d 9. b 10. c
B.   1. Circe 2. Book of the Dead (Nekuia) 3. Telemachus 4. Eumaeus 5. Telegonus

Chapter 19
A.   1. c 2. b 3. d 4. a 5. b 6. c 7. a 8. d 9. b 10. a
B.   1. the Danaids 2. Hypermnestra 3. Amymone 4. drops of Medusa's blood 5. Argos

Chapter 20
A.   1. d 2. b 3. a 4. d 5. b 6. d 7. c 8. c 9. d 10. b
B.   1. parerga (or incidental deeds) 2. Deianira 3. Heraclidae 4. within the Peloponnese and outside of the Peloponnese (or elsewhere) 5. athloi

Chapter 21
A.   1. c 2. b 3. d 4. c 5. a 6. b 7. d 8. c 9. d 10. b
B.   1. Daedalus 2. Icarus 3. Glaucus 4. Cnossus 5. Erechtheum

Chapter 22
A.   1. b 2. d 3. a 4. c 5. b 6. d 7. b 8. c 9. d 10. a
B.   1. Argonauts 2. clashing rocks 3. Hecate 4. struck by a piece of wood from the Argo. 5. Phrixus and Helle

Chapter 23

A. 1. c 2. c 3. b 4. d 5. b 6. c 7. b 8. c 9. d 10. b
B. 1. Arethusa 2. Atalanta 3. Meleager 4. choral song in honor of Dionysus 5. Rhodes

Chapter 24

A. 1. c 2. b 3. c 4. a 5. d 6. c 7. b 8. a 9. b 10. d
B. Sibylline 2. Apollo 3. Lucretia 4. Dido 5. Vergil, <u>Aeneid</u>

Glossary of Mythological Words
and Phrases in English

Many of us talk the language of myth without even realizing it. Myth encompasses a tradition, a repository of images, themes, motifs, and archetypes which can serve to give human speech resonance beyond its immediate context. When Hamlet compares his murdered father to his uncle as *Hyperion* to a *satyr*, he speaks a powerful shorthand; the images conveyed by these two personages do more to express his inner state than if he were simply to speak admiringly of the one and disparagingly of the other. Often we use mythological references in our everyday speech, blissfully unaware that many of our common everyday expressions find their origin in the mythic traditions of Greece and Rome; one can use the word *chaotic* without knowing its ultimate source.

The following list is designed to explain briefly the original mythological meaning of some of the more common terms that have entered our language. Cross-references to Morford and Lenardon's *Classical Mythology*, by page number in the parentheses following each entry, offer access to more lengthy discussion of the myths.

Achillean/Achilles' heel/Achilles' tendon: Achilles was the son of the mortal Peleus and the nymph Thetis. A warrior of legendary prowess in battle and the hero of Homer's *Iliad*, he was essential to the Greek war effort against Troy. To describe someone as *Achillean* is to mark that person as invincible or invulnerable, or nearly so. Achilles himself had one vulnerable spot. His mother dipped the infant Achilles in the magical waters of the river Styx in a vain attempt to render him immortal; she grasped him by the heel in order to submerge him in the stream, thereby leaving one spot on his body susceptible to injury. Paris took advantage of this weakness and with Apollo's help delivered the fatal arrow. An *Achilles' heel* refers to the one assailable feature or weakness a person may have, and in anatomy the *Achilles' tendon* stretches from the heel bone to the calf muscle. (M/L 367-368, 371-390)

Adonis: Adonis was such a handsome youth that Aphrodite herself found him irresistible. A capable hunter, he disregarded the warnings of the goddess to retreat in the face of a boar which stood its ground and sustained a fatal injury from the charging boar's tusk. A grieving Aphrodite sprinkled nectar on the blood-soaked ground and the anemone blossomed forth. To call a man an *Adonis* is to draw attention to his beauty. (M/L 132-134)

aegis: The aegis is the shield of Zeus (originally a "goat-skin"), which thunders when he shakes it. Athena also bore the aegis, often tasseled and with the head of Medusa affixed, its petrifying power still intact. This divine shield afforded safety and security, and so to be under the *aegis* of an individual or of an institution is to be favored with protection, sponsorship, or patronage. (M/L 79, 122-125, 622 n. 4)

Aeolian harp or lyre: Aeolus was put in charge of the winds by Zeus. He kept watch over his subjects in a cave on the Island of Aeolia. An *Aeolian harp* is a box-shaped musical instrument across which strings are strung, which vibrate when wind passes across them. (M/L 71, 395-396, 501, 541)

Amazon: The Amazons were a warrior-race of women from the north who joined battle with a terrifying war-cry. They were the equal of men in the field. They came to be seen as haters of men, women who sought foreign husbands, only to kill their sons and raise their daughters as Amazons. Later tradition has it that they cut off their right breast to become better archers. A vigorous and aggressive woman today might be deemed an *amazon*, while also conveying the idea of enormous physical stature. Often it is a derogatory term. The *Amazon ant* is a species of red ant that captures the offspring of other species and turns them into slaves. (M/L 119, 383, 465, 503-504)

ambrosia/ambrosial: The Greek gods on Olympus took food and drink as mortals do. But since the gods are of a different order from mortals, so too is their sustenance. Ambrosia, culled from the regions beyond the

Wandering Rocks, served variously as food for the gods, as unguent or perfume, or as fodder for horses. It is often coupled with nectar, which provided drink for the Olympians. Both words derive from roots which indicate their power to bestow immortality and stave off death. Today *ambrosia* can refer to a dessert of fruit and whipped cream or, especially when joined with nectar, any gourmet masterpiece. Generally, *ambrosial* has come to indicate anything fit for the gods or of divine provenance. See *nectar*. (M/L 93, 257)

aphrodisiac: According to Hesiod, Aphrodite was born of the foam around the severed genitals of Uranus, a fitting beginning for a divinity whose concern is the sexual. From her name comes the noun *aphrodisiac*, denoting anything that has the power to excite the sexual passions. (M/L 128-156)

Apollonian: Apollo had as his purview the arts, prophecy, and healing. At his chief shrine at Delphi the watchword was "know thyself," the beginning and principal aim of human understanding. He is the god of rationality, harmony, and balance, known by the epithet Phoebus, "bright" or "shining," by which he is equated with the sun and more broadly the order of the cosmos. The adjective *Apollonian* describes that which partakes of the rational and is marked by a sense of order and harmony. Its opposite is *Dionysian*, which describes unbridled nature, the frenzied and the irrational. These polarities, the *Apollonian* and the *Dionysian*, were recognized by the Greeks as twin aspects of the human psyche. See *bacchanal*. (M/L 169-199)

apple of discord: To the wedding of Peleus and Thetis all the gods and goddesses were invited, save one, Eris, or "Strife." To avenge this slight, this goddess of discord tossed into the wedding hall a golden apple with the inscription "For the Fairest." It was immediately claimed by three rival goddesses: Hera, Athena, and Aphrodite. Zeus refused to decide the issue, but instead gave it to Paris, the son of Priam, king of Troy, to settle. The *Judgment of Paris*, as it has come to be known, bestowed the apple on Aphrodite, who had promised to Paris the most beautiful woman in the world, namely, Helen, wife of Menelaus, king of Sparta. The abduction of Helen by Paris was the cause of the ten-year siege and destruction of Troy under the onslaught of the Greek forces, pledged to wreak vengeance on the seducer. The *apple of discord* describes any action or situation that causes dissension and turmoil and is more trouble than it is worth. (M/L 352-358)

arachnid: Arachne was a common girl with a remarkable skill in weaving. She won such fame that Athena, slighted and envious, challenged Arachne to a contest. Athena wove themes, including the fate of foolish mortals who dared to vie with the gods. Arachne depicted the gods' compromising love-affairs. Outraged, Athena struck the girl with her shuttle and, after Arachne hanged herself, in remorse transformed Arachne into a spider, so that she and her species might practice her art of weaving forever. An *arachnid* refers to any of the various arthropods of the class Arachnida, including the spider. (M/L 123-125)

Arcadia/arcadian: Arcadia is the central mountainous region of the Peloponnese. Often it is described in idyllic terms: the ideal land of rustic simplicity, especially dear to Hermes, the home of Callisto (the favorite of Artemis), and the usual playground of Pan; for the bucolic poets, Arcadia is a place where life is easy, where shepherds leisurely tend their flocks and pursue romantic dalliances. Thus *Arcadia* becomes that imagined primeval terrain, when human beings lived in contentment and harmony with the natural world. *Arcadian* refers to any place or time signifying the simple, rustic, pastoral life of a golden age lost. (M/L 163, 200, 244-245, 316)

Atlas/Atlantic/atlantes/Atlantis: Atlas was a Titan who opposed Zeus in the battle between the Olympians and the earlier generation of Titans. The defeated Titans were condemned to Tartarus, but Atlas was punished with the task of supporting upon his shoulders the vault of the heavens, thereby keeping the earth and sky separate. Through a mistaken notion that this vault, sometimes depicted as a sphere, was actually the earth, Atlas has given his name to that particular kind of book which contains a collection of geographical maps. It was not until the Flemish cartographer Gerhardus Mercator (1512-1594) depicted on the frontispiece of his *atlas* the Titan carrying the earth that the association became fixed. The plural of atlas has given us the term *atlantes*, which refers to support columns formed in the shape of men, corresponding to the maiden columns known as caryatids. Atlas endured his torment at the western edge of the world and so has given his name to the ocean beyond the straits of Gibraltar, the *Atlantic,* as well as to the *Atlas* mountains in northwest Africa. The mythical island of *Atlantis* was located, according to Plato, in the western ocean. (M/L 53, 55, 60, 415-416, 429-430, 432)

aurora australis/borealis: Aurora was the Roman goddess of the dawn (the Greek Eos). The sons of Aurora and the Titan Astraeus were the four winds: Boreas, who blows from the north, Notus, the southwest, Eurus, the east, and Zephyrus, the west. The streaks of light which appear in the sky at night are a result of the effect of the particles of the sun's rays on the upper atmosphere. Seen especially at the poles, in the northern hemisphere they are called the *northern lights* or the *aurora borealis,* and in the south, the *aurora australis,* Auster being the Roman name of the southwest wind. (M/L 43-44, 46, 89, 141, 384, 453)

bacchanal/bacchanalia/bacchanalian/bacchant/bacchante/bacchic: Dionysus, the Roman Bacchus, was the god of wine, frenzied music and dance, and the irrational. He presided over ecstatic, sometimes orgiastic, rites, which involved initiation and drove the participants into another plane of perception, as they became possessed by the deity. He is usually represented in the midst of a retinue of female worshipers, known as *maenads, bacchae,* or *bacchantes* (the feminine singular is *bacchante;* a male follower is a *bacchant,* plural *bacchants*); he is also attended by male *satyrs,* mischievous and lecherous creatures, half-human and half-animal. Wine proved a powerful conduit to the ineffable, amidst rituals that included the rending of a sacrificial victim and the eating of its raw flesh. The *Dionysiac* or *Dionysian* experience is the antithesis of the *Apollonian,* characterized by moderation, symmetry, and reason. Dionysiac rites among the Romans became known as *Bacchanalia,* and the sometimes extreme behavior of the initiates provoked the Roman Senate to outlaw them in 186 B.C. Thus we derive the words *bacchanal* and *bacchanalia* to refer to any debauched party or celebration. *Bacchanal, bacchant, bacchante,* and *bacchae* can be used to characterize an overzealous party-goer. The adjectives *bacchanalian* and *bacchic* describe any exuberant, drunken revelry. See *Apollonian.* (M/L 218-250, 190-191, 304-310, 461-463, 504-506, 522-523, 575, 584-585)

boreal: Boreas, the north wind, has given us this adjective, which refers to the region of the world from which his blasts come. See *aurora australis.* (M/L 56, 71, 73, 456, 478)

by Jupiter/by Jove/jovian/jovial: Jupiter was the Roman counterpart of Zeus, the supreme god and father. He was a god of the sky and his name is derived from Indo-European roots dyaus/pitr, which literally mean god/father. In Latin the common oath "by Jupiter" would be rendered "pro Jove" (Jove being a different form of his name). In the Christian tradition there is no religious significance to this exclamation, but English writers, by using it as an expression of surprise or pleasure, avoided taking God's name in vain; thus "by Jupiter" or "by Jove" was used to replace the offensive "by God." To describe someone or something as *jovian* means that one partakes of that awe-inspiring majesty that is particular to a supreme god. Many mythological names found a new existence in the field of astrology. Since it was felt that the heavenly bodies influence the life of humans on earth, celestial bodies were given appellations drawn from mythology, for example, Jupiter became the name not only of a god but a planet. Those who were born under the influence of the planet Jupiter were said to be of a cheerful disposition, hence the meaning of the adjective, *jovial.* (M/L 49-82, 94-96, 516-519, 541, 561-562)

caduceus: In Latin the herald's staff was known as the *caduceum,* derived from the Greek word *keryx,* or herald, and his staff the *kerykeion.* Hermes, as divine messenger, was invariably depicted with the *caduceus,* which was variously represented as a staff with white ribbons or intertwined snakes. The white ribbons may have indicated the inviolability of his office. The image of intertwined snakes may have been drawn from the Near Eastern use of copulating snakes as a symbol of fertility, for Hermes was a fertility god. The staff of Hermes became confused with the staff of Asclepius, the renowned mythic physician and son of Apollo, because some stories about Asclepius did involve snakes, and the reptile has the ability to slough its old skin and seemingly be "reborn." (M/L 213-214, 185-186)

calliope: Calliope was one of the nine Muses, who gives her name to the musical instrument the *calliope*, made up of tuned steam whistles and played like an organ; it is also the name for the California hummingbird. See *Muse.*

Cassandra: Trojan Cassandra, daughter of Priam and Hecuba, was amorously pursued by the god Apollo. Having at first agreed to succumb to his advances, she was awarded the gift of prophecy, but later, when she changed her mind and refused him, Apollo punished her. She would remain a prophetess, but would never be believed. Cassandra's predictions were invariably of disaster, foretelling the murder of Agamemnon by Clytemnestra or the destruction of Troy through the ruse of the Wooden Horse. A *Cassandra* today is anyone who utters dire warnings of the future, regardless of their truth. (M/L 179, 344-345, 360, 365, 386, 388, 583)

Calypso/calypso music: Calypso ("she who hides or conceals") was the daughter of Thetis and either Atlas, Nereus, or Oceanus. Odysseus was detained on her island home of Ogygia for seven years with the promise that she would make him immortal. Though he enjoyed her bed, each day he would weep and look with longing over the sea to his homeland Ithaca. Eventually Zeus sent Hermes to inform Calypso that she must give up Odysseus. *Calypso music*, derived from the name of the nymph, originated on the islands of the West Indies and treats of topical or amusing themes. (M/L 393-394, 400-401)

catamite: Zeus was so impressed with the beauty of the Trojan youth Ganymede that he took the form of an eagle and brought him to Olympus to become the cupbearer of the gods. The Latin rendering of Ganymede's name was *Catamitus*, and his relationship with Zeus (or Jupiter) was interpreted by some as overtly homosexual, to lend divine authority to ancient pederastic practices; today a *catamite* is still the designation for a boy used for pederastic purposes. (M/L 82-83, 140-141, 155, 574)

Cerberus: Cerberus, the hound of the Underworld, stood guard at the gates of Hades and prevented those not permitted from entering. He is usually described as a beast with three heads and the tail of a dragon. When Aeneas journeyed to the lower regions under the guidance of the Sibyl, he brought along a medicated cake to drug the animal and insure their safe passage. *To throw a sop to Cerberus* means to give a bribe and thereby ward off an unpleasant situation. (M/L 81, 115, 154, 288, 430)

cereal: Ceres (the Roman counterpart of Demeter) was goddess of grain and the fertility of the earth. From her name is derived the Latin adjective Cerealis (having to do with Ceres and the grain), from which comes our English word *cereal*. (M/L 52-53, 251-270, 307-310, 523)

chaos/chaotic: Whether Chaos is to be understood as a void or a primordial, formless, undifferentiated, and seething mass out of which the order of the universe is created, it is the starting point of creation. This unformed, initial beginning is contrasted with later creation, a universe called the cosmos, a designation meaning, literally, harmony or order. The sky and the stars, the earth and its creatures, and the laws and cycles which direct and control creation seem to exhibit the balance, order, and reason which the mind discerns in the natural world. For us *chaos*, together with its adjective *chaotic*, simply means a state of confusion; *cosmos*, on the other hand, refers to the universe and all that is ordered and harmonious. The study of *cosmology* deals with the origin and structure of the universe. The adjective *cosmic* may designate the universe beyond and apart from the earth itself, or it may in a generalized sense describe something of vast significance or implication. Akin to the word *cosmos* are various English words derived from the Greek adjective *cosmeticos*. *Cosmos* means not only order and harmony, but also arrangement and decoration; thus *cosmetic* is a substance which adorns or decorates the body, and *cosmetician*, the person involved with cosmetics. (M/L 38-39, 285, 306)

chimera: A wild, hybrid creature, the Chimaera had the head of a lion, the body of a goat, and the tail of a serpent, and it breathed fire. It was killed by the Corinthian hero Bellerophon on one of his journeys. Today a *chimera* is a fantastic delusion, an illusory creation of the mind. It can also refer to a hybrid organism, usually a plant. (M/L 115, 286, 503)

cornucopia: The Latin *cornucopia* means "horn of plenty." There are two stories about this horn, which bestows upon the owner an endless bounty. Zeus, in his secluded infancy on Crete, was nursed by a goat named Amalthea, which was also the name of the goddess of plenty. One of the horns of this goat was broken off and became the first cornucopia. The horn of plenty is also associated with Hercules. In order to win Deianira as his bride, he had to defeat the horned river-god Achelous. In the struggle, Hercules broke off one of the horns of the river-god but after his victory returned the horn and received as recompense the horn of Amalthea. Ovid, however, relates that in fact the horn of Achelous became a second horn of plenty. Today the *cornucopia* is a sign of nature's abundance, and the word comes to mean a plenteous bounty. (M/L 49-51, 435-436, 641 [note 19])

cosmos/cosmic/cosmology/cosmetic/cosmetician: See **chaos**.

cupidity: The Latin word *cupidus* (desirous or greedy) gave rise to *Cupido*, Cupid, the Roman equivalent of the Greek god of love, Eros. In early representations he is a handsome youth, but becomes increasingly younger and develops his familiar attributes of bow and arrow (with which he rouses passion both in gods and mortals) and wings, until he finally evolves into the Italian putti or decorative cherubs frequently seen in Renaissance art. From the same root is derived *cupiditas* to denote any intense passion or desire, from which we derive *cupidity* (avarice or greed). To the Greeks Eros was one of the first generation of divinities born from Chaos; he was also said to be the son of Aphrodite and Ares. From the Greek adjective *eroticos* we derive *erotic*, which describes anyone or anything characterized by the amatory or sexual passions. *Erotica* is a branch of literature or art whose main function is the arousal of sexual desire. *Erotomania* is an obsessive desire for sex. (M/L Cupid: 151-155, 180, 215; Eros: 38-39, 142-143, 147-151, 306-307, 357)

cyclopean: There were two distinct groups of giants called the Cyclopes, whose name means circle-eyed and indicates their principal distinguishing feature, one round eye in the center of their forehead. The first, offspring of Uranus and Ge, were the smiths who labored with Hephaestus at his forge to create the thunderbolt for Zeus and other masterpieces. The second group of Cyclopes were a tribe of giants, the most important of whom is Polyphemus, a son of Poseidon, encountered by Odysseus. The word *cyclopean* refers to anything that pertains to the Cyclopes or partakes of their gigantic and powerful nature. Thus the Cyclopes were said to be responsible for the massive stone walls which surround the palace-fortresses of the Mycenaean period. And so *cyclopean* is used generally to describe a primitive building style, which uses immense, irregular stone blocks, held together by their sheer weight without mortar. (M/L 21, 40-41, 47-48, 53, 83, 108-111, 187, 394-395, 521)

cynosure: The constellation Ursa Minor ("little bear") was called Kunosoura ("the dog's tail") by the astronomer Aratus, who saw in it one of the nymphs who raised the infant Zeus. Long a guiding star for seafarers, it has given us the word *cynosure*, which can describe anything that serves to focus attention or give guidance. (For the story of Callisto and Arcas and the constellations see M/L 163-165)

demon/demoniac/demonic/demonology: In Greek *daimon* was a word of rather fluid definition. In Homer the Olympians are referred to as either gods (*theoi*) or *daimones* ("divine powers"). In later literature the daimones became intermediate beings between gods and men, or often the spirits of the dead came to be called daimones, especially among the Romans. *Daimon* could also denote that particular spirit granted to each mortal at his birth to watch over its charge. This corresponds to the Roman *Genius*, a vital force behind each individual, originally associated with male fertility and particularly with the male head of a household. Later it became a tutelary spirit assigned to guide and shape each person's life. With the triumph of Christianity, all pagan deities were suspect, and daimon, viewed solely as a power sprung from the devil, became our *demon* (any evil or satanic spirit). As an adjective *demoniac* or *demonic* suggests possession by an evil spirit and can mean simply fiendish. As a noun *demoniac* refers to one who is or seems possessed by a demon. *Demonology* is the study of evil spirits. As for *genius*, it has come to denote a remarkable, innate, intellectual or creative ability, or a person possessed of such ability. Through French we have the word *genie*, which had served as a translation of *jinn*, spirits (as in the Arabian Nights) which have the power to assume human or animal form and supernaturally influence human life. (M/L 282)

Dionysian: See **Apollonian** and **Bacchanal**.

echo: There are two major myths which tell how the acoustic phenomenon of the *echo* arose. According to one, Echo was originally a nymph who rejected the lusty advances of the god Pan. In her flight she was torn apart by shepherds who had been driven into a *panic* by the spurned god Pan. The second version involves the mortal Narcissus. Echo had been condemned by Hera to repeat the last utterance she heard and no more. It was in this state that Echo caught sight of the handsome Narcissus. Narcissus, a youth cold to all love, rejected the amorous advances of Echo, who could now only mimic Narcissus' words. Stung deeply by this rebuff, she hid herself in woods and caves and pined for her love, until all that remained of the nymph was her voice. As for Narcissus, too proud in his beauty, he inevitably called down upon himself the curse of a spurned lover. Narcissus was doomed to be so captivated by his own reflection in a pool that he could not turn away his gaze, even to take food and drink. He wasted away and died. From the spot where he died sprang the *narcissus* flower. *Narcissism* has come to mean an obsessive love of oneself. As used in psychoanalysis it is an arrested development at an infantile stage characterized by erotic attachment to oneself. One so afflicted with such *narcissistic* characteristics is a *narcissist*. (M/L 244-250)

Electra complex: See **Oedipus**.

Elysian Fields/Elysian/Elysium: In Vergil's conception of the Underworld there is a place in the realm of Hades reserved for mortals who through their surpassing deeds and virtuous life have won a blessed afterlife. It is named the *Elysian Fields* or *Elysium*, and the souls who inhabit this paradise live a purer, more carefree and pleasant existence. The adjective *Elysian* has come to mean blissful. (M/L 284-297)

enthusiasm: In cultic ritual, particularly Dionysiac, the initiate was often thought to become possessed by the god and transported to a state of ecstatic union with the divine. The Greeks described a person so exalted as being *entheos*, "filled with the god," which gave rise to the verb *enthousiazein*. Thus the English word *enthusiasm*, meaning an excited interest, passion, or zeal. See *bacchanal*.

erotic/erotica/erotomania: See **cupidity**.

eristic: Eris was the goddess of "strife" or "discord," responsible for all the dissension arising from the apple of discord, which she threw among the guests at the wedding banquet of Peleus and Thetis. Thus is derived the term *eristic*, which as an adjective means pertaining to argument or dispute, as a noun, rhetoric or the art of debate. See *apple of discord*.

Europe: Europa was the daughter of Agenor, king of Tyre in Phoenicia. Zeus, disguised as a white bull, enticed the girl to sit on his back and rushed into the sea and made his way toward Greece. When they reached Crete, Zeus seduced Europa, who bore a son named Minos and gave her name to a foreign continent. The word *Europe* itself may be of Semitic origin, meaning the land of the setting sun. (M/L 317-319)

Faunus/faun/fauna/flora: *Faunus*, whose name means one who shows favor, was a Roman woodland deity. He was thought to bring prosperity to farmers and shepherds and was often depicted with horns, ears, tail, and sometimes legs of a goat; therefore he was associated with the Greek god Pan and also Dionysiac satyrs. A *faun* comes to be another name for a satyr. Faunus' consort was *Fauna*, a female deity like him in nature. *Flora* was another, though minor, agricultural deity, a goddess of flowers, grain, and the grapevine. When we talk of *flora and fauna*, we refer, respectively, to flowers and animals collectively. (M/L 522-526)

Furies/furious/furioso: The *Erinyes* (Furies) were avenging spirits. They sprang from the severed genitals of Uranus, when drops of his blood fell to the earth. They pursued those who had unlawfully shed blood, particularly within a family. They were said to rise up to avenge the blood of the slain and pursue the murderer, driving the guilty to madness. As chthonic deities they are associated with the Underworld and are charged with punishing sinners; they are usually depicted as winged goddesses with snaky locks. In English *fury* can refer to a fit of violent rage or a person in the grip of such a passion, especially a woman. The Latin adjective *furiosus* has given us our adjective *furious* as well as a musical term *furioso*, which is a direction to play a piece in a turbulent, rushing manner. (M/L 48, 71, 289-296, 343-349)

Gaia hypothesis: Gaia (or Ge), sprung from Chaos, is the personification of the earth. Her name has been employed in a recent coinage, the *Gaia hypothesis*, a theory that views the earth as a complete living organism, all of its parts working in concert for its own continued existence. (M/L 38-42, 45-52, 79-80)

genius: See **demon**.

gorgon/gorgoneion/gorgonian/gorgonize: The Gorgons were three sisters who had snakes for hair and a gaze so terrifying that a mortal who looked into their eyes was turned to stone. Medusa, the most famous of the three, was beheaded by Perseus, aided by Athena and Hermes. Perseus gave the head to Athena, who affixed it to her shield (see *aegis*). The head of the Gorgon was often depicted in Greek art in a highly stylized manner; this formalized depiction is called a *gorgoneion*. Today a *gorgon* can mean a terrifying or ugly woman. There is also a species of coral known as *gorgonian*, with an intricate network of branching parts. The verb *to gorgonize* means to paralyze by fear.

halcyon/halcyon days: The mythical bird the *halcyon* is identified with the kingfisher. Ceyx and Alcyone were lovers. Ceyx, the king of Trachis, was drowned at sea. Hera sent word to Alcyone in her sleep through Morpheus, the god of dreams, that her husband was dead. Alcyone in her grief was transformed into the kingfisher; as she tried to drag the lifeless body of Ceyx to shore, he too was changed into a bird. The lovers still traverse the waves, and in winter she broods her young in a nest which floats upon the surface of the water. During this time, Alcyone's father, Aeolus, king of the winds, keeps them from disturbing the serene and tranquil sea. Today, the *halcyon days* are a period of calm weather during the winter solstice, especially the seven days preceding and following it. *Halcyon days* can also describe any time of tranquillity. (M/L 493)

harpy: The Harpies ("snatchers"), the daughters of Thaumas and Electra, were originally conceived of as winds, but came eventually to be depicted as bird-like women who tormented mortals. The Argonauts rescued Phineus, the blind king and prophet of Salmydessus, whose food was "snatched" away by these ravenous monsters. Today when we call someone a *harpy* we evoke images of these vile, foul-smelling, predatory creatures; or *harpy* simply means a shrew. (M/L 113-114, 478, 539)

hector: Hector was the greatest warrior of the Trojans, who was defeated by his counterpart on the Greek side, Achilles. To *hector* means to bluster and bully. The noun *hector* denotes a bully. The connection between the noble Hector and this later conception originated in the Middle Ages, when Hector was portrayed as a braggart and bully. (M/L 360, 371-383)

heliotrope/heliotropism, etc.: Helius was a god of the sun. The Greek root *trop-* refers to a turning in a certain direction. *Heliotropism* is a biological term which refers to the growth or movement of an organism toward or away from sunlight. A *heliotrope* is a genus of plant that behaves in that manner. Several scientific or technical words derive from the name of the sun-god, for example: a *heliostat* is an instrument that uses a mirror to reflect sunlight; *heliotherapy*, treatment by means of the sun's rays; *heliotype*, a photomechanical process of printing a plate, or the printing plate itself produced in this fashion; *heliograph* is an instrument used to photograph the sun; and *heliocentric* refers to anything that has the sun as a center or is relative to the sun. (M/L 43-45, 495-496, 506-507)

Hercules/herculean/Hercules' club: Hercules, in Greek Heracles, was the greatest hero in the ancient world, who wore a lion skin and brandished a club and achieved countless remarkable exploits. He is most famous for twelve canonical labors. To describe someone as *herculean* is to liken him to Hercules in strength and stature. Any effort that is *herculean* requires a tremendous exertion or spirit of heroic endurance. The *Hercules* is a constellation in the northern hemisphere near Lyra and Corona Borealis. A shrub indigenous to the southeastern United States and characterized by prickly leaves and large clusters of white blossoms is known as *Hercules' club*. (M/L 420-448, 521-522, 533-534, 580)

hermetic/hermeneutic/hermeneutics/hermaphrodite: The god Hermes became associated with the Egyptian god Thoth and received the appellation Trismegistus ("thrice-greatest"). A number of works on occult matters, known as the Hermetic Corpus, were attributed to Hermes Trismegistus; today *hermetic* refers to occult knowledge, particularly alchemy, astrology, and magic. From this notion of secret or sealed knowledge *hermetic* comes to mean completely sealed; a hermetic jar is one closed against outside contamination. From Hermes' primary function as a bearer of messages came the Greek *hermeneus* ("interpreter") and the phrase *hermeneutike techne* ("the art of interpretation"). *Hermeneutics* is the science of interpretation, and *hermeneutic*, as adjective or noun, connotes an interpretive or explanatory function. Hermaphroditus, the beautiful son of Hermes and Aphrodite, was bathing in a pool, when the nymph Salmacis caught sight of him and was filled with desire. She plunged into the water and entwined her limbs around him. He fought her efforts to seduce him but her prayer to the gods that they might become united into one being was granted. A *hermaphrodite* has the genitalia and secondary sexual characteristics of both male and female. (M/L 200-217, 244-245, 530-531)

hydra: Heracles' second labor was to encounter the Hydra, a nine-headed serpent which would grow back two heads for every one that was severed. Every time he clubbed off one of the heads, the stump was cauterized so that another could not grow. A *hydra* is a polyp with a cylindrical body and tentacles surrounding an oral cavity, and it has the ability to regrow itself from cut-off parts. A hydra can also be a destructive force that does not succumb to a single effort. The *Hydra* is a constellation in the equatorial region of the southern sky near the constellation Cancer. (M/L 425)

hymen/hymeneal: Hymen was the god of marriage and was invoked during the wedding ceremony with the chant "O Hymen, Hymenaeus"; thus he was the overseer of *hymeneal* or marriage rites. Originally the Greek word *hymen* referred to any membrane, but today the *hymen* is a membranous fold of tissue which covers the outer orifice of the vagina. (M/L 298, 357, 370)

hyperborean: The Hyperboreans were a mythical race that inhabited a paradise in the far north, at the edge of the world, "beyond" (hyper) the reach of the north wind (Boreas) and his arctic blasts. In English *hyperborean* merely means arctic or frigid. (M/L 413, 425-426)

hypnosis/hypnotic, etc: Hypnos, son of Nyx (Night) and brother of Thanatos (death), was the god of sleep and father of Morpheus, the god of dreams. *Hypnosis* is a sleep-like condition in which the person becomes susceptible to suggestion. *Hypnotic* as an adjective means to pertain to or induce hypnosis and as a noun refers to the person hypnotized, something that promotes hypnotism, or means simply a soporific, that which induces sleep. *Hypnogogic* refers to a drug that produces sleep or describes the state immediately preceding sleep, while *hypnopompic* refers to the state immediately preceding awakening; both states may be marked by visual or auditory hallucination as well as sleep-induced paralysis. *Hypnophobia* is a pathological fear of sleep.

I fear Greeks even when they bear gifts: The fall of Troy was finally accomplished by a ruse of the Greeks. They constructed an enormous, hollow, wooden horse, into which they hid some of their best fighters. The horse was left behind as the rest of the Greek host sailed off to the nearby island of Tenedos and waited. The treacherous Sinon convinced the Trojans to drag the gift into the city, despite the warnings of Laocoon, a priest of Poseidon. In Vergil's account, Laocoon implored his countrymen not to bring the treacherous horse into Troy, crying *"I fear Greeks even when they bear gifts" (Timeo Danaos et dona ferentis)*. Two serpents emerged from the sea to strangle Laocoon and his two sons. The Trojans were convinced that they should accept the horse and thus wrought their own destruction. Laocoon's utterance has become a warning to beware of treachery and look for the hidden motives behind even the most fair-seeming generosity. (M/L 385-390)

ichor: Gods, although immortal, can suffer wounds; but from those wounds flows not human blood but instead a clear, rarefied liquid, divine ichor. In English *ichor* can refer to a fluid, like blood, or, in pathological terms, a watery substance discharged from wounds or ulcers. (M/L 93)

iris: Iris was the goddess of the rainbow (the meaning of her name). The adjective *iridescent* describes anything which gleams with the colors of the rainbow. The *iris* is the colored portion of the eye, which contracts when exposed to light. It is also a genus of plant which has narrow leaves and multi-colored blossoms. (M/L 113-114, 171, 259, 478)

Junoesque: Juno was the mighty and majestic queen of the Roman Pantheon, wife and sister of Jupiter, identified with the Greek Hera. To describe someone as *Junoesque* is to liken her to the goddess in stature and stately bearing. (M/L 68-69, 78-80, 163-164, 218, 353-358, 409, 422-424, 513, 519, 538-545)

labyrinth/labyrinthine: In Crete, King Minos had Daedalus construct a maze in which to imprison the monstrous Minotaur. Theseus' greatest achievement was to kill the Minotaur and, with the help of Ariadne's thread, find his way out of the maze, which was known as the *labyrinth*. Excavations of the complex and vast palace of Cnossus in Crete with its network of rooms seem to substantiate elements of this legend. A *labyrinth* is a maze, and the adjective *labyrinthine* describes something winding, complicated, and intricate. *Labyrinth* can also denote anatomical features marked by connecting passages, in particular the structures of the internal ear. (M/L 460-461, 468-469)

lethe/lethargy/lethargic: Lethe was the river of "forgetfulness" in the Underworld. From it souls would drink and forget their experiences upon being reincarnated. *Lethe* refers today to a state of oblivion or forgetfulness; *lethargy* and *lethargic* denote a state of persistent drowsiness or sluggishness. (M/L 282-283, 292-295)

lotus/lotus eater: Odysseus was driven to North Africa and the land of the Lotus Eaters, who consumed the fruit of the lotus and lived in a continual state of dreamy forgetfulness and happy irresponsibility. Today a *lotus eater* is anyone who succumbs to indolent pleasure. The *lotus*, a small tree of the Mediterranean, produces the fruit supposedly consumed by the Lotus Eaters; it is also an aquatic plant indigenous to southern Asia. (M/L 394)

maenad: See **bacchanal**.

March/martial: Mars was the Roman god of war, equated with the Greek Ares. He personified the conflict of battle in all its brutality and bloodshed. The adjective *martial* means of or pertaining to battle; when the military authority usurps the power of civil authority, the population is said to be under *martial law*. Also the name of the month *March* is derived from Mars. (M/L 86-90, 513-516)

matinee/matin: Matuta was a minor Roman deity, the goddess of the dawn (in Latin dawn is *tempus matutinum*). Through French, we have *matinee* (a theatrical or cinematic performance given in the daytime) and *matins* (also called Morning Prayer), the first division of the day in the system of canonical hours of the monastic tradition.

Medusa: See **gorgon**.

mentor: In Book 1 of Homer's *Odyssey*, Odysseus' palace is ravaged by suitors for the hand of his wife, Penelope. His son, Telemachus, daydreaming of his father's return, is incapable of action. Athena, in the guise of Odysseus' trusted counselor, Mentor, comes to Ithaca to rouse Telemachus and give him advice and hope. Thus *mentor* means a trusted guardian and teacher.

mercury/mercurial: Mercury was the Roman equivalent of the Greek Hermes (see *Hermetic*). This fleet-footed messenger of the gods has given us the word *mercury*, a silver metallic element, which at room temperature is in liquid form, also called "quicksilver" because of the nature of its movement. In astrology, *Mercury* is the name given to the planet closest to the sun, around which it completes one revolution in 88 days. In botany, it refers to a genus of weedy plant. To describe someone as *mercurial* is to impart to the individual craftiness, eloquence, cunning, and swiftness, all attributes of the god. It can also simply mean quick or changeable in temperament, either from the nature of the god or the influence of the planet.

Midas' ass's ears and golden touch: Apollo and Pan entered into a musical contest. When Apollo was judged victorious by the mountain-god Tmolus, Midas, the king of Phrygia, disagreed. For his lack of perception Apollo transformed Midas' offending ears into those of an ass. To have *ass's ears* means that one lacks true musical judgment and taste. On another occasion, the god Dionysus granted Midas' wish that whatever he might touch be turned into gold. To his despair, Midas found that even as he put food and drink to his mouth it was transmuted into gold. Dionysus granted him relief by telling him to bathe in the river Pactolus, whose bed became golden. To have the *golden touch* means to be successful in any endeavor. (M/L 188–189, 242)

money/monetary: In the Temple of Juno Moneta ("money," "mint") was housed the Roman mint. *Moneta*, through the Old French *moneie*, has given us the word *money*; the adjective *monetary*, "pertaining to money," comes from the stem *monet-*.

morphine: Morpheus was the god of dreams, or more particularly the shapes (*morphai*) that come to one in dreams. Later he became confused with the god of sleep, and it is from this confusion that the meaning of *morphine* comes. *Morphine*, an addictive compound of the opium plant, is used as an anesthetic or sedative. The compounds which include the stem *morph-*, such as *metamorphosis* (a transformation into another shape or state of being), are drawn from the Greek word *morphe* ("shape" or "form") and not the god Morpheus.

Muse/music/museum/mosaic: The nine Muses were the daughters of Zeus and Mnemosyne ("memory"), whose province was inspiration in the arts, particularly poetry and music; from *muse* we derive the word *music*. The Greek word *mouseion* ("place of the Muses"), in Latin *museum*, has given us *museum*, a place for displaying works of artistic, historical, or scientific interest. From the adjective *mousaicos* ("pertaining to the Muses") comes *mosaic*, a picture or design made up of small colored tiles or stones. (M/L 37–38, 43–45, 90–91, 192, 198–199)

narcissism/narcissist/narcissistic/narcissus: See **echo**.

nectar: Nectar is the special drink of the gods, usually paired with their food, ambrosia. *Nectar* has come to mean any refreshing drink, the pure juice of a fruit, or the liquid gathered by bees from the blossoms of flowers, used in making honey. (M/L 93, 206)

nemesis: Nemesis is the goddess of vengeance, who brings retribution on those who have sinned, especially through hubris ("over-weaning pride"). A *nemesis* denotes: the abstract idea of retributive vengeance; the agent of retribution; an invincible rival in a contest or battle; or a necessary or inevitable consequence. (M/L 60, 98)

nestor: Nestor, the oldest and wisest of the Greek kings at Troy, lived to see three generations of heroes. A brave and strong warrior when young, in old age he was prized for his good counsel and his oratory. Homer tells us that his speech flowed more sweetly than honey. When a politician or statesman today is called a *nestor*, it is these qualities of wisdom, good counsel, and oratory that are emphasized. (M/L 21-22, 364, 403, 434)

nymph/nymphomania/nympholepsy: Nymphs are beautiful, idyllic goddesses of wood and stream and nature, often the objects of love and desire. A *nymph* today may simply mean a remarkably attractive young woman, but if she were to suffer from *nymphomania* ("nymph-madness"), she would be suffering from sexual promiscuousness. *Nympholepsy* (from *lepsis*, "a seizing"), on the other hand, refers to the madness which assails one who has glimpsed a nymph. It can also denote a strong desire for what is unattainable.

ocean: In mythology the world is a disc circled by a stream of water, the god Oceanus, who is the father of the Oceanids, i.e., all the lesser rivers, streams, brooks, and rills that flow over the earth. Today *ocean* can refer to the entire body of salt water or any of its major divisions covering the globe. (M/L 42-44)

odyssey: Homer's *Odyssey* recounts the return of Odysseus to Ithaca, his wife, Penelope, and his son, Telemachus. After ten years of war at Troy, Odysseus found the day of his return postponed for another ten years by the god Poseidon. On his extended travels he overcame many challenges of every sort before winning his homecoming. An *odyssey* has come to mean a long, tortuous period of wandering, travel, and adventure, often in a quest, both literally and spiritually. (M/L 393-408)

Oedipus/oedipal complex: King Laius of Thebes was given a prophecy that his wife, Jocasta, would bear a son who would kill his father and marry his mother. They did have a son whose name was Oedipus, and when he grew up he killed his father and married his mother, despite all that was done to avert the prophecy and destiny. Sophocles' masterpiece *Oedipus the King* inspired Sigmund Freud to crystallize one of his major, defining ideas on the nature of the human psyche (q.v.) and infantile sexual development, the Oedipus complex, the term used to describe the natural progression of psycho-sexual development, in which the child has libidinal feelings for a parent of the opposite sex and hostility for the parent of the same sex. The term *Oedipus complex* refers to the male child; comparable in the development of the female is the *Electra complex*, a psychotic attachment to the father and hostility toward the mother, a designation also drawn from myth. Electra was the daughter of Agamemnon and Clytemnestra, a young woman obsessed by her grief over the murder of her beloved father and tormented by unrelenting hatred for her mother, who killed him. (M/L 323-334; 343-349)

Olympian: The Greek gods had their homes on the heights of Mt. Olympus in northern Greece, and so were called the Olympians. The term *Olympian* carries with it notions of the new order ushered in by Zeus and his family and also distinguishes these gods in their sunlit heights from the *chthonic* ("of the earth") deities, who have associations with the gloom of the Underworld. Therefore *Olympian* means towering, awesome, and majestic, akin to the gods of Olympus. The adjective can also refer to one who competes in or has won a contest in the *Olympic games*, but this designation is derived from the ancient Olympic games, celebrated at *Olympia*, which was a major sanctuary of Zeus in the Peloponnese. (M/L 80-82, 93-95)

paean: Paean was an epithet of the god Apollo, invoked in a cry for victory in battle or for deliverance from sickness. A *paean* thus became a song of thanksgiving. Today it refers to a song of joy or praise, whether to a god or a human being. (M/L 22, 185-186, 535)

palladium: As a child Athena had a special girlfriend named Pallas, with whom she used to play at war. During one of their skirmishes Athena inadvertently killed Pallas, and in her memory she built a wooden statue of the girl. This statue was thrown down to earth by Zeus, where it became known as the *Palladium* and became for the Trojans a talisman for their city; so long as they had possession of it, the city would stand. Thus the English *palladium* means a protection from harm for a people or state, a lucky charm. (M/L 121-123, 364, 521)

Pandora's box: Pandora was the first woman, given to mankind as punishment for Prometheus' theft of fire. Sent with her was a jar, which, when opened, released all the ills that now plague human beings. Later this jar became a box, and now *Pandora's box* refers to something that should be left unexamined, lest it breed disaster. (M/L 63-65)

panic: See **echo**.

procrustean: Procrustes (the "one who stretches") was encountered by Theseus. He would make unwitting travelers lie down on a bed. If they did not fit it exactly, he would either cut them down or stretch them out to size. The adjective *procrustean* refers to someone or something that aims at conformity through extreme methods. A *procrustean bed* decribes a terrible, arbitrary standard against which things are measured. (M/L 459)

Prometheus/Promethean: The god Prometheus ("forethought"), son of the Titan Iapetus, was the creator of mankind and its benefactor. He bestowed upon mortals many gifts that lifted them from savagery to civilization; one of his most potent benefactions was fire, which he stole from heaven in a fennel stalk to give to mankind, a boon expressly forbidden by Zeus. As a result of his championship of human beings in opposition to Zeus, Prometheus was bound to a rocky crag, and a vulture ate at his liver, which would grow back again for each day's repast. Thus the name *Prometheus* becomes synonymous for the archetypal champion, with fire his symbol of defiance and progress. The adjective *Promethean* means courageous, creative, original, and life-sustaining. Beethoven's music may be called Promethean, and Mary Shelley subtitled her gothic horror novel *Frankenstein, A Modern Prometheus*. (M/L 57, 60-70, 426, 430, 574)

protean: Proteus was a sea god who could change shape and who possessed knowledge of the future. To obtain information, one had to grapple with him until his metamorphoses ceased. *Protean* means of changeable or variable form, or having the ability to change form. (M/L 112, 624 n.2 [ch.5])

psyche/psychology, etc.: The Greek word for the soul was *psyche*. For Freud *psyche* means mind, and psychic refers to mental activity; many English derivatives describe the study of the mind and the healing of its disorders: *psychology, psychiatry*, etc. In *psychoanalytic* terms, the soul is the mind, the seat of thoughts and feelings, our true self, which seeks to orient our lives to our surroundings.

python: Apollo established the major sanctuary for his worship and his oracle at Delphi, but to do so he had to kill the serpent which guarded the site. He named his new sanctuary *Pytho*, from the rotting of the serpent after it had been killed (the Greek verb *pythein* means to rot); or the serpent's name was Python. A *python* today belongs to a particular family of non-venomous Old World snakes. (M/L 175-177)

rich as Croesus: Croesus was the king of Lydia who possessed great wealth that became legendary. Thus to emphasize the possession of extreme riches, we describe a person as *rich as Croesus*. (M/L 98-107)

saturnalia/saturnine/saturnism: The Titan Saturn (equated with the Greek Cronus) castrated his father, hated his children, devoured them, and was castrated and overthrown by his son Zeus. After his defeat, Saturn ruled over the Golden Age of the world; according to Roman mythology, he fled to the west and brought a new golden time to Italy. Originally Saturn was an old Italic deity of the harvest; the Romans built a temple to Saturn on the Capitoline hill and each December celebrated the winter planting with the *Saturnalia*, a time of revelry and the giving of presents. *Saturnalia* today denotes a period of unrestrained or orgiastic revelry. *Saturn* gives his name to the sixth planet from the sun, the second largest planet in the solar system, after Jupiter. Anyone born under the influence of Saturn may have a *saturnine* temperament, which is to say, gloomy or melancholy, characteristics of the god who castrated his father and was overthrown. *Saturnian* simply means pertaining to the god or the planet Saturn. The planet Saturn was also associated with the element lead, and so the term for lead poisoning is *saturnism*. (M/L 47-51, 58, 522-523)

satyr: Satyrs were male woodland deities who were part man and part animal and worshiped Dionysus (Bacchus), god of wine, often in a state of sexual excitement. A *satyr* today is nothing more than a lecher. A man who has an excessive and uncontrollable sexual drive suffers from *satyriasis*. (M/L 238)

siren: The Sirens were nymphs (encountered by Odysseus) often depicted with bird-like bodies, who sang such enticing songs that seafarers were lured to their death. A *siren* has come to mean a seductive woman. It can also denote a device which uses compressed steam or air to produce a high, piercing sound as a warning. A *siren song* refers to something bewitching or alluring that also may be treacherous. (M/L 399-400)

Sisyphean: see **Tartarean** (M/L 276, 290, 295-296, 501-502)

sphinx: The sphinx terrorized Thebes before the arrival of Oedipus (see *Oedipus*). She was a hybrid creature with the head of a woman, body of a lion, wings of an eagle, and the tail of a serpent. She punished those who failed to answer her riddle with strangulation (the Greek verb *sphingein* means to strangle). At some point the Greek Sphinx became associated with Egyptian iconography, in which the sphinx had a lion's body and a hawk's or man's head. When we liken someone to a *sphinx*, we have in mind the great riddler of the Greeks and not the Egyptian conception. A *sphinx* is an inscrutable person, given to enigmatic utterances (the Greek word *ainigma* means a riddle). (M/L 325)

stentorian: Stentor was the herald of the Greek army at Troy, who could speak with the power of fifty men. Today we may liken a powerful orator to *Stentor* and designate the effect of his voice as *stentorian*.

stygian: Across the river Styx, the "hateful" river that circles the realm of the Underworld, the ferryman Charon transports our souls to Hades. The gods swear their most dread and unbreakable oaths by invoking the name of the river Styx. *Stygian* describes something to be linked with the infernal regions of hell, something gloomy or inviolable. (M/L 286-288, 295, 297)

syringe: Syrinx ("pan-pipe") rejected the god Pan and was turned into a bed of reeds from which he fashioned his pan-pipes. A *syringe* is a device made up of a pipe or tube, used for injecting and ejecting liquids. *Syringa* is a genus of plants used for making pipes or pipe stems. (M/L 244)

tantalize: see **Tartarean.** (M/L 275, 290, 296, 299, 338-342)

Tartarean: Tartarus is the region in the realm of Hades reserved for the punishment of sinners, among whom are those who have committed the most heinous crimes and suffer the most terrible punishments. The adjective *Tartarean* refers to those infernal regions. Tantalus, who through hubris tried to feed the gods human flesh, is punished by being in a state of perpetual thirst and hunger, food and drink always just beyond his reach. To *tantalize* is therefore to tease and tempt without satisfaction. There too is Sisyphus, condemned to roll an enormous rock up a hill only to have it fall back down, endless labor for revealing the secret of one of Zeus' love affairs. A *Sisyphean* task has become a term for work that is difficult, laborious, almost impossible of completion. (M/L 38-39, 55-56, 284-297, 634 n. 11)

terpsichorean: From Terpsichore, one of the nine Muses, comes the adjective *terpsichorean*, which refers to her special area of expertise, dancing. See *Muse*.

titan/titanic: The twelve Titans, the second generation of gods, born of Ge and Uranus, were of gigantic stature, most of them conceived of as natural forces, and although defeated and punished by Zeus, virtually invincible. Their massive strength is preserved in the adjective *titanic,* which was also the name given to an ocean vessel thought to be unsinkable. To call someone a *titan* is to emphasize that person's enormous mastery and ability in any field or endeavor. (M/L 42-47)

typhoon: Zeus' struggle with the dragon Typhon (also named Typhaon or Typhoeus) was the most serious battle that he had before finally consolidating his rule. Typhon had a hundred heads and tongues, fire shot out of his eyes, and terrible cries bellowed from his throats. The word *typhoon,* meaning a severe tropical hurricane which arises in the China Sea or the western Pacific Ocean, comes from the Chinese *ta* ("great") and *feng* ("wind"), but the form of the word is influenced by the name Typhon. (M/L 55-56; 195-196)

venereal/venery/veneration: Venus was the powerful Roman goddess of love, equated with the Greek Aphrodite, who was born from the foam around Uranus' castrated genitals. Her dominant sexual aspect is made clear by the nature of her origin. The adjective *venereal* denotes a sexually transmitted disease, and the noun *venery* means indulgence in sexual license. *Veneration,* however, is the act of showing respectful love, adoration, or reverence. (M/L 128-156, 526-527, 541, 543)

volcanic/volcano: The Roman god Vulcan, identified with the Greek Hephaestus, was the supreme craftsman of the gods. His helpers were three Cyclopes (see *Cyclopean*), and his forge was located in various places but most often under Mt. Etna in Sicily, or similar *volcanic* regions, which betray its presence. A *volcano* is a vent in the earth's crust which spews forth molten material and thereby forms a mountain. (M/L 83-89, 146-147, 379, 520-521)

Wheel of Fortune: Fors or Fortuna was an Italic fertility goddess who controlled the cycles of the seasons and became associated with the Greek conception of good or bad fortune (Tyche). She is often represented holding the cornucopia (q.v.) in one hand and a wheel in the other, to signify the rising and falling of an individual's prospects. From that iconography comes *wheel of fortune,* a device used in a game of chance.

zephyr: Zephyrus is the west wind (see *aurora borealis*), which signals the return of spring. Today a *zephyr* is a pleasant, gentle breeze, as well as a reference to any insignificant or passing thing. (M/L 56, 130, 152, 523-524).

Discography

This list of works on classical themes available on compact disc (we have not included cassette tapes) is by no means complete; additions to the catalogue appear daily, both new recordings and performances originally issued on 78s, LPs, or tape; but unfortunately some CDs are deleted all too quickly, although one may hope for their reissue. Every performance of individual works is not listed, especially those recorded many times; one should always consult the most recent issue of the Schwann catalogue for classical music (*Opus*) and for popular music (*Spectrum*).

1. "Achilles Last Stand." Rock song. *Led Zeppelin. Presence.* Swan Song SS 8416-2.

2. ALBERT, STEPHEN (b. 1941). *Into Eclipse.* Song cycle about *Oedipus.* Gordon. 20th Century Consort, cond. Kendall, Electra/Nonesuch CD 9 79153-2; Lakes. Juilliard Orchestra, cond. Schwartz. New World NW 381-2.

3. ANFOSSI, PASQUALE (1727-1797). *La Maga Circe (The Enchantress Circe).* Opera. Baker-Genovesi et al. Il Gruppo di Roma, cond. Colusso. Bongiovanni GB 10001/2-2.

4. BABBITT, MILTON (b. 1916). *Philomel,* for soprano and synthesized sound. Beardslee. New World Records 80466-2.

5. BACH, JOHANN CHRISTOPH FRIEDRICH (1735-1782). *Ino.* Cantata for soprano and orchestra. Schlick. Das kleine Konzert, cond. Max. Capriccio 110 303.

6. _____. *Pygmalion.* Cantata for bass and orchestra. Van der Kamp. See previous entry.

7. BACH, JOHANN SEBASTIAN (1685-1750). Cantata 295, "Der zufriedengestellte Aeolus" ("Aeolus Propitiated"). Concentus Musicus Wein, cond. Harnoncourt. Teldec 8.42915.

8. BACH, P. D. Q. (PETER SCHICKELE, b. 1935). *Oedipus Tex & Other Choral Calamities.* Humorous cantata. The Greater Hoople Area Off-Season Philharmonic and Okay Chorale, cond. Newton Wayland. Telarc CD-80239.

9. BARBER, SAMUEL (1910-1981). *Andromache's Farewell,* for soprano and orchestra. *Samuel Barber.* Arroyo. The New York Philharmonic, cond. Schippers. Masterworks Portrait (Sony). MPK 46727. *Barber, Scenes and Arias.* Alexander. The Netherlands Radio Philharmonic, cond. de Waart. Etcetera KTC 1145.

10. _____. *Antony and Cleopatra.* Opera. Hinds et al. Spoleto Festival Orchestra, cond. Badea. New World Records NW 322/23/24-2. Two scenes: *Leontyne Price Sings Barber.* New Philharmonia Orchestra, cond. Schippers. RCA Victor (Gold Seal) 09026-61983-2. See also *Barber, Scenes and Arias,* in the previous entry.

11. _____. *Medea.* Orchestral Suite from the ballet *Cave of the Heart.* New Zealand Symphony Orchestra, cond. Schenck. Koch 3-7010-2. Also Eastman-Rochester Orchestra, cond. Hanson. Mercury 432-016-2. *Medea's Meditation and Dance of Vengeance.* Another orchestral piece derived from the ballet. London Symphony Orchestra, cond. Schenck. Musical Heritage Society MHS 419503 (original Academy Sound & Vision Recording ASV CDDCA-534, distr. Harmonia Mundi). The original version entitled *Cave of the Heart. Music for Martha Graham.* The Atlantic Sinfonietta, cond. Schenck. Koch 3-7019-2.

12. _____. *Music for a Scene from Shelley's Prometheus Unbound.* The New Zealand Symphony Orchestra, cond. Schenck. Stradivari Classics SCD 8012.

13. BEDFORD, DAVID. *The Odyssey.* Popular. Blue Plate CAROL-1199 2.

14. BEETHOVEN, LUDWIG VAN (1770-1827). *The Creatures of Prometheus.* Ballet. Orpheus Chamber Orchestra. Deutsche Grammophon 419 608 2. See also 222. *Prometheus, the Myth in Music.*

15. BELLINI, VINCENZO (1801-1835). *Norma.* Opera. Callas and Corelli et al. Orchestra and Chorus of Teatro all Scala, Milan, cond. Serafin. EMI CMS 7 63000 2. Several other excellent recordings are available.

16. BERLIOZ, HECTOR (1803-1869). *La Mort de Cléopâtre.* Cantata. Baker. London Symphony Orchestra, cond. Gibson. Angel CDM 69544.

17. _____. *La Mort d'Orphée.* Cantata. Garino et al. Dutch Radio Symphony Orchestra, cond. Fournet. Denon CO-72886.

18. _____. *Les Troyens.* Opera. Vickers et al. Orchestra of the Royal Opera House, Covent Garden, cond. Davis. Philips 416 432-2; Lakes et al. Orchestre Symphonique de Montréal, cond. Dutoit. London 443 693-2.

19. BERNSTEIN, LEONARD (1918-1990). *Serenade,* after Plato's *Symposium. Bernstein Conducts Bernstein.* Deutsche Grammophon 423 583-2. Several other recordings are available.

20. BLISS, ARTHUR (1891-1975). *Hymn to Apollo.* Ulster Orchestra, cond. Handley. Chandos CHAN 8818; London Symphony Orchestra, cond. Bliss. Lyrita SRCD 225.

21. _____. *Morning Heroes,* for orator, orchestra, and chorus. Blessed. London Philharmonic Orchestra, cond. Kibblewhite. Cala CACD 1010; Westbrook, Liverpool Philharmonic Orchestra, cond. Groves. EMI CDM 7 63906 2.

22. _____. *The Olympians.* Opera. Ambrosian Singers and Soloists, Polyphonia Orchestra, cond. Fairfax. Intaglio INCD 7552.

23. BLITZSTEIN, MARC (1905-1964). *The Harpies.* Rees et al. Adirondack Chamber Orchestra, cond. Smith. Premiere Recordings PRCD 1009.

24. BLOW, JOHN (1649?-1708). *Venus & Adonis.* Masque. Argenta et al. London Baroque, cond. Medlam. Harmonia Mundi HMA 1901276.

25. BOITO, ARRIGO (1842-1918). *Nerone.* Opera. Nagy et al. Hungarian State Opera Orchestra, cond. Queler. Hungaroton HCD 12487-89-2.

26. BON, ANDRÉ (b. 1946). *The Rape of Persephone.* Opera. Vassilieva et al. Orchestre de l'Opéra de Nancy, cond. Kaltenbach. Cybelia (Musique Française) CY 861.

27. BONINI, SEVERO (1582-1663). "Lamento d' Arianna" in stille recitatio. See 140. *Lamento d'Arianna.*

28. BRITTEN, BENJAMIN (1913-1976). *Metamorphoses after Ovid,* for solo oboe. Zubicky. Simax PSC-1022. The six metamorphoses are: Pan, Phaethon, Niobe, Bacchus, Narcissus, and Arethusa.

29. _____. *Phaedra,* Dramatic Cantata for mezzo-soprano. Baker et al. English Chamber Orchestra, cond. Britten (includes *The Rape of Lucretia*); Palmer. Endymion Ensemble, cond. Whitfield. EMI CDC 7 49259 2.

30. _____. *The Rape of Lucretia.* Opera. See entry above; Rigby et al. City of London Sinfonia, cond. Hickox. Chandos 9254/5.

31. _____. *Young Apollo,* for piano and strings. Evans. Scottish Chamber Orchestra, cond. Serebrier.

32. BUCK, DUDLEY (1839-1909). "The Capture of Bacchus." *Songs of an Innocent Age, Music from Turn of the Century America.* Sperry and Vallecillo. Albany Records TROY 034-2.

33. BUSH, GEOFFREY (b. 1920). "Echo's Lament for Narcissus." *An Album of English Songs.* I. and J. Partridge. Musical Heritage Society 414531K (An Original Academy Sound & Vision Recording).

34. CALDARA, ANTONIO (ca. 1670-1736). *Medea in Corinto.* Cantata for alto solo. Lesne. Il Seminario musicale. Virgin Classics VC 7 91479-2.

35. "Calypso." Popular song. *Suzanne Vega, Solitude Standing.* A & M Records CD 5136.

36. CAMPRA, ANDRÉ (1660-1774). *Achille Oisif, Arion, Daphné, Didon, Hébé. French Cantatas.* Nicolas. Cond. Chapuis. Pierre Verany PV.786101 (distr. Harmonia Mundi).

37. _____. *Arion, La Dispute de l'Amour et de l'Hymen, Énée & Didon.* Feldman et al. Les Arts Florissants, cond. Christie. Harmonia Mundi HMA 1901238. 35.

38. _____. *Silène.* Koningsberger. Academy of the Begynhof, Amsterdam. Globe GLO 5055.

39. _____. *Idoménée.* Opera. Deletré et al. Les Arts Florissants, cond. Christie. Harmonia Mundi HMC 901396.98.

40. CARTER, ELLIOTT (b. 1908). *In Sleep, In Thunder.* Six poems of Robert Lowell. *Elliott Carter, The Vocal Works (1975-1981).* Ciesinski et al. Speculum Musicae. Bridge BCD 9014.

41. _____. *The Minotaur.* Ballet. *Elliott Carter.* New York Chamber Symphony of the 92nd Street Y, cond. Schwarz. Elektra Nonesuch 9 79248-2.

42. _____. *Syringa. Elliott Carter.* DeGaetani et al. American Masters CRI CD610. See also 40. *Elliott Carter, The Vocal Works.*

43. "Cassandra." Rock song. *Steve Hackett. Guitar Noir.* Viceroy Music VIC8008-2.

44. CATALANI, ALFREDO (1854-1893). *Dejanice.* Opera. Basto et al. Orchestra Lirico Sinfonica del Teatro del Giglio di Lucca, cond. Latham-Koenig. Bongiovanni GB 2031/32-2.

45. CAVALLI, FRANCESCO (1602-1676). *La Calisto.* Opera. Piscitelli et al. Gioioso Players, cond. Moretti. Stradivarius STR-13606/07; Bayo et al. Concerto Vocale, cond. Jacobs. Harmonia Mundi HMC 901515.17.

46. _____. *Didone.* Excerpts from the opera. Anfuso, accompanied by Renaissance Harp. Auvidis A6118.

47. _____. *Giasone.* Opera. Dubosc et al. Concerto vocale, cond. Jacobs. Harmonia Mundi HMC-90-1282/84.

48. CHABRIER, EMMANUEL (1841-1894). *Briséis ou Les amants de Corinthe.* Act 1 of an unfinished opera. Rodgers et al. BBC Scottish Symphony Orchestra, cond. Ossonce. Hyperion CDA66803.

49. CHADWICK, GEORGE WHITEFIELD (1854-1931). *Euterpe: Concert Overture for Orchestra.* The Louisville Orchestra, First Edition Encores, cond. Mester. Albany Records TROY 030-2. Includes Converse, *Endymion's Narrative.*

50. CHARPENTIER, MARC-ANTOINE (1643-1704). *Actéon.* Opera. Visse et al. Les Arts Florissants, cond. Christie. Harmonia Mundi HM 90.1095.

51. _____. *Médée.* Opera. Hunt et al. Les Arts Florissants, cond. Christie. Erato 4509-96558-2.

52. _____. *Orphée Descendant aux Enfers.* Cantata. Soloists with the Ricercar Consort, cond. Ledroit. Ricercar RIC 037011.

53. CHERUBINI, LUIGI (1760-1842). *Medea.* Callas et al. Orchestra and Chorus of La Scala Opera House, cond. Serafin. EMI CMS 7 63625 2; also on Denon C37-7336/37. Callas in one of her greatest roles. Live performances by Callas are also available; Magda Olivero is another Medea to contend with!

54. _____. *Pigmalione.* Opera. Borghi et al. Orchestra Sinfonica e Coro della RAI di Milano, cond. Gerelli. Melodram CDM 29501.

55. CHRISTINÉ, HENRI. *Phi-Phi.* Abridged version of the operetta. Bourvil et al., cond. Rys. EMI CDM 7 63342 2.

56. CIMAROSA, DOMENICO (1749-1801). *Gli Orazii e i Curiazi.* Dessy et al. Orchestra Sinfonica di Sanremo, cond. Bernart. Bongiovanni GB2021/22-2; Vercelli et al. Orchestra Sinfonica e Coro della RAI di Milano, cond. Giulini. Melodram CDM 29500.

57. CLERAMBAULT, LOUIS-NICOLAS (1676-1749). *Médée.* Cantata. See 79. *French Cantatas of the 18th Century.*

58. CONVERSE, FREDERICK SHEPHERD, (1871-1940). *Endymion's Narrative: Romance for Orchestra.* See 49. Chadwick.

59. COSTA, FRANCESCO ANTONIO (16th/17th cent.). "Pianto d'Arianna," a voce sola. See 140. *Lamento d'Arianna.*

60. DEBUSSY, CLAUDE (1862-1918). *Nocturnes,* for orchestra and chorus. Part 3: *Sirènes.* Los Angeles Philharmonic Orchestra, cond. Salonen. Sony Classicals SK 58952.

61. _____. *Prelude à l'Après-Midi d'un Faune.* NBC Symphony Orchestra, cond. Toscanini. RCA Victor 60265-2-RG (Vol. 37 of The Toscanini Collection). Many recordings are available.

62. _____. *Syrinx,* for unaccompanied flute. Bourdin. Philips 422 839-2.

63. De Paul, Gene. *Seven Brides for Seven Brothers.* Lyrics by Johnny Mercer. Original London Cast. First Night Records. OCRCD 6008.

64. DESSAU, PAUL (1894-1979). *The Condemnation of Lucullus (Die Verurteilung des Lukullus).* Opera. Bauer et al. Rundfunk-Sinfonie-Orchester Leipzig, cond. Kegel. Berlin Classics BC 1073-2.

65. DIEPENBROCK, ALPHONS (1862-1921). *Elektra.* Symphonic Suite; and *Marsyas.* Concert Suite. Residentie Orchestra The Hague, cond. Vonk. Chandos CHAN 8821. Also includes his Overture to Aristophanes' *The Birds.*

66. DITTERSDORF, CARL DITTERS VON (1793-1799). *Six Symphonies after Ovid's Metamorphoses.* Cantelina, cond. Shepherd. Musical Heritage Society MHS 522223A (originally Chandos CHAN-8564/65). The Symphonies are subtitled: The Four Ages of Man, The Fall of Phaëthon, The Transformation of Actaeon into a Stag, The Rescuing of Andromeda by Perseus, The Petrification of Phineus and His Friends, The Transformation of the Lycian Peasants into Frogs.

67. DONIZETTI, GAETANO (1797-1848). *L'Esule di Roma.* Opera. Alaimo et al. Orchestra Sinfonica di Piacenza, cond. Bernart. Bongiovanni GB 2045/46-2.

68. _____. *Il Pigmalione.* Pellegrini and Rigacci. Orchestra da Camera dell'Associazioe In Canto, cond. Maestri. Bongiovanni GB 2109/10-2.

69. _____. *Poliuto.* Opera. Corelli, Callas et al. Coro e Orchestra del Teatro all Scala, cond. Votto. Verona 289993/4 (with an English translation of the libretto); this great live performance has also been issued on Arkadia CDHP 520.2 and Virtuoso 2697212; Carreras, Ricciarelli et al. Vienna Symphony, cond. Caetani. Legato Classics LCD-129-2. 64.

70. ELGAR, EDWARD (1857-1934). *Caractacus.* Cantata. Howarth et al. London Symphony Orchestra, cond. Hickox. Chandos CHAN 9156/7.

71. "The End." Oedipal rock song by Jim Morrison. *The Doors.* Elektra 74007-2.

72. ENESCO, GEORGES (1881-1955). *Oedipe.* Opera. Van Dam et al. Orchestre Philharmonique de Monte-Carlo, cond. Foster. EMI CDS 7 54011 2.

73. FAURÉ, GABRIEL (1845-1924). *Pénélope.* Opera. Norman et al. Orchestre Philharmonique de Monte-Carlo, cond. Dutoit. Erato 2292-45405-2; Crespin et al. Orchestre National, cond. Inghelbrecht. Rudolphe RPC 32447/48.

74. "Flight of Icarus." Rock song. *Iron Maiden. Piece of Mind.* Capitol C21Y-46363.

75. FOSS, LUKAS (b. 1922). *Orpheus and Euridice.* Menuhin and Michell, violins. Brooklyn Philharmonic, cond. Foss. New World Records NW375-2.

76. "The Fountain of Salmacis." Rock song. *Genesis. Nursery Cryme.* Atlantic 82673-2.

77. FRANCK, CÉSAR (1822-1890). *Les Eolides.* Symphonic Poem. Concertgebouw Orchestra, cond. Van Otterloo. IMP Collectors Series IMPX 9037. NBC Symphony Orchestra, cond. Toscanini. Music & Arts ATRA-274 (includes "Psyché et Eros").

78. _____. *Psyché.* Symphonic Poem. Orchestre de Paris, cond. Barenboim. Deutsche Grammophon 431468-2 GGA; BBC Welsh National Orchestra and Chorus, cond. Otaka. CHAN 9342; Final section: "Psyché et Eros." NBC Symphony Orchestra, cond. Toscanini. RCA Victor 09026-60322-2. See also Toscanini in the previous entry.

79. *French Cantatas of the 18th Century.* Baird. American Baroque, cond. Schuktz. Koch, International Classics 3-7096-2 H1. Includes Clerambault, *Médée* and Montéclair, *La Mort de Didon,* and *Pan et Sirinx.*

80. FUX, JOHANN JOSEPH (1660-1741). *Dafne in Lauro.* Van der Sluis et al. Orchestre baroque du Clemencic Consort, cond. Clemencic. Nuova Era 6930/31.

81. GADE, NIELS W. (1817-1890). *Kalanus.* Oratorio. Gedda et al. Collegium Musicum, cond. Rasmussen. Danacord DACOCD 310.

82. GAGLIANO, MARCO DA (1582-1643). *La Dafne.* Opera. Ensemble Elyma, cond. Garrido. K617 (made in France) K617058.

83. GAGNEUX, RENAUD (b. 1947). *Orphée.* Extracts from the opera. Lara et al. Philharmonic Orchestra of Strasbourg, cond. Schnitzler. Cybelia CY 865.

84. GLIERE, REINHOLD (1875-1956). *The Sirens.* Symphonic Poem. Slovam Philharmonic Orchestra, cond. Gunzenhauser. HK Marco Polo 8.220349.

85. GLUCK, CHRISTOPH WILLIBALD (1714-1787). *Alceste.* Opera. Norman et al. Bavarian Radio Symphony, cond. Baudo. Orfeo C-027823 F. Live performance by Flagstad, Orchestra of the Danish Radio, cond. Hye-Knudsen. Eclipse EKR CD 17; live performance by Callas, Orchestra del Teatro alla Scala, cond. Giulini. Melodram MEL 26026.

86. _____. *Echo et Narcisse.* Opera. Boulin et al. Concerto Köln, cond. Jacobs. Harmonia Mundi HMC 905201.02.

87. _____. *Iphigenia in Aulis.* Opera. Revised version by Wagner. Moffo et al. Munich Radio Orchestra, cond. Eichhorn. Eurodisc 7796-2-RG. A very fine performance of one of Gluck's best works.

88. _____. *Iphigénie en Tauride.* Opera. Montague et al. Orchestre de l'Opéra de Lyon, cond. Gardiner. Among several other recordings is a live performance with Callas et al. La Scala Orchestra, cond. Sanzogno. Melodram MEL CD-26012.

89. _____. *Orphée et Eurydice.* Unabridged original French version for tenor. Simoneau, Danco et al. Orchestre des Concerts Lamoureux, cond. Rosbaud. Philips 434 784-2. A great performance. Many fine recordings are available in various versions, including the revision by Berlioz, with Orpheus usually sung by a mezzo-soprano. The concert performance of Act 2 (Merriman et al., NBC Symphony Orchestra, cond. Toscanini) is a revelation. RCA Victor 60280-2-RC (Vol. 46 of the Toscanini Collection).

90. _____. *Paride ed Elena.* Cotrubas et al. ORF Symphonie Orchestra, cond. Zagrosek. Orfeo C 118 842 H; Alexander et al. La Stagione, cond. Schneider. Capriccio 60 027-2.

91. GOEBBELS, HEINER (b. 1962). *Herakles 2,* for five brass players, drums, and sampler. Ensemble Modern, cond. Rundel. EMC New Series 1483.

92. GOLDMARK, KARL (1830-1915). *Penthesilea.* Overture. Rhenish Philharmonic Orchestra, cond. Halász. Marco Polo 8.220417.

93. GOUNOD, CHARLES (1820-1889). *Sapho.* Opera. Command et al. Nouvel Orchestre de Saint-Etienne, cond. Fournillier. Koch/Swann 3-1311-2. Ciesinski et al. Nouvel Orchestre Philharmonique, cond. Cambreling. Rodolphe RPC 32453/54.

94. *The Great Opera Singers of the XVIIIth Century.* In tribute to the castrato Guadagni and sung by a countertenor, arias are drawn from several operas, including Hasse's *Il Trionfo di Clelia*, Piccinni's *Tigrane*, and Traetta's *Iphigénie en Tauride*. Zaepffel, Ensemble Stradivaria, cond. Cuiller.

95. GRÉTRY, ANDRÉ-ERNEST-MODESTE (1741-1813). *Le Jugement de Midas.* Excerpts from the opera. Devos et al. Chamber Orch. from the Nouvel Orchestre de la R.T.B.F., cond. Zollman. Koch/Schwann 3-1090-2; Elwes et al. La Petite Bande, cond. Leonhardt. Ricercar RIC 063033.

96. HAEFFNER, JOHANN CHRISTIAN FRIEDRICH (1759-1833). *Electra.* Selections from the opera: *Gustaviansk Opera (Gustavian Opera)*. Musica Sveciae (Swedish Music Anthology) MSCD 426.

97. HANDEL, GEORGE FRIDERIC (1685-1759). *Aci, Galatea e Polifemo.* Dramatic cantata. Kirkby et al. London Baroque, cond. Medlam. Harmonia Mundi HMC 901253-4. 89.

98. _____. *Acis and Galatea.* Masque on the same theme as the previous entry and more famous. Burrows et al. English Baroque soloists, cond. Gardiner. Deutsche Grammophon (Archiv) 423406. Some may prefer the work as arranged by Mozart: Bonney et al. English Consort and Choir, cond. Pinnock. Deutsche Grammophon 4257922.

99. _____. *Agrippina.* Opera. Bradshaw et al. Capella Savaria, cond. McGegan. Harmonia Mundi HMU 907063.65.

100. _____. *Alessandro.* Opera. Terzian et al. Sinfonia Varsovia, cond. Nowakowski. Studios Classique CD SC 100 303.

101. _____. *Apollo e Dafne.* Cantata. Alexander and Hampson. Concentus Musicus Wein, cond. Harnoncourt. Teldec 4509-98645-2. Nelson et al. Philharmonia Baroque Orchestra, cond. McGegan. Harmonia Mundi 905157.

102. _____. *The Choice of Hercules.* Cantata. Zaeppffel et al. Neues Bachisches Collegium Musicum Leipzig, cond. Pommer. Capriccio 10019.

103. _____. *Hercules.* Opera. Tomlinson et al. The English Baroque Soloists, cond. Gardiner. Archiv Produktion 423 137-2.

104. _____. *Julius Caesar (Giulio Cesare in Egitto).* Opera. Treigle, Sills et al. New York City Opera Orchestra and Chorus, cond. Rudel. RCA Victor 6182-2-RG. Several other excellent recordings are available.

105. _____. *Scipione.* Opera. Ragin et al. Les Talens Lyriques, cond. Rousset. FNAC Music 592245.

106. _____. *Semele.* Oratorio/Opera. Battle et al. English Chamber Orchestra, cond. Nelson. Deutsche Grammophon 435 782-2.

107. _____. *Teseo.* Opera. James et al. Les Musiciens du Louvre, cond. Minkowski. Erato 2292-45806-2.

108. HANSON, HOWARD (1896-1981). *Nymphs and Satyr Ballet Suite.* Rochester Chamber Orchestra, cond. Fetler. Bay Cities BCD-1005.

109. _____. *Pan and the Priest, Symphonic Poem.* World Youth Symphony Orchestra, cond. Howard Hanson. Bay Cities BCD-1009.

110. HARBISON, JOHN (b. 1938). *Ulysses' Bow.* Ballet. Pittsburgh Symphony Orchestra, cond. Previn. Nonesuch 79129-2.

111. HARRISON, LOU (b. 1917). *Ariadne,* for flute and percussion. *Lou Harrison.* Leta Miller, flute, et al., cond. Davies. Music Masters MMD 60241X.

112. _____. *Solstice.* Suite from the Ballet. See above.

113. _____. *A Summerfield Set,* for solo piano. See above.

114. HASSE, JOHANN ADOLF (1699-1783). *Cleofide.* Opera. Kirkby et al. Cappella Coloniensis, cond. Christie. Capriccio 10 193/96.

115. _____. *Piramo e Tisbe.* Opera. Schlick et al. Capella Clementina, cond. Müller-Brühl. Koch/Schwann 3-1088-2; La Stagione, cond. Schneider. Capriccio 60 043-2.

116. HAYDN, FRANZ JOSEPH (1732-1809). *Arianna a Naxos.* Cantata for soprano and keyboard. Bartoli and Schiff. London 440297-2.

117. _____. *The Creation.* Oratorio. Seefried et al. Berlin Philharmonic Orchestra, cond. Markevitch. Deutsche Grammophon (Double Series) 437380-2.

118. _____. *Orfeo ed Euridice.* Sutherland, Gedda et al. Scottish National Orchestra, cond. Bonynge. Verona 28018/19, also Myto MCD 905.29.

119. HENZE, HANS WERNER (b. 1926). *The Bassarids.* Opera. Armstrong et al. Radio-Symphonie-Orchester Berlin, cond. Albrecht. Koch/Schwann 314 006.

120. _____. *Orpheus behind the Wire. To Orpheus.* The New York Virtuoso Singers, cond. Harold Rosenbaum. CRI CD 615

121. HOFFMANN, E. T. A. (1776-1822). *Aurora.* Opera. Soloists with the Jugendorchester Bamberg, cond. Dechant. Bayer Records BR 100-276-78.

122. HOLST, GUSTAV (1874-1934). *Hymn to Dionysus,* for women's chorus and orchestra. Royal Philharmonic Orchestra, cond. Willcocks. Unicorn-Kanchana DKP(CD) 9046.

123. _____. *The Planets.* The Toronto Symphony, cond. Davis. EMI CDC 547417. Several excellent recordings are available.

124. HONEGGER, ARTHUR (1892-1955). *Antigone.* Incidental music. Serres et al. Orchestre National, cond. Roux. Bourg BGC 17.

125. _____. *Phèdre.* Suite. The U.S.S.R. Ministry of Culture Orchestra, cond. Rozhdestvensky. Olympia OCD 212, also Melodiya MCD 212.

126. HOVHANESS, ALAN (b. 1911). *Meditation on Orpheus,* for orchestra. Seattle Symphony Orchestra, cond. Schwarz. Delos DE 3168.

127. _____. *String Quartet No. 1, "Jupiter." Spirit Murmur.* The Shanghai Quartet. Delos DE 3162; *Prelude and Quadruple Fugue.* Delos DE 3157.

128. _____. *Symphony No. 25 (Odysseus).* Alan Hovhaness, Polyphonia Orchestra, cond. Hovhannes. Crystal CD 807.

129. *A Hundred Years of Italian Opera.* Opera Rara ORCH 103. This album (with an informative booklet) covers the years 1810-1820, and among its selections are: Pucitta, *La Vestale;* Rossini, *Il Trionfo di Quinto Fabio;* Manfroce, *Ecuba;* Mayr, *Medea in Corinto;* Mercadante, *L'Apoteosi d'Ercole.*

130. IBERT, JACQUES (1890-1962). *Bacchanale.* Orchestre Symphonique de Montréal, cond. Dutoit.

131. "Icarus." New Age music. *Paul Winter Consort.* Living Music LD0004. Ralph Towner, the composer, has his own recorded version.

132. "Icarus Ascending." Rock song. *Steve Hackett. Please Don't Touch.* Carol 1861-2.

133. "Icarus—Borne on the Wings of Steel." Rock song. *Kansas. Masque* Kirshner ZK 33806.

134. IRELAND, JOHN (1879-1962). *Tritons.* Symphonic Prelude. London Symphony Orchestra, cond. Hickox. Chandos CHAN 8994.

135. JOMMELLI, NICCOLÒ (1774-1774). *Didone Abbandonata.* Opera. Röschmann et al. Stuttgarter Kammerorchester, cond. Bernius. Orfeo C 381 953 F.

136. KEISER, REINHARD (1674-1793). *Croesus.* Opera. Klietmann et al. Orchestra Baroque du Clemencic Consort, cond. Clemencic. Nuova Era 6934/35.

137. KOCÁB, MICHAEL (b. 1954). *Odysseus.* A Mysterium on the Motifs of Homer's *Odyssey.* Setting of texts in ancient Greek. Supraphon 110403-2.

138. KOECHLIN, CHARLES (1867-1950). *Songs by Charles Koechlin.* Leblanc and Sharon. Hyperion CDA66243. Includes "Le Cortège d'Amphitrite" and "Hymne à Vénus."

139. KORNGOLD, ERICH WOLFGANG (1897-1957). "The Diary Song," from the opera, *The Ring of Polycrates.* Janowitz. The Austrian State Radio Orchestra, cond. Loibner. Cambria CD 1032; Baker and Calusdian. Entr'acte ESCD 6502.

140. *Lamento d'Arianna.* Compositions by Claudio Monteverdi, Severo Bonini, Claudio Pari, Francesco Costa, Antonio il Verso, Francesco Maria Rascarini. The Consort of Musicke, cond. Rooley. Editio Classica, Deutsche Harmonia Mundi 77115-2-RG. See also 181. Monteverdi.

141. LAMPE, JOHN FREDERICK (ca. 1702-1751). *Pyramus and Thisbe.* A Mock Opera. Padmore and Bisatt. Opera Restor'd, cond. Holman. Hyperion CDA66759.

142. LANDI, STEFANO (1586-1639). *La Morte D'Orfeo*. Opera. Elwes et al. Currende, cond. Stubbs. Accent ACC 8746/47D.

143. LANG, DAVID (b. 1957). *Orpheus, Over and Under*, for two pianos. *Are You Experienced?* Niemann and Tilles (Double Edge). CRI CD 625.

144. LARSSON, LARS-ERIK (1908-1986). *God in Disguise*. Cantata. Söderström et al. Swedish Radio Symphony Orchestra, cond. Westerberg. Swedish Society SCD 1020.

145. LAZAROF, HENRI (b. 1932). *Icarus* (Second Concerto for Orchestra). Henri Lazarof. Seattle Symphony Orchestra, cond. Gerard Schwarz. Delos DE 3069.

146. LECLAIR, JEAN-MARIE (1697-1764). *Scylla et Glaucus*. Opera. Brown et al. Monteverdi Choir and English Baroque Soloists, cond. Gardiner. Erato ECD 75339.

147. LEHRER, TOM. "Oedipus Rex." Humorous song. *An Evening Wasted with Tom Lehrer*. Reprise Records 6199-2.

148. LEKEU, GUILLAUME (1870-1894). *Andromede*. Cantata. Bryant et al. Orchestre Philharmonique de Liege, cond. Bartholomée. Ricercar RIS 099083.

149. LEONCAVALLO, RUGGIERO (1858-1919). *Edipo Re*. Opera. Fioraventi et al. Orchestra e Coro del Teatro San Carlo di Napoli, cond. Parodi. Italian Opera Rarities LO 7723.

150. LERDAHL, FRED (b. 1943). *Eros*. Variations for mezzo-soprano and chamber ensemble. Mezzo, Beverly Morgan, Collage, cond. Fred Lerdahl. CRI CD 580.

151. LIDHOLM, INGVAR (b. 1921). *Nausicaa Alone*. Söderström. The Swedish Radio Symphony Orchestra, cond. Westerberg. Caprice CAP 21366.

152. LIEBERMANN, ROLF. *Penelope*. Opera. Goltz et al. Weiner Philharmoniker, cond. Szell. Orfeo C 328 931 B.

153. LISZT, FRANZ (1811-1886). *Orpheus*. Symphonic Poem. Czech Philharmonic Orchestra, cond. Kosler. Supraphonet 11 1112-2. Includes *Prometheus*. Several recordings of both are available.

154. _____. *Prometheus*. Symphonic Poem. See the previous entry and 222. *Prometheus, The Myth in Music*.

155. LLOYD, GEORGE (b. 1913). *The Vigil of Venus (Pervigilium Veneris)*. James and Booth. Orchestra and Chorus of the Welsh National Opera, cond. Lloyd. Argo 430 329-2.

156. LLOYD WEBBER, WILLIAM. (1914-1982). *Aurora*. Tone poem. London Philharmonic Orchestra, cond. Maazel. Philips 420 32-2.

157. LOEVENDE, THEO (b. 1930). *Venus and Adonis*, for five instruments. Nieuw Ensemble. Etcetera KTC 1097.

158. LOEWE, FREDERICK. *My Fair Lady*. Lyrics by Alan Jay Lerner. Andrews, Harrison et al. Original Broadway Cast. Columbia CK-5090.

159. LULLY, JEAN-BAPTISTE (1631-1687). *Atys*. Opera. Mey et al. Les Arts Florissants, cond. Christie. Harmonia Mundi HMC 901257.59.

160. _____. *Phaëton*. Opera. Crook et al. Les Musiciens du Louvre. Erato 4509-91737-2.

161. MAGNARD, ALBÉRIC (1865-1914). *Hymne à Vénus. Du Crepuscule à L'Aurore*. Orchestre Philharmonique de Liege, cond. Bartholomee. Ricercar 030005.

162. MANCINELLI, LUIGI (1842-1921). *Cleopatra*. Orchestral Suite. Warmia National Orchestra, cond. Silvano Frontalini. Bongiovanni GB 5505-2.

163. MANFROCE, NICOLA ANTONIO (1791-1813). *Ecuba*. Opera. Antonacci et al. Orchestra Filarmonica Italiana, cond. Bernart. Bongiovanni GB 2119/20-2.

164. MARAIS, MARIN (1656-1728). *Alcyone*. Opera. Smith et al. Les Musiciens du Louvre, cond. Minkowski. Erato 2292-45522-2.

165. MARTINU, BOHUSLAV (1890-1959). *Ariane*. Opera. Lindsley et al. Czech Philharmonic Orchestra, cond. Neumann. Supraphon 10 4395-2.

166. MASCAGNI, PIETRO (1863-1945). *Nerone*. Opera. Tcholakov et al. Radio Symphony Orchestra di Hilversum, cond. Bakels. Bongiovanni GB 2052/53-2.

167. MASSENET, JULES (1842-1912). *Cléopâtre*. Opera. Harries et al. Nouvel Orchestre de Saint-Etienne, cond. Fournillier. Koch/Schwann 3-1032-2.

168. MAW, NICHOLAS (b. 1935). *Odyssey*. Symphonic Work. City of Birmingham Symphony Orchestra, cond. Rattle. EMI CDS 7 54277 2.

169. MAYR, GIOVANNI SIMONE (1763-1845). *Medea in Corinto*. Opera. Eaglen et al. Philharmonia Orchestra, cond. Parry. Opera Rara ORC 11.

170. MENDELSSOHN, FELIX (1809-1847). *Antigone*. Incidental Music. Hämer et al. Radio-Symphonie-Orchester Berlin, cond. Soltesz. Capriccio 10 392.

171. _____. *Ödipus*. Incidental Music. Sander et al. Radio-Symphonie-Orchester Berlin, cond. Soltesz. Capriccio 10 393.

172. MENOTTI, GIAN CARLO (b. 1911). *Errand into the Maze*. Ballet. *More Music for Martha Graham*. The Atlantic Sinfonietta, cond. Schenck. Koch 3-7051-2 H1 (includes *Night Journey*).

173. MERCADANTE, SAVERIO (1795-1870). *Orazi e Curiazi*. Opera. Miricioiu et al. Philharmonia Orchestra, cond. Parry. Opera Rara ORC 12.

174. *Metastasio's Kings and Heroes*. Palacio. Salieri Chamber Orchestra, cond. Pál. Arkadia CDAK 137.1. Tenor arias from operas with texts by Metastasio, including: Johann A. Hasse, *La Clemenza di Tito*; Nicolò Jommelli, *Temistocle*; Leonardo Leo, *L'Olimpiade*; Leonardo Vinci, *Catone in Utica*.

175. MILHAUD, DARIUS (1892-1974). *Les Malheurs d'Orphée*. Matrix Ensemble, cond. Robert Ziegler. ASV CD DCA 758.

176. _____. *Trois Opéras-Minute: L'enlèvement d'Europe, L'abandon d'Ariane, and La délivrance de Thésée*. Ensemble Ars Nova, cond. Siranossian. Arion ARN 68195; Capella Cracoviensis, cond. Rickenbacher. Koch 3-1139-2.

177. _____. *Les Choéphores* and *Les Euménides*. Cond. Milhaud. Sacem (Archives Sonores de la Phonothèque Nationale) 150 122.

178. MONDONVILLE, JEAN-JOSEPH CASSANÉA DE (1711-1772). *Titon et L'Aurore*. Opera. Fouchécourt et al. Les Musiciens du Louvre, cond. Minkowski. Erato 2292-45715-2.

179. MONK, MEREDITH (b. 1942). *Atlas*. Meredith Monk et al. Orchestra, cond. Hankin. ECM New Series ECM 14991.

180. MONTÉCLAIR, MICHEL PIGNOLET DE (1667-1737). *La Mort de Didon* and *Pan ct Sirinx*. Cantatas. See 79. *French Cantatas of the 18th Century*.

181. MONTEVERDI, CLAUDIO (1567-1643). "Lamento d'Arianna" a voce sola and "Lamento d'Arianna" a 5; "Pianto della Madonna" a voce sola. See 140. *Lamento d'Arianna*.

182. _____. *L'Incoronazione di Poppea*. Opera. Donath et al. Concentus Musicus Wien, cond. Harnoncourt. Teldec 8.35247-2. Several recordings give different realizations of the score.

183. _____. *L'Orfeo*. Opera. Berberian et al. Vienna Concentus Musicus, cond. Harnoncourt. Teldec 35020. Several recordings give different realizations of the score.

184. _____. *Il Ritorno d'Ulisse in Patria*. Opera. Vienna Concentus Musicus, cond. Harnoncourt. Teldec 35024 ZB.

185. MOROSS, JEROME. *The Golden Apple*. Three songs,"Lazy Afternoon," "Wind Flowers," and "By Goona-Goona Lagoon," are reissued on *Original Casts, The Fifties, Part 1* (Metropolitan Opera Recording) MET 805CD. We hope that the entire LP original cast album (RCA Victor LOC-1014) of this classic American musical will eventually appear on CD.

186. MOZART, WOLFGANG AMADEUS (1756-1791). *Ascanio in Alba*. Opera. Sukis et al. Mozarteum-Orchester Salzburg, cond. Hager. Philips 422 530-2.

187. _____. *Apollo et Hyacinthus*. Opera. Johnson et al. Mozarteum-Orchester Salzburg. Philips 422 526-2; Dickie et al. Rundfunk-Sinfonie-Orchester Leipzig, cond. Pommer. Berlin Classics 0210 010 (includes *Bastien und Bastienne*).

188. _____. *La Clemenza di Tito*. Berganza et al. Vienna State Opera Orchestra, cond. Kertesz. London 430106-2.

189. _____. *Idomeneo, Rè di Creta*. Opera. Popp, Pavarotti, et al. Vienna Philharmonic Orchestra, cond. Pritchard. London 411805-2.

190. _____. *Mitridate, Rè di Ponto*. Opera. Gabry et al. Salzburg Mozarteum Orchestra, cond. Hager. Memories HR 4156/57.

191. _____. *Il Sogno di Scipione*. Opera. Schreier et al. Mozarteum-Orchester Salzburg, cond. Hager. Philips 422 531-2.

192. *Music of Ancient Greece.* By Christodoulos Halaris. Orata Ltd. ORANGM 2013 (Athens, Greece). Among its selections: Pindar's first Pythian; Stasimon from Euripides' *Orestes*; First and second Delphic hymn; Exercises for cithara (by Contrapollinopolis); Tecmessa's lament; Paean to Asclepius; Epitaph of Sikelos; Hymns (to the Sun, the Muse, Nemesis, the Holy Trinity); Prosodic chant to Apollo. The Second Delphic Hymn appears on another recording by Halaris, *Enorgana, Instrumental Greek Music Vol. 1* (Antiquity, Middle Ages, Post-Byzantine Period). Orata Ltd. ORORG 001. Yet another recording by Halaris, *Hellenic Elegies* (Orata Ltd. ORM 4012), includes the stasimon from Euripides' *Orestes* and Tecmessa's lament; See *Music of Greek Antiquity*.

193. *Music of Greek Antiquity.* By Petros Tabouris. F. M. Records (Athens, Greece) 653. Some of the same pieces as those in *Music of Ancient Greece* (see previous entry) are reconstructed on this recording, which contains a much more informative booklet. Among the selections are: Lament by Simonides; First Pythian Ode of Pindar; Ithyphallic song; Entrance song of the Phallophoroi; Partheneion by Alkman; Epithalamium and Hymeneal by Sappho; First and second Delphic hymn to Apollo; Instrumental fragment from Cantrapollinopolis; Encomium by Ibykus ; Double aulos; Fragment from the tragedy *Aias* (Tecmessa's lament); Hymns by Mesomedes of Crete (to the Sun, the Muse, Nemesis); Fragment from Aristophanes' *Birds;* Fragment from the *Iliad*; Stasimon from Euripides' *Orestes*.

194. NAUMANN, JOHANN GOTTLIEB (1741-1801). *Amphion*. Aria from the opera. See Haeffner.

195. NEVIN, ETHELBERT (1862-1901). "Narcissus." See 32. Buck.

196. NIELSEN, CARL (1865-1931). *Pan & Syrinx.* Pastorale for Orchestra. Beethoven Academie, cond. Caeyers,

197. NONO, LUIGI (1924-1990). *Prometeo.* Opera. Ade-Jeseman et al. Ensemble Modern, cond. Metzmacher. EMI CD55 55209-22. *Prometheo*, Suite. See 222. *Prometheus, The Myth in Music.*

198. _____. *Fragmente-Stille, An Diotima*, for string quartet. LaSalle Quartet. Deutsche Grammophon 437 720-2.

199. OFFENBACH, JACQUES (1819-1880). *La Belle Hélène.* Operetta. Nancel et al. Orchestre et Ensemble des Bouffes-Parisiens, cond. Calvi. Accord 290002; Sung in German: *Die Schöne Helena*. Rothenberger et al. Münchner Rundfunkorchester, cond. Mattes. EMI CMS 5 65366 2 (Angel CDMB 65366).

200. _____. *Orpheus in the Underworld (Orphée aux Enfers).* Operetta. Sung in German: *Orpheus in der Unterwelt.* Rothenberger et al. Philharmonia Hungarica, cond. Mattes EMI CMS 5 65384 2 (Angel CDMB 65384). It is amusing to hear performances of Offenbach in clever English translations, which can convey the brilliance and universality of his wit. Some are recorded and should be searched out.

201. ORFF, CARL (1895-1982). *Antigonae.* Opera. Goltz et al. Bayerisches Staatsorchester, cond. Solti. Orfeo C 407 952 1; Borkh et al. Members of the Bavarian Symphony Orchestra, cond. Leitner. Deutsche Grammophon 437 721-2. Fisher et al. Die Weiner Philharmoniker, cond. Fricsay. Stradivarius STR 10060. We hope Orff's setting of *Oedipus* and *Prometheus* will appear on CD.

202. _____. *Carmina Burana* and *Catulli Carmina*. Individual recordings of these two works are available (many of the popular *Carmina Burana*). See next entry.

203. _____. *Trionfo di Afrodite.* Scenic Cantata. Soloists and chorus. Prague Symphony Orchestra, cond. Smetácek Supraphon 11 0321-2; Leipzig Radio Orchestra, cond. Kegel. Berlin Classics BER 2047. Both recordings include *Carmina Burana* and *Catulli Carmina*.

204. *Orpheus Suite.* Popular. Composed, conducted, and produced by Chip Davis. Performed by Mannheim Steamroller. *Fresh Aire VI.* American Gramaphone AGCD-386.

205. PACINI, GIOVANNI (1795-1867). *Saffo.* Opera. Gencer et al. Orchestra e Coro del Teatro San Carlo di Napoli, cond. Capuana. Hunt CD 541.

206. PAINE, JOHN KNOWLES (1839-1906). *Oedipus Tyrannus-Prelude. John Alden Carpenter, Skyscrapers, and Other Music of the American East Coast School.* London Symphony Orchestra, cond. Klein. EMI CDC-7 49263 2.

207. Pan flute, played by masters of the modern pan flute. *Budd, Kevin, Tender Pan Flute Favorites.* The Beautiful Music Company BMD 1-106. Budd performs popular music. "Syrinx" Simion Stanciu, *Concertos for Flute and Orchestra.* I Solisti Veneti, cond. Scimone. Erato ECD 88166. "Syrinx," plays music by Bach, Quantz, and Mozart. Orchestre de Chambre de Lausanne, cond. Jordan. Musical Heritage Society MHS 11185T (originally Erato 75187 LP). *Zamfir, Opéra.* Philips D 103218. Zamfir plays arias from popular operas. Many of his recordings are available.

208. PARI, CLAUDIO (16th/17th cent.). "Il Lamento d'Arianna" a 5. See 140. *Lamento d'Arianna.*

209. PARRY, HUBERT (1848-1916). "Blest Pair of Sirens." Choral song. London Philharmonic, cond. Boult. EMI CDC 7 49022 2.

210. _____. *The Lotus Eaters*, for soprano, chorus, and orchestra. Jones. London Philharmonic Chorus and Orchestra, cond. Bamert. Chandos CHA 8990.

211. PARTCH, HARRY (1901-1976). *Castor and Pollux.* Dance. *The Music of Harry Partch.* Gate 5 Ensemble of Sausalito. CRI CD 7000.

212. _____. *Daphne of the Dunes. Newband, Microtonal Works 2.* Mode 33.

213. _____. *Revelation in the Courthouse Park.* Opera/Theater. Tomato 2686552-2.

214. PERGOLESI, GIOVANNI BATTISTA (1710-1736). *L'Olimpiade.* Opera. Bizzi et al. Transylvania State Philharmonic Orchestra, cond. Armiliato. Arkadia CDAK 129.3.

215. _____. *Orfeo.* Cantata for Soprano, Strings, and Continuo. Faulkner. Camerata Budapest, cond. Halász. Naxos 8.550766.

216. PERI, JACOPO (1561-1633). *L'Euridice.* Opera. Bonay et al. I Solisti di Milano, cond. Ephrikian. Rivo Alto CRA2 89151.

217. PERLE, GEORGE (b. 1915). *Sonnets to Orpheus*, from *Songs of Praise and Lamentation*, for orchestra and chorus. See 119. Henze.

218. PHILIDOR, FRANÇOIS-ANDRÉ DANICAN (1726-1795). *Carmen Saeculare.* Cantata. La Grande Écurie et la Chambre du Roy, cond. Malgoire. Erato 2292-45609-2.

219. PICCINNI, NICCOLO (1728-1800). *Didon.* Opera. Tucci et al. Orchestra "A. Scarlatti" di Napolii della Rai, cond. Rossi. Arkadia CDHP 596.2.

220. _____. *Iphigénie en Tauride.* Opera. Baleani et al. Orchestra e Coro dell'Ente Artistico Teatro Petruzzelli, cond. Renzetti. Fonit/Cetra CDC 32.

221. PORTER, COLE (1891-1964). *Out of This World.* Greenwood et al. Original Broadway Cast Recording. Sony Broadway SK 48223.

222. *Prometheus, The Myth in Music.* Martha Argerich et al., Berliner Philharmoniker, cond. Abbado. Sony Classical SK 53978. Includes Beethoven, *The Creatures of Prometheus*; Liszt, *Prometheus*; Nono, *Prometeo*; Scriabin, *Prométhée, Le Poème du feu.*

223. PUCCINI, GIACOMO (1858-1924). "Hymn to Diana." *The Unknown Puccini.* Domingo and Rudel. CBS MK 44981.

224. PURCELL, HENRY (ca. 1659-1695). *Dido and Aeneas.* Flagstad et al. The Mermaid Singers and Orchestra, cond. Jones. EMI CDH 7 61006 2. Outstanding among the many versions available.

225. RAITIO, VÄINÖ (1892-1945). *Antigone.* Tone-Poem. Finnish Radio Symphony Orchestra, cond. Saraste. Ondine ODE 790-2.

226. RAMEAU, JEAN-PHILIPPE (1683-1764). *Les Boréades.* Opera. Smith et al. English Baroque solists, cond. Gardiner. Erato 22922-45572-2.

227. _____. *Castor et Pollux.* Opera. Souzay et al. Concentus Musicus Wien, cond. Harnoncourt. Teldec 8.35048 ZB.

228. _____. *Dardanus.* Opera. Von Stade et al. Choeurs & Orchestre du Théâtre National de l'Opera de Paris, cond. Leppard. Erato 4509-95312-2. *Dardanus.* Orchestral Suite. English Baroque Soloists, cond. Gardiner.

229. _____. *Hippolyte et Aricie.* Opera. Fouchécourt et al. Les Musiciens du Louvre, cond. Minkowski. Archiv 445 853-2.

230. _____. *Orphée.* Cantata. Schlick et al. with harpsichord. Musikproduktion Dabringhaus und Grimm (distr. Koch International) L-3131.

231. _____. *Platée.* Opera. Sénéchal et al. Orchestre de la Société des Concerts du Conservatoire, cond. Rosbaud. EMI CMS 7 69861 2.

232. _____. *Pygmalion.* Acte de Ballet, which includes a text. Les Arts Florissants, cond. Christie. Harmonia Mundi 901381. The recording includes *Nélée & Myrthis*, a tale set in antiquity: Nélée, a victor in the Argive games, puts the love of his Myrthis to the test.

233. RASCARINI, FRANCESO MARIA (ca. 1645-1796). "Reciproco Amore: Lasciatemi Morire" a 3. See 140. Lamento d'Arianna.

234. RAVEL, MAURICE (1875-1937). "Air d'Alcyone." Excerpt from a cantata. Atger, Orchestre Philharmonique de Monte-Carlo, cond. Constant. Valois V 4644.

235. RESPIGHI, OTTORINO (1879-1936). *Lucrezia.* Opera. Remor et al. Marco Polo 8.223717.

236. RODGERS, RICHARD (1902-1979). *The Boys from Syracuse.* Musical. Nelson et al. Chorus and Orchestra, cond. Engel. Sony Broadway SK 53329.

237. _____. "Jupiter Forbid," from *By Jupiter.* Norma Doggett, chorus, and orchestra, cond. Setzer. Original Cast, The Sixties: Part 2 (Metropolitan Opera) MET 808CD. Reissued from the original cast LP album RCA Victor LOC-113070 (which we hope will be reissued in its entirety on CD).

238. *Roman Heroes.* Domingo. National Philharmonic Orchestra, cond. Kohn. EMI CDC 7 54053 2. Includes arias from Bellini, *Norma*, Handel, *Giulio Cesare in Egitto*, Mascagni, *Nerone*, Spontini, *La Vestale.*

239. ROSSI, LUIGI (1597-1653). *Orfeo.* Opera. Mellon et al. Les Arts Florissants, cond. Christie. Harmonia Mundi HMC 901358.60.

240. ROSSINI, GIOACCHINO (1792-1868). *Edipo a Colono.* Cantata for bass, chorus, and orchestra. Ghiuselev. Philharmonia Orchestra, cond. Scimone. Fonit Cetra (Italia). CDC 68.

241. _____. *Ermione.* Opera. Gasdia et al. Orchestre Philharmonique de Monte-Carlo, cond. Scimone. Erato ECD 75336.

242. ROUSSEL, ALBERT (1869-1937). *Bacchus et Ariane.* Ballet Suite. Orchestre National de France, cond. Prêtre. EMI CDC 7 47376 2.

243. ROZSA, MIKLOS (b. 1907). *Quo Vadis.* Film music. The Royal Philharmonic Orchestra and Chorus, cond. Rózsa. London 820 200-2.

244. SAINT-SAENS, CAMILLE (1835-1921). *La Jeunesse d'Hercule, Phaéton,* and *Le Rouet d'Omphale.* Symphonic Poems. Philharmonia Orchestra, cond. Dutoit. London (Jubilee) 425021-2 (includes all three works).

245. _____. "Bacchanale" from the opera *Samson et Dalila.* CSR Symphony Orchestra (Bratislava), cond. Gunzenhauser. Naxos 8.550138 (includes *Le Rouet d'Omphale*).

246. SALIERI, ANTONIO (1750-1825). *Les Danaïdes.* Opera. Marshall et al. Radio-Sinfonieorchester Stuttgart, cond. Gelmetti. EMI CDS 7 54073 2.

247. SATIE, ERIK (1866-1925). *Socrate.* Work for voice or voices and chamber orchestra or piano. Cuenod and Parsons. Nimbus NI 5027.

248. SCHOECK, OTHMAR (1886-1957). *Penthesilea.* Opera. Dernesch et al. Austrian Radio Chorus and Symphony Orchestra, cond. Albrecht. Orfeo C364941B. Orchestral Suite. Swiss Youth Symphony Orchestra, cond. Delfs. Claves CD 50 9201.

249. _____. *Venus.* Opera. Popp et al. Philharmonische Werkstatt Schweiz, cond. Venzago. Musikszene Schweiz (Suisa) MGB CD 6112.

250. SCHUBERT, FRANZ (1797-1828). *The Hyperion Schubert Edition 14.* Hampson, McLaughlin, and Johnson. Hyperion CDJ33014. Contains on one CD many classically inspired songs: "Die Götter Griechenlands," "Amphiaraos," "Gruppe aus dem Tartarus," "Hippolits Lied," "Memnon," "Fragment aus dem Aeschylus," "Philoktet," "Lied eines Schiffers an die Dioskuren," "Orest auf Tauris," "Der entsühnte Orest," "Der zürnenden Diana," and "Uraniens Fluckt," and the two duets, "Antigone und Oedip," and "Hektors Abschied."

251. _____. *Lieder.* Fischer-Dieskau and Moore. Deutsche Grammophon 437 215-2. Vol. 1 (of three volumes) contains "Amphiaraos," "Fahrt zum Hades," "Fragment aus dem Aeschylus," "Ganymed," "Memnon," "Orpheus," "Lied eines Schiffers an die Dioskuren," "Philoktet." Vol. 2: "Atys," "Dithyrambe," "Elysium," "Der entsühnte Orest," "Die Götter Griechenlands," "Gruppe aus dem Tartarus," "Heliopolis I," "Hippolits Lied," "Der Musensohn," "Orest auf Tauris," "Prometheus," "Der zürnenden Diana." Vol. 3: "Der Atlas." For "Uraniens Fluckt" (omitted in this "complete" collection of solo songs) and the duets "Antigone und Oedip" and "Hektors Abschied," see previous entry.

252. SCHUMAN, WILLIAM (1910-1992). *Night Journey.* Ballet about Jocasta. *More Music for Martha Graham.* The Atlantic Sinfonietta, cond. Schenck. Koch 3-7051-2 H1 (Includes *Errand into the Maze*).

253. _____. "Orpheus with His Lute." Fisk, guitar, and Robison, flute. Musicmasters 70838-2-C; also Musical Heritage Society, CD 11239Y.

254. SCOTT, STEPHEN (b. 1944). *Minerva's Web* and *The Tears of Niobe*. The Colorado College New Music Ensemble. New Albion Records NA 026 CD.

255. SCRIABIN, ALEXANDER (1872-1915). *Prométhée, Le Poème du feu.* See 222. *Prometheus, The Myth in Music.*

256. SIBELIUS, JEAN (1865-1957). *The Dryad.* Tone-Poem. *The Complete Tone Poems.* Scottish National Orchestra, cond. Gibson. Chandos CHAN 8395/6.

257. _____. *The Oceanides.* See previous entry.

258. *Sirens.* Popular. Composed, conducted, and produced by Chip Davis. Performed by Mannheim Steamroller. *Fresh Aire VI.* American Gramaphone AGCD-386.

259. SKALKOTTAS, NIKOS (1904-1949). *The Return of Odysseus, Symphony in one movement.* Danish Symphony Orchestra, cond. Caridis, Koch Schwann Musica Mundi CD 311 110.

260. SMITH, JOHN STAFFORD (1750-1836). "Blest Pair of Sirens." *The Romantic Muse, English Music in the Time of Beethoven.* Invocation, cond. Roberts. Hyperion CDA66745.

261. SONDHEIM, STEPHEN. "Fear No More." Song from *The Frogs. A Collector's Sondheim.* RCA Red Seal RCD 3-5480. (Note also a cassette recording: *A Stephen Sondheim Evening,* cast recording. RCA CBK2-4745. Includes "Invocation and Instructions to the Audience" from *The Frogs* and selections from *A Funny Thing Happened on the Way to the Forum.*)

262. _____. *A Funny Thing Happened on the Way to the Forum.* Mostel et al. Original Broadway Cast Recording. Broadway Angel D 120609.

263. "The Song of the Sibyl" ("El Cant de la Sibilla"). Obsidienne vocal ensemble, cond. Bellsolà. Opus 111 OPS 30-130.

264. SPONTINI, GASPARE (1774-1851). *Olimpia.* Opera. Varady et al. Berlin Radio Symphony Orchestra, cond. Albrecht. Orfeo C 137862 H; Lorengar et al. Orchestra e Coro del Teatro alla Scala, cond. Molinari-Pradelli. Giuseppe di Stefano GDS 21021.

265. _____. *La Vestale.* Opera. Huffstodt et al. Orchestra e Coro del Teatro alla Scala, cond. Muti. Sony S3K 66357; Callas, Corelli et al. Orchestra e Choro del Teatro alla Scala, cond. Votto. Melodram MEL 26008 and Great Opera Performances GOP 741.

266. STRAUSS, RICHARD (1864-1949). *Die ägyptische Helena.* Opera. Jones et al. Detroit Symphony Orchestra, cond. Dorati. London 430 381-2; Rysanek et al. Bavarian State Opera Orchestra, cond. Keilberth. Melodram MEL 2706. The "Awakening Scene" is magnificently sung by Leontyne Price in a collection of Strauss arias. RCA Gold Seal 60398-2-RG.

267. _____. *Ariadne auf Naxos.* Schwarzkopf et al. Philharmonia Orchestra, cond. Karajan. EMI CMS 7-69296 2 (Angel CDMB 69296). A stellar cast makes this a classic. Watch for a reissue of the complete recording conducted by Leinsdorf, with the splendid Rysanek and Peerce, one of the few tenors who could really *sing* Bacchus.

268. _____. *Daphne.* Popp et al. Bavarian Radio Orchestra, cond. Haitink. EMI CDS 7 49309 2 (Angel CDCB 49309); Güden et al. Wiener Symphoniker, cond. Böhm. Deutsche Grammophon 445322-2 (formerly 423 579-2).

269. _____. *Elektra.* Nilsson et al. Vienna Philharmonic, cond. Solti. London 417345-2LH2 (Nilsson's vocalism is extraordinary); also excellent is Borkh et al. Dresden State Orchestra, cond. Böhm. Deutsche Grammophon 445329-2 (formerly 431737-2).

270. _____. *Die Liebe der Danae.* Opera. Kupper et al. Die Wiener Philharmoniker, cond. Krauss. Melodram MEL 37061.

271. STRAVINSKY, IGOR. (1882-1971). *Apollo (Apollon Musagète).* Ballet. Orchestra of St. John's, Smith Square, cond. Lubbock. ASV CD DCA 618. This is the 1928 version; the work was revised in 1947. *Orpheus* also is included.

272. _____. *Oedipus Rex.* Opera-Oratorio. Norman et al. Saito Kinen Orchestra, cond. Ozawa. Philips 438 865-2.

273. _____. *Orpheus.* Ballet. See *Apollo* above.

274. _____. *Perséphone.* Perséphone, 1934. A melodrama, for speaker, tenor, orchestra, mixed chorus, and boy's chorus, 1934. London Philharmonic Orchestra and Chorus, cond. Fournet. Virgin Classics 59077; The Orchestra of St. Luke's et al., cond. Craft. MusicMasters 01612-67103-2.

275. "Stupid Cupid," by Neil Sedaka. Popular Song recorded by Connie Francis. Among the reissues on CD are Polydor 827 569-2 and Mercury 832 041-3.

276. SUPPÉ, FRANZ VON (1819-1895). *Die schöne Galathée*. Highlights from the operetta. Moffo et al. Münicher Rundfunkorchester, cond. Eichorn. Eurodisc 258 376.

277. "Tales of Brave Ulysses." Rock song by Clapton and Sharp. *Live Cream, Volume II*. GEMA 823 661-2.

278. TANEIEV (TANEYEV), SERGEI (1856-1915). *The Oresteia*. Chernobayev et al. Chorus and Orchestra of the Belorussian State Opera, cond. Kolomizheva. Olympia OCD 1w95A/B.

279. TELSON, BOB. *Gospel at Colonus*. Musical. Original cast recording. Fountain and the Five Blind Boys of Alabama et al. Electra/Nonesuch 79191-2.

280. TERRASSE, CLAUDE (1867-1923). *Les Travaux d'Hercule*. Operetta. Rey et al. Orchestre Lyrique de la RTF, cond. Cariven. Musidisc 201792 MU 744.

281. TIPPETT, MICHAEL (b. 1905). *King Priam*. Opera. Bailey et al. London Sinfonietta, cond. Atherton. London 414 241-2 and Chandos CHAN 9406/7.

282. UTTINI, FRANCESCO ANTONIO (1723-1795). *Thétis and Pelée*. Selections from the opera. See 96. Haeffner.

283. VACCAJ (VACCAI), NICOLA (1790-1848). *Andromeda*. Cantata for soprano and orchestra. Ferrante. Grande Accademia Vocale e Strumentale Ensemble Seicentonovecento, cond. Colussi. Bongiovanni GB 10005-2.

284. "Venus." Popular song. *The Best of Frankie Avalon*. Varèse Sarabande VSO-5594.

285. "Venus in Blue Jeans." Popular song. *The Very Best of Jimmy Clanton*. Ace Records 2039.

286. VERSO, ANTONIO IL (1560?-1621). "Lasciatemi Morire" a 5. See 140. *Lamento d'Arianna*.

287. VINCI, LEONARDO (ca. 1690-1730). Soprano arias from his operas, including *Catone in Utica, Didone Abbandonata, La Feste di Baccho*. M. A. Peters. String Quartet of the Orchestre Internazionale d'Italia, cond. Carraro. Memories DR 3109. See also 174. *Metastasio's Kings and Heroes*.

288. WAKEMAN, RICK, and RAMON REMEDIOS. *A Suite of Gods*. Relativity/President 88561-1026-2. A classical new age recording for tenor, keyboards, and percussion. Songs are entitled: "Dawn of Time," "The Oracle," "Pandora's Box," "Chariot of the Sun," "The Flood," "The Voyage of Ulysses," "Hercules."

289. WALTON, WILLIAM (1902-1983). *Troilus and Cressida*. Opera. Baker et al. Chorus and Orchestra of the Royal Opera House Covent Garden, cond. Foster. EMI CMS 5 65550-2 (Angel CDMB 65550). Howarth et al. English Northern Philharmonia, cond. Hickox. Chandos CHA 9370.

290. WEILL, KURT (1900-1950). "One Touch of Venus," the title song of his operetta sung by Greta Keller. *Kurt Weill, American Songbook Series, Smithsonian Collection of Recordings*. Sony Music Special Products. "I'm a Stranger Here Myself." *Stratas Sings Weill*. Y Chamber Symphony, cond. Schwarz. Nonesuch E2-79131.

291. WINTER, PAUL. *Missa Gaia (Earth Mass)*. New Age Music. Paul Winter Consort. Living Music LD 0002.

292. WOLF, HUGO (1860-1903). *Penthesilea*. Symphonic poem. Orchestre de Paris, cond. Barenboim. Erato 2292-45416-2.

293. _____. "Ganymed." Song. *Songs of Hugo Wolf*. Holzmair and Palm. Collins Classics 14022.

294. XENAKIS, IANNIS (b. 1922). *Oresteia*. Suite, for chorus and orchestra with baritone and percussion solo. Salabert/Actuels SCD8906, distributed by Harmonia Mundi.

295. _____. *Phlegra*. For chamber orchestra. Ensemble Intercontemporain, cond. Tabachnik. Erato 2292-45770-2.